melly william (handwritten signature)

THE JERSEY GUARDIAN

Book One of the Jersey Demon Trilogy

By the same author:

Animal High, The Book Guild, 1994

THE JERSEY GUARDIAN

Book One of the Jersey Demon Trilogy

Holly Williams

Book Guild Publishing
Sussex, England

First published in Great Britain in 2005 by
The Book Guild Ltd
25 High Street
Lewes, Sussex
BN7 2LU

Typesetting in Palatino by
Keyboard Services, Luton, Bedfordshire

Printed in Great Britain by
Antony Rowe Ltd, Chippenham, Wiltshire

A catalogue record for this book is
available from the British Library

ISBN 1 85776 918 X

*Dedicated to the memory of my Gramps, Harry Hill,
who introduced me to the magical world of books,
and to my best friend, Michele Hawkes,
who was Elsa to my Jess.*

Chapter 1

The Meeting of the Elders

A pale, silvery moon casts its light over the stillness of Greve de Lecq bay. Along the coastal road the slightly neglected, white-washed shops and café that cling to the skirt of the rocky cliff stand abandoned for the night by the few tourists that still choose to visit this mystic isle. In the imposing shadow of jagged black cliffs that embraces the shoreline, the dark, green sea crested by ghostly ripples of surf caresses the seaweed-strewn rocks that jut their weather-beaten faces from beneath the smooth sand.

Along the almost overgrown path that snakes its way steeply down the cliff-side, a lone, stocky figure moves haltingly among the long grass like some comical, overweight mountain goat as he picks his way down towards the beach. But Jim Hellily knows that the purpose of his journey is far from a light-hearted one. For he is one of the few who remember, a true island person. His blood runs thick with salt water and magic. Jersey has become so diluted through the centuries that many who make their home here nowadays don't believe in the spirits; the magic has been forgotten. Christianity came to this place ages ago and many of the locals abandoned the ancient ways to join the new faith. Through the years the magic folk have had to keep themselves hidden because so many islanders were now unfriendly to the faeriefolk and merpeople. But a few stayed strong. Through wars and invasions they kept the old ways alive, the magic that protected Jersey. Unfortunately, among the believers there were those who followed the dark side of the magic. Witches, warlocks and Black Trolls who worship the dark spirit that lurks beneath the isle also live in these parts, although

1

many of them had been driven to the mainland after the failed uprising fourteen years ago. Jim pulled his moth-eaten cap down over his wild, grey hair and shuddered. It wasn't pleasant to speculate on followers of the dark side, especially when you had been in such close contact with them as Jim had. It caused him great grief to remember the responsibility his family held to the island. On dark nights when storms lash down on the island and the wind howls across the beach near his home at St Ouens, the nightmares still haunt his brain, jolting him awake, crying like a child despite his sixty-six years. He lost his sister to the wicked ones over thirty years ago, a bloody unplanned attack to break the sacred, magical chain that had protected Jersey for centuries. Thank God her daughter survived to carry on Iris's work. Jim remembered his niece with a smile; Emma had been a headstrong girl and an intelligent woman. She knew well the power that coursed through her veins and was eager to banish the evil that had destroyed her mother. When the uprising came she did everything in her power to stop it. The battle she put up had been talked about in hushed whispers among the island folk ever since. Thirteen witches and warlocks against one mortal, each one bent on waking the Dark One from his cold, stone grave. But Emma sent them fleeing; she'd keep the island safe even if it cost her life. No, with a family history like that Jim wasn't one for reminiscing.

He was a good way down the cliff side now, about twenty feet from the smooth black tarmac of the road. He was about to bring his heavy, work boot down upon a clump of long grass that was in the centre of the path when a small, yellowish white light no bigger than a tennis ball, shot up out of the clod at such a speed that it almost made him fall backwards. The glowing ball, which to an unbeliever might have appeared like a rather large firefly, hovered a few inches in front of Jim's round, ruddy nose jiggling about from side to side, obviously quite cross about nearly being trodden on. Jim, having recovered from the initial shock, grumbled to himself and searched in the pockets of his overcoat for his glasses. Finding them under a handkerchief and several toffee wrappers, he put them on and peered into the golden light to see if it was anyone he knew. The faerie, for that was what the strange glowing creature was, glared back at him angrily. She was young, although ageing

2

faeries was never easy as their skin never betrayed any signs of maturity (nor, Jim thought, did their character), with silvery-white complexion and long willowy limbs. Her short, reddish blonde hair was pulled back from her face, which made her already sharp features appear even more pointed. On her back, a pair of delicate, translucent wings fluttered so frantically it was barely possible for the human eye to see them. Her pale blue eyes burned into Jim with fury.

Jim batted his huge, rough-skinned hand waving the creature away but she remained floating in front of his face. 'Silly girl, you frightened the life outta me!'

The faerie, who seemed far from afraid of Jim, placed her hands on her hips and glared at him.

'Frightened!' she stated, her voice high and very musical like all faeries. 'You nearly crushed me alive!' She did a neat pirouette in mid-air just to check her wings hadn't been damaged. 'Luckily I'm the quickest of the faeriefolk this side of the island, I can easily dodge a great lug like you!' She flicked a microscopic speck of dust from her simple white garment.

Jim sighed and looked at her with his dark, crinkly eyes.

'You mind your manners little missy,' said Jim, waggling his finger as if telling off a young faerie was the most normal thing in the world. 'A girl like you should be tucked up in bed by now, not hiding in the grass ready to play a magic prank on some old man. I have a good mind to tell Old Oaky, your elder, on you. He knows what to do with wayward sprites, he'd clip your wings!'

The faerie wasn't at all threatened by Jim's remarks and continued to do an odd dance before him, flying to and fro, her graceful limbs spread out like a ballerina.

'Old Oaky's my grandfather,' she said in that strange sing-song voice of hers. 'I'm Rosehip, his favourite grand-daughter. He wouldn't do anything to me, so there!' She finished her dance and flew up to perch on the peak of Jim's cap so he couldn't see her. Crossly, Jim tried to brush the young sprite off his hat but she sat firm.

'And what, pray tell, would your grandfather say if he knew you were being very rude and disobedient to one of his oldest friends?' said Jim, still trying to dislodge her.

Amused that her antics were annoying Jim and pleased that

he was too large and slow to catch her, Rosehip knelt firmly on the rim of his cap, giggling mischievously as the old man tossed his head from side to side trying to knock her off. Placing her tiny delicate hands on the edge of the brim she peered down under it, her strange magical glow illuminating the craggy creases in Jim's leathery, tanned face. 'He told me to wait for you.' She laughed. 'Old Oaky said it was very important that you should be at the meeting and I should make sure you arrived, and when you did, get Keela to take you to the elders.'

Jim pursed his thin lips and gazed at the upside-down face hanging from his hat. 'I'm not a child. I do know how to find my way to the Gathering Place.'

Rosehip made a small 'humph' sound and leaped from Jim's hat so she was once again fluttering in front of him.

'I don't care!' she said indignantly. 'My grandfather told me to make sure you were coming so that's what I did!'

With that she shot away until she was about three feet ahead of Jim before hovering, waiting for him to follow her. Sighing deeply and muttering something about the youth of today having no respect, Jim stepped from the cliff path onto the dark, hard surface of the main road. If he was completely honest, Jim thought as he watched Rosehip's pale light reflect in the small puddles that dotted the tarmac here and there, he found the faeriefolk of Jersey highly annoying. It was very difficult to hold a sensible conversation with a faerie; they were frustratingly impatient creatures, always flying about, never taking much notice of what you said. Old Oaky, the six-hundred-year-old leader of the faeries, Jim could stand. He was mature enough to listen to what you said and too ancient to buzz about pestering you. No, on the whole Jim much preferred merfolk to faeries, although he was in a minority. For some reason that had never been clear to Jim, a great many of the islanders were slightly afraid of the strange, green-skinned, dark-haired half-fish-like people who made their home in the sea surrounding Jersey. To him they were the most pleasant and respectful individuals one could hope to meet. He guessed that people had been made wary of the merfolk because of their connections with the shipwrecks of old. It was true that in the past young mermaids would sit on the cliffs at Corbiere luring lonely sailors to crash their ships on the jagged rocks hidden beneath the foaming waves, watching them drown for amusement. But, as Jim's aquatic friend Keela often said, how many innocent merchildren were caught in the nets and speared by the harpoons of those very vessels? Rosehip's bright light brought him out of his thoughts and together the two beings travelled along the black, man-made river until it turned downwards into the bumpy, cobbled slip road leading onto the beach. Tide was out and Jim had to be careful not to lose his balance on the damp sand-covered path. Rosehip darted about back and forth with annoyance as Jim edged his way onto the sand.

'Come on, come on!' she twittered as she zoomed about in front of him, 'We're going to be late! Everyone's waiting for you!'

She fluttered down to land on one of the blackish-brown rocks that littered the beach. Jim stood on the shore for a moment to catch his breath. A cool, pleasant breeze blew off the sea and in the sky above them, a million stars shone down, each one as clear and perfect as a diamond.

'Well?' asked Rosehip impatient as ever, 'are you going to stand there all night? Call Keela!'

Tired of being badgered by the young faerie, Jim stooped and selected a smooth, round stone from the beach and tossed it as far as he could out into the dark water, crying the name, 'Keela!' The pebble landed with a satisfying plop about twenty feet from the beach. Jim and Rosehip were silent for a moment as they both searched the rippling waves of Grave de Leq bay for a sign of the merman. After what seemed like an age in the still night, a head emerged from beneath the swells of the cold ocean not far from where the stone had landed. It bobbed there for a few seconds, too far away for anyone on the shore to make out its features, before moving swiftly and smoothly through the dark water towards where Jim and Rosehip were. The creature swam fast and with such expertise it was obvious that it couldn't possibly be human. For one thing a human swimmer would leave a trail of ripples in his wake but this creature swept through the water without so much as disturbing the surface. In a matter of seconds it was not ten feet from the beach and Jim could see the face of Keela his friend. The merman's thick, glossy greenish-black hair was swept in deep curls close to his scalp by salt water. His jade skin shone with the silver glow of

5

the moon. Huge, golden eyes swept across the beach as he searched for his friend who was waving to him from the sand. His mouth formed a welcoming smile, revealing a row of dagger-sharp, pearly teeth as he waved a muscular arm and called out in a deep voice. 'Ahoy there, Jim! 'Tis good to see you!'

With that, he powered himself toward the sands until the water was shallow enough for him to bank himself on the seabed. There he rested and allowed the waves to break over his smooth, hairless torso and silver, scaled tail. Jim waded through the shallows, water filling his boots and soaking his trousers until he reached Keela's side, Rosehip fluttering behind him. Keela flipped himself over onto his back, flicking his powerful tail in the breaking waves.

'Keela, it has been an age. I trust you have been keeping well?' Jim extended his hand towards the merman who grasped it in his nail-less green fingers and shook it warmly.

'Fare as the sea breeze,' replied Keela tossing back his thick mane to gaze up on the full moon. 'Although, I will be glad when summer has past and the seas and beaches are more deserted. It isn't often safe for our folk to come inshore this time of year what with the tourists and all.'

Jim nodded in agreement as Keela scooped a piece of jagged driftwood from the water and began to use it to groom his hair and neat goatee beard. 'I know what you mean. Winter is a lot more peaceful for all of us. No doubt Reeni will be glad when it is safe to let the little ones swim where they like without having to worry if they are spotted?'

Keela let out a hearty belly-laugh and slapped his tail causing large sprays of water to soak Rosehip who had been flying around, rather cross that she was being ignored.

'Yes,' Keela smiled. 'My wife, she is a worrier. Pod and Coona are old enough to swim away from her now; just when she thinks one is safe the other has slipped out and is headed for the shore. They are quite a pair!'

He chuckled again but was quickly silenced by Rosehip swooping down and pulling at his hair.

'Tell him!' she hissed not quite quietly enough for Jim not to hear. 'He has got to know.'

The sharp-toothed smile fell from Keela's face and the golden glow within his huge eyes seemed to grow dim. He took a deep breath and gazed gravely at Jim. 'I was trying to break it to you gently, old boy, but missy here seems to think I should tell you straight. You know what the meeting's about?'

Jim felt the colour drain from his face. He stuck his hands deep in his pockets and pulled his coat around him. Suddenly, standing knee deep in water, he felt very cold and scared. 'I've been trying to pretend I didn't but I have a pretty good idea,' he said dryly.

Keela looked at the water lapping around him and sighed. 'You knew how dangerous it was to let her go. You were putting everyone one in Jersey, perhaps more, at peril. I thought you were wrong to let her father take her in the first place.'

Jim threw his friend a bitter look and swallowed, but the foul-tasting lump in his throat wouldn't go down. 'Maybe if your family had been through what mine had, maybe if you'd watched your sister and your niece die in such vile ways, you would have sent her away too. She is my only living relative; I wanted her to be safe.'

Keela squeezed his glowing eyes shut as if he was about to cry and clenched his fists. 'I know Jim, I know. But it is her destiny, and it is your duty to let her know who she is.' He opened his eyes and looked at Jim. 'It is not my place to argue with you. I was just sent as a Gatekeeper. The others are waiting, I must take you to them.'

With that, Keela looked out into the black waters of Greve de Lecq and raised his thick, muscle-bound arms before him. When he next spoke his voice rang out through the still night.

'Hear me, mother ocean,' he cried. 'I call upon you to open your majesty to three believers who wish to battle the forces of evil. Give us passage to the sacred arena where our forefathers met throughout the ages and guard them from what evil we may face.'

Almost immediately after Keela had spoken the water surrounding Jim's legs began to ebb away. As if being cut in two by some enormous invisible ship, the sea drew back towards the rocky cliffs encircling the bay, leaving the seabed before Jim and Rosehip exposed. Waves rolled back on themselves as if drawn by a force stronger than the current itself, so the water formed two enormous walls either side of the newly exposed path, their surfaces as smooth and flat as if they were behind glass. Jim peered down the long, damp tunnel and saw that after 30 feet or so it widened out into a large open space where a few figures were already seated on the rocks of the seabed. He looked back to Keela but the merman looked away.

'You know what you have to do Jim,' he murmured sadly before dragging himself through the wall of waves and swimming away.

Breathing deeply and with Rosehip hovering unnaturally quiet beside him, Jim Hellily started the long walk towards the sacred circle. Between the great walls that towered above him, the air was cool and the white spray that bubbled on the crest of the magical partitions fell down upon him like a fine, misty rain. As he gazed through the transparent water, Jim could see Keela along with dozens of other merfolk dart agilely through the sea, their wild hair flowing behind them, beautiful metallic scales of their tails glistening through the eerie underwater light, all of them heading towards the meeting spot. Jim wanted to turn and run back to the shore, back to a life where he didn't carry this sombre responsibility, a life where his family was safe. But he knew he couldn't. It was only a matter of minutes now before he knew for sure what his great-niece's sacrifice would be.

He had reached the end of the passageway now and was so far from the land the air that surrounded him was as icy as mid-winter. The great arena stood before him shining with a strange light that alternated from gold to blue to green then back to gold. The area was filled with islanders, most of whom were around Jim's age and nearly all of whom he knew. Every one of them wore a solemn expression and many started to murmur once he entered the circle. Directly in front of him, seated on three raised rocks, were the elders of Jersey, one from each of the peoples who lived on and around the island.

Arthur LeBlanc, the ninety-seven-year-old representative of the humans who dwelt on Jersey, looked old and frail in his baggy tweed suit. His face was drawn and his intelligent blue eyes rested deep in their sockets. What little remained of his thin, white hair was sleeked back and his pale face looked as weathered and hardy as the cliffs of Jersey itself. To his left, radiating a pale white light, was Old Oaky, the ancient leader of the faeries. He was wrapped in a cloak of red sycamore leaves and his long silver beard was as soft and white as clouds. The final place was occupied by the imposing black-skinned figure of Xandu, most respected and feared of the merfolk. His hair and beard were emerald green and unruly and his long navy tail curled under him. His eyes glowed like the most brilliant of golden flames and his face was set in a cold scowl.

Through the water that surrounded the arena hundreds of merfolk floated, gazing expectantly at Jim. Above the assembly, a halo of light spun, humming melodiously; it was this that lit the arena and Jim knew it was formed of faeries.

Jim removed his cap and wrung it in his hands. 'You wanted to see me?' he said, sounding like a child called to the headmaster's office.

Arthur cleared his throat and spoke solemnly. 'Yes Jim, we did.' The old man looked slightly lost for words and gazed down at his knees.

Impatiently Xandu threw him a look from the corner of his glowing eyes. 'In Neptune's name, man, spit it out. He is the only chance we've got – him and the girl.'

Arthur quavered for a moment beneath Xandu's blazing gaze. Slowly his thin-lipped mouth fell open. 'Witches,' he said quietly. There was a sudden murmur of panic amongst everyone in the circle. People looked at each other in horror and disbelief and the faeries above spun more frantically in their ring emitting an ear-splitting squeal. Rosehip, who up until now had been floating quite happily beside Jim's left shoulder shot forward towards her grandfather who wrapped her in his arms.

Jim blinked in amazement. 'You're joking!' he said.

Arthur, who seemed to have regained the power of speech, shook his head. 'I would not joke about something like that. We have the proof. All the old gathering places have been uncovered again: the dungeon at Gorey, St Peter's graveyard, the Petrified Forest, even Devil's Hole.' He went ghostly pale. 'Faeries and merfolk have seen activity in all of them. There's no doubt about it. Followers of the Dark One are returning.'

Jim swallowed hard and looked bewildered; many of the islanders had tears in their eyes and in the sea surrounding the circle merfolk darted back and forth, too panicky to keep still. Somehow he found his voice. 'Do ... do you know who they are?' he asked.

Arthur shook his head sadly. 'Not a clue. We don't know whether they are old islanders returning or pagans from the mainland.'

Old Oaky looked up from comforting Rosehip who was weeping by his side. 'Seven faeries have already been found dead near the magic places,' he said in a scared but musical tone. 'You know our blood is prized in the practice of the Black Arts. We can deny it all we want but if witches have returned they have one aim in mind – raising the Dark Lord.'

From the crowd that had assembled within the arena a woman let out a scream. Quickly, others gathered round to comfort her.

Arthur's cobalt eyes locked with Jim's. 'You know that there is only one way to stop them, don't you Jim?' he said dryly. 'That's why you sent for her. You told me, remember, her plane lands in three days.'

Jim felt as if all the blood had drained out of him into the damp sand. 'No,' he said quietly, 'I won't allow it. She's too young, she's only fourteen.'

Arthur clenched his fists so tightly his bony knuckles turned white. 'Jim,' he said sternly, 'it isn't like you have a choice in this.'

Jim puffed out his chest and jutted out his chin. 'That's where you're wrong,' he stated firmly. 'I didn't have a choice with Iris or Emma; twice I had to watch the blood of my family spilled. But not with Jessica; she is my only living relative and I shall not put her in danger. If she doesn't know what is asked of her then there is nothing she can do.'

Xandu regarded the old man with glowing golden eyes. 'You are a fool, Jim Hellily. When her mother died it was her duty to stay in Jersey; you should never have let her go with her father. She is the last in the line, eldest child of an eldest child, descendant of the banisher of the Dark Lord. Didn't it ever enter your mind that this is why the evil is returning? Because the Guardian left?'

Jim met Xandu's wide-eyed, angry gaze. 'You were there, Xandu,' he spat. 'You saw it all, the birth and the death, Emma writhing with agony as that wickedness was poured into her swollen stomach. That creature that polluted her womb.' He stopped himself and looked away. He hadn't wanted to mention the child.

10

But Xandu had heard. The merman lent forward, his face contorted with fury. 'It lives,' he spat vindictively. 'My people took it in when you abandoned it. It leads a lonely existence in a sea cave not far from this very bay. Alone it is, and in pain but not a monster!'

'Then you should be able to see why I don't want Jessica to meet the same fate,' Jim retorted. 'I cannot allow her to die, or worse, end up like that poor being.'

Xandu was about to launch into another verbal attack when Arthur put up his hand to stop him.

'Jim,' he said simply, 'the options are clear. Either you tell the girl who she really is and what is expected of her, or Jersey, everyone in it, and perhaps the world, is doomed.'

Jim gazed at the wet seabed and tears filled his eyes. 'Ay, I know. I was just hoping she wouldn't have to go through this.'

Arthur took a deep breath. 'She won't face this alone, the Elders have decided that already.' The old man looked into the crowd of frightened faces. 'Jake,' he called, a hint of woe in his voice.

From the group of islanders stepped forth a young boy, not more than seventeen years old. He, like Arthur, was tall and thin with piercing blue eyes. His hair was jet black and unruly and his nose slightly too big for his otherwise delicate features. He came to stand next to Arthur, who rested a hand on his shoulder. 'Yes, grandfather?' he asked, sounding slightly nervous.

Arthur turned to the boy. 'Are you completely sure about this?' he asked gently.

Jake nodded slowly but did not answer.

Arthur turned back to Jim. 'This is Jake, my youngest grandchild. As a mark of faith in your family he has agreed to go with Jessica when she faces the witches.'

Jake looked to Jim and half smiled. 'I will do all I can to protect her and the island,' he said quietly.

Arthur turned to his left. 'I believe my fellows are willing to make a similar gesture.'

Old Oaky motioned to Rosehip to get to her feet. 'The faeriefolk of this isle have agreed they will use whatever power they have to guard your great-niece and I appoint Rosehip here as the girl's personal sentinel.'

11

Upon hearing this, the young faerie took off and started to buzz around Jim's head. 'You'll see, Jim, Jessica will be safe with me around,' she chirped proudly.

'Oh great!' muttered the old man unenthusiastically.

Arthur then turned to Xandu who had been glaring at Jim silently. 'And you, my friend. What offer of aid do you extend to the Guardian?'

Xandu's hypnotic eyes flitted from Jim to Arthur and then back again. 'I think,' he stated bitterly, 'considering that we have raised and protected the other child for the past fourteen years, the merfolk's support is clear. But as we are all fighting under the same flag, you have my oath that no harm shall befall the girl under the waves of Jersey.' He met Jim with a steely glare.

Arthur clapped his hands on his knees. 'Then it is settled. The girl has our unwavering support.' He gave Jim a serious look. 'I have your word you will tell her what is expected of her, don't I, Jim?'

He held eye contact with Jim in such a way the younger man knew he didn't have a choice. 'Ay,' he muttered. 'She will know soon enough. Just trust me to tell her in my own time.'

Arthur smiled contentedly but at his side Jim could see Xandu silently fuming.

Arthur turned his pale face to the indigo sky. 'Then there is nothing more to say,' he uttered in a voice that sounded like an echo from a time long gone. 'We have prepared for the darkness and the fates have placed the standard of our battle in the hands of a child. She alone has the power.'

Xandu made a sound that showed he wasn't entirely in agreement with what Arthur had said. 'If that is the case I suggest we all return home and do what we can to ready ourselves,' he stated dryly.

Arthur nodded and the merman slithered off the rock and, using his powerful arms, hauled himself across the sand and through the wall of water, whereupon he and the other merfolk swam away in the blink of an eye.

Old Oaky stood up heavily and with a polite nod to Arthur and Jim, spread his slightly tattered wings from beneath his cape and took to the sky to join the golden band of light high above. In a matter of seconds the magical circle broke into uncountable pieces and each one zipped away into the night.

Without the brilliant glow of the faeries the gathering place was suddenly very cold and dark. People began heading along the vast tunnel leading back to the land.

Jim gazed down at his feet as he shuffled towards the beach trying to figure out how he could bring himself to break the news to his great-niece, who, he guessed, never thought of herself as anything but an ordinary girl, never dreamt that the destiny of this isle, perhaps the world, was in her hands.

Chapter 2

Welcome to Jersey

The small jet plane descended from the cloudy grey sky and landed with a gentle bump on the tarmac of Jersey Airport's runway. At her window seat, Jessica Kent peered up from the article in the magazine she was reading and gazed unenthusiastically at the island on which she and her father would be staying for the next two weeks. The sky was as grey as when they left Gatwick an hour ago and she couldn't imagine that any place that only took that long to fly to had anything of interest for a teenager from South London.

'Jersey's boring!' she said decidedly as she went back to her article. In the seat beside her, her father Martin sighed and placed the bookmark in the page he was reading.

'Well done, Jess! You lived with it for all of two seconds,' he muttered, getting to his feet and pulling open the luggage compartment.

Jessica stood up and crossed her arms. 'I know it is,' she stated in the voice that announced, as her father was over twenty-five, he knew nothing about anything. 'All that comes from Jersey is cows, potatoes and that cruddy old detective series that used to be on. There'll be nothing for me to do.'

Her father ignored her and threw her denim shoulder bag in her direction. Jessica caught it with a grunt and pulled it on.

'Stacy's going to Ibiza. Her family's got a villa, she said I could come. Why did you drag me to this crummy place anyway? And her mum let her have her belly button pierced,' she whined as they pushed their way down the aisle.

Martin gave his daughter a stern look. 'Jessica, as I told you before, we are very lucky your great uncle invited us to stay

14

with him. I can't afford to take you on holiday until I sell my book to a publisher. I'm not sending you to a foreign country with people I hardly know, especially when they allow their children to make holes in themselves willy-nilly!'

Jessica let out a long drawn-out sigh as they shuffled to the front of the plane. The letter had arrived two months ago. Until then Jessica hadn't even been aware she had a Great Uncle Jim. As far as she knew her only family was her father. She knew her mother had died giving birth to her and that she had come from the Channel Islands. Her father had met her mother when he had been on holiday there in the early eighties. He had been (still was) an out-of-work writer looking for inspiration. They had married and moved to London a short time later. Apart from that her early years were a mystery to her. She sometimes asked her father what her mother had been like but he was always unwilling to divulge any details. There was no doubt, however, in Jessica's mind that he must have loved her a great deal as their house was full of photographs of the attractive young woman whose dark brown, almost black, eyes were so like Jessica's own. She wished that she had more information about the woman who had given life to her, apart from the photographs and the fact she came from this place. She felt so lost at times. Despite the fact most of her friends' parents were separated, they at least knew who their families were. Maybe, she thought, this Uncle Jim could tell her something about her mother. She hoped so; at least it would stop this holiday being a complete wash-out.

The two of them stepped out of the plane and descended the steep flight of stairs that led down to the runway.

'What kind of place, 'Jessica wondered, 'had an airport where you had to walk across the runway?' It wasn't a good sign. A pale, watery sun was shining from behind the grey clouds, trying desperately to warm the bitterly cold wind that blew around them. The breeze caught Jessica's shoulder length, bushy, light brown hair and she pushed a few wayward strands out of her face. She hated her hair, in fact she hated the way she looked altogether. Her father said she was pretty but that didn't count as he was biased. She knew that her eyes and hair were nondescript, that no matter how much she spent on creams and potions the rash of acne still dotted her chin. If only she had

15

long blonde locks and brilliant blue eyes like Hannah Turner. All the boys fancied her and, Jessica thought crossing her arms self-consciously across her chest, she didn't have to stuff her bra!

They entered the terminal building through a sliding glass door and followed the signs for 'Baggage Reclaim'. The airport was tiny compared to Gatwick. The long corridor snaked ahead of them, echoing with the noise of trolleys being pushed and suitcases being loaded on to them. The walls were dotted with large illuminated posters of Jersey's leading attractions. On one a naked woman knelt smothered by golden chains under the words, 'Jersey Gold'; from another the grinning face of the actor John Nettles stared out beside the words, 'Come and Experience Jersey's Living Legend!'. Jessica smirked, as she wondered just how old he must be to be called a 'legend' and just what it meant to *experience* him.

Martin and Jessica soon found themselves in a larger area where three or four carousels revolved aimlessly, laden with bags and suitcases of every description. People were milling around them, struggling to grab their possessions before they once again disappeared behind the flapping black plastic curtains. Martin found an empty trolley and he and his daughter pushed their way to Carousel One where their flight's luggage was being unloaded.

'So who is this Uncle Jim, anyway?' asked Jessica as she spotted her case and hauled it off the moving belt on to the trolley.

Her father's brow creased. 'If I'm honest with you Jess, I don't have that much of a memory of him. He was your grandmother's younger brother. Emma lived with him when her mother died. An odd job man, if I remember correctly. Always doing this and that for people. One week a painter, the next doing someone's garden, the next helping the farmer calve.'

He stopped to collect his case from the belt while Jessica surveyed the sea of holidaymakers wondering which was her long-lost uncle. Suddenly she spotted a chubby, elderly man in a ragged, navy jumper that looked as if he had knitted it himself. He was waving at them frantically and called, 'Hey, Martin, over here!'

Jessica tapped her father on his shoulder and pointed to the man who was now pushing his way through the crowd. 'Dad, is that him?' she asked.

Her father regarded the man making his way towards them. 'Yep,' he sighed. 'That's your great uncle Jim, all right!'

The man had now squeezed his way through the throng and was standing next to them. He was a stocky figure, almost as wide as he was tall. Apart from the jumper, he had on a faded pair of baggy jeans, which his enormous stomach hung over the belt of, and some very dirty, very battered work boots. His eyes were dark and twinkled merrily under bushy grey brows. What remained of his hair was wild, grey and frizzy and his face was a craggy map of wrinkles and rough stubble. He smiled warmly at Jessica and her father and gripped her father's hand in a firm handshake.

'Martin, good to see you after all this time.'

He had the oddest accent Jessica had ever heard. His voice was soft and slightly lilting as if he were French but at the same time had the brisk pronunciation of someone who came from South Africa. Jess liked it.

Martin gave Jim an oddly strained smile as he let go of his hand. 'You too, Jim. I can't thank you enough for allowing Jess and me to stay with you. I don't think our budget would have stretched to a holiday this year if it hadn't been for your kind offer. I trust we're not being too much of a hindrance?'

The old man waved his hand dismissively. 'Not at all! I'm glad of the company. I have friends of course, but at the end of the day I'm all alone in that big old house. And,' he added turning his twinkling gaze to Jessica, 'I wouldn't miss the chance to meet my great-niece for the world. The last time I saw you was just after you were born. You *have* grown a lot since then, haven't you? How old are you again?'

'Fourteen,' said Jessica, wanting to make it absolutely clear that she wasn't a child. 'Fifteen in October.'

Jim smiled and looked back to Martin. 'Fourteen years,' he breathed. 'Time goes by so fast. Isn't she the image of her mother too? Almost identical to the way she looked at that age.'

A sudden, very uncomfortable air fell on the group that Jessica wasn't quite able to understand. Jim was gazing at her father as if he expected him to make a comment but Martin said nothing. It only lasted for a moment but there was definitely

17

something between the two men that neither was willing to disclose. Jim sighed and then the mood was warm once more.

Jim took the trolley and began to wheel it towards the exit. Martin and Jessica followed. 'My house is in St Ouen's; it's not that far,' he called to them as they left the airport and made their way through the rows of cars. 'It's really too big for me now but my family has lived there so long I don't have the heart to sell it.'

The trio came to a halt beside a rather grubby white truck. Both Jessica and Martin stared at it in disbelief. The paintwork, the windows, the wheels, everything was smeared with dried mud, and lying in the back was a large collection of fishing equipment. Jim swung the two cases into the back and yanked open the driver's door.

'I shan't bother to strap that lot down,' he said, nodding to the cases. 'This old wreck doesn't go fast enough for them to come out.'

He hauled his robust frame in behind the wheel as Martin and Jessica cautiously approached the passenger side. Tentatively, Martin pulled open the door and being careful not to touch too much of the vehicle, climbed aboard. Jessica followed him unwillingly. Inside, the cab was as much of a mess as the exterior. The seats were of cracked black plastic and despite the coldness of the wind outside, were sticky and hot. The floor was littered with old newspapers and sweet wrappers and the dashboard covered with odd scribbled notes and adorned with an old margarine tub. From the rear view mirror hung a strange wooden doll with black bead eyes and green hair. But the most overpowering thing about the cab was the vile smell! The disgusting odour was a mixture of manure and dead fish. Jessica covered her nose and opened the window.

'Ew, what is that smell?' she said as Jim started the engine with an almighty judder.

'I'd been doing a bit of fishing this morning,' he explained as they pulled out of their parking place, 'and I had to fertilize Mrs MacDonald's garden for her!'

Jessica shuddered and kept her hand to her nose.

The ancient truck chugged along the narrow twisting roads of Jersey, throwing its passengers about every time Jim hit the slightest bump. Jessica gazed out of the window and marvelled at the beautiful scenery. Beyond the pinkish stone walls that ran parallel to the road, lush green fields spread out like a multi-coloured patchwork to the sapphire sea beyond. Now and then they passed picturesque houses of the same pink brick with neat gardens of hydrangeas and tall, orange flowers, the like of which she had never seen on the mainland.

'You like fishing?' asked Jim as they turned down yet another avenue.

Jessica shrugged. 'Never been,' she said. 'I doubt you're allowed to in Hyde Park – not without a whopping great permit anyway!'

The old man laughed. 'I'll take you and your dad. Your mum loved fishing when she was a girl. I'd take her out in my rowing boat on the sea and we would sit there till it got too dark to see. A right tomboy was your mum – fishing, climbing trees, playing on the cliffs. Quite the thrill seeker!'

Jessica looked away from the window and regarded the old man. 'Will you tell me about her?' she asked directly. 'You know, what she was like. The places she used to go. Stuff like that.'

She noticed her father shift uncomfortably in his seat but ignored him. It was her right to know who her mother was, after all, and if he wouldn't tell her maybe Uncle Jim would.

Jim smiled broadly. 'Of course I will. I'll tell you anything you want. It's good you're interested in your heritage.'

Martin looked decidedly ill and Jessica wondered whether it was the smell of the fish or something else. Whatever it was Jim saw it too and said, 'But not today, we'll talk about her later.'

The cab fell silent but for the rumble of the engine once again and Jessica returned to gazing out the window. They passed a field of golden-coloured Jersey cows with large liquid brown eyes and several more large house before the road turned onto a long straight boulevard bordered on one side by shrub land stretching out to the pale sand of what looked like an un-welcomingly cold beach.

'Not far now,' grunted Jim.

Sure enough, after just a few minutes trundling up the road a moderately sized house encircled by a wall of that same pink stone loomed into view. The van pulled into the gravelled courtyard and Jessica gazed up at the building. The ruddy stonework was overgrown in lush green ivy and four windows with pristine white painted frames stared out like friendly eyes. The front door was of solid oak with a shiny black knocker and letterbox and screwed to the wall was an iron sign in scrolled letters. Jessica read it out loud.

'Maison de l'hache?' she said quizzically. 'I thought they spoke English here?'

Jim put on the handbrake and switched off the engine. 'We do now but there are a lot of French influences here in Jersey, especially place names. This house is called House of The Axe. Our family have lived here for generations.'

He opened the cab door and got out. Jessica and Martin, eager to get back into the fresh air, did the same. Jim fetched the luggage from the back of the truck and the three of them approached the large front door. Resting the bags for a moment, Jim rummaged in his pocket searching for the key. Jessica wondered if the inside of Jim's house was as untidy as his van. The old man unlocked the door and booting it open with his foot, carried the suitcases inside, nodding for Jessica and her father to follow.

Once inside, Jessica was pleasantly surprised to find herself in a decidedly neat, if old-fashioned, passageway. The walls were slightly uneven and painted a shade of creamy white with dark beams of wood visible, running through the pale plaster. Here and there were hung idyllic rural paintings of cows, farms and seascapes. Against the wall to the right of them was a well-polished narrow chestnut table on which was placed an expensive-looking crystal vase containing five or six pink and white lilies. At the end of the corridor were two heavy wooden doors, one on either wall and a craggy old staircase that led to the first floor. It was all quite different from Jessica's South London semi. Sidling between Jess and her father, Jim lugged the cases down the corridor which, with his less than svelte frame, seemed a near impossible task.

'I'll take these upstairs and then while you're getting unpacked I'll see if I can rustle you up some dinner,' muttered Jim as Martin and Jess followed him up the ancient stairs which creaked and groaned with every step they took.

The upstairs landing was wider than the hallway from where they had come and had a ceiling of wooden beams that slanted upwards into the roof. It was lit by a single window at the end of the landing, adorned with frilly lace curtains. There were four doors leading off the landing, all of that same heavy wood.

'Mine's the nearest,' said Jim nodding to the door closest to them on the right. 'Across the hall there's the bathroom. Martin, you're in the far left one and that one's yours, Jessica.' He carried the bags across to the far right hand door before adding, 'It used to be your mother's room.'

A cold feeling ran up Jessica's spine but she tried to ignore it. Jim opened the door and he and Jessica went inside.

The bedroom was large, though slightly too femininely decorated for Jessica's tastes. The flowery wallpaper was pink and green to complement the salmon-coloured carpet. There were two chests of drawers, a wardrobe with a fine, mirrored door, a prettily carved dressing table and a bed, all in the same matching antique pine. The bed had been made with powder pink sheets and a soft green quilt and pillows. Jim placed the suitcase on the bed and glanced at Jessica who was staring around.

'Yeah, no doubt about it,' he said staring out of the window. 'Best room in the house, this is.'

Jess frowned slightly. 'Then why don't you sleep here if you have the place all to yourself?' she asked.

A small smile played on the old man's lips. 'Not my place,' he said with almost a chuckle. 'It was your mother's room; now it is yours.'

Once again Jessica felt that icy prickling run up her spine. In the short time she had known her great uncle he seemed a pleasant and jovial chap but there was something about the way he spoke about her mother that unnerved her. It was almost as if he thought she had come here to take her place.

The old man turned to go, saying, 'I'll leave you to unpack,' and Jessica found herself alone in the empty room, an odd gnawing feeling in her stomach. She had come to Jersey to find out who her mother was but now she was here, in the room where she had slept, in the house she grew up in, it was as if a part of Jessica that up until now had been just beyond the edge of her imagination was suddenly becoming very real and solid. Her mother had been a living, breathing person, not just a picture in a frame or the few scraps of information her father had given her. This place seemed to have soaked up her essence,

21

drawing Jessica to it, to fill in the missing parts of her life. It was an exciting prospect but also frightening. She was stepping into the unknown.

Sighing deeply, Jessica unfastened the straps that secured her suitcase and undid the lid. There, on top of the slightly crumpled clothes was the object she had packed last thing that morning: the framed photograph of her mother. Jessica took it out and cupping it in her hands gazed down into the face of the young woman whose life she hoped to uncover. It was Jessica's favourite photograph, taken ironically on the rocky beach not far from here. It showed a beautiful healthy girl in her mid-twenties, with warm, brown, lively eyes and thick shoulder-length dark hair. She was perched, relaxed and laughing, on a rock, the wind tugging at her mane. As in most pictures that Jessica had seen of her she had on a faded pair of jeans and in this one, a loose red shirt. Jessica ran her finger over the glass and felt a hard lump come to her throat. She wondered, as she had a million times before, what her voice had been like, how she had sounded when she laughed? Did she hate cabbage as much as Jessica did? Was she able to touch her nose with the tip of her tongue? Tiny things that were insignificant to everyone else but that meant the world to Jess. Most of all Jessica wondered whether, in the short time between giving birth to her and dying, she had even held her in her arms and told Jessica she loved her. She hoped she had; it helped her to think that just for the briefest of moments she had felt a mother's love.

Jessica placed the photograph on the chest of drawers beside the bed and whispered to it, 'I'll find out who you were Mum. I promise.' Then, wiping her damp eyes with the back of her hand, she proceeded to unpack her clothes into the drawers and wardrobe. By the time she had finished Jessica was feeling slightly happier and unsure what to do next, climbed onto the bed and peered out of the window.

Below her, at the back of the house, she could see Jim's neat garden. There was a green lawn edged with borders of large blue and pink hydrangeas and long stems of agapanthus with balls of pale pastel flowers spurting from the top of each one. Poking through the masses of green and blue were statuesque cannas with their sharp rusty brown foliage and bright orange petals. To the back of the garden, up against the stone wall, grew a medium-sized willow tree, its silver-green leaves rustling in the wind and making shadows on the grass in the late afternoon sun. In the far left corner, almost hidden behind a mass of hydrangea blossoms, Jessica could just make out a small pond surrounded by rocks and greenery.

She was just wondering whether to go downstairs and have a better look at the garden when there was a sharp rap on the door and her father called out, 'Can I come in?'

Jessica climbed down from her kneeling position and went to answer the door. Martin stepped inside and glanced around as his daughter had done before him.

'Some things never change,' he murmured, running a hand across the dressing table. 'This furniture was here when I stayed here. What? Sixteen years ago. In my room you can still see the stain on the carpet where I spilt my tea on my first morning.'

He laughed quietly but there was a sadness in his eyes. Jessica sat on the bed and regarded her father thoughtfully. It was obvious he wanted to say something to her but seemed unable to find the words.

Finally he asked, 'What do you think of Jim?'

Jess sighed deeply and hugged her knee to her chest. It took her a few seconds to answer.

'Different,' she said bluntly. 'I don't know. Maybe people on Jersey are slightly stranger than people in London.'

Martin crossed the room and sat down beside his daughter but didn't look at her. Instead he fixed his eyes on the photograph of Emma.

'Not strange Jess,' he muttered, 'just special. Theirs is a life more in touch with the land and sea. Their spirits are free.'

The room fell silent for a moment. Jessica looked at her father who seemed to be unaware of her, lost, perhaps, in a world where the woman he loved was still alive.

Then, as if suddenly brought out of a trance, he turned to her and said, 'Promise me something, Jess. Promise you won't go around asking Jim too many questions about your mum.'

Jessica blinked with shock. She knew it hurt her father deeply to speak of his late wife but she never thought he would want to stop her finding out who she was.

'Why Dad? I honestly don't think Jim minds. He seems almost

23

grateful that I want to talk about her. How about if I do it when you're not around; then you won't get upset.'

Martin shook his head and clasped his hands in front of him. 'You don't understand,' he said almost angrily. 'There are things ... things that are in the past ... that we can never reach again. And sometimes,' he paused and stood up to gaze out of the window, 'sometimes it's better that way.'

Jessica felt puzzled and a little cross with her father. She loved him but there were times, like this, when she knew that he was keeping a vital part of who she was from her.

'What is it about Mum that you're frightened of me finding out? Why do you never answer my questions? She was *my* mother. I have a right to know.'

Still Martin did not meet her gaze. He had one hand on the bedstead, gripping it so tightly Jessica could see his knuckles turning white.

'It would do you no good to ask things that might lead you to places you couldn't handle. One day, when you're old enough, you will realize that the past is gone and we can gain nothing from it but experience – not love, not comfort, just the lesson we are taught.'

Jessica looked at her father, then back to the pale green bed cover. She wasn't at all sure it was possible for her to make that promise, not when she had a golden opportunity to find out where she came from. What could be so awful in her family's past that discovering it would hurt as much as her father said? Some terrible crime? A dark secret concerning her mother's identity? An almost twisted fascination bubbled inside her, an unhealthy combination of trepidation and excitement that there was something here, more than just a life ended before its time – a reason for her to dig. But for now, if she was going to find out anything it was vital she kept her plans from her father.

'I promise,' she said quietly so that the guilt in her voice could not be heard.

Martin faced her and forced a smile. 'You're a good girl,' he said softly. 'You are what you made yourself, not who I or your mum was. Make your own choices in this life. Never go by what people say you are. Always remember that.'

With this he turned and, without waiting for her to reply, left the room. Jessica sat for a moment, contemplating what had just been said. She didn't for a second intend obeying her father, not out of stubbornness but simply because the quest to find out about her mother was set so resolutely in her mind it was impossible to shift it. She'd waited fourteen years for this opportunity and she was not going to give it up. An idea struck her. She remembered something she had half heard in an English lesson which at the time had seemed very boring and utterly pointless, something that Mrs Rennals had called 'Brainstorming'. Quickly, Jessica opened one of the drawers in the dresser and pulled out her diary. She then climbed back onto the bed and, sitting cross-legged, turned to the back page which was reserved for 'Notes' and at present was blank. Maybe, she thought sucking the end of her pen, if she wrote down everything she knew about her mother and added to it what information she could obtain from Jim throughout the holiday, by the end of the fortnight she would have a kind of written picture of who her mother was. Removing the lid from her pen and smoothing out the white paper, Jessica printed 'Emma Hellily' in large black letters directly in the centre of the page. Then under it in slightly smaller writing: 'Born 21.4.63, died 15.9.86'. She paused for a second, unsure what to write next, then added: 'Married Martin Kent 25.3.84 and moved from St Ouens, Jersey to Southwark, London'. She was just about to add her own date of birth when it hit her that it was the same as the date of her mother's death. Not wanting to dwell on this, she simply scrawled, 'One daughter, Jessica'.

That was it, Jess thought – well, all she knew for sure. She gazed at the still fairly blank page and tapped her pen on her teeth. There were things she had sort of worked out for herself, which she guessed she should add. 'Always wore jeans' and 'Lived with uncle Jim' were added to the page and, remembering the conversation she had had in the van earlier that day, she wrote, 'Liked fishing, climbing, walking'. She was just searching her brain for something else to write when a strongly accented voice echoed up the stairs. 'Dinner's ready.'

Tucking the diary under a pile of T-shirts in her drawer and wondering when she would get the opportunity to question Jim without her father knowing, Jessica headed downstairs for dinner. The house being as compact as it was, it didn't take her long to discover that the door on the left downstairs was the kitchen-cum-dining room and the one on the right was the living room.

The kitchen was an odd mix of Victorian furniture, well-worn surfaces and modern appliances. Almost the whole of one wall was a huge unused brick fireplace which now housed a cooker and cupboards. Above, on the chimney breast, hung a collection of brass pans and horse brasses. Along the opposite wall was what looked like a fairly new counter top that seemed to have been fitted onto the original wooden cupboards. Set into the worktops was a huge old-fashioned china sink. The floor was blood-red terracotta tiles and right in the centre of the room was a large farmhouse pine table and chairs. The room was filled with the delicious aroma of freshly cooked plaice which made Jessica realize she hadn't eaten since lunch and was now very hungry indeed. Jim stood in front of the oven, a slightly stained apron stretched across his bulging stomach, dishing breaded fillets onto three plates. At the table sat Martin, idly flicking through the *Jersey Evening Post*. Jessica entered and took the empty seat beside her father.

'Unpacked, have we?' said Jim cheerily, taking off his apron and carrying the three plates across to the table.

Jess nodded and regarded the meal in front of her.

Jim took up his knife and fork and nudged her. 'That's good grub, that is. A proper Jersey meal. Fresh fish, boiled Jersey Royals with lots of black pepper and butter and home grown peas. Eat up while it's hot.' He stabbed a large potato and shovelled it whole into his mouth.

Jessica cut into the crisp, golden breadcrumbs of her fillet to reveal flaky white flesh. Tasting it she discovered that this had to be the most delicious fish in the world; it melted in her mouth. The three of them were silent for a good few minutes, eating hungrily.

Eventually, Jim wiped some butter from his lips and said, 'So, Jessica, I bet you didn't know you even had a great uncle!'

Jess swallowed a soft earthy lump of potato. 'Dad told me Mum came from Jersey,' she said, being careful not to seem as interested as she really was in front of her father. 'Never said I had any other relations over here though.'

Jim's eyes flitted to Martin for a second, conveying a look of hurt and anger. Jessica had become quite used to the fact that

26

there was no love lost between the two men, though she guessed both would deny it adamantly. She wondered what it was that drove this wedge between them.

'Your family has lived on Jersey ... well, since records began,' Jim continued, waving his fork. 'Yes, right back over a thousand years ago.'

Jessica raised her eyebrows. 'Wow, it must be one of the oldest families on the island,' she gasped. 'You would've thought in all that time they would've moved – well, Mum did. But, still, it's pretty impressive.'

Jim nodded as he chewed a lump of fish and looked thoughtful. His shiny black eyes had come to rest once again on Martin with that same interrogatory stare. 'People in our family did visit the mainland,' he said softly. 'It's not like we haven't travelled, it's just Hellilys always return to Jersey. The island is in their blood. Why, even your mother came back just before you were born. It was the last time I saw her. I do miss having family around. That's why I was so happy to hear you were coming.'

Jim was cut short by Martin coughing so loudly that Jessica practically jumped out of her seat. She glanced at her father who, much to her surprise, looked positively livid. His normally pale cheeks were scarlet and he was glaring at Jim with fury.

A fine holiday this was going to be, Jessica thought to herself. Martin swallowed deeply and tried to cool his anger.

Jim glanced at Jessica and shook his head. 'Your father doesn't like talking about Emma; it's upsetting for him. Let's change the subject. Do you like school?'

The remaining time at the dinner table was spent making idle chit-chat about Jessica's school, Jim's garden and the trouble Martin was having with his editor, none of which held much interest for Jessica, especially when the mystery and tension surrounding her mother was so tantalizing. It seemed as if the more difficult it was for Jim and her father to discuss, the greater Jess's fascination grew. However, as long as Martin was present the matter seemed strictly taboo. Jessica was itching to get Jim on his own so she could ask him the hundreds of questions that were whizzing through her brain but she knew that within the confines of the small house this was too dangerous. She would have to wait.

The evening dragged on and with dinner over and the pleasant violet twilight creeping over the sky the three of them retired into Jim's cosy sitting room. The room was warm and pleasant with a pair of comfy armchairs, a slightly worn sofa and walls filled with dozens of old black and white photographs. Jim lit a fire in the brick grate and the two men chatted about this and that (mainly the various jobs Jim did for people around the island) while Jessica stared at the photographs, getting increasingly bored. Her belly was full and this, combined with the warm room and the dull conversation, contributed to a gradual drowsiness. By nine o'clock Jim and Martin were decidedly more chummy than they had been for the most of the day – no doubt helped by the bottle of port that had appeared after dinner. As Jim began yet another story about fishing, Jessica decided to go to bed.

Despite the events of the day and her fascination with what had happened to her mother being fresh in her mind sleep came so swiftly Jessica didn't even have time to think about what had gone before. Perhaps if Fate had allowed her to slumber for the remainder of the night things would have turned out very differently. But Fate has a way of guiding people where they need to go and, in the hazy spirit world that Jessica knew nothing about, Fate had placed her on a very important and dangerous road indeed.

At a quarter to eleven, Jessica woke up. She wondered for a moment what had roused her before realizing that it had been the voices coming from downstairs – angry, arguing voices that were muffled by the heavy wooden door of her bedroom. Curious as to the cause the argument and aware that it could very well be about her mother, Jessica slipped out of bed and cautiously crept into the hallway. The landing was almost pitch black apart from the light that came from the open living room door downstairs. Jessica could hear Jim and her father arguing as clearly as if they were standing before her. She leant against the wall and held her breath so as to catch each word.

'This is ridiculous! I can't believe I'm even hearing it!' Her father was practically shouting, his voice filled with incredulity. 'No, no! I refuse to start this idiotic practice again.'

Now Jim, sounding calmer but firm. 'Why did you think I called you? Martin, believe me, I am as unwilling to bring Jess into this as you are, but you don't know the way of these things. We don't have a choice.'

Jessica's breath caught in her throat. What on Earth was happening? What ulterior motive could Jim have for inviting them to this place?

Her father's voice was low and menacing. 'You're a sick, sick man, Jim Hellily. This is the twenty-first century, for God's sake. Sane people don't believe in magic and omens. I'm not allowing my only child to be dragged into some outdated pagan ritual that is at best ridiculous and at worst...' He stopped.

Jessica stood silent and confused in the near darkness not wanting to know what would be said next but unable to stop herself listening.

'At worst what, Martin? 'Jim was almost whispering now so Jessica strained her ears to hear. 'Go on. At worst meet the same fate as her mother. That's what you were going to say wasn't it? For someone who thinks the old ways are a lot of mumbo-jumbo you seem pretty afraid.'

There was another tense pause and when Jim spoke again it was with such force and certainty Jessica jumped.

'Let's face facts, Martin. You saw what happened the night Emma died. You know as well as I do this is far from a load of rubbish. That's why you're so defensive. You're too scared of what might happen if you let Jessica face her destiny. But, believe me, whatever you can imagine happening if Jessica stays here is nothing compared to the awful things that will happen if she leaves.'

Jessica heard the scraping of a chair as someone stood up.

'I'm not listening to any more of this!' growled Martin.

He left the room and Jessica had just enough time to slip back inside her bedroom before he turned to climbed the stairs. Inside Jessica squeezed her eyes shut to stop the tears of fear from flowing. She felt frightened and alone and very confused about what she had just heard. She came here looking for her mother but now she wasn't completely sure she wanted to know how she had died. Was she to follow her in some awful pattern? What was this terrible secret Jim and her father shared? Jessica wished she was back home. Back in London where everything was safe and familiar. She didn't understand about pagans and magic, only from the fairytales her father had told her as a child. But this was something very different and dangerous. Rushing across the room she dragged her suitcase from under the bed. They had to leave Jersey – tomorrow if possible. Get away from Jim and this strange world.

It was then that something out of the bedroom window made Jess stop in her panic, something so unusual and enchanting that she forgot about escaping and climbed onto the bed for a better look. In the furthest corner of the garden beside the pond, the hydrangea bush appeared to be on fire. Not with bright orange flames as if it had been torched, but with a gentle silver-white glow that pulsed through the leaves as if emulating from the heart of the plant itself. The light was so magnificent and beautiful that just watching it filled Jessica with a joy and happiness she had never known before. Without the slightest twinge of fear Jessica open the window and on the soft night breeze heard the sweet music that filled the garden. The sound was unlike anything man could play. A thousand voices rang out like chiming bells, each one with its individual melody yet all weaving together in perfect harmony. Totally calm and relaxed now, Jessica heard the words of the song as if they were already in her mind.

> *Your fate is set, your path is laid,*
> *Open your heart, don't be afraid,*
> *For back to us you've come at last,*
> *From blood to blood; the duty's passed.*
> *Soon shall come your greatest test;*
> *Take not your flight, your life is blessed,*
> *For of your forebears, take no shame;*
> *Instead Their wisdom, task and name.*
> *Have faith in friends, you're not alone,*
> *Throughout this Isle; your name is known;*
> *Those who dwell within the sea*
> *Have pledged to help and succour thee*
> *And We, of tree and bush and flower*
> *Will aid you now with all our power.*
> *The Demon if you don't defeat*
> *For all our Folks the future's bleak;*
> *So face the evil, take your place*
> *You alone can meet Its face.*

The song ended there but still the mystical voices drifted with wordless melodies through Jessica's head. She felt dizzy but very peaceful. She no longer wished to leave Jersey. She was still aware of the danger Jim's and her father's words had carried but it had been softened by the beautiful song. It was as if the music was an old friend returning from a long journey. For perhaps the first time since she arrived, Jersey felt like home. Jessica quietly settled down in the soft bed and almost immediately fell asleep.

In the garden, behind the thick leaves of the hydrangea bush, Rosehip finished chanting her spell and opened her eyes. She wasn't used to using her faerie magic so powerfully and felt quite exhausted. She doubted Old Oaky or any of the other elders would approve of Jessica's first knowledge of the magic world; it would have been better if Jim had told her face to face. For the present a simple faerie music would do to soothe her fears. Jessica would not leave the island now. Feeling more than slightly pleased with her efforts, Rosehip spread her wings and flew into the night.

Chapter 3

A Visit to St Helier

When Jessica awoke the next morning it was to the warm sunlight pouring through the open window and the tantalizing smell of bacon wafting up from the kitchen. She lay still for a moment trying to come round. She had the feeling something had happened that was very important but whenever she tried to think about what it was ridiculous notions came into her head: Jim and her father rowing about paganism? A glowing bush singing in the garden? It was so stupid Jessica had to laugh. 'Only dreams,' she said, getting out of bed, 'only dreams.'

The delicious smell of breakfast was too much for her to resist. Jessica dressed and hurried downstairs. A place was already set for her at the table and both Martin and Jim smiled warmly as she entered.

'Good morning!' cheered her great uncle as she sat down. 'Sleep well, did ya?' He pushed two plump sausages and a rasher of bacon onto her plate.

'Kinda,' she said with a shrug as Jim took his place at the table. 'Kept having the weirdest dreams though.'

Martin looked at her and smiled. 'Must be the sea air,' he added, pouring himself a cup of coffee. 'What kind of dreams?'

Jessica laughed and cut into her sausage. 'Really strange – and they seemed so real. First I dreamed you and Uncle Jim had a big fight about me being magical. Then I thought that the hydrangea bush I can see out my window was glowing silver and singing to me.'

She looked to Jim, almost expecting him to say it was true but he just laughed.

'Dreams are funny things,' he said dismissively.

Jessica took a bite of bacon and chewed it thoughtfully. She wondered if any of this was connected with her mother and made a mental note to ask Jim about her today.

'What are we doing today?' she inquired.

Jim dunked a wedge of fried bread into the runny yellow yoke of his egg.

'I got to do some shopping for Mrs Noir so we're heading into St Helier, the main town. I take it you like shopping?'

Jessica nodded and shovelled another piece of sausage into her mouth. Jim glanced across the table to Martin. 'Are you coming?' he asked.

Jessica's father shook his head. 'I have work to do on an article. You go ahead.'

Jim smiled at Jessica, 'Looks like it's just going to be the two of us,' he said, his black eyes twinkling.

After breakfast, Jessica helped wash up while Jim loaded the truck. Then, having put the crockery away, she wandered into the garden on the pretext of enjoying the early morning sun. She wanted to examine the hydrangea bush that had featured in her dream. She discovered, to her disappointment, that the plant was green and healthy, without a scorch mark in sight.

Around ten-thirty, having said goodbye to Martin, Jessica climbed into the cab of Jim's truck and they were off to Jersey's main town. Although St Helier lay on the other side of the island, it wasn't a long journey and Jessica soon found that instead of the rambling lanes they had travelled along the day before, they were trundling along a straight dual carriageway that ran parallel to the deep, broad bay of St Helier in which floated several small sailing boats. On a rocky outcrop stood a proud castle.

'What's that?' she asked, pointing to the fortress.

'Elizabeth Castle,' Jim replied knowingly. 'Built by Sir Walter Raleigh and named after Queen Elizabeth I of England.'

'Oh,' said Jessica indifferently. History was not her favourite topic. On the other side of the road stood row upon row of expensive looking flats, interspersed now and again with smart hotels and wine bars.

'Yuppies!' sniffed Jim as they past. 'There used to be nice little guest-houses all the way along here. That was before people started going abroad on holiday. Nearly all Jersey's hotels have been bought up and turned into flats now.'

'Did you prefer it when there were more tourists?' asked Jessica.

Jim pulled a face and shrugged.

'Better the devil you know,' he sighed. 'Can't say I *liked* the tourists but at least we had the winter without them. I always preferred the company of true islanders to that of people born on the mainland. We look at things differently.'

Jessica looked at Jim and felt slightly hurt. 'So, you don't like me?' she asked crossing her arms.

Jim chuckled and placed a spade-like hand on her shoulder. ''Course I like *you*,' he laughed. 'You're special. You have Jersey blood in you.'

They carried on along the carriageway a little further before Jim turned off down a narrow road lined with close packed houses. They parked on one side of the road and Jim led Jessica through a maze of winding streets to the main precinct. The main street of St Helier was broad and cobbled with silver-grey stones. Tall shops lined each side and the whole area was pedestrianized. To Jessica's relief, most of the shops were branches of those in London, apart from a number of jewellers and perfumeries. The street was packed with shoppers; somewhere in the distance Jess could hear the faint strum of a busker playing a guitar.

'Right,' said Jim, 'I don't expect you want to hang round with an old codger like me, so why don't I leave you to explore while I do Mrs Noir's shopping. If you keep to this road there's plenty of shops and you shouldn't get lost. I'll meet you back here around one-ish.'

He was just about to turn away when a voice rang out above the hubbub of the crowd that made both Jim and Jessica turn around. A tall boy of about seventeen with untidy, dark hair and a slightly hooked nose was pushing his way through the crowd calling Jim's name. Spotting him, the old man waved back cheerily and called out, 'Hello Jake!'

The boy reached them and smiled warmly. Jessica looked up at the lad. He was quite different from the boys she went to school with. Jake was getting on to be six feet tall and was so gangly and thin it looked as if he had been stretched. His hair looked as if it hadn't been brushed for days and his friendly, azure eyes seemed full of life.

'Watchya, Jim! How are you?' He had the same unusual accent as Jim, so Jessica guessed he must be one of the 'real Jersey people' Jim talked about.

Jim smiled and nodded. 'Fine, Jake lad, fine. Your folks okay?'

Jake buried his hands in the pockets of his rather baggy jeans. 'Dad's gone to the mainland to see about selling some cattle,' he said. 'Grandpa sends his regards to you.'

Jim raised his hand. 'Thanks lad,' he said. 'By the way, this is Jessica, my great niece.'

A glimmer of recognition ignited in Jake's eyes as he turned to Jessica. Her stomach tightened. Did Jake fancy her? He was definitely not her type. Not only was he not the handsomest boy she had ever met but there was a peculiar odour about him reminiscent of Jim's lorry.

'Jake LeBlanc,' he said, sticking out a grubby-nailed hand. 'Pleased to meet you.'

Jess stared at the boy's dirty hand and decided not to take it. 'Jessica Kent,' she muttered, forcing a smile.

Jake grinned at her as if she'd introduced herself as some sort of celebrity. 'Oh, I know who you are,' he stated. 'Jim's told everyone about you. You are Emma's daughter after all!'

Jessica frowned slightly. What an odd thing for someone to say! She caught Jim looking meaningfully at him and a fleeting expression of realization darted across Jake's face. What a strange bunch these Jersey people were. But then she was getting quite used to Jim's quirky mannerisms.

The old man glanced at his watch. 'Well,' he said with a sigh, 'I really must get on with Mrs Noir's shopping. Maybe Jake could show you around if he isn't too busy.'

Jake shook his head. 'I wouldn't mind at all, Mr H. With Dad away I have nothing to do until the cows need milking this evening. That's if Jessica's cool with it?'

Unsure what to say to this strange boy and not really wanting to be rude, Jessica smiled and nodded. Seeming pleased, Jim waved the two of them goodbye and headed into the throng.

Jake rubbed his hands together and sighed. 'Right,' he said. 'What d'ya want to do?'

Jessica shrugged. 'Don't really mind,' she said. 'What *do* you do in Jersey for leisure?'

Jake combed his fingers through his shaggy hair. 'We've got shops,' he said bluntly. 'Modern stuff, like what you have on the mainland; it's not all that old fashioned. And we don't have to pay tax so it's all a bit cheaper. That's why people come here, to stock up on duty-free booze and ciggies. And there's a cinema and a theatre, only they don't have much on – just plays and musicals, no bands. Or sometimes we take the cows down to the harbour and give them swimming lessons!'

Jessica's eyebrows shot up. 'What?' she gasped. 'You're joking?'

Jake threw back his head and chuckled merrily. "Course I am!' he chortled. 'I just wanted to see if you were a Bean or not.'

He turned and strolled up the High Street. Bewildered, Jess followed him, but with Jake's lanky legs and long stride she had to trot along at a fair pace to keep up.

'A what?' she asked.

Jake looked at her and raised his eyebrows. 'A Bean. Dad's a Bean, I'm a Bean but me Mum's a Donkey.'

Jessica creased her forehead. 'You're crazy,' she declared.

Jake laughed again and Jessica felt slightly cross that he seemed to think she was stupid.

'Beans are people born in Jersey, Donkeys are born in Guernsey. It's just local slang. But now I realise you're neither. You're a Grockle, you're from the mainland.'

This did not make Jessica feel the slightest bit better. She felt 'Grockle' was something slightly insulting and that Jake saw her as somewhat naïve because she came from England. She wanted to prove him wrong.

'I'm only part Grockle, or whatever you call it,' she said, staring into the window of the jewellers they were passing. 'My mum came from Jersey, remember. She was Jim's niece.'

She turned to face Jake who was giving her the most puzzled look. He leant against the shop window, a small frown creasing his forehead.

'Well, that's why you're here, isn't it?' he asked. 'Because of your mother.'

Jessica gazed at him confused. She still hadn't made up her mind whether she liked Jake or not. People on Jersey seemed to have an infuriating habit of speaking in riddles. She chewed her bottom lip and picked at the glossy black paint of the window frame. 'My mother's dead,' she said softly, hoping Jake would show a bit of sympathy. 'I never knew her; I suppose I came here to find out what she was like.'

She expected Jake to looked saddened, or even shocked, by what she had said but instead he stuck his hands in his pockets, sighed and carried on up the road with a flippant, 'I know.'

Jessica's blood boiled. Jake was far too cocky for someone who spent his days mucking out cattle. If he knew that her mother was dead he could show a little more compassion. She once again followed him up the cobbled hill.

'You could say a little more than "I know",' Jessica snapped bitterly. 'It isn't very nice. If you *do* know something about her you could tell me because I know practically nothing!'

Jake stopped for a moment and looked back at her as if he was about to say something, but shook his head. 'If that's really true,' he said in a voice that had just a hint of panic in it, 'I would start trying to find stuff out. Mind you, it'll do no good asking me, as I never even met her and it's not my place to say things.' He glanced over his shoulder as if he thought someone might be eavesdropping on their conversation. Then Jake took Jessica firmly by the arm and directed her into the doorway of a department store that bore the name 'DeGrudy'.

This guy, Jessica thought as they stood in the shade of the shop's sign, is a total nutcase.

Jake's eyes were flitting about as if he were about to divulge some matter of national security.

'Okay,' he muttered when he was sure the coast was clear. 'Okay. I'm going to tell you this and only this because I think you should know.'

Jessica rolled her eyes. 'Is this how you chat up people in the Channel Islands? Force them into doorways and give them the CIA routine?'

Jake looked exasperated. 'Look, do you want to find out about your mother or don't you?' he said through gritted teeth.

Jess sighed and decided she hadn't got anything to lose. 'Go on then, 007. What's the big secret?'

Jake took a deep breath and began. 'There are people you can trust and those you can't,' he muttered ominously. 'Folks round here aren't always what they seem.'

Jessica looked at him in disbelief. 'Really?' she said sarcastically. 'I come from East London and you can trust everyone from there! I'd better be careful those nasty old Beans don't try and trick me!'

Jake either didn't realize the sarcasm in her voice or wasn't taking any notice because he went on, 'Look, a lot of people know about your mother but they weren't all her friends. She had quite a name for herself – and so do you.'

Jessica sighed. It was the first day of her holiday and already she was lumbered with the local weirdo.

'Is there anything else?' she asked, deciding she wanted to lose Jake as soon as possible.

The boy bit his lip and looked nervous. 'It's okay,' he said. 'I know you don't believe me. You won't until you find out for yourself. But if it's any help...' He paused and breathed in. 'Ask your uncle about St Helier. Ask him what he did, who he was. And be careful. I'll be around if you need me.' With that he backed away and left Jessica feeling confused and uneasy.

'Nutter,' she muttered to herself as she watched Jake leave.

Jessica decided to look around the town on her own. Not wanting to get lost she kept to the main street and spent a pleasant couple of hours wandering in and out the perfumeries and jewellers as well as DeGrudy's. In the latter, a rather grand department store, she treated herself to a new pair of denim shorts out of the money she had saved up. By the time she had paid for them it was getting on for one o'clock so she decided to stroll back to where she had said she would meet Jim. The old man was waiting for her, two bulging shopping bags in his hands.

'Have a good time with Jake?' he asked with a smile.

Jessica shrugged.

'Yes and no. I ditched Jake not long after you left. He kept making weird comments about my mum. It kinda creeped me out.'

Jim's leathery face creased into a frown. 'What exactly did he say?' he asked, sounding slightly annoyed.

Jessica scuffed her feet and leant against a streetlight.

'Really weird stuff. Said I was here, in Jersey, because of Mum and that not everyone could be trusted. When I asked what he meant he said I should talk to you about St Helier. At that point

I figured he was totally loony and went off on my own.' She wrinkled her forehead. 'Do you know what he meant?'

Jim bit his lip as if he wanted to say something but didn't. 'People should mind their own business,' he said angrily, flashing his gaze around the crowd as Jake had done. 'Jake had no right to say anything to you. This family can look after itself – me, you, Emma. There's enough going on as it is without...' He paused as he realized that Jessica was staring at him.

He shook his head. 'I don't like people saying things about Emma, that's all.' He sighed and for a moment Jessica thought she saw sadness in his eyes. Jim must miss his niece even more than she did.

Jim studied her face with suspicion and wet his lips. 'Do you *want* to know about St Helier?' he asked.

'I don't mind,' she said, the quaver in her voice betraying her bewilderment.

Jim glanced at his watch. 'I have a little time before we have to go to Mrs Noir.' He motioned for Jessica to follow him and together they proceeded down a side street that led them out to the sea front. After crossing the road, Jim directed Jess up to the sea wall. She looked out over the bay. A fine, grey mist lay across the water making the rocks and Elizabeth Castle no more than ghostly shadows. Jim pointed a chubby finger towards the skyline where a pale yellow sun silhouetted one of the larger rocks that jutted out from the sea. 'Can you see that small island?' he asked her.

Jessica nodded, still wondering what the point of this whole exercise was.

'Many years ago that was the home of Helier the hermit.' Jim bit his lip and took a deep breath. 'Now back then almost the whole of Europe was Pagan. Witches and warlocks practised freely through England, France and Belgium. Some say spirits of darkness and evil roamed the lands, terrorizing simple folk in ways you cannot imagine.' He looked at Jessica, his dark eyes glistening with menace. 'Let me tell you, a real witch or warlock – one whose heart is as black and dull as midnight – is a terrible thing to cross. The power lives within them like some venomous serpent coiled in the pit of their stomach. Witchcraft can be used for good, to heal and protect, but if it gets hold of you, seeps under your very skin, then you become a mere vessel for pure

39

evil. People become hooked on the power it brings them and will stop at nothing to control the spirits of darkness.'

A cold wind blew off the water making Jessica shiver. 'It's just a story,' she told herself, 'nothing else.' She was wishing that Jake had never mentioned Helier. There was something in Jim's voice that filled her with dread.

Jim continued his story. 'Now there was one such warlock by the name of Sigebert living in Belgium around fifteen hundred years ago. Powerful was he and many feared both him and his wife. They were said to have under their control a Dark Spirit in the form of a great black hound with eyes redder than burning coals. Yet for all their power Sigebert and his bride Lusegard were not blessed with children. Seven long years they tried, making sacrifice after sacrifice to the pagan idols, chanting endless spells and concocting the most difficult and complex of potions. Sigebert was tormented. What good was his great power if he had no heir? So in his desperation he turned to a Christian teacher called Cunibert who lived nearby. Cunibert agreed to pray to God to bless them with a child but only if Sigebert and Lusegard gave up their pagan ways and brought up their child as a Christian. Sigebert agreed and not long after Lusegard conceived and in due course gave birth to a boy. But within Sigebert's heart his lust for power was great. As a warlock he had wielded so much might, why, the beasts of the forest understood and obeyed him. Mortals had all but worshipped him out of fear. Now, as a mere man, he felt he was worth nothing. The black magic had consumed his soul. Soon he turned his back on the promise he made to Cunibert and returned to his pagan ways.'

Jim paused and wet his cracked lips. Jessica crossed her arms and leant against the sea wall. She was so captivated by the tale that she had totally forgotten it was Jake's nonsensical ramblings that had made her ask him about Helier in the first place. The tale was so fascinating she could almost picture Sigebert's huge, midnight-black dog with its glowing eyes charging through the cold mist.

Jim took a deep breath and started again. 'Now, when the boy was seven years old, he was struck down by a terrible illness, the like of which neither warlock nor apothecary had ever seen.'

Jessica looked up from the swelling waves that rippled beneath them. 'What's an apothecary?' she asked, wanting to be clear on every detail of the story. (She wished they would teach things like this in school, warlocks and demon dogs were a damn sight more interesting than the facts they were given in history.)

'Oh, an apothecary? Well, that's like an old-fashioned doctor who used plants and herbs and stuff. Anyhow, Sigebert's son was very ill, dying almost, and Sigebert tried everything to heal him. But once again all his spells, sacrifices and potions failed him and, against his will, he was forced to turn to Cunibert for help.'

'I bet Cunibert wasn't very happy about that! What with Sigebert being a warlock again,' said Jessica.

Jim clapped a hand on her shoulder. 'Too right there!' he said. 'Cunibert was livid that Sigebert had lied to him. He knew that he could no longer trust him with the child's welfare. Sigebert begged Cunibert to save his son, for if there was one good thing to be said about Sigebert, it was that he cherished that child dearly. Finally, after much arguing Cunibert agreed he would try and heal the child on the condition that he could take him away from his pagan parents to live a Christian life. Sigebert was heart-broken at the thought of losing his only son but, unable to watch him suffer, the warlock handed the child over to the Christian and Cunibert took him to a church far, far away from his parents and in time he was healed. Cunibert renamed the child Helier and together they lived in the church.'

'And the church was here on Jersey, right?' asked Jessica, suddenly hoping very much Jim would take her to the place where Cunibert and Helier lived.

Jim shook his head. 'No, Helier didn't come to Jersey until he was a man. As a boy he lived with Cunibert on the continent. Cunibert taught him about Christianity and of the love of God; he cared for Helier and was more of a loving father than Sigebert would ever have been. Helier was very happy. That was until things began to happen – things that people found difficult to explain.'

'What things?' enquired Jessica.

Jim leant against the wall. 'Helier was a kind-hearted and sensitive boy,' he said. 'Very often Cunibert would find him in the garden of the church talking to the rabbits, who seemed to understand every word. In fact some say that Helier negotiated with the rabbits so they could share the vegetables that grew there. He seemed to understand and love all the creatures on God's earth. He could persuade the ox to pull a plough without the need for it to be whipped; he charmed a snake from one man's throat when it slithered there while he slept. He even worked towards bringing harmony between the humans and the faeriefolk.'

Jessica sniggered. 'Faeriefolk? Isn't that taking things a bit far. Witches and warlocks I can go along with but you don't seriously expect me to believe fairies existed.'

A small smile played on Jim's wrinkled face. 'Believe in what you can,' he replied. 'Anyway, all the people knew Helier was blessed with strange and mysterious powers. Some said he was blessed by God, a messenger to show His love, and healed in Jesus' name. But others were wary of him. They knew he was the son of the warlock Sigebert and said these deeds were a sign that evil blood ran in his veins. Such talk reached across the countryside, back to where Sigebert mourned the child stolen from him ten years earlier. Enraged at the thought that Helier might have witchcraft in him that Cunibert had stolen from him, and determined to find his heir, Sigebert summoned his great red-eyed hound and set off across the countryside as if possessed by the Devil himself. He rode through many villages spreading death and terror wherever he went, his mind set upon finding his son.'

Jessica's eyes were wide with amazement. Gazing at the horizon she could picture Sigebert on a midnight black steed, that awful demon dog by his side, riding, his heart filled with fury, to find Cunibert and Helier. 'But he didn't find them, right?' she asked, her voice trembling with fear. 'They got away, didn't they?'

Jim shook his head, his eyes as dull and as dark as coals. 'Oh, I'm afraid Sigebert did find them,' he said quietly. 'One night, Sigebert and a small band of warlocks stormed Cunibert's church and although the teacher stood up to him Cunibert was murdered by Sigebert. Then the warlock turned to face his son. "Child," he said "blood of my blood, I have come for you. You have been given great power and under my guidance you and I can rule the world." But Helier, seeing how heartlessly he had murdered Cunibert and wanting only to do good, defied him and fled. Some, those who believe Helier really did have warlock blood in him, say it was Helier's pure love that allowed him to turn his magic against his father and escape, but all that is known for sure is that Helier escaped Sigebert and from that day Sigebert faded into time without further trace.'

'And then he came to Jersey, right?' interrupted Jessica once again.

Jim shook his head, 'You are too impatient, my girl. The less you interrupt the quicker I can finish the story and then you'll know what happened. Anyway, Helier was distraught as he fled from his home. Cunibert, the man who was all but a father to him was dead and the arrival of Sigebert had made him doubt that the powers he possessed were a blessing of God. He knew now that by the right of his birth he was a warlock but in his heart he wanted nothing to do with the dark arts. All he wanted was to live a good, Christian life. He wandered for many years, heartbroken, so they say, until God directed him to Nanteuil in the Cotentin, where he found a holy man by the name of Marculf. Helier spoke with Marculf at great length of what had happened to Cunibert and how he doubted his abilities were a gift from God. Marculf was very wise and told Helier that any gift, even magic, if used unselfishly and with love was a gift of God. He witnessed how Helier spoke to the beasts and saw him heal a great many people. He told Helier to use his powers for the greater good of his fellow man and, after baptizing him, sent him to live here in Jersey where Marculf said he was needed. So, along with a man called Romard, who he had met during his travels, Helier set sail for Jersey and started life as a hermit on that rock.'

Jim gestured once again to the small island out in the bay. Jessica stared for a moment at the rock, and wondered if it had somehow absorbed some of Helier's mysterious powers.

'Was he happy here?' she asked. 'Did people like him and were they okay about his father being a warlock?'

Jim took a long deep breath. 'To be honest, the people on Jersey back then had a great deal more to worry about than Helier. Jersey then was a terrible, rocky wasteland, plagued by all manner of wicked atrocities. Only thirty humans lived here at that time and most of them were pagans, but not powerful witches and warlocks like Sigebert. They dabbled in the Dark

43

Arts just to try and make their crops grow but it brought all manner of evil spirits to Jersey that they could not control.'

'What? Like Sigebert's hound?' said Jessica, sensing the story was getting exciting again.

Jim leant close to her, his eyes glistening. 'And worse,' he said in a hushed whisper. 'They say a demon roamed Jersey in those times, so hideous and powerful not even Sigebert himself could've controlled it. At the mere sight of it crops would wither, livestock would die and any man who saw it would be cursed. No-one who witnessed the beast could even speak of what its form was. Its very presence on the isle was like a beacon to all people whose hearts were black and evil. Because of it, Vikings were lured to Jersey and they robbed and slaughtered the islanders. Eventually, not knowing where else to turn, the inhabitants visited Helier and Romard on their rock and begged Helier to aid them in some way. After much consideration and prayer to God as to what he should do, Helier left his rock and prepared to face the great demon.'

Jessica's eyes were as wide as saucers as she waited for Jim to conclude his tale. The old man turned his weather beaten, leathery face towards the yellow light of the horizon.

'It was a dark, stormy night when Helier stood on the rocks that now overlook Devil's Hole to face the demon. He was an old man by now and the islanders doubted he would have any power over such a malevolent beast. The hermit said a short prayer for God to give him strength in his task, and raised his staff towards the sky. Suddenly the creature appeared before him, twisting and turning like some unholy snake. Its fangs were red with the blood of its latest meal and it glared at Helier with loathing. Helier held his rod before him and spoke to the beast.

'"I am Helier," he shouted clear and loud above the roar of the thunder. "In the name of God, cease the torment of these innocent people and be forever encased in the rock of this island, taking with you the wicked plunderers who lay siege to this place." There was a flash of white light from the tip of Helier's staff and the waves of St Ouens began to rise, thrashing and engulfing both the Demon and the Viking ships and dragging them down to the sea floor where they were imprisoned. Those Vikings who survived sailed far away from Jersey never to return. The island was saved. Helier returned to live his simple life with Romard on his rock and in time the islanders learnt of Christianity from him and prospered, knowing as long as Helier lived the island would be safe. But Helier knew his time on this world was growing short so, after much prayer, he turned to his faithful companion Romard and said, "Dear friend, faithful servant, this isle needs to be guarded from evil and soon I will no longer be here to protect it. Since you have been as a son to me it is your bloodline that will safeguard Jersey. When I depart from this earthly plane, take the weapon of my slayer and keep it within your family. As it bears my blood you will be my son and your descendants will be blessed by God to guide this tiny isle." Not three days later a ship of Vandals landed on this beach. One discovered Helier's hiding place and with an axe decapitated the holy man. It is said the body of St Helier stood and, picking up his severed head, walked into the sea where Christ greeted him and took him up into Heaven. The Vandals fled and Romard took the axe into his home. A short time later Romard married and throughout the ages his descendants had the power to heal. As long as they live in Jersey no real harm can befall her.'

Jim smiled and stood up. Jessica looked at him, more than slightly impressed. It had completely slipped her mind that it was Jake who had made her ask about St Helier. 'That,' she said, 'was a totally brilliant story.'

Jim gathered up his shopping bags and looked modest. 'Brilliant or not it's what I was told as a boy; 'course it might've got a bit altered through the centuries but as far as I'm concerned that's the true story of St Helier.' He glanced at his watch. 'What with all this story telling we're late dropping off Mrs Noir's shopping. Come on.'

The old man started heading back towards the truck. Jessica followed him but not before glancing over her shoulder one last time at the rocky outcrop Helier had once called home.

'That Romard bloke, Helier's companion, do his descendants still live in Jersey?' she asked.

Jim had his back to her so Jessica did not see him flinch as he murmured, 'Yes, Jessica, they do.'

Chapter 4

The Old Woman and the Girl

Jessica had thoroughly enjoyed Jim's tale of St Helier with all its links to witchcraft and darkness – so much so, in fact, that she spent the short journey from St Helier to Mrs Noir's home in the pleasant seaside parish of Gorey, re-running it through her head. It was indeed a fascinating story. She pictured Sigebert's fury at losing his son; the evil spirit that terrorized Jersey; Helier confining the demon and the Vikings to a watery grave. It would make a great film, she thought. She wondered if when she got back to school and had to write a 'What I Did in my Holiday' piece they would let her do the story of Helier. One thing was for sure, if Uncle Jim had any more great stories like that the holiday wouldn't be so bad after all.

Gorey was, like St Helier, on Jersey's coastline and also had an impressive castle, although this fortress was more inland than Elizabeth Castle. It was perched atop a steep hill overlooking the small village. A long promenade stretched along in front of the wide shallow bay and curled round beneath the imposing castle. Several tourists were strolling along it in the warm early afternoon sunshine. The bay itself was wide and sandy but the great numbers of small sailing boats resting on the sand suggested to Jessica it was more popular with fishermen than holidaymakers. In the shadow of the hill, clinging close to the bottom of its rocky slopes, were a long row of smart white-fronted houses that, once the path crooked round to enclose the bay, became hotels, shops and in the case of one, a welcoming pub. Jim parked the truck on the side of the road so it faced out to the bay and he and Jessica got out and carried Mrs Noir's shopping along the coastal path towards the private houses. The sun was

46

now quite warm and, gazing at the light reflecting off the rippling sea, Jessica thought that, with such a pleasant view, Gorey must be the ideal place for an elderly woman to live.

'Here we are,' said Jim as he stopped outside one of the tidy residences. He juggled the shopping as he tried to get the key from his pocket. 'Mrs Noir has given me a key because she has trouble answering the door. She's eighty-three and barely leaves the house. I have no idea how she copes.'

He pushed the door open and they stepped inside. Jessica stared around the hallway and felt an inexplicable shiver run up her spine. The house couldn't have been more different from Jim's homely abode if it had tried and the happiness Jess felt moments before suddenly evaporated. The wallpaper bore a garish floral design of deep fuchsia and moss green that was barely visible through the layers of grime and smoke residue that had built up over the years. To the right, just inside the doorway, stood a deeply carved oak hallstand, its mirror ancient, tarnished and freckled with dark brown spots of rust. The hooks were of discoloured brass and fashioned, most oddly, in the shape of human hands. The stand was empty apart from four items: a long, cape-like tweed coat, a matching hat with a brown suede band and greenish feathers, an old-fashioned black umbrella with a duck head handle and (which struck Jessica as odd) a child's navy-blue duffle coat. She was still staring at the coat wondering why an old woman would have such an item when something out of the corner of her eye made Jessica jump with fright. Mounted on the wall next to the hallstand was a deer's head, its glass eyes staring lifelessly ahead. Once again Jessica shuddered; she hated stuffed animals and there was something about this house that made her very nervous. The only sound was the rhythmic tick of an unseen clock. The air had the strangest odour. It wasn't the same stench that filled Jim's truck but something more stale and claustrophobic. Cat hair was part of it and cigarette smoke, also old perfume and a pungent smell of some sort of herbs cooking.

A voice, old and cracking, with an accent not quite Jersey and not quite French, drifted into the hallway. 'Jim? Is that you?' it called.

Seemingly unaware of Jessica's nervousness Jim took off his cap and hung it on the hallstand.

'Hello, Agatha. Yes, only me. I've got your shopping. Shall I put it away for you?'

'No, no,' the voice replied. 'It can be done later. Come in and have a cup of tea.'

Jessica prayed that Jim would say they were too busy; she didn't like this house one bit. But Jim called out, 'That would be lovely. I have my great-niece Jessica with me. You know, Emma's girl. Would you like to meet her?'

There was a long pause, as if the old woman was trying to remember something, before the voice called, slow and thoughtful. 'That would be wonderful. Do show her in. I'm in the living room.'

Placing a hand on her shoulder Jim guided Jessica through a door to the left of them into the elderly lady's sitting room.

As they entered Jessica hugged herself. The room was cold compared to the sunny outside. The sitting room, like the hall, was dusty and unwelcoming. The walls were lined with velvety flock wallpaper to which dirt clung like a magnet. An ornate stone fireplace, surrounded by old-fashioned metal spoons and forks dominated the small room, but no cheery fire glowed in it. Above the fireplace, just under the mantel, was carved a grotesque face, like some gargoyle, its mouth open in a ghoulish grin. Large oil paintings hung on the walls depicting figures from long ago, all of them with blank, soulless eyes, the canvases filthy with dirt. Hanging above the fireplace was a huge mirror framed in gold leaf that had long ago lost its lustre; in front of it stood a collection of green glass bottles of varying shapes and sizes. To the back of the room, opposite the window, was an ebony glass-fronted bookcase containing row upon row of dusty leather-bound books. In front of the window crouched a monstrous oak dining table and six carved chairs, their backs twisted with deeply chiselled spiral designs. A tall vase containing faded silk flowers stood petrified in the centre of the table. In front of the fireplace a leather settee and armchair, both battered and worn, completed the depressing scene. The whole room had the appearance of a bric-a-brac shop. It was not at all hospitable.

In the winged chair to the left of the fireplace, looking as if she hadn't moved from that spot for a great many years, sat the plump figure of Mrs Noir. Her hair was greyish white and pulled high atop her head in a neat bun. The deep wrinkled skin of her face was plastered with pale make-up and a smear of orange lipstick formed what would have been an otherwise barely visible mouth. She had abnormally thin, highy arched eyebrows that looked as if they had been over-plucked and little, narrow eyes the colour of seaweed. A navy-blue blouse with tiny white dots struggled to contain her ample frame, assisted, not very competently, by a straight blue skirt, navy well-polished patent leather shoes and thick, creased stockings. Fastened at her throat was a Victorian brooch of black opal in a gold setting. Her eyes rose to greet Jim and Jessica as they entered the room and her thin orange lips parted in a polite smile – a smile, Jessica noted, that did not extend to her eyes.

'Good day to you, Jim,' said Mrs Noir, her words blunted by her unusual accent. Jim nodded politely.

'Afternoon, Agatha. I left your shopping in the hall. Is that okay?'

The old woman clasped her pale, bony hands together. 'You are too good to me. Do sit down and have something to drink.'

Jim settled himself onto the ancient sofa. Mrs Noir's eyes then fell upon Jessica who had been trying to conceal herself behind Jim's portly physique. The old woman gazed at her and, for the briefest moments, Jessica felt herself freeze to the spot. The thin lips again formed a chilly smile, revealing a set of very white, obviously false, teeth.

'And who is this pretty young lady?' she asked still smiling at Jessica.

Jim grinned. 'That's my great niece, Jessica,' he said proudly. 'Emma's daughter. Her and her dad are over here on holiday.'

Mrs Noir, her eyes never leaving Jessica, tilted her head to one side. 'Jessica,' she murmured quietly. 'What a lovely name. Why don't you sit down and we can have a nice cup of tea.'

Every nerve in Jessica's body was tense and she didn't know why. She didn't like this house, that nauseating odour was stronger in here than it had been in the hall and her skin goose-pimpled from the coldness. She really didn't want to stay in this place very long; it was as if the house was stuck in a time warp, not quite of this world. In particular, Jessica felt ill at ease whenever the old lady looked at her. But she knew it would be impossible to make an exit without Jim and from the way he had settled down into his seat she feared they were to be here for some time. Reluctantly, Jessica sat down beside her great uncle and stared into Mrs Noir's piggy eyes.

The old lady sighed contentedly and smiled at Jessica. 'Would you like some tea?' she asked, indicating the floral china tea service that was neatly set on a small wooden table beside her. Jessica noticed that although Mrs Noir seemed to have been alone until they had entered the house, there were three cups and saucers laid out upon the silver tray. How odd!

'Thank you,' she managed to reply.

Mrs Noir's dainty hands darted quickly about the tray. 'Oh yes,' she murmured softly as she poured the brew through the tea strainer, 'I know all about you, Jessica. Jim very often talked about how he wished you would visit and now, here you are.'

She offered cups of tea to Jessica and Jim. Jessica took hers apprehensively and gazed down into the cup. Steam rose from it in pale white curls while the beverage itself had a greenish tinge that Jessica had never seen before in tea. Her eyes flitted from the cup to Mrs Noir's face. The old woman was staring at her expectantly, perfectly still, waiting for her to take a sip. Slowly, Jessica raised the cup to her lips. It did not taste like the tea she drank at home; it was bitter with a distinctly herby tang.

'It's my own secret recipe,' the elderly woman said encouragingly.

Jess smiled nervously and placed the cup on the floor beside her feet; she didn't intended to finish the remainder. As she did so something warm and furry brushed against her arm making her jump and almost spill the tea. Looking down she saw the sleek, well-groomed form of a Siamese cat slip round from behind the sofa. It padded gracefully onto the rug in front of the fireplace before curling round to gaze at Jessica with large sapphire eyes, swishing its tail elegantly. Slowly Jessica reached out her hand to pet the creature's chocolate-patched ears. However, before she had even touched the animal's silky fur, the cat arched its back and hissed viciously at her. Quick as lightning Jessica drew back her hand just before the Siamese could claw her. Mrs Noir chuckled.

'Do not be afraid of Magiver,' she said as the feline leaped skilfully onto her broad lap. 'It sometimes takes him a while to trust people, though he is usually a very good judge of character.'

The cat coiled itself into the old lady's skirt purring contentedly. Jessica again felt very uncomfortable in the presence of Mrs Noir. Magiver's attack had startled her slightly and even now, as he lay cosseted by the old woman, his large, blue eyes bore into Jessica with what looked suspiciously like loathing.

Mrs Noir sat, her teacup in one hand, stroking Magiver with the other and stared fixedly at Jessica. 'So, have you been on the island long?' she asked, her voice deep and melodic.

Jessica shook her head. 'No, I only arrived yesterday. I'm staying with Jim. Dad's here too but he's back at the house.'

Agatha Noir grinned and fingered the handle of her teacup. 'You didn't tell me they were arriving so soon, Jim,' she murmured.

Jim scratched his balding head. 'Must've slipped my mind,' he muttered, slurping his tea. 'They're staying two weeks.'

Mrs Noir put her teacup back on the tray and twisted a stray lock of grey hair round her bony fingers.

'Splendid,' she said quietly. 'I expect you are going to have a wonderful time. Jersey is such a beautiful island to explore.' Her voice trailed off as she finished her sentence and she seemed to enter a world of her own for a few seconds, gazing into the empty grate. Then, just as Jessica began to wonder whether she had dropped off to sleep, the old woman's dark eyes snapped very suddenly back to life and she gazed once again at Jessica. 'I expect you will want to find out about your mother while you're here. No doubt her identity is somewhat of a mystery to you.'

Jessica blinked with shock. Since arriving in Jersey, no-one (not Jim nor Jake nor her father) had tackled the doubt hanging in her mind so directly. She wondered for a moment how Mrs Noir knew that was the real reason she'd come to the island.

'Yes, yes I do want to know about her,' said Jessica earnestly.

At her side, Jim choked on his tea with surprise. He threw the old woman a shocked glance.

'Agatha, as I made clear to young Jake LeBlanc earlier today I am perfectly capable of telling Jessica all she needs to know about her mother.' His voice was tinged with anger.

Mrs Noir pouted her thin, orange mouth and flapped her hand as if to bat away Jim's comment. 'Don't be such a spoilsport,' she laughed coldly. 'I only want to help the girl if I can.'

In her lap, Magiver was suddenly alert again, his blue eyes glinting menacingly, the tip of his tail twitching. Jessica wondered if he'd seen a mouse. Mrs Noir regarded Jessica and smiled.

'Your mother was a sweet girl,' she said coyly. 'Very kind – and you look so much like her! She was intelligent too, you know; always right on the ball. She would've done well on the mainland. It was such a shock when she died. But we all did get to see her one last time.'

As the old woman spoke Jessica began to feel, despite the room remaining bitterly chilly, very hot indeed. In her chest, an unexplainable panic rose; it was as if she were drowning. The room began to spin and pain seared through her head. She was about to faint when a sound outside the living room brought her back to her senses. Someone was coming downstairs from the top floor of the house. As Jess regained her composure the door swung open and in stepped a young girl. All three of them turned to look at her.

The girl couldn't have been more than eleven or twelve but her almost painfully thin frame made her look younger. Her face was pale and sullen, as if she had recently recovered from a serious illness. Dark circles lay under her watery blue eyes giving them the appearance of belonging to a woman more than three times her age. There was no youth or vitality in those eyes, just the haunted, empty stare of someone who had been scarred by a great tragedy. Her shoulder-length blonde hair was as fine as a baby's and tied back in a thin ponytail. Her clothing looked as if it belonged in a bygone age. She wore a simple, white cotton blouse with a frill down the front and tiny pearl buttons, what appeared to be a hand-knitted cardigan of bluish-grey wool and a knee length skirt. It was all much too big for her which added to her malnourished appearance. She surveyed the room with lonely eyes before glancing timidly at Mrs Noir. The old woman wore a look of utter annoyance on her wrinkled face, as if the girl's presence had interrupted something very important.

'Elsa, how many times must I tell you? Knock before entering a room. We have guests.'

The girl tipped her head slightly with shame and approached Mrs Noir's chair.

So, thought Jessica, this is the owner of the duffle coat.

Elsa began straightening the tea things on the tray, her ghostly white hands as quick and dexterous as Mrs Noir's had been.

'I'm sorry, grandmère. I didn't know. I came to get the tea things.' Her voice was barely audible and she kept her eyes fixed upon the china as she spoke.

The old woman grunted as Elsa picked up the tray. 'Have you done your studies?' she asked briskly. The girl nodded her head, stiffened and turned to Jim and Jessica. 'Good afternoon, Mr Hellily,' she murmured. Her eyes locked with Jessica's for a few seconds and Elsa's mouth dropped open slightly. Jessica too was surprised. There was something deep within the young girl's eyes that made Jessica's blood run cold: a black and terrifying torment extinguished the carefree spark of youth which normally glows in the eyes of someone of her years.

Mrs Noir seemed to notice the connection between the girls. 'Elsa!' she reprimanded, 'Don't daydream!'

Elsa jumped, causing the china on the tea tray to rattle. Jessica had begun to feel very sorry for her. She had never known either of her grandmothers but she imagined that a grandma should be kind and loving. Mrs Noir had not said a pleasant thing to Elsa since she had entered.

The elderly lady drummed her fingers on the arm of her chair. 'Mr Hellily and his great-niece have brought me my shopping. When you've washed up, you can put it away – and try not to break anything. You are so clumsy, girl.'

Elsa lowered her eyes sadly. 'Yes, grandmère,' she whispered turning towards the door. Quickly, Jessica jumped to her feet. Mrs Noir was Jim's friend so she couldn't very well say she thought she was being cruel but... 'I'll help Elsa put the shopping away,' she said with a smile.

Jim, Mrs Noir and especially Elsa herself looked astounded by this offer. The old woman stared at her amazed, a flame of annoyance sparking momentarily in her eyes.

'Thank you, Jessica,' she murmured, recovering her composure. 'You girls go off, I want to speak with Jim anyway.'

Jessica placed a hand warmly on Elsa's slim arm. 'Hi!' she grinned cheerfully at the bewildered girl. 'You can call me Jess. Where's the kitchen? I'm a dab hand at clearing up, we'll have the shopping sorted in no time.'

Elsa looked as if she'd just met an alien. 'Thank you,' she gasped. 'It's right through here.'

The two of them left the room. Jim and Mrs Noir were deep in conversation. Just as the door was about to swing close, Magiver roused himself from the warm indentation he had made in Mrs Noir's skirt, leapt delicately down to the floor and padded after them. In the hallway, Jessica collected the shopping bags and followed Elsa down to the end of the corridor and through a large wooden door into Mrs Noir's kitchen.

If Jessica thought Jim's kitchen had been old-fashioned and odd, then this was practically archaic! She could not see one appliance more recent than the fifties larder refrigerator that stood humming and clattering loudly at the back of the room. The cupboards were of dark oak with leaded glass fronts, some cracked in places or missing altogether. The room, in contrast to the rest of the house, was unbelievably hot, owing to the fact that there was a glowing fire crackling in the black wood-burning stove which dominated one whole wall of the kitchen. As in Jim's home, there was a sturdy brick fireplace but, far from being adapted into storage, it appeared it was still very much in use for a small pile of blackened ashes smouldered on the grate. Jessica sniffed the air. The herby, antiseptic smell positively reeked in this room and when she glanced up at the ceiling she understood why. From the oak beamed ceiling hung row upon row of dried herbs and plants, so bunched together it was virtually impossible to see the ceiling itself. Some of them Jessica recognized; others were new to her eyes.

Magiver brushed against Elsa's legs and mewed impatiently. The girl tutted and placing the tea tray beside the white porcelain sink, bent down to pet him. Magiver's sapphire eyes fell upon the back door and he padded over to it, scraping at the panelled wood with his claws. Elsa took a large brass key off the hook beside the doorframe.

'You want to go out?' she asked the cat, her voice sounding slightly more confident than when she had addressed her grandmother. The Siamese gazed up at her and mewed again. Sighing, Elsa unlocked the door and Magiver slipped out into the garden beyond.

'And no more bringing back dead birds and stuff, okay? It's not nice.' Elsa called after him before locking the door.

54

Jessica deposited the shopping on one of the worktops and started to unpack while Elsa returned silently from the doorway and began to fill the sink with water. Jessica noticed that the girl made no effort to talk as she scrubbed the tea things and kept her eyes fixed upon the frothy suds. What an odd girl, she thought as she placed a packet of biscuits in the cupboard. They remained like that for a few minutes until Jessica couldn't stand the silence any longer. She was going to be friendly to Elsa, whether Elsa liked it or not.

'So,' she said trying to think of something to say, 'I'm in Jersey for a fortnight. Do you know any cool places to hang out?'

Elsa stopped washing the teacup she had in her hand and looked at Jessica, not sure what to say.

'No, I...' she murmured timidly, 'I don't go out much.'

Jessica took a pint of milk out of the bag and crossed to the fridge. 'Oh,' she said pulling the door open. 'But you must go out sometimes. What do you like to do? Do you like music? Films?'

Elsa turned from the sink and gave Jessica that curious look as if she had said something in a foreign language. She paused for a few seconds, trying to find an answer.

'I like my books,' she said very slowly and softly. A small smile played on Elsa's dry, pale lips and for the first time since Jessica had met her she looked almost cheerful. 'Sometimes,' she continued wistfully, 'when grandmère has a nap, I take my book into the garden and read it, under the apple tree.'

Jessica smiled back at Elsa, glad that there was at least some small pleasure in her life. But then as quickly as the joy had appeared in Elsa's face it vanished. She turned and started to put away the tea service. 'But I've got to look after grandmère,' she said sharply as if lecturing herself. 'Grandmère is old and she needs me. Needs me to take care of her and the house. It's important, you see. Grandmère looks after me when I get sick. I get so very, very sick. Grandmère makes me better. So it wouldn't be right if I didn't care for her. I must be a good girl. I must always be good.'

Jessica stared with uneasy concern as Elsa stacked the china away muttering to herself in this nervous manner. The girl seemed to be very anxious and she couldn't help but wonder if Mrs Noir's austere manner was putting pressure on her out of

55

all proportion to her years. She put a comforting hand on the girl's bony shoulder.

'Hey,' she said gently, making her turn to face her. 'It's okay, don't get up tight. I'm sure you're doing just great.'

Elsa's pale eyes softened slightly and she didn't look so afraid.

'I'm sorry,' she sighed, turning her attention to the remaining unpacked groceries. 'I get in a panic sometimes. Grandmère isn't so bad.'

She began unloading tins and stacking them in one of the cupboards. Jessica bit her tongue. From what she had witnessed Mrs Noir seemed very awkward indeed.

'Can't you tell your parents about how you feel? I'm sure they would be worried.'

At the mention of her parents Elsa's diminutive frame crumbled with woe. She hung her head and her fine blonde hair fell limply across her face.

'They're dead,' she murmured, her voice layered with sadness. 'They were killed in a car accident when I was three months old. I've lived here with grandmère all my life. She's the only family I've got.'

Jessica felt a familiar stab at her heart. She knew, to an extent, how Elsa felt. But at least, Jessica thought, I have one parent who loves me. What did this poor girl have apart from a strange old woman who showed more love to her cat than her granddaughter?

'I guess I know how you feel,' Jessica said softly. 'I never knew my mum. She died just after I was born. I don't even know what killed her. That's why I came to Jersey. She grew up here and I wanted to find out who she was.'

Elsa glanced over her shoulder. 'Then you know what it's like,' she said quietly. 'There's like a big hole in the centre of your life and you do what you can to fill it in but because you don't remember it's hard.'

Jessica nodded slowly, her eyes moistening. She didn't want to cry but Elsa had put into words exactly how she felt about her mother. 'You wonder what they were like. How they spoke and acted. Don't you?'

Elsa bit her lip as if she were fighting back a lifetime's worth of tears. Jessica regarded the sorrow in her companion's face. Maybe this is the connection I felt between us, thought Jessica.

A sympathy for each other's loss and mourning. Perhaps, even if she couldn't find out about her own mother, befriending Elsa might just ease the grief. She certainly believed now that her own situation could be a lot worse.

Then, as if suddenly realizing that she had let her emotions get the better of her, Elsa wiped her eyes on the sleeve of her cardigan. 'I am so, so sorry,' she said leaning against the counter. 'I shouldn't cry like that, especially in front of strangers. Grandmère says it's wrong.'

Jessica put a hand comfortingly on Elsa's shoulder. 'Everyone cries sometimes,' she said gently. 'I still get upset about my mum from time to time.'

Elsa shook her head and picked a stray thread from her skirt. 'Grandmère doesn't cry,' she muttered sadly. 'I've never seen her upset about Mum and Dad.'

Jessica chewed her bottom lip. 'Yeah, I could see that,' she murmured wryly. She was getting a very clear picture of the kind of woman Mrs Noir was. 'But that doesn't mean it's wrong for *you* to cry. Look, I know we've only just met but how would you like to hang round with me while I'm in Jersey? I'm sure Jim and your grandmother won't mind.'

She had begun to feel increasingly sorry for Elsa and believed it would do the girl no harm to get out of the house once in a while.

A small smile tweaked the corners of Elsa's mouth. 'I would like that,' she whispered quietly, lifting her chin slightly. 'And I can show you the island.'

Jessica shrugged. 'Sure!' she replied cheerily. 'You could tell me all about Jersey, or if you feel upset about your parents and want someone to talk to, I don't mind.'

In Elsa's dull black pupils Jessica thought she saw a tiny spark of excitement.

'I'd like that,' she breathed enthusiastically. 'We'd be like friends, right?'

Jessica thought for a moment and then nodded. 'Yes, why not.'

Elsa clasped her hands and grinned broadly. 'I've never had a friend before,' she gushed excitedly. 'People at school think I'm strange and I don't really like leaving grandmère on her own. But if I'm with Jim, it'll be okay.'

The news that she could spend some time with Jessica definitely seemed to lift Elsa's spirits and the shopping was soon packed away. Much to Jessica's surprise the old woman seemed positively eager to allow Elsa to visit Jim's home in the near future and with his consent it was arranged that Elsa would come to tea the day after tomorrow. With that, Jim and Jessica said their goodbyes and headed homeward.

As she reclined in the worn passenger seat of Jim's truck, Jessica looked back on her first full day in Jersey. It had certainly given her a lot to think about. The folk of Jersey, as far as she could see, were a peculiar bunch. First she'd met Jake, who definitely seemed off his rocker. Although she had enjoyed the tale of St Helier, she still didn't know why he had brought it up when she'd asked what he knew about her mother. The boy did seem to have some knowledge about Emma but, like everyone else she had asked about her, he seemed unwilling to tell her anything. And what did he mean when he said not all people who knew her mother were her friends? It didn't make sense. The only person who was willing to talk openly about her mother was Mrs Noir. To be honest, Jessica wasn't sure she wanted Mrs Noir to tell her anything about anything. From the moment she entered the house Jessica had had the creeps and from her odd appearance and manner, not to mention the way she spoke to Elsa, Jessica was more or less decided she didn't like Mrs Noir one little bit. The only person she had met that Jessica felt a real affinity for was Elsa. Ironically, Elsa hadn't given even the slightest clue towards the identity of her mother but through her Jessica found a real connection to what she had lost. She was glad Mrs Noir had allowed her to visit them. Despite her shyness and sheltered life, Jessica thought that Elsa might prove to be a true friend.

Chapter 5

The Dweller

A pale silver moon, cloaked in wisps of violet cloud, threw its gentle white light onto the rippling waves of Corbiere as they beat against the jagged cliff. Night in Jersey. While humans slept peacefully in their beds, faeries and merfolk were free for a few hours to move about the sea and island without fear of being spotted by unfriendly eyes. Deep beneath the surf, in water so dark human vision would be useless, the powerful, sleek body of Keela the merman zoomed through the water, his huge golden eyes peeled for his prey. In his nailess fingers he carried a crude spear with a stone tip and wooden handle and his mind was alert and focused on the hunt. Suddenly a shimmer of silver scales darted in front of him. Grinning broadly, Keela beat his strong, burnished tail against the water and shot after the fish; the chase was on. The fish flitted this way and that through the icy depths, trying to escape its pursuer, but the merman kept close on its tail, his eyes fixed unblinking on his quarry. With a burst of energy, Keela gained on the creature and, quick as lightning, pierced it with his weapon. A small cloud of scarlet blood billowed from the creature's wound as Keela ripped it from his spear and clasped it securely in his razor-sharp fangs. With a flick of his tail, Keela swam up to the surface. He broke through the waves with a splash and rested for a second, the moonlight gleaming on his glossy, black hair.

Keela loved to fish. True, it was a necessary task for him and his family to survive but that didn't stop the thrill he got when he was pursuing his prey. The simple things gave his life meaning. Fishing, playing with his two young children, Coona and Pod, in the thick seaweed; sitting alone on a rock in the moonlight with his darling wife Reeni singing their hauntingly hypnotic song; chatting with his good friend Jim when he sometimes rowed his boat out to see him, bringing a bottle of that delicious land drink called brandy for them to share. These were the things that made Keela happy. He did not care that much for the delicate social politics that joined together the three races of Jersey. There were some who believed that merfolk, faeries and humans should not mix. For instance, he had once heard it said (no doubt by Xandu, the leader of Jersey's merfolk) that if a merperson saw a human fall overboard, even if it was someone who knew of their existence, he should do nothing to save him. To Keela this seemed ridiculous and cruel. He bore no grudge towards human or faerie. If Keela had his way, all three would live together openly and peacefully.

Keela smiled sadly to himself and looked upon the moon riding high in the dark sky. It had been his tolerant views on all creatures that had saved the life of the strange beast, for whom he had captured the fish, on that terrible day fourteen years ago. Keela remembered that day as if it had just passed: The agonising screams of its mother tearing the air as she died and that unnatural, cursed creature crawling from her womb into the bubbling ocean. It had been a wretched sight. Keela thought back to the look of disgust on his friend Jim's face and remembered the words he had spoken. 'It is nothing human,' he had growled furiously, 'nor faerie nor merperson. It is a demon, a creature of darkness and evil. I shall not recognize it. Kill it, and end the madness.' Some merfolk agreed. The animal was indeed repulsive in appearance, with its skin of dark olive, blemished with warts and boils that oozed pus, its hair thick and slimy. But there was something in the babe's liquid brown eyes that told Keela the child was far from evil. Keela had not the heart to murder the child so, after much discussion with Xandu and the other merfolk, it was agreed the child would be placed in a cave within these very cliffs and Keela, being the one who had objected most to killing it, would feed and care for it until a date when a better plan could be formulated. Such a plan had never come about and the child, known to less accepting merfolk as 'The Dweller', still lived in its secret hiding place.

The dead fish still clamped between his teeth, Keela began

the swim towards the jagged rocks of Corbiere. The water was choppy around the cliff and unwelcoming, even to merfolk. Twisting first this way then that between the sharp rocks, Keela followed the secret waterway known only to him and a few other merfolk who were tolerant of the creature. If the truth were known, Keela held the poor animal in an almost fatherly affection. It had shown no evil intent or aggression and from time to time he had even allowed Pod and Coona to play with it as if it were a sibling. It was he who, knowing the animal would be hurt if it knew it was called simply The Dweller, christened it with the human name Marina, meaning 'of the sea'. In return the creature had developed a genuine fondness for him.

Finally, Keela came level with the actual cliff face and working his way along the apparently solid wall of rock came to the small opening, about four feet wide and three feet high, and slipped inside. The cave itself was of a good size, domed high above. The walls were thick with green algae and stalactites hung from the roof dripping water into the enclosed pool. Around the edge of the cave a wide shelf of stone jutted out about five feet and to the back there was a smaller tunnel burrowed deep into the rock face in which Keela knew he would find Marina. The cave was pitch black and the merman was thankful for his phenomenal eyesight as he swam across to the stone ledge.

Removing the fish from his mouth and placing it on the side near the dank opening, Keela hauled himself out of the water and perched on the outcrop, his glistening tail dangling in the water. Once he was comfortably seated the merman removed the crudely fashioned, leather flask he wore around his body and placed it next to the fish carcase.

'Marina,' he hissed into the darkness of the inner cave. 'Dinner time.'

From within the dank catacomb, there came a strange, wet, snuffling, like a new-born animal trying to clear the liquid from its lungs. This was shortly followed by the sound of a heavy, damp, scaled body being dragging along the rocky cave floor. Keela sat in silence for a moment, waiting for the creature to emerge. Soon, out of the shadows of the grotto, an ugly head materialized and stared at the merman with huge, shining eyes.

61

The mouth was all but a thin crease in the scarred skin and its nose broad and flat with narrow slits of nostrils.

Marina's eyes shone when she saw the merman who had become her surrogate father and her wrinkled mouth formed a smile revealing a row of sharp white fangs. 'Keelie!' she croaked, her voice thick and gravelly. 'My Keelie come. It is goodly to see you, Keelie.'

The merman smiled as the creature shuffled out of its hiding place. Her body was slender and greasy and marked by carbuncles. She had enormous hands, way out of proportion with the rest of her and her fingers were long and tapered. Her torso ended not in legs like a human or a tail like a merperson, but in an odd mixture of the two. A pair of snake-like limbs replaced the legs of a normal human and slithered behind her as she crawled forward to sniff the dead fish hungrily.

'Goodly good yummings,' she muttered enthusiastically, regarding the corpse and licking her lips with a thick, black tongue. 'Rina be very, mighty hungry. Um's stummy gnarling. Thanky, Keelie.'

The merman laughed good-heartedly. Marina had never really learnt to speak properly. The first years of her life the only sound she could utter was a bubbling, crackling squeal that she would make when she wanted to communicate. The problem was that a hungry squeal was very much like a happy squeal, which was a lot like a scared squeal. That and a lot of gesturing with those huge hands was Keela's only clue to what she wanted. He was glad of what little other language she did have.

He picked up the flask and shook it playfully. 'And look what I've got. Mermilk.'

Marina squeaked with joy and clapped her oversized hands. 'Milky, milky, milky,' she sang happily. 'Rina is liking yumsome milky. It is um's favouritest thing. It is umsome yum and goodly in the stummy!'

She snatched the flask from Keela's hand and raised the teat to her wrinkled mouth. An off-green, creamy liquid, like turned cow's milk flowed out. Marina greedily lapped it up with her black tongue. She would have gulped it all down at once if Keela hadn't stopped her.

'Hey, take it easy,' he said, placing a hand on her scarred arm. 'Don't drink it all at once. The mermaids only have their young on milk for a few summer months and you're very lucky someone has spared you some. So put it away like a good girl and eat your fish.'

Marina nodded her head and corked the flask again, tucking it carefully behind a rock. She then grabbed the fish in her huge hand and bit a chunk out of it with her sharp teeth. Curling her serpent-like hind quarters up in front of her and gripping her dinner between her huge hands, Marina set about devouring the fish with her tiny pointed fangs. From time to time, she made contented, hungry growls as she tore the flesh from the bone.

Keela reclined against the wall of the cave and gazed at her thoughtfully. He knew that it was up to him to explain to the child the confusing changes that were taking place above her dark hideaway but found it difficult to find words she would understand. It was hard enough for anyone to conceive of the evil that lurked in Jersey now, let alone explain to a creature with such limited knowledge. He had always been as honest as he could with her without hurting her feelings. Marina understood Keela was not her real family, that her mother was dead and the rest of her relations lived on the land. But the merman hadn't had the heart to tell her Jim rejected her and that outside the cave her life would be at peril. But now he must try and explain that things were about to change.

'Marina,' he said gently, stroking the tip of her right fin, 'we need to talk and you must try very hard to understand what I am going to tell you.'

Marina sucked the fish's eyeball from its socket and swallowed it. 'Talksies?' she asked, tilting her head to one side. 'Is beings what about?'

Keela sighed. 'About Uncle Jim. Do you remember I told you about Uncle Jim?'

The girl stared at him with those unnaturally beautiful brown eyes and nodded, fish scales hanging from her chin.

'Ya,' she murmured, sounding slightly awestruck, 'Keelie tell um about him. Uncy Jim, he live uppy 'bove. He real family. Is he come see me? You say lot of time, one day Uncy Jim come and see Rina but no way yet. No Uncy Jim. Rina sometime think Keelie tell fibby lies.'

She frowned and her blemished face creased up even more.

Keela lowered his golden eyes. He wanted Jim to accept Marina and love her as much as he did, but the old man hadn't softened in his decision to cut Marina out of his life. He always hoped that one day he could keep his promise.

'I am not lying Marina. I am going to try and bring Uncle Jim to see you very soon but right now I must try and explain this to you.' He looked towards the exit of the cave. 'A few days ago your Uncle Jim had a visit. The rest of your family have come back to Jersey.'

Marina's wrinkly mouth fell open and she dropped what remained of the fish. She let out a high pitched scream and began jumping about the ledge in the most comical manner, clapping her hands and slapping her fins on the rock. She threw her arms around the merman's neck and planted a big, wet, fishy kiss on his cheek.

'Fabatolical news!' she screeched, smiling broadly. 'Jecica is back. Oh muchly, muchly good goodly. Is being muchly happy time. Rina is remembering what Keelie is tellings me. You say when Jecica come back to Jersey, all is going to be okay. Ya, Jecica come then Uncy Jim come see Rina, then Jecica make all Bla-Bla go bye-bye and then' (she let out a deep blissful sigh) 'Rina be beautifully lady like in piccie book and Jim and Jecica and Rina and Da all be family on land and happy.'

Before Keela could comment Marina had scrambled back into the gloom of the narrow passageway and dragged out an ancient, sodden, dog-eaten fairytale book that Keela had found lying on the beach some time ago. On the front was a drawing of a princess with long golden locks and rosy cheeks – the only human Marina had ever seen. Keela sighed sadly as Marina tapped the book with a long, green finger.

'See,' she said proudly, 'Rina be pretty, pretty when Bla-Bla gone.'

Keela frowned puzzled. Marina had invented many words to describe the life she knew and mostly he could understand her. But 'Bla-Bla' was unfamiliar and something told him it was going to be bad news.

'Marina,' he queried slowly as the girl tenderly ran her fingers across the book cover, 'what is Bla-Bla?'

Marina looked up from her book, a mixture of fear and confusion in her eyes. 'Is not nice,' she said quietly. She looked left and right, an expression of confusion etched on her face as she struggled to find the right words to describe her fear. She held her long fingered hand up so it was about four feet above the ledge where they were sitting. 'Bla-Bla is beings about yea highly big,' she explained. 'Them got muchly squinty little black eyes and icky crusty skin like rock. Bla-Bla them is havings fierce stabsome sharp teeth and little fisty scratchum hands. Them ain't any good. Muchly badsome is them. Rina is being sleepsing in her grotty at night when she hear Bla-Bla come all shuffly down the cliff. They go snarling with muchly of the gnashing of teeth. Muchly scary. Bla-Bla is beings sniffling around outside Rina's cave. Rina lay still then Bla-Bla not be seeings and go way.'

She wrapped her arms around her fins and peered at Keela timidly. The merman's stomach tightened. It was quite clear to him what had frightened Marina so terribly. In her innocent and faltering way she had perfectly described Black Trolls – unholy, foul creatures that lived deep within the rocks and were always hypnotically drawn to where there was Dark Magic. There hadn't been any in Jersey for a great number of years but with the signs of witchcraft returning to the island it wasn't much of a surprise the trolls had followed. It wasn't a welcome occurrence. Keela placed a hand on Marina's wart-covered skin.

'You were right to tell me about the Bla-Bla,' he said gently to the child, who was shivering slightly at the thought of the horrible creatures. 'Just keep hiding if they come back. Everything's going to be okay. Jessica will take care of them.'

Marina made an odd, upset snuffling noise and rubbed her flat nose on the back of her hand. 'Rina no likey Bla-Bla,' she mewed sadly again. 'All Rina is wanting is to be with Jecica and Da and Uncy Jim and be pretty, pretty lady.'

She was looking suddenly very tired and Keela knew all the exciting news had been too much for her. Besides, he had to find a way of getting a message to Jim about the Black Trolls returning.

'Come on,' he said softly, 'I think it's your bedtime.'

Wearily, Marina nodded and the merman followed her as she shuffled inside the entrance to the tunnel. There, just inside, was a small pile of ropes, seaweed and other flotsam that made up Marina's bed.

The child gave a snarl-like yawn and crawled in among the debris, making a nest for herself with her fins. Keela tenderly covered her with a large piece of fishing net and tucked her beloved fairytale book in beside her. Marina snuggled down into the jetsam and closed her enormous brown eyes. Keela gazed at her sadly. He didn't know if her dreams of beauty and a real family would ever come true. He wasn't even sure if Jessica was capable of the task that would save them all from the dark magic. All he knew was that he had to aid them both whatever way he could and right now that meant telling Jim about the Black Trolls.

He leant over and planted a small kiss on the sleeping Marina's blistered cheek. She didn't deserve to live the rest of her days in a cold, dank cave, whatever she looked like. One day, he would keep his promise and bring Jim to see what a kind-hearted, gentle girl she was. With that thought, the merman crawled silently out of the grotto and dived gracefully into the sea.

Chapter 6

The Boy Beneath the Waves

After what had undoubtedly been an interesting and eventful first day in Jersey, Jessica had been looking forward to a good night's sleep and the possibility of a lie-in the next day. Meeting with Jake, Mrs Noir and Elsa had certainly given her lots to ponder on. She had come to the conclusion that most 'true islanders', as Jim would put it, were slightly strange. She had heard somewhere that enclosed communities such as Jersey were a bit odd because everyone was married to everyone else and there was a very good likelihood that you could end up dating your cousin. Still, whatever the cause, Jessica had quickly discovered that although practically everyone she talked to knew who her mother was, most were very cagey about disclosing cold, hard facts. It therefore seemed a great waste of her time to pester people when it might be a more useful strategy to lie back and hope someone like Uncle Jim would let more information slip that she could follow up on her own. She already knew she had been wrong about one thing; her holiday in Jersey was looking far from boring.

At half past seven the next morning, Jessica's hopes for remaining in bed were dashed when she was rudely awakened by the sound of Jim's ancient truck rumbling and chugging outside. Wondering what the old man was doing up so early, she quickly dressed and hurried downstairs into the courtyard at the front of the house. Just as she suspected, her great uncle was sitting in the cab of the truck, manoeuvring it very carefully out of the garage. The vehicle seemed even more lumbering than usual as Jim edged it slowly forward. Martin, Jessica's father, had also been woken by the noise and was standing on the doorstep watching the scene in the cool, slightly damp morning mist.

'What is he doing at this time of the morning?' Jessica asked her father as Jim nudged the lorry another centimetre out of the garage.

Martin shrugged. 'Don't ask me,' he said. 'I just got here!'

Just then Jim poked his head out of the van window. 'Hello there!' he called cheerily, his breath forming little clouds in the cool air. 'I see you're up at last; I've got a little surprise for you.'

As he spoke, he momentarily lost his concentration and the van scraped against the wall of the garage, making a nerve-jangling grating noise and adding another scratch to the already tarnished bodywork.

Jessica laughed and ran forward. 'What on earth are you doing?' she asked.

Jim turned off the engine for a moment. 'Well,' he replied, 'as you seem so interested in the kind of stuff your mum did, I thought you would like to have a go at one of her favourite pastimes. I'm taking you and your dad fishing.' He chuckled and glanced back into the garage. 'Go in the kitchen and have breakfast. There's a pot of porridge on the stove and I've made us a packed lunch.'

With a smile, Jessica and her father headed back inside the house. Sure enough, in the kitchen they found a saucepan bubbling on the cooker. Together they settled down to a warm and filling breakfast, which they felt even more grateful for after their brief encounter with the cold morning air. After washing up they found a large cooler box in the corner of the kitchen containing three rounds of sandwiches, crisps, some oranges, a packet of chocolate biscuits and a bottle of lemonade. Martin found a thermos flask in one of the cupboards, which they filled with piping hot coffee and the two of them carried the provisions out to where Jim was.

The old man had by this time managed to get the truck out and Jessica now saw what had hindered his driving so much. There was a small trailer attached to the tow bar of the vehicle on which rested a small fishing boat just big enough for three or four people. It was a pretty little thing, painted white with its name in clear black letters on the stern. The glossy paint shining in the early morning sunlight made it look quite the most jolly and pleasant sight and even Jessica had to admit it made her feel quite cheerful even if she wasn't completely sure she wanted to go fishing. She walked over to have a better look and saw that the sign on the back read 'Friendship of the Waves'.

'Oh what a lovely little boat!' she said, running her hand along the smooth wooden side.

Jim grinned and pushed up the peak of his cap. 'Yeah, she's my pride and joy,' he said happily.

Martin stood with his hands in his pockets regarding the vessel. 'Yes,' he said thoughtfully, 'I remember going out in this old tub with Emma. She adored it. Spent most of her spare time out in it.'

He smiled. It was one of the rare times Jessica had seen him looking happy when he talked about her mother. Martin rested his hand on the side of the boat.

'We used to row all the way round the island together. She was always most contented when she was on the sea.' His voice trailed off and, sensing her father was again feeling a pang of grief, Jessica gently squeezed his arm.

Jim sighed sadly as if he too suddenly remembered the loss of his beloved niece. 'Come on,' he murmured quietly, 'let's get the tackle loaded up.'

Silently Jessica headed back inside the house and collected the two long fishing poles and bait basket from inside the doorway. Placing them carefully inside the boat she and Martin climbed into the cab of the lorry and the three of them set off.

Jersey in the early morning light was like a completely different island. The roads were practically empty and it almost seemed as if they were the only people on the island. A cool, grey mist hung in the air making everything they passed seem moist and clean. Dew spread like a magical silver veil across the green fields and hedges, dressing them with tiny, sparkling jewels of clear water. Now and again they would pass a herd of cows grazing lazily in the ever-growing light. The sky was beautiful – a dull, powdery blue with the very last visible stars twinkling above while on the horizon an angry, orange sun was turning the edge of the sky a burnished copper. Jessica wrapped her jacket around herself; without the sun fully risen the air was bitterly cold. Jim turned on the heater and a blast of welcome warmth wafted into the cab.

Jessica glanced out of the back window. 'Why have you only brought two rods, Jim?' she asked.

Her father tapped his breast pocket and smiled. 'I've got my book to read,' he chuckled. 'Your mum used to try and teach me to fish but I was awful. I'll leave catching tea to you and Jim.'

All three of them laughed and Jim headed the truck in the direction of St Brelade's Bay.

St Brelade's was totally different from Gorey and St Helier and to a town-dweller like Jessica it was just what a beach should be. Golden sand stretched down to the edge of the aquamarine shoreline, clean and unspoilt in the early morning light. Along the promenade, a row of neat, white shops and cafés stood ready and waiting for the day's arrival of tourists. Opposite the beach, across from the main road, was a park with bright flowerbeds and lush green lawns. The place was almost deserted as it was so early, apart from one couple who were strolling along the beach, a black Labrador bounding along at their side.

Jim drove along the road parallel to the beach and backed onto the slip road that led down to the sand. The truck bumped about even more than usual as they backed onto the empty beach.

'Come on you two,' he laughed, turning off the engine. 'Let's get this beauty on the sea.'

He passed Jessica and Martin a pair of wellies each and opened the lorry door.

Jessica regarded her new footwear with puzzlement. 'I'm wearing flip-flops,' she said as Jim and Martin went round to the back of the lorry and unhooked the *Friendship of the Waves* from her trailer.

Jim laughed. 'Fine, wear them if you want to get your toes froze off,' he chuckled.

Jessica looked towards the sea; the water was a deep, cold, navy-blue with ripples of white surf breaking on the surface. It didn't look very welcoming. She perched on the step of the lorry.

'Perhaps you have a point,' she muttered, pulling on the boots.

By the time she had her wellies on Jim had unhitched the boat and loaded the fishing tackle and cooler box into it. Jessica wandered round to the back of the truck and looked at the small vessel lying in the sand. There was a pregnant pause. Finally Jim turned to her and chuckled.

'Well, don't just stand there and gawp. I believe in sexual equality. You can help your dad get her down to the water while I park the truck. Be back in a jiffy.'

With that Jim got in the truck and drove it up the slip road towards the car park. Jessica stared at her dad in amazement.

'Cheek!' she snorted, hands on hips. 'Equal rights, indeed. More like he's a lazy old codger.'

Martin bent down to lift the boat and laughed. 'What? You're saying you're too much of a girly to do it?' he teased good-heartedly.

Jessica frowned jokingly. 'If there's anyone who's too weak it's you, old man. You don't get muscles typing articles on a laptop!'

They both laughed and together they lifted the boat. It was surprisingly light to carry between them and Jessica found herself in an unexpectedly good mood as they headed towards the ocean. The sea wind smelt fresh and wholesome in her nostrils and overhead seagulls called loudly. She knew that must have been how her mother felt, way before she'd been born – carefree and alive in the early morning, surrounded by nature. Twenty or so years before it would have been Emma who had woken early in the cottage to accompany her uncle on a fishing trip. Emma, who had sat in the passenger seat of the battered old truck watching the sun rise. Emma who, as Jessica now, helped carry the *Friendship* down to the sea, ready for a beautiful day on the water. It helped Jessica to think of that; of her mother doing the same things she was on a day like this. It made her seem real, alive, as if her spirit walked beside her on the unspoilt golden sand. It was probably the closest Jessica had felt to her since arriving on Jersey; not a sad or spooky feeling at all but one that filled her with joy. Today, she was following in the footsteps of the mother she had lost but who now felt so close at hand that she could almost hear her voice in the fresh sea breeze.

Finally, Jessica and Martin reached the edge of the water where the waves from the sea broke across the sands casting up shiny,

71

round pebbles like jewels upon the beach. Together they waded in and rested the boat in the shallow water, being careful not to let it float away. The *Friendship* bobbed about merrily in the shallows and the waves gently broke over it. Then, just as Jessica looked round for Jim, a breaker, slightly bigger than the others, splashed over the top of her boots, drenching her bare shins with icy water. She let out a yelp of surprise and nearly fell backwards into the water.

Martin laughed. 'Looks like Jim was right about you needing those wellies!' he chuckled.

Playfully, Jessica splashed his bare legs. 'Shut up,' she giggled. 'It's freezing, see!' She splashed him again making him nearly lose his grip on the side of the boat. 'I wonder where Jim is?' She turned to look up the beach. Sure enough, she was just in time to witness Jim's portly figure waddling towards them, leaving a third set of footprints beside the tracks Martin and Jessica had already imprinted in the sand. He looked even more chubby than usual in the bright orange lifejacket he had on. He carried two more of these under his arms.

'Here,' he said, passing them to Jessica and Martin. 'You'd better put these on. We don't want any men overboard, do we?'

Jessica pulled on her lifejacket as Jim and Martin manoeuvred the boat into slightly deeper waters and climbed in. She splashed through the water to the side of the vessel.

'Take my hand,' instructed Jim. 'You can't be too careful when you're around boats.'

Cautiously, Jessica gripped her great uncle's hand and climbed into the boat. Her legs shook as she stood on the curved wooden bottom and as quickly as possible she sat down on the plank that lay across the boat.

Jim clapped. 'Done like a true sailor,' he said chuckling. 'You're a natural!'

Jessica smiled. 'I don't know about that! I nearly fell over a minute ago.'

Jim took up the oars and began to paddle the *Friendship* away from the beach. Day was dawning and the air already felt warmer than when they had departed from the cottage. The sun had risen and it looked as if they were on the threshold of a pleasant day. The sky turned from a dusky indigo to a bright, pale blue with just one or two puffy white clouds floating in it, like abstract sheep grazing upon a periwinkle field. All around the boat, tiny beams of silver and gold sunlight reflected off the shimmering water. Jim sat squat upon the centreboard, paddling rhythmically out from the bay. The old man was grinning happily to himself and after a few moments in silence began to warble an odd sea shanty in his gruff Jersey accent.

'O take me out on the waves of blue,
Where Helier lived, and the fiend was slew.
The catch is plenty and the air is sweet
And on the breeze floats a faeriefolk beat.
There is a maiden of the sea
And her heart and love she's sworn to me;
With skin of emerald and eyes of gold
She knows the legends that were told.'

Jessica laughed at her great uncle's off-key singing and fiddled idly with one of the fishing rods.

'What a funny song!' she remarked. 'Really, what sort of a man would want a woman with green skin?'

The old man chuckled as the fresh ocean wind tussled his fine, grey hair. 'Quite a few if they had been on a ship with two hundred other men for six months,' he said, his black eyes glinting cheekily. 'That's an old Jersey sea shanty that is. Sung by sailors in these parts for centuries. Many a seaman would've been grateful of the company of a mermaid, even if it meant risking his life.'

Jessica smiled and peered over the side of the boat. 'And the rest of the song's about Helier, right?' she asked, quite proud of her recently acquired knowledge of Jersey. 'Uncle Jim told me all about St Helier yesterday, Dad.' She grinned happily.

Martin looked up from his book, an expression of irritation on his face.

'You said nothing about that,' he said. It was clear from his voice he again disapproved.

Jessica gritted her teeth. She was quickly growing sick and tired of her father's uncomfortable manner towards Jim. If he disliked him this much, she thought, why are we on holiday with him? She squinted her eyes from the sea spray and looked at her father.

'Wasn't a big issue, Dad,' she said bluntly. 'Just a cool story, that's all. And since when did I have to tell you everything?'

Martin clicked his tongue and turned back to his book. 'No,' he muttered resentfully. 'Why should you tell me anything? I'm only your father.'

Jessica sighed angrily, if he was going to be like this, there wasn't any point arguing.

Jim paused from rowing for a second. 'I only told her an old folk legend, Martin, nothing more. It looks to be a fine day, let's not spoil it by quarrelling so early.'

His voice was even softer than usual and his dark eyes rested upon Martin's face. The younger man, his face still displaying offence, shrugged and continued reading. Disheartened, Jessica met Jim's face in hope of some comfort. Not a word was spoken between them but both knew the writer well enough to realize it would just ruin things for the rest of the day if the argument continued over such a small issue. Jim straightened his back and forced a smile.

'Come on, Jess,' he said gently. 'I'll show you how to row.'

Smiling, and making a decided effort to ignore her father's attitude, Jessica very carefully shifted her position in the boat so she sat, rather squashed up, beside Jim. The old man smiled, obviously happy to be fishing with company for a change. 'Right,' he said. 'I think the best thing would be if I take the left oar and you take the right. We can row together.'

Jessica did as Jim told her and, mimicking the old man's movements, drew the oar through the water. It was decidedly difficult at first and Jessica's arms quickly began to ache. But after a while she got quite used to it. Once again she began to feel the joy of being out in the fresh morning air despite her father's somewhat gloomy attitude. In fact, when Jim began to warble the sea shanty again, Jessica felt only to happy to join in with him.

The tiny vessel with its three passengers carried on bobbing away from the shore until Jessica could barely make out the tourists who had begun to fill the beach. Then Jim drew the oars inside the boat and picked out a small, hook-like anchor attached to a length of rope, the other end of which was tied to the stern of the vessel. Jim lowered the anchor over the side of the *Friendship* and it sank to the bottom.

'Right,' murmured Jim, giving the rope a good tug to make sure they were fixed securely. 'That'll hold us for the morning. Now let's see if we can catch some fish.'

He picked up the two rods and handed one to Jessica. 'First we need some bait.'

He rummaged in the wicker bait basket, cupped something in his huge, shovel-like hand and held it up for Jessica to see. A pile of creamy white grubs squirmed and wriggled in his palm. Jessica wrinkled her nose in disgust.

'Ugh, they're horrible!' she squealed, turning her head away.

Jim laughed. 'They're worms,' he said, 'and there's nothing better for catching fish. Now what you have to do is get one of these beauties and skewer it on your hook, like this.' He took one of them between his thumb and forefinger and pierced it onto his hook. 'Now you try,' he encouraged.

Jessica shuddered. 'No thanks!' she said stiffly.

Jim shrugged and sighed. 'Your mother did it all the time.'

But Jessica pulled a face and firmly shook her head.

'Okay,' he said, 'I'll do it this time but by end of this holiday I want to see you doing it yourself.'

Jessica squinted as Jim baited her hook for her.

He then sat squarely back on the plank, his fishing pole gripped firmly in his hands. 'Now we cast our lines,' he said. 'Watch this.'

With a skilful flick of his wrist, Jim cast his line out over the sea. Jessica watched him and, taking her own tackle, attempted to mimic the same movement. The line flicked out from the rod rather haphazardly but landed all the same in the green-blue sea. She smiled proudly at Jim.

'Pretty good,' complimented her great uncle. 'Now we sit here, enjoy the sun and see if today's our lucky day.'

He settled himself as comfortably as he could on the narrow wooden seat and looked out into the distance.

Eager to see whether she could catch anything and prove herself a true Jersey person, Jessica did the same and the two of them sat back to back as Martin contentedly read his book and the sun rose high in the sky.

For the first hour or so Jessica found fishing quite enjoyable, sitting in the warmth as the boat bobbed merrily about on the waves. She liked watching the line as it joggled about, waiting for it to go taut so she could reel in some monster of a fish. But as the morning drew on and nothing happened at the end of her or Jim's line the novelty began to wear thin. Her father was deeply engrossed in his book and Jim had remained completely silent since they had cast off. At one point, Jessica had glanced over her great uncle's shoulder to see that he had his eyes closed and was snoring quietly. The day got hotter and hotter and Jessica was beginning to feel quite claustrophobic in her life jacket, not to mention very bored. She began to wonder whether Jim had ever caught anything or if he just rowed out here for a bit of peace and quiet. At about eleven o'clock she rummaged in the cooler and helped herself to her sandwiches, shifting about on the seat because her bum was beginning to ache. She finished her lunch still holding onto her rod one handed but her bait tempted no fish.

She was staring into the water, chewing on a melted chocolate biscuit and wondering whether to wake Jim and ask him if they could row back to shore, when something caught her eye, something very odd indeed.

Staring back up at her from about five feet below the rippling waves was a boy, not more than five or six years old. He was floating quite happily below the waves, upright, as if he were standing on something. His head was tilted back as he grinned up at Jessica and far from seeming in any distress, the child seemed relaxed and happy. Jessica blinked hard. She simply couldn't believe what she was seeing. She opened her eyes again and the boy was still there, smiling broadly. His skin was a pale mint green; his eyes were gold and looked almost too large for his face. A mane of curls floated about his head like a halo and his cheeks glowed not rosy pink like a normal child's but bottle green. Jessica could not make out the lower half of the child's body as the water was too dark but he was bare-chested and his green skin was perfectly smooth without a blemish. She leant over the side of the boat for a closer look. The boy, happy that Jessica had noticed him, grinned broadly and gracefully turned in a half circle so that he was still staring up at her, only now upside down. Jessica was amazed, how could this be possible? A child, without a guardian in sight, was swimming in the open sea beneath the waves and in no more distress than he would be paddling in the shallows. But if she had been

76

astonished before, Jessica was dumbstruck by what she saw as the boy twirled beneath the waves. He was propelling himself not with his legs as a normal human child might, but by moving a tail of delicate royal blue scales like a fish. Jess shook her head. It couldn't be happening; it just couldn't. Mermaids didn't exist. They belonged in the pages of children's books with wicked witches and dragons. You did not see them swimming about in the sea off family seaside resorts! But this was no figment of her imagination – there was a little boy with green skin and a tail floating about under the water beside the boat. The child raised a chubby fingered hand towards the surface of the water and waved merrily at Jessica. Unable to contain her disbelief any longer Jessica looked away from the child to the two men sharing the boat.

'Dad! Uncle Jim! Quick, look! You are never going to believe this!'

Jim snorted loudly as he woke from dozing, nearly dropping his rod as he did so and Martin looked up from his book, his face red from sunburn.

'What is it, Jess?' asked Jim, groggily rubbing the sleep from his eyes.

Jessica quickly rested her rod against the side of the boat. 'A boy!' she said animatedly, her eyes flicking between their confused faces. 'A little boy with green skin and a blue tail like a mermaid. He is swimming right by the boat!'

She peered into the waves again, as did her relatives but the sea was empty. The child had vanished.

Jim pushed back his cap. 'I don't see nothing,' he said shrugging his shoulders.

Martin looked slightly peeved and pushed his glasses onto the bridge of his nose. 'Of course she didn't see anything. It was probably just a trick of the light on the water!' His voice sounded slightly strained, tense even.

Jessica hit the side of the boat in frustration. 'I know what I saw and it wasn't a trick of the light! I sat here looking into the water and I saw a child floating just *there*, not two feet away!' she pleaded angrily. 'He was like a mermaid or something. He was there for a good two minutes. He even waved to me. I know it sounds crazy but I know he was there.'

Jim was staring intently into the sea. 'Well, he ain't there now!' he said, poking into the waves with his hand. 'I expect he's swum off.'

Martin closed his book and fixed Jim with his most intellectual stare. 'Jim,' he said sounding slightly patronizing, 'you can't honestly believe there was anything remotely like a child in the sea this far out. And, Jessica dear, I thought you were too old and mature to make up stories about mermaids.'

Jessica blinked indignantly. 'I only said what I thought I saw and I am not making it up. If you had seen it you would have sworn it was a mermaid!' she declared.

Martin's blue eyes flickered and he leant forward. 'Listen,' he said firmly, 'there are no such things as mermaids. You saw something – it was a trick of the light – maybe the sun got to you but I am telling you it was nothing more. Only children believe in mermaids and unless you want me to treat you like a child you will leave the matter alone.'

His voice was strong and serious as if he were scolding Jessica for saying something rude or offensive. Jessica couldn't believe she was being told off. Okay, it sounded highly unlikely that a small boy could have been swimming in the sea this far from shore but even if she was mistaken (which she knew she wasn't), she couldn't see why she was getting into trouble for saying what she truly believed was there. Angrily she crossed her arms and reclined sulkily in the boat, glaring at her father. Jim, who was still gazing into the waves as if he really expected to see the boy, sighed and looked between the father and daughter.

'It's too hot,' he said, squinting skywards, 'and I doubt we'll catch any fish now. Let's head back to shore.'

He reeled in the lines and packed away the tackle while Jessica sat silently, her eyes trained on the sea, hoping the child would reappear. She knew what she had seen wasn't a trick of the light; the child had been real. Jim rowed back to the beach but, sensing the mood, didn't sing. No-one spoke. Martin returned to reading his novel as Jessica strained to catch the slightest glimmer of movement in the water, but she saw nothing. The *Friendship* grounded on the soft gold sands and Jess and Martin climbed out. The beach was full of people by now, all wearing shorts and swimming costumes, enjoying the beautiful weather. Jess pulled off her life jacket and wellies and dumped them in the boat before helping Jim and her father carry the vessel back up the beach, being careful not to bump into the holiday-makers. She was seething with anger at her father's rebuke and the image of the boy's face still burned fresh in her brain. Whatever she'd seen had been as real and alive as she was. She'd *seen* the fleshy chubbiness of his cheeks and fingers, watched the thin stream of bubbles rise from the corner of his mouth and pop on the surface. Figments of the sun-stroked imagination didn't have such clarity, nor did they remain in the mind so clearly for so long. She glanced at her great uncle as they trudged up the beach. A strange thought entered her head. Her father had clearly disbelieved her when she said what she saw but Jim hadn't actually made any comment to dismiss the vision as just a daydream. In fact, now that Jessica thought about it more, Jim had said the boy wasn't there *now* when he had looked in the water. Did that mean he perhaps believed he *had* been there when Jessica looked? It could be that Jessica was just over-reacting. It could be that Jim was just humouring her. Jessica wasn't sure but there was a possibility that Jim believed her.

They came to the street just off the promenade where Jim had parked the lorry. They placed the boat onto its trailer and Jim began to tie it securely in place. Martin wandered back to the promenade and gazed out at the sea. Jessica glanced at him to make sure that he was out of earshot. Then she leaned over to Jim as he tied the boat in place.

'You believe me,' she whispered, before her better judgement could stop her. Jim looked up, his eyes sparkling like opals, confusion on his face.

'Believe what?' he said, his voice hushed as if he knew Jessica didn't want her father to hear.

She leaned on the boat and picked at the peeling paint. 'It's no good denying it – I know you do. You believe I saw something out there on the sea, a little boy.'

She felt as if she had finally broke into the secret world that Jim and every other Jersey person seemed to inhabit. The old man went back to arranging the oars and tackle in the boat.

'People see a lot of things, specially in these parts. Most people are too sceptical to believe them. That's the trouble with the world today, too many sceptics. Me, I live life with an open mind – less surprises that way. If you say you saw a little boy swimming under the water and you say you ain't lying, who am I to say otherwise? You've got to believe what is true to you.'

He straightened up and Jessica met his gaze. 'So you're saying you believe me?' she asked defiantly. 'I want to hear you say it.'

Jim looked uncomfortable and fiddled with a bit of rope from the boat. He opened his mouth and was about to answer when another voice cried out from up the street.

'Ahoy, sailors! Caught anything today?'

Jessica looked up to see the gawky figure of Jake, the grandson of Jim's old friend whom Jessica had met the day before, lolling towards them. The ungainly farmer's son had on a pair of baggy Bermuda shorts adorned with bright red and blue flowers that made his long, bony-kneed legs look even more comical and a slightly dirty, white vest shirt with a cartoon surfer shark on it and the words 'Bite The Surf' emblazoned on the front. He strolled leisurely over to Jim and Jessica and gazed into the boat.

'Hi, Jessica. Hi, Jim. I see you have been fishing for the famed Jersey Invisible Trout,' he said with a laugh. Jim chuckled. Jessica threw the young lad an icy look as she remembered their first meeting. Jake stuck his hands in his pockets and grinned at her.

'You're certainly looking less like a Grockle today, Jess.'

Jessica pushed a flyaway strand of her thick hair behind her ear. 'Thanks, I've been out fishing with Dad and Jim all morning. I guess that makes me a bit more of a Jersey person.'

Jake shrugged. 'Works for me,' he replied.

Jim gazed at the boy with suspicion. 'Shouldn't you be back at the farm, helping?' asked the old man.

Jake kicked a loose stone on the road and watched it roll downhill lazily. 'Probably, but it's too nice a day to be working. I've fed the cows and chicks already this morning. All work and no play makes Jake a dull boy.'

Jim sighed but Jake's laid-back manner made Jess laugh. He was so comical, with his lanky, white legs, hooked nose and cheesy jokes, she could feel herself warming to him.

Jake looked at her, narrowing his eyes in the bright sunlight. 'Want an ice cream or something?' he asked. 'Café's just along the front.'

Jessica looked at Jim for approval and the old man shrugged. 'Go ahead, you two. I expect Jessica's fed-up. She's been stuck with me all morning. Fishing isn't the most interesting of activities. I'll let your dad know where you are.'

So, leaving Jim to finish off tying up the boat, the two young people strolled back down the hill and along the seafront to the joint café and shop. Inside, the air was cool and refreshing and several plastic tables were laid out. They sat at one near the front window so they could watch the holidaymakers. They glanced at the slightly dog-eared menu and made their selections. Jessica chose a strawberry and vanilla sundae while Jake plumped for a mint choc chip one. Soon a middle-aged waitress with bleached blonde hair and a slightly worn expression approached them and took their order. They then waited, staring absent-mindedly out of the window.

'I think I owe you an apology,' said Jake finally.

Jessica looked away from the large bluebottle buzzing in the corner of the pane.

'For what?' she replied.

Jake played with the salt and pepper shakers on the table and looked embarrassed. 'For yesterday. What I said about your mother. It was none of my business and I was bang out of order for even mentioning her. And I'm sorry if I didn't seem very sensitive about her dying.'

'Oh,' said Jessica quietly.

She wasn't sure what else to say. She had been hurt by Jake's words but now she wondered if she had been too thin-skinned. She had just been angry that he had started talking about her and then left her with a lot of loose ends, like everyone else did. Maybe he had been thoughtless, but no less so than anyone else had been.

'I forgive you,' she answered finally, seeing the guilt in Jake's eyes. 'I just don't understand what you meant. I want to know about her; if you can help me please do. What did you mean about people in Jersey not being what they seemed? And why has my mother got a name for herself?'

Jake had begun to look shifty again, as he had in the doorway of DeGrudy's. Jessica was about to get cross with him but something stopped her. She thought of the child she had seen in the water this morning. Maybe the whole thing did make sense. Jim had said he lived life with an open mind; perhaps if she began to do the same she could start to understand.

81

She leant back in her chair. 'Go on,' she encouraged, keeping her tone flat.

The smile had fallen from Jake's face. 'Okay, I guess I owe you,' he said softly, before adding in a more determined voice, 'but understand, I'm not going over the mark. Like I said, it was none of my business in the first place but I am in it now so I guess I can't back out. And promise you'll take what I tell you with an unbiased mind and don't push me for any more than I can give. Promise?'

Jess nodded. 'Promise,' she said firmly.

Jake took a paper napkin out of the dispenser on the table and slowly unfolded it as he spoke.

'People on Jersey,' he began slowly, 'are different from people on the mainland. You must understand that, Jessica. It comes from living cut off on an island. We have ways of living, rules that govern us deeper than any law. You can't comprehend them right now, not with your head. But in your heart, you know. You have Jersey blood in you so you know. These rules, they cannot be broken, it is they that guide our life. One of the rules is believe in family, trust in family. This is why I can't tell you all; it must come from your family. Family is what binds us all, you especially. Who you are is in your heart.'

Jake's pale blue eyes dropped sadly and he said no more. The words he spoke seemed not to be his but an echo of a time and a place that Jessica felt was just out of reach. He was right – she didn't understand what he had meant by rules, but then there was so much she didn't understand: the boy beneath the waves, the song she had heard the first night she had arrived in Jersey, the unbridgeable gulf between her father and her great uncle. She didn't know what these things meant. She looked at Jake who was once again staring out of the window, a rather melancholy look on his face.

'I ... I don't understand, Jake. You're right, and I don't know where to look for answers. Don't worry I'm not asking you for any more help. A promise is a promise.' She looked out of the window, at the families passing by. Fathers, children, mothers – were they from Jersey? Did they understand the rules that Jake spoke of? She couldn't say. 'Mum's dead,' she said simply, stating a fact, not asking for pity, 'and Dad and uncle Jim won't speak about her. They tell me nothing. What they do say makes no sense. I wish Jim would give me a straight answer. I *know* he knows more than he's letting on?'

Jake sighed deeply and smiled a crooked half smile. 'I expect he will, given time. Olds are funny that way.'

Just then the blonde waitress returned carrying two tall glasses of delicious Jersey ice cream, which she plonked on the table in front of them. 'One strawberry and vanilla and one mint choc chip,' she said cheerily; then looked at their glum faces. 'Ah, cheer up, you two. I don't see why two healthy young 'uns like yourselves are looking so miserable on a lovely sunny day like today. You wanna try being on your feet since nine this morning in a boiling hot kitchen while everyone is out on the beach!' She sighed and tore a bill from her pad. 'That's four pounds, fifty – and cheer up!' She turned and waddled away.

Jake grinned and took up his spoon. 'She has a point,' he said, shovelling a lump into his mouth, 'and this is very good ice cream. Let's drop the subject for now.'

Jessica smiled and nibbled at the wafer. 'Thanks for being honest with me. I don't pretend to understand it all but I am going to make an effort to.' She grinned and picked up her spoon. 'To tell you the truth yesterday, when I first met you, I thought you were a bit strange but things have happened since then that have opened my eyes.'

Jake patted some of the melted green ice cream from his lips. 'I kind of figured that you found me a bit a of nutter; most people do. But what changed your mind?'

Jessica wrinkled her forehead. A lot of things had happened in the past day that made Jake's somewhat eccentric manner seem not so odd. Primarily her vision this morning. After all she couldn't really call someone weird when she herself was seeing mermaids. But her meeting with the strange Agatha Noir and her haunted grand-daughter Elsa had also made her realize there were people on this island a lot more disturbing than Jake. But Jessica still wasn't sure even Jake would believe her about the mermaid. So instead she decided to mention only the Noirs.

'Just met someone yesterday that made me realise you weren't so much of a loony,' she said drolly, taking a spoonful of ice cream.

Jake leant his elbows on the table. 'Who?' he asked.

Jessica squished the melting ice cream about in the glass

playfully before meeting his interested gaze. 'Do you know an old woman called Mrs Noir? Jim helped her with her shopping yesterday and took me with him. Boy! Her and that grand-daughter of hers are peculiar.' She shuddered at the memory.

Jake's eyes widened and he put a hand to his throat in mock terror. 'You made an understatement there, Jess,' he said in hushed tones. 'That old biddy's an urban legend round here. Dad jokingly calls her the Curse of Gorey! Your great uncle's one of the few people who has anything to do with her. There are loads of stories about her. They say she killed her husband.'

Jess chuckled. 'You're kidding!' she said. She knew that Jake had tricked her before – swimming cows indeed!

But the boy shrugged and toyed with his spoon, clinking it in the glass. 'Like I said, it's all hearsay but everyone knows the story – just that no-one can prove anything. I'll tell you if you like.'

Jessica needed no encouragement. 'Go on,' she said grinning.

Jake clasped his hands in front of him and began.

'Well, back in the late fifties Agatha was married to a man called Philippe Noir. Now, apparently Philippe was a bit of a ladies' man and was constantly cheating on her. He would go out, get drunk and chase any young thing in a skirt. Agatha ignored it. Some say she didn't know, others that she was too proud to admit it. Divorce was frowned on back then, so leaving him was out of the question. Anyway the story as I heard it goes: Philippe begins a particular passionate affair with a young milkmaid on the farm where he's a labourer. Lily Treq was her name – just seventeen and very pretty. Now Agatha is pregnant at the time with his child but that's not going to stop Phil. He thinks he's got it made – cushy life at home and a bit on the side. That is until it comes out that Lily, unmarried, is also pregnant! The poor girl is right up a gum tree, 'cause having a baby out of wedlock back then was really shameful. Her father tells her to marry the father or get rid of the baby, but as far as anyone knows Lily has no boyfriend. But tongues are wagging about Philippe and word gets back to Agatha. Now things get interesting.'

'What?' said Jessica. She wasn't that keen on Mrs Noir and was glad her gut feelings seemed to be correct. Jake took a couple more mouthfuls of ice cream to moisten his throat and

84

then continued. 'The story gets a bit fuzzy here so I'm only saying what I was told. One night Philippe and two mates take a boat out to do a bit of night fishing. Philippe has with him a hip flask of brandy and all night he is swigging away, having a great time. Suddenly he begins to feel ill. I mean *really* sick. His skin turns green and begins to come up in blisters; he is foaming at the mouth and clutching his chest. His friends are really worried and they are about to turn back to shore when Philippe staggers, stands up in the boat, wobbles a bit and plunges overboard, sinking like a stone. The friends row back to Gorey and raise the alarm but though the police do a search all round the island, there's no body. Official verdict, accidental death; unofficial verdict, murder by poison. All those herbs in Mrs Noir's back garden – everyone thought Lily's pregnancy was the last straw and she spiked his brandy. But the flask vanishes with the body, so where's the proof?'

Jessica gasped, open mouthed. 'Wow, you're kidding,' she said.

Jake grimly shook his head. 'And that's how the legend started: Agatha Noir, Multiple Murderess. Not that I believe the other deaths have anything to do with her. Or even that she killed Philippe. But where that family's concerned there's been some bad luck – if you can call it that.'

Jessica blinked in disbelief. 'Hang on, what "other deaths"? How many?'

'Four in all. If you believe the stories, which I don't. Even if she's as nutty as a fruitcake, things like that just don't happen in Jersey.'

Jessica gazed at him, her heart throbbing with grim excitement. There was nothing she liked better than a good story, especially a macabre one. 'Well,' she enthused, 'who do they say she killed?'

Slowly he counted off the names on his fingers. 'Philippe Noir, Lily Treq, Katrina Noir and Bill Green. But, I mean, look at the evidence on Lily's death. Suicide. The girl knows her fate – the father of her unborn child is dead, she'll live in shame for the rest of her life. Then she sees the only way out. Climbs to the top of Gorey Castle, onto the battlements, and jumps.' He let a dollop of ice cream drop from his spoon into the glass with a splat as if to illustrate his point.

Jessica grimaced. 'That's horrible,' she said, covering her mouth, 'but hardly murder.'

'That's what I'm saying. And the same with Katrina and Bill. Murder? No way.'

'Who were they?' she asked looking at her sundae with new disgust.

Jake crossed his arms. 'Katrina was Agatha's daughter, born shortly after the whole messy Lily-Philippe business. Apparently Agatha made her the centre of her world; she was all she had. Very protective of her – never let her go to school, taught her at home. She was always with her. Still lived at home when she was thirty.'

Jess was quiet for a moment. She thought of Elsa, obviously Katrina's child. History seemed to be repeating itself. Did Katrina suffer as much then as her daughter seemed to be suffering now? 'Go on,' she said dryly.

Jake took a deep breath and looked slightly pale. 'Anyway, as you can imagine Katrina ended up really resenting her mother and finally she starts to rebel. She begins to date a kindly shop-keeper by the name of Bill Green. Agatha hates it but Katrina's thirty and she's an old woman so how can she stop her? So Kat and Bill begin to get serious and finally Bill is offered a better-paid job on the mainland so he, knowing the hold Agatha has over Katrina, proposes and suggests they move back to England. Kat is overjoyed and agrees, but her mother is livid. She does not want her daughter to leave Jersey and the two have a blazing row, in which Katrina tells her mother she wants nothing else to do with her and leaves. She and Bill move away from the island and are married. Soon they have a baby girl, Elsa, and the future looks peachy.'

'Good for Katrina, I say!' said Jessica.

Listening to Jake's story had made her dislike Mrs Noir even more. She didn't know if she was a murderer but even if she wasn't she could believe the rest of the story was true. But the young lad shook his head. 'Not as good as you think. When Elsa is three months old, the family is out on a drive in the country when a car that was never identified overtakes them on a narrow lane forcing Bill to swerve and crash headlong into a wall. Both Bill and Katrina were killed on impact but, miraculously, baby Elsa was found sleeping unharmed among the wreckage.'

86

Jessica frowned. 'Poor Elsa. But what are you saying? Mrs Noir somehow arranged for her daughter and her son-in-law to be killed? Sounds a bit far fetched if you ask me.'

Jake smiled. 'I know – my point exactly. But some people believe it. Not me, or your uncle, but some do. The story is that Mrs Noir's a bit of a control freak, can't stand people undermining her – to an extent I can see that. But if you swallow all the gossip you have to accept that Mrs Noir hired a hit man to make the deaths look like an accident. Rubbish, if you ask me. She was at least seventy and where would she find a hit man? Mind you, she wasn't too upset by their deaths – didn't even go to the funeral; never forgave Katrina for leaving, see? The only real interest she showed was in getting custody of Elsa, which she did. Worse luck. That girl would've been better off in care. And I know first hand what she's like with her. I find it a lot more believable and a lot more frightening than any horror stories about Mrs Noir being a murderer. Weird set-up, just weird.'

Jessica nodded in agreement. From her one, brief meeting with the pair she was sure Elsa wasn't at all happy with her grandmother and Jake seemed to be confirming her fears.

'What is it with them?' she asked, supping the melted ice cream from the bottom of her glass.

Jake reclined in his chair. 'Everyone can see it. It's in Elsa's eyes. She's practically a prisoner in that house. Agatha lets her go to school but apart from that she never leaves her grandmother's side. She's scared to. Some say Agatha beats her to make her stay, others that she knows what happened when her mother crossed her grandmother. But she is frightened. Just sits in class, staring at everything with those haunted eyes. People try to befriend her but she backs away, says grandmère wouldn't like it. I bet grandmère wouldn't, barmy old bat!'

His face was etched with bitterness and Jess could not blame him. She believed Jake, for all his joking and riddles; she believed Elsa was in trouble and a voice in the back of her head urged her, if she had the chance, to help the girl when they next met. She had begun to feel, what with all that had happened that day, that Jersey was enveloping her in its dark labyrinth of whispers and secrets and that maybe, just maybe, there was some force that drew her to it – perhaps to save Elsa. She was in deep now, too deep to turn away, whatever her father and Jim said. She would discover the truth.

Jake turned back from the window and stared at Jessica with deep, blue eyes. 'She's ill too,' he continued. 'God knows what is wrong with her. Did you see how painfully thin she was? Wears clothes made for a six year old. That old bag doesn't give her hardly enough to eat. My cousin works as an assistant in her class and she says there have been several times at school when she's fainted or had a coughing fit. But Agatha refuses to take her to a doctor, treats everything with herbs and stuff from her garden. No-one will do anything because people who have crossed Agatha Noir have a very nasty habit of ending up dead!'

Jess felt suddenly very angry. Maybe there was a reason for her being in Jersey. Maybe it was to stop someone else dying too young as her mother had. Maybe the boy beneath the waves was an icon, a symbol of Elsa needing to be rescued. She stood up and placed her hands on her hips.

'I'll help Elsa. I'm not scared of some mean old woman,' she said.

Jake looked up at her shocked. 'Please, Jess,' he said. 'You don't understand. There's more at stake. You could get in a lot of trouble.'

She turned to the boy and cocked an eyebrow. 'I thought you said you didn't believe Mrs Noir was a murderer.'

Jake looked uncomfortable. 'I don't but you shouldn't barge into other people's business when you don't know everything. Remember what I said about family, you gotta get things straight in your own life before you can help others.'

'I understand that family's important over here but you yourself believe Elsa's being mistreated. Surely that's more important than the fact Mrs Noir's her grandmother? Are you behind me or not?'

Jake dropped his eyes. 'Yes,' he said quietly, 'I am behind you. You have to do what you feel is right.'

Jessica rummaged in her pocket and pulled out the change to pay for the sundaes.

'Well, good!' she said abruptly, before adding in a softer voice, 'I'm glad of your help, Jake.'

She turned and left the café to look for Jim and her father.

Jake watched her go but didn't follow. He had promised his grandfather he would help Jessica all he could and from what he knew of this headstrong girl – she would certainly need it.

Chapter 7

Calling of the Dark One

It was a cold, misty night in Gorey. As the previous day had brought warm sunshine and fair breezes, nightfall had claimed its hours with a biting chill and a clammy, wet wind that blew in from the sea causing the boats moored in the bay to toss about like startled horses pulling at their halters. Tourists had departed with the sunlight, drawing into the safe warmth of cosy hotels and boarding houses away from the night, and even hardier islanders in the small town had returned home to their beds extinguishing the lights from the windows of their houses. The night was pitch, as dark as a raven's feather, as dark as death itself. Not even the moon dared shed its glow on Gorey, for this was a night for witchcraft, a night for evil.

Two lone figures, however, struck out on such an unholy night towards the steep hill that led to the castle. One sat, squat and fat, in an ancient wheelchair, a battered leather doctor's case clutched preciously on its lap, tweed coat blowing in the wind; the other, young and painfully thin, with hair like a babe's that flew out behind her as she pushed the chair, much too heavy for her tiny frame. An odd pair with a midnight mission that would strike fear into any mortal heart. Through the darkness and the wind they trudged, heading up to Gorey Castle.

Elsa's spindly legs gave way as she stumbled on the gravel path causing the chair to skid. Agatha Noir glared over her shoulder at her granddaughter, her eyes burning with contempt.

'Honestly girl! Be careful. You nearly tipped me out. Don't you dare try it, you useless bag of bones!' The old woman's voice was heavy with a loathing that made the brisk tones she used towards Elsa in company seem like a loving purr.

90

The child dipped her head in fear. 'I'm sorry, Grandmère, my foot slipped. It ... it won't happen again.'

Her tone was a timid mew, barely audible above the howling wind.

Mrs Noir snorted with scorn and jabbed at the girl with a bony finger.

'You just see that it doesn't, my girl, or it's a week in the attic without food!' she cackled.

Elsa chewed her bottom lip and lowered her pretty, pale eyes. She knew better than to cross her grandmother, especially on a night like this. She feared the ritual that they were to perform, more than her grandmother, more than a week in the attic, but she knew that it was best she did what she was told or God knew how she would be punished. Summoning all her strength she took hold of the wheelchair and heaved it forward.

They had reached the top of the hill by now and Gorey Castle loomed over them like some dark and imposing monster, shadowy in the blackness. Agatha gazed up at it and her little green eyes gleamed with almost demonic joy. 'Yes,' she croaked to herself, her thin painted lips spread in a reptilian smile. Elsa too regarded the castle, wariness shining in her eyes. She knew its secrets, her grandmother had showed her first hand the hidden passageways where the bravest of hearts feared to roam. Not that Elsa was brave. Her will was not her own; it was enslaved to her grandmother. She had no choice in whether she went forward or back. Agatha's seaweed-coloured eyes glanced at Elsa.

'You know the place,' she barked, half questioning, half ordering.

Elsa nodded silently and pushed the chair up towards the castle's sandy wall. The old woman's eyes flickered across the uneven surface for a moment before regarding the leather holdall in her lap. Fingers slightly trembling, like a child about to unwrap a birthday gift, Agatha's quick hands unfastened the clasp on the case. The bag opened and from the interior pulsed a pale, golden light, quite beautiful, that illuminated the old hag's creased face. But the source of the light wasn't what Agatha was interested in at that moment. She reached into the satchel and dipped her fingertips into a purple velvet purse, smothering them with a powder like mustard. Snapping the bag shut, the

91

old woman turned her attention back to the wall of the castle and in particular one large stone, slightly paler than the rest. Elsa took a couple of steps backwards in fear as her grandmother scrawled on the stone slab with her fingers, leaving odd marks and symbols in the yellow powder. When she was contented she sat back in her chair and began to chant in a strange low voice:

'Sentinels of stone and rock,
You, who have stood for countless years,
As watchmen over the place of coven's home land,
Lay down your guard to me.
I come to step upon the footways of Brisoue the Fearful
The all-powerful Warlock who fathered the magic makers
of this isle
Who placed you within this pitiful barricade,
As guardians for the foolish and the ignorant
So they may not find this place.
I wish to act upon the mystical arts –
Yield to me!
Show me your secret!'

The very second Agatha had finished speaking, the marks she had drawn upon the stone began to glow a dull green. Elsa scrunched up her eyes and drew her head deeper inside the hood of her duffle coat. She didn't like it when her grand-mother did magic but she knew this spell was merely a playful conjuring trick compared with what was to come. The odd symbols continued to shine for a few moments before slowly fading away. As they did so, the sturdy stone upon which they were written began to shimmer and become transparent. In a matter of seconds it had disappeared completely and the stones surrounding the gap began to dissolve away. One by one, the stones that made up the wall of the castle glowed eerily before vanishing into the cold, night air. Within about a minute, the spell was complete and before Agatha and Elsa there stood a dark and foreboding tunnel that led straight into the wall of the castle, just wide enough for Agatha's wheelchair to get through.

Elsa quaked. She didn't want to enter the ghostly passageway.

It was dank and tight and full of ancient secrets. Agatha smiled at her slyly.

'The time has come, child,' she croaked, gleeful to see Elsa's distress.

The child shuddered but, knowing it was best to get the awful deed over with quickly, she took hold of the wheelchair and crept through the sinister arch.

The tunnel was claustrophobically narrow, the width barely enough to get Agatha's chair past the solid stone walls and the roof so low the ancient cobwebs that hung from it became tangled in Elsa's blonde hair. Once they were a few feet inside, the magical doorway that had opened up became once again transformed into solid rock, leaving them trapped deep within the castle wall with no way to go but forwards. Warily, Elsa trudged along the narrow passageway, wheeling her grandmother's cumbersome weight ahead of her. The night outside had been dark but it was as bright as the midday sun compared to the blackness of the tunnel. It was as if she had been suddenly blinded, so impenetrable was the blackness. Elsa wanted to close her eyes to block out the horror of her situation but with her eyes closed she was no less afraid than when they were open. Her other senses still told her what a wicked place this was. She could feel the slimy algae that clung to the walls rub wetly against the back of her hands as she pushed the wheelchair; hear the slow, cold dripping of water as it oozed from the ceiling; smell the repugnant odour that filled the cramped walkway, a stench of decay and death that made her want to retch. She knew there were creatures living in this underground burrow, disgusting things like rats and spiders that scurried around near her. She was sure there were other beings that did not have physical forms, or even names, lurking ready to strike. But still she went on, through the darkness.

Agatha remained silent. Elsa knew this was not because she was frightened, but because the old woman was deep in contemplation of the supernatural ritual she was to perform when they reached their journey's end. Elsa knew her grandmother was very clever. Not kind, not good-natured, but possessing a seemingly bottomless pit of knowledge incomprehensible to lesser mortals. This was one of the reasons Elsa was so scared of her: she was never quite sure of what her grandmother was capable.

The passage seemed to snake on for ever, burrowing ever downwards in a tightly coiling spiral into the hard, dark rock of the mountain. Elsa thought they had been walking for a good hour before any sign of their destination was visible. But as they rounded a twisted corner in the passageway a chink of moonlight illuminated the blackness, shining through the end of the tunnel. Elsa was almost joyous to see it – almost. For although she was more than glad to be coming out of the awful, dank blackness she knew that what was awaiting them was far worse than the gloom of the tunnel.

The passage ended in a particularly steep and bumpy downhill slope and Elsa had to lean back with all her feeble strength to stop the weight of Mrs Noir's wheelchair running away from her. The passageway emerged onto a stone outcrop cut into the side of the hill a good fifty feet below the castle. The shelf was round and perfectly smooth as if it had been fashioned into the mountain by man rather than nature. All around the edges of the tunnel entrance and around the ledge itself green wild grasses and bracken grew which meant it was almost completely hidden from anyone on the sea. Right within the centre of the outcrop was a shallow pool about three feet wide and a foot deep, filled with seawater and surrounded by a ring of jagged rock that curved in over it like claws. The wind whistled even more fiercely out here on the mountain and it chapped Elsa's cheeks. But Agatha Noir couldn't seem happier in this strange place if she tried. Her dark green eyes glistened insanely in the dull moonlight and her orange painted mouth formed a malicious smile. She took off her tweed hat and her silver-white hair trailed behind her in the wind like ghostly, pale vapour.

Chilled by the bitter night air and fearful of the impending wizardry, Elsa pulled her duffle coat around her more tightly and began to edge slowly inside the passageway in the hope that she could hide while her grandmother performed the evil task. But Mrs Noir's shifty eyes fixed on her just as she began to back away.

'And where do you think you're going?' barked the old woman in a voice so accusing it nailed Elsa to the spot.

Elsa played nervously with the toggles on her jacket and stared at the toes of her shoes. 'I don't like magic, you know that, Grandmère, and I am no good at it,' she mumbled timidly.

'Can't I just wait in the tunnel until you're finished, please?'

A wicked grin spread across Agatha's face and she slowly shook her head. 'Oh no,' she purred, her voice quiet but threatening. 'No, no, no, my girl. You are going to stay here and help me as you always do.' She paused for a moment to let the fear sink deep into her grand-daughter's spirit before snapping. 'Now, get back here and light the candles!'

Elsa jumped with fright and scuttled back to her grandmother's side. Mrs Noir threw the huge leather satchel roughly into Elsa's arms, nearly knocking her backwards. The girl, eyes wide and watery with terror, placed the bag on the smooth stone ground and knelt beside it. She flicked the catch and as the case opened once again the eerie golden light glowed from within it. This time, however, it was accompanied by a tiny, high-pitched cry.

'Please,' the little quaking voice begged. 'Help me, let me go!'

Elsa's face crumbled with pity but she knew she could do nothing. She glanced at her grandmother and then back inside the bag. 'I'm sorry,' she whispered, her voice filled with compassion. 'I can't. I don't want her to hurt you but I must do what I am told.' The tiny voice began to weep pitifully.

Agatha glanced down at her grand-daughter. 'Girl,' she roared. 'Don't talk to the sacrifice! Get the candles.'

Quickly Elsa reached inside the satchel and pulled out four large, white candles and a box of matches before snapping the case shut. The light still remained in the bag crying bitterly. Trying to repress her feelings of guilt and distress, Elsa stood the four candles around the pool in the centre of the ledge. Her tiny, slender fingers trembling with fear, the girl took one match from the box and struck it. The little orange flame sprung to life at the end of the taper and flickered in the wind beneath the shelter of her cupped hand. Careful not to let the flame become extinguished by the bitter breeze, Elsa lit the candles one by one under the watchful eye of the old woman. Miraculously, despite the strong wind, once each candle was lit the flame that glowed from it remained still and tall without so much as a flicker in the cold air. They illuminated the dark arena and sparkled in the reflection of the black pool. It was a still, almost golden light that automatically made the stone ledge seem sacred and pagan.

Elsa stood back up, the leather satchel in her hands, her body tense and nervy. 'Do ... do you want the ingredients, Grandmère?' she asked quietly.

The old woman glared at her. 'Of course I do, stupid child! Did you make sure to bring everything? The wormwart? The widow's cap?'

Elsa nodded stiffly. She didn't dare forget anything; she would be in grave trouble if she did. Her grandmother had taught her well of the mystical properties the plants that grew in the unkempt back garden of their home had when they were mixed together with skill. However, Mrs Noir made sure that Elsa never had the opportunity to develop magical skills of her own. That would give her too much power.

The girl once again opened the ancient bag. Almost immediately the strange golden light shone brightly from inside it and the high crying was audible. This time though, Agatha heard the soft wailing and sneered disapprovingly.

'Shut it, you pathetic little firefly,' she barked. 'You have only a few more minutes to live. Don't waste it grizzling!'

Elsa tried to block out her grandmother's cruelty as she unpacked the other items. She didn't want to think about what was going to happen to the poor creature inside the bag.

One by one Elsa passed the odd collection from the satchel to Agatha. First there was a large, shallow dish of brown earthenware. It looked ancient and was very chipped around the edges and marked both inside and out with strange symbols like the ones Mrs Noir had made on the castle wall. Accompanying this was a small marble pestle both of which the old woman grabbed eagerly. Next came a long, thin, black glass bottle that reeked of rotten fish. Agatha took this and, removing the cork with her teeth, poured the oily contents into the bowl. More strange things were to follow as Elsa blindly unpacked them, trying hard to be dispassionate. A pouch of red leather containing some moss-coloured powder, several bundles of leaves and sticks tied up with string, a trio of small bright blue bottles each containing a different coloured liquid, an old jam jar, with some foul matter congealing around the neck, in which lurked something that looked like mud but moved of its own accord. All these unusual and unpleasant items were poured into the dish by Mrs Noir and crushed with the pestle, the old hag cackling and muttering to herself.

As the last item was added to the unholy brew, the mixture within the bowl turned a deep shade of purple, bubbling as if it had been boiled. Mrs Noir stirred it lovingly with the pestle before turning back to her grand-daughter, who stood hugging the satchel for comfort.

'Now girl,' she croaked urgently. 'The faerie. Bring it to me so I can make the sacrifice.'

She held out a ghostly pale hand towards her. Elsa took a half step backwards, still clutching the bag.

'Why?' she whispered, tears in her pale eyes. 'I don't understand. I'll never understand. Why are you doing this?' She looked at the dark pool and the candles shimmering around it. 'It's evil,' she stated, her voice small with fear. 'That thing is evil. And you keep feeding it. Why?'

Agatha's face was dark, her voice low; she spoke not in anger but in a tone cold and emotionless.

'It is the way of nature,' she muttered to the quaking Elsa. 'So many things have been forgotten because of man's blindness to the spirits of night and nature. People like us, we keep the one true power alive. What Helier did was a crime against mother earth. The spirit that is imprisoned within the rock of Jersey – it is right that it is released. Then the isle shall return to a state of pure magic and blackness. Nature shall reign.' She smiled, her eyes dancing demonically in the candlelight. 'And we, my child, we shall be rewarded with powers beyond our wildest dreams.' She glanced back to the bowl that rested on her knees and sighed. 'But to do that, the guardian of Jersey must be destroyed. I failed once to end the bloodline Helier blessed. I shall not fail again.'

Elsa still didn't move. She stood still, her arms wrapped around the bag, shivering with cold and fear. Agatha caught her frightened gaze.

'Give me the sacrifice.'

The child remained motionless, her tiny, frail chest rising and falling in short, scared gasps.

The aged hag's eyes filled with rage at this act of silent defiance. She turned her open hand over so that her gnarled fingers formed a claw.

'I said give me the faerie, you useless cretin!' she roared fiercely. As she did so a bolt of jagged white-blue lightning shot

97

from her fingertips, piercing the darkness momentarily before shooting into Elsa's arm in a star-like explosion. The young girl let out a bloodcurdling scream, dropped the bag and clutched her forearm with pain. Mrs Noir leant heavily on the arm of her wheelchair as if the last spell had drained her energy.

'You want another one?' she spat at Elsa, who knelt beside the bag nursing her wounded limb, tears filling her eyes. The scrawny child shook her head silently. Without further orders from her grandmother, she began to open the mysterious satchel again. Once more, the beautiful golden light flooded out as Elsa reached inside the bag, sobbing. Slowly and ceremoniously, Elsa lifted the source of the light from the bag, letting it illuminate the broad stone. Inside an ornate gilded cage, like those used to imprison songbirds in days of yore, quivering with fear and crouched into a tiny ball was the figure of a weeping faerie, its wings brutally crushed so that she could not fly. She glowed, as all faeries did, but Elsa knew that her light would soon be extinguished. Quickly, Elsa passed the cage to her grandmother who stared at the magic creature with morbid fascination.

'The ceremonial dagger,' barked Mrs Noir, her green eyes never leaving the frightened elf. Grimly, Elsa reached inside the bag for the last time and pulled out a bundle of dirty, white rags, which she reluctantly unwrapped. Inside lay a very beautiful, very deadly dagger. Its blade was short and pointed, fashioned out of a cold, silver metal that gleamed in the firelight. The handle was beautifully crafted in the form of a rampant snake, its scales made from tiny diamonds and sapphires. The serpent's eye was a glistening emerald that looked so lifelike Elsa was sure it could blink. She shuddered as Agatha grabbed it from her hand and slowly began to mutter some inaudible chant to herself.

Elsa shut her eyes tight. She did not want to think about what her wicked grandmother was doing to the poor elf. She could hear its high-pitched cries for help and cursed herself for not having the courage to do anything. Soon the air became eerily quiet and timidly Elsa opened her eyes. The golden glow of the faerie was no more and her grandmother sat in her wheelchair, wiping the silver elf blood from the knife on the rags. In the vessel resting on her lap, the potion was no longer rich amethyst but shone like cut crystal with a million tiny rainbows. Elsa gulped. She knew it was now her turn. This was the reason her grandmother had brought her up here to this evil place ever since she was a babe. She was a living sacrifice to the Dark One.

'Come here!' growled the old woman grabbing hold of Elsa's wrist. She roughly rolled up the girl's sleeves. Elsa gritted her teeth and prepared for the pain that was to come. Her gaunt, pale arm was exposed revealing the patchwork of scabs and scars upon her skin. The old woman eyed her disfigured flesh and almost gently placed the silver blade onto it.

'The final ingredient,' she hissed menacingly. 'The fresh blood of a young witch!'

Elsa squeezed her eyes tightly shut. Inside her head she began to chant her own mantra of which her grandmother knew nothing. It was the one act of rebellion she could muster to detach herself from the blood she was forced to give. I do this unwillingly, she thought angrily. The Dark One is evil, Grandmère is evil. You take my body but never my soul ... never, never, never!

The sharp slice of the dagger pierced her forearm, making her gasp with the familiar agony, but still she silently chanted. Agatha gripped the girl's arm, squeezing it. A strong trickle of scarlet oozed into the bowl hissing violently as it met the silver brew. When there was enough, Agatha flexed her fingers over Elsa's wound and quickly a new black scab appeared to staunch the flow. She cast the girl roughly to one side. Elsa yelped and lay rubbing her injury.

Agatha gazed into the bowl and chuckled evilly. The potion had once again changed appearance and was now bright red, hissing and crackling like some angry beast wanting to be released. A thin plume of black, foul-smelling smoke had begun to rise from it. Elsa turned her eyes skyward. Dark clouds had begun to form overhead. The wind howled even more strongly in Elsa's ears as she crouched low on the rock. Laughing maniacally, Agatha Noir slowly rose to her feet, the bubbling liquid foaming wildly in the dish. She threw her head backwards and her long, grey hair streamed out.

'Hear me, Dark Demon,' she cried as she slowly begun to pour the foul brew into the black pool:

'I am a child of darkness.
I summon ye from your stone prison
To gain knowledge.
Show your face and advise me on my quest to defeat
The bloodline that incarcerated you
Within the rock of Devil's Hole
So together we may reign again.'

The last of the boiling liquid flowed from the bowl deep into the dark water of the stone pool. As it vanished, the water began to churn and foam, forming images under the flickering candlelight. Soon a face emerged from the bubbles, gazing up out of the hole with dark soulless eyes. Its cheeks were sunken and its brow heavy with wrinkles. A wide, thick-lipped mouth could be seen containing row upon row of long, dagger-like teeth. The face floated as if unattached to any body below the surface of the swilling water. The old woman gazed down at the foul apparition floating in the pool and chuckled to herself. Elsa lay hidden within the shadows, head buried in her arms, wailing and rocking to and fro for comfort. The demon licked its thick, black lips with its serpentine tongue and then spoke, its chilling voice hollow and echoing as if from within a mighty stone cavern.

'Thou hast summoned me, Agatha Noir. For what foul purpose?'

The hag's green eyes glistened in the wavering candlelight.

'The time has come, oh being of darkness,' she whispered, the icy wind tugging at her hair and clothing. 'The heir of Helier is in Jersey once more. A girl – Jessica, they call her. She is the last in the line descended from Romard and she is within our grasp.'

The face half closed its dull, dark eyes and groaned. 'Yes,' the voice echoed as if remembering something from long ago. 'I believed my ancient senses detected the presence of my mortal enemy. The holy enchantment laid upon her at her birth ebbed into her blood from her mother's womb. I feel it tighten my shackles once again.'

The old woman nodded her head in agreement. 'I sensed it too on meeting her, oh foul one.'

Suddenly the sky cracked with silver lightning and thunder roared in the clouds above. The pool of water bubbled violently;

100

bright red sparks of flame shot from it making Elsa scream with terror. The demon's black eyes blazed with fury.

'You have encountered this deadly foe and yet she is not destroyed,' it boomed fiercely as another clap of thunder shattered the air. 'What treachery is this? I am relying on you, Noir, as the last true black-hearted witch on this pitiful isle. I have been fair and reasonable, old hag. I have granted you every desire your tainted soul has called for. You requested justice when your husband wronged you; it was given. You asked that his lover and her child be punished and did I not crush them? When your child proved weak-willed to carry on the legacy of the dark arts was she not suitable chastised? And yet you have proved a grave disappointment. The bloodline is not ended!'

A tongue of scarlet flame lashed from the fizzing waves and singed the hem of her coat. Mrs Noir stumbled backwards into her wheelchair.

'I did the best I could, Your Evilness,' she breathed, her voice trembling with fear. 'I did try and terminate the heir of your defeater, end the inheritance of Helier. I killed Iris, didn't I? And when that dratted daughter of hers, Emma, stood up to my coven, yes we were beaten but not before making her pay with her life and cursing her baby.'

The demon glared at her from within its foaming window. 'But this Jessica – she bears no scar, no ailments of a curse,' it barked. 'I have a sense for these things. Her presence is untainted by your magic. She has inherited the blessings of Helier, the sight of merfolk and faeries, ability to heal and that which we fear most, white magic. She may be little more than a child but she has the power to destroy us!'

Agatha leant forward in her chair and peered over the stones surrounding the pool. 'Yes,' she murmured, a wicked smile playing on her lips. 'If she knew she had these powers, but she doesn't.'

Elsa stopped her weeping and lay very still. She did not like the sound of this one little bit. In its dank cavern, the Jersey demon was quiet, its thick lips forming a curious smile.

'Go on,' it purred evily.

The old hag shifted her bulk excitedly in her chair. 'Well, when I destroyed the girl's mother, her father, a Grockle, was so horrified that he took the child to the mainland. She has had no contact with the fool, Jim Hellily, until three days ago and even he's worried about telling her the truth. Poor baby! She knows nothing of who she is or the powers she possesses.' Agatha cackled. 'She even thinks faeries and merfolk belong in story books.'

The demon laughed deeply and as it did so a crack of thunder shook the atmosphere. 'This could not be better,' it growled. 'The Guardian is defenceless. But we must act fast. She has many allies in this isle and if we are not swift she will learn the truth. We must do away with her before she learns of our existence. A simple aqua charm should do the trick.'

The old woman chortled wickedly. 'What do you want me to do?' she asked eagerly rubbing her hands.

The fiend looked thoughtful and then a smile spread across its hideous face.

'Not you,' he murmured slowly. 'The girl has the ability to sense evil; she might not know why but she will not trust you. We need someone pure, untainted by any sign of evil but over whom we have complete power. Somebody nearer to her age to befriend her, win her trust before she plants the spell.'

Both demon and witch smiled as their minds focused on the same frightful idea.

Then the demon whispered low, 'Show me the child.'

Elsa too, had realised what they were plotting and it made her nauseous. As long as she could remember she had unwillingly been part of her grandmother's twisted scheme but nothing could match the awful plan she was now being woven into. She could not kill the girl who, just two days before, had shown her such kindness and sympathy. Quickly, but trying to make no sound, she stood up and began to shuffle towards the entrance of the tunnel. However, Agatha was too fast for her and, quick as a flash, reached out and grabbed the hood of her coat, yanking the poor child onto her knees before the swirling pool. Elsa's eyes grew wide with fear as her grandmother held on tightly to the back of her clothing, forcing her to gaze into the demon's evil face.

The fiend regarded the terrified child with interest. 'So,' it crowed, 'this is the pitiful being whose blood has kept me nourished these past twelve years. What a puny specimen!'

Mrs Noir shook Elsa roughly by the scruff of her neck. 'Yes,

Dark One, this is she. My sorry excuse for a grand-daughter. But she has no magic power. How will she destroy our enemy?'

The demon laughed as lightning tore the sky. The rain was falling now, thick and cold, soaking Elsa's thin hair and slicking it to her head.

'The child is merely a messenger,' the creature crooned. 'Tomorrow you will send this pathetic girl to the house of Jim Hellily on the pretence of being a playmate for this Jessica. Whilst there she shall give the child the charm as a token of friendship. That night the spell will take hold of her, drawing her from her bed, out the house and down to the shore. Once in the sea, the currents will carry her below the waves to a watery grave.'

The evil face cackled wildly and as it did so the surface of its black pond bubbled and spat even more ferociously. Bright green foam formed over the top of the water, covering the demon's features completely. Purple and blue sparks flew from it, exploding like miniature fireworks. After a few minutes, an object could be seen to rise from the froth, floating eerily abreast of the green cloud. It was a pendant, a blood red gemstone enclosed within a golden frame of intertwined serpents and suspended from a thin gold chain. It was skilfully fashioned and the detail was exquisite. The old woman snatched it up in her free hand and grinned maliciously.

'Perfect,' she hissed and the cloud over the pool cleared again to reveal the dark spirit's features.

Elsa quaked under her grandmother's vice-like grip, her eyes saucer-large and brimming with tears.

'No,' she whispered shaking her head. 'I can't do it.'

Agatha and the demon stopped their chuckling and glared at the small child with spite. 'What?' screeched the hag, her features distorted with rage.

Blue flames flickered from the demon's inhuman eyes as it glared at her from within its prison. 'You dare defy the Dark Spirit of Jersey!' it howled, its voice so low and echoing it burned Elsa's ears to hear it. 'For this disobedience, you must be disciplined!'

At that moment a fork of lightning sliced open the clouds, diving into the sea beyond the edge of the shelf. The waves breaking on the rocks below swelled and churned black-green.

They began to spin, slowly at first, but then faster and faster until a small but fierce whirlpool formed.

Elsa screamed but already sparks of purple had begun to rise from the pool forming a heavy violet mist that spiralled around her tiny frame like a huge fist. Mrs Noir cackled maniacally and released the girl's clothing, allowing the thick vapour to lift her off her feet into the air.

Elsa cried out as the magic of the Dark Spirit dangled her in mid-air high above the raging whirlpool. She struggled, but where could she go? Thunder boomed around her as the demon's voice filled her head.

'Now, you wayward brat! Do you still rebel against my power and that of your grandmother?'

Elsa's blonde hair flew about her in the wind as she was tossed to and fro.

'I ... I ... I just don't want to hurt anyone.'

She peeped from within the dark spinning fog. More lightning shook the atmosphere.

'Wrong answer!' bellowed the fiend.

The mist suddenly thinned and Elsa found herself plummeting towards the green vortex whirling below her. She fell a good eight feet before the cloud reappeared, holding her fast in the air. One of her shoes became dislodged from her foot and fell crashing onto the rocks before being sucked deep into the whirlpool.

The demon chuckled at Elsa's horror. 'Now what do you say, my girl?' it taunted.

Elsa gasped with fear. 'I'll do it,' she pleaded. 'I'll give Jessica the pendant. Just, please, don't drop me!'

She heard the creature laugh again before the vapour whisked her back up to the outcrop, dumping her roughly on the hard stone. Agatha shot her a look of disappointment and threw the pendant at her before turning to look again into the pool. The purple cloud had evaporated and the sea was once again calm. The face reflected in the pool was fainter now, its features more dim. When it spoke, the voice was but a whisper.

'I am weary,' it uttered. 'Disciplining the girl has drained my powers. I must rest.'

Mrs Noir nodded solemnly. 'I understand. But soon the Heir of Helier will be no more and you can return to your glorious self.'

The demon shut its eyes and let out a tired groan before the water shimmered and it disappeared. Mrs Noir turned to face Elsa who was still lying, ashen-faced on the ground. 'Don't just loll there, you lazy thing,' she barked. 'You have a big day tomorrow.'

Silently, Elsa tucked the cursed pendant in her pocket and began to pack up the magical tools. Her heart felt like lead in her chest. She had no idea how Jessica could avoid her fate. The girl had shown her nothing but kindness and she wished that she knew of her heritage so she would stop this awful plot. But Elsa dared not go against the Demon again. As always she would have to bury her feelings and do as she was told. She prayed Jessica would discover the truth before it was too late.

Chapter 8

Adventures in the Cellar

Jessica had a disturbed night following her strange fishing trip the day before. Nightmares swamped her brain making her toss in her sheets and several times during the night she woke in panic. She was almost completely sure that they were connected to her vision of the boy in the sea and the weird tales that Jake had told her about Mrs Noir. She dreamt that she witnessed the alleged murders of Philippe and Katrina Noir and that of Lily Treq – saw them as if she were a ghost, knowing what would happen but defenceless to stop it. She heard Mrs Noir laughing cruelly as they breathed their last. In another dream she was in Jim's fishing boat, alone on the open sea. She had looked into the waves and seen Elsa turning and twisting as if she were being pulled down by a great beast. She tried to save her but woke too soon. Finally, in the early hours of the morning she settled into a more restful slumber, free from the terrors of the night.

When she awoke it was late morning, yet outside her window it was still dark. Rubbing her eyes Jessica sat up in bed and pulled back the curtains. Heavy charcoal cloud blanketed the sky hurling down shafts of cold rain that bounced powerfully off the garden pond and dribbled miserably down the window pane. Rough winds howled outside, whisking the elegant branches of the willow into a wild dance. Jessica groaned. She had been hoping to persuade Jim to take her on another boat ride in the hope of spotting the mysterious underwater child again. Now that was definitely out of the question. As she dressed in the warmest clothes she'd thought to bring, Jess wondered what she was going to do all day. Being stuck in the cottage with her dad and her great uncle with no computer games or anything seemed a boring prospect, especially as she knew she wasn't allowed to ask any questions about her mum.

She clomped downstairs to find that breakfast was over and Jim and her father were sitting quietly in the lounge reading the papers as the morning TV droned unregarded in the background.

'It's raining,' she said. It was a statement of the obvious but the rain had dampened her mood so she didn't really care.

Her father peered over the top of the paper. 'You've missed breakfast,' he remarked equally obviously.

Jess shrugged and stuck her hands in the pockets of her denim jacket. She still hadn't completely forgiven him for telling her off yesterday. 'Not hungry,' she sniffed.

Strangely enough it was true; she wasn't in the mood for one of Jim's huge cooked breakfasts. She wandered across the room and perched on the arm of one the large armchairs and regarded her great uncle who sat in the chair closest to the fireplace prodding at the burning logs with a brass poker.

She sighed deeply, blowing the air from her lungs so that it caused her lips to vibrate, making a satisfying 'raspberry' noise. 'What do you do in Jersey when it's raining?' she queried.

Jim gazed at the roaring blaze. 'Rains a lot over 'ere,' he muttered.

Jess shuffled her feet on the hearthrug, making the pile go the wrong way. 'Yeah, but what do you do?' she asked, almost whinily.

Jim drummed his fingers on the arm of his chair. 'Well,' he began, 'your dad told me he gotta finish that article of his, so that's what he's doing. And I've got some housework to be getting on with, so that'll keep me busy.'

Jess groaned. What a way to spend your holiday! She knew she would probably end up back in her bedroom, reading her magazines and hoping the weather got better soon. Jim grinned that craggy grin of his. 'Bored, huh?' he asked, placing the poker back beside the grate. 'Typical teenager. Don't worry, I've made sure you've plenty to keep you amused. Mrs Noir rang this morning. Remember, we arranged for Elsa to come over today.'

Jessica's ears pricked up at the mention of the girl's name. She had totally forgotten about the visit. She had promised herself she would try and help the girl any way she could. She was almost convinced that Jake's stories about Mrs Noir mistreating her grand-daughter were true. She hadn't told Jim or her father, especially after yesterday; she was sure they would not believe her. But that did not mean she wasn't going to talk to Elsa and maybe find out if she was being hurt, perhaps persuade her to get some help, even if it was only someone to assist with the care of her grandmother.

Martin closed his newspaper. 'Who is Elsa?' he asked.

Jim cocked his head slightly to one side.

'The grand-daughter of one of the people I help out. An old girl who lives in Gorey. Her daughter and son-in-law were killed in an accident, and she's had to bring up the child herself. Very sad, very difficult for her.'

Jess made a quiet 'tsk' noise to show she didn't completely agree with this but neither Jim nor Martin heard her.

Jim continued. 'Her and Jess really hit it off when I popped into drop off Agatha's shopping on Monday. I thought it would be a friend for Jess while she's on the island – invited her for tea. Poor scrap of a thing doesn't go out much, weak chest. And, well, you know, with them both losing their mums they may be able to console each other.'

Jess glanced round to look at her dad, half expecting him to go into one of his strange moods at the mention of her mother, but he didn't seem bothered. 'How is she getting here?' he asked. 'Are you picking her up?'

The old man shook his head. 'Nah, coming on the bus.'

Jessica blinked hard. Yet more proof Mrs Noir didn't give two hoots about Elsa. Here it was, a thunderstorm raging outside, and the old bat had sent her twelve year old grand-daughter across the island on her own by bus. She was about to voice an objection but her father beat her to it.

'She's coming on a bus by herself?' he asked in disbelief. 'All the way from Gorey, in weather like this?'

Jessica glanced at him feeling slightly cross. She didn't want her father to agree with what she was thinking, not when she was still angry with him from yesterday. Normally she would've taken the opposing view just out of spite. But her pity for Elsa was too great for her to argue. Instead she folded her arms across her chest.

'Doesn't seem safe to me,' she declared to Jim, elevating her chin slightly. 'Not for someone like Elsa. Dad doesn't let *me* catch the bus unless I'm with a friend and Elsa doesn't seem very mature, even for a twelve-year-old.'

'I wouldn't say that,' Jim said softly. 'Elsa is a very responsible young lady. She catches the bus everywhere – has to. Mrs Noir is housebound, see – can't go out without a wheelchair. And she manages to take care of that big old house and look after her grandmother. 'Course, I help when I can, but Elsa's very capable.'

Martin cleared his throat and rustled the pages of his newspaper. 'Let's just drop the subject,' he muttered, knowing it was no good arguing with Jim. Jess too bit her lip. She had her own opinion about the way Elsa was treated and she was going to help her, no matter what Jim thought.

'But what are we going to do?' she asked.

Back in London she had computer games and videos to keep her amused. What were they going to do?

The old man's eyes twinkled merrily, as if he held a great secret that he knew would thrill Jessica.

'I thought you two might like to go through the old store boxes in the cellar. There's lots of interesting stuff down there, half of which I've probably forgotten about. Old records, clothes, toys, and tons of photos of our family. You two girls can have a rummage, kinda like a treasure hunt – see what you can find.'

Jessica's heart leaped excitedly in her chest. She could not believe her luck. It appeared that her patience in finding out about her mother's past was going to pay off. The cellar was likely to be a treasure trove of information: photos of her to go along with the one she treasured so dearly, old school reports, and letters perhaps that would fill in precious details of her character – items she had touched, played with, real and solid that Jessica could now feel for herself.

'Yes,' he said gently, getting to his feet. 'That's what you've been waiting for, Jess. I stored a load of your mum's stuff down there. Guess it hurt me too much to throw it away. Maybe I knew you would like to see it one day.'

Jess nodded, smiling through her tears.

'Dad,' she said quietly. 'You don't mind, do you? Me going through Mum's old stuff. Just to get to know her a bit better.'

She held her breath, half expecting him to snap at her again, as he had about the mermaid.

Martin's face wore that same, pale, worn expression Jess had seen so many times before whenever her mother was talked about. His blue eyes were far away, as clouded and disturbed as the rainy sky outside.

Jim spoke. 'Photographs, Martin. Photos and old clothes, that's all there is down there. Nothing more – I swear on her grave. Let Jess see them; it'll do her no harm.'

Martin bit his lip. 'I guess I can't say no,' he muttered. 'You know it's there now. But remember what I've said. I don't believe in digging up the past – it can cause a lot of heartache and hurt. Just have a look, find out what you feel you need and then leave it be. Don't go pushing too hard.'

He removed his glasses and wiped the moisture from his eyes. Jess threw her arms around his neck and hugged him warmly.

'Thanks, Dad,' she whispered. 'I think I'll go upstairs for a little while, before Elsa arrives.' In truth, she needed to be alone with her thoughts.

Returning to her bedroom, she sat silently for some time. Once the initial feeling of overwhelming joy had passed and she had dried her tears, she allowed herself to fantasize about what exciting discoveries she might make. Maybe one of her distant relatives had been a Jersey smuggler and there was a stash of gold and precious gems under the house; or perhaps a noble sailor who had sailed bravely into battle against the French. She wondered, caught up in the excitement of it all and letting her imagination run wild, if her own mother had been a secret agent of some sort. Anything was possible. But then her thoughts returned to the poor girl who was coming to join her in her quest. Jessica knew Elsa had lost both her parents. She didn't suppose for a second that the cold-hearted Mrs Noir had kept any souvenirs of her late daughter and son-in-law for Elsa to remember them by. She wondered, since Jersey was such a small island and Jim knew the family quite well, whether there might be something in the cellar that related to Elsa's own history. If so, perhaps Jessica could give it to her. She was happily pondering this when she heard the doorbell ring and heard her great uncle go to answer it. Jessica hurriedly clattered downstairs, eager to greet her guest.

110

She found Elsa standing in the hallway, looking as lost and shy as ever. She had on the blue duffle coat Jessica had seen hanging on Mrs Noir's hallstand, the hood pulled so far forward her face was barely visible, and a pair of dark green wellies that looked three or four sizes too big. She had been soaked by the foul weather and this, combined with her painfully thin frame, gave her the appearance of a malnourished kitten that someone had attempted to drown. Her diminutive figure seemed even tinier next to Jim's portly physique as he helped her off with her jacket.

'I am grateful for you inviting me to come to your house, Mr Hellily,' the child mumbled, hanging up her coat and taking her boots off. 'It was very nice of you. I am sorry I am late, only I had to make sure grandmère was okay in the house on her own, and the bus was a bit late.' Her pale blue eyes flickered, as if she expected to be reprimanded. But Jim, of course, wasn't bothered.

'Don't worry,' the old man laughed. 'Where would we go on a day like this anyway?'

A shy smile flickered across Elsa face and her eyes fell on Jessica.

'Hello,' she said quietly.

Jessica descended the last few stairs and grinned at the girl warmly. 'Hi,' she said. Elsa's attire was dull and old-fashioned as it had been the first time they met. Today she had on a light blue long-sleeved blouse, buttoned almost chokingly up to her neck, and a dark navy pinafore dress with neatly ironed creases in the skirt and two small pockets. The outfit looked like a school uniform and Jessica wondered if she had ever owned a colourful piece of clothing in her life. Her thin, blonde locks hung in two limp pigtails that made her face look even more drawn.

Unsure what to say for a moment, Elsa fiddled with the hem of her skirt. Then, as if her memory had suddenly come back to her, she picked up a cake tin that was resting on the side table.

'I brought you some biscuits to say thank you for having me,' she said politely, pulling off the lid. 'Would you like some?' Inside, arranged beautifully on a paper towel, were about two dozen delicious-looking biscuits, baked golden brown. Jessica could see big chunks of chocolate set mouth-wateringly in each one. It made her stomach rumble and she remembered she hadn't eaten since yesterday – but the thought of the foul tea she had drunk at Elsa's grandmother's made her hesitate. Jim, however, thanked her kindly and took one, biting into it eagerly.

'Delicious!' he declared.

Elsa blushed at the compliment and looked back to Jessica.

'Don't you want one?' she said, her voice wavering slightly as if she was worried about causing offence. Jessica was suddenly reminded of *Snow White*. She had watched the Walt Disney cartoon as a child and been terrified when the wicked witch gave Snow White the poisoned apple. What an odd thought! Why should she imagine that Elsa would try to hurt her? She searched the girl's eyes for a glimmer of malice. However, all she saw was that lonely, haunted stare that made Jessica pity her so.

Slowly, Jess reached inside the tin, selected a small biscuit and raised it hesitantly to her lips. She bit into it; the taste was appetizing and sweet. The chocolate melted over her tongue, velvet confection. She swallowed and held her breath almost in terror, waiting for her stomach to churn, her breath to fail, her pulse weaken – but nothing happened. She felt fine.

Jessica shook her head. How ridiculous and cruel to think such awful thoughts about a sweet, shy girl like Elsa! She was not trying to harm her – why would she? Jess chided herself for being so suspicious; she had promised to be kind to Elsa.

'Do ... do you like it?' Elsa asked, the smile once again falling from her face.

'Yes, it was lovely.'

Elsa grinned again, relieved she had won Jessica's approval.

Just then the door to the living room swung open and Martin stepped into the hallway.

'Hi Dad,' said Jessica, 'this is Elsa.'

'Hello, Mr Kent,' she mumbled. 'Would you like a biscuit? I baked them fresh yesterday.'

Squatting down so he was level with Elsa's face, Martin took one of the biscuits and bit it.

'Mmm. Thank you very much, Elsa. Did your Gran help you make these?'

Elsa looked at the cookies but didn't take one. 'No,' she sighed, 'I cooked them myself. Grandmère can't cook now she's old.'

Both Jessica and Martin looked rather worried. Jessica had seen Mrs Noir's huge, old-fashioned range and wondered how a tiny thing like Elsa could manage it. But it was Martin who voiced their concern.

'Kitchens can be dangerous places if you're not careful, Elsa? Doesn't your grandma realise you could get hurt?'

A clap of thunder exploded outside the cottage making everyone, especially Elsa, jump. The pale skinned girl squeaked with fright and nearly dropped the tin.

'It's all right,' Jess said gently. 'It's only a bit of thunder.'

She put her hand comfortingly on Elsa's arm. Elsa breathed heavily. She was shaking with fear.

'I know it's the storm. I don't like thunder, that's all. I just don't like thunder. And I manage in the kitchen fine, thank you. I am careful. I know how to do things right.'

Her tone was the same brisk, nervous, almost angry one Jessica had heard her use before. Both she and her father were unsure what to say.

'Well, thank you very much for the biscuits, Elsa,' Jim said. 'It was a nice thought and we can have some more later.' He took the tin from her and replaced the lid. 'Now, I thought, as it's such a horrible day, you and Jessica might like to go down to the cellar and look through all the store boxes. I have loads of old photos and things.'

Jessica smiled encouragingly at her younger companion. 'I thought I might find some things that belonged to my mum and maybe, as Jersey is such a small place, there could be something connected to your mum and dad. Would you like that?'

Elsa shyly nodded her head. Jessica's father had disappeared back into the living room as soon as the cellar was mentioned, leaving the girls to Jim, who headed towards the kitchen, beckoning for them to follow him. He rummaged in one of the kitchen cupboards muttering to himself, 'Where did I put that blasted key?'

After a brief moment he exclaimed, 'Here it is,' and produced from the cupboard a large, black, iron key. He shuffled over to the far side of the unused fireplace to an old-fashioned wooden door. Jessica had not noticed it before. Inserting the key in its cavernous lock, he opened the door.

'Well,' he sighed as the hinges creaked, 'there you go – the cellar. Do be careful going down the stairs. There are no banisters.'

He flicked a switch on the wall and the dark cellar was suddenly filled with light. Jessica and Elsa peered inside. A flight of about fifteen steep, wooden stairs led downward into the underground room. It was quite a large space, filled with pieces of old furniture and storage boxes. The walls were rough, red brick and the floor, ancient wooden planks covered in a thick layer of dust. The room was bitterly cold compared to the rest of the house and the air musty and slightly damp. A bubble of nervous excitement rose in Jessica's stomach. This place was an Aladdin's Cave of artefacts from the Hellily family and her fingers itched to rummage through the boxes and uncover her mother's past.

The three of them descended the creaky staircase and Jessica gazed around. She could see better now the contents of the room. An old-fashioned bicycle leaned up against the crumbling brickwork, its large wicker basket frayed and broken. Against the far wall was a long, squat oak bookcase filled with damp-stained leather volumes. Behind the mountain of packing cases, almost blocked from view, was a mahogany wardrobe, its front mirror cracked. Everything surrounding them seemed broken and forgotten, as if Jim really had stopped thinking about what was here. Elsa stared around her, her pale face expressionless as if she was frightened but didn't want to show it. Jim began to head back upstairs. 'Well, I've got housework to do. I'll let you two explore. And, Jessica,' he added as he paused to look back down at them, 'if you want to keep anything, just ask.' With that he was gone.

Jessica was eager to get started but her gaze fell upon Elsa's nervous face and she suddenly remembered the horrible tales Jake had told her the day before. This was the perfect opportunity to find out if Elsa was really okay. She certainly didn't look it. Her face was drawn and her eyes flickered about the room uneasily. Suddenly, she sat down on the bottom step and seemed to be gasping for air. Worried, Jess sat down beside her and put a hand on her knee.

114

'Is everything okay?' she asked gently. 'The dust isn't affecting your chest, is it?'

The girl quickly shook her head. 'No,' she smiled nervously. 'I'm fine really. I just had an attack last night and I'm a bit worried about it happening again. But I'm sure it won't.'

Jessica bit her lip thoughtfully. This was the opening she had been looking for. It was her chance to find out just how badly Mrs Noir treated Elsa.

'Oh,' she said, trying to sound casual, 'I expect your grandmother called the doctor then, to make sure you were okay?'

Elsa poked her feet in the dust, drawing circles so she didn't have to meet Jessica's gaze.

'No,' she whispered, 'I don't need the doctor. Grandmère looks after me. She uses plants to cure me. I'm okay now.'

Jessica regarded the child's dark-rimmed eyes and sallow complexion. She wasn't at all convinced that Elsa was in the best of health, and she didn't see how the old woman could make her better simply with herbs. She looked at Elsa's stick-like legs and wondered just what kind of illness she had.

'You know, Elsa,' she said carefully, 'going to the doctor's might not be such a bad idea. He could see if your chest was okay, and maybe get someone to help you look after your grandmother.'

A clap of thunder sounded high above them. Elsa jumped up from the step so quickly it was as if she had been struck by lightning. It shocked Jessica. The girl stood, bolt upright, with her back to Jess.

'I don't want to go to a doctor,' she stated firmly as Jess stared at her. 'Don't think just because grandmère's old she isn't capable of looking after me, because she is. She is very, very, capable. And I am capable of looking after the house.' She stopped suddenly, inhaling deeply.

Jessica had begun to realise that these half-angry, half-nervous outbursts were a recurring part of Elsa's personality. They were disturbing. It was obvious that if Elsa didn't want to talk about her home life there was no way Jessica could persuade her to, even if it was for her own good. She would just have to hope the child would warm to her during their time together and tell her the truth bit by bit.

115

Slowly Elsa turned to face Jess again, her eyes filled with sadness. 'I'm sorry,' she murmured. 'My illness is inherited. My mum was ill. I think that's what killed her. I don't know, I can't really remember. All I know is she was ill and I am too.' She gripped her forearm tightly as if in pain.

Jessica furrowed her brow in puzzlement. What Elsa had just said didn't make any sense. Both Jake and Elsa herself had said that Katrina Noir had been killed in a car accident. Now she was telling her that her mother had died of some sort of disease. Why? Was she lying to her? Did she just forget? Did Mrs Noir make up the story of an inherited illness to scare Elsa? It made no sense. But she guessed that after Elsa's outburst it would be futile to press for answers. Maybe they would come in time.

'I'm sorry, it was none of my business,' she said.

Elsa's tense features relaxed. 'It's okay, I guess you were only trying to help.'

'Shall we see what we can find in this lot?' Jessica surveyed the mountain of packing cases. 'I don't know where to start.'

She stood up and strolled over to the pile, then glanced down into one of the cardboard boxes. 'Hey, look! Records – and an old player. Help me lift it out.'

Elsa scurried over and together they lifted the heavy turntable onto the floor and dusted off the cobwebs. Jessica stared down at the old piece of equipment with its huge, black disc and thin metal arm. She checked the sides of its case but could not find an electric lead. 'Where do you plug it in?' she asked Elsa.

Elsa laughed and knelt on the floor beside it. 'You don't! You wind it up! See? Here's the handle. Pass me a record and I'll show you.'

The girl began to crank the small handle at the side of the box. Jessica rooted through the packing case to find a suitable disc. 'Perry Como, Buddy Holly, Gene Pitney. Who are these people?' she asked, looking at the creased sleeves. 'Ah, Elvis. I know who he is! Put this on, Els.'

Elsa paused from winding up the record player and looked at Jess, silent for a moment.

Jessica met her gaze with puzzlement. 'What?' she asked.

Elsa grinned slightly. 'What did you call me?'

Jessica shrugged her shoulders. 'Els. Why? Don't you like it?'

The child shook her head and giggled. 'No, I like it. Sounds friendly. Nobody's ever called me Els before.'

Jess grinned at her. 'Then I will, and you can call me Jess. Put the record on, Els.'

Elsa chuckled mischievously, her pale eyes glowing. 'Okay, Jess, I will!'

She slipped the disc from its slightly stained paper cover and placed it carefully on the turntable resting the needle carefully in the groove. The voice of the long dead rocker warbled from the machine, muffled heavily by a sea of hisses and cracks. Jessica wrinkled up her nose.

'Ugh, sounds terrible!' she said. 'Glad I've got my CDs.'

Elsa sighed, staring at the record as it spun lazily on the gramophone. 'I bet this belonged to Jim, or your grandmère. Too old to be your mother's.'

Jessica gave up looking at the records and turned her attention to the bookcase at the back of the cellar, dusting away the thick layer of grime from the books that were stacked there.

'Perhaps these were Mum's,' she murmured, as much to herself as to Elsa. 'The Famous Five, The Wind In the Willows, Little Women.'

She squatted down to look at the hardbacks stacked on the lowest shelves. These appeared older and more well-read than the others, their spines cracked and pages torn. Jessica squinted to read their titles. 'The Witch Hunter's Almanac, Dark Forces: A Guide to Protection, From Black Trolls To Wilting Crops: Signs of Dark Magic, A History of Magical Beings in Jersey,' she read amazed. 'What the heck are these doing here?'

She reached out to inspect the strange books more clearly but before she had the chance to remove them from the dust-covered shelf, a squeal of excitement from Elsa made her spin round.

The girl was kneeling beside one of the open packing cases, her hands buried deep inside it.

'Jess!' she called, her tone shrill with pleasure. 'Oh, come over here and take a look at this!'

Disappointed she hadn't got the chance to examine the strange library further, Jessica crossed the cellar to Elsa and peered into the box.

Elsa's face was alight with joy, such as Jessica hadn't seen before. Carefully, she lifted the object from among the other débris packed in with it. The item was a doll, the old-fashioned kind, with a fine china face and limbs slightly marked by the grime that had built up over the years. It had a wig of real chestnut hair in tight ringlets and delicately painted baby-blue eyes and rose pink, Cupid's bow lips. It was dressed in a burgundy and moss-green floral smock, with a matching white lace apron and bloomers. On its feet were tiny, black leather shoes. Jessica herself wasn't too keen on the doll; even as a child she'd had no great passion for them. However, Elsa seemed completely enraptured by the discovery, sitting it carefully on her lap, fussing about with its dress and hair.

'Isn't she beautiful?' she enthused, studying the toy's fragile face and hands.

Jessica shrugged. 'It's okay. I've never been really interested in dolls. I've always been a bit of a tomboy.' Jessica doubted the toy had belonged to her mother anyway as, from what Jim had told her, she too had had little time for what were considered traditional feminine pursuits.

Elsa sighed, clasped the tiny figure between her dainty hands and held it up to the light.

'I wish I had a beautiful dolly like this,' she sighed. 'Grandmère doesn't like me having toys. She says playthings make hands lazy and the mind unfocused.' She breathed sadly and sat the doll back on the dirty wooden floor. 'I wonder what her name is? If she was mine I would call her Rosie and play with her every day.'

Jessica gazed at Elsa who was carefully wiping the grime from the toy's cheeks. It was the first time she had actually seen Elsa talking and acting like a normal child. It was both a joyful and a saddening experience to watch. Jessica wondered just how old Elsa had been when she had had to start caring for her grandmother. Was it as soon as she could walk? Before she'd started school? Had the girl had any childhood at all before it had been swallowed up by looking after that nasty old woman and worrying about the house? It didn't seem fair on her that Elsa had no help. Jessica wanted to make her situation better but still couldn't figure out how. She looked at the doll sitting up against the packing case staring out at them with her unblinking blue eyes.

'Would you like to keep her?' Jess asked, looking at Elsa. 'To take her home with you?'

Elsa looked round and stared at Jess, half in joy, half in shock. ' Do ... do you really mean that, Jess?' she asked.

Jessica shrugged. 'Sure. I don't really enjoy playing with dolls and I think Jim's a bit old for them. He said I could keep anything I wanted. I'm sure he wouldn't mind if you took her.'

Elsa grinned broadly for a moment then looked down at the dust-covered floor and frowned.

'Oh no, I'd better not. Grandmère doesn't like me having toys,' she repeated quietly.

Once again, Jessica felt her dislike of Mrs Noir rise. How dare she deprive a sweet girl like Elsa of her childhood! She was sure it wasn't because the old woman couldn't afford toys for her grand-daughter. She just wanted her to spend less time playing and more time taking care of her. She put a comforting arm around Elsa's thin shoulders.

'You know,' she said quietly, 'sometimes you don't have to tell grown-ups everything. Adults keep things from kids, so why shouldn't we have secrets? You could take Rosie home under your coat and hide her. That way your grandmother wouldn't know.'

Elsa chewed her bottom lip thoughtfully and gazed longingly at the beautiful old doll. 'Grandmère would be so cross if she found out,' she murmured to herself. 'But you said you don't mind, so it isn't really stealing, and she is such a beautiful dolly.' She stroked the skirt of the doll's dress.

Jess leaned closer and whispered in Elsa's ear. 'I bet Rosie has been sitting in that horrible cardboard box for years, just waiting for a little girl to come along and play with her again.'

She picked up the doll and placed it gently in Elsa's arms. The child looked up at her and smiled warmly.

'Thank you very much, Jess,' she said putting her arms around the older girl's neck and hugging her tightly. 'I promise I'll take good care of Rosie. Now let's see if there's anything down here for you.'

They drew apart and returned to searching the box. There didn't appear to be much else of interest in it, just an old, chipped glass vase, a few bundles of boys' comics and some Dinky toys with their wheels missing. But then something right at the bottom caught Jess's eye – an ancient leather-bound book.

'Hey!' she exclaimed excitedly. 'A photo album! I'll bet there's some pictures of Mum in here!'

She pulled out the book as Elsa settled back on the floor with Rosie on her lap. The scrap-book came out of the box in a shower of dust and cobwebs and as it did so, a photograph fell from its pages and landed in Jessica's lap. She placed the album itself to one side for a moment and studied the loose picture.

The photograph was older than she had expected. In fact, it was so old Jessica wondered if even Jim would know who it was. The man in it looked Edwardian. He had a completely bald head and a bushy but neat beard. He was dressed in a sombre three-piece suit and seated at a wooden roll-top desk, a pen resting in his hand as if he were about to write a very important letter. His expression was pensive. His eyes, like Jim's, were dark and full of intelligence. Jess wondered who he could be. Thoughtfully, she twisted the small, sepia photograph over in her hands. There, on the back, among the dirt and stains of age, she saw elegant writing so faded it was barely readable.

'William Edward Hellily.' She read out loud slowly. '1897. Guardian of Jersey and Witch Hunter Extraordinaire.' Her heart leapt but she had no idea why. All she knew was that this photo meant something. But what? She thought of the books she had found stacked at the bottom of the bookcase. Had they belonged to him? Surely no-one believed in witches, even a hundred years ago. And what was the Guardian of Jersey? The title sounded familiar, even though she had never heard of it before. She looked up at Elsa to see if she had any thoughts on the matter.

Elsa was sitting completely still on the floor, her face more ghostly than usual. Panic glimmered in her eyes. 'Elsa,' Jessica asked, 'you've lived in Jersey all your life. Have you ever heard of the Guardian of Jersey?'

Elsa shook her head and tried very hard not to look worried. Jessica could swear there was an air of guilt in her expression, as if she had uncovered some secret Elsa would rather have kept hidden. However, when she spoke she seemed all too eager to dismiss any thoughts that the photograph was important.

'No. It's probably some outdated government title. I've never heard of it.'

She laughed – a hollow, nervous laugh and Jess noted that she did not meet her gaze.

Jessica still held the picture, face down in her palm. 'Witch Hunter,' she repeated quietly. 'I thought people stopped believing in witches ages ago. People in Jersey must have been a bit backward then. There couldn't have been much for him to do.'

'There wasn't!' snapped Elsa suddenly, making Jessica jump. Her nimble hands fiddled with the doll's lace apron, as if they were looking for something to do. 'I mean, why should there be? There weren't any witches on the island then. And there are definitely no witches on Jersey now, no way.'

She giggled, an almost hysterical high-pitched giggle, her eyes shining, and looked at her companion suspiciously. Jessica was struck by the thought that Elsa might be suffering from some kind of mental illness.

'It's okay,' Jessica said quietly, trying to defuse Elsa's obvious panic. 'There are no such things as witches. I expect this William Hellily just thought people who were a bit odd were witches. Let's put him away and look at the other photos, shall we?' She smiled nervously and tucked the photo into her pocket.

Elsa relaxed again. 'Silly,' she sighed. 'Of course witchcraft isn't real. Why should I think it was.'

She crossed the floor and sat down beside Jessica. Together they turned the first page and gazed at the black and white photographs. The first depicted a handsome young man in his twenties. He had a ruddy, strong-jawed face and sandy hair swept back in a quiff. He was wearing a white shirt and knitted tank top and wheeling a bicycle that looked suspiciously like the one leaning against the cellar wall. He grinned at them broadly.

'*He* ain't bad,' said Jess humorously.

Elsa pointed to the writing underneath. 'Look. James Michael, August 1958. It's Jim! Your Uncle Jim.'

Jess laughed in amazement. 'You're right! He looks so thin and young. Wow!'

Elsa tapped the photograph on the opposite page. 'And this must be your grandmère.'

Jessica looked at the photograph. A woman, maybe in her mid-twenties, with dark hair bobby-pinned in place and wearing a floral dress with a wide skirt was leaning on a gate. To her left, still grinning, was the young Jim and to her right, his arm protectively round her waist, was another man, with dark hair.

Jess touched the photograph sadly. 'Wow!' she breathed. 'Jim, Iris and Iris's fiancé, Freddie Kerr. These are my grandparents. I always wondered what they looked like.' She felt suddenly melancholy knowing that these photos were all she knew them by. 'She's beautiful,' Jess murmured to herself.

Elsa looked at her. 'You look like her,' she said, as they turned the page, before adding, 'Why was your mother's name Emma Hellily and not Emma Kerr?'

Jess shrugged. 'I'm not sure. I think Jim changed it back when he adopted her.'

The next page bore a collection of photographs of Iris and Freddie's wedding and the date April 4th 1961. Iris looked beautiful in a straight-skirted ivory gown embroidered with pearls. Jessica was admiring the detail of it in one photograph when something unusual caught her eye. Under her bouquet, perched on the back of her hand, Jessica could make out a tiny figure not two inches tall. A girl, with fine, long blonde hair and transparent wings was peeking out from behind one of the roses. Jess blinked and put her face closer to the picture to study the image more clearly. Sure enough, odd as it seemed, the fairy, for Jessica knew not how else to describe it, could be seen as plainly as anything in the photograph. She nudged Elsa and tapped the photo.

'Look, Elsa. Right by my grandma's hand, do you see anything?'

Elsa squinted at the picture in the dim light and shook her head. 'Only the flowers in her bouquet.'

Jessica frowned. 'No, you *must* be able to see it,' she insisted, her eyes never leaving the album. 'It looks like a little girl, sitting on her hand. Can't you see it?'

Elsa carefully took the book from Jessica's hands and studied the page, her long, tapered fingers resting just beside the place where Jessica had seen the image.

'No,' she said gently. 'These old photographs are covered in grime and the focusing is so bad,' she swirled her index finger across the image. 'See! It's just the shadow of the flowers on her hand.'

She passed the album back to Jess. Jessica gazed once again at the picture but this time the girl's face was nowhere to be

122

seen. She felt a tightness in her forehead like the beginning of a migraine. What was happening to her? This was the second time in as many days that she had witnessed a strange vision she could swear was as clear as day, only for it to disappear and for her to be told she'd imagined it. She felt as if she was going crazy; something in the air of Jersey was clouding her mind and making her dream things that could not be. Children with fishtails, fairies in old photographs – it wasn't in her nature to imagine such fantasies. These things had been as clear to her watching eye as they had been mysterious to her sceptical mind. She closed her eyes and rested her fingertips against her temple.

'I think I'm getting a headache,' she muttered. 'I don't know if I want to look at these photos right now.'

Elsa viewed Jessica with concern. But before she could say anything the cellar door opened and Jim entered carrying a tray laden with goodies.

'Lunch time,' he called out as he creaked down the stairs. 'I brought you down the rest of Elsa's delicious cookies, some cakes, a couple of bags of crisps and some lemonade.'

He reached the bottom and Elsa met his eyes with a worried gaze. 'Jessica's not feeling very well.'

The old man's face filled with concern as he placed the tea things on an upturned packing box.

'You all right?' he asked anxiously, kneeling down beside Jess and offering her a glass of lemonade.

Jess sighed deeply and smiled. 'I'm fine, don't worry. I just had a little tension headache. I've had nothing to eat except a biscuit and I got myself all excited about going through Mum's old stuff, that's all.'

She took the soft drink and sipped it quietly. It was not a lie; the pain in her temple had indeed passed and she felt better now, if a little hungry. She felt it wasn't worth saying anything to Jim about what she thought she had seen in the wedding photograph. Telling him of the mermaid was one thing, but he might think her a bit weird if she was forever 'seeing things'.

'We were just looking at these old photographs,' she continued, indicating the album on her knees. 'There's loads of really old ones but I haven't found one of Mum, not yet anyway.'

The old man lifted the ancient volume from Jessica's lap. 'There should be some in here somewhere,' he mused, flicking through the grimy pages. 'Here you go. Her and your grandma and grandpa on the beach at Greve de Lecq, 1963.' He looked suddenly sad. 'That was just a little while before Iris died.'

He handed the album back to her and Jessica studied the black and white photograph. Iris and Freddie were seated on a tartan blanket, smiling happily at the camera. On the sand in front of them, playing with a bucket and spade, was a chubby baby girl in sunhat and dungarees with plump, rosy cheeks and thick, dark curls. Jess knew that the child was her own mother.

The family looked so happy, so normal, Jessica's heart ached to think how it had been torn apart by the death of her grandmother shortly afterwards. It pained her even more to think her own mother had herself known the great emptiness Jessica felt inside from growing up without a parent. It wasn't fair that not one but two generations of the Hellily lineage had been scarred by the untimely demise of a young mother who would never see her daughter enter adulthood. Jessica pondered for a moment whether, when and if she had a child, she too would fall prey to this curse that seemed to plague her family.

'How did she die?' asked Jessica softly, still looking at the photograph. 'You were her brother; you must remember.'

Jim bit his bottom lip and his dark eyes glistened. 'Mugged,' he said blankly. 'She was walking home one evening and someone attacked her. She shouldn't have been alone. Women never walked alone at night back then. But that one time ... Iris...'

He pulled a handkerchief from his pocket and dabbed his eyes. 'I'm sorry. She was my big sister and I loved her dearly.' He regained some of his composure. 'But, my word, there was those that took her loss a great deal worse than I did. Your grandfather for example.'

Jessica placed a comforting hand on Jim's arm. 'What happened to him?' she asked.

Jim frowned. 'Took her death awfully, he did. I remember it as if it was yesterday. Went completely mute, he did. Then two days after the funeral he packed his bags, dropped Emma off with me and left the island. Told everyone he needed time to get over losing Iris. Everyone waited for him to come back but he never returned. No-one saw him again, not on the island at least. I brought your mother up as you know, but I never stopped hoping he would come back for her. Family's family – she'd lost her mother and, thanks to him, she never had a father either.'

There was distinct bitterness in Jim's voice. Who could blame him? She knew from her own father how deeply the tragic loss of a partner can haunt a man, but to abandon a daughter as Fred Kerr had done seemed unthinkable. Jim sensed Jessica's distress and shook his head.

'It does no good for either of us to think about what happened when Iris died,' he said, turning the page in the album. 'Just believe me when I say that even without a mum and dad your mother had a good life. I made sure of that.'

Instinctively Jessica's eyes flickered to Elsa who had remained silent all this time. The girl was squatting beside the tea tray, watching Jessica and Jim with those lonely, blue eyes. She had already munched her way through a bag of crisps and half the biscuits Jim had brought down and only paused from devouring another Kit-Kat when Jessica met her eye.

The pale child blushed guiltily and wiped the brown, chocolate evidence from around her lips.

'Sorry,' she breathed softly.

'It's all right, you go ahead,' Jessica grinned. She thought the girl needed all the sugary treats she could get to keep her strength up.

For the next half hour or so Jim Hellily turned the pages of the old book. Jessica watched and listened enthralled as her great uncle revealed through words and pictures more about her mother than she'd ever known before. She watched the old black and white portraits become colour and her mother turn from a chubby-faced baby gurgling on her uncle's lap to a dark-haired, tomboyish child in ragged jeans and shirts and finally to a beautiful but still somewhat masculine young woman amongst the boats and fishing gear at various ports around Jersey. Through the snapshots of a time long before she existed, Jessica witnessed her mother opening her birthday and Christmas presents, in her school uniform, ruddy cheeked and dirty from climbing trees and exploring the coves around her island home. But soon Jim turned to a page where there was just one final picture. It was of Jess's mother, attired in a dress of black velvet, a sparkling diamond ring on her finger. Jess's dad was pictured too, younger and more carefree than she had ever seen him, his arm around Emma's waist, nibbling playfully on her earlobe.

'And that's your mum and dad at the engagement party I threw them before they left for the mainland,' said Jim with a sigh.

Jessica felt a wave of sorrow wash over her. This was the last photograph Jim had of her mother; this was where her life ended in the album and Jessica could see no more of what was or what might have been. She wished with all her heart that there were photographs of her mother holding her as a baby, of the three of them on holiday, of her and her mother as Jessica was now, two pairs of the same dark eyes.

'Why did she have to die, Jim?' she asked quietly, knowing in her heart he did not have the answers.

'Because this world is unfair and there are powers in it that are sometimes too great for us to control,' he said quietly.

Jessica closed the photo album and gave her great uncle a sad smile. 'Thanks for showing the photos to me.'

She hugged him. The old man returned her embrace.

'That's fine,' he murmured. Jim got to his feet and brushed the dust from his jeans. 'Well, back to work,' he said, picking up the tea tray and departing upstairs.

Elsa shuffled over and sat next to Jessica. 'You okay?' she asked timidly, brushing a stray white-blonde hair from her face.

'Yeah,' she said, chuckling slightly. 'Not happy, but okay. I guess I got what I wanted, to know more about Mum. Doesn't stop me missing not having her around though.' She hugged the battered old album to her chest. 'But at least I've got something to remember her by now.'

Elsa looked upset and lowered her hollow eyes to the ground as she fiddled with the hem of her skirt. 'I don't,' she said quietly, almost as if she didn't want Jessica to hear.

Jess blinked out of her own sorrow and looked quizzically at the younger girl. 'Surely your grandmother must have some photographs of your mum and dad stored away in that big, old house of hers. Maybe she's like my dad and doesn't like having them on display – ask her.'

Elsa shook her head and began to pack away some of the items Jessica had removed from the box when she'd retrieved the photo album. 'I know for sure she doesn't – not one. She got rid of them all, you see.'

Jessica looked at the waif-like child in disbelief. It seemed every time she heard something about Mrs Noir, it made the elderly lady's character worse.

'What do you mean, got rid of them?'

Elsa shrugged and closed the packing box. 'She burnt them. Everything belonging to Mum she burnt when she was killed. The photos, her books, her clothes, everything ... everything.' Her voice, tinged with sadness nevertheless had a matter-of-fact tone that deeply disturbed Jessica. It seemed that this extraordinary reaction of Mrs Noir to Elsa's mother's death was as usual to Elsa as placing flowers on her grave. Upsetting for her, yes – but, nonetheless, a fact of life.

'Your grandma burnt everything your mother owned?' Jess repeated, unable to hide her shock and repulsion. Elsa nodded silently and sat the doll atop the box.

Jess was quiet for a minute. 'Who told you that?' she asked finally, not quite wanting to believe the horrible story was true. She thought it might be some cruel childhood prank fed to Elsa in the playground, for she knew from personal experience how heartless some children can be.

'Grandmère said,' she muttered. 'She told me that when mum and dad died and I came to live with her as a baby, she got all the things belonging to mum in a big pile in the garden and set fire to them. She said that, as I had come to live with her, she didn't need mum's stuff any more. Oh look! Monopoly.' Elsa pulled out a games box while Jessica sat there agog at what she had just been told.

'That's ... that's just awful!' exclaimed Jessica. 'I'm sorry, Els, but normal people don't burn their relatives' possessions when they die.' She actually felt physically sick for she imagined how appalled and upset she would feel if Jim or her father had set what had remained of her mother's belongings ablaze.

Elsa looked up from the Monopoly box and shrugged. 'Some do,' she stated. 'Grandmère did – that's just the way she is.'

Jessica regarded Elsa with pity. 'Your mother and grandmother didn't get on very well, did they?'

Elsa's eyes flamed with annoyance and her thin lips formed an angry pout.

'Who told you that?' she barked hoarsely, in a voice reminiscent of her grandmother's brisk tone. 'It's not true. None of it's true.' She banged the board game down roughly.

'I'm sorry,' Jessica said gently. 'I'd just heard rumours.'

Elsa's white-skinned hands formed fists and she glared at the older girl with fury. 'Well, they were wrong. Who told you, anyway? It's none of their business. And it's none of yours either. Why do you keep asking questions about my family? I don't ask you about yours. I could, but I don't.'

She got to her feet and buried her hands in the pockets of her pinafore dress. She looked to the stairs leading up from the cellar as if she was about to leave but didn't move. Outside, the thunder still rumbled.

'I'm really sorry,' Jessica repeated earnestly. 'I keep asking you about your grandma, don't I? You're right, it's none of my business. After all, I only met you two days ago. I promise I won't do it any more.'

'Promise?'

'Promise,' said Jessica.

Elsa took a half step forward as if she did not completely trust her. 'And you won't say any more horrid things about my mother or grandmère?'

'I promise.'

Jessica lifted the lid off the Monopoly box and started to unpack the game. 'Would you like to play Monopoly?' she asked Elsa, hoping this would lighten the atmosphere between them and restore their fragile friendship.

Elsa nodded and sat down.

For the next two hours or so the girls were happily engaged in their game. Jessica let Elsa beat her. She had a great deal more on her mind than paper money and miniature hotels. She still wanted to help the girl achieve a better life but it was difficult to aid someone who didn't want help. Jessica also thought about the photo album and her own family. She had indeed got what she wanted – more information about her mother. But had it really helped her? The pictures seemed only to make her mother more real and the more real she felt the more Jessica missed her. It physically hurt to know she was gone forever. The album had also raised questions about the rest of her family. Where did Uncle Jim fit in now, after all this time, and were there other relatives her father had 'forgotten' to tell her about?

Elsa's success in the game cheered her up and, as they played together, her anger and mistrust of Jessica seemed to diminish. In fact, by the end of the game the pair seemed more at ease with each other than they had ever been. Afterwards, Jessica packed the board away.

'Now, where did this go?' she asked Elsa. 'It was behind that packing box,' she said, getting to her feet and brushing herself down.

Jessica shifted the packing case where she had found the photograph album out of the way. It was then she saw the chest. It was oddly shaped, about a foot wide and the same deep and three feet long. Its lid wasn't flat but came to a high triangular peak so the top formed a long prism shape. It was beautifully crafted of maple wood, richly inlaid with marquetry pictures in light pine and dark chestnut, depicting birds and flowers. It had a metal lock and handles at either end so it could be carried.

'Elsa!' Jess called, still studying the delicate patterning on the case. Elsa approached and gazed at the beautiful object.

'I wonder what's inside?' she said as Jessica ran her hands over the lid.

'Help me lift it out so we can open it.'

Together the two girls took hold of the handles and heaved. The chest was incredibly heavy and it took all their combined strength to haul it out of its hiding place into the centre of the floor. It was then that the weight of it got too much for the pair and they dropped the casket with a loud bang. The box shook as it hit the ground and the rusty lock fell open. Cautiously Jessica knelt beside it and lifted the lid.

Inside, stacked perfectly one after another, was a line of thick leather-bound journals. Jessica pulled one out and let it fall open in her hands. On the wrinkled, white paper was a child-like script:

April 3rd 1972. At school today Brian pulled my hair and called me a stinky head. I hate him, I hate him sooooooooooo much. Don't want to tell Uncle Jim cos that'll make me look like a baby. Walked down to the beach to talk to Keela about it. He said when his brother teases him he slaps him with his tail. It's not fair! Merfolk don't have to go to school and I do!

129

Jess felt the colour drain from her face as she realized what these books were. They were her mother's diaries, from her childhood to the year she died. They were the key. These books could tell her everything she needed to know about the identity of the woman who had given birth to her. Jess felt weak. Her hands trembled and her throat went dry. Should she actually read these diaries? She ached to with all her heart but somehow it felt as if she would be trespassing on her mother's past by doing so.

'Jessica, Jessica, are you all right?' Elsa's voice broke into her thoughts. The child was looking at her with grave concern. 'What are they?' she asked.

Jessica blinked hard. 'Elsa,' she murmured. 'They're my mum's diaries.'

Elsa gasped and her body stiffened but Jessica barely noticed. She was re-reading the page. Who was Keela? A childhood friend. But a friend with a tail? And who or what were Merfolk? An image sprang into her mind. The boy in the sea she'd seen the previous day. Could it be that this Keela was somebody similar? Had she inherited some sort of sight for these creatures from her mother?

Jessica looked back to Elsa and noticed the girl was holding something in her hands. She closed the diary and leaned forward to examine the small, glittering item in Elsa's outstretched palm. It was a ruby pendant suspended on a long, fine gold chain. The gemstone was perfectly cut and almost glowed in the dim light of the cellar. Two skilfully crafted, gold serpents were entwined around the blood-red jewel. Jessica was mesmerized; never before had she seen a piece of jewellery so unusual and beautiful.

'Where did you find that?' she murmured to Elsa, her eyes never leaving the pendant.

'In the chest, under that diary,' she whispered, with lowered eyes. 'It must've been your mother's.'

She held the necklace by its chain and it swayed slightly from side to side. Jessica watched it for a few seconds and then very slowly she reached out and took it. Brilliant reds glowed within the precious gem and she suddenly felt a great urge to put it on. Her eyes left the pendant for a moment and she looked at her friend sitting opposite. 'Elsa,' she asked quietly, 'do you think it would be creepy if I wore this?'

There was no answer but Jessica didn't really care. She had already undone the clasp on the chain and fastened it around her throat. Elsa watched intently. She opened her mouth as if to say something, but closed it again.

The chain around her neck, Jessica now turned her attention back to the diaries in the wooden case. She ran her fingertips across their spines and pondered what to do. She once again looked at Elsa who had gone very pale. 'I don't know whether to read these.'

Elsa fixed her with a stare. 'I think I'd better go home now,' she said quietly, getting to her feet. 'Grandmère will be waiting for me. Goodbye, Jessica.' With that she turned on her heel and walked quickly up the cellar steps without looking back.

Jessica heard her say goodbye to Jim, and the front door shut. She looked again at the diaries. Before she could change her mind she had put those of 1983 to 1986 in a cardboard box and hidden them with the photo album. Then she tucked the pendant inside her shirt and left the cellar, not noticing that Elsa had gone without taking the doll.

Chapter 9

The Gem and the Journal

When Jessica emerged from the cellar carrying the box, she found her father and great uncle were sitting in the kitchen. The air was steamy and filled with the scent of roast chicken and the room seemed unbearably light to her eyes in comparison with the dingy cellar. Jessica felt the solid bump of her mother's pendant dig against her chest. She decided not to mention it or her discovery of the diaries to her uncle and father. She had made up her mind that if they knew about the journal it would only hamper her finding out the truth about her mother. She was definitely sure neither of them would approve of her reading her mother's old diaries.

Jim looked up from the oven where he was tending to the chicken.

'What got into Elsa? She left awfully quickly. Practically ran out.'

Jessica shook her head and shifted the box awkwardly in her arms. The books were heavier than she'd anticipated.

'She said her grandmother would be waiting for her, then just took off.'

Jim frowned as he began to carve the plump bird. 'I thought she was staying for dinner.'

Martin too looked perplexed. 'Very strange child,' he said. 'She struck me as a little backward.'

Jessica nodded. She wasn't sure her father's assessment was correct but she was convinced there was something definitely wrong with Elsa, physically and emotionally.

Martin looked over his shoulder at Jim. 'I have a friend who's a very understanding child psychologist. I could get her referred

132

if her grandmother would agree, just to give the girl someone to talk to.'

Jessica knew that Mrs Noir would definitely not approve of a psychologist prying into Elsa's thoughts. It might expose to the world what a strange and rather vicious old lady she was. Perhaps it wasn't only Elsa who needed psychiatric help!

Jim shook his head. 'Elsa's fine. Just a little eccentric, like her grandmother. You get characters like that in Jersey.'

'Yeah, but when does eccentric become nutty?' she said, although as soon as she uttered these words, a voice in her head retorted. 'When you start reading your dead mother's diaries without anyone knowing, and seeing fairies in old photos!' It scared her, to think Jersey was making her weird. But it wasn't enough to override her curiosity.

Almost as if he were reading her thoughts, her father changed the subject and said, 'Did you find anything interesting in the cellar? What's in the box?'

Jessica swallowed hard and her pulse quickened. She wasn't a bad liar but then she had never had to lie about anything that seemed this important. She definitely wanted to keep the diaries secret; if her father knew she had them it could blow everything apart and then she'd be back to square one with no more leads on her mother.

She shrugged.

'Not a lot, just some photos and old clothes. I was going to go through them tonight.'

She held her breath, hoping she knew her father well enough to be sure he wouldn't want to go through his deceased wife's things with her.

'Do you want us to sit with you, like I did earlier, Jess?' her great uncle asked.

She shook her head and edged towards the kitchen door.

'If you don't mind, Uncle Jim, I'd like to go through these alone. Get to know mum on my own.'

Her great uncle smiled understandingly at her as she carried the packing box through the door. Jessica practically ran upstairs and into her bedroom. Once alone she breathed a heavy sigh. Her secret was safe. She checked inside the box just to make completely sure her discovery of the diaries wasn't wishful thinking. To her relief the three leather volumes were

133

still safely stored inside. These three simple books held the key to what had happened in her mother's last days. Carefully she hid the box and its contents beneath her bed and returned downstairs.

As usual, Jim had prepared a delicious dinner but, despite having barely eaten all that day, Jessica couldn't finish it. Her stomach was in a knot from wondering what questions the journals answered. Who was her mother? What was she like? What did she think and feel? Maybe they could even tell her why her mother's life had been cut so tragically short and why her husband and uncle refused to talk about her. All the uncertainty that filled Jessica's heart might be put to rest by the diaries.

After the meal she helped clear away the plates and then slipped upstairs without saying goodnight. It was still early evening but because of the storm that had raged all day a murky twilight had already begun to fall. The thunder and lightning that had battled all day had quietened but the rain still fell in heavy sheets and now a bitterly cold wind blew the dark clouds across the sky and tore at the leaves and branches of the willow tree.

Jessica drew the curtains across her bedside window to block out the foul weather. Then, with trembling hands, she lifted the battered cardboard box out from its hiding place and laid it carefully on the green bedspread. She seated herself comfortably against the pillow and almost ceremoniously removed each of the identical leather books from the packing case and placed them before her. Switching the bedside lamp on she gazed at the journals and took a deep breath. There was no turning back now. She was about to uncover who Emma Hellily really was. She gently took the 1983 diary in her hands and opened it at the very first page. There, under the year, was written in bold blue ink her mother's name and the following words:

This is the chronicle of Emma Hellily, friend of faeriefolk, companion of Merfolk, Guardian of Jersey. Let the events recorded here be a legacy for those who go after me.

A chill ran up Jessica's spine. There was that title again, just as on the back of that photograph of Williams Edward Hellily.

134

Had her mum held the same office? Elsa had said that title had been outdated but this diary was only twenty years old. And what was the meaning of faeriefolk and merfolk? It sounded like something from a fairytale. Why would a grown woman write about them in her diary? The whole passage sounded like text from an ancient legend. She turned the page, hoping the diary entries would give her more clues. Her mother's elegant handwriting spread out before her on the paper as clear and as legible as the day it had been written.

January 1st
New Year, a new start. Once again I make the promise I will carry on the tradition laid on my family through the ages and finish my mother's work. Things are so different now Martin is here. I love him dearly and one day hope to spend my life with him but he isn't an islander and doesn't understand my duty to Jersey. He went back to London today and as always made me promise I will give up what he calls 'those ridiculous ways'. I can't do that. The dark forces took my mother and I fear they will take me if I am not prepared.

The key, I believe, lies in the caves off Plemount. I have already begun mapping the hidden tunnels of it and aim to finish before the spring. So long have they been unused I am finding it difficult to know how many Magicroutes are under this island. They must spread everywhere but so far I have yet to encounter any signs of witchcraft in them. I have a feeling a coven still exists in Jersey but where it is and who are involved still elude me. The faeries said they have seen nothing but then, as Uncle Jim says, when can you rely on a faerie's judgement? Still, as long as their numbers do not diminish it means that there is little witchcraft on the island. Powerful Dark Magic needs faerie blood.

I have also talked at great length with Keela and the other Merfolk. As always their friendship and wisdom aid me greatly although, as I predicted, their knowledge on Magicroutes is limited as they are familiar only with the caves and grottos that lead in from the sea. I am pretty sure all of these are clear and unused by witches. It is the inland passageways that worry me more as they have been all but forgotten by true islanders and would make perfect thoroughfares for those wishing to travel in secret. I plan to explore and record my findings here as soon as possible.

135

Jessica stared at the page in disbelief. She understood the words written in the diary but it all sounded like fiction. It didn't seem right for her mother to be recording tales of fairies and merpeople in such a real way. She felt strangely cheated by the diaries, angry at them for not giving her what she was hoping for and even angrier at herself for not being able to make sense of what had been written. Frustrated, she flicked through the pages, hoping to find something that made sense. More entries met her confused eyes, detailed accounts of what her mother called Magicroutes burrowing under the island:

January 26th
Have uncovered the primary chamber by travelling through a narrow crack in the cave wall off the public area. I thank God for blessing me with the skill to see such well hidden ways. The connecting passage is unbelievably restricted, not more than a couple of feet across, and I have to edge along it sideways to get through. But the main chamber is magnificent. Even I have to marvel at the interweaving of Mother Nature and other elements of magic to create such a spectacular sight. The roof is at least a hundred feet high and hung with uncountable stalactites of all conceivable shapes and sizes. The cave itself seems to consist of at least three levels, each one leading into a honeycomb of tunnels going off in all directions. From what I have read, many of these could be dead ends but at this stage it is impossible to tell which. Access to the levels is granted by several small stairways, clearly not formed by nature, carved deep into the rock.

Page after page followed in which Jessica's mother described in meticulous detail her explorations of the various tunnels, interspersed with accounts from her daily life in Jersey – living with her uncle, working in a shop in St Helier and fishing in her spare time. Jessica enjoyed these ordinary accounts more than she did the frequent reports of what her mother found (or more commonly didn't find) in the catacombs off Plemount. They were difficult and boring to read, full of long paragraphs about different types of rocks and the dimensions of the various tunnels. They were also all written with an air of deep frustration. Her mother kept mentioning searching for signs of witchcraft but nearly every cave account ended with the words: '*This search was unsuccessful;*

136

no signs of Dark Magic. But I know the coven is close.' It worried Jessica to think of her mother being so obsessed with something that clearly wasn't real. There was no mention of Jim's concern for his niece while Emma's accounts of the caves and of the merfolk and faeriefolk she met were so clear and well documented it was only logic that stopped Jessica believing they were real. Also recorded in the journals were the visits Jessica's father made to Jersey and the passionate relationship he and her mother seemed to have. It was clear Emma's love for him continued to grow but she also wrote angrily about the way he mocked her explorations even though she recounted how he himself had met with her supernatural friends. But eventually it appeared that her fruitless searches and Martin's scepticism finally wore her down and she decided to leave Jersey to marry him:

August 17th
Today, while we were out on the sea, Martin proposed to me. In a funny way it wasn't a surprise. Dear Martin – I know him so well. How he loves me and longs to give me a happy, secure life. There would have been a time when that would be the last thing I wanted – to leave my island home, my life intertwined with nature and magic – but not now. Experience has softened my character, made my lust to search for evil weak. It is not that I underestimate my responsibility to Jersey. It is just that I am finding it harder and harder to believe witchcraft is still being practised here. All my research ends up with nothing concrete and devoting all of myself to the island leaves my heart empty. When I'm with Martin that emptiness goes away and part of me longs to start a new life with him. That's why I have said yes. I truly believe I am not needed here, for the present at least. If I were, of course, I would return. But for now, as always, I will follow my heart and that rests with Martin.

Jessica closed the diary and sighed sadly. There was such melancholy in her mother's words. She didn't understand Emma's obsession with the caves under Jersey nor her visions of magical creatures but they had clearly been her passion. It was clear that her parents had been deeply in love but it almost seemed that by marrying Martin and leaving Jersey Emma had been giving up part of herself forever.

She looked at the other two journals lying before her on the bed. The first diary had explained quite a bit about her mother but Jessica still wanted to know why she had died. Maybe her final entries would fill the gap between where Emma's life had ended and Jessica's had begun. With some trepidation Jessica picked up the 1986 diary and flicked through it. The entries in this journal were not as concise as the first, as if Emma's departure from Jersey had left a great hole in her life. Her words seemed happy and contented but bland in comparison to her earlier records. She wrote excitedly of her new home in London and the impending birth of the child she was carrying. From time to time though, it seemed as if her mother were pining for her old life in Jersey. She wrote wistfully of fishing and exploring and wondered whether her unborn child would ever see her native isle. It was sadly ironic to Jessica to realize that she sat reading her mother's wishes for her to see Jersey in the very place she had been dreaming of. It was almost as if they were looking at each other from either side of a mirror of time, neither one quite able to see the other. Suddenly she came across an entry which made her stomach churn with fear. The writing on this page was more jagged, as if her mother had been in a great hurry or distress:

19th October
The day that has haunted my nightmares ever since I left Jersey has arrived. Uncle Jim has written to me with word that the coven has been actively trying to raise the Dark One and that I must return to Jersey to battle them. I know, as I have always known, that this is my true destiny. It has been so since the task was laid upon my family, before memory began. And yet I am scared. I am not convinced that my life is as blessed as legend says it is. I carry within me the next link in our chain and although motherly instinct binds me to protect this child, I can feel the powers that I have possessed all my life drain from my body into hers. I don't know if I have the power still in me to defeat the coven. My mind tells me to flee from this challenge in order to save my child and myself but if I do that darkness shall surely reign. I have no choice but to take up my destiny as so many have done before me and return to Jersey. The flight is booked for tomorrow and against his principles, my darling

138

husband has given his blessing. He knows it is not in his power to make me stay. The rest lies with me alone. As I sit here and nurse my swollen belly I pray to God he grants me the strength to defeat this evil and save the child who will bear this legacy and whom I love above all things.

A bitter chill came over Jessica, a burning coldness that pricked at her skin. This was the last thing her mother had written. It held so much dread and foreboding it seemed to tear everything Jessica had thought to be true to shreds. Suddenly merfolk, fairies and witchcraft were no longer the stuff of children's books. They were very real and very close. The diary had more or less spelt it out for her. Emma had been killed by magic. Jessica felt very ill. Coloured lights danced before her eyes in swirls of green and purple. Her head throbbed and swam as the room whirled before her hypnotically. She was overcome by a great urge to sleep. Jessica flopped backwards against the pillows and fell immediately into a heavy slumber.

She didn't know for how long she slept. But the slumber, although deep, was far from restful. It was as if a huge, dark cloud had descended on her and was slowly squeezing the very essence of life from her soul. Then, just as suddenly as Jessica had fallen asleep, she found herself wide-awake and conscious that a terrible spell seemed to have been cast on her.

A pain, deep and flaming, pierced her chest. The room was bathed in a bright, red light that flickered like a million reflecting pieces of scarlet glass. With every flicker the pain in Jessica's chest flared; then she realized why. The throbbing that burned her so excruciatingly emanated from the ruby and gold pendant she was wearing around her neck, as too did the unearthly light. Slowly, for even the smallest move made her muscles contract with agony, Jessica lifted her head and looked at the jewel resting on her chest. The gem was glowing as if it was a red hot coal and to her absolute horror, she could see black burning marks as it charred her clothing. She tried to move, to throw it off, but her body seemed paralysed with pain. She tried to scream but her jaw was clenched tight shut and she couldn't open it.

Then she heard it. A cruel, hissing voice, vicious and not altogether human, that seemed to come from deep within her brain.

139

'Get up off the bed,' it hissed. Her body was no longer her own. She found herself sitting up and climbing out of bed, though every movement caused a wave of agony to pulse through her. However much she willed herself to stay still in the hope the pain would ease, her body seemed to respond only to the low jeering tone in her head.

The spell that had completely taken hold of her body kept her bolt upright so she could not slip back into unconsciousness. A fiery, steel rod seemed to have been driven through her legs and spine, forcing her to stand in agony.

'Walk out of the room and down the stairs,' the voice inside her brain continued. Each time her feet touched the floor, the pain shot from the very tips of her toes all the way up her body to her scalp, as if she were being engulfed in flames. She wanted to scream but her mouth and throat were as hard and motionless as granite. She reached the door of her bedroom to find it flung open by unseen hands.

The landing was pitch black and silent, apart from the gentle breathing of Jessica's father and great uncle as they slept. She prayed that this was a nightmare, but the terror she felt was too real to be a mere dream. The hex spun her around so she faced the stairs. The steps wobbled and twisted before her and she stumbled down them, clinging to the banisters for support. She willed her body not to move any further but a sudden thump between her shoulder-blades made her tumble to the foot of the stairs in a shaking heap. As soon as she landed, Jessica felt the power within draw her again to her feet. The front door opened magically and Jessica was flung out into the tempestuous night.

The rain and wind lashed at her as she stumbled blindly away from the house. Her sight was so distorted by now that in the blackness of the late hour she was all but blind. Her body was in such pain that she was completely unaware of where she was heading. All she knew was that she seemed to be travelling at immense speed, far faster than she could normally run. Across fields and roads she flew, her feet barely touching the ground until the demonic voice in her mind began chanting three words over and over again: 'Off the cliffs! Off the cliffs!'

Faster and faster she flew, her body ignited like a living flame. She felt as if some monstrous bird had her gripped tightly in its talons. Then suddenly Jessica stopped dead in mid-air. Her vision cleared and she found herself high above the sea off St Ouens Bay, the rain and wind swirling around her. She gazed down to see the tumultuous ocean crashing beneath. Then she dropped.

The fall seemed to take forever. Jessica braced herself and shut her eyes as she plummeted into the angry water like a stone. The impact forced the air from her lungs. She began floundering wildly to keep her head above the waves, but the dark current grabbed her like a great sea-serpent and her weak form was swiftly engulfed. Her arms and legs moved wildly as she tried to swim but her pitiful attempts were no match for the tide.

Deeper she sank, her nose, mouth and lungs filling with the icy water, but, just as she was on the brink of death, a force stronger than the current seemed to grip her around the waist and drag her upward like a torpedo. Someone, or something, had a firm hold of her limp form and was pulling her swiftly to the surface. It powered her out of the water and into the oxygen-filled night air.

Jessica lay, bobbing in the creature's arms, coughing the salt water from her lungs and gasping for air. She looked at her rescuer groggily. The burning was still in her chest but it was now just a dull pain.

'Jessica Hellily, are you okay?' The young man supporting her body was speaking, his voice strong and full of concern.

Jess tried to reply but all she could manage was a weak moan. Her eyes were foggy and she couldn't make out her rescuer's features.

She felt his fingers lift the chain around her neck but was too tired and confused to comprehend what was happening. He gasped in horror as he examined the pendant.

'It's a drowning curse,' he murmured. Jess felt her body shake suddenly as the man grabbed the chain, snatched it from her and hurled it deep into the sea. Almost immediately the burning stopped and her eyesight cleared. Despite the bitter cold she felt normal again. Gratefully she turned to face her rescuer but the creature that met her eyes was definitely not human.

His shoulder-length hair was a lush mossy green and framed his strong features in sweeping natural curls. His nose was large

141

and hooked, his lips thick and slightly pouting. He had the most hauntingly beautiful eyes Jessica had ever seen, wide and clear with golden irises that sparkled like antique coins in the moonlight. He was bare-chested apart from a dainty string of shells that hung around his neck and his skin glistened aquamarine.

Despite her fear and confusion, Jessica was at the same time fascinated. There was something oddly familiar about his appearance. Then it hit her – the boy in the sea off St Brelade's. This man had the same otherworldly look. She hadn't been dreaming.

The man regarded her with grave anxiety. 'Jessica,' he said, 'that amulet you were wearing had a curse on it. You could have been killed.'

As he spoke his thick lips revealed sharp, dagger-like teeth. Jessica shuddered. The creature had saved her from a watery grave but for what purpose? With razor sharp fangs like that it seemed very likely she could be his supper. But what could she do? She wasn't a strong enough swimmer to break free and escape to the shore. She shivered in the icy water and gazed fearfully at the stranger.

'Who are you?' she begged timidly.

The sea-man cocked his head to one side and a lock of his glorious mane streamed out in the ocean breeze.

'My name is Inggot,' he said soothingly. He raised an elegant, long-fingered hand and touched her cheek in an effort to calm her. His hand was cool and smooth as silk – and had no fingernails.

Jessica breathed deeply. It was clear he meant her no harm; he simply floated serenely in the cold ocean, his powerful arms supporting her against the waves. Finally, she mustered the courage to speak again.

'What are you? How do you know my name?'

He looked quizzically at her and gently ran his fingers across her forehead as if he was worried she might have been concussed and lost her memory.

'I'm a merman,' he said softly. He fixed her with an inquisitive stare and Jessica noticed how his eyes seemed to generate a gentle yellow light of their own. 'You do know what a merman is, don't you?'

142

Jessica shook her head. 'Not really, no.'

Now that the awful heat that had agonised her minutes before had departed, she was left feeling bitterly cold. She wished Inggot would take her back to the shore but the merman seemed to be more concerned about her memory and discovering what she did or didn't know.

He licked his greenish lips nervously. 'You do know what your title is, don't you? Tell me, Jessica. Don't play games. Tell me who you are?'

Nothing this strange creature was saying was making any sense. She had no title as far as she knew and she hadn't thought it possible that mermen existed, even though she had just been rescued by one. She shook her head violently

'I don't know what you're talking about,' she cried, gripping Inggot's smooth blue shoulders angrily. 'I am Jessica Kent. My father is Martin Kent. My mother was Emma Hellily, but she is dead and I don't know who she was. I don't know what my title is and I want you to take me back to the shore!'

She was cold and angry and nothing around her made any sense. Inggot held her firmly but gently and spoke to her in such a caring and velvety tone it calmed her fury.

'Okay Jessica,' he soothed. 'I understand now and I am going to help you. I will call Keela. He's a good friend of your Uncle Jim and he will help you.'

He looked out over the rippling ocean and inhaled deeply. 'Keela!' he cried and, as he did so, his voice seemed to ripple through the water, penetrating its murky depths.

Jessica watched in disbelief as three more heads broke the surface of the bay and began swimming quickly and steadily towards them. As they drew closer she saw these were more merfolk.

The largest was about the same size as Inggot but looked slightly older. His hair and beard were inky green and his skin a smooth emerald. Behind him came another smaller creature with elegant long arms and a mane of the most brilliant sapphire tresses spreading out behind her as she swam. Her face was elfin and her flesh the colour of newly budded leaves. She kept stopping every few feet or so and looking back at the tiny figure who was zig-zagging along behind her at an amazing speed. Jessica recognized the smallest figure as the blue-haired boy she had seen on her fishing trip. The group drew level with them and surrounded the pair. Both the older merfolk wore worried expressions when they saw Jessica but the child bobbed about excitedly, obviously recognizing her. All had beautiful gold eyes.

Inggot turned to the other merman. 'Keela! Thank Neptune you came quickly. You won't believe what happened. This is Jessica Hellily.'

Keela placed a graceful hand on Jessica's wet hair and smoothed it back gently. 'I know,' he said softly. 'She has her mother's eyes. Go on, Inggot.'

The younger merman continued. 'She fell off the cliffs. I was swimming nearby and saw her. I brought her to the surface. Keela, she had a drowning curse on her! It was woven by a pendant around her neck. I got rid of it.'

Keela was regarding the human all the while Inggot spoke. His gold eyes were full of kindness and he looked at her as an old family friend would look at a young person they hadn't seen for a great many years.

'Jessica,' he said gently, 'didn't Jim tell you to be careful of magic omens?'

Jessica shook her head. She was still very confused and scared but the gentle, fatherly presence of Keela made her feel safer. Inggot, however, was most agitated. He placed a firm hand on Keela's arm.

'That's what I'm trying to tell you,' he insisted. 'She doesn't know anything. I'm worried, Keela. She said she'd hadn't heard of merfolk and she doesn't even realize she's the Guardian.'

Keela's bright eyes filled with horror. He looked broodingly into the sea as if some great betrayal had just taken place.

Meanwhile, the female had swum over to Jessica and was carefully examining her face with small elegant hands. Her touch was soft and Jessica was astounded by the beauty of her features, despite their odd colouring.

'She's cold,' the mermaid told Keela. Her voice was melodic and calm, like a combination of a sea-breeze whispering and the hollow tune of an oboe. 'Husband, humans are warm blooded; she shouldn't spend any longer out here. It'll make her ill. Take her back to Jim.'

The merman was still deep in thought. He looked at Jessica, with anger and concern. 'Jessica,' he said in a low voice, 'tell me. Have you heard or seen anything strange since you've been in Jersey? Have people talked about your mother or said things that didn't make sense to you?'

'Yes,' she replied, glad to meet someone who seemed to understand at last. 'There were these strange lights in the garden the first night I arrived and I heard singing. I came to Jersey to find out who my mother was but no-one will really tell me anything. They all seem to have known her but when I ask questions they go all secretive. Uncle Jim's especially like that. Everyone knows who I am too; even you know my name. I don't understand it.' She looked at the small boy who was swimming about excitedly nearby. 'Your son,' she added anxiously. 'I saw him too. Two days ago Uncle Jim took me fishing and I looked down into the water and he was there, waving at me.'

Keela threw the merchild a stern glance. 'Is this true?' he asked gruffly.

The little boy nodded excitedly. 'Yes, dada,' he gushed. 'I was swimming on my own and I looked up and there was a fishing boat and Jessica was sitting in it and I saw her and I waved.' He clapped his chubby hands excitedly, grinning broadly.

Keela fixed his son with a serious stare. 'Pod, how many times have I told you, don't swim inland during the daytime. And never wave at boats!'

The small boy pouted moodily and crossed his arms. 'Not fair,' he sulked. 'I knew she was the Guardian so it was okay and still I get in trouble.'

Reeni, the mermaid, swam over to her child. 'Your father's right, dear. An outsider could have seen you and then we'd all be in a lot of trouble.' She took her son by the hand and turned back to her husband. 'I'll take him back to bed, Keela. I think it's best if you take Jessica back to the shore. She does look bitterly cold.'

The merman nodded thoughtfully. 'Yes, Reeni dear. I intend to. I want to speak with Jim anyway.'

Reeni half-smiled and together she and Pod dived gracefully under the waves. As they did so, Jessica saw the moonlight glimmer on their silvery tails.

'Do you want me to come with you?' Inggot asked.

Keela shook his head. 'No, Inggot, I would prefer to do this alone. I understand your concern and indeed, this is a matter for the whole community but I know Jim Hellily well. I would appreciate it if you didn't mention this to anyone, not even Xandu. It would only cause unnecessary panic.'

Inggot lowered his shining eyes and nodded. 'I understand,' he murmured. 'I wish you good luck, Jessica Hellily.'

Keela touched Jess gently on her arm. 'Do you think you could climb on my back and I'll swim you to shore?' he asked.

Jessica nodded silently. She was struggling desperately to take in everything that was happening. Not only had she nearly drowned that night but her rescue had transported her to a world she wouldn't have thought could possibly exist. It seemed clear to her that her quest to discover the true identity of Emma Hellily was reaching a conclusion, but it was one more complex and unexpected than she could ever have imagined.

Carefully Inggot helped Jessica climb onto Keela's back before disappearing below the ocean. Jess wrapped her arms around the merman's neck and gripped him tightly with her thighs. Once he was sure that the girl was holding on securely, Keela swam towards the rocky beach of St Ouens Bay and the truth of Jessica's destiny.

Chapter 10

The Heir of Helier

Keela cut through the cold black water with a speed and effortlessness that Jessica could scarcely believe. Her ignorance seemed to stretch beyond simply her mother's identity and she wondered just how many other people knew of the merfolk's existence. Then there was Jake. At first she had found him very odd but now she begun to wonder about some of the things he had said. 'People on Jersey are different.' They had been his words. Did he mean that the people on this island were in touch with mermaids and the like? Did Jake too know about Keela, Inggot and the others? If so, why was she, someone who had been raised on the mainland, saved from drowning by them? What special value was there in her life?

Keela groaned crossly to himself as his strong body cut through the icy swells. 'This is wrong,' he said mournfully.

Jessica stopped pondering everything that had happened as she heard the merman's words. She could only see the back of his head, his dark green mane entangled here and there with sand and seaweed, but she could tell he was frowning. There was great anger in his voice, as if he felt some vast injustice had been done. Jessica thought for one awful second she herself had infuriated him and the merman was about to abandon her.

'Have I done something wrong?' she asked nervously.

Keela shook his head heavily. 'It's not your fault, Jessica,' he said. 'I am just so angry that you had to find out this way. You should never have been put in such danger. What was Jim thinking? He should have told you the truth from the start.'

Jessica blinked the salt spray from her eyes. 'You know my

great uncle well?' she queried as they drew into the shallow waters of the bay.

'I've known Jim Hellily since we were both young,' he replied fondly with a shake of his inky locks. 'He's a dear friend of mine. As good a human as a merman could hope to meet. Of course, there are certain matters on which we disagree but I am still proud to call him a friend.'

Jessica peered over his shoulder at the rapidly approaching beach. Her eyesight had grown quite accustomed to the blackness by now and she could clearly make out the sheer rock-face of the cliff, the seaweed-strewn sand of the shoreline and the jagged rocks that jutted out from the sea. She realized with a shudder just how lucky she had been not to fall onto the hard rocks and be crushed to death. She thanked God for the sea and its kind inhabitants, and held more tightly on to Keela's back.

'I am so glad that your friend, Inggot, rescued me when I fell,' she said, staring up at the treacherous cliffs. 'I would've drowned for sure. I never knew curses existed – or merfolk for that matter.'

Keela inhaled deeply. 'It would appear there are a lot of things you don't know that you should have been told about.'

Jessica nodded sadly. The merman seemed to know the extent of her frustration. He appeared to think it vital that Jessica should have been told about the existence of his species. Moreover, Jessica was struck by the fact that his fury was directed at Jim who, as far as she was aware, knew nothing of magic and legends apart from the songs and tales with which he had entertained her. That Keela claimed to be a good friend of Jim astounded Jessica and made her wonder, after the supernatural events of that night, whether or not the merman had also known her mother. She thought back to the journals and remembered Keela's name had featured in them.

They were in the shallows by now, not more than ten or fifteen feet from the shore. The merman had slowed down a great deal as the tide became lower, clearly finding it difficult to move when he could not swim. Sensing his awkwardness, Jessica climbed off his back and waded through the waves towards the sand. Her clothes were heavy and dripping with salt water, her hair plastered cold and damp to her head. She

148

shivered as she walked out of the sea; the air around her was even more chilling. Unsure what to do, she sat down on a large rock and gazed back out to the shallows where Keela was dragging himself slowly but surely from the sea towards her. Hugging her sopping denim jacket around her to retain what little body heat she still had, she felt lost and alone. What new revelations were coming her way? She wanted to cry, to have someone tuck her safely into bed and tell her it was all a dream.

Keela had hauled himself up the beach and settled on his back, half leaning against the rock where Jessica sat. She gazed down at him and his magnificent fishlike tail as it lay outstretched on the sand. It began about an inch or so below his navel and was covered by row upon row of tiny, silver scales that shone and glinted in the moonlight like delicate panels of silver plate. At the end it spread out into a splendid pair of fins, translucent with fragile veins of whitish grey running through them like the supporting struts of a fan. He was a striking and wondrous presence.

The merman looked up at Jessica as she sat shivering on the rock. 'You can't stay here like this,' he said gently. 'You'll catch cold. I'll call Rosehip to go and fetch your uncle.'

She couldn't imagine who or what Rosehip was, but Keela had shown her such concern and care she doubted it could be anything dangerous. He stroked her cheek tenderly, to calm the obvious panic Jess was expressing. The merman turned his shining eyes towards the top of the cliffs and let out a long, sweet whistle, more melodic than Jess had ever heard from a human. The night wind seemed to carry it far up above their heads into the mainland of Jersey.

Jessica followed Keela's gaze but could see nothing save the ominous rock face and dark night sky.

'She's a faerie,' he explained.

This was yet more information from a realm she was having difficulties comprehending – first merfolk and now faeries. The whole thing was becoming more and more like a fable.

'You're finding this all a bit hard to take in, aren't you, Jessica?' Keela said, a hint of disappointment in his voice.

'Quite frankly, yes! I mean, can you blame me? Curses and magic – I thought they were just superstition. And, no offence, but I never believed merfolk existed.'

149

She rubbed her cold nose on the back of her hand.

'There are more things in this world than today's human sciences can explain or understand. Ways of beauty and wonderment as well as of darkness, and evil forces that this world has dismissed and forgotten. In the past it was easier; humans were not so hungry to control and explain everything. They accepted there were creatures and powers in nature with whom they had to co-operate, and that we are all part of one whole. Thank God there are still places like Jersey, remote from the modern sceptical world, where merfolk and faeries can live in relative harmony with mankind. True Jersey people accept us for what we are.'

Jessica sat in silence as the merman spoke of the hidden world, so new and strange to her. She had been shocked by the existence of such mystical beings and magical ways and yet a part of her that had felt empty and lost for as long as she could remember seemed to be put to rest. This ancient and supernatural world of which Keela spoke seemed to Jessica not completely alien at all, but rather like a lost memory. It seemed to be a link to a past she had spent so long searching for, to the mother she had never known. In the darkest recesses of her mind, knowledge had begun to awaken, a knowledge she had been born with but until this moment had been unable to use. She felt as if she had come home.

'So,' she asked quietly, her eyes returning to the rocky headland above them. 'Is it all real, then? Everything in legends and folklore. Elves, faeries, witches and dragons. They all do exist.'

The wind ruffled Keela's dark hair, making it fly out in long unkempt strands as he spoke. 'Dragons I don't know of in these parts, but elves and faeries are commonplace in Jersey. You have the skill to see them, as you do my kind; it comes from your mother. The faeries will aid you, as will merfolk. That I can promise.'

A tiny shiver ran up Jessica's spine as she remembered some of the passages from her mother's diary. Passages filled with concern and frustration as she wrote about the caves of Plemount and her elusive search for witchcraft. 'And what about witches?' she asked, not altogether convinced she wanted an answer.

Keela's face darkened. 'There are humans,' he started slowly, 'who possess certain powers which allow them to do terrible deeds. But those powers come at a great price. They are in

150

league with dark spirits who fill their hearts with hatred and a lust for power. I am afraid to say that your destiny is linked with such cruel-hearted people, but I shall speak no more on that until your family is present.'

A chill shot through Jessica, more biting than the cold she felt from her wet garments. She thought about the last entry in her mother's diary. How she had spoken of her duty and the fear she had for the life of her unborn child. After a respite of fourteen years would her mother's fear finally be realized? Jessica did not want to ponder this thought and didn't have the opportunity, for a strange sight on the top of the cliff caught both her and Keela's attention.

A tiny pinprick of light was hovering above the cliff, subtle and uncertain as a glow-worm. In the starless night the radiant dot glistened quite beautifully, growing in power until its soft golden beams illuminated the craggy rock face. It floated motionless for a few moments, as if looking for something, then quickly leaped into life. It shot upwards a few feet before descending towards the beach in a golden arc like a miniature comet falling from the heavens with a fiery tail of white light behind it. Jessica watched in amazement as the glowing sphere stopped its descent a foot or so above the sand and hovered there before floating slowly towards them, bobbing merrily up and down and illuminating the beach as it approached. The glistening globe emitted a soft tinkling sound as it went, like tiny chimes, but as it got closer Jessica realized that the tinkling was in fact a little high voice muttering worriedly to itself.

'Oh dear,' it muttered. 'Now I'm for it, now I'm in trouble!'

The light drew level with Jessica and Keela and revealed itself as a tiny female figure whose pale, silvery skin was wonderfully luminescent. She was unbelievably delicate and beautiful, with graceful, long limbs like a ballerina and a halo of short strawberry-blonde hair. Her eyes were the lightest shade of china blue and her features pointed and elfin. She had on a simple white dress of silky material and on her back fluttered a fragile pair of transparent wings. Jessica stared at her. Never before had she seen anything so fragile and beautiful. The faerie perched on the damp sand and stared back, first at Jessica and then at the merman.

'Well?' she asked, her tiny musical voice filled with concern.

151

'Is she hurt? Oh dear, oh dear! They said "Look after her" and if she is hurt it's my fault. I saw it happen but I couldn't stop it.' She kicked the grains of sand around nervously.

Keela sighed exasperatedly. 'Rosehip,' he said, 'look at her. Does she look hurt?'

The faerie screwed up her pointed nose and examined Jessica closely for a few seconds. Then she stood up and walked over to her, her hands resting on her narrow hips. Still not confident enough to make a judgement, Rosehip fluttered her cobweb-thin wings and floated into the air, circling the astounded girl before landing on Keela's shoulder. It was only then she gave her answer.

'No. No, she doesn't look hurt,' she declared.

Keela groaned and clapped his hands slowly. 'Another triumph for faerie intelligence,' he sighed sarcastically.

Rosehip hopped down off his shoulder back onto the sand. 'Yes, but I saw her, Keela. I saw her stumble out of the house and I saw the dark magic carry her to the cliff. It was a curse, I think – black magic. Then she fell off the cliff.' She danced about wildly as she spoke, flapping her arms.

Keela watched her patiently, waiting for her to finish.

'And what did you do?' he quizzed, sounding like a teacher waiting for a naughty schoolgirl to catch herself out.

Rosehip drew a tiny circle in the sand with her foot. 'Well, first I thought I have to stop her 'cause she's the Guardian and if she gets hurt we're all in trouble. But then I thought the curse must have been cast by a witch or a warlock and, do you know what they do to faeries? They tear off your wings and cut off your head and squish you into itty-bitty pieces. And I didn't want that.'

'So what did you do?' he repeated.

Rosehip looked slightly ashamed and played with the hem of her dress. 'I hid,' she muttered quietly.

Keela rolled his shining eyes disappointedly and crossed his muscular arms. 'That wasn't a very responsible thing to do, was it?'

The small sprite looked up at him angrily. 'It's all right for you,' she squeaked, flying up and buzzing crossly in his face. 'Big, old fishy thing like you. They couldn't mush you up. I was scared!' She grabbed hold of a long strand of his dark hair

152

and pulled it. 'And I *have* been trying to help. The first night she was here she wanted to go home, but I cast a peace spell. I made her stay.'

Keela relented and held out the back of his hand for Rosehip to perch on.

'I guess there was nothing you could do, and Jessica's fine now. The curse is gone.' He looked at the faerie, who was sitting lightly on his wrist. 'But I need you to fly to Jim and tell him what has happened. Bring him here at once.'

Rosehip nodded willingly and jumped to her feet, her beautiful, fine wings outstretched. 'You can count on me,' she squeaked eagerly. 'I'll be back quicker than a sparrow, faster than moonlight on the sea, speedier than lightning! You won't know I'm gone.' She hopped into the air and hovered for a moment in front of Keela's face, looking slightly confused. 'Where am I going again?'

The merman groaned in exasperation. 'Jim's house, Maison de l'hache. Now hurry.'

The vital information finally clear in her brain, Rosehip zoomed away up the beach and swiftly soared over the cliff tops. Jessica watched her vanish. Keela noted her wonderment. 'Faeries are amazing magical beings,' he said. 'Just don't credit them with too much intelligence. There's only so much you can keep in a head the size of an acorn!'

Without Rosehip's magical light, the deserted beach was once again plunged into near blackness. Jessica's clothes felt slightly drier against the cold wind but there was still a dampness about them that clung to her skin. She could hear the wild ocean crashing on the shore a few feet away and taste the fresh salt that coated her chapped lips. The cove of St Ouens felt a very lonely place to be and now that Keela had fallen silent Jessica had a moment to reflect upon the strange events of that night.

Jersey, it would seem, was an island of mysteries and secrets and Jessica had come to realize that her own family must be part of that shadowy world. Indeed, she had now come to see that right from the moment she landed she herself had entered unknowingly into a land more mystical than she first thought. She had worked out that the glowing bush in her great uncle's garden had been caused by Rosehip's faerie spell. But why? And then it hit her. The dream she had had of Jim and her father arguing about magic. It hadn't been a dream. They really had been fighting, disagreeing about whether or not to tell her the truth about the magic that existed all around them. She had trouble remembering the exact content of the argument – Rosehip had probably seen to that – but they had both been deadly serious. They knew about Keela, Rosehip and the others and had been lying to her all the time. Her mother, the woman whose life had been so carefully hidden from Jessica, knew about the merfolk and faeries, they had been a close part of her life, that was why her family refused to tell her the truth.

She turned to Keela, who was staring out to sea. 'You knew her, didn't you?' she said. 'You were friends with my mum. Tell me, Keela. Who was she and why has everyone been lying to me?'

The merman turned to face Jessica. His eyes glimmered like two perfect round discs of gold filled with the sadness of a secret he had kept for too long. 'You're right,' he murmured woefully. 'I was close to Emma Hellily. We all were. The merfolk who swim in Jersey's waters and the faeries who are nature's own servants. That's why I am so angry with Jim for lying to you all these years. Your mother was a brave woman, one of the last humans who could rightly be called a hero. When she died, a darkness fell on this island.'

Jessica took the merman's cool, smooth hand and gripped it tightly. 'So you do know what happened to her. I found her diaries today. She was coming back to Jersey, coming back to complete something. What was that?'

Keela's beautiful eyes filled with tears of anger and pain, not clear, watery tears such as a human would cry but tears as white and creamy as pearls. 'She gave up everything for her duty, her heritage. Yet this is how she is repaid, with lies. It wasn't Jim's choice to make; it certainly wasn't your father's. I know it's cruel but it's the only way; that's why she did what she did.'

Jessica felt she wanted to scream. Nothing made sense any more. All she asked was a straight answer to what had ended her mother's life but not even Keela would tell her. She was about to beg him to state what had happened in cold, hard facts when the sound of voices made her spin around. Once again the tiny golden light of Rosehip was visible, bobbing through the chill night, leading two human figures along the beach towards them.

154

Jessica could make out the outlines of her father and great uncle, still in their pyjamas, their coats wrapped around their bodies, trudging along the damp sand. She stood up and ran towards them, desperate for them to own up and reveal what they had kept from her. Martin broke into a dash when he saw his daughter alive and well. He threw his arms around her and cried with relief. Jim was soon behind them but hung back when he saw Keela glaring at him menacingly. Martin saw the furious merman and realized his daughter now knew the truth about Jersey. Keela's eyes bore into Jim's and his voice was bitter.

'It was a drowning curse, Jim. The girl found it on a pendant with some of Emma's old stuff, she had probably been studying it. Just what the hell do you think you were playing at? She should've known. You said you would tell her.'

Jim looked ashamed and put a protective hand on Jess's shoulder. 'The moment never arose. It wasn't an easy thing to say.'

Keela shook his head. His eyes then flickered to Martin and he sneered. 'And you,' he spat. 'I don't even want to look at your mainland face. It was your fault in the first place. If you had remained with Jess on the island she could've grown up knowing the truth.'

Martin's face darkened with wrath at the merman's words. He stepped past Jessica and glared down at him. 'I,' he stated clearly, 'was trying to save my daughter, as I tried to save the woman I loved. What good came when Emma got involved with your kind? Witches and warlocks. If she hadn't come back to Jersey she might still be alive.'

Jessica was amazed. It was one thing that Jim, someone whom she barely knew and who seemed deeply connected to Jersey, knew Keela, but a non-Jersey man like her father? The world seemed to have gone crazy. She felt disgusted – her father, the man who had brought her up, whom she believed had not talked about her mother because of agonizing grief, had been lying to her all her life. The death of her mother was part of some huge secret involving the magic folk she had just discovered.

Keela was livid. 'When will you humans see that there is more to this world than the preservation of your own lives?' he raged. 'Emma was a dear friend of mine and if you think I was happy to see her killed you are very wrong. But if Emma had not given her life then the Dark Ones would have seized control and this land as we know it would've been destroyed. That is the legacy of Helier's Heir.'

Jessica's stomach lurched. So that was it. Her mother's death was no mere accident. She had been murdered. She pushed between Keela and Martin, not knowing at whom to look for an answer. Fear and confusion bubbled inside her and her head swam with a million questions. She looked at her father and saw he had tears in his eyes. Tears of grief, but also of shame for the horrible secret he had kept from her.

'Dad,' she said softly, her voice holding a firmness that made it clear she would stand no more lies. 'What happened to mum? Why is Keela so cross? What have you kept from me?'

Martin's face was ashen with despair.

Behind them, Keela sat, as cold and fixed as the dark cliffs that towered above. 'It's not his place to say,' he declared coolly. 'Nor is it mine. Jim, you're the one. Tell her of her legacy.'

Jim knelt before Jessica. His eyes that usually shone so brightly were dull and his voice was filled with fear.

'This world,' he said softly, 'is more mysterious and dark than you can possibly realize. Centuries ago, man knew of the existence of faeries and merfolk and had less power to control the world around him. He was happy to live as part of nature. But as man became greedier he began to depart from the power of the earth. We abandoned our fellow beings and slowly they have been forgotten. It is only in close communities like Jersey, where magic is still respected, that faeries and merfolk can find refuge.'

Jessica sighed in frustration. 'Keela told me that already. And you might as well know I've found Mum's diaries, down in the cellar. I know she was friends with Keela and the others. I just want to know what killed her and why you haven't told me about the magic before.'

Jim gripped her shoulders firmly. 'This isn't a game, Jessica,' he said through gritted teeth. 'You may think it's cute and fun to know there are merfolk and faeries in Jersey, but this is not a children's fairytale. There are dark forces surrounding us and you especially must be aware of everything that is happening.'

Jessica glanced at her father sitting on the rock. He was sobbing quietly to himself, seeming not to want to hear what Jim was saying.

'Why me?' she asked the old man sternly. 'Why am I so important? I've never even been to Jersey before. And what do you mean by Dark Forces?'

'As long as man has walked upon this earth, there have been those who would do anything, and I mean anything, for power. They bear deep within them a lust to harness the magic of the world and use it for their own ends. No good can come of such unnatural desires. As you become more capable of working with the dark arts, you begin to give up your humanity. The demons that supply you with such deadly skills take away your compassion, your love for your fellow man. You do terrible, terrible things. That's what it means to become a witch or warlock.'

Jessica felt the blood drain from her face. 'No,' she cried, 'Mum wasn't like that. She loved Dad.'

'Of course she wasn't,' he soothed. 'Emma was no witch. She was a good girl, a kind woman. But it's vital you know about the witches, Jessica, because the lives of such cruel and brutal people are directly linked to your own destiny – and your mother's. Do you remember I told you the legend of St Helier? It's true. No-one knows for sure whether his powers came from his faith in Jesus or from his heathen parentage. But I believe that Helier's faith and pure heart allowed him to turn his witchcraft to good, thus saving Jersey.'

Tears of frustration ran down Jess's cheeks. 'Why are you telling me about Helier again?' she screamed. 'I just want the truth about Mum.'

Keela, who had been silent for some time, growled with anger. 'Silly girl! Can't you see? Don't the pieces fit yet? Helier knew it was he and he alone who stood between the warlocks and the demon he'd banished into the rocks of Jersey. He knew that once his mortal life was through the followers of the Dark Side would rise up and take the island. He had to provide a safeguard that would last beyond his years – a legacy, an heir.'

Jim continued. 'When his loyal servant Romard took the axe that slew St Helier, he received the duty and the power to protect Jersey from the Evil One. For the past five hundred years the direct descendants of Romard have had the power to stop the warlocks and witches reclaiming Jersey and releasing that wicked demon again. As soon as the first child of a new generation

157

is born to the eldest child of the previous one, they take on the legacy to guard the island. They alone can do it. If the bloodline ends then Jersey will fall into darkness.'

It was as if someone had unlocked a door in Jessica's mind and her real identity had flown through it. She lifted her head, tall and proud, her fear and confusion vanishing. At last she knew who she was. When she spoke her voice was calm and soft.

'Hellily, from the name Helier. Our family are the descendants of Romard. My grandmother was your older sister, Jim; Mum was her only child. That's what happened, wasn't it? I see it now. Mum was the Heir of Helier!'

Suddenly Martin got to his feet and wiped the tears angrily from his eyes. 'Happy now?' he barked at Jim. 'You've got what you wanted. She knows what happened to Emma. I should never have brought her here. She could've been happy. She could've got on with a normal life and never had to get involved with this awful curse. But you begged and pleaded to see your great-niece.'

Martin met his daughter's amazed stare. 'Emma told me, as soon as our relationship began getting serious. She explained who her ancestors were and their legacy. At first I didn't believe her but then she introduced me to the merfolk, showed me her research into the caves at Plemount – which I take it you've seen, Jess. I soon realized just how dangerous these witches were. They killed your grandmother to try and end the bloodline. That's why Emma was so bent on finding them and stopping their evil. Every day she remained in Jersey her life was in danger. I adored your mother, Jess. I wanted to keep her safe. That's why I finally persuaded her to marry me and live in London.'

From his seat on the damp sand, Keela the merman glared up at him. 'And that's how you almost sealed all our fates, you fool!' he snapped angrily. 'While Emma was away the followers of the Dark Side banded together to raise the demon again. It was a fearful time for Jersey. Not knowing what else to do and with the coven powers at their strongest, Jim wrote to Emma and begged her to return.'

Martin buried his face deep in his hands. 'I knew it was no good trying to talk her out of it,' he wailed. 'Emma was determined to fulfil her duty to Jersey, even though she was pregnant at the time. She caught the first plane over here and prepared to confront the witches. I can't tell you what happened – it was too horrible.'

'The details are too painful to speak of,' said Jim. 'Your mother faced thirteen witches and warlocks single handed as they prepared to raise the demon of Jersey. She bore the terrible spells they cast on her, using her very body as a vessel of white magic, the blessing of her blood. It dispelled the coven's magic and sent them fleeing but it also cost her her life. After the battle she had just enough strength to give birth to you before her agony was ended.'

Tears filled Jessica's eyes as she realized the awful price her mother had paid. But a sense of purpose now resided in her and although she felt very unsure as to what her duty actually meant she knew she had to do something. 'What must I do?' she asked. 'I won't let Mum's death be in vain.'

'No!' exclaimed Martin. 'You don't have to do anything.'

Keela silenced him with a stare. 'No more lies,' he ordered. 'Jessica, Jim wrote to your father because there have been signs in Jersey that indicate witches are returning. Only you have the power to find who they are and stop them before it's too late. You won't be alone. Rosehip here has been appointed to help you.'

The small faerie fluttered from her seat on the sand to Jessica's shoulder. 'Don't worry,' she whispered, 'I promise I won't let you get hurt again.'

Jessica smiled unsurely and looked back to the merman. The sky had begun to lighten with the rays of the rising sun.

'I suggest the three of you go home and get some sleep,' Keela said. 'I am always here if you ever need me. A great fate has been placed on your shoulders, Jessica. I pray you have the strength within you to carry it through.' He flipped onto his stomach and crawled down the beach, back to his aquatic home.

Silently the three humans and Rosehip returned to Jim's small dwelling and went to their beds. Jessica knew her life would never be the same. She couldn't go back to being just Jessica Kent from East London, wandering through her life without really knowing or caring where she was heading. She was now part of a great and complex tapestry of magic and heritage. She couldn't begin to comprehend what was expected of her. She didn't know how she would go about finding a witch or what she would do if she did find one. But she knew she would do everything she could to stop these awful people who had stolen her mother away so cruelly.

Chapter 11

Something in the Caves

Emotionally and physically exhausted, Jessica crawled beneath the sheets of her bed and fell asleep. She did not think it could be possible, after all that had happened that night, for her brain to switch off and let her rest but as soon as her head hit the pillow she fell into a deep, restful slumber. It was as if her body knew that she needed this time to come to terms with what she had discovered and file all the new and disturbing information away until she was good and rested to deal with it. In fact Jessica slept soundly until lunchtime the next day when she awoke, rather shocked, to find Rosehip sitting cross-legged on her chest. Jessica blinked hard, not fully remembering what had happened, and stared at the sprite trying to figure out what it was.

'Hi!' squeaked Rosehip, flexing her delicate silver wings and staring into Jessica bloodshot eyes. 'You've been asleep for ages. Jim's got all your mum's old stuff out downstairs. Come and see.'

Jessica groaned and shook her head. 'You're ... you're a faerie,' she muttered drowsily, rubbing her eyes.

Rosehip got to her feet and padded softly about in a small circle on the bedcover. 'Yep,' she chirped. 'Your own personal faerie guardian. Now, get up. There are things to be done.'

Jessica's head flopped back onto the pillow. It was hard to believe the events of the night before had actually been real and that she was the saviour of Jersey. But the faerie pacing about on her chest, not to mention the pile of wet clothes beside the bed, proved that she was now part of a different world altogether. She rolled over onto her side. On the bedside table, the three

161

volumes of her mother's journal lay just where she had left them. She picked one up but didn't open it.

'The Heir of Helier,' she murmured thoughtfully. 'I'm the last in a long line of witch hunters, the Guardian of Jersey.' Rosehip wasn't listening, she had become distracted by the mirror that hung above the dressing table and was flitting about in front of it looking at her reflection. Not that Jessica was bothered anyway. She was too busy trying to comprehend what was going to become of her life now she had, as Keela put it, a great fate resting on her shoulders. Jessica got out of bed. Rosehip stopped admiring herself in the mirror and flew back.

'Where are you going?' she asked, hovering just above Jessica's right shoulder.

What a pointless question! Jessica had begun to realize that faeries were not the most intellectual of creatures. 'I'm going to the bathroom to get changed. As you said, there are things to be done.'

Jessica picked out her sturdiest pair of jeans and one of her older t-shirts and went to the bathroom to wash and dress, shutting the door quickly behind her so that the faerie wasn't able to follow. She had decided it was best to dress for exploring because although she wasn't completely sure what she would be asked to do, as Guardian of Jersey, from what she knew of her mother's adventures, it would probably involve a lot of physical effort. She had decided that she really wanted to go down to Plemount as soon as possible because that was the place her mum had felt held the key to the Jersey witches. She really didn't know where else to start, unless Jim had a better idea.

Once she had dressed, Jessica and Rosehip went downstairs and into the kitchen where she made herself a large cheese sandwich (it was lunchtime after all) and a cup of tea. She could hear the voices of Jim and her father in animated conversation in the living room and carried her meal through to see just what Rosehip had meant when she'd said they had all her mum's old stuff out.

She found the two men sitting side by side on Jim's sofa surrounded by various items that had clearly been brought up from the cellar. The old wooden chest Elsa and Jessica had discovered lay open on the floor. The triangular lid was tilted back to show the remaining volumes of her mother's diaries but Jessica also noticed the flat inside of the lid had been removed, exposing a hidden cavity. This secret chamber was packed with rolls of paper like old treasure maps, some of which Jim had begun to spread out on the floor. Apart from the casket and its contents, Jessica noticed there was a pile of ancient leather books stacked on the arm of the sofa. Both the men were poring over the rolls of parchment so intently they didn't notice Jessica until she sat down beside them and coughed politely.

Jim looked up from the paper he was studying and smiled awkwardly. It was obvious that after the emotional exchanges of the night before the old man felt uncomfortable about speaking to Jess.

It was up to Jessica to break the silence. 'Morning,' she murmured softly. 'Rosehip told me you'd found some of Mum's old stuff. I guess this is it.'

She glanced at her father.

'Are you all right?' he asked gently. Rosehip, chirpy and eager to show off as usual, landed on the arm of the sofa and gazed up at Jessica.

'She's fine,' the sprite squeaked merrily. 'I wove a healing spell over her while she was asleep.'

'You didn't tell me that,' she said, unnerved that Rosehip had been using magic on her without her knowing.

Rosehip shrugged and sat down. 'You never asked.'

Jessica turned back to Martin. 'I'm all right, really,' she said reassuringly. 'I know why you did what you did. I'm not angry any more. You were just trying to help me.' She frowned slightly. 'But now, dad, I've decided I want to carry on where mum left off. I want Jim to teach me to be the Guardian. I know it might upset you, I know it could be dangerous, but it's something I have to do – for mum.' She gave his hand a gentle squeeze.

'I understand,' he murmured quietly. 'Just be careful. You don't know what you're dealing with. The life of the Heir of Helier is a very dangerous one.'

Jessica looked at the masses of paper laid out around them and then at her great uncle as he rummaged through yet more scrolls.

'Jim,' she said firmly, 'explain to me what I have to do. How do I hunt witches?'

The old man muttered as he stretched out the scroll he was

163

scrutinizing so Jessica too could see it. 'To be a good witch-hunter you have to understand witchcraft, know the signs. Take a look at this.'

Jessica regarded the manuscript. It appeared to be a map or, more accurately, a complex of interlinking pathways, twisting and turning in such intricate patterns it made Jessica's head hurt to look at it. Here and there, in between the lines of the maze, tiny, neat notes had been made in bright blue ink. Jessica squinted as she read one of them:

6.79 Slight scraping on east passage wall 3 ft from floor. No clear runes.

She looked at Jim, puzzled. 'I don't understand any of this. What is it? What do the notes mean?'

'It's a map your mother made of the secret caves and passageways of Plemount, a record of the signs of magic and witchcraft she found there.'

'Magicroutes!' she exclaimed. 'I read about them in Mum's old diaries. But I'm not sure what they are.'

Jim traced one of the pathways marked on the map with his stubby finger. 'Deep in the caves at Plemount and Corbiere there are tunnels leading all over the island. Some of them are formed by nature but others were created by witches and warlocks in the dark ages as thoroughfares to travel about Jersey without normal folk spotting them. They even took over some of the natural tunnels and caves and used them as Magicroutes. When witches wanted to hide and cast spells without people knowing they would disappear into the Magicroutes and perform their witchcraft there.'

'So Magicroutes are like secret meeting places for witches,' she said. 'If they performed spells there recently there would be signs that someone had been there. Eyes of newts, toes of bats, that kinda thing.'

Jim looked at her, impressed with how quickly she was working everything out. 'Not exactly eye of newt,' he responded. 'But part of witchcraft is writing spells and hexes in symbols known as runes. They are like an ancient code witches have used for centuries.'

He put the map down on the floor and picked up a slim,

164

black, leather book from the arm of the sofa. The volume was well-thumbed. The gold leaf that lined the edges of its dog-eared pages had flaked away in places and the corners had begun to curl. On the front, in clear gold script, were printed the words: *A Complex Guide to The Symbolic Meanings of Runes by D.Q. Westbrook.*

'This,' he told her, tapping the book lightly, 'is your guide to understanding the language of witches. Runes are a very obscure and abstract way of writing.'

Jessica took the book from him and gently flicked through the crinkly old pages. On each one was an odd minimalist drawing made up of lines and shapes with an explanation of what it represented underneath. It all appeared vague and mysterious. For instance, three wavy lines on top of each other were said to mean water, but they could also mean sea, river, underwater, wave or pool. Jessica wasn't sure that if she saw a set of runes carved in the rock of Plemount she would know what they meant.

'This is all very confusing,' she sighed, shutting the book. 'I don't know if I understand any of it. Do you use runes, Rosehip?'

The faerie huffed indignantly and stood up. 'Faeries don't need all this mumbo-jumbo,' she squeaked, arms crossed defensively on her chest.' We *are* magic. We don't make potions or write down stupid symbols. Our magic comes from nature itself. That's why witches want to squish us, so they can use our blood to cast their wicked spells!'

Jessica grimaced. It was horrible to think of somebody wanting to murder something as beautiful and magical as a faerie just to use its blood. 'That's not true, is it?' she asked Jim, horrified.

Jim nodded sadly. 'I'm afraid Rosehip is absolutely correct,' he said. 'Faerie blood is very potent and witches often use it to complete their spells. Some people even say that faerie blood is liquid magic. That any enchantment, no matter how extravagant, can work with faerie blood. That's another sign that witches have been using the Magicroutes recently. If you see a glistening, silver liquid on any of the rocks, that's faerie blood and it means witchcraft has been practised there lately.'

Jessica sighed with despair and slumped back on the sofa, gazing miserably at the papers and books that lay in front of her. 'You see,' she groaned, 'I don't know anything. How can I be the Guardian of Jersey? Mum had all her life to learn about witchcraft and magic. I've only just discovered faeries and merpeople exist.'

Jim placed a comforting hand on her knee and looked at her with his dark, glittering eyes. 'Have faith,' he said gently. 'I know all this is new to you and it's a lot to take in. But being the Guardian of Jersey is all about knowing what witchcraft involves. It isn't facts and figures. It's about something deep in your heart that guides you to do what is right. That's the true magic. And I know you have that in you.'

Jessica looked at her father who was smiling at her sadly. 'It's true,' he sighed. 'Even I know that. Even when your mum knew that coming back to Jersey could kill her she did it because the legacy of Helier drew her to do what was right for the island. I see her goodness in you in so many ways. I know you have the strength to carry on her work.'

Jessica smiled gratefully. 'Thanks,' she said. 'I am going to do my best even if I don't know as much as mum did.'

Jim grinned at her proudly. 'I know you will, both your father and I have every faith in you. But if you're going to explore Plemount you will need to be prepared. I'm afraid that these maps your mother drew up are completely out of date. Who knows what has changed in the caves in the last fifteen years? You'll have to start making records all over again. It's going to be difficult for you. I am too old to be scrambling about in caves and that. But I may have a few things that could help you.'

'Like me,' chirped Rosehip, sitting on Jessica's shoulder. 'After what happened last night, I'm not going to leave your side.'

She nodded confidently but Jim looked doubtful.

'I was thinking more of something like this.' He rummaged among the papers in the open casket until he came across what he was searching for. Carefully he sco-oped up the item in his huge hands and held it out for Jessica to see.

Lying in his palm was a long golden chain from which was suspended a round, clear lens, about two inches in diameter and half an inch thick, framed with a thin ring of gold. The glass was mottled and uneven, like that in a very old window, making everything viewed through it look distorted. It looked like a giant monocle.

166

Jessica eyed the glass cautiously. The last item of jewellery she had discovered in her mother's casket had been the pendant that had nearly killed her so she was understandably wary.

'What is it?' she asked, making no motion to touch the object.

Jim held the warped lens between his stubby fingers. 'Don't worry,' he said, knowing exactly why Jessica was unwilling to touch it. 'This isn't witchcraft – well, not the bad kind anyway. This is a magascope. Been in our family for two hundred years. This the best friend you could have going down in them caves.'

He passed it to Jessica who handled it as if the item was a burning coal. 'What does it do?' she queried, holding the chain and letting the glass swing from side to side.

Jim cleared a small space on the floor in front of them.

'Let me show you. Rosehip, just stand in front of Jessica if you will.'

'Certainly,' the faerie squeaked. She fluttered down from Jess's shoulder and landed gracefully in the spot on the floor that Jim had cleared for her. There she stood as poised and elegant as a ballerina.

'Now,' continued the old man to Jessica, 'take the magascope between your thumb and forefinger and look through it at your dad.'

Carefully Jessica held up the glass. Gazing through the twisted lens she saw the features of her father, slightly misshapen by the flaws in the glass.

'Tell me what you see?' said Jim.

'Nothing unusual,' she muttered, twisting the lens slightly. 'I can't see him very well but that's just because the glass isn't flat.'

'Exactly,' smiled Jim. 'Your father is just a human. He has no magic in him. So when you see him through the lens it's like looking through a slightly uneven window. Now, take a look at Rosehip through the magascope.'

Jessica turned her hand to hold the mystical glass before the faerie. As soon as she did so, the magascope lit up like a sunbeam shining through cut diamond. The glass glowed with a soft, silver light and here and there where the glass was dented, tiny rainbows formed, glistening like precious gems. Right in the centre of the sparkling lens, Jessica could see the outline of Rosehip, pure white and gleaming. 'Oh,' she gasped. 'How beautiful!'

Rosehip giggled, flattered. 'Thank you,' she squeaked. 'I know I am.'

Jim tapped the magascope gently. 'Now can you see, what it does?' he asked. 'A magascope shows what kind of magic is within a creature, any creature. Faeries like Rosehip here, are pure magic so the magascope will always glow silver or white when they're near. The magic of a merperson is directly in tune with the ocean so the magascope will show them as a deep green or blue. However,' he paused and placed the golden chain of the magascope over Jessica head, 'if the glass turns black or dark grey then it is a warning that you are near a witch or some other evil. When you're in the caves, if any thing like that happens, get out as soon as you can. I mean it Jessica – run for your life. You're not ready to face dark magic yet.'

Jessica looked at the glass, which was once again perfectly clear and nodded solemnly. 'I understand,' she said grimly. 'Is there anything else I should know before I start?'

The old man shook his head and shrugged. 'Nothing that I can tell you. Everything is so out of date in these maps. I'm afraid I can offer you no more help. But I mean what I say, Jess. If that lens turns dark, or if you get the feeling something isn't quite right, get away from the caves as soon as possible.'

Jessica nodded and collected up the books her great uncle had shown her, as well as the map of Plemount. She glanced at her father who still looked a little unnerved. 'Are you coming with me?' she asked.

'No,' he said quietly. 'It wouldn't be right. I want to but, not being an islander, I would be of no help to you. Just remember what Jim said – if you start to feel something may not be as it seems, get out. Jim'll be waiting for you near the surface.'

Jessica looked down at the books cradled in her arms. She felt dejected and alone knowing that her father could not accompany her on her great mission. It made the prospect of exploring the caves seem even more dangerous, even if Rosehip was with her. The faerie might be pure magic but from the short time she had known her Jessica wasn't convinced that she'd be much help if anything went wrong. Still it was no good thinking such negative thoughts. As she saw it, she didn't have much of a choice about whether she should continue her mother's research or not so she might as well try and stay positive.

She stood up and looked at her relatives. 'I'm going upstairs to pack the stuff I need,' she said confidently.

'Don't be too long,' Jim advised her. 'We've wasted a lot of daylight as it is. It's not a good idea to be down in the Magicroutes once dusk falls.'

Jess forced a smile and made her way out of the room, Rosehip tagging behind her. Jessica found her rucksack and began to pack the provisions she'd need for the day. She found it very difficult to know what to pack, as she wasn't exactly sure what she would be facing in the dark caverns of Plemount. The first things she made sure she had was the map Jim had given her and the collection of books that she hoped might give her some useful information on anything odd she might discover on her journey. After that she was pretty unsure what else to bring. She tried very hard to picture her mother preparing to investigate witchcraft all those years ago and think what she might have used, but that was both difficult and upsetting. In the end Jessica just tried to plan the expedition practically. She put in her bag a pen and pad in case she needed to make notes, as well as her mother's 1983 diary as it described the caves at Plemount a lot more clearly than the more complicated map Jim had given her. She also included a small torch that she attached to her key chain, as she didn't know just how dark the caves would be. Rosehip 'helped' by dropping in useless items like nail varnish and hair clips!

After a short time Jessica headed back downstairs and into the kitchen just to check if there was anything useful in there she could pack. There was a small, sharp fruit knife on the draining board beside the sink. Jess looked at it thoughtfully. She didn't like to think she would need a weapon to protect herself but not knowing what to expect it seemed slightly foolish to head into the haunts of witches and the like without some sort of defence. It couldn't hurt to be prepared so, wrapping a wad of kitchen paper around the blade to make it safer to carry, she slipped it in the front pocket of her bag.

Jessica was just about to do one final check of the kitchen for useful items when, to her surprise, she heard a brisk rapping on the front door. She frowned. With such an important venture it seemed unlikely that Jim would've invited visitors. She wondered who it was. In the hall she heard Jim answer the

169

door. Jessica hauled her rucksack onto her back and turned to Rosehip who was doing handstands on the tap.

'Wait here,' she told her.

The faerie finished her acrobatics and straddled the faucet, swinging her legs playfully. 'Why?' she asked.

It seemed you had to explain everything to Rosehip. 'Because it might not be an islander and then we'd all be in trouble,' she said, exasperated by the elf's silliness.

Rosehip shrugged and watched the drips from the tap plop into the sink below. 'Okay,' she said, not sounding at all bothered. 'Just don't dare leave without me!'

Jessica turned her back on Rosehip and headed into the hall to see who the visitor was. To her utter amazement she found her great uncle standing in the passageway with none other than Jake LeBlanc. The lanky farmer's son was wearing a pair of tattered, dusty jeans with holes in the knees, a cotton shirt with gaudy red and yellow checks and a pair of heavy, leather walking boots. Over his shoulder was slung a rucksack and he grinned merrily at Jessica as she entered.

Jessica eyed him, unsure what to say. She had enough on her mind and Jake, whom she found pleasant enough if a little strange, was the last person she expected to see.

'What are you doing here?' she asked cautiously, glancing at Jim for some clue.

The beak-nosed youth frowned at her. 'That's not a very nice way to greet someone who's come to lend you a hand,' he said.

Jessica warily looked from him to Jim and back again, fingering the strap of her bag. Neither Jake nor Jim spoke and there was a very long, very awkward silence as Jessica pondered just what the boy meant and how she should reply. Jake whistled quietly and contemplated the cracks in the ceiling.

Finally, unable to bear the silence, Jim explained. 'Jess, Jake knows about who you are.'

The boy gave her a lopsided grin. 'Sure do,' he laughed, making a comical bow. 'Hail, oh powerful Guardian.'

Jessica coloured with anger. She had realized that people in Jersey probably knew who she was, but it peeved her that Jake could make a joke out of it. It annoyed her too that he had almost certainly known about what had happened to her mother and about the faeries and merfolk long before she had.

170

'That's not funny, Jake,' she snapped, angrily brushing a stray hair behind her ear. 'My mother died because of who she was. You just don't know when to shut up!'

Jake held up his hands in mock defence. 'Whoa, easy tiger. Save some for the witches.' Then, seeing she was really annoyed, 'Okay, sorry; no more jokes. I'm here to help you.'

Jessica still had no idea what Jake was talking about. She glanced at Jim in the hope he would explain. 'Shouldn't we be off?' she asked, tugging at her bag crossly. 'I mean, what is he doing here?'

'I asked him to come with us,' Jim muttered quietly. 'I phoned him this morning.'

'Why? First you tell me this is a highly serious matter, and then you ask the local comic along. What good can he do?'

Jim turned to Jake. 'I think you better explain,' he said, backing out of the front door. 'I'll go and get the truck ready.' He quickly shut the door behind him.

Jess sighed and leaned against the wall. 'Okay,' she breathed heavily. 'You might as well tell me. Why are you here?'

Jake ran a hand through his unruly, dark, hair as he tried to think how to explain the situation. Absentmindedly, Jessica fingered the magascope that hung round her neck, bringing it up to peer at Jake through it. The boy noticed and laughed nervously.

'Oh, no,' he said. 'It's nothing like that. I'm not a warlock or anything.'

Jessica dropped the lens. 'Pity,' she said wryly. 'This doesn't detect idiots.'

Jake chewed the inside of his cheek for a second. 'Okay,' he began. 'You know about the Council of Elders?'

'No,' she said, trying hard to keep her patience.

'Well,' explained Jake, rubbing his hands together, 'each of the three races that live on and around Jersey appoints the wisest of their kind to represent them and they meet in times of trouble.'

Jessica rolled her eyes. She wanted to get down to Plemount, not listen to yet another story. 'Don't tell me,' she said sarcastically, 'you're the wisest man in Jersey, I don't think!'

'No,' said Jake, waving his hand, 'but my grandfather, Arthur Le Blanc, is. There was a big meeting last week, at which they discussed telling you the truth about your birthright. Things ain't going to be easy for you being Guardian and all. It was decided you'll need some help. The faeries appointed Rosehip, then Keela was elected to keep an eye out for you, and...' he smiled, his chest puffing slightly with pride, 'you've got me as your bodyguard.'

Jessica groaned. 'Well, that's just lovely. I'm setting off on a great quest to save Jersey and who's watching my back? You, the court jester. Excuse me if I'm not impressed, Jake.'

'Hey,' he barked, shrugging his backpack on roughly. 'Just what is your problem? What's wrong with me? You can't take these things lightly – witch-hunting is a dangerous business. You're going to need all the support you can get. Since the first time we met you've looked at me like a country bumpkin and all I've been trying to do is give you a little advice.'

Jessica snorted, unimpressed. She wasn't in the least convinced that having Jake along on the trip would aid matters in any way.

'Number one, you *are* a country bumpkin, Jake; and number two, what advice? All you've done is make stupid jokes and talked in riddles. I'm better off alone.'

She tried to push pass him to go outside but Jake called after her.

'Who told you to ask about St Helier?'

Jessica stopped dead. It had been Jake who had prompted her to ask Jim about the hermit whose legacy she now carried. She thought back over her past two meetings with him. At the time most of what he said had sounded like nonsense but now, after everything had changed so drastically, maybe she did understand.

'Family's what binds us,' she murmured quietly.' That's what you said. And you were right.'

Jake approached her but Jessica didn't turn around. 'I was trying to explain,' he said, his voice returning to its soft, Jersey tone. 'No-one could tell you what happened to your mum but Jim, and I kinda guessed you would have to prise it out of him. Call it planting the seeds of doubt in your mind. I am a farmer's son, after all.' He put a friendly hand on her shoulder. Jessica turned to face him. A country bumpkin, Jake may be, she thought, but stupid he definitely wasn't. He knew more about Jersey than she did and apart from anything else she didn't much fancy heading down to Plemount alone.

'What did the Elders have in mind?' she asked. 'Do you have any powers?'

Jake shrugged. 'Nope,' he said bluntly. 'I told you, I'm not a warlock. But I've lived in Jersey all my life. I know it, know about the magic creatures. Plus, I'm quite strong – I can protect you if there is a fight.'

Jessica snorted. 'Well, let's make some ground rules, for a start. I'm not your damsel in distress type, so don't think you have to come on all macho because I'm a girl. If I need protecting I'll let you know. And no corny jokes either; you're not as funny as you think.'

Jake smirked. 'Fine. I'll do that and you can stop treating me like I've got hay between my ears.'

Jessica offered him her hand. 'Deal,' she said as he shook it firmly. There was no turning back now. Like it or lump it, Jake was on the team. She turned back down the corridor and headed towards the kitchen. 'I just need to get something.'

She opened the door and called Rosehip's name. The tiny sprite zoomed out and perched on Jessica's shoulder.

'Are we off, then?' the faerie chirped. 'I've been waiting ages.'

Jessica nodded and checked her backpack was securely on her shoulders. Rosehip gazed at Jake suspiciously.

'What's he doing here?' she asked, pointing at the youth.

'Don't even ask,' Jessica said wearily.

The unlikely trio headed out into the early afternoon sunlight. The fierce rain of the night before seemed to have gone and although the sky was blanketed in heavy, grey clouds, a sallow sun shimmered high above. The truck was ready and waiting outside the garage.

'About time,' Jim muttered. 'I told you, you've got to be outta the caves by nightfall.'

Jessica glanced over her shoulder at Jake, who was scraping the gravel about with the toe of his boot. She wondered how on earth this gangly individual was meant to protect her from anything.

Jim started the engine and soon they were making their way down Rue de Landes in his ancient lorry. Rosehip was rummaging through the junk on the dashboard, Jake was whistling tunelessly to himself and Jessica was pondering the situation that lay ahead of her. She thought of all the fairy stories and fantasy books she'd read as a child. The heroes always seemed to be accompanied by wise and skilled companions to aid them on their quest – knowledgeable wizards who cast complex spells, brave warriors who helped them defeat their foes. What had she been given when faced with immeasurable evil? A small, immature faerie who was at present losing a fight with an empty crisp packet and a farm hand whose only threatening skill was a seemingly endless supply of awful jokes. It was hardly *Lord of the Rings*. But then who was she to talk? She had been nearly killed last night and now she was willingly heading into the Magicroutes of Plemount when she hadn't the skills to defeat even a small witch. At least Jake and Rosehip seemed to have faith in her and under the circumstances. That in itself was brave indeed.

Kindly, Jessica reached forwards and removed the crisp packet from Rosehip. The small sprite fastidiously brushed the salt and grease from her tiny body.

'Do you three have a plan?' Jim asked. Jessica shook her head.

'Not really. I'm hoping to find the main chamber today but I don't expect to get any further. I'm not that experienced. I'm quite glad Jake and Rosehip are with me.'

Jake looked at her and raised his eyebrows. 'That's not what you said earlier. More or less told me to boil my head when I first offered to help you.'

Rosehip was sitting on the dashboard, licking a toffee wrapper. 'They were fighting, Jim,' she sighed. 'I heard them. Jess was dead cross at him. I was listening at the door.'

Jessica glared at the faerie. 'I wish you wouldn't do that,' she said. 'Eavesdropping is very rude.'

Rosehip shrugged and wrapped the foil around her shoulders like a cape. 'Don't care,' she chirped rudely.

Jess ignored her. 'I didn't much fancy going down into the caves on my own,' she admitted.

'Good,' said Jake with a defiant nod. 'Coz I wasn't going to let you anyway!'

'And neither was I,' added Rosehip, fluttering up to land on Jess's shoulder.

The truck rounded a bend in the road and Jim put on the brakes suddenly. 'What's going on here?' he muttered.

All three passengers stared through the windscreen. A small girl was half running, half stumbling up the road towards them.

She seemed exhausted, her painfully thin legs almost buckling beneath her and her fly-away blonde hair stuck to her head with sweat. She was wearing a cotton, floral shift dress that looked at least a size too big for her and waving her frail arms to get them to stop. Her ghostly features were etched with fear as she called out, 'Stop! Wait!'

'It's Elsa!' Jessica cried.

Jake threw open the door as Mrs Noir's feeble grand-daughter drew level with the vehicle. She stooped double, gasping for breath, her chest wheezing audibly.

Jake looked at the exhausted child in amazement. 'What on earth are you doing here?' he asked incredulously. 'You look as if you've run all the way from Gorey!'

Elsa shook her head, still gulping for air. 'Caught the bus to St Martin's,' she panted. 'Ran here from the bus stop.' She stood up, her pale skin flushed a ruddy pink.

Jim eyed the girl with concern. 'Why? Has something happened to your grandmother?'

Elsa leaned wearily against the side of the truck. 'Grandmère's fine,' she gasped. 'But I heard, I heard everything. Everything that happened last night. The pendant. Are you okay, Jessica? I thought ... oh God help me what I thought – terrible, terrible things.'

She closed her light blue eyes and seemed on the brink of tears.

Rosehip gazed at her from Jessica's shoulder.

'She's crazy,' the faerie said in her tactless manner. 'That's what I think – she's crazy.'

Jessica hushed the elf and turned to comfort Elsa.

'I'm fine,' she soothed. 'The pendant did have a curse on it but the merfolk saved me. I wasn't hurt. But how do you know what happened?'

'Everyone will know by now,' interrupted Jim, quietly. 'All the true islanders; so will the faeries and merfolk. You're the Guardian. Anything happens to you and the news gets around the island pretty quick.'

Elsa nodded. 'Grandmère and I heard first thing this morning. I feel so guilty. If only I hadn't shown you the pendant.' She had begun to wring her small white hands together, the way she always did when she was anxious. Jessica leaned across and touched her shoulder.

175

'Please don't blame yourself,' she said reassuringly. 'My mother was probably studying it.'

Elsa became calmer. She stopped wringing her hands and looked at Jessica. 'So, you know?' she said quietly.

Jessica nodded and laid her hand on Elsa's. 'I know,' she answered solemnly. 'Uncle Jim explained after I was rescued. I can't say I was prepared to be the saviour of Jersey but I'm going to do the best I can. I'm heading down to Plemount right now to explore the old Magicroutes. Jake and Rosehip are coming along to help.'

An expression of utter horror appeared in Elsa's sallow face. 'You can't do that!' she exclaimed in panic. 'It's too dangerous. I mean, anything could happen!' She grabbed hold of the handle above the truck door and started to pull herself aboard. 'I'm coming too, to make sure everything is okay.'

Jessica and Jake looked at the small girl in horror. Elsa was fragile and timid, not to mention suffering from who knew what debilitating ailments. The Magicroutes were filled with unknown horrors.

Jake put his hands on Elsa's bony shoulders as she tried to climb in the cab. 'Easy,' he soothed. 'I don't think this is such a good idea, do you Jess?'

Jessica shook her head. 'Too right,' she agreed. 'Elsa, you don't know what you're getting into. We don't know what's down in those caves. From what Jim said it could be very nasty.'

Elsa struggled to get past Jake. 'I don't care,' she said firmly. Her tone was unusually bold and she seemed remarkably determined.

'Elsa,' Jim said, 'I really do think it's best if you go back home. I mean, what would your grandmother say?'

Elsa dropped back from the cab but kept one foot resting on the step. 'She said the Guardian's more important than anything,' she replied. 'She said we should all keep an eye on Jessica. Besides, Jessica's my friend – I won't let anything happen to her.'

'May I talk to Jim and Jake alone for a moment,' she asked Elsa gently.

The girl stepped back. 'Okay, but I'm going to hold on to the side of the truck so you can't just drive off and leave me here.'

Jessica chuckled to herself. That sounded rather like the silly kind of thing Rosehip would say. She watched Elsa walk to the back of the lorry and lean against it, arms dangling over the side, Jake shut the door and looked at Jessica quizzically.

'You're not seriously thinking of letting her come along, are you?' he asked, raising his eyebrows.

Jessica slumped back into the seat and stared blankly out the window in front of her. 'I don't know,' she said softly. 'She seems so determined.'

Jim leant across and looked at his great-niece. 'A lot of people are worried about the safety of the Guardian; that doesn't necessarily mean that they should come along with you.'

Jessica chewed her lip thoughtfully. 'I know,' she breathed. 'But I have this feeling about Elsa. I don't know.' She paused for a second. 'Do you believe in fate?'

Jim's eyes twinkled thoughtfully as he gazed at her. 'Yes, I do,' he replied. 'If you've got a gut instinct about Elsa, I suggest you go with it.'

Jessica glanced at Jake. 'What do you think?' she asked.

'That you're probably mad if you think having Elsa come along will help any of us – Elsa included,' he said dryly. 'You said to me yourself you wanted to protect her, sending her down to Plemount is not protecting her in the slightest.'

Jessica looked out of the back window at Elsa reclining against the lorry. Something told her that if Elsa didn't come with them it would be a terrible mistake.

'Elsa's part of this,' she said quietly. 'I know it, don't ask me how but I just know.'

'I'm not sure,' Jake said doubtfully. 'As I told you, I think Elsa's more than a bit odd and God knows how much living with that barmy old grandmother of hers has affected her. Going down the caves could be the thing that cracks her.'

'Maybe,' she said. 'But you also said I needed all the help I can get.'

Perhaps it was the fact that Elsa too had lost her parents, but Jessica felt that if she was the Guardian of Jersey her strong empathy with Elsa wasn't just a coincidence.

'I've decided,' she said quietly.

She leant across Jake and opened the door. Seeing this as an encouraging sign, Elsa walked back towards them.

'Well?' she asked, in her soft, timid voice.

'I've made up my mind. You can come.'

Eagerly, Elsa squeezed into the cab beside Jake. Jessica fixed her with a sombre stare.

'I don't want you getting hurt,' she told her. 'So if I feel that things are getting dangerous, I'm going to send you back to the surface with Rosehip.'

Elsa nodded but the faerie slumped back sulkily against Jessica's shoulder.

'I don't want to be a babysitter,' she pouted. 'I'll miss all the good stuff!'

Jessica fixed Rosehip with a stern glare. She was getting quite used to being head of the team. 'I don't care,' she told her. 'Elsa's too young, I don't want her getting hurt.'

The cab remained silent as they drove the short distance to Plemount. Each of the three young people pondered silently on what fate might have in store for them in the dark grottos of the mysterious bay. Soon they arrived at the pleasant little beach that was the unlikely entrance to the world of witchcraft. Jessica looked at the golden sands encircled by pinkish granite cliffs and caves and couldn't help feeling slightly disappointed. She had expected something more threatening than this – a wild cove with rocky outcrops jutting from the sea and black waves beating the shore perhaps. Plemount looked no more sinister than any other beach she had seen in her short time on the island. She glanced at Jim doubtfully.

'Are you sure this is the right place?' she asked.

'The beach is as safe as houses,' he said. 'That's the beauty of the place. It was chosen to look as innocent as possible so if someone saw a witch heading down here no-one would think anything of it. That's a popular trick of witches, using the innocuous to mask evil.'

Elsa suddenly shuddered and Jessica gave her a worried look.

'Everything okay?' she asked.

The pale, young girl smiled timidly. 'I just felt a little nervous,' she said.

'Elsa's right to be wary,' Jim told them. 'The beach is perfectly safe but once you get down in the Magicroutes, you're at the mercy of whatever's down there. Be very careful.'

He unlocked the truck door and looked back towards them. 'I suggest you let Rosehip get in your rucksack, Jessica. We don't want anyone spying her.'

The sprite pouted angrily. 'Why should I?' she squeaked.

Jessica picked up her bag and opened it. 'So none of the non-islanders will see you,' she explained.

Rosehip crossed her arms and grumbled to herself but she fluttered inside the knapsack. Jessica pulled the drawstring shut and she, Jake, Jim and Elsa got out of the lorry and walked down the cliff path to the waiting sand. The day was bright but there was a decidedly cold breeze so there were only a handful of people on the beach, mainly families with very young toddlers who had whined to be brought down to play on the sand. A couple of teenage boys were there too, splashing in the water a little way from the shore, struggling with surfboards to catch the incoming waves. The four adventurers hung back from the sand, walking parallel with the rocky inlets and caves that shaped the shoreline. Jim led the way, striding surely across the uneven ground, now and again stopping to peer into one of the caves. Jess followed close behind, nervously glancing for signs of anything out of the ordinary. Jake strolled along behind her whistling merrily, his rucksack slung over one shoulder. A few feet behind them, Elsa dawdled nervously seeming very unwilling to be on the adventure despite her earlier insistence that she be included.

There were many inlets and Jessica wondered whether after so many years Jim would remember which one housed the hidden entrance to the Magicroutes. Finally they came to a large cave set well back from the sea in a small cove of its own. The entrance was angular in shape, one wall almost perfectly straight and flat while the other sloped steeply inwards with rocky protuberances that looked like sharp noses carved into the ruddy pink granite. The sandy ground was covered with uneven boulders and the cave gradually became narrower as it bore into the solid cliff.

The four travellers peered curiously inside. Despite the bright sunlight they could not see where the cavern ended for dark shadows hid its true depth. Jessica squinted into the gloom doubtfully.

'So this is it?' she asked Jim. 'I thought it would be more disguised than this.'

The old man leant against the rock face, the salty wind teasing his thin white hair. 'The tunnel leading to the great chamber is

179

hidden deep inside, near the back. Not many mortals can find it.'

Jessica looked at him hesitantly. 'Then, will I be able to find it?' she asked.

Jake placed a hand on her shoulder as they gazed into the dank cave. 'If anyone is able to it'll be you,' he said. 'You're the Heir of Helier, remember? You have the skill to detect magic.'

Jessica half smiled at his faith in her and edged a few inches into the cave entrance. Nervously, Elsa crept forward and watched as the older girl stepped with trepidation into the cavern.

'Be careful,' she piped timidly, chewing the cuff of her blouse.

Cautiously, Jessica made her way forward into the grotto. The many uneven rocks that scattered the floor of the cave made walking difficult and she had to pick her way among them carefully to avoid stumbling. She cast her eye over the dappled patterns of the reddish pink stone in search of some of the symbols from the book of runes carved into the rock but could see none. The cave narrowed the further she went into it and after she had travelled forty or fifty feet from where her friends were standing she realized that she had reached the back of the cave and that solid rock prevented her from going any further. She ran her fingertips across the damp, uneven stone in the hope they might encounter some sort of hidden button or catch that would unlock the entrance but she felt nothing. Back on the beach Jim, Jake and Elsa strained their eyes to see what she was doing.

'Well?' Jim asked in a hushed whisper that echoed down into the cave. 'Have you found it?'

Jessica rubbed her palms against the solid granite. 'There's nothing here,' she replied. 'There isn't a door or a tunnel or anything. It's a dead end.'

Jake edged into the cave and beckoned Elsa to follow him. Jim looked frustrated. 'I know this is the place,' he muttered. He stood silent for a few seconds; then he remembered. 'Jessica,' he called, 'look at the wall. See the entrance?'

The girl frowned. 'I've told you,' she called back. 'The rock is solid. There's no way through.' She pushed at the wall with her whole body weight to make sure.

Jim leaned deeper into the mouth of the cave. He could still just make out the figures of Jake and Elsa as they ventured into the gloom but Jessica was too far in for him to see. 'Forget what you know,' he ordered firmly. 'The toughness of the rock is an illusion. You have the power to break it. Stand back from the wall and look for a way in. Trust what your eyes are trying to see.'

Jessica didn't understand how this would help her. She had touched the stone with her hands; it was solid. There was no way a door or tunnel could open in it. However, she took a pace back from the wall and looked directly at it.

'Relax your eyes,' came Jim's voice again. Jessica blinked hard and studied the freckled blotches of the stone. In the dim light of the cave she could see the cracks and crevices snaking across the dappled surface. Suddenly, to her complete disbelief, she saw these very same clefts and splits expand and grow as if the cliff was breaking open like an enormous eggshell. They grew and joined together until there was one huge split in the rock face just under a foot wide and five feet high. Shrugging off her rucksack, she unzipped it and searched for her torch. Straightaway, Rosehip zoomed out of her hiding place, nearly scaring Jessica to death.

'So, what have I missed?' the faerie asked brightly, her soft golden glow illuminating the dark stone. She turned and stared in wonderment at the magical gateway in the granite. 'Say!' she gasped, fluttering forward to examine it. 'You've found an entrance to the Magicroutes. That's pretty cool for a beginner.'

'I know,' said Jessica, still rummaging in her bag. She found her flashlight and shone its beam inside the narrow crevice. It appeared to be the opening to a long, dark tunnel leading deep into the rock. She could just make out the jagged stones that hung from its roof like vicious daggers waiting to drop. A faint odour of dampness and rot seeped from the hollow and the prospect of going inside didn't exactly fill Jess's heart with joy. She heard footsteps behind her and spun around to see that Jake and Elsa had joined her in the darkness. Their faces looked eerily white in the light of the torch.

Jake's eyes fell on the ominous crack in the stone. 'Wow!' he said softly. 'You did it, Jess. You've opened the doorway to the Magicroutes. You really are the Guardian.'

Jessica shrugged. 'Jim told me to look at the wall and when I did all the cracks in the stone began to open up. I don't know how.'

'You did it,' Elsa whispered. 'Everyone knows the Guardian has the power to undo witchcraft.'

Jess was quiet for a moment. It made her feel odd to think that she had mystical powers. Even after she had learnt about her destiny, Jessica didn't feel that she was any different from an ordinary human being. Now, for the first time, she herself had caused something magical to occur.

'Is everything all right?' Jim's voice echoing from outside, broke her reverie.

'Yes,' she called back. 'We've found the way in.'

There was a slight pause and Jess could tell her great uncle was unwilling to let her enter the mystical portal. 'You need to go inside,' he told them at last, trying to sound calm. 'Once inside the witchcraft will be too strong for us to talk. You will be able to get back out the way you came in as long as it is daylight, so don't be too long. Be *very* careful.'

Jessica gazed at the narrow opening and swallowed hard. 'Okay,' she replied, trying to hide her fear. She glanced round at the faces of her three companions. 'We'd better get going,' she told them. 'Rosehip, I want you to fly in there ahead of us and scout it out.'

The sprite raised her fine arched eyebrows in surprise. 'Me?' she squeaked in horror. 'Why'd you pick on me? There could be witches or anything down there.'

Jessica looked at her grimly. 'I know,' she said. 'I know how dangerous it is. But you're the smallest and the quickest. If there is any danger you'd be able to get back in a hurry and warn us.'

Rosehip looked doubtful and fluttered just inside the tunnel. 'Don't fancy it much,' she muttered. 'Do I have to?'

Jessica sighed and shook her head. 'No,' she uttered sadly, 'you don't, Rosehip. I'm the Guardian, it's up to me. If any of you want to go back now I'm not going to stop you.' Jessica didn't like the thought of being alone in the caves but the idea of putting innocent lives in jeopardy was a lot worse. She felt responsible for her friends, especially for Elsa who was the least able of them all.

Jake looked at her crossly. 'No way,' he announced. 'We're in this together, no matter what. I promised the Elders I would look out for you, Jess, and I'm not going back on that. Rosehip,

182

you should be ashamed of yourself. You were appointed Jessica's faerie lookout and fat lot of good you've been so far. She nearly died last night because you were a coward.'

Rosehip looked defiant and flew close to Jake's face. 'I am not a coward,' she chirped angrily. 'I'll go down there, just you watch.' With that she gracefully back-flipped away and zoomed into the dank passage. Soon she was completely out of sight. Jessica smiled appreciatively at Jake.

'That meant a lot to me, Jake,' she told him.

The lad shrugged and grinned. 'I told you, you're stuck with me and Rosehip, whether you like it or not.'

'And me,' added Elsa. 'I'm not going back now.'

She took the older girl's hand and squeezed it reassuringly. Jake placed his palm over their hands.

'Partners,' he told them, 'from here on in. Whatever happens, you've got us, Jess.'

Jessica managed a smile. 'Okay,' she told them. 'I suppose we'd better head off. I'll go in first. Jake, you follow me. Elsa will bring up the rear so if there's anything nasty ahead she can get out first.'

Taking a deep breath, Jessica cautiously edged her way inside the dark tunnel. It was an incredibly tight fit, just as her mother's diary had said, and she had to shuffle down it sideways to get through. The walls seemed to press in on her and the air was cold and damp. She placed her hands on the wall just inches away from her face and used it to ease her body through the cramped passageway. Jim had indeed been correct; she could hear no sound from the beach, only the careful footsteps of Jake and Elsa as they crept along with her. She turned her head in the direction she was travelling and strained her eyes but the blackness that surrounded her was so complete she was all but blind. Her key-chain torch did little good as it only showed the distance a few inches ahead of her. Suddenly, something soft, dry and clinging caught her face, sticking to it like a ghoulish hand. Jessica screamed and clawed at the horrid thing but it disintegrated beneath her fingertips into a fine, tacky mess.

Jake, hearing her, cried out, 'Are you okay?'

Jessica wiped the tangled strands on her jeans. 'A cobweb,' she called back, her breath caught in her chest. 'Just a cobweb.'

She was shaken though. The passage was a dark and eerie

place and her encounter with the cobweb had filled her imagination with horrific thoughts of what might be in the darkness ahead. She heard Jake chuckle and felt a flare of annoyance.

'Shut up,' she muttered back to him, as Jake's giggle echoed through the damp air. 'It could've been a ghost, or God knows what!' She could almost picture Jake's mocking grin.

'Yeah, but it wasn't,' the young lad chortled. 'It was an incy-whincy spider.'

Jessica inched herself forward through the narrow tunnel. That was going to be one incident Jake wouldn't let her live down. 'Is everything all right back there?' she asked him.

She could still hear the footsteps of Jake and Elsa and knew they weren't far behind. The boy's voice rang out to her in the cavern.

'We're fine,' he said. 'The entrance closed behind us once we were through it though. I hope you can open it again when we get back. If we get back that is.'

A stab of fear went through Jessica. She knew that now the entrance to the passageway was closed, their safety depended upon keeping their wits about them within the caves and her ability to recover their safe passage to the surface.

'Don't say things like that,' she muttered. 'You'll scare Elsa. How are you doing back there, Elsa?'

There was a moment of silence before Jessica heard the girl reply and the only sound was the gentle shuffling of the travellers' feet. Then Elsa spoke. 'I'm okay, Jessica,' she called out, sounding as if she was trying to convince herself that she wasn't scared.

Jessica smiled at the child's courage and determination. 'We are going to be all right,' she told her companions as she eased herself between the rocks another few inches. 'It can't be much further.'

'Have you seen any sign of Rosehip yet?' called Jake.

'No,' she sighed. 'We'll just have to keep going.'

She prayed that nothing had happened to the faerie.

They carried on along the passageway for what seemed like hours in the pitch-blackness. The walls pressed in on them as they squeezed along the trail. The atmosphere was musty, the cavern air cold and clammy on their skin. It bore the faint odour of rotten meat. The only sounds were their footsteps on the

184

uneven ground and Jake whistling 'Incy-whincy spider' to himself. He had the sickest sense of humour.

Suddenly Jessica became aware of another sound; it was very faint and she had to strain her ears to hear it. Rosehip was calling them. Jess shushed Jake and edged forwards. The faerie's high, musical voice was alive with excitement. 'I've found it!' she piped. 'Jessica, it's right down here. The main chamber. Just wait till you see it.'

Spurred on by Rosehip's excitement, she pushed her way through the passage. After a few more feet, she found that the tunnel widened and sloped upwards towards a small arch. Through the gateway she could see the pale golden glow of Rosehip's faerie light. She stretched her stiff limbs, grateful for the new space within the tunnel and gazed at the opening.

'I think we've found it!' she called to her friends. Her legs trembled, partly with fear, partly with anticipation as she scrambled up the stony hill toward the entrance to the main chamber. Once at the top, Jessica found herself standing beside Rosehip on a long flight of crude stone stairs overlooking the great chamber.

The cavern was vast and Jessica felt quite intimidated. The roof was at least a hundred feet high and hung with countless stalactites of various lengths like the swords of ancient stone warriors. The chamber itself was a huge well, the damp stone walls curving down to the floor. The great rock staircase on which they were standing spiralled up and around the walls and hundreds of dark caves like the one they had just emerged from, led off in all directions. Tiny waterfalls trickled down the rock, their splashing echoing through the vast space of the grotto; everywhere clumps of faintly luminescent fungi clung to the damp granite. The air was icy and wet; Jessica could already feel her clothing becoming moist on her body. The whole place reeked of decay and death. Even with Rosehip's faerie glow and Jessica's torch, it was hard to see everything in the huge cavern. Jess gazed at the pit below them. She could just make out the outline of a large object down there, still and eerie in the blackness, but she was unable to determine what it was. She took a step closer to the edge of the staircase and peered down, flashing her torch beam into the darkness. The light, however, was too faint to reveal any more detail. A sudden

185

sound behind her made her jump back from the ledge in fear, her heart thumping in her chest. She spun around and shone her torch in the direction of the sound. Framed in the dark archway stood the figures of Jake and Elsa.

Jessica gave a sigh of relief. 'Don't ever do that again!' she hissed. 'You scared the living daylights out of me!'

Jake sniffed but Elsa hid timidly behind him.

'Is there anything you're not scared of?' he asked and Jessica glared at him crossly. 'I mean some Guardian you are if...'

He stopped suddenly and gazed at his surroundings for the first time in amazement. 'Blooming heck!' he murmured. 'Where are we?'

His voice echoed off the gigantic walls.

Jessica shrugged off her rucksack and began to rummage through it once more.

'The main chamber,' she told them, pulling out the books Jim had given to her earlier. 'I read something about it in my mum's diary.'

She opened *A History of Magical Beings in Jersey* and flicked through the index.

'Main chamber, main chamber,' she muttered to herself, as she studied the ancient pages in the light of her torch. 'Ah, this sounds promising. The *Great* Chamber, page 128.'

Jake and Elsa gazed up at the threatening stalactites as Jessica found the correct page and began to read aloud. 'The Great Chamber or Main Chamber or Grotto de la Grande is, and has always been, an intrinsic part of the dark magic of Jersey. Believed to have been created by the notorious warlock, Triconious Stoneeagle, in the seventh century, it has long been known as the meeting place and refuge of witches and warlocks through-out the island. Many stories and legends are attached to the infamous cave and it is now very difficult to determine where truth ends and folklore begins. The truth about the Chamber is made even more difficult to grasp by the fact that only users of black magic and the Guardian of Jersey are able to gain access. This much is definitely known: the Chamber has been used on various occasions for the past thousand years as a gathering place for witches and an area for practising witchcraft. It houses a pagan altar for the sacrifice of animals, humans and faeriefolk.'

186

Jessica looked up from the book and shuddered. Rosehip, who had been seated quite happily on the staircase, suddenly turned very pale and flew up into the air.

'That's it!' she chirped nervously. 'Faerie sacrifice. I'm out of here!'

She zipped off in the direction of the tunnel but Jake's arm shot out and grabbed her tightly before she could get away.

'Faerie *and* human sacrifice,' he told the elf, as she struggled to escape his grip. 'We're all at risk. Don't be such a coward. The four of us are in this together now. Besides you can't get out without Jessica, so there's no point even trying.'

He opened his hand and reluctantly Rosehip flew out.

'We're dead,' she piped glumly. 'I hope you realize that. We are all dead.'

Jessica was leaning against the wall of the cave looking puzzled. 'This doesn't make sense,' she pondered out loud. 'If the Guardian could gain access to this chamber ever since it was built, why hasn't it been destroyed to stop the witchcraft?'

Jake wandered over to her and glanced at the book.

'Look, it says why right here.' He pointed. 'In 1659, the Guardian of Jersey, a Samuel Hellily, proposed a scheme to demolish the Chamber once and for all by setting off charges of dynamite in the rock face which would cause the cavern to collapse. However, as he began researching the scheme, he discovered that the destruction of the cave would result in the geological collapse of Jersey itself. It would seem that Triconious created the chamber using such deep and penetrating magic that the very existence of it and the network of tunnels leading from it prevented Jersey crumbling into the sea.'

Jessica shut the book and sighed. 'You've got to give it to those witches,' she said. 'They're pretty damn crafty.'

She looked at Elsa who had barely uttered a word since they entered the chamber. The girl was hugging herself gently and looked very pale and nervous.

'Don't like it here,' she whispered very quietly, scraping her toe on the step.

Jake threw Jessica a look that said, 'I told you you shouldn't have brought her along.'

But Jessica ignored it. She walked across to the girl and softly touched her arm.

'None of us does,' she reassured her. 'But if we are going to stop the witchcraft, we have to find out its source.'

She gave the child a half-hearted smile, which Elsa shyly returned. Jessica wandered over to the edge of the step and peered down into the darkness. She could still see the faint outline of something large and motionless in the black shadows.

'There's definitely something down there,' she murmured, shining her tiny flashlight into the gloom. 'But I can't see what.'

Jake unzipped his bag and rooted inside. 'Well what do you expect with a wimpy little girl's torch like that?' he laughed. He reached inside his rucksack and pulled out a large, yellow flashlight. 'Thank God, I came prepared.'

Jessica glared at him crossly. 'You could've told us you had that with you earlier.'

Jake smirked and raised an eyebrow. He turned his torch on. The bright beam shone out from the large bulb and straightaway the cave seemed less gloomy. Jake gave Jessica a smug grin and she sighed exasperated at his cocky attitude. Jake shone the torch down over the side of the staircase and the four companions peered over to see what had been hidden in the shadows of the cave.

The beam shone down, showing that they were about twenty or so feet above the floor of the cave. Below them, illuminated in the light of Jake's torch was a large disc of pale grey stone, perfectly round and about ten feet in diameter. On the surface, engraved deeply into the stone was the symbol of a five-pointed star that stretched across the top of the circle. Around the table, seemingly growing out of the very floor of the chamber, were a dozen smaller mounds of rock, each with a flat smooth top. Jessica gazed in eerie wonderment at the sight. She had never in her life seen anything like it. The circle seemed to emit a mystical power. 'What is it?' she asked softly.

'It looks like a table and chairs,' Jake said, his voice sounding puzzled. 'Check the book.'

Jessica leafed through the pages but as she did so Elsa spoke very softly, her eyes never leaving the stone disc. 'It's a sacrificial altar for a coven,' she said blankly.

Jessica and Jake gazed at her in amazement. 'Elsa, how could you possibly know that?' asked Jessica.

'The meetings of the Elders,' she said quickly. 'I heard my

grandmère say the witches, if they came back, would try and find this place to perform their spells.'

'Oh yeah,' Jake said. 'I remember, grandpa told me. See, there's thirteen stools. A coven has twelve witches and a lead warlock or senior enchantress.'

Jessica gazed down at the sacred stone. 'We should go down and investigate, see if anyone has been casting spells,' she said, trying not to sound afraid.

The other three nodded and together they made their way very slowly, very carefully down the broad, stone steps that spiralled around the chamber. No-one spoke and their footsteps echoed off the solid rock walls and were amplified in the huge space of the cave. The beam from Jake's torch shone out in front of them like a pale, golden pathway, exposing the cracks and formations of the dark granite to their eyes. It seemed to take forever to reach the foot of the stairs but when they finally stepped into the great chamber itself the party stopped still and all four of them stared in fearful respect at the altar.

After a few seconds of complete silence Rosehip spoke. 'To think,' she whispered, 'All those faeries and humans who have been murdered on that table.' She gave a little shudder.

A cold sensation ran through Jessica's body as if someone had walked over her grave. 'It doesn't bear thinking about,' she told them, taking a half step towards the altar. 'We'd better take a look at the table.'

Jessica slowly began to approach the stone circle. She tried very hard not to think about all the wicked crimes that had been committed in this evil place. Elsa and Jake followed with caution, the farmer's son shining the torch in the direction of the stone table. The broad, bright beam illuminated the surface, showing every scratch on the whitish granite.

Slowly Jessica came level with the huge tablet and stared down at its smooth, even surface. In the light of Jake's torch she could see that the tabletop appeared to be derelict, unused for many years. The growth of fungi showed that for some time no-one had put this place to noticeable use. The pentagram that adorned the surface of the altar was still clearly visible, deeply engraved in the stone with clear, sharp grooves about an inch deep. There were other carvings too, scratched crudely on the rock as if made with the tip of a dagger. Some were runes;

others indicated vicious stabbing motions as if someone had tried to gouge something on the altar but missed. All of these marks were clearly decades old and held no clues to the present. In the centre of the disc, marring the delicately piebald stone, was a large ancient stain, red-brown in colour like claret wine that had been left to seep into the granite over many years.

Jessica swallowed the sickening lump in her throat as she gazed at the dark blemish in the middle of the five-pointed star.

'I think that's blood,' she said edgily, her skin prickling with unease. Her legs felt like jelly and she longed to turn and run but she knew that getting out of the cave would do nothing to destroy the evil that stalked the island.

'Something – or someone – has been killed on this table,' she declared hoarsely. Behind her Elsa clung onto Jake's arm as if her life depended on it. The young lad had become very pale and although his mind hated to acknowledge his fear, the bright torch shook in his grasp. Rosehip hovered just above Jessica's right shoulder making small, frightened squeaks. Jessica had begun to sweat. Her body shook and despite her brain urging her not to, the impulse to flee was getting stronger. Then she felt a heavy hand on her shoulder.

'Take it easy,' Jake reassured her. 'We are all together. Nothing is going to happen as long as we stick together.'

Despite her fear, Jessica almost laughed. Jake sounded strangely like her great uncle right now and in spite of their bickering earlier in the day she was very glad he was here.

'Besides,' he continued, swallowing hard. 'It's animal's blood, I'm almost sure of it. I've seen it on the farm. And it's old, so there's no need to get wound up.'

Jessica inhaled and tried to calm herself. The stain did indeed look ancient. Slowly she raised her arms and held them out over the table. She squeezed her eyes tight shut and blocked all thoughts of evil and murder from her mind. Gradually, Jessica lowered her hands until her fingertips rested upon the cold, damp stone of the altar. She stood there silent for a moment, her body tense as she waited for something terrible to happen. But nothing did. Mystified, she opened her eyes and stared down at the stone. It was still as old and as pale as it had been before.

'Nothing happened,' she said.

'It probably won't,' Jake told her. 'I bet you anything there are some sort of magic words or enchantment you have to say for anything to happen. Check what the book says.'

Jessica reached into her rucksack and pulled out *A History of Magical Beings in Jersey* as she went to perch on one of the stone stools that surrounded the altar. Suddenly Elsa let out a terrified scream and rushed forwards. Leaping on Jessica, she pushed her onto the hard ground away from the stool. Jessica cried out in shock as she hit the floor. Rosehip, determined not to let Jessica come to any harm, flew at the smaller girl, grabbing her thin, blonde locks. Jake stepped forward, bewildered at this odd outburst and shone his torch into the tangle of arms and legs.

Jessica sat up, winded but okay as Elsa tried to bat an angry Rosehip away from her face. Jake crouched beside them and looked worriedly at Jess who was clutching her arm and groaning.

'Are you all right?' he asked placing the torch on the floor.

Jessica winced and flexed her fingers to check her arm wasn't broken. 'Yeah,' she gasped. 'No thanks to you, Elsa! Why in God's name did you do that?'

The white-faced child sat breathing heavily on the cold, hard ground. Her light-blue eyes flitted back to the stool on which Jessica had been going to sit.

'It wasn't safe,' she uttered between gasps. 'The seats. I guessed. That's what protects the altar.'

Jake and Jess looked at each other. The younger girl got to her feet and picked up a small stone from the cave floor.

Rosehip glared at her suspiciously and fluttered close to her face. 'You were attacking Jessica,' she accused in an angry voice. 'You were trying to hurt her. I saw.'

Elsa's narrow, shoulders slumped and she glanced warily at Jessica. 'I wasn't,' she murmured softly, her eyes pleading with them.

Rosehip circled Elsa's head very slowly, glaring at her. 'I am going to be keeping a very close eye on you, young lady.'

The child began to quake with unease under the small sprite's stare. She bit her lip and looked as if she were about to burst into tears.

Jessica, who had recovered from the shock of her fall, got to her feet and dusted herself off. She looked angrily at Rosehip, who seemed to be revelling in Elsa's torment. 'Rosehip,' she said sternly, 'stop winding Elsa up. She hasn't been given a chance to say why she pushed me out of the way.'

Rosehip zoomed off and sat sulkily on Jake's rucksack. 'Taking her side because she's human,' she mumbled crossly to herself.

Gently, Jessica placed her hands on Elsa's shoulders. The child was glancing this way and that in the darkness as if searching for invisible demons.

'I didn't do wrong,' she gibbered to herself nervously. 'I was trying to help.'

'No-one's saying you did.' Jessica soothed her, stroking her thin blonde hair. 'Rosehip is just over-reacting. It's this place, it's making everyone jumpy. Now, just explain what you meant by the seats protecting the altar.'

Elsa gazed into Jessica's eyes with a long, lonely look. 'I don't want to make anyone mad.'

'No-one's going to be cross,' she reassured the child.

Elsa lowered her eyes and took a step back from Jessica. 'It makes sense really,' she explained softly, turning towards the stone table. 'If you, the Guardian, couldn't sense anything from the altar itself, well the enchantment *had* to be in the chairs. Watch.'

She raised the hand in which she held the pebble and held it above the small stone mound. She dropped the rock and it landing with a slight bounce on the flat stool. Jessica and Jake watched in horrified silence as the granite seat glowed a sickly green and bubbles began to foam from it as if it were being attacked by acid. In a few seconds, the solid surface had been transformed into a hissing green that emitted a foul-smelling smoke. The group watched in terror as the stone sank slowly into the frothing sludge, turning black as it went. When the pebble had completely disappeared the green liquid also vanished and the seat was whole again. Jessica shuddered.

Jake raised his eyebrows and placed a hand on her shoulder. 'Flipping Nora!' he exclaimed. 'That could have been your bum, Jess!'

Jessica swallowed hard and nodded. She glanced at Elsa, who had backed away from the altar and was staring at the stool with great reverence. 'Elsa,' she breathed, 'You ... you saved my life!'

The small girl looked from the stone to Jessica but didn't say a word. Her face looked even more drawn than normal and her pale lips puckered slightly as if she were holding back from saying something.

Jessica spun to look at Rosehip. The faerie was hovering in mid air, her mouth open in wonderment. 'You see,' she exclaimed to the amazed sprite. 'Elsa wasn't trying to harm me at all. If I had sat on that rock, I could've been killed!'

Rosehip didn't answer. She continued fluttering in mid-air, her face fixed with an expression of shock.

'Stool, magic, bubble, rock, gone, witchcraft,' she muttered in amazement. Then, suddenly, the faerie's eyes fluttered closed and with a sigh she fell from the air and landed with a gentle plop on the ground.

Jessica gazed at the elf with concern as Jake stooped to pick her up in his cupped hands. 'Is she all right?' she asked the boy as he looked at the golden light glowing in his palms.

Jake looked up and half smiled. 'Yeah,' he laughed. 'She's just fainted, that's all. I told you she was a coward.'

The farmer's son prodded the faerie gently with his finger. 'Come on,' he encouraged. 'Wakey, wakey!'

Slowly Rosehip stirred in Jake's rough palm murmuring softly. She soon sat up and dopily shook her head.

'If you're going to flake out every time we encounter something odd on this trip you might as well stay in the bag!' Jessica told Rosehip as the faerie stretched her wings.

Rosehip hopped off of Jake's palm and flew over to Jessica's shoulder. 'I panicked,' she chirped defensively.

Jessica picked up the book from where it had dropped as she fell. 'I know,' she murmured thoughtfully. 'What we've got to find out is whether it's an old spell or someone has been down here recently.'

The others gathered around her as Jessica turned the pages to the passage that spoke about the great chamber.

'It says about it!' she exclaimed excitedly, as Jake shone the torch onto the page so she could read. Jessica cleared her throat and began to read from the book.

'In the centre of the Main Chamber stands a large, granite altar of black magic measuring approximately twelve feet in diameter. The surface is engraved with a pentagram, sacred symbol of witchcraft. The altar is one of the last remaining dark circles in Britain today, matched only by the legendary Stone Henge (which has long since been abandoned by witches owing to unwanted public attention). Created in France at the turn of the 10th Century and carried to Jersey, many believe, on dragonback, the table is the official gathering place of a complete coven. Note the small rounded stones, thirteen in all, that surround the altar.' Jessica paused and grimaced. 'We certainly did that!' she said before continuing. 'These are what is widely referred to as Witches' Stoops, enchanted stools created from the stone floor itself and so well guarded by magic that any mortal, even the Guardian, would have their flesh dissolved by sitting on them. The altar can only be used for witchcraft when a full coven of thirteen are seated on the stoops. Until this condition obtains, the altar remains cold and devoid of all magic energy.'

Jessica shrugged. 'Well, now we know,' she told her friends. 'If a full coven is in Jersey this is where they would meet and there would be signs of witchcraft. I'd better check with the magascope.'

She lifted the small golden-framed lens from where it hung about her neck. Her fingers trembled as she held it out before her to gaze at the granite altar. Jake shone the torch beam onto the great stone circle to aid Jessica's vision. Jess felt the fear in her stomach rise as she slowly brought her eye line up to the mystical glass, searching for some supernatural indication of whether the altar had indeed been used recently. The yellow torchlight glistened through the ancient, mottled glass like sunbeams on rippling water. Jessica strained her pupils to find something other than the electric glow mirrored in the tiny lens but could detect nothing. She felt Elsa nervously draw close to her side and glanced at her. Jessica lowered the magascope and sighed.

'Nothing,' she told them. 'Well, not as far as I can see. It just looks like a table.'

She didn't know whether to feel relieved or disappointed by the lack of magical energy given out by the altar. She didn't fancy coming face to face with a coven of witches but after discovering the centre of Jersey's black magic so soon she couldn't help but feel a little let down that her great find and near death had been for nothing. She closed *A History of Magical Beings in Jersey* and tucked the volume back in her rucksack.

Jake stuck his hands in his pockets and creased his forehead in puzzlement, but Elsa looked understandably relieved.

'Well, that doesn't make sense at all!' exclaimed the farmer's son, strolling around the great stone altar. 'My grandpa and the other Elders are convinced that there are witches in Jersey at this very moment. I mean why would they have called you back here if there weren't?'

Jessica gazed up at the huge stone ceiling of the Great Chamber, at the countless number of tunnels that ran off it in all directions. 'Who said there weren't?' she asked. 'Remember what the book said? Only a full coven can activate the altar. Who's to say there aren't just one or two witches or warlocks acting alone? Not a coven.'

Her eyes dropped from the monstrous roof of the cave and she looked at her friends. The younger girl looked even more pale and sickly than normal in the dim light of the grotto.

'Do you have any idea who they might be?' she asked timidly, her light blue eyes flitting around the foreboding cave.

Jessica gave a loose stone on the ground a gentle kick. 'Of course I don't,' she mused. 'I only found out I was the Guardian last night. It could be anyone in Jersey as far as I know.'

She looked up again at the many openings that pierced the walls of the chamber and thought hard. 'But I bet you anything my mum was right, about the answer lying in these caves. If witches and warlocks still use the Magicroutes to move about and do spells, I bet this magascope could pick them up.'

She fingered the lens once again as she wondered what directions the witches would come from. She noticed Jake fixing her with a dubious stare and gazed back at him. 'What?' she asked.

The boy shrugged and regarded the tunnel where they had entered the Great Chamber.

'I don't know if that's such a good idea,' he muttered. 'I mean, directly following a trail of dark magic on your first hunt. It sounds risky.'

Both Elsa and Rosehip nodded in enthusiastic agreement. Jessica played with the magascope in her hands.

'Why?' she asked, surprised at her own bravery. 'There is no organised coven and it's pointless standing here all day.'

Jake solemnly shook his head. 'Even one witch or warlock can be very powerful. I don't want you getting hurt.'

195

But already Jessica had lifted the magascope and was scanning the cave entrances for signs of magic. She knew that what Jake was saying was right but if they turned back to the beginning now the whole trip would seem useless. What kind of guardian would she be if she didn't even try to find out who the witches were?

She studied each of the dark holes in the rock face carefully. But none of them showed anything through the enchanted lens except still and complete blackness. Suddenly, as she placed the glass in line with one particular opening, a strange apparition materialized within the warped lens. Jessica squinted at it carefully. Within the magascope a faint light grey cloud had appeared, swirling slowly like a miniature typhoon framed within the cave entrance. The vision was very dim, like smoke from a far away fire, and floated like a wispy serpent from the tunnel. Jessica swallowed hard and, eyes still fixed on the cave, lowered the lens. To her naked eye, the cave now appeared completely empty and as nondescript as any of the others. A slight tingle of fear pricked her skin but she knew what she had to do. She secured her rucksack on her shoulder and glanced at her worried looking friends.

'That one,' she told them firmly, pointing to the aperture. 'I knew there had to be signs of magic in one of them. I can see a grey cloud coming from it when I look through the magascope. I'm going to see what it is.'

She pulled on her rucksack and proceeded to head towards the foot of the granite staircase. Jake looked concerned and started after her.

'Are you mad?' he asked. 'Remember what Jim said. We don't know what's up there.'

He caught her arm and spun her round to face him. Jessica fixed him with a weary stare.

'Look,' she told him bluntly, 'if you want you can wait here with Elsa and Rosehip. Make sure they're safe. I'm pretty sure nothing's going to happen in the Great Chamber so the three of you should be safe.'

Jake looked offended and squared his shoulders. 'Don't you talk to me like I'm scared of this place,' he told her defensively. 'And besides, if you think I am going to let you saunter around the Magicroutes on your own, you had better think again. I was sent to look after you and that is what I'm going to do.'

Jessica cocked her head. 'So you keep reminding me.' Jake's 'big, protective man' act was beginning to wear thin and she wished he would drop it. She looked back at her two other friends huddled close together in the dank cave and sighed. 'You two,' she called out. 'Are you coming or not?'

Both the faerie and the young girl looked unsure. Despite the fact that the Great Chamber seemed relatively safe, Jessica didn't much fancy leaving the delicate Elsa alone with only Rosehip for protection. Having said that, taking her into a tunnel where an unknown magic force was present wasn't the safest option either. She had begun to wish even more that Elsa hadn't accompanied them, but now she was here it seemed there was safety in numbers. Besides – Jessica glanced at the ominous witches' stoops that surrounded the altar – Elsa had proved slightly more shrewd than she appeared and Jess did need all the information about Jersey that she could get. She took a step forward.

'I think it's best that you come with Jake and me,' she told her, offering Elsa her hand. 'That is, if you want to.'

The child shuffled towards her. 'I do,' she murmured shyly. 'I'm just nervous.'

She joined them at the foot of the huge stone staircase. Jessica smiled at her.

'I know,' she said, her voice wavering slightly. 'We all are.'

Rosehip remained where she was, seated, legs crossed on the cold stone floor of the cave.

'I'm not coming,' she told them defiantly. 'Like Jake said, there's unknown magic up there and I'm not taking any chances!'

She nodded and folded her arms across her chest.

Jessica shrugged and turned to climb the steps. Rosehip had proved even less help than Jake and at this point Jessica was almost glad that she could investigate the caves without the faerie's childish whining. The three humans began to climb the stone steps, leaving Rosehip beside the altar. However, after just a few seconds the faerie called after them.

'Hey,' she piped, her normally bold tone laced with fear. 'You're not going to leave me alone down here, are you?'

Jessica stopped climbing and glanced over her shoulder. 'Why, yes,' she said. 'Jake doesn't want me going into the tunnel without him and I need to keep an eye on Elsa.'

Rosehip made a small high-pitched whine and looked around her, kicking her heels against the floor.

'Didn't realize I would have to wait here on my own,' she complained nervously. 'Something might come out of one of these tunnels and eat me.'

She began to wrap a strand of her strawberry blonde hair around her fingers. Jessica sighed and motioned to the others to carry on up the staircase. Rosehip got to her feet and spread her wings.

'Well, I've changed my mind, thank you very much,' she squealed, flying up quickly to land on Jessica's shoulder.

Jess sighed at Rosehip's fickleness but made no further comment and the four of them continued to climb towards the cave.

Soon they reached it and stood around the wide entrance, gazing in with trepidation. To the naked eye the tunnel looked no different from the others leading off from the Great Chamber. It was broader than the one they had entered through, about five feet wide and tall enough for a full-grown man to walk along without stooping. The walls were very damp and covered with a thick film of bluish green algae and like the rest of the cavern the atmosphere was cold and damp. Without the magascope there was no sign of anything unusual about the cave but everyone, especially Jessica, knew that there was some unknown magical power lurking in the darkness.

Jake took the light and its beam flashed around the walls of the foreboding tunnel. 'Is this it?' he asked unsurely.

Jessica fiddled with the small lens that hung about her neck. 'According to the magascope,' she said. 'But I'll check again.'

Once more she lifted the warped glass to her eye and gazed through it down into the depths of the wet passageway. Jake and Elsa also looked into the twisted lens to see if there was any sign of mystical activity emanating from the eerie darkness. Sure enough, framed in the antique gold casing, a small spiral of light grey vapour twisted away into the blackness.

Jessica felt a small hand rest upon her shoulder as she gazed at the slowly coiling vortex. Elsa swallowed timidly.

'What do you think is causing it?' she asked.

Jessica shook her head and lowered the magascope. 'I have

no idea,' she muttered. She put her head inside the cave and took a small sniff of the stale air. A faint odour filled her nostrils, not quite strong enough for her to distinguish what it was. 'Can you smell something?' she asked her companions.

Jake took a step inside the passageway and breathed in the damp air. 'Yes,' he murmured softly, 'and I recognize it, but I can't quite remember from where.'

Jake took a few more steps inside the tunnel, moving his torch this way and that around the sodden walls. Jessica, Elsa and Rosehip remained just outside the entrance trying to summon up the courage to venture inside. Jake was gazing at the walls of the cave, his piercing blue eyes searching for any sign that something was amiss.

'Is it safe?' Jess hissed as Jake stared up at the rounded ceiling.

The farmer's son glanced back at her, a half smile on his lips.

'Probably not,' he stated. 'But we already knew that. If what you're asking me is can I see any runes or signs of magic, the answer is no.' He was silent for a second, regarding the unnerved expression on Jessica's features. 'Look, it was your idea to explore this tunnel so I suggest you get in here and try and find out what was giving out those signals we saw in the magascope.' He sucked his cheek and gazed into the darkness of the passage. 'That is, if you're not too scared.'

Jessica glared at him. 'I was just building up my courage.' She began to walk slowly towards him. Nervously, Elsa and Rosehip followed.

Jessica looked upon the heavy stone that surrounded them very closely. She strained her pupils in the glow of the torch to spot any symbols or carvings in the brown granite, but nearly every inch of the stone was covered with a thick blanket of the rotten bluish moss. If there hadn't been the threat of something terrible occurring in this cave the plant would've been quite beautiful; its foliage was a rich sapphire colour with tiny sprouts like miniature dandelions. The floor of the passageway sloped downwards. Jessica could still hear and feel the water trickling in tiny ripples beside her feet. Liquid dripped from the ceiling high above them, echoing as it splashed heavily upon the stone. Now and again an icy droplet would fall onto Jessica's clothing or bare skin making her shiver with cold. She shrugged up the

199

collar of her jacket to stop the bitter wetness dribbling down her neck.

'Why is everything so wet in these caves?' she complained out loud.

Rosehip fluttered up beside her and gave her tiny form a vigorous shake. 'I'm soaked to the skin,' she chirped.

Jake shone his flashlight into the depths of the cavern. 'Moisture,' he informed them, 'from the surface. All the rain that falls must drain down into these tunnels. As there's no sunlight down here to evaporate it I guess it just takes longer to empty away.'

'Oh,' said Jess. She wasn't really interested in how the tunnels retained so much water. She just wished she could keep dry.

They had been following the tunnel for what seemed a very long time now, Jake and Jessica in the lead and Elsa and Rosehip close behind them. The gentle slope seemed to lead them deeper into the solid rock of Jersey's structure and when Jessica looked back she could no longer see the entrance to the Great Chamber. The lush moss that had covered the walls of the cave had more or less vanished as they travelled deeper and now only hung in rough patches here and there on the dark rock. The strange smell that Jessica had detected on first entering the cave had continued to grow stronger and now, deep below the surface, the wet air positively reeked of it, although neither Jessica nor Jake could recall what it was. It was a stagnant, putrid stench, like something that had badly gone off, and it hung heavy in the clammy air. They had come to a sudden bend in the tunnel, almost a right angle in fact, where the path they had been travelling was blocked by a solid wall of stone and the passageway itself twisted off to the left into a narrow crack in the cave wall. The company stopped for a moment and assessed the situation.

Jessica regarded the constricted gap. It wasn't quite as narrow as the one that had led to the Great Chamber but was still barely big enough for a man to pass through. She could see in the light of the torch that, rather than a continuation of the passageway, the opening was more of an arch leading into a bigger cave. Jake stepped forward and peered into it, running his hands down the side.

'Well,' he muttered, 'either this is a dead end or we go through this archway.'

Jessica gazed around the tunnel and sniffed the pungent air.

'That smell has got to be coming from somewhere down here,' she stated. 'It's getting stronger.'

Jake squared his shoulders and clasped the flashlight firmly in his hand. He looked at the narrow opening in the rock and nodded. 'Okay,' he said firmly. 'I'm going to see what's there. If you hear me shout, go back.'

Both girls nodded and slowly the young man ventured through the archway. He fitted inside easily and soon Elsa and Jessica were unable to see him. There was a moment of tense silence as the group waited for a sign that everything was all right. Rosehip fluttered forward into the tunnel and called out to him in a high-pitched whisper. 'Is everything okay, Jake?'

In the still damp of the cave the friends could hear Jake breathing in short, nervous gasps. Finally he spoke.

'It's fine,' he gasped, sounding extremely tense. 'This isn't a dead end. There's a way we can get through but we have to be very, very careful.'

Elsa, Rosehip and Jessica looked at each other with concern. Then they heard Jake continue.

'Come through the gap, one at a time, but whatever you do, keep close to the rock, the pathway is narrow. Take two steps forward and then one directly to your right. Do you understand?'

They could see the beam of his flashlight darting about through the arch and his voice sounded panicky. Jessica took a deep breath and shuffled forward. 'You wait here,' she informed Elsa and Rosehip.

Steeling herself, she edged inside, her hands gripping the cold, wet stone. Her eyes fixed directly in front of her, she took two tentative steps through the archway. Before her, the cavern opened out into a wide, high-roofed cave, similar to, but smaller than, the Great Chamber. The roof was hung with stalactites and she could hear the familiar sound of trickling water. Jake, however, was nowhere in sight.

'Jake,' she called out.

Then, for the first time she glanced downwards and gasped in horror at what she saw. A gaping drop of at least twenty feet loomed below her and vicious looking stalagmites dotted the cave floor like upturned knives. She was, in fact, standing on a ledge of stone, not one foot in width. Jessica's head swam and she gripped the wall for dear life. The space below her seemed

201

to twist and she felt as if she were plummeting as she had done the night before off the cliffs at St Ouens. Just as she felt she was about to drop, a strong hand gripped her right arm. Jessica broke her gaze away from the deadly fall to see Jake standing on the ledge beside her, his body rigid against the stone wall of the cavern. His face was a ghostly white and he was sweating profusely. She gulped for air and leaned as far against the rock face as she possibly could. Jake kept a firm hold of her wrist.

'I told you the path was narrow!' he squeaked through gritted teeth. 'I nearly fell down there.'

He nodded in the direction of the edge of the overhang on which they were perched. Jessica could feel her body trembling with fear as her fingertips gripped the wall she was standing against. She glared at Jake.

'Why didn't you warn us?' she hissed at him.

The boy shuffled his feet so he was further away from the edge. 'I panicked!' he exclaimed. 'I couldn't think straight. Besides, I had to get you through here somehow.'

'Why?' she protested in an angry whisper. 'It's a death trap. I've already been thrown off a cliff in the last twenty-four hours. I don't want to repeat the experience!'

Jake looked in the opposite direction and Jessica followed his gaze. She saw that the narrow ledge they were balanced on led all the way around the circumference of the cave where it widened out into another tunnel on the far side.

'Look,' explained Jake, 'whatever is giving out those magical signals must be down there. This is the only way out of the tunnel. We are going to have to edge along until we reach the other side.'

Jessica took another very quick glance at the drop in front of her and then gazed along the ledge to the apparent safety of the tunnel on the far side. It seemed impossibly far away and she felt very doubtful that she could bring herself to pick her way along the treacherous rim of the cave to the other side.

Jake met her eyes and held her nervous gaze. 'We've got to do this,' he whispered. 'You said it yourself. We have a duty to find out what is causing the black magic.'

Jessica took a deep breath and nodded. She gripped tight hold of Jake's hand and together they inched their way along the narrow stone shelf towards the exit. They had travelled only a matter of a few inches when a familiar tiny voice echoed from the passageway Jessica had recently vacated.

'I'm scared here on my own,' it squeaked. 'We're coming through – Rosehip and me.'

Jessica and Jake glanced at each other in horror. What with their own fear of falling off the edge they had completely forgotten to warn Elsa. If she came into the cavern without looking she could easily slip off the ledge. Before either of them had a chance to cry out a warning, the slim figure of Elsa emerged from the darkness of the passageway, stepping within centimetres of the deadly drop.

Jessica let out a cry of terror as she glanced back to see a terrified Elsa teetering on the cliff edge, her pale blue eyes filled with horror. In that instant, Jessica forgot her own vertigo and shot out her one free arm to grab the thin cotton of Elsa's dress and pulled her to safety. The sickly girl's face had turned even paler and her huge blue eyes were staring in complete horror over the side of the cliff. She clung on to Jessica's hand and gulped for air.

'I nearly fell,' she murmured, leaning heavily against the wall of the cave.

Jessica nodded grimly. 'I know,' she told her. 'Both Jake and I had a similar experience. Are you okay?'

Elsa's eyes flitted nervously around the cave and then back to Jessica's face. 'You saved me,' she whispered timidly, her soft voice echoing in the hollowness of the cave. She sounded awestruck, as if she'd almost expected Jessica to let her plummet to her death. However, Jessica was feeling far from heroic.

'Well, you saved me when I nearly sat on that witches' stoop,' she replied, taking hold of her hand.

Just then a small, twittering ball of light emerged from the archway and hovered before the three of them. Rosehip had a bemused expression on her face and gazed at her companions impatiently. 'What's all this shouting and screaming about?' she chirped, staring at the humans clinging close to the rock face.

Jake glared at her crossly. 'There's a twenty-foot drop below us!' he exclaimed.

Rosehip glanced down and shrugged calmly. 'So?'

If Jessica hadn't been holding on tightly to Elsa's and Jake's hands, she would have grabbed the faerie out of thin air and thrown her against the stone wall. She blinked angrily at her.

Rosehip merely giggled and flexed her delicate wings. 'Oops!' she laughed. 'I forgot you can't fly. Silly me.' She fluttered off away from the group and perched just inside the cave entrance on the other side. 'I'll just wait here while you cross.'

Jake gritted his teeth. 'Faeries,' he muttered quietly. 'Can't shut them up!' He straightened his back and, leaning firmly against the stone wall, reached out with his one free hand to grab a good secure hold on the rock face. 'Come on,' he told the two girls. 'We've got to get to the other side.'

Jessica swallowed and, gripping her friends' hands as tightly as she could, she and Elsa began very cautiously to creep sideways after Jake along the treacherous route. It was slow going. Every inch had to be approached with the utmost caution as they had no way of telling whether the fragile outcrop of stone would bear their weight. As the three of them tiptoed sideways, Jake searched out shallow finger holds with his right hand to give him a better grip on the stone. All the time, Jessica held her breath and listened in the near darkness. Above the heavy breathing of her companions she was sure she could hear the light rumble of stones falling away from their perch. She began to wonder just how long this route had remained unused and whether the unexpected pressure of their bodies upon it would cause it to give way. That really didn't bear thinking about. She tried to concentrate on getting across to the other side. The air in the cave was filled with the odd, rancid stench they had smelt earlier and the atmosphere was moist and clammy. The golden beam from the torch shone through the darkness, jogging uneasily in Jake's nervous grasp. Suddenly, in the blackness below them Jessica was certain she saw a movement, a scuttling among the rocks at the bottom of the cavern. Once again she glanced downwards in a vain effort to discover what it was. Her feet shuffled the smallest distance towards the edge of the overhang as she searched the dark below for what might have caused the disturbance.

Almost in an instant, the section of granite shelf she was perched on began to crumble beneath her toes and Jessica found herself slipping into the abyss. She felt Elsa's thin hand slip from her grasp as her legs flailed against the quickly vanishing outcrop. She screamed as she fell towards the cruel spikes of stone below. Suddenly she stopped, suspended dangerously in mid-air, her right arm grasped in a vice-like grip as her legs still scrambled against the rock face. She glanced up to see Jake, crouched on what remained of the stone shelf, both his hands clasped firmly around her forearm. He had just managed to catch her in time. The torch he had been carrying clattered from his hand and rolled into the darkness, its light extinguished. Jessica began to sweat as Jake's fingers slipped slowly down the limb they grasped, trying desperately not to let go. She clung to the sleeve of his shirt with her fingertips, hoping she would find the strength to hoist herself back onto the ledge.

The farmer's son gripped her arm for dear life but with every moment he felt her growing heavier and heavier. Slowly, carefully, he lowered himself so he was almost lying on the outcrop clasping Jessica with all his might. His palms were quickly becoming clammy and he was sure that if she didn't find a way of regaining her foothold he would drop her. Jessica struggled in mid-air, her heels floundering against the rock face.

Straining against the onset of cramp in his arm, Jake cried out, 'Climb up me.'

Glancing downwards, Jessica felt the floor of the cave swim up to meet her. 'I can't!' she gasped.

Jake gritted his teeth. 'You've got to,' he told her. 'I don't know how much longer I can hold onto you like this!'

Suddenly there came a ripping sound and Jessica gazed up in horror as she realized the sleeve of Jake's shirt had begun to tear. It came away in her hand as she desperately grabbed hold of his bare arm. She gasped, panting with fear, and with all her might hoisted herself further up the cave wall using Jake's body as a rope. Somehow she managed to grasp Jake's shoulders with both hands and the farmer's son heaved her onto what remained of the outcrop. Jess perched there for a moment or two, gasping for breath and staring down at the jagged rocks that had very nearly sealed her fate. Exhausted, Jake slumped against the wall of the cave, his eyes closed.

Jessica regarded the gap in the shelf through which she had nearly plummeted. She felt her heart pounding in her chest as she thought about how close she had come to losing her life. She glanced at Jake.

'You saved me,' she murmured, aware that it had been the second time in a matter of hours that one of her new found friends had helped her narrowly elude death.

He sat up flexing the aching muscles of his bare arm and smiled grimly. 'Don't mention it.' He looked over to the far side of the chamber where Rosehip had perched all the time watching. 'And a fat lot of good you were,' he called. 'As far as I can see your presence on this venture has been as much use as a chocolate teapot! I thought you had magical powers. Couldn't you have stopped her falling?'

The young faerie got to her feet and pouted angrily, hands on hips. 'I *do* have magic powers,' she squeaked. 'They're just not strong enough to carry a human.'

Jessica shook her head. 'Leave it, Jake. It's not worth the aggravation.'

Rosehip, however, was not willing to leave it. 'What about her?' she piped, wagging a tiny finger in the direction of Elsa. 'She let go of your hand. She didn't try to help you.'

Jake and Jessica glanced at each other in horror. In the panic caused by Jessica's fall and rescue, they had forgotten all about the small girl still perched on the stone overhang. Jessica looked back in the direction they had just come. There was now a large gap in the natural bridge where the rock had crumbled away, leaving a hole of two or three feet between the ledge where she and Jake were seated and the narrow shelf on which Elsa was perched. The child had obviously been quite disturbed by her friend's near scrape with death. She was standing up close against the wall, her china blue eyes flitting from the drop to Jessica, to the faerie, to Jake. She had begun to wring her hands nervously as she very often did at times of stress.

'I didn't mean to let you fall, Jessica,' she murmured. 'I'm sorry.'

Jake had slowly managed to get back to his feet and was standing against the cave wall, glancing around with a nervous look in his eye. 'I've got a very strong feeling,' he informed Jessica, 'that this place isn't going to be safe for very much longer. This bridge has already begun to fall apart. I think we need to get off of it as soon as possible. There's something else I'm worried about but now's not the best time to mention it.'

Jessica battled to keep calm. She slowly planted her feet on the secure stone of the ledge and edged herself up the cave wall until she was standing beside Jake.

'Okay,' she asked, trying to sound in control, 'what now? What do we do about Elsa?'

Jake looked at the short distance the two of them had to travel to the safety of the tunnel on the other side of the cave and then back again to Elsa clinging to the cave wall on the other side of the crumbled ledge. He met Jessica's eyes and she noticed just the smallest glimmer of doubt in his pupils.

'She's going to have to jump across and I'll have to catch her.'

Jessica's jaw dropped. 'What?' she hissed. She lowered her voice to a whisper. 'Jake, tell me you're not serious? You said yourself Elsa is ill. We have no idea if she could jump that far. What if she falls? What if you drop her?'

Jake fixed Jessica with a stern stare. 'Look,' he said quietly. 'I said it was a bad idea to let her come in the first place but now she's here I'm not going to argue about it. We have no ropes with us and if she goes back through the Great Chamber without you she can't open the exit to the surface. The only way forward is for her to jump across that gap.'

Jessica looked at Elsa leaning pitiful and nervous against the wall of the cave. She was softly muttering to herself words that Jessica couldn't hear. She could see the child's painfully thin legs beneath the hem of her skirt and wondered if such puny limbs could jump across the break in the outcrop. The gap was only a matter of a few feet but for someone as weak as Elsa they might as well be asking her to jump the Grand Canyon.

'I promise I'm not going to let her fall,' Jake said.

A bubble of dread sat in Jessica's stomach. The young girl looked at her with expectant eyes. Jessica forced her lips into a calming smile. 'Elsa,' she murmured softly, 'we need to get you across to this side of the bridge. This means you're going to have to jump and Jake will catch you.'

The child shrunk back. 'No,' she squeaked with fear. 'Don't want to. Don't want to.'

Jake stretched out his arms towards her. 'Come on, Elsa,' he encouraged. 'I won't drop you. I promise.'

Elsa remained rooted to the spot on the opposite side of the gap and turned her pale face against the wet stone so that all her companions could see was her long, fine, blonde hair.

Jessica stood just behind Jake on the ledge and reached out to the girl. 'He won't,' she persisted gently. 'He didn't drop me, now did he?'

Elsa didn't move. She stood as still as a statue, her face buried against the rock. When she spoke her voice was even quieter than normal, so soft that Jessica could barely hear.

'You're important, Jessica. You're the Guardian. I'm nothing.'

Jessica took a tiny step forward. 'Don't say things like that,' she implored. 'This has nothing to do with me being the Guardian. We're in this together. Remember what we said earlier? Nothing's going to happen as long as we stick together.'

She paused for moment in the hope that her words of encouragement could persuade the young girl that she and Jake would not let her perish. Elsa, however, seemed determined to stay where she was. She had pulled herself in close to the rock face, her trembling hands gripping it for dear life. She did not look at Jessica or Jake but kept her face turned against the wall, her whole body shaking with fear.

Jessica's mouth felt very dry. She realized now that, whether she liked it or not, she was linked to both Elsa and Jake in a deeper way than she'd ever thought possible considering she barely knew them. Not only had they chosen of their own free will to accompany her on this dangerous quest, but in the space of a few short hours they had each on separate occasions saved her life. She believed that Jake had the ability to catch Elsa if she would only trust him enough, and knew it was up to her to persuade the child she would come to no harm.

From her safe perch just outside the passageway on the other side of the cavern, Rosehip watched the scene with curiosity. She decided she would help Jessica to encourage Elsa. The tiny sprite got to her feet and cupped her delicate hands around her mouth like a miniature megaphone. 'Come on, Elsa,' she squeaked. 'You can do it! Jump, jump, jump!'

Elsa quickly turned her head to look at the faerie. Her pale eyes were filled with terror and her chest rose and fell erratically with fear. Jessica glared over her shoulder.

'Would you shut up!' she hissed angrily, aware that Rosehip's chanting was causing Elsa to panic even more. Rosehip stopped abruptly and sulked.

'I was trying to help,' she said defensively. 'You know, build up her confidence.'

'Well, you're not,' Jessica replied. 'Look, isn't there a spell or something you can cast to help her?'

Rosehip looked thoughtful for a minute and played with her skirt. Suddenly, she let out an excited squeak and fluttered her wings. 'I know!' she piped. 'I could cast a bravery spell.'

Jessica looked doubtful. Jake glanced back but didn't drop his arms from their outstretched position ready to catch Elsa.

'We've got to hurry,' he said. 'A lump of this ledge has already fallen away. It's not a good place to hang around.'

Jessica nodded stiffly. 'Do it, cast your spell,' she ordered the faerie.

'You sure?' queried Rosehip, quite taken aback that Jessica had listened to one of her suggestions.

Jess shot her a filthy look for wasting time. 'Yes!' she yelled with fury.

Her voice echoed around the chamber, shaking the ancient stone. A few rocks fell away from the stone shelf on which they were standing and Jake quickly shuffled backwards away from the edge.

'Might not be a good idea to shout,' he muttered tensely.

Jessica felt tiny beads of sweat forming on her forehead but knew for Elsa's sake she must stay calm. The faerie began at once. She waved her long, willowy arms in front of her in mystical and complex patterns. Tiny, glittering sparks of golden dust flew from her fingertips, crackling in the stale, damp air of the cave. She did an elegant pirouette and clapped her hands three times.

'There,' she said brightly, 'now she won't fall.'

Jessica studied Elsa closely. There appeared to be no change in her nervous demeanour. She still clung petrified to the wall. Jess cleared her throat and spoke gently.

'Elsa, Rosehip has cast a bravery spell to help you get across to us. Now please jump and, I promise, Jake will catch you.'

Elsa held Jess's gaze with wide and frightened eyes, one hand still clinging to the rock. Jessica felt the panic in her rise again. She didn't know whether or not the bridge on which they were standing would continue to hold their weight.

'Elsa, please,' she begged. 'I am your friend and friends don't let each other get hurt.'

Elsa regarded her intently and Jessica saw the fear in her eyes die away. The child took a deep breath and closed her eyes. Jessica stooped low behind Jake to help him when he caught Elsa. She watched the girl's wasted muscles tense in preparation. Then, with all her might, Elsa threw her body forward towards them, her scrawny limbs flailing about as she left the safety of her perch. Jake leant forward and stretched his arms out as far as he could. With a slight jolt the child landed safely and he rolled backwards into Jessica. A few more fragments of granite tumbled from the ledge into the darkness below them. Jake sat up with Elsa still clutching him.

'You okay?' he asked the girl sitting on his lap.

Elsa barely moved. She remained hunched up in a ball, her arms locked around his neck and her head bowed. Stiffly she nodded, but said nothing. Jessica peered over the young man's shoulder and smiled.

'You did it!' she cheered softly, placing a hand on the child's blonde hair. 'I knew you could!'

Slowly, Elsa raised her head and looked at her two friends with amazement dancing in her blue eyes.

'You're right,' she gasped, a note of pride in her hushed voice. 'I did it. I jumped. All by myself.' She gazed up at Jake. 'Thank you for catching me,' she said earnestly.

Jake gave her a lop-sided grin. 'Don't mention it,' he joked. 'Two damsels in ten minutes; I'm getting good at this hero lark!'

Both Jess and Elsa chuckled but in a second the grin faded from Jake's lips. 'We've gotta get out of here,' he muttered anxiously.

It took them only a matter of moments to traverse what remained of the rapidly crumbling ledge and reach the safety of the broad stone outcrop in front of the tunnel where Rosehip was sitting. This area was a good ten feet deep, flat and felt a great deal more sturdy than the narrow pathway. Jake fell to his knees with exhaustion and let out a deep sigh. Both Jessica and Elsa also collapsed on the cool rock to recover from their eventful journey.

Jake closed his eyes and threw his head back with a tired groan. 'I can't believe we've made it across here alive,' he breathed.

Jessica patted him on the shoulder. 'Well, we probably wouldn't have if it hadn't been for you.'

The farmer's son opened his eyes and gazed at her with his familiar cheeky grin. 'I guess you need a man to take care of you after all,' he laughed, still sounding exhausted from his ordeal.

Jessica bit her lip and smiled. She hated to admit when she was wrong and hated even more to appear the helpless girl, but Jake was right. She didn't like to think about what would've happened to Elsa and her if Jake hadn't been there. She made a mental note not to be so hard on him next time he made one of his quirky comments.

Elsa, meanwhile, was crouching on the cold stone gazing back at the sizeable gap she had somehow managed to traverse.

'I can't believe I was brave enough to jump across,' she muttered.

Jessica smiled at her. 'Thank God for Rosehip's bravery spell.'

'Really!' the faerie said incredulously. 'That's weird because there isn't such a thing as a bravery spell.'

Jessica's jaw dropped and Elsa's face lost what little colour it had managed to regain.

Jessica blinked hard. 'What do you mean, there isn't such a thing?' she asked.

Rosehip shrugged as she played with a strand of her reddish coloured hair. 'Made it up.'

Elsa groaned weakly and slumped against Jake.

'What were all the sparks about?' Jessica asked.

Rosehip got to her feet. 'Faerie glitter,' she informed them. 'I can do it any time I want to. Look.' She clicked her fingers and sent bright sparks of light darting into the air. 'Doesn't mean anything. I just gave her the confidence she needed to get across. Pointless waiting around all day.'

There was a pause. Then Jake said, 'It's best we move on, that is if Elsa's feeling strong enough.'

The slight girl was still overcome by her major achievement. She stared at the crumbling remains of the ledge, the tiniest smile visible on her lips. 'I did it,' she murmured softly to herself. 'All by myself.'

Whether what the faerie had done was magic or not was beside the point really. It had given Elsa faith in herself and that was indeed magical.

Elsa tore her eyes away from the ledge and gazed at Jessica. There was a light shining in the girl's eyes that Jessica had not witnessed before. For the first time since Jessica had known her, Elsa seemed truly thrilled by something. 'Let's go,' she said.

Jake strained his eyes as he peered into the dark shadows of the tunnel. 'Looks like we've got no choice but to go down here,' he announced, unwillingly.

Jessica gripped the strap of her rucksack. 'Then forward we go,' she said firmly. Elsa's new-found confidence had rubbed off on Jessica and after making it across to this side of the cavern she felt there was nothing the four of them couldn't face. The party headed into the gaping passageway.

The tunnel was wide and tall, very much like the one they had passed through earlier. The walls were uneven and so damp it seemed their entire surface lay behind a curtain of water. There were large, shallow puddles on the floor of the tunnel. Jessica felt drained as they trudged along in the gloom. They seemed to have been below ground forever and she suddenly felt a great need to see the sun. She gazed about and tried to gain some bearing on where they were. The tunnel they were travelling down was oddly square compared to the others she had seen. The walls on either side of them were practically vertical and the ceiling was almost perfectly flat. Jessica took a deep breath and straightaway wished she hadn't. The air was foul. The rotten odour that drifted through the caves was definitely becoming more noxious. She cupped her hands over her nose and mouth.

'What is that smell?' she exclaimed. 'It's getting worse!'

Jake stopped dead in his tracks. 'Ah!' he said quietly.

Jessica sneered at him in disgust. 'Phew, Jake!' she said backing away. 'You could at least say, "pardon".'

The boy spun to face her, his face anxious in the gloom. 'I don't mean it's me!' He looked worried. 'That's what I meant back on the ledge when I said there was something I had to tell you.'

Jessica stopped. Jake was gazing around the cave in a very unsettling manner.

'What do you mean?' she asked nervously. She felt Elsa's hand tremble in her grasp.

Jake swallowed and took a deep breath.

'About two months back,' he explained, 'Dad and I went into the cattle shed, like we do every morning, and found one of the cows slaughtered in the most horrible way. I'm not squeamish but what happened to that animal made me feel physically sick. Blood and guts everywhere. I've seen cows that dogs have killed before and believe me, this was no dog attack. One cow and only one, torn completely open. Everything had been eaten – flesh, organs, even the head – just the skin and bone was left.'

Jessica's stomach began to churn. She didn't want to know where this story was heading.

He sniffed the foul smelling air. 'And there was this awful smell, like God knows what. The same smell that's here. I think whatever did that to our cow is down here.'

Jessica felt sheer terror rise in her chest and she leaned against the tunnel wall for support. Rosehip covered her face with her tiny hands and squealed. Elsa clung to Jessica's arm for support.

'We've got to go back,' Jessica stated, trying to sound firm.

Jake gazed back down the tunnel in the direction they had come from. 'And cross that crumbling bridge again? Face it, Jessica – you know it won't take our weight a second time.'

Elsa buried her face in Jessica's sleeve and began to cry softly.

Rosehip fluttered squeaking. 'We're dead,' she cried.

Jessica glared at the nervous faerie. 'Will you stop saying that whenever we find ourselves in a difficult situation?' she growled.

She remained staring at the elf for a few moments still very unsure about what to do but knowing that as the Guardian it was her responsibility to get them to safety. Her eyes wandered to the cave wall directly behind Rosehip and she spotted something that momentarily drove all other thoughts from her mind. In the rock were carved two crude symbols. One was a perfect square with two lines curving upwards from the top corners. The other was a diagonal cross with round dots marking the four sections. Jessica took a step closer and studied the unusual markings with fascination.

Jake, who had not yet noticed the magic carvings, sighed and gazed around edgily. 'We can't stay here,' he told her.

Jessica hushed him abruptly and reached into her rucksack. 'Runes!' she explained, pointing her finger at the symbols engraved in the rock. 'And I think they're fresh. This could be a clue.'

She pulled out the leather-bound volume Jim had given her that morning, *A Complex Guide to The Symbolic Meanings of Runes* by D.Q. Westbrook. Jake gazed over Jessica's shoulder. 'Be quick,' he said. 'This isn't a place I fancy hanging around in for a long time.'

Elsa, too, stared at the symbols, then quickly shrank back towards Jake.

In Rosehip's dull glow, Jessica studied the ancient pages of the book, searching for an explanation of the encrypted message. Her fingers trembled as she turned the crinkled pages until, after a few minutes, she found the definition of the first rune.

She read it aloud but was aware that neither Jake nor Elsa was listening. '*Haish*; noun, meaning creature of the ground, cow or cattle, pig, sheep, troll, meat-eater of non-human birth.' She frowned, trying to make sense of the vague description. 'Does that mean anything to you, Jake?' she called back still flicking through the book.

'Jess,' he whispered hoarsely, 'I think we'd better leave, now!'

Jessica shook her head. She could hear a terrible laboured breathing and guessed it must be Elsa. She knew the girl had a weak chest but she had never heard her wheeze like this before. She would find out what the second rune meant and then it would probably be best if they headed back above ground.

'In a minute,' she replied, as she leafed through the volume in her hands. Finally her eyes fell on a drawing that resembled the second mark. '*Ourin*; adjective, to be devoid of colour or goodness, black, evil, dark or darkness, to draw on what is evil.'

She tipped back her head and pondered what the message could mean, all the time Elsa's heavy breathing ringing in her ears.

'Sheep black, cow evil – this is nonsense.'

She turned to face her friends but they did not meet her gaze. Both Jake and Elsa were transfixed with terror at what they saw illuminated in Rosehip's pale glow.

Jake swallowed hard and spoke. 'It makes sense all right,' he whispered. 'It's a warning – Black Trolls!'

Jess looked at him in confusion and then realized that it wasn't Elsa's breathing she'd heard rasping in the darkness. It was, in fact, the repulsive creature that lay not three feet away from them. Her pupils grew wide with horror as she gazed at the hideous animal whose lair they had stumbled upon. A ghastly pale skin covered its huge fat frame, puckered here and there with great hairy warts. Its skin, rough and wrinkled, was covered in sweat which seemed to be the source of the cave's foul stench. Its limbs were short and stubby but proportioned like a human's rather than those of a four-legged beast. The hands and feet were fist-like with three small chubby digits on each and long, black claws. From the crown of its head to its rear there was a crest of rough, black hair that bristled like wire. The face was the stuff of nightmares, fat and covered with short, black stubble. From the bottom jaw jutted a vicious pair of fangs resembling those of a boar, tinged pink with what could only be blood. Its snout was long and creased, ending in two upturned nostrils that flared with its awful snoring. The eyes were closed beneath heavy black brows and its forehead was long and protruding.

Jessica gasped and took a step backwards from the unholy sight. Somehow, her hands found those of her friends and she gripped them tight. She didn't know what a Black Troll was and from looking at the animal slumbering before them, she didn't want to find out.

Jake took a deep breath and spoke very softly. 'If we leave very, very quietly, it won't wake up and we'll be okay.'

Both the girls nodded and slowly began to back away. However, at that moment Rosehip, who had been studying the runes carved on the cave wall, turned to see what everyone was looking at. She saw the troll and before anyone could stop her let out a scream of terror. The faerie's high-pitched, musical voice echoed through the cave as clearly as a bell and in a flash the troll was awoken from its slumber and opened its bloodshot red eyes.

Snarling, the beast quickly scrambled from where it lay and bared vicious teeth. Black, dagger-like claws clattered upon the wet rock and from its jaws a ferocious bellow came.

The beast fixed them with its evil red eyes. Jessica shuffled backwards in a vain attempt to flee but the moment she moved the troll pounced forward. Without another thought the four travellers spun on their heels and fled through the tunnel. The troll emitted a blood-curdling roar and bounded after them, its wiry mane raised in fury. They ran for their lives, Rosehip zooming in front of them. But, despite the creature's heavy build, it hounded them with the fleetness of a fox, its powerful limbs propelling it forward, sometimes on two legs sometimes four, its razor-sharp teeth snapping at the air. The humans' feet threw up splashes of water as they tore through the puddles that dotted the cave floor, slipping this way and that, their toes struggling to carry them swiftly through the wetness. The troll, however, seemed to suffer no such handicap; its sturdy claws gripped the moist rock with natural purchase.

The group stumbled onwards in the near darkness, frantic to escape. Suddenly, Jessica realized Elsa had fallen behind. She glanced over her shoulder and saw the small child practically crawling on her hands and knees, the troll bearing down on her. She stopped dead in her tracks.

'Elsa!' she screamed, her voice shrill with terror.

Before Jake could stop her she was heading back at top speed to where the hungry troll was pawing at the unconscious child. Rosehip, too, paused in mid-flight and turned back. 'She needs light!' she piped.

It took the two females a matter of seconds to reach Elsa. The troll was crouched beside her, panting hungrily, its sharp fangs and jaws dripping with saliva. Its claw-like front paws were clasped around Elsa's right forearm. The only sign of life from the girl was a slight fluttering of her eyelids and a barely audible moaning. The creature wheeled round to face Jessica, its fangs exposed in an angry snarl. Instinctively, Jessica reached back into a pocket of her rucksack and drew out the small kitchen knife she had put there. Adrenalin was pumping through her veins and all thoughts of her own safety vanished as she saw that her friend was on the verge of death. With a cry of anger, she hurled herself at the hissing monster, pushing its body away from Elsa. The animal tumbled backwards, roaring and spitting. Jess lashed out wildly with the blade but in the dimness of the tunnel it was impossible to see her foe clearly.

One of the beast's black talons tore through the material of her T-shirt, shredding it as easily as tissue paper and scratching her skin inches from her throat. Jessica gasped at her near escape and once again slashed the knife she was gripping at the troll's flesh. The blade hit its mark and drove itself deep into the creature's shoulder. It roared in agony. Her hand still on the handle, Jessica felt a gush of warm, inky liquid spurt onto her skin. It scalded like acid and she released the weapon. The troll, with the knife embedded in its breast reeled back hissing with pain.

Exhausted, and her hand still throbbing from the strange sting of the troll's blood, Jessica scrambled to her feet and looked around her. Elsa still lay on the floor, her face twitching, while Rosehip hovered high in the air, seeming unsure what to do. She swooped down to Jessica's shoulder just as the girl gazed around to see the troll rise up once more, blood still streaming from its wound. It threw its head back and let out a roar that seemed to echo through the whole labyrinth of caves. Jessica took a frightened step backward and glanced at her faerie friend.

'It won't die!' she screamed with fear.

A determined look came over the elf's face. 'Maybe not,' she said, her blue eyes gleaming, 'but I can hold it back. Get Elsa.'

Jessica was too desperate and too scared to argue. The faerie reached her arms out in front of her as if pushing a great weight away from her tiny body. A ball of golden sparks no bigger than Jessica's thumbnail shot out like a lightning bolt in the direction of the troll. It zoomed straight into its hideous face and exploded like a miniature firework. The creature howled in pain and backed away. Rosehip looked at Jessica urgently.

'Hurry,' she urged. 'I can't hold him off for ever.'

Still shaken from her battle, Jessica scrambled over to Elsa. The child still appeared very pale but her eyes were now open and she was gazing around her in a daze. Jessica crouched beside her and helped the girl sit up. Elsa's eyes rolled up in her head as she tried to focus.

'I don't think I can walk,' she murmured. 'Leave me, Jessica. Leave me and go.'

Jessica shifted the child's weight onto her lap. 'Don't talk nonsense,' she whispered, trying to ignore the agony in her own hand. 'I'll carry you.'

With that she mustered all the strength she could and got to her feet, Elsa cradled in her arms.

From behind them there came another roar and Jessica knew that the troll had regained its strength. The faerie spun in mid-air and shot another fireball at the troll, sending the creature reeling for a second time.

Jessica forced herself forward. For once she was grateful for

217

the child's wasted physique as it made it easier to carry her as they struggled through the tunnel. Rosehip fluttered this way and that, from time to time glancing behind to send another orb of brilliant light at the troll. But despite her valiant efforts to keep it back, the hideous beast still struggled after them, roaring in pain.

After what seemed like an age, Jessica saw the end of the tunnel open out into the cave that they had crossed. On the ledge overlooking the chasm, stood Jake, his face pale. The youth's eyes grew wide in amazement as his three travelling companions emerged from the gloom. Rosehip was zooming frantically ahead shooting sparks back into the cave every few feet. At her side, Jessica stumbled, her clothes in shreds, her face and arms scratched and bruised. Her right hand appeared to be encased in some kind of smouldering black resin and in her arms, blinking with fear, was Elsa. Jake ran forward to meet them. Jessica gently deposited Elsa on her feet and collapsed against the cave wall exhausted. Elsa lent against an astonished Jake for support and Rosehip hovered, still staring back in to the tunnel.

'I thought you two were goners,' said Jake.

'Well, thanks for helping us,' replied Jessica sarcastically.

Jake flinched. He cautiously took Jessica's wounded forearm and examined it. 'Sorry,' he murmured. 'But when Elsa went down I didn't honestly think there was much point. Black Trolls are ferocious killers. I was trying to get you as far away from it as possible. When you went back to save her I heard this awful commotion; I thought it had got both of you and was coming after me. I'm so sorry – I was terrified.'

Jessica winced as a shooting pain gripped her fingers. 'I forgive you,' she groaned. 'You can't be the hero all the time. At least you didn't completely leave us.'

Jake looked back into the cavern. 'I didn't have much choice,' he murmured quietly. 'Look.'

He pointed to the left wall of the cave where the ledge they had crossed had been. The rocky overhang had crumbled away; all that remained were two or three clumps of granite that hung precariously to the wall. Jessica swallowed hard and shuddered.

'When the troll roared, it echoed all the way through here,' Jake explained. 'The ledge just fell away with the vibrations.'

Suddenly, another terrible troll howl reverberated from the tunnel. Rosehip shot another bolt into the darkness. The faerie's face was slowly being drained and Jessica knew that all the spells she was casting were weakening her. She took a deep breath and gazed around. The remaining fragments of the ledge were clearly too fragile to take their weight. Behind her, the dark passage echoed with the grunting of the monster hot on their tail. The only safety they had at that moment was the tiny plateau of rock on which they stood and she knew that once the troll had recovered from Rosehip's magic that also would be in danger. She looked at her three companions. 'We're trapped.'

Jake's face hardened. 'No we're not,' He said firmly. 'There's one way we can go.' He glanced over the cliff edge. 'Down.'

'Are you mad?' Jessica screamed. 'You're suggesting we jump off a cliff onto rocky ground. We'll be killed!'

Jake crouched down and eased his legs over the side of the ledge. 'I hate to remind you of this,' he muttered, 'but when that troll reaches us we are going to be killed anyway. At least this way we stand *some* chance of getting out of here alive!'

Jessica edged closer to the rim of the cliff and peered over. On closer inspection, the fall was not a sheer drop after all but a very steep slope dotted with bumps and stones. It levelled out at the bottom to form the floor of the cave. It would be possible for someone to slide down it but even then the sheer angle and the uneven surface of the incline would make it a treacherous and uncomfortable ride.

The growling of the troll echoed throughout the cavern again. It was getting nearer. She knew that her companion was right. Their only route of flight was downwards.

Jake spread his arms and motioned for Elsa to come to him. 'I'll take her on my lap,' he explained softly. 'That way the fall won't be so dangerous for her. You will have to slide down on your own. Rosehip, how many of those fireballs do you think you have left in you?'

The faerie fluttered round to face him. Her magical glow was growing dimmer and her tiny chest was heaving with tired gasps.

'I think I could manage a couple more,' she breathed wearily. 'But not many.'

Jake gathered Elsa into his arms and placed her securely on

219

his lap, his arms folded across her. He threw Jessica a scared glance. 'This is it,' he said. 'Once we've gone, sit on the edge and slide down after us. Keep your arms in and your legs together. Try and relax your body; you'll be less likely to break anything.'

Jessica nodded. 'Good luck!' she said.

Jake took a deep breath and launched himself off the ledge, tumbling downwards towards the cave floor twenty or so feet below. In the dim light it was only a matter of seconds before Jessica lost sight of them in the darkness; then, with a nervous gulp, she seated herself on the cliff edge.

'Go,' she told the faerie. 'Fly down and see if they're okay.'

'Don't you need me for light?' Rosehip asked.

Jessica shut her eyes tight and shook her head. 'No,' she muttered. 'Quite frankly I don't want to see what's coming.'

Rosehip dived into the cavern, leaving Jessica in utter darkness. She shrugged off her rucksack and hugged it to her chest so the straps wouldn't snag on the way down.

Squeezing her eyes shut, she allowed her body to go limp and slipped down the slope. She kept her eyes firmly shut as she skidded this way and that downwards. Sharp stones caught on her clothing, ripping it as she fell and making painful cuts and grazes on her shins and back. She spread her feet to try and slow her descent but the angle of the slope was too steep. Dust and gravel was thrown up all around her as she tumbled, stinging her face and eyes. The drop seemed to go on for ever. Suddenly, she hit a large bump in the ground and felt her body being thrown into the air, only to land again with a painful jolt at the foot of the slope.

She lay there in the silent blackness for a moment feeling every excruciating ache that throbbed in her body. The fall had left her T-shirt ripped to ribbons and the skin of her back was a mass of lacerations. It felt wet and sticky. Her hand was still burning inside the black cocoon of troll's blood – so much so it was barely possible for her to move her fingers. An agonizing pain immobilized her left calf and she guessed she had twisted her ankle.

Gritting her teeth, Jessica hauled herself up to a sitting position and opened her eyes. She found that she was at the very bottom of the cavern. All around her huge stalagmites reached up to the cave roof like hideous gothic columns.

'There she is.'

Jessica looked to her right to see Jake, face scratched and clothes ripped, limping towards her. Just behind him Elsa trotted, slightly less dishevelled thanks to Jake's protection but still with a large bruise near her right eye. Rosehip hovered near her, not visibly injured but looking weak from the amount of magic she'd used up on the troll. Jake knelt by Jessica's side.

'Are you all right?' he asked, placing a hand around her shoulders.

She winced and reached down to rub her wounded leg. 'No. I think I've twisted my ankle.'

Jake moved to examine his companion's injured limb but the moment he laid his hands on it Jessica cried out with pain.

'It could be broken,' he muttered gravely. 'Don't worry, I'll carry you.'

He was just about to lift her when Elsa let out a scream of horror and pointed to the cliff they had just descended. 'Look!'

Clinging to the rock face, its dagger-like claws gripping the granite with perfect ease and purpose, was the troll. It was crawling swiftly on all fours, down the slope, its fangs bared, white drool dripping from its jaws. The creature's scarlet eyes glowed maliciously and its nostrils flared as it sniffed its prey. It threw back its foul head and howled. The sound rang through the cave, and from behind stalagmites and within hidden grottos, came answering snarls and roars. The friends looked in horror as all around them more creatures emerged, like phantoms evolving from the darkness. The trolls swiftly circled the group, hackles raised, claws poised, ready to kill and feed.

The frightened companions clung to each other unable to move. There were at least six trolls in all, each one driven to a frenzy by the odour of Jessica's bleeding wounds. There was no escape. Jess joined hands with her friends and prayed her death would be swift.

Then, out of nowhere, a cry echoed out in the cave, so different and startling compared to the trolls' hungry snarls, that Jessica opened her eyes. The scream was gruff and husky, almost as if the creature making it was being drowned. But however odd the call was it wasn't the mere baying of an animal; it was a voice shouting.

'Bla-Blas no!'

Behind the trolls, arched up on its stomach, was an animal quite unlike any the friends had ever seen. Its skin was a deep shade of olive green and scarred with thousands of warts and carbuncles. Its arms were strong and lean and ended in huge hands with long, tapered fingers. Its head, held high and proud, was crowned with an unruly mane of greenish-black hair. It had a flat, snub nose and its eyes were large and a beautiful shade of chocolate brown. Behind it, two, long snake-like tails thrashed angrily. It bared its sharp white teeth and hissed.

The trolls, turned from their prey and growled evilly at the odd stranger. The creature's brown eyes shone with momentary fear but it gritted its teeth and prepared to fight.

'Bla-Bla no hurtings huming-beings. Muchly badsome. Rina hurtings nasty Bla-Blas if they bitey at huming-beings,' it snarled, eyeing its foes.

The trolls snapped their jaws at the strange creature and began to advance on it.

'What is it?' Jessica whispered to Jake, as the mysterious, green-skinned creature whipped its tails from side to side.

The youth just stared and shook his head. 'I have no idea,' He muttered. 'I've never seen anything like it before.'

Just then, the largest of the trolls leapt forward and pounced on the beast. The animal let out an angry hiss and sunk its sharp white teeth into the troll's flesh. The troll howled out for its brothers to come to its aid and the whole pack rushed on the animal snarling. The creature was not deterred, however. It lashed out with every weapon it had on its malformed body, spitting and punching. Its serpent-like limbs thrashed around like leather whips, striking the trolls whenever they could. Again and again it bit its enemy, leaving deep, black fang marks in the greasy skin. The huge hands struck out with fierce slaps and punches as the trolls piled on top of it. They grabbed at its arms and legs with their blade-like talons and battled to pin it to the cave floor but the animal was too agile and wiry. It slipped from their grasp, flailing its tails about and screeching throatily. Then, pouncing at the head troll, it bit it squarely on its snout. The stocky creature squealed in agony and leapt back from its attacker. Startled, it yelped several times and the other trolls quickly drew back. Realizing that the unusual animal was not an easy target, they fled to the wall of the cave and claws

222

clattering against the granite, scrambled up into the safety of the tunnel above.

The strange being made no attempt to pursue them but instead remained where it was, squealing angrily and barking.

'Bla-Blas right, Bla-Blas running goodbye! No be back or Rina be bitings ya.'

The creature then slumped wearily on its side and with a gentle sigh, began to lick a wound on its right forearm with a long, black tongue.

Jessica and Elsa sat perfectly still, transfixed by the extraordinary apparition. Quietly, Jake began to gather together their belongings.

'Let's get out of here!' he muttered nervously.

Jessica tore her eyes away from the animal to look at him. 'Why?' she asked. 'That thing, whatever it is, saved our lives. Don't you think we should at least thank it?'

'Look,' Jake told her, 'whatever it is, it just saw off six trolls single-handedly. It could just be after us for its dinner and I don't much fancy being trapped in a cave with a ferocious something that is as strong at least as six trolls!'

Elsa nodded timidly in agreement. 'It's scary,' she whispered.

Rosehip picked herself up from where she had been sheltering in a fold of Elsa's skirt. 'You saw how fierce it was,' she piped to Jessica, examining her wings to make sure they hadn't been crushed. 'It could shred us to little pieces!'

Jessica gazed back to the creature and studied it closely. Right at that moment, it didn't look ferocious at all – in fact, it looked rather hurt and small. Its head was stooped low over its injured forearm as it cleaned the wound and it was making little snuffling sounds to itself. Its rear limbs, which had moments before been deadly weapons, were curled around its lower body in a sort of hug. In a matter of seconds, the monster that had attacked the evil trolls had disappeared and in its place was a creature who looked as passive as a kitten.

Jessica stared at it intently. The being was indeed hideous, with its rough, blemished skin and seaweed-like hair, but as Jessica watched a strange feeling of peace rushed through her and she knew instinctively that the animal would not harm them.

The creature finished lapping the gash in its flesh and lifted its head to regard the group. Realizing it was looking at them, both Jake and Elsa started back in fright but Jessica remained seated on the floor watching to see how it would react. The animal cocked its head to one side and gazed at them, its beautiful brown eyes twinkling with curiosity.

'Peoples?' it croaked with interest, unwinding its snake-like lower limbs. 'Huming-beings? Oh.'

The creature seemed as fascinated by the young people as they were by it. Its brown eyes were fixed on the group as it clumsily crawled towards them, dragging its snake-like body over the rock with its huge hands.

Jake made a high-pitched squeak as the animal crept level to them. 'It's thinking about who to eat first,' he muttered tensely.

Jessica rolled her eyes. It seemed clear to her that the creature was simply keen to find out who they were. 'Don't be such a big baby!' she scolded.

The animal circled the group, examining them closely. Its nostrils flared as it sniffed their scent. It slowly nudged closer to Jake who was frozen to the spot with fear. Gently it pressed its snub nose against his hand and sniffed it. Jake squealed but was too petrified to move away.

The creature gazed up at him and made an interested huffing sound. 'Is beings boy,' it decided, looking up at the tall youth. 'And is beings muchly tallsome.'

It shook its head and circled round behind him. Jake relaxed as the creature crawled away from him and shuffled its way towards Elsa. The child's pale eyes grew wide with horror as the animal crouched back on its serpent-like limbs and gazed intently at her. It reached out a long-fingered green hand, softly brushed her fine blonde hair and touched the material of her dress. 'Girl,' it uttered softly, wrapping a strand of hair around its tapered digit. 'Muchly tinysome and nicely hair.' The creature constricted its foul face in what could loosely be called a smile. 'Oo is beings muchly prettily,' it said to the terrified Elsa.

Beside Elsa's knee, Rosehip fluttered nervously.

'That thing better not get near me,' she squeaked. 'I heard things like "whatever that is" eat faeries!'

The elf's flickering and musical speech caught the creature's attention and inquisitively it stooped its head low to see the brightly shining being better.

'Oooh!' it uttered, fascinated by Rosehip's golden glow. 'What

224

is beings this? Muchly, muchly beautifully and icky bitsys. Oo is being all shinisome and muchly nicely, bitsy glowsy one.'

Rosehip backed away from the enquiring creature, her tiny chest rising and falling with fear.

'Keep away,' she threatened. 'Keep away or I'll cast a spell on you.'

The stranger didn't understand, or else it was not scared by Rosehip's threats. It began to reach out with long fingers towards the faerie. 'You is havings beautifully fluttersome wingys,' it uttered coming closer.

The faerie let out a petrified scream and shot into the air, waving her arms and frantically shooting golden sparks at the beast. Terrified of the bright light, it hissed and shuffled quickly away, its huge hands covering its face. It curled itself into a frightened ball and began to make a gurgling sound.

'Rosehip!' Jessica barked crossly as the faerie landed on her left shoulder. 'You frightened it! What did you do a thing like that for?'

Rosehip crossed her arms angrily. 'Me? Scare it?' she cried. 'That thing was trying to rip my wings off!'

Jessica scooped the elf into her hand and held her in front of her face. 'It wasn't,' she stated. 'Look at it.'

Both of them regarded the terrified being quaking behind one of the stalagmites. It still had its face buried in its hands and was paddling its tails nervously up and down on the rock and whining as if it was crying.

'Nasty glowy bitsys thing!' it squealed. 'Why you go all flashy, flashy, hurty, hurty? Rina is fightings Bla-Blas to be saving you and you now is makings nasty all ouchsome sparksies at me? Is not goodly at all, you is badsome icky glowy thing!'

Jessica gently placed Rosehip on the ground beside her and looked directly into the frightened creature's wide brown eyes. The animal stopped its squealing and peeped through its long fingers. It was odd, but from the first moment Jessica had laid eyes on the strange being she had felt no fear of it. Something deep inside told her that this creature meant no harm. It was as if Jessica felt an empathy with the creature, an understanding that this was more than some heartless beast. Wincing from the pain that still gripped her leg, Jessica shuffled forwards a little and reached out to the frightened animal.

'She didn't mean to harm you,' Jessica told it softly. 'You scared her, that's all.'

The creature lowered its hands from its face and gazed at Jessica. She felt as if as if she was gazing into the eyes of a long-lost friend. She didn't know how, perhaps it was one of the gifts the Guardian of Jersey possessed, but Jessica understood this creature and she was sure it understood her.

Jake, Elsa and Rosehip however, did not have such faith. All three of them remained frozen to the spot. The animal brushed a long strand of thick hair from its face and edged closer.

Jake stooped. 'Let's get out of here, while it's still scared of Rosehip,' he whispered in her ear.

Jess shot him an angry glance. 'And do what? Wander round until another troll finds us? She won't hurt us; she only wants to know what we are.'

Jake raised his eyebrows. 'She?' he queried. 'You know what sex it is now?'

Jessica brought her finger swiftly up to her lips to hush him. 'It's a she. Don't ask me how I know, but it is, okay?'

Jake shrugged. Jessica turned back to the inquisitive animal and cleared her throat. 'I know you understand me, or at least I think you do,' she said clearly, as the creature crept timidly towards them. Jessica paused for a moment and then continued. 'We want to say thank you for saving us from the trolls – you know, the Bla-Blas.'

The animal stopped in her tracks and regarded the group carefully, her huge eyes flicking from one face to another. Jessica swallowed and decided to try a different approach.

She pointed to Jake and said very clearly, 'This is Jake, Jake.' She glanced up at him and muttered, 'Say hello.'

The boy looked very pale and gave a weak wave. 'Hi,' he muttered, unwillingly.

The animal stared at him and raised a finger. 'Ake,' she repeated.

Jessica smiled, proud that the creature knew what she was saying. 'Very good,' she encouraged.

The creature pulled back its lips into a grim smile and crawled a few inches closer. Jessica's heart beat faster at the realization this strange animal knew what she was saying. She slowly placed her hand on Elsa's shoulder.

'And this, this is Elsa, El-sa.'

Elsa said nothing but looked positively terrified. The creature gazed at the girl.

'Elly-sa,' it croaked. She hopped forward a little way. 'Elly-sa is beings muchly prettily.'

Jessica chuckled and looked back at Elsa.

'She thinks you're pretty,' she told the stunned girl.

Elsa's eyes flicked to Jake. 'What is Jessica doing?' she asked him.

Jake gulped. 'I think Jess hit her head when she landed and may have gone a bit insane,' he told the child.

Rosehip huffed in amazement. 'She'll get us all eaten and I'll be first. You mark my words,' she squeaked.

The faerie was just about to spread her wings and make a bid for freedom when Jessica cupped her in her hands and held her out for the creature to see. 'And this is Rosehip,' she explained. 'She's a faerie – Rose-hip.'

The animal stopped where she was at the sight of the small elf and glanced at her warily. Her slit-like nostrils flared as she sniffed the air.

'Bah!' she said crossly. 'No, Wos-ip badsome, she is makings flashy, flashy, muchly hurtsome, bah!'

Jess was holding Rosehip's wings gently but firmly between her finger and thumb so she couldn't fly away.

'Let me go!' she complained. 'It'll eat me, you watch. One snap of those ugly fangs and it's bye-bye Rosehip.'

Jessica sighed. 'She doesn't want to eat you,' she informed the angry faerie. 'And Rosehip didn't mean to scare you. We're all friends. Friends don't hurt each other.'

Rosehip tutted and crossed her arms and the creature made a dismissive little snort.

Jessica lifted her hand up in front of her face and glared at the faerie.

'Rosehip,' she said sternly, 'say you're sorry.'

Rosehip stuck her upturned nose in the air and crossed her legs. 'I don't want to be friends with a horrible, wart-covered, fishy, monster,' she squeaked sulkily.

Jessica shrugged. 'Fine,' she said. 'You can go back in my bag if you don't want to speak to her!'

Rosehip squealed in protest as Jessica flipped open the rucksack on her knees and popped her inside.

The creature muttered something unintelligible and turned her head sadly away. Jess felt a pang of pity for the animal.

'Ignore her,' she said. 'Faeries are silly sometimes. But I'll be your friend. Would you like to know my name?'

The creature was very still for a moment, gazing at the floor of the cave. Then, very slowly, she raised her head and stared into Jessica's eyes. Jessica felt a strange tingling sensation all over her body, just the same as when she'd discovered her mother's diaries. She suddenly felt that it was no accident they had encountered this being; it was fate. Somehow this creature was connected to her destiny as the Guardian of Jersey.

The animal's eyes grew wide with amazement and its puckered mouth fell open as it said one word. 'Jecica?'

Jessica let out a gasp of astonishment. 'She knows my name.'

Jake and Elsa momentarily forgot their fear. Jake shifted his feet awkwardly.

'How on earth did it know who you were?' he asked in a hushed voice.

Elsa looked up at him. 'Perhaps it's because Jessica's the Guardian,' she said. 'They say every creature in Jersey knows about the Guardian. What do you think, Jessica?'

Jessica, however, was not listening. She sat transfixed by the creature, gazing deep into her huge, dark eyes. She felt a great empathy with the odd being seated before her and it was all Jessica could do not to cry. It was as if a great joy and an equally powerful sorrow had exploded within her and she could tell by the wide-eyed gaze of the unusual being that it was feeling the same.

The creature was clearly as moved as Jessica. Very slowly, she reached out with her long, olive-coloured finger and ever so gently touched Jessica's face as if she was trying to convince herself that the girl was real. Jessica didn't reject this gesture despite the hideous appearance of the scarred hand. She allowed the beast to trace her profile with her fingertip, from her forehead, down the bridge of her nose, across her lips to her chin. To Jessica's surprise, the skin of the creature was not as slimy as it appeared, but soft and smooth like good quality leather. The animal then placed her finger to her own features and traced them in the same manner. The creature smiled.

'My Jecica,' the being murmured, its croaky tones strained with emotion. 'My Jecica is comings back to me.'

She clutched Jessica's hand in hers and brought it to her mouth where she smothered it with wet kisses. Jess turned back to her companions and looked at them bewildered. The creature was slapping it snake-like limbs on the cave floor and making excited high screams. Unsure what the creature was so pleased about, Jessica shifted herself away from it slightly. Sensing her confusion, the animal stopped her thrilled shouts and clutched her large hands together, muttering quietly to herself as if trying to find a clear explanation. Finally she placed a hand on her chest and said as clearly as she could, 'Um is beings Rina.'

Jessica gasped. 'Rina!' she stated. 'Your name is Rina.' She nudged a confused Jake. 'See,' she enthused. 'I told you she was a girl.'

Rina nodded enthusiastically.

'But why did she save us and why is she so excited to see you?' he asked.

The strange being glanced up at him, 'I beings tellings you, Ake,' she gasped, clearly eager to explain herself. 'Rina is beings havings muchly odd feeling for way long time now. Rina is knowings ma muchly special Jecica is comings back to be with Rina. Keelie is tellings me. Rina is asking ma Keelie bring Jecica see me but Keelie he is say "no". Always he is goings "later, later", making Rina muchly crossly. But um is knowings it be very, muchly, muchly important for Rina to be seeings Jecica. So now, um is beings in um's grotty asleepsies and is hearings the Bla-Blas shuffly around. Muchly, muchly biggy noises. And,' she paused for dramatic effect and grabbed Jessica's hand before continuing, 'um is hearings screamsies of the huming-being, Rina now knows is Ake, Elly-sa and my Jecica. Rina be thinkings "that might be ma Jecica in muchly trouble!" And um is not letting nasty Bla-Blas hurting my Jecica so is gettings teethsy all way nashy sharp and handsies ready for go bam on Bla-Bla and savings Jecica and all new friends.'

Rina stopped and gave the bewildered group a broad grin. Jessica blinked hard and shook her head. Rina had chattered away at a great speed and with her odd manner of speech it was nearly impossible to understand what she was saying. She understood that the odd being had overheard their screams and rushed to their aid but she still wasn't clear why. However, one word in Rina's barely intelligible story struck Jessica.

'Keelie,' she gasped, clutching the creature's huge leathery hand. 'Do you mean Keela, the merman? I know him.'

She felt a rush of excitement at the thought of Rina being somehow connected to the outside world and a being that could possibly give her a clearer explanation as to why the snake-like girl was so pleased to see her.

Rina nodded her head enthusiastically, leaping up and down on the cave floor. 'My Keelie, my Keelie, my Keelie,' she repeated. Her face creased with concentration and it was clear that she was trying to find words to explain what the merman meant to her. 'My Keelie is beings muchly nicely to um. Is teachings Rina, is talksies to Rina, is givings Rina fishies to eat. Keelie is all Rina is knowing.' She paused for a second and gazed at Jessica with her huge brown eyes. 'But Jecica musts be promisings no tell Keelie she sees Rina. No, no, no. Keelie is nicely but he be muchly crossome with Rina if he is knowings um be comings out um's grotty. Promisings, Jecica, promisings.'

Rina looked very concerned that the merman might be cross with her and Jessica knew that even though she owed the merman a great deal, she must keep their meeting a secret from him, and indeed from everyone else.

'I promise,' she reassured the creature.

Jessica shuffled forward a few inches to get closer to the beast but once again the piercing agony in her shin flared and she yelped in pain. Concerned, Jake crouched down beside her and examined her limb. Elsa gazed over Jessica's shoulder, her pale face harrowed with anxiety.

Rina looked worried. 'Jecica hurting?' she queried Jake as he placed a hand on Jessica's calf.

Before he realized what he was doing Jake had answered, 'Yeah, she caught her leg when she jumped.'

He stopped abruptly, stared at the creature and shook his head. 'Now I'm talking to it,' he muttered incredulously.

Rina's scarred face wrinkled with concern for Jessica's plight. She looked at the leg Jessica was gripping in pain and also at the foul, crusted residue that encased her right hand. She made a sympathetic gurgling purr and lowered her head towards Jessica's hand. Jessica drew back.

'No,' she explained. 'This is the troll's blood – remember Bla-Bla. You could catch something from it.'

But Rina took no notice. Carefully, she extended her black tongue and began lovingly to lick Jessica's scarred hand. Through the disgusting black scab that sheathed her fingers Jessica could feel the warm wetness of Rina's tongue as she lapped at the dry blood. A tingling sensation spread through her hand as if it was being bathed in very warm water. Tiny cracks begun to appear in the uneven, dark scar and Jess watched as the foul shell crumbled away, freeing her hand. In relief, she flexed her fingers and momentarily forgot the pain in her leg.

'How did you do that?' she asked.

Rina, however, had not finished and now turned her attention to Jessica's injured leg.

The creature seemed to be almost in a trance as she went to work healing her newfound friend. She did not speak or make a sound but moved very slowly, almost gracefully down to Jessica's wounded limb. Her huge, dark eyes regarded the leg as she sat perfectly still for a moment. Slowly, she bowed down and rested her wart-covered forehead on the exact spot that was the centre of the pain. Jessica gritted her teeth as the throbbing in her limb erupted again. However, the agony lasted only a few seconds before it was replaced by an intensely warm pressure, like someone putting a hot towel on her wound. The heat seemed to be coming directly from Rina's forehead as the odd animal crouched beside Jessica rocking her head from side to side ever so slightly. Jessica felt wave after wave of soothing, gentle heat wash through her wound, soothing all hurt and injury. Both Jake and Elsa gazed at her, unsure what to do. Jake's instinct was to stop the creature but it soon became apparent that, far from harming Jessica, Rina was helping her in some way.

After a few minutes, the warmth in Jessica's leg diminished and Rina lifted her head and shook it slightly as if she had just woken. Cautiously, Jessica shifted her leg a few inches and was amazed to discover there was no pain in it. Jake stared in utter bewilderment.

'You okay?' he asked her as Jess bent her knee and flexed her toe.

'Yes,' she murmured. 'In fact, I think I can stand.'

Tentatively, and with one arm around Jake's shoulder, Jessica got to her feet. She was scared at first to put any weight upon her newly healed leg, but once Jake had helped her stand she quickly discovered it was perfectly healthy and as stable as it ever was. She took a few steps to make sure she was completely okay and was amazed to discover she felt no pain or weakness in the limb that moments before had been immobile.

Elsa took a step forward and regarded her friend's healed leg. 'But how?' she murmured. 'It must be magic.'

Jake scratched his head and looked down at Rina, who was squatting dog-like, on her back fins. 'Merfolk can't heal, nor can faeries – well, not like that anyway,' he muttered. 'How did she manage to do it?'

Jessica touched Rina's thick, dark hair. It felt wet and slightly rubbery like lengths of seaweed. 'Thank you,' she said softly, 'I don't know what you did but thank you.'

The mystery being made a purring sound and shrugged her scarred shoulders as if to say she didn't know how she'd healed Jessica either.

Jake glanced down at his watch. 'Just gone seven o'clock,' he said. 'No wonder the trolls attacked. I bet the sun's beginning to set already. Remember, Jim said be out by nightfall. We've got to find a way back to the surface.'

He began gazing around the cavern looking for an exit.

'Maybe Rina knows how we can get out,' suggested Jessica.

The creature's beautiful, brown eyes grew large and her puckered mouth opened in a tiny 'Ooo'. She pointed a long, green, nail-less finger up to the roof of the cave.

'Ake and Elly-sa and Jecica is wanting to go uppy 'bove?' she questioned.

The trio nodded. Rina swiftly turned away from them and began to crawl, using her muscular arms to propel herself. After a few feet she stopped and glanced back at them.

'Oo come, oo come this way!' she enthused, beckoning with her huge, green hand. 'Rina is knowings the way.'

Jessica picked up her rucksack with Rosehip still screaming inside and set off after Rina. 'Come on!' she told the others.

Elsa blinked her pale eyes in confusion. 'Do you think we should?' she asked timidly.

Jessica sighed, not wanting to get cross with Elsa but eager to get out of the cave as soon as possible. 'If she wanted to hurt us she would have done it by now, and like Jake said, we've gotta get to the shore before sundown.'

Jake and Elsa gave each other a nervous look but both knew if they tried to find their own way out they could easily run into more trouble.

Jake swallowed and took Elsa's hand. 'Once more unto the breach, dear friend; once more, we follow our unfaltering leader,' he said, displaying a glimmer of his trademark sense of humour.

With Elsa trotting nervously at his side, Jake followed Jessica through the gloomy blackness of the cavern. All round them, the mighty stalagmites reached up to the domed roof like malformed, wizards' hats. Jessica kept in hot pursuit of Rina as she shuffled swiftly among the imposing stone giants. The creature moved remarkably quickly despite her ungainly manner. The humans followed her as she rounded a stalagmite and stopped to rest before a mighty opening in the cave wall, about ten foot wide and twenty high. Jessica gazed into the gap. From the very top, a narrow shaft of pale sunlight shone, illuminating the rocky slope that led out of the cave. The hill was steep and made up of rough, uneven stone. Jessica's face broke into a joyful smile as she gazed up at the tiny window of light that would surely end their journey through the hellish Magicroutes.

'There!' she cried to her friends, pointing into the opening. 'I can see sunlight. We're almost out.'

Rina seemed to share her excitement. She made a series of playful little leaps, slapping her large hands and fins on the cold rock. 'Uppy 'bove, uppy 'bove!' she gurgled happily. 'Rina help see, see?'

She scuttled forward and began to climb up the pile of rocks.

Jake and Elsa joined Jessica at the foot of the slope and gazed up at the chink of light.

'I don't believe it!' murmured Jake, his eyes fixed on the shaft of brightness flooding the dank shadows of the cave. 'She's found a way out.'

Jess tutted and shook her head. 'What did you expect?' she told him. 'I knew Rina was trying to help us. Now let's get out of here!'

Hastily, Jessica, shaking from tiredness and excitement, began to climb up to the light. Jake and Elsa, who were feeling more than a little worse for wear after their harrowing experience, felt their energy renewed at the prospect of returning to the safety of the outside world. Pulling themselves together, they started to pick their way up gradually through the jagged boulders. Rina was having no trouble scaling the steep mound, however, and her gravelly voice came in short eager cries, egging them on.

'Come Jecica, come Ake, come prettily Elly-sa. Almost all done, almost uppy 'bove.'

The creature dragged herself with relative ease up the rocks while the three companions scrabbled behind her and soon all four beings were at the top.

Jessica took a deep breath and gazed at the outside world. The outlet led into a small sea cave filled to about five feet below the gap she was looking through with seawater and with a stone ledge running round the edge. Through the entrance of the cave she beheld the still sea stretching out before her and the bright, orange sun dipping into it on the horizon.

She laughed with joy as she placed an arm around Elsa's shoulder. 'We made it.'

Rina chuckled and clapped her hands. 'Now all go uppy 'bove now,' she cried.

Eagerly, Jake and Jessica scrambled through the hole on the ledge and breathed in the sweet, sea air to clear the stench of the caves from their lungs. They took hold of Elsa's hands and hoisted the tiny girl out beside them. Rina smiled broadly but remained just inside the tunnel.

'Jecica go home now,' she enthused. 'And Ake and Elly-sa all be safeness.' She regarded Jessica and her deep, chocolate eyes softened. 'Jecica be back soon, talksies to Rina,' she said in a deep voice, filled with emotion.

'I promise,' she whispered, so low neither Jake nor Elsa could hear. 'Thank you, Rina, for everything.'

Jessica glanced at the sunset for a moment, but when she turned to face the cave again, she found that Rina had vanished into the murky darkness.

Chapter 12

Recovery and Research

'She's vanished,' Jessica said sadly, staring back into the tiny gap in the cave wall where moments before Rina had been.

Jake stood up on the narrow ledge where they were all perched and stretched, inhaling the fresh sea air. 'Well, at least we're out alive,' he said. 'I'll be honest with you now – there were times back there when I didn't think we'd make it.'

He helped Elsa to her feet and brushed some of the dirt and grime from her dress. Jessica, however, remained seated beside the narrow entrance, running her fingertips around the fissure in the rock. She definitely did not want to re-enter the domain of the Black Trolls, but she felt disappointed that the odd creature who had saved and healed her had disappeared into the dank depths of the Magicroutes without her truly knowing who, or what, she was.

'I never got a chance to say goodbye,' she murmured, caressing the damp stone.

Elsa blinked and brushed a straggly length of blonde hair from her face. 'To the Black Trolls?' she asked in bewilderment.

Jake snorted.

'No,' said the older girl. She got to her feet and leant against the cave wall. 'I wanted to say goodbye to Rina.'

Jake wiped his dirty hands on his equally filthy jeans. 'I saved your life too, remember?' he said. 'And so did Elsa, back in the main chamber. Why are you so taken with ... well, whatever she was?'

Jessica stared down at her arm, which had been burnt by the troll blood but now, thanks to Rina, was completely healed. 'I know,' she admitted, looking at her friends, 'and I'm very

235

grateful, believe me. But Rina...' she shook her head, 'I don't know. There was something about her. Do either of you know of a creature that could mend a twisted ankle by touching it?'

Jake and Elsa shook their heads.

'Faerie blood has some healing properties but nothing that powerful,' Jake said. 'Look, all I know at the moment is the sooner we get out of this cave, the sooner we can get home. Quite frankly, Jess, you look like death warmed up!'

Jessica smirked. 'You're one to talk,' she retorted, 'and Elsa's not much better! We all look like we've been dragged through a hedge backwards.'

It was true. The three of them were cut and bruised and their clothes were tattered and filthy. Jessica had a stinging graze on her right cheek and her hair was tangled with dirt, dry blood and débris. Her T-shirt hung off her shoulders in shreds and her back and arms were covered with a criss-cross of weeping cuts from her uncomfortable descent from the troll. Jake's face too was grimy from the dirt of the cave and there was a deep slash above his eyebrow. His chequered shirt, though it had looked old and worn that morning, was now fit only for the dustbin. A large bruise tattooed his exposed arm. At his side, looking without a doubt the worst of the three, stood Elsa. Her dress was so filthy with algae and mud that the floral pattern was barely visible. Her skin was paper white, tinged with green, as if she were about to be sick. Her hands, face, legs and neck were covered in tiny cuts and bruises and her hair was almost grey with dust. Around her right eye, a dark purple swelling had begun to form. She was breathing in shallow pants and Jess could hear a rattling wheeze in her chest. The child did not look well. Jessica knew the terror of the troll attack and the dampness of the cave environment could have done nothing to help the mysterious illness that plagued Elsa.

She glanced at Jake. 'You're right,' she said seriously. 'We need to get home and fast. Elsa looks very weak. D'you think you can carry her?'

Jake was clearly exhausted but he took off his rucksack and slung it to Jessica. 'Sure,' he breathed. 'Come on, little one – piggy-back time.'

Sighing wearily he bent down and allowed Elsa to clamber onto his back. The tiny child wrapped her spindly arms and legs around him as Jake hoisted her up. Jessica tucked Jake's bag under her arm and the three of them trudged along the ledge out onto the uneven rocks that skirted the breaking waves. The air was fresh and full of spray as they picked their way among the ridges and rock-pools at the base of the towering cliffs. In the sky above, noisy seagulls screamed and against the angry, flaming light of the setting sun a tall, thin tower was silhouetted, protruding straight and proud from the waters of the bay.

Jake gazed at the structure as it stood like a giant soldier, guarding the coastline of Jersey. 'Grosnez Lighthouse,' he announced, pointing at the prominent edifice. 'We're only about a quarter of a mile from Plemount.'

Jessica sheltered her eyes with her hand. 'How are we going to get there?' she asked him.

'Quickest way would be by sea. Plemount is literally round the corner from here. It's nearly dusk so we could call Keela or some of the others and they could take us.'

Jessica gripped Jake's rucksack to her chest and shook her head. It wasn't that she didn't trust the merman, far from it. The kind and honourable sea-dweller had shown her perhaps more aid and been more truthful than anyone else on the island when he had rescued her from drowning and forced Jim to reveal what had really happened to her mother. It was that she kept remembering the crudely spoken words Rina had uttered to her in the caves. 'No tell Keelie.' Rina had been adamant that Jessica was not to let the merman know they had met. Keela had struck Jessica as a creature with a good, quick mind and if they told him they had been exploring the Magicroutes he would be bound to ask them what they found. Jessica did not think that, at present, she had a convincing enough lie to offer him.

She shook her head. 'I don't think that's a good idea. It's still light and he might be spotted. Besides, Rosehip is still in my bag and she would drown if we went back by water, not to mention what the cold would do to Elsa's chest.'

She glanced at the small child hanging limply onto Jake's shoulders, her head resting wearily against the boy's dark hair. Jake looked as if he was about to agree with Jessica, when their eyes met and he gazed at her suspiciously.

237

'Oh now I remember,' he said wryly. 'Now I know what you're doing. This isn't about it being too light, being worried, or about Rosehip or Elsa. You're scared Keela's going to find out about us seeing Rina!'

Angrily Jessica brushed her hair from her eyes. 'No, it's not that at all!' she said defensively. She steadied herself on the rocks and rested her hands on her hips. 'Okay, so what if I don't want him to know about her? What harm can it do?'

'I just don't understand why you are so taken with such an odd creature?'

'I don't know either!' she replied crossly. 'Why are *you* so against her. I just think that we don't know enough about her to go around telling everyone. I don't want anyone to know about her, okay?'

'What are you frightened of, Jessica?' he asked. 'Why should she mean so much to you?'

Jessica shut her eyes. An image of Rina making her way back through the Magicroutes to the place she called home swam into her mind and she seemed to know what Rina was doing and feeling as clearly as if she was there herself.

'She's scared,' she uttered bluntly, eyes still closed. 'Keela told her to stay, stay where it was safe. She'd been impatient. The time was coming soon when we would meet. She'd done what she thought was right but if Keela knew, if anyone knew, she'd be in trouble.'

Jessica opened her eyes and looked at her companions. The vision had lasted only a matter of seconds and now it had vanished completely. 'We don't understand enough about her. I just know she's good and I don't want her hurt.'

'Okay,' Jake murmured. 'No-one will hear about her from me.'

'Nor me,' Elsa whispered, her voice faint with weakness and fatigue. Jessica glanced around the craggy shoreline. A steep wooden staircase clung to the granite about twenty feet from where they were standing. Not quite a ladder, it reached the fifty or so feet up to the cliff-top and was constructed from thick chunks of barnacle-encrusted wood. Despite its odd location it looked safe and sturdy. She nudged Jake and pointed. 'What about that over there?' she asked, drawing his gaze towards the wooden steps. Jake looked.

'The old scavenger's ladder?' he queried. 'Yeah, that'll take us up to the cliff top, right onto the five mile road. It'll be perfect, come on.'

He held Elsa firmly to make sure she didn't slip from his back and he and Jess made their way along the stony outcrop towards the flight of stairs that would lead them home.

Running up either side of the stairway was a thick rope banister which Jessica clung to gratefully as they climbed. The journey was slow and slightly awkward owing to the fact she was still carrying Jake's rucksack for him whilst trying to grip the loose ropes for support. Jake too, picked out his footing with care, clinging to the slack barrier with his left hand while hanging onto Elsa with his right. The climb was steep and their legs throbbed with weariness.

'I'm glad that it's here,' Jessica puffed, 'but this is a funny place for someone to build a staircase.'

Jake looked up from a few steps below her. 'I told you, it's a scavenger's ladder – or a replica one anyway.'

'What's a scavenger's ladder?'

'The water in this area is very shallow. Before the lighthouse was built, a lot of cargo ships got wrecked around here. When a ship went down, it was seen as ... well ... acceptable to some of the more unscrupulous islanders to come down and steal what they could of the cargo washed up at the bottom of the cliff. They made ladders so they could climb down. This isn't an original – it's too sturdy. The real ones were made of rope so they could be rolled up and hidden from the authorities.'

'What a load of cut-throats and thieves you Jerseymen are!'

Jake chuckled. 'Yes, and yours is the oldest family on the island so I wouldn't be surprised if there weren't past guardians who had rogues as siblings!'

Jessica raised her eyebrows but said nothing. The three of them clambered to the top of the steps and out onto the cliff-top overlooking Grosnez. They found themselves on a barren grey expanse of rough heathland, stretching parallel to the straight five mile road that skirted the coast around this corner of the island. The whole area was an odd mix of sparse, natural beauty and half-derelict man-made structures. Clumps of bristly, dark gorse blanketed the flat land, looking almost dead apart from the small yellow flowers that bloomed among the snagging thorns. The grass all around them was unkempt and rippled in

239

the chill, dusk wind like the waves of the sea. To their left, along the coastline, they could see a large shabby building, its formerly gleaming white walls now dull and stained from the rigours of the coastal weather. The windows were dark and lifeless, like those of so many abandoned tourist haunts up and down the island. In front a notice, barely readable through the grime and peeling paint, declared it to have been 'The Watersplash Nightclub'. Cars droned monotonously up and down the straight expanse of road. It was hard for Jessica to believe that the ancient and mystical realm of the Magicroutes had ever existed.

The small troop trudged through the grass and, upon reaching the road, turned east towards 'The Watersplash'. Above them, the sky was a clear silky violet, pricked here and there with emerging stars.

Jessica and Jake hobbled slightly with tiredness and the pain of their minor wounds. Elsa lolled exhausted on Jake's back, drifting in and out of shallow slumber. Every few seconds, Jessica would glance at the child's sallow face to check she was still okay. Jake, battling hard against his own tiredness, focused on the cliffs of Plemount that rose in front of them, growing ever closer as they marched onwards. Jessica hugged herself for warmth against the bitter chill and gazed wistfully out at the rippling waves. During their silent journey along the cliff, her thoughts had once again turned to the odd creature, Rina, who had shown such bravery and kindness towards her. Her ignorance of the magic creatures of Jersey hadn't particularly troubled her until now. Rosehip seemed to have a knowledge that was of little use, but Keela and the merfolk were articulate and wise enough to explain their role in the life of the Guardian of Jersey. But the more she pondered about Rina (and without a doubt, the being's existence haunted her persistently), the more of an enigma she appeared to be. She was clearly a creature of magic and yet a true islander such as Jake had been totally unaware of her presence. Her crude speech and uncivilized manner told Jessica she should be a lower life form, not as intelligent as a human or merperson, and yet she knew clearly who Jessica was and probably realized she was the Guardian. She also knew Keela well. Jessica gazed down at her left leg as they strolled along. She was sure the fall had fractured her calf but, just by resting her hideous head upon the wound, Rina seemed to have mended the bone. What kind of creature could heal but remain so ugly it would surely be ostracized from society? What bothered Jessica the most was the powerful feeling of empathy and compassion for Rina that so overwhelmed her.

'I wonder if she's cold,' she murmured quietly, almost unaware the words had left her mouth.

Jake turned wearily, his eyelids drooping. 'What?' he muttered as Elsa too lifted her tired head to look at Jess. 'Who?'

'Rina,' explained Jess. 'I was just imagining how cold those caves must be after dark. Not to mention dangerous, with all those trolls running about and God knows what else.'

'From what I saw,' Jake said dully, 'Rina, or whatever she was, could well take care of herself.'

'You really don't know what kind of creature she was, Jake?'

'You've got a bee in your bonnet about this one now, haven't you, Grockle?' he chided wearily. 'No, I haven't got a clue what it was. It was hideous and bizarre and I've never seen anything quite as weird in my whole life.'

'Don't speak about her like that, it hurts our feelings!' she barked.

'I'm sorry,' he protested, shocked by the ferocity of her outburst. He paused. 'Did you just say "hurt *our* feelings"?'

'I meant her, hurt *her* feelings. Anyway, you seem to have missed the point. What I'm trying to say is don't you think it's a little strange that there's a creature like that living in Jersey who knows me but wants to keeps itself completely secret and that even you know nothing about? I mean, what could it possibly be?' She quickly turned her eyes away, unnerved by the realization that he was indeed correct and she had said 'our'.

Jake bit his lip and stared thoughtfully at the horizon. 'It is odd,' he agreed, his voice softening. 'Whatever she is, she's clearly a creature of magic.'

Jessica stopped walking and pointed at the sea.

'She said she knew Keela. Perhaps she is a mermaid.'

Jake was far from convinced by this theory. 'She didn't look anything like a mermaid,' he said dismissively. 'All those warts, that thick sea-weedy hair and two tails? When have you seen a mermaid looking like that?'

He had continued strolling along the cliff path as Jessica stopped and tried to put her thoughts into order. Now she had to jog along for a few metres to catch up with him. She reached his side.

'Until yesterday I didn't know what a mermaid looked like at all,' she informed him. 'I'm just making guesses here. Maybe she's a mermaid who is ill in some way, disabled or something, and the others put her in that cave to get better.'

Jake paused for the briefest of moments and for a second Jessica thought he was impressed. Then he spoke.

'Do you ever listen to yourself when you speak?' he asked. 'Do you know what complete and utter garbage you talk at times? I can't believe you are the Guardian! You know nothing about merfolk or magic!'

Jessica glared at him. Jake was using the same patronizing tone she'd heard him use before. She gave him an angry shove which woke Elsa from her slumber.

'I never claimed I knew anything about magic creatures,' she growled, rage boiling inside her. 'I just believe we should find out what she is. I was simply making a suggestion. If it is misguided don't insult me without saying why you think I'm wrong.'

'Lesson one in merfolk,' Jake began. 'They are a deeply compassionate and caring race. If a child is born with any deformity, and note that in their species that's about one in a million, it is aided and nurtured by the whole community and treated the same as any other merchild. Merfolk parents never, ever abandon their offspring.'

As he spoke Jessica gazed thoughtfully at the scrawny figure of Elsa clinging weakly to his shoulders. Her skin was still very pale and her eyelids kept fluttering open and closed as she struggled to keep awake. Jessica placed a concerned hand on the child's back and to her horror, realized that through the threadbare material of her dress she could feel the bony ridge of her spine. If Jake was right, disabled merchildren had a far better chance in life than some unfortunate humans.

Jake groaned, aware that he did not have Jessica's full attention. 'Are you listening to me?' he asked, impatiently.

'Yes I am,' Jessica said loudly in his ear.

Jake ignored her anger. 'Lesson Two: merfolk depend on the sea for their survival. It is the environment that their bodies are designed to live in. It is virtually impossible for a merperson to

242

survive long periods out of water. If that creature had been an abandoned mermaid, she would have wanted to get back in the sea as soon as possible, not, as she did, return to the caves. And while we're at it, Lesson Three: merfolk cannot heal.'

'So, she's not a mermaid.'

Jake glanced at her out of the corner of his eye. 'That's what I told you in the first place,' he said with an air of superiority.

Jessica scraped her feet along the pavement. In the rucksack hanging loosely from her shoulders she could feel the gentle fluttering of Rosehip and she knew that the impertinent sprite was eager to be released. However, the bluish glow of twilight still bathed the cliffs of Jersey and the cars that zoomed up and down the road beside them at frequent intervals meant that it would be impossible to release the faerie without someone spotting her.

'Well,' said Jessica, 'I am guessing Rina was too big to be any kind of faerie. Am I right?'

Jake nodded but remained silent, trudging steadily along.

Jessica stared up at the early evening sky that seemed to be darkening before her very eyes from a powdery mauve to the deep navy of night. Nothing was said for a few moments. Then Jake's pace slowed and an odd expression came over his angular features, as if he had just remembered something.

'It's a long shot of course,' he began, 'but she could be...' He stopped and shook his head.

'Go on,' she said. 'Could be a what?'

'It's stupid!' he told her. 'I don't know why it even entered my head. It's even worse than some of your ideas, Grockle. Totally ridiculous.'

Jess raised her eyebrows and gazed at him. 'Being told I'm descended from St Helier, that's ridiculous,' she said dryly. 'Being saved from a cursed pendant by merpeople, that's ridiculous; us getting attacked and nearly eaten by Black Trolls, that's ridiculous. I'm telling you Jake, after what I've been through in the last twenty-four hours, ridiculous is beginning to be what I trust the most.'

'You won't believe me,' he sang. 'You will think I'm crazy, I know you. You are a logical, sceptical, town-dwelling Grockle and you will fly off the handle the moment I say it. A Jersey boy like me even finds it hard to believe.'

Jessica threw back her head and let out a groan. 'Look,' she said honestly, 'I'm the Guardian of Jersey, protector of the island, friend to all the magic creatures, even the incredibly annoying ones. It has come as a bigger surprise to me than anyone, but fate says that's what I am. So, like it or not, I have to say goodbye to old cynical, non-believing London Jessica and take on board whatever magic and myths that apparently are real. So tell me what you think it is?'

Jake made a weak little sigh and scowled as if anticipating Jessica's explosion of incredulity. 'Now I'm not saying I think it could be this,' he said. 'I mean it is virtually impossible. Like you, I'm just making a suggestion. But there is a very, very, very small chance that it might be...' He paused and took a deep breath, 'A dragon.'

'A dragon!' she gasped, so loudly Elsa was shaken from her fitful slumber.

The child rubbed her weary eyes and looked at Jessica in confusion. 'What?' she murmured sleepily.

Jessica pointed at Jake. 'He thinks that Rina's a dragon!'

Elsa was suddenly very much awake, her eyes wide with disbelief. 'That can't be,' she whispered. 'Dragons have been extinct for centuries.'

Jake hung his head and sighed in exasperation.

'I never said I thought it was a dragon,' he explained, trying to keep his patience. 'I said there was a tiny, microscopic possibility that it could be. It was a stupid suggestion and there are plenty of reasons why it couldn't be a dragon.'

He bit his lip and hoisted the now wide-awake Elsa further up his back. The fragile girl gazed down at Jessica from her perch.

'They're extinct, you know,' she reiterated softly as they continued their journey.

Jake looked straight ahead wearing a look that said he greatly regretted mentioning the idea of dragons and thus giving Jessica something else to be obsessed about.

'The last record of a dragon living in Britain was in the twelfth century,' he explained to a thoughtful Jessica. 'It was quite common for knights to slay a dragon to prove their bravery. I'm sure even you have heard of that. Too many knights plus too few dragons meant that the dragons died out. The big pity of the whole story is that people didn't really start researching the habits of dragons until they were all gone. That's why there is so little written about them. There was a school of thought that saw them as more than fire-breathing monsters. The greatest researcher into dragons was a man called Christen Robert Hiegman – great believer in the supernatural, lived in the early 1800s. Travelled all over Britain researching the magical creatures – very famous in certain circles. He believed dragons had great intelligence and many powers.'

Jessica mulled over what Jake has said. The name Christen Hiegman struck a chord in her brain; she was sure she had seen it recently. But the possibility that the animal that had saved their lives was indeed a dragon seemed too far-fetched even to be part of the magical heritage of Jersey. However, she was determined to keep an open mind.

'It's a very small dragon if it is one,' she stated. 'Correct me if I'm wrong, but aren't dragons meant to be huge?'

Jake nodded. 'True,' he said. 'A good thirty feet tall if you believe the records. But I was thinking that if a dragon laid an egg and it got lodged deep in those caves many years ago, there could be a possibility that it survived there for centuries and only recently hatched.' He paused. 'It's a stupid idea. The chances of it being a dragon are one in a million.'

Jessica fixed him with a sly look. 'So about the same odds as it being a disabled mermaid,' she observed dryly.

Elsa hugged her spindly arms around Jake's neck and gazed down at Jessica, her right eye nearly closed.

'Dragon breath can heal,' she told them softly. Both Jessica and Jake looked at her amazed that the child should know anything about the long vanished creatures of magic.

'How did you know that?' asked the boy.

The child blinked her huge eyes in momentary confusion as if she didn't quite know how to answer. 'In a book,' she whispered. 'I read it in a book.'

Jessica gave an interested little grunt and raised her eyebrows. 'Do you remember if the book said anything else?' she asked.

Elsa looked thoughtful and rested her head against Jake's shoulder. 'The stab of a dragon's claw can kill anything instantly,' she said as the wild evening wind tussled her fine hair. She closed her eyes. 'That's all I remember.'

Jake gave Jessica a wry glance, as Elsa seemed to drift back

245

into slumber. 'You're going to fixate over this now, aren't you?' he said dryly. 'You're going to go on and on about dragons and because I'm meant to be looking out for you, I'm going to get dragged along on a wild goose chase, or is that goosed along on a wild dragon chase!'

The silly pun made Jessica smile but she knew that Jake had a point.

'I just think we should follow up every possible avenue – and, anyway, you were the one who brought up dragons in the first place.'

Jake gritted his teeth. 'Yeah,' he said ruefully, 'and don't I regret it.'

They continued to walk as they discussed the possible beings Rina might be and by now, almost without realizing it, had reached the car park overlooking Plemount. The bay looked very different now from the bright seaside resort they had left behind earlier that day. The golden sand now appeared muddy in the dim light of dusk and was blemished here and there by the ruins of proud sandcastles and footprints of departed tourists. They could hear the rush of the sea as it washed the shoreline. The coast was deserted now apart from one lone squat figure who sat hunched up close to the cliff wall, his curly, grey hair ruffled in the breeze.

Jessica gazed down. 'It's Jim,' she told her companions, her voice filled with joy.

During their dangerous venture into the Magicroutes of Jersey, they had seemed miles away from any other humans and Jessica was glad to see her great uncle still waiting patiently for their return. Jake followed her gaze and his face broke into a lop-sided grin.

'Good old Jim,' he muttered. 'I knew he'd be waiting for us.'

The lanky youth was just about to trot down the wooden steps that led to the beach when Jessica caught his arm.

'Remember what we agreed,' she muttered to him and Elsa who had just re-awoken. 'Jim can't know about Rina – not for the moment anyway.'

Jake was becoming a bit weary of Jessica always telling him what to do. 'Okay!' he groaned.' But what are we going to say?'

Jessica bit her lip thoughtfully. 'I don't know,' she said. 'I'll think of something.'

Then, unable to control her excitement at being reunited with the human world, she turned and quickly clambered down the staircase, Jake hot on her heels.

The old man who, until now, had been sitting forlornly on the sand, his eyes trained on the cave through which the young people had disappeared, was shaken by the sudden sound of eager footsteps on the steps leading down to the beach. He was surprised and overjoyed to see his great-niece and her two friends ambling towards him. 'Thank God, they've made it,' he murmured, before getting up and jogging merrily towards them, his short, chubby legs sinking in the soft sand.

He met them with a happy shout and flung his arms around his young relative in a great bear hug which Jessica was more than pleased to return. He then stood back and gazed at them, his ruddy face glowing with pride.

'Jess love, Elsa, Jake, my lad. Thank goodness you're all here. I was beginning to think you'd had your chips!'

He glanced from one young person to another his eyes glowing. Then he looked up to the cliff top. 'But how did you get up there? I was waiting for you to come back through the cave.'

Jake lowered Elsa to the ground but kept a steadying arm around the weak girl. 'We found another way out from the Magicroutes,' he explained, slightly out of breath. 'From a cave in the cliff at Grosnez. We climbed up the scavenger's ladder and walked along the cliff top.'

Jim stood still for a second staring at them and scratching his balding brow. The old man seemed unable to believe that the three young people had returned in one piece. Then his eyes filled with concern as he noticed their shabby appearances.

'Look at you!' he said. 'You all look as if you've been dragged through a hedge backwards, stared Death in the face, shook his hand and said "Howd'ya do?".'

He began fussing about the three young people in a surprisingly maternal manner that contradicted his rough, weathered appearance. 'Are you okay?' he asked earnestly, as his examination flitted from Elsa's black eye to Jake's bruised arm to the graze on Jess's face. 'Any bumped heads? Twisted ankles? Broken bones?'

Jess caught hold of her great uncle's broad wrist to stop his clumsy nursing. 'We're fine,' she told him. 'Just a little bumped and bruised, that's all.' She took a deep breath and paused before adding, 'We were attacked by trolls.'

An expression of absolute dismay formed upon the old Jersyman's aged features. 'My God!' he said. 'They're back.' The old man seemed momentarily lost in shock as he struggled to digest the news. 'That means there are definitely witches on the island again. But Keela said nothing. Does he know?

'When did this happen? How many were there? Did they bite you?'

His questions were frantic and earnest and Jessica struggled to keep up. She was very aware that if she wished to keep the existence of the mysterious Rina a secret she would have to come up with a plausible explanation about what happened in the Magicroutes and how she and her friends survived their blood-chilling ordeal.

'We were exploring one of the tunnels when we accidentally woke one up,' she explained honestly, trying desperately to assemble her thoughts into some kind of logical order. 'It chased us into this big cave. Elsa was nearly bitten, on the arm, but Rosehip and I managed to fight it off.'

Jim listened to her gabble anxiously, his eyes flitting from Jessica to Elsa. The young girl clung wearily to Jake's arms and half buried her face in his shirt.

'There were lots,' she murmured, almost unconsciously. 'Lots of trolls. Scary.'

'How many?' demanded Jim.

Jessica tried to defuse the situation, aware that her great uncle was getting flustered. 'It wasn't that many really,' she said. 'No more than eight.'

Jim fixed her with a fearful stare. He had crouched down on one knee to speak to Elsa and was now taking off his jacket to wrap around the girl.

'Eight!' he exclaimed. 'You may not realize this, Jess, but eight is a lot of Black Trolls. How on earth did you get out alive?'

Jessica quickly glanced at her two friends and uttered the first thing that entered her head.

'Jake saved us,' she exclaimed.

Jim looked shocked as did the young lad Jessica had named as their hero. She caught Jake's bewildered stare and shot him

248

a look that conveyed most clearly that he should go along with anything she said.

'Is that right, Jake lad?' asked the old man.

Jake himself had been shaken by Jessica's sudden announcement that it was he who had fought off the viscious beasts. Despite his active boasting that he would protect Jessica whatever foe she faced, Jake found himself short of an explanation when pronounced a hero. Confused, he stood there rubbing the back of his neck.

'Yeah, er ... I, well, er ... I saved them,' he muttered stiffly. His wide, blue eyes flew to Jessica for support as he fought for words.

Exasperated at Jake's lack of imagination, Jessica took the opportunity to punch him swiftly on the arm while Jim was fastening his coat around Elsa's bony shoulders.

'He was ever so brave!' she told her great uncle. 'There we all were, the four of us, surrounded by Black Trolls when Jake leaps forward, rips the arm from his shirt, pulls out a box of matches from his pocket, lights the material and hurls it at the trolls. They were so afraid of the fire they ran off and we managed to escape.'

Jim's face wore a mixture of disbelief and admiration as he studied the youth. Jake kept his eyes firmly on the sandy ground, still unsure what to say. He could feel his face turning scarlet and prayed that Jim would think that it was because of his noble modesty and not in fact because he hadn't a clue what Jessica was getting him in to.

The old man caught his gaze with his penetrating dark eyes.

'That's very brave of you, lad,' he murmured, his voice hushed in bewilderment.

Jake took a deep breath and composed himself just enough to make what he hoped was a credible statement. 'Well, needs must in the call of duty,' he said. 'I swore I would protect the Guardian and that I did.'

He crossed his arms and took up what he considered to be a suitable heroic pose. Jessica glanced at Jake from the corner of her eye and allowed herself to emit a small groan of despair. Jake's victory speech had been full of the false masculine waffle the farmer's son always seemed to use when he was desperately trying to regain control of a situation that had been snatched suddenly away from him.

Jim eyed the young man with moderate suspicion. He liked Jake. The lad was honest and trustworthy but he had never struck Jim as being especially courageous. Still, he could think of no other plausible explanation of how the three young people had escaped a vicious troll attack. Jake was healthy – it was possible that with the aid of fire he could have frightened the evil creatures away.

He looked at Elsa. The child was shivering and her pale blue eyes seemed to have a vacancy about them as if she were struggling to concentrate on the world around her. Jim gathered her up in his arms and looked at her fellow travellers.

'I want to get Elsa back to our house as soon as possible,' he told them. 'I'm going to make up a batch of witch-hunters' broth. It's the only thing to calm you after a Black Troll attack, drives the evil from the blood. You could all do with some, but especially Elsa.' He paused for a second and regarded Jake intently. 'Well done, lad. What you did was very brave. You should be proud of yourself.'

He then turned his back on the pair and proceeded to walk towards the wooden staircase with Elsa cradled snugly in his arms.

When he was far enough away, Jake spun to face Jessica and gave her a confused and angry glare. 'What you go and do that for?' he hissed, losing his air of valour.

Jessica slung his rucksack back to him. 'Do what?' she asked.

'Why did you tell Jim I rescued you from the Black Trolls?'

'I needed an explanation of how we escaped unharmed. I told you I don't think Jim should know about Rina, not yet anyway. It was the best I could come up with at short notice.'

She gave a little shrug and began to stroll after Jim. The lanky lad gave a tired whimper and followed her, still unsatisfied with his role of rescuer.

'Yes,' he continued, 'but why me? Why not Elsa or Rosehip, or you for that matter? I am not a good liar, as well you know.'

Jessica continued her steady pace, unaffected by Jake's pleas.

'I don't know why you are making such a fuss about it,' she said. 'You're the one who's always saying it's his job to protect me, how I need a man to look after my well being. So now I'm agreeing with you – as far as Jim is concerned it was your quick wits and bravery that saved Rosehip, Elsa and me from being troll food. You should be happy.'

Jake pulled a face as if he had just swallowed something very unpleasant and shook his head.

'Well credit where credit's due, I did save you once today – the ledge, remember? So at least it's a half-truth. But I still think we should have agreed on a story before.'

They had reached the steps and Jessica had begun to climb back up to the car park. She paused and glanced over her shoulder.

'My mum was the Guardian so I inherited the skills of a witch-hunter,' she said coolly. 'But my dad's a writer so I know a thing or two about spinning a story when I have to. If you can't think on your feet that's your problem.'

'Bloomin' know-it-all Grockle!' Jake muttered as he climbed after her.

The pair reached the car park to find that Jim had already placed Elsa in the passenger seat of his truck and was climbing in behind the steering wheel. The elderly Jerseyman had clearly taken the news about the Black Trolls very seriously as he still wore a tense and nervy expression when Jessica and Jake climbed into the cab.

Jessica glanced at Elsa who was lying slumped on the plastic seat, her skin ghostly pale in the dim early evening light. Her eyelids were drooping and she looked as if she was about to fall asleep. Noticing this, Jim gave the child a gentle shake to awaken her. The girl's eyes flickered open and she gazed around her in a dreamy manner.

Jim slipped the key into the ignition and the truck juddered to life in a cloud of diesel fumes. He nodded at Elsa and addressed his great-niece.

'Keep her awake,' he said sternly as they drew out of the car park. 'Until we can get some witch-hunter's broth in her at least.'

Jessica took hold of Elsa's skeletal hand. 'You okay?' she asked gently.

The girl struggled to focus on Jess's face. 'I'm all right,' she murmured softly, squeezing her friend's fingers. Jessica looked at Elsa's pale lips as she spoke and noticed with horror that the inside of her mouth was tinged black. She glanced up at Jim with worry. The old man sensed her concern.

251

'She'll be fine,' he told them gruffly. 'The troll didn't actually bite her, did it?'

Jess shook her head and propped Elsa further up in her seat.

'Then she'll be fine,' Jim reiterated, 'once she has the witch-hunter's broth down her. I want you and Jake to have a healthy dose too, even if you feel fine at the moment. Nasty things, Black Trolls – not nice at all.'

Jessica shuddered and put her arm around Elsa's shoulder. She didn't need Jim to tell her that.

'Bad news, eh?' she said.

The old man nodded. They were out on the road that led back to Maison de l'hache at St Ouens now and despite the age of the battered vehicle they were in, Jim was driving at quite a swift speed to get home.

'The worst,' he grumbled. 'You have no idea how lucky you are to escape from those awful things. As bad as a witch or warlock in some cases.'

He gave a little shudder as if the very thought of meeting a Black Troll chilled his blood.

Jessica stared out of the window at the winding road ahead of them. Night had enveloped the island completely by now and the sky was a bluish black, a dark backdrop upon which was hung a moon of light gold. Stars peppered the heavens, winking and blinking from behind the strands of clouds that floated eerily in the sky. Jessica shifted her arm gently to make sure Elsa didn't drop off to sleep on her shoulder.

'What are they?' she asked with genuine interest, looking at her great uncle. But it was Jake who answered.

'Black Trolls? Nobody knows for sure. I don't anyway. Jim's right though – we were fortunate to get away from them alive. Lucky you had me to fight them off!'

Jessica glanced at him wryly. For someone who moments ago was complaining about being cast as a hero, Jake had certainly regained his cocksureness.

Jim chewed his bottom lip as he rounded a corner in the road. 'Not completely true, Jake boy. I know a little about them.'

'You do?' he said, surprised.

'When you have had four generations of Guardians in your family, you tend to know a thing or two about black magic.'

252

Jessica sat up in her seat, eager to add to the knowledge she needed as Guardian. 'Tell us then, about Black Trolls.'

Jim looked very serious and took a deep breath. 'They are a lower form of magical creatures,' he explained. 'Less intelligent than faeries or merfolk, practically animals really. We can't be sure of their origins but it is commonly believed they are descended from humans cursed by witches and warlocks many centuries ago. They live deep within the earth, in deeper caves and crevices than the Magicroutes normally, the wetter and darker the better. They have very few magical powers of their own but...' He paused for a second and looked slightly uncomfortable.

'But what?' she asked.

The old man looked at her out of the corner of his eye. 'Black Trolls are like vampires,' he explained coldly. 'But instead of living off the blood of other beings, they gain all their energy from drawing upon black magic. They are quite literally the embodiment of pure evil.'

Elsa stirred in her seat, blinking restlessly and tossing her head. Jessica glanced down at her with concern.

'Hold on,' she murmured to her sickly friend. 'We're nearly home.'

Jim went on. 'Black Trolls are irresistibly drawn towards witchcraft of any kind. Even witches wear protective amulets when they travel in the Magicroutes to drive trolls away. Normally they hate being near the surface. They will only come up as far as the caves you were in if they sense there is witchcraft in the air.'

Jessica's skin prickled with goose bumps. She hadn't realized just how evil the hideous creatures she had encountered were.

'That means they must be sensing witchcraft in Jersey,' she exclaimed, thinking out loud.

Jim grunted. 'That's what I'm worried about. It's just what the elders feared: there are witches or warlocks on the island again. And no doubt they are planning to raise the demon Helier banished.'

Her head resting on Jess's arm, Elsa struggled uncomfortably, pulling a face as if in great pain. Her pale lips moved revealing black tinted gums. She was trying to say something but couldn't form the words. Jessica stroked her cheek and tried to calm her.

'It's all right,' she soothed. 'You'll be fine once you have some witch-hunter's broth.' She looked at the old man driving the truck. 'Why did they have to attack Elsa?' she asked. 'She's weak enough as it is.'

'Black Trolls are pure evil,' he emphasised. 'No logic, no morals, just pure murderous intent. If one bites you you're cursed for life and a drop of their blood on your skin will leave you with a scar that can never heal.'

These words hit Jessica hard and she struggled not to show her shock. When she had fought the troll in the cave, its dark blood had scalded her arm like acid and yet now her skin was flawless and without pain. She had also witnessed with her own eyes the wicked trolls' attack on the odd creature, Rina, and how they had sunk their long fangs into her flesh. Yet after the fight she seemed to recover. Jessica longed to question Jim on how this was possible but she was sure that revealing the existence of the mysterious animal wasn't a good move. Instead she asked, 'There wouldn't be a way of healing yourself if you got troll blood on your skin then?'

The old man shook his head. 'Impossible. You would have a black crust over that area of your body for life. Your great-great-grandfather William Edward Hellily battled a Black Troll once – got its blood on his forearm. Had a mark the size of a lamb chop on his skin till the day he died. I've got a photo somewhere. I'll look it out for you.'

Jessica quickly slipped her hand over the spot on her own forearm where the troll's blood had injured her and briskly shook her head.

'No thank you,' she told him before pausing to add, 'and no creature would be okay after it was bitten by a troll? Not even a merperson or faerie of some kind?'

Jim frowned. 'Nah,' he said. 'Anyone would be cursed until they died. Terrible sicknesses, nightmares, haunting depression, awful bad luck – no-one would want to be near them.' He stopped. 'Why? Do you think it might have bitten Elsa?'

Jess firmly shook here head. 'No, definitely not. I fought it off.'

Jake let out a loud cough and glanced at Jessica who quickly corrected herself. 'I mean, *we* fought it off before it had the chance.'

Jim nodded seriously. 'Good, or I wouldn't like to think what could happen.'

The truck turned off the road and drew onto the gravel drive of Jim's family home, Maison de l'hache, and the old man switched off the engine. Jessica gazed at the house. A golden light was shining in the downstairs window and she knew that her father, Martin, was waiting anxiously inside for them. Sure enough, almost as soon as they had parked, the front door opened and the tall, sandy-haired writer stepped outside.

Jim, Jake and Jessica quickly clambered down from the truck and Jake carefully lifted Elsa and stood her on her feet. Martin rushed over to the group, his face etched with worry.

'Where have you been? I didn't expect you to take this long. Jess, are you okay?'

Jessica hugged her father. 'I'm fine, Dad, really. The explorations took longer than we expected.'

Jim fixed the younger man with a sombre stare. 'They got attacked by trolls,' he explained curtly. 'Jake here fought them off and managed to find a way back to the surface, thank God.' He began to bustle the group towards the house.

'Jess and Jake are fine, but I'm worried about Elsa. She seems to have taken the attack badly. I'm going to make some witch-hunter's broth; they need the evil washed from their bodies as soon as possible.'

All five of them bustled into the hallway of Jim's home. Martin wore an expression of great anxiety and kept glancing at his daughter with grave concern to check she was okay. Jessica felt fine in herself but her mind was awhirl with questions of what her next move should be. She shrugged off her rucksack and looked down at it. She could see the slight movement of Rosehip fluttering about inside and knew it was cruel to leave the tiny faerie trapped for so long, even though she was enjoying life without her insane twittering. However, Jess was unwilling to release her in front of Jim and her father. For such a tiny creature Rosehip had a big mouth. Jessica decided it was best that she went up to her bedroom and told the faerie of her plan. The others were already heading for the kitchen when Jessica began climbing the stairs. Jim glanced at her.

'Where are you going?' he asked. 'You must have some broth right away.'

255

Jessica stopped half way up. 'I've got to make sure Rosehip is all right,' she said. 'I'll be down in a minute.'

With that she trotted upstairs and made her way to her bedroom. Once inside, Jessica carefully placed her rucksack on the bed and unzipped it. Rosehip's pale golden glow flooded out onto the bedspread and the tiny figure of the young elf climbed out. She stood up and stretched her delicate wings, brushing the creases from her simple white dress.

'About time too!' she squeaked angrily as Jessica knelt at the side of the bed so she could look Rosehip in the face. 'I was in that stinky old bag ages! Why did you have to do that?'

Jessica's face softened. She knew it was vital that she kept Rosehip on her side or the faerie would surely tell Jim everything about what had happened in the cave and about Rina.

'I'm sorry,' she said, as Rosehip settled crossed-legged on the bed. 'But you and Rina weren't getting along so I thought it was for the best.'

The small sprite wrinkled her angular face into a disgusted sneer. 'Rina,' she said. 'That thing has a name,' she shuddered.

'Yes, she has a name and for your information she wasn't trying to hurt us. In fact, she showed us how to get back to the surface and healed my hand and leg.'

Her voice drifted off at the end of this sentence as she remembered the odd feeling of familiarity she had felt in the beast's company. However, Rosehip didn't pick up on Jessica's wistful mood. Instead she looked at her with bright blue eyes and chirped eagerly, 'Did you kill it? Whack it on the head with a spade? You're the Guardian. You're meant to get rid of black magic.'

Jessica stared at her, appalled.

'Rosehip!' she exclaimed. 'That's a wicked thing to say! No, I certainly did not whack her on the head with a spade. She led us to the surface and then disappeared down into the Magicroutes.'

Rosehip stood up and straightened her dress, resting her hands cockily on her hips.

'I would have killed it,' she told Jessica, 'especially if it could do magic. It wasn't a merperson. It definitely wasn't a faerie and it could do magic. Therefore, it must have been some kind of witch.'

Jessica wondered whether all faeries had this ruthless, violent streak or whether Rosehip was unique. She reached inside her rucksack and pulled out *A History of Magical Beings in Jersey* and lazily flicked through its pages.

'That's exactly the reason I didn't kill it, you bloodthirsty little imp!'

She got to her feet and walked over to the chest of drawers to get a jumper. Rosehip padded across the bed, dived into the air and fluttered across to land on Jess's shoulder.

'What kind of a witch-hunter doesn't get rid of witches?' she sang, sounding as if Jessica was a grave disappointment to her.

Jessica paused, pulling the warm, white sweater she had just retrieved from the drawer over her arms. 'Look,' she explained to the faerie, 'whatever Rina was, she probably saved all our lives. She also knew who I was and helped me. If you are right and she was some kind of witch wouldn't she kill me when she had the chance? I think she's someone special.'

Jessica gently brushed Rosehip from her shoulder and tugged on her jumper. She then looked at the elf, expecting her to make another foolish comment. But Rosehip had suddenly gone very quiet. She hovered in mid-air, her transparent wings beating slowly and with a deep thoughtful expression on her face. Jessica regarded her curiously.

'What?' she questioned.

Rosehip looked towards the bedroom window. 'I just remembered something,' she said, her high-pitched voice unusually soft. 'Something my grandfather told me a long time ago.'

She began to fly towards the window and, puzzled, Jess followed her.

'What?' she repeated.

Rosehip shook her strawberry blonde curls. 'I'm not sure. I must speak to my people. Will you open the window, Jessica?'

Still without any idea what was going through Rosehip's mind, Jessica reached for the window catch. Pausing, she said, 'Promise me you won't tell my Uncle Jim about Rina.'

Rosehip nodded and turned back towards the pane of glass. Happy that Rosehip had agreed to keep Rina secret, Jess opened the window and the tiny elf flew off into the still night. Jess sighed and closed the window. It seemed that the odd creature in the caves had affected Rosehip almost as much as herself.

She wondered what had caused the faerie to change her mind. She climbed off the bed and, tucking *A History of Magical Beings in Jersey* under one arm, headed back downstairs to the kitchen.

As she entered, Jessica was hit by a hot gust of steam that carried a strong smell like burning rubber. The room was a hive of activity. Jim stood at the stove stirring a large saucepan of boiling water. Every few seconds he would look over to Martin and Jake who were holding a practically unconscious Elsa on her feet and marching her up and down to keep her awake. The girl's face was ashen and, to Jessica's horror, the dark tint she had noticed on her gums had spread to her lips.

Jessica shut the door. 'Is she all right?' she asked, gazing into the girl's unfocused eyes.

Martin glanced at his daughter. 'Hopefully,' he murmured. 'If Jim hurries with the broth.' He nodded to the old man who now had his full attention on the cooking pot. Jessica bustled over and gazed at the bubbling, brown liquid.

'What's in there?' she asked.

Jim gave the brew a vigorous stir. 'Bones of a Black Troll,' he explained. 'Killed in 1622 and used by this family ever since for witch-hunter's broth. Add a clove of crushed garlic, tablespoon of honey, chopped mint, three live black beetles, a handful of soil, a little seawater, a splash of vinegar and a good glass of brandy.'

Jessica grimaced and looked at the foul concoction. 'That's revolting!' she exclaimed.

'Exactly!' he said. 'But, believe me, it takes something this awful to drive black magic from your body.'

'It'll kill her,' she said, shaking her head.

'Taken like this, you're probably right,' he said bluntly. 'It needs one final ingredient.

'What's that?' she asked, not really sure she wanted to know.

'You have got to spit in it!' Jim told her.

In her short time as Guardian she had heard some astonishing things but what Jim was telling her now seemed just ludicrous.

'You want me to spit in this and then it'll save Elsa?'

From across the kitchen Elsa let out a weak moan. Martin caught his daughter's incredulous gaze.

'You've got to do it,' he said. 'That's the only way.'

'The Guardian of Jersey has the power to turn black magic

against itself,' said Jim. 'Your spit will turn the magic in the troll's bones against the magic in Elsa.'

Jessica couldn't believe what she was hearing. But then nearly everything in the last four days had been beyond comprehension. Taking a deep breath, Jessica leant close to the foaming pot and spat into its contents. The stew hissed violently. Picking up the ladle, Jim scooped out a generous dose.

'Quick!' he told Jessica. 'Go to the sink and fill a tall glass with water.'

Too confused to argue, Jess rushed to the tap and taking a beaker from the draining board filled it while Jim carefully made his way towards Elsa with the witch-hunter's broth stewing in the ladle. Jessica was quickly at his side with the water and slowly Jake and Martin lowered Elsa onto one of the kitchen chairs. The girl's eyelids were drooping heavily and Jake held her chin to stop her slumping forward.

'Now,' instructed Jim, 'I'm going to give her the broth. Straight afterwards she must drink the water. Make sure every drop goes down, okay?'

Jessica nodded and with Jake holding her nose to keep her mouth open, Jim poured the thick, brown liquid down Elsa's throat. The child struggled violently, her eyes rolling. Her pale cheeks suddenly turned deep pink and billowed as if she was about to vomit. Quickly, Jessica held the glass of water to Elsa's pursed lips and poured it swiftly down after the brew to make completely sure the girl didn't bring the healing tonic straight back up.

'Good girl, Elsa. Make sure it's all gone.'

The child gulped eagerly, desperate to wash the repugnant taste from her mouth. She finished the water and Jessica and the three men stepped back. Elsa looked slightly dazed for a moment, her pupils no longer rolling but staring straight ahead like a rabbit caught in the beam of a car's headlights. The ruddy pink had faded from her cheeks. She blinked a couple of times and then opened her mouth to emit a long and very loud belch that was accompanied by a wisp of malodorous grey smoke.

Elsa gazed round at the worried group surrounding her. 'We're at Jim's house,' she declared in a soft voice. 'We were at Plemount. Jake carried me. Now we're here.' She stared at the tarnished material of her floral dress and looked very confused. 'That's all I remember.'

Jess crouched down beside Elsa. 'How do you feel?'

The girl raised a slim hand to her forehead. 'Nightmares,' she whispered, her face creasing into a frown. 'I had the worst nightmares, trolls everywhere. My body hurts so much.'

She rubbed her arms as if they still ached now. Jessica hugged her friend. She felt immense relief to see Elsa fully conscious and speaking again. She had begun to think that by allowing the waiflike child to accompany her on her perilous adventure she had made a grave mistake and that Elsa might not survive her ordeal with the trolls. But now her heart filled with joy to see she was recovering.

Jessica leant back and looked at the girl. 'And now you're okay?' she asked hopefully.

Elsa wet her thin lips and rested her hands in her lap. 'I feel a little better,' she said quietly, 'but my body still aches and I'm tired.'

Jessica glanced up at her great uncle. 'Is that natural?' she asked.

'Perfectly,' he said. 'It will take a couple of days before the black magic is out of her system – then she'll be fine. I'll take her home, but first I want to make sure you and Jake have some broth too, just in case.'

Jessica grimaced at the thought of sampling the horrible concoction and got to her feet. She glanced at Elsa sitting still and quiet on the kitchen chair and asked, 'What is it like? Is it really bad?'

The small girl wrinkled her nose. 'It's disgusting,' she said with a shudder.

Jim returned to the pot hissing and steaming on the stove.

'You won't need as big a dose as Elsa,' he told Jake and Jessica, 'because you didn't get as close to the trolls as she did.'

Jessica nervously sat down at the kitchen table as Jim filled two beakers with tap water and rummaged in a drawer for a desert spoon. She watched as he dipped it into the heaving brown liquid. The potion swilled and gurgled in the bowl of the spoon just as it had done in the ladle. With the bubbling spoon in one hand and a glass of water in the other, Jim turned towards the two teenagers.

'Right,' he said bluntly. 'Who's first?'

Jessica and Jake exchanged glances. They played a game of stalemate for a few seconds. Finally, Jake squared his shoulders and stepped forward.

'I'll go first,' he said.

'Best to try and swallow it quickly and then gulp down the water,' Jim advised.

Jake took a deep breath and opened his mouth. Being careful not to spill a drop, Jim poured the steaming potion down Jake's throat. Almost immediately, the young man's jaws snapped shut and his hand shot to his neck. Lips tightly together, he emitted a series of desperate grunting sounds, his cheeks bulging like two red balloons. It looked as if he was going to spit out the broth but he quickly brought the water to his lips and drank it; his scarlet face returned to its normal hue. He finished the water with a loud burp of grey smoke and almost collapsed against the kitchen cabinet gasping, an expression of utter revulsion on his face.

'Ack!' he spat, trying to get the taste out of his mouth. 'That was terrible! I've never tasted anything that bad.'

Jessica knew it was her turn next.

'I feel fine,' she said brightly. 'I honestly don't think I need any witch-hunter's broth.'

She laughed nervously and reached for the door handle. But Jake spotted where she was heading and rushed forward. Before Jessica realized what was happening, Jake had grabbed her in a bear hug, pinning her arms to her sides.

'Jake, what are you doing? Let me go, you idiot!'

She struggled but the healthy farmer's son was too strong for her.

'Now, Jim!' he called to the old man; then hissed in Jess's ear, 'This is for dropping me in it earlier.'

Jim hurriedly scooped some of the potion out of the pan and dashed across the kitchen to dump it in Jessica's screaming mouth. The boiling liquid filled her throat with a heat and foul taste the like of which Jessica had never experienced. It scalded her tongue and throat and was so repugnant Jessica could almost feel her taste buds draw away from it in horror. The texture of the liquid was such that it felt almost alive on her tongue, like hundreds of crawling maggots twisting and turning inside her.

261

Wriggling free of Jake's grasp she rushed to grab the glass of water that was still standing by the sink. She gulped it down and as she did so felt a great cloud of steam fill her head, hissing violently in her ears. The water gushed down her throat forcing the churning potion down into her stomach like a smooth stone.

For a second Jessica leant wearily against the sink trying to catch her breath. Then she felt a movement in her belly like a serpent uncoiling. Before she knew what was happening it was forcing its way at a fiercely swift speed into her mouth, scorching like boiling steam as it went. It escaped in a hearty belch of smoke and Jessica slumped back against the table, an exhausted heap.

Elsa blinked at her timidly from her seat. 'See,' she whispered. 'I told you it was nasty.'

Jessica straightened her back and paused for a second. After such an intensely abominable experience she had expected to feel quite ill but in fact her body was in no pain or discomfort whatsoever.

Jim opened one of the kitchen cupboards and took out a funnel, a thick, brown glass bottle and some rather dirty looking rags.

'I'm sorry that it was so rough on you, Jess,' he told her, placing the funnel in the neck of the bottle and pouring the brown liquid inside. 'But Jake did the right thing. You had to take the witch-hunter's broth or who knows what effect the trolls would have had on you. Don't worry, the first time's always the worst.'

Jessica watched Jim as he emptied the last of the broth into the bottle, corked it and then tipped the remaining contents of the pan onto the rag. He wrapped the small collection of stubby, black bones, up in the white cloth carefully and placed them and the bottle back in the cupboard.

Jim now turned his attention to Elsa. The girl looked very tired and the purple bruises still ringed her eye.

'I think it's time for you to go home now. Your grandma will be worried,' he said gently.

Elsa slowly nodded her head. Jim took her hand and helped her to her feet. 'I'll tell Agatha what happened and tell her to put her straight to bed,' he said, as he and the tiny girl shuffled into the hallway. 'She'll need plenty of rest but a couple of days and she'll be fine.'

Elsa glanced over her shoulder to look at Jessica as she and Jim left but remained silent. Jessica doubted Elsa would be treated properly by the uncaring Mrs Noir, and she had had a very harrowing experience. But she made no comment. They heard the front door open and close and knew that the old man and Elsa had left.

Martin gazed around the kitchen seeming lost for words. 'Well,' he said, 'thank God that's all over. Nasty business, Black Trolls being back in Jersey.' He looked at Jessica expectantly. 'So that's it, Jess? Nothing else happened today? Nothing else Jim and I should know about?'

Jessica perched on the edge of the table and swung her legs guiltily. A crystal clear image of Rina flooded into her mind and she had physically to struggle not to tell her father the truth. She gazed down at the tiled floor and shook her head.

'We checked the main chamber,' she told him, still staring at the floor. 'The altar isn't active so we know there isn't a full coven in Jersey.' She stood perfectly still for a second, feeling as guilty as she had done when she'd taken her mother's diaries without anyone knowing. The room was silent and it was this silence that prevented Jessica from meeting her father's gaze. She knew if she raised her eyes to meet his he would see she was withholding something from him. The kitchen remained hushed for a few seconds.

'Well,' Martin breathed, 'that's one good thing at least. There's not a full coven.' His voice was light but Jessica detected a note of vague doubt that told her that even the prospect of one witch on the island was a grim notion. At last she raised her eyes to look at him.

'I want to speak to Jake,' she said, 'before he goes. Recap what happened today.' She was aware that the last phrase sounded as vague as the ones Jake himself used at times. The boy looked momentarily surprised but his expression quickly changed as he realized what Jessica wanted to see him about.

'Right,' said her father. 'I take that as a hint you don't want me around. I'll leave you to it. Goodnight, Jake.' The man smiled and left the two teenagers alone.

The minute the kitchen door swung shut, Jessica hopped from her perch on the table and swiftly slapped Jake's arm.

'That's for jumping on me and letting Jim pour that horrible stuff down my throat,' she hissed, half playfully. 'Happy now you've had your little revenge on me for making you into a hero?'

Jake rubbed his arm. Jessica's blow had been harder than she'd intended and had caught him right on his bruise. 'All right, I did enjoy seeing you suffer a bit Grockle, especially since islanders from here to St Helier will now be quizzing me on how I saw off six Black Trolls. Can we just say we're even and forget about it?'

Jess gazed up at him for a second. 'Yeah, we're even,' she said. She turned back towards the table and scooped up the book she had left there. 'Besides, I want you to look through this with me. I want to make absolutely sure Rina isn't a dragon.'

She began to leaf through the pages. Jake looked exasperated and edged towards the door. Jess caught his eye. 'What?' she demanded defensively.

'I think you're crazy obsessing over that thing in the cave and one off-the-cuff remark I made about it being a dragon – that's what. Far be it from me to tell you what the Guardian's job is but I think you should be concentrating on finding witches, not looking for dragons.'

Anger flared inside Jessica but she fought to repress it and said calmly. 'Look, Jake, I've been thinking.' She pulled out a chair from the table and sat down. 'I've been away from Jersey all my life. No-one seems to know what that creature is. What if it's linked to me being the Guardian? What if me coming back sort of woke it up? Like the trolls coming back because witches are around.'

She sat quietly at the table, the book in front of her and gazed at Jake hoping he wouldn't walk out. She needed a sounding board, someone who had witnessed the remarkable events of the day and knew, as she did, that they were real. She wanted to talk to someone to try and make some sense of the overpowering feelings of longing she had felt ever since laying eyes on Rina. Rosehip had gone, full of whimsical ideas of her own that Jessica wasn't convinced were any use to her anyway and Elsa was too ill even to think about what had happened. Though he might never agree with her, Jake was Jess's only confidante.

The boy stood framed in the doorway, his strong-featured face more serious than Jessica had ever seen it. 'So you do think it's something to do with black magic?' he said, his voice drained of both anger and compassion. 'Then you should've done something when we were down in the cave!'

'You sound like Rosehip,' she told him. 'That's just what she said.'

'Well there's no need to be *that* insulting.'

'Does that mean you'll look with me?'

Jake's resolve ebbed away. He slunk over to the table and sat down. 'I just want to make it clear that this is all I'm doing to help you on this subject and I'm only doing it to prove how wrong you are. I still think we should concentrate on finding who's doing witchcraft. If you continue to go on about this, I don't want to be involved.'

Jessica held her hand up. 'Fine, anything else to do with her I'll deal with myself.' She flicked the book open to the first page and straightaway something caught her eye. *A History of Magical Beings in Jersey* by C.R. Hiegman,' she read aloud. 'That was the name you mentioned, Jake. The researcher who found out about dragons! This book is bound to tell us whether Rina is one or not.'

Jake nodded. 'Well, you're right about that. There hasn't been another person who knew more about dragons than Christian Hiegman.'

Together they flicked through the crinkled pages of the book until they came to the index. Jessica ran her fingertip down the list until she reached the Ds. 'Dogwood, drachm...' she muttered as she search for the reference she needed. 'Here it is – Dragons, page seventy-eight.'

Beside her, Jake edged closer.

Jess turned to the appropriate point in the volume and studied the words that lay before her. On the facing page there was an intricate print of a dragon, looking, much to Jessica's surprise, almost identical to the ones she had seen in her childhood storybooks. Its long, willowy neck was bent low and it was seated back on its hind legs, like a dog begging for a treat. Its face had been skilfully drawn so every detail from its narrow, black eyes and reptilian snout to its tiny scales and numerous horns was clearly visible. On its back was a pair of magnificent

265

leathery wings, half unfurled. Jessica's heart sank with disappointment. The illustration bore not even a passing resemblance to the creature in the caves. Still hoping for an explanation she began to read aloud from the passage on the opposite page:

'As in most parts of the United Kingdom and Ireland, Jersey had once been the home of dragons. In fact, it is common knowledge that the Lord of Hambye in Normandy slaughtered such a beast many centuries ago and another dragon, perhaps an ancestor of the noble creature, carried the enchanted altar to the main chamber of the Magicroutes.

'However, owing to the practice of murdering these beautiful and mystical creatures as a mark of a knight's courage, it is my sad belief that a dragon has not lived in Jersey since the 14th century. My fury at the complete extermination of these wondrous animals before Man fully understood their magical and gentle qualities – their high intellect, ability to communicate without speech and healing abilities – is inexpressible.

'As always, it had been my hope that a dragon egg would have survived, but that is just fancy. An infant dragon would need the heat of molten lava to hatch and would quickly grow too large to live undetected on this tiny island.'

Jessica sighed wistfully and shut the book. Looking at Jake she saw the boy wore a pitying and complacent expression that told her the passage had done little more than confirm what he already knew. Whatever had saved them in the Magicroutes, it had certainly not been a dragon. Sensing Jessica's deep disappointment, he resisted the temptation to gloat and simply got to his feet.

Jessica gazed up at him. Dwarfed by the lad's height, she felt very tiny both physically and spiritually. She placed the book on the table and shoved it aside as if it had gone out its way to betray her.

'You were right,' she said, her voice sounding as timid as Elsa's.

Jake sucked his lips and shrugged but said nothing. Jessica knew that this was as close as Jake got to being sympathetic when he knew he had been right from the start. He collected his bag from the kitchen floor. As he moved towards the door she caught his arm.

'You're not a bad friend, Jake,' she confessed gently. 'Not a great one, but not bad.'

The lanky boy gave her a smile. 'And you're not a bad Guardian. Not a great one, yet, but not bad.'

Jessica grinned at him, pleased that she had his support even if they struggled to see eye to eye. Jake caught her gaze and held it, his face taking on a knowing expression as if he was reading her thoughts. When he spoke, Jess was shocked to realize he had succeeded.

'You're going to go down there tomorrow, aren't you? You're planning on heading back to Grosnez to find out what Rina is?'

Jessica nodded, struck not only by the fact Jake had realized exactly what she was going to do but that he had chosen for the first time to address the creature by name. Jake laughed and waggled his finger.

'You're a crazy lady, Jessica Kent. But I like you.' With that he headed into the hallway and, after saying farewell to Martin, left for home.

Jessica stood silently in her great uncle's house, her spirits in quiet turmoil. The day had been one of startling adventures. The sun had set and she felt greatly inclined to put away all that had happened until tomorrow. But it was Rina's scarred face she saw in her dreams.

Chapter 13

The Iris of the Ancestors

Jessica was in a light but restful slumber when she found herself woken by an urgent tapping on her window. She lay in the warmth of her bed, eyes shut tightly, trying to ignore the sound, but it was persistent.

Rolling over, she strained her weary eyelids open and fumbled for her watch on the bedside cabinet. The face screamed at her that it was 5:30 in the morning and she let out a groan of exasperation as she pondered who would have the nerve to wake her at such an ungodly hour, especially after the trauma she had been through the day before. Her body still not fully awake, she turned over and shoved the curtain out of the way to look out. Rosehip was standing on the windowsill beating the glass furiously with her tiny fists, her sharp features etched with frustration. Jessica lifted herself up on one elbow and fiddled with the catch on the windowpane. It flew open and Rosehip fluttered inside on the cold morning air. Jessica shuddered with the chill of the dawn breeze and quickly shut the casement.

Rosehip had landed delicately on Jess's bedspread and was hopping and jumping about in an even more excited manner than usual. Jessica slumped back onto the pillow and gazed at the elf through heavy, half-closed eyes.

'It's the middle of the night, Rosehip,' the girl groaned as the faerie stood staring at her from atop a crease in the covers. 'After yesterday, I think I deserve a bit of a lie in.'

The faerie's back arched slightly with annoyance and she stamped her dancer-like foot on the bed. 'But this is important,' she squeaked. 'Really important.'

Jessica ran a hand through her knotted hair and looked

doubtful. In the short time she had known Rosehip, Jessica had discovered that most of what she said was irrelevant, a lot of it was annoying and none of it was important. However, from the expression Rosehip wore it was clear that she would not leave Jessica alone before she'd said her piece.

'Couldn't it wait until morning?' she asked, already knowing the answer.

Rosehip crouched so she was sitting in her favourite position, cross-legged. 'I did,' she stated, her voice as shrill as a piccolo. 'It's dawn already. I realized late last night, but I let you sleep. I couldn't wait any longer.'

Jessica frowned, not fully awake and barely able to focus on what the small elf was saying. 'What?' she groaned.

Rosehip gave a huge sigh at Jessica's slow wit and got to her feet so she could see her face more clearly. 'I mean I know where you can find out about that ugly old thing we saw in the caves yesterday, though why you want to is a mystery to me – it was horrible.'

Suddenly Jessica felt very much awake. The image of Rina and the strange compulsion Jessica had to find out more about her had returned the very second Rosehip had uttered the words. She knew in her heart that there was a possibility that Rosehip could be offering her another red herring, like Jake and his dragons, and Jessica didn't want to get her hopes dashed for a second time. But she felt it would be foolish to turn down the opportunity of finding out something more. She sat bolt upright, all thoughts of going back to sleep vanishing and gazed at Rosehip.

'You remembered something about us – I mean her?' she urged, clasping her hands in excitement. 'Tell me?'

Rosehip hopped gracefully from one foot to the other a thoughtful look on her face. 'I don't *know* anything,' she explained. 'It's just that when you said you didn't think that thing we saw was a witch I remembered about something my grandfather said, about the Iris of the Ancestors.'

Jessica shifted her weight from her bed and swung her feet onto the floor. 'The what?' she asked. Her mind quickly beginning to shake off the dull shrouds of sleep.

Rosehip too seemed to be filled with excitement brought on by Jessica's interest. She spread her cobweb-like wings and fluttered up to Jessica's shoulder, her golden light glowing.

'It's Jersey's memory pool,' she explained as Jessica shuffled around the bedroom trying to gather together some appropriate attire. 'We, the faeries, guard it; keep it safe and healthy. It records important events from the island's past and can repeat them, so people can learn from what has happened before. It knows everything.'

Jessica was just about to pull her jumper on when she paused for a second and looked at Rosehip quizzically. 'So it will tell me anything, anything I want to know?' she asked, a million questions about her mother and her past flooding her mind.

Rosehip shook her head. 'Grandpa says that's not how it works,' she piped. 'He says it will not give knowledge unless the person asking for it really needs to know. It is only there to show what is of value now and what the person asking must not forget.'

Jessica put on her sweater and looked puzzled. 'I don't understand,' she said.

'I didn't quite understand when my grandpa explained it to me either,' Rosehip confessed, 'but there's always a chance that it might tell you about what that creature is.'

Jessica grinned and swung her backpack on. 'Then let's go and find out.,' she said, feeling very excited.

Together, Rosehip and Jessica made their way through the still house. It was still early and both Jessica's father and great uncle were asleep. The only sounds to be heard were the soft ticking of the grandfather clock and the dawn song of the birds. Jessica resisted the temptation to slip into the kitchen to make herself breakfast as it might wake her relatives but paused at the hall table to scribble a note, explaining that she was with Rosehip doing some research, before taking the key from the hook and creeping outside into the crisp morning.

A misty, blue light illuminated the sky as Jessica stepped cheerfully onto the road outside Maison de l'hache and following Rosehip's lead, headed down the road towards the cliffs. The air around her was fresh with dew. The sky above them was a soft blanket of powder blue clouds, not heavy enough to hold rain but still devoid of the warmth of the rising sun. Very few stars were visible in the wide expanse of cool light and those that still remained were quickly fading. Everything in Jersey at this early hour seemed clean and fresh as if the moisture which clung to every blade of grass and tree branch had some magical quality that washed away all the harm and tiredness of the previous day. Jessica inhaled deeply; her nostrils were filled with the sweet invigorating odour of the early morn – newly cut grass, wild flowers, and the sea. She felt completely at home.

After about half an hour of following the empty road flanked on one side by the sturdy walls of pink granite and on the other by thick bracken and heather, Rosehip darted into the dense undergrowth. Jessica paused for a second having been daydreaming for some time about the beauty of the Jersey countryside and gazed around not quite sure what to do. Noting the human's lost expression, Rosehip re-emerged from the thick, woody tangle of branches and hovered just above them.

'You follow the path,' she explained to Jessica, her high, musical voice sounding even crisper than usual in the clear morning air.

The faerie pointed to the bracken and Jessica noticed for the first time that there was a very narrow, winding path, not more than a foot across cutting through the dark purplish-brown brushwood like the twisting track of a large snake.

'Oh,' Jessica exclaimed. She stepped from the firm, man-made road that they had been following onto the tiny, sandy path. 'I head this way, do I?' she asked.

Rosehip nodded.

Jessica took a deep breath of the fresh air and began to cut her way through the tangle of branches that were knotted over the well-hidden pathway. It was relatively slow going. Every few minutes it seemed Jessica had to stop to disentangle a thorn or piece of bracken that had become caught on her jeans. Rosehip, however, had no such problems and darted quickly ahead, weaving in and out of the shrubs until she left Jessica so far behind that all the girl could see of her was her bright light glowing among the plants. Undeterred Jessica steadily picked her way onwards. Suddenly, Jessica heard a familiar musical murmuring. She looked up and realized that among the deep undergrowth there were dozens of patches of golden light, giggling and quivering. She was surrounded by faeries.

Jessica stood perfectly still and gazed around. Although she couldn't see them, she was aware of scores of tiny, bright eyes staring at her and little voices whispering.

271

'Hello,' she ventured, her voice loud in the still morning air. 'I'm with Rosehip. We're looking for the Iris of the Ancestors. My name is Jessica, Jessica Kent.'

The moment that she mentioned her name the whispers and giggles that had echoed among the plant life ceased and were replaced by awestruck murmurs that seemed to repeat themselves over and over. 'Jessica,' they went. 'It's the Guardian, the Guardian of Jersey. She has come. What does she want?'

After a few seconds of confused muttering, there was a gentle rustle from the heather on Jess's left side and a faerie fluttered up to greet her. It flew up and floated in front of her face and stared at her with wide green eyes. The elf was similar to Rosehip only slightly chubbier with fat red cheeks. Its hair was glossy black and it wore an outfit of heather. It beamed dumbly as if Jess were some sort of celebrity. Finally it spoke.

'Are you the Guardian?' it sang timidly.

Jessica nodded. The faerie clutched its tiny hands to its cheery face and squealed with joy.

'It's the Guardian,' she squeaked excitedly. A tiny gasp rustled the heather making Jess glance round. She saw that several small heads had emerged from the bracken and were regarding her, their mouths open in amazement. Jess was a little overawed herself in the presence of such a large number of faeries. Dealing with Rosehip was enough of a struggle; she didn't have a clue how to address a whole crowd of the creatures. Licking her lips nervously she turned back to the round-faced elf fluttering at her shoulder and decided it would be best to try and strike up a conversation.

'And you are?' she asked politely.

The elf seemed to glow with pride at being addressed personally. 'I'm Cowslip,' she sang clearly.

Jessica smiled but before she had the chance to gain any information as to where Rosehip or the Iris of Ancestors was, dozens of voices from all around chimed in, all introducing themselves at once.

'I'm Nettle,'

'Bluebell, that's me.'

'Hi! I'm Primrose.'

'Burdock, and don't you forget it.'

'They call me Crocus.'

272

'And I'm Heather.'

The air was filled with the musical jumble of dozens of faerie voices all chattering away at the same time. There were faeries everywhere, sitting cross-legged on the ground, hiding under the bracken, hovering in the air. Some of the females had flowers and bird feathers plaited in their hair and one or two older males stood around smoking tiny wooden pipes. All were blessed with delicate wings and sharp, clear features and they were all talking at the same time. The noise was almost deafening, like hundreds of tiny bells being struck simultaneously and Jessica was forced to clap her hands over her ears to muffle the sound.

'Please,' she begged, straining to be heard above the un-melodious symphony. 'I can't understand if you all talk at the same time.' Placing a finger to her lips she let out a long 'shhhhhhhh' until the singing and chattering finally stopped.

Cupping her hand she allowed Cowslip to settle in her palm. 'Now Cowslip,' she breathed, before adding in a louder tone, 'and *only* Cowslip. Will you please tell me where the Iris of the Ancestors is? I need to ask it something.'

The apple-faced faerie gazed up at her with sparking, emerald eyes and pointed a chubby finger towards a small hillock a few feet away.

'It's over there,' she chirped merrily, 'and so is Old Oaky. He'll tell you about it. Old Oaky knows everything.'

Jessica smiled gratefully as the elf launched herself into the air and fluttered away. Then she turned towards the small mound in the bracken and headed towards it eagerly. It only took her a few strides to reach the bank and mount it but as she found herself looking down at the mystical pool she felt somewhat disappointed with what she saw.

At the bottom of the narrow slope was a dirty and rather stagnant pond. Jessica had been expecting a pretty faerie dell with glistening springs surrounded by wildflowers. The pool that lay before her now was far from picturesque. It was about ten feet in diameter and so dank and muddy that Jessica was sure no life could survive in it. Around the edge, the ground was stony with clumps of moss here and there. Jessica was gazing at the dirty water with acute disappointment when a high-pitched shout made her look up.

'There you are! I've been waiting here for ages!'

Jess saw that Rosehip had re-appeared and was standing on one of the rocks beside the pond. Jessica stepped out of the bracken and edged her way around the pool to where the faerie was.

'I'm sorry,' she said, 'I didn't know which way to go and I got caught up speaking to some of your friends.' She stopped and glanced back at the cloudy expanse of water that lay near her feet. 'So this is it,' she breathed, unable to hide her disillusionment, 'The Iris of the Ancestors. I've got to be honest with you, Rosehip, it sounded more magical than it looks.'

Rosehip's mouth tightened into a pout. 'You should never judge by appearances. This memory pool has been here for over a thousand years.'

Dubiously, Jessica crouched on the moist ground and leant over the pool. Her reflection in the misty water stared back up at her with the same weary expression.

'You faeries could've done a better job at keeping it clean,' she said.

Rosehip sighed and tapped her tiny, pale toes. 'It's not meant to be clean,' she explained. 'All that gunk and slime in there holds millions of memories.'

Jessica was not altogether convinced that Rosehip knew what she was talking about. Curious, she stretched her hand out towards the murky water to see if anything magical would happen if she touched the surface but Rosehip quickly flew up and buzzed at her fingers.

'Don't touch it!' she sang crossly. 'You'll mess with the memories and make it forget something.'

Jessica swiftly withdrew her hand and glanced at the faerie hovering near her. 'Then what do I do?' she asked, beginning to wonder if the whole thing was a wild goose chase. 'Is there a spell or something I'm meant to say?'

Rosehip had landed back on her rock and was pacing purposefully away from Jessica towards a large clump of leaves near the edge of the pool. 'I'm not sure what you're meant to do but Grandpa will know.'

She stopped beside the pile of leaves and placing her hands on it began to shake it gently, calling, 'Grandpa Oaky, Grandpa Oaky, wake up.'

The leaves emitted a soft groan, then began to shift and fall apart to reveal the figure of a very old faerie. His face was leathery and etched with creases as if carved from the wood of some ancient tree. He had a long, silvery-white beard and small, crystal blue eyes that sparkled like precious gems. He was somewhat larger than Rosehip and the other faeries with a round face and belly that reminded Jessica of her own great uncle. The elf rolled over and rubbed his eyes muttering sleepily to himself. Rosehip took hold of his hand and with an almighty heave, aided him into a sitting position. The tiny old man gave himself a little shake to wipe off his sleepiness and flapped the leaves that surrounded him so they folded out into a cape.

'What's this? What's this? Why have you woken me up?' he muttered.

Rosehip sat cross-legged at his side. 'Jessica,' she explained, pointing to the girl, 'the Guardian. She wants to use the Iris of the Ancestors. She needs advice.'

The old elf picked a piece of dirt from his beard and regarded Jessica with his shining eyes. 'Oh yes,' he said kindly. 'You must be Jessica – a fine young human if I may say so myself and very much like your mother in looks.' He had a pleasant calming voice, lower than that of the other faeries Jess had met. It was reminiscent of bamboo wind chimes.

Jessica nodded politely. She was rather taken with the elderly faerie.

Old Oaky clasped his tiny, gnarled hands together and stared into the pool of water in front of him.

'And you are wanting to consult the Iris; there's something on your mind.'

Jessica looked uncomfortable. She didn't want to tell Old Oaky about Rina; she didn't want anyone to know about the kind but odd creature who had saved her the day before in case the discovery put Rina's life in peril. She opened her mouth to say that she did have something on her mind and Rosehip had advised her to come here but the portly elf held up his hand to stop her.

'Don't say a thing, young lady, not a word. You have no duty to explain yourself to me. The Iris already knows what has passed in your young life. Now have you ever looked into a memory pool before?'

'No,' Jessica replied, gazing once again at the muddy pond and wondering what secrets it could possibly hold.

Old Oaky shifted his cape around him and looked a little perturbed. 'No,' he sniffed, 'of course you haven't. You've been living in the blinkered world of man and are only now learning about the true magic world. Messy business with you being the Guardian and all, put the proper line of things right out of whack. Still what is done is done.' He stopped, aware that he was rambling and scratched his pointed nose. 'A memory pool,' he began slowly, spreading his fingers to illustrate his point, 'is ... well it's like a living book. A record of a certain place and what has happened there. It remembers things that have passed.'

He stopped. It was clear the human hadn't a clue what he was talking about. He groaned and slumped back onto his rock to begin again. 'Have you ever been to a place like a very old building and felt it had a memory of its own, that it had seen a great many events in its time and could recall them to itself?'

Jessica nodded. She had had that feeling many a time when she had visited castles and old buildings with her school. Old Oaky gave a gummy grin of relief and said, 'That means there was probably a memory pool nearby. They absorb sights, sounds and experiences of the people who live near them and draw them deep into their depth, locking them away so they will always remain fresh, long after man, faerie or merperson has passed on. They hold onto what should never be lost.' As he spoke this last sentence, the elderly elf's eyes grew wide and Jessica's brain filled with understanding.

'So it knows everything, everything about Jersey,' she gasped. 'It could tell me who the witches are and what happened to my mother.' Eagerly she studied the surface of the water gleaming in the early morning sun but still all she saw was her own reflection there.

Old Oaky sighed and Jessica looked back at him.

'It's not that simple,' he said softly. 'There are two strict rules you must understand when you look into the Iris of the Ancestors. The first is that it does exactly what its name says: it will only allow you to see and know what *your* ancestors did, not those of other islanders.' He stopped for a moment, his wrinkled features deadly serious. 'The second is that whatever it reveals to you is wholly and completely what you need to know – nothing more, nothing less. What you may see might not be

276

pleasant, it might not even make sense to you but it will be the information you need.'

'You mean I might see something horrid?' she asked.

Old Oaky shrugged his shoulders and gently opened and closed his tattered wings. 'It is impossible for me to say. Only the Iris knows what it will show to you and you alone know what advice you are requesting of it.'

Jessica gazed at her image reflected in the still, brown water and knew in her heart she must discover the true identity of the creature who had risked its life for her.

'What do I do?' she asked, not raising her eyes from the pool.

Old Oaky's melodious voice came to her in a hushed whisper carried on the still, dawn air. 'Think of the question that is in your heart. Look into your own eyes. The truth of your family's past and the answer you seek lies there.'

Silently, Jessica studied the reflection of her own features glistening on the surface of the enchanted pool. She stared deep into the eyes of the Jessica who seemed imprisoned beneath the glassy surface of the Iris and saw in them the troubled question that filled her heart and mind. She let the thought, and only that thought, flow through her and pour like a waterfall from her eyes into the shining water.

'Who is Rina?' she asked silently. 'Why did she save me?'

Her thoughts seemed to flow like a river from her mind into the magical Iris. The air around her had become suddenly still and she could no longer hear the gentle sounds of the early morning headland. It was as if they had faded away into the background leaving her in a void with nothing but the mystical pool for company. Yet still all she saw in the water were her own dark eyes and anxious face. Then, to her quiet amazement, Jessica witnessed a small alteration in the image floating on the water. Not a drastic metamorphosis by any means, but a shift in her features so slight it took her a few seconds to realize anything was happening. It started with her eyes: they became darker, almost black and their shape became more almond-like beneath the gentle ripples of the water. Tiny waves seemed to spread out from those dark irises, disturbing the reflection of her face and making it reform into someone else's. Jessica remained as still as a statue, frightened that if she moved the slightest bit it would break the spell that was being cast. She watched the reflection as its face and skin aged from that of a teenager to a young woman in her twenties and the hair turned from mousy brown to glossy ebony. The water surrounding the image began to change as well. It shimmered in the dawn light to reveal that the woman was seated in a rowing-boat off St Ouens bay. Finally, as the last ripple reached the perimeter of the pool, the new image settled into a vision that was strangely familiar to Jessica. She let out a gasp as she realized the girl reflected in the pool was Emma Hellily, her mother.

She was exactly as Jessica had pictured her, beautiful, with dark features, haunted russet eyes and flowing hair. She appeared to have an easy, almost manly air and was strong and healthy. She was wearing ragged jeans and a checked shirt and staring, not directly at Jessica, but at another figure in the vision – Martin. She looked troubled. Jessica felt an overwhelming desire to reach into the water and touch her mother but she knew it was simply a picture, a memory, no more truly alive than a photograph. Then a voice from the still water pierced her thoughts. It was both clear as crystal and miles away. Within the pool her father was speaking. He sounded urgent.

'Have you thought any more about it?' he asked gently. 'You promised you would.'

Emma bit her lip and looked out to sea. 'Yes, of course I have. But it can't change anything. I've explained that.'

Jessica felt herself shake. It was the first time she had ever heard her mother's voice. She had a strong Jersey accent, wise and soft. She watched her father dip his head in despair and sigh.

'I don't understand,' he said bitterly. 'It's been hard enough for me to accept that these...' he paused, 'these things exist, but I tried to, for you. But it hurts me to think they, this island, is more important to you than I am. Don't you love me?'

Emma turned to face him, her thick mane flying in the breeze. 'Of course I love you,' she said tenderly, placing a hand on his cheek. 'I adore you, you're the only man I'll ever love. I want to marry you, to be with you, to have your children.' She stopped and dropped her eyes from his face. 'But my duty is to Jersey and it always will be. There's nothing I can do. I am the Guardian. If the dark ones ever return it's up to me alone to face them.'

Jessica felt a pang in her heart. There was such sadness in

her mother's eyes and a stubborn determination to do the right thing, even if it broke her heart. It was made even more tragic by the fact that Jessica knew that all her heartache had been in vain and that the witches had taken her life anyway. In the watery apparition, Martin took Emma's hand and squeezed it.

'And have they returned?' he asked gently, as Emma bowed her head in defeat.

The young woman remained silent for a brief moment, then taking a heavy breath she answered.

'You know I've been unable to find any signs of black magic in the Magicroutes,' she said, sounding as if she had come to the end of a long and arduous battle. 'To my knowledge there are no witches in Jersey, not at the present time anyway.' She placed a hand on her brow as if she was suffering from a painful headache. 'I get so tired and frustrated at times,' she said angrily as her fiancé put a comforting arm around her shoulder. 'If there is witchcraft being practised in Jersey it is my duty to stop it. But I can find nothing, nothing that proves my work is worthwhile.'

Jessica watched as her father embraced her mother. She suddenly knew that the mantle which had rested with her mother and now had been placed into her hands was greater than she realized. She wondered for a second, whether when her two-week holiday was up, it would be wise to return to her former home on the mainland. It was something that she would have to speak of with her father and great uncle. But for now Jessica forced such ideas to the back of her mind. The concept held too much weight for her to deal with at this moment and there were other matters she had to contend with first.

In the pool, Emma looked at Martin, her face wearing the same determined expression Jessica herself had when her mind was set on something. 'I've made up my mind. There has to be more to my life than searching for evil that might not even exist. I want to be something more than just the Guardian of Jersey. I want a home and a family. I love you Martin and I want to be your wife. I've decided to accept your proposal and come to London.'

Jess's father's face broke into a joyous smile and he kissed his love tenderly, but after a few seconds Emma broke away and fixed him with a serious stare. 'Martin,' she told him firmly, 'I want a life with you but that doesn't mean I can give up my

279

obligation as the Guardian. There will always be a part of me that belongs solely to Jersey and the magic. If this island needs me, I must come back. Remember, too, that our first-born child will become the Guardian when I die and he or she must know the truth.'

Martin's eyes were filled with both love and sorrow. 'I understand,' he whispered unwillingly.

His words echoed from the depths of the pool and as they reached Jessica's ears she saw the image of her parents begin to dissolve. Their faces swam in the murky water, getting fainter and fainter until they resembled a bright, swirling cloud.

'Is that all?' she asked, not raising her eyes from the swirls of colour that danced beneath the surface of the water.

Old Oaky's voice came to her through the air. 'Keep watching, young lady, I believe the Iris has more memories to reveal to you.'

Jessica studied the billowing clouds in the water, searching for something that might guide her. The image of her parents had been pleasant but it told her nothing she hadn't already learnt from her mother's diaries. It certainly gave her no further information about Rina. 'Come on, magical Iris,' she willed silently. 'Show me, help me.'

The haze in the Iris whirled slowly, changing colour from green to black to blue, making tiny spirals beneath the still, mirror-like surface. The water barely moved but in its depths the hidden memories of Jersey's past twisted in and out of each other with flashes of pure, white light. Slowly, a new image shimmered to the surface.

Jessica found herself staring at the hallway of her great uncle's home. She could see the stocky figure of her great uncle pacing the floor, head bowed, face ashen with worrying. Suddenly, the front door swung open and Emma burst in, her face streaked with grief. Jessica could now tell that this scene had taken place a few years after the preceding one. Emma looked older, but what shook Jessica was that Emma's belly was now swollen with pregnancy. She realized quickly that the child her mother was carrying was herself. Behind her stood Martin, his face grim. Jessica watched as Emma approached her uncle and placed a concerned hand on his arm.

'I came as fast as I could. I got the first plane,' Emma said, her voice deep with worry. 'What has happened? Is it what we feared?'

The old man's round, tanned face looked unusually ghostly and drawn as he gazed up at his niece. 'It's the coven,' he uttered chillingly. 'They have reformed. I had no idea. If I had, I would have called you sooner.'

Emma looked back to the front door and took a deep breath. 'Do you have any names?' she asked, closing her eyes as if to prepare for the horror she had to face. 'Any clues as to who they are?'

Jim shook his head. 'I think it's a mix – some mainlanders, some Jersey folk. I cannot believe some Jersey people would still practise black magic in this age, it makes me so ashamed.'

Emma stooped down and picked up a small bundle that lay on the floor. Jessica lent closer to the still water and strained to see what it was but the distorted nature of the image made it impossible to see. Emma tucked the package under her arm and looked from her uncle to her husband. 'I'm going after them,' she said surely. 'I know I can stop them.'

Jim's face was filled with dismay. 'You can't,' exclaimed the old man. 'It's too dangerous.'

In a flash, Martin dashed to his wife's side and put his arms around her. 'What about the baby?' he whispered. Emma looked as if she was about to crumple with grief in his arms. Jessica saw her bite her lip to fight back the tears. Instinctively, her hand shot to her swollen belly and she caressed it lovingly.

'I don't want to hurt our child, Martin,' she murmured, adding in a firmer voice, 'But if I don't stop the witches there won't be a world for our baby to be born into.'

She swiftly drew away from his embrace and straightened her back.

Jim was gazing round him as if he was struggling to comprehend what was going on. 'No Guardian has ever faced a coven when pregnant,' he said under his breath. 'You are carrying the next heir within you, Emma. You know you are passing your powers onto her. It'll weaken you.'

Emma embraced herself and bowed her head. 'I know,' she replied quietly. 'But tell me, uncle, do I have a choice? Is there another way to fight them? I believe there is not.'

281

Jim shrugged and lowered his eyes. 'It's the only way; it has always been.'

Emma stepped away from the two men and headed towards the door. 'Then I must fight them,' she said, as she stepped outside. 'I ask you both to pray for me.'

Her voice seemed to get fainter and once again the shining mist that lay dormant in the lowest depths of the Iris rose up and dissolved the sad face of the young woman, leaving her daughter feeling frightened and alone. Inside the Iris, mists churned and billowed, angry scarlet in colour like the spilt blood of her mother, flowing fresh again after fourteen long years. Yet still the two bright, brown eyes of Emma Hellily remained floating still and hypnotic in the gory water. Jessica wanted to look away, to shut her own eyes before the terrible vision of her mother's demise appeared in the pool. But all she could do was stare frozen with horror as the young woman's eyes filled with agony. She heard Emma's desperate cries, weak with fear and pain as she called out to some unseen foe. 'Your evil deeds shall not harm this isle, in the name of Helier I banish you. You shall take my life but never my child; the legacy shall remain.' Jessica clapped her hands over her ears as a dreadful shriek of death rose up like a white flame from the pool, shattering the dawn air.

'Please,' Jessica whispered in her mind, 'don't make me watch her die. Show me something else, anything.'

Then, as if in mercy, the waters answering her prayers, began to transform. The violent, crimson clouds darkened to a deep forest green and the storm that raged within the Iris calmed until the thick, mossy mist was simply twirling like wisps of vapour. Jessica became more composed and although she had been shaken by the nightmarish image of her mother's final hours she no longer felt compelled to look away. She still saw a pair of eyes staring back at her from the glistening water but now they had changed. They remained dark brown but where her mother's beautiful clear skin had been there was now the wrinkled face of a man in his fifties. His hair was silver and curly and Jessica recognized him straightaway as her great uncle. His expression was that of fury and he was crouching on a rocky outcrop by the sea.

Jessica saw another familiar figure, seated beside the old man, its long shimmering tail dipping into the gentle waves. It was

Keela. The merman looked younger and was clean shaven. His arms formed a tender cradle and within them he nursed a creature with tarnished, olive skin and wild, black hair. A pair of snake-like limbs flopped weakly over his arm and the creature was gurgling noisily. With a gasp, Jessica recognized that the animal must be Rina as a baby. Keela was rocking her very gently and stroking her blotched skin with his long, soft fingers. Hopefully, he turned to Jim and spoke.

'Hold her,' he said softly, extending the malformed infant towards Jim. 'Just for a minute or two, then you will see she's not evil.'

The old man shrunk away from the crying creature, a look of revulsion on his face. 'That thing is not natural,' he spat viciously. 'It belongs not to any species of creature that lives on this isle. It is a curse, a symbol of black magic, the same black magic that killed my niece. There is nothing good in its heart.'

The being in the merman's arms let out a shrill cry of hunger and Keela drew it closer to his chest, hushing its cries. 'You know where she belongs, Jim Hellily,' he said. 'It is the proper thing that she lives with you, is cared for by you.'

Jim fiercely shook his head. 'Keela, that mistake of nature has nothing to do with me,' he growled angrily. 'I refuse to have it become part of my world. It is a remnant, a foul discharge of an evil deed that robbed Emma of her life. If you let it live it could grow into something that may have the power to destroy us all. If you care for Jersey, you will kill it now.'

The merman winced and his face grew dark. 'I believed you were an honourable man, Jim. I believed that you knew well the responsibility your family holds unto this isle. You may not be the Heir of Helier but you have a duty to guide the ones whose destiny it is to drive away the black magic. Are you so blinded by the marks that scar this child to see her goodness?'

Jim remained still, his back towards the merman, his features twisted with anguish. 'What do your people say should be done with it?' he asked. 'What does Xandu advise?'

Jessica saw Keela's body fold around the child in his arms as if to protect it. He placed a soft kiss on the babe's scarred brow. 'My people are split on the matter,' he said. 'Some say, like you, that this poor being is an omen of wickedness, that her light should be crushed before she has the chance to prove her soul for herself.' He paused and ran his fingers through the infant's mass of rough hair. 'But there are those of us who see more in this child than an abnormal body and cursed form, who see hope in her eyes and purity in her heart.'

The infant had stopped its bawling and Jessica saw it was reaching out with long leathery fingers to grip the merman's thumb. Keela smiled sadly down at her. 'She needs guidance, Jim. A wise mind who knows the secrets of this island. With your help she could do great things.'

Jim's eyes were filling with tears. However, he didn't look back at Keela.

'Bah,' he said angrily. 'My mind is made up. It'll receive no help from me. Do what you will with it.'

'And what of Jessica?' Keela asked. 'Where is she now?'

Jessica felt her blood run cold. This last vision had caused her much distress. She knew already that Keela was somehow connected to Rina but it shocked her that it seemed to be Jim who was responsible for the creature. Why had he not spoken of her existence to her and what was it that caused him to have such animosity towards a creature that Jessica knew from her own experience was harmless? But the question that chilled Jessica most was – why did Keela speak as if she and Rina were somehow connected?

Within the pool, Jim hung his head. 'I've sent her back with her father,' he sighed wearily. 'Back to the mainland. It's not safe for her in Jersey now.'

Keela's eyes narrowed with fury. 'You did what?' he hissed. 'You let Emma's daughter leave Jersey and now you expect me to murder this poor innocent! Have you taken leave of your senses? Do you want black magic to destroy us all?' The merman shuffled to the edge of the rocks, pressing the baby to his chest. 'Jim,' he said firmly, 'you are experiencing great grief at this time and I know in your heart you realize what is right for Jersey. But at present I must do what I can to aid you, even if you can't see it. The child comes with me.'

Placing a protective hand on the child's head he slipped gracefully off the rocks into the water. Jim looked back to the merman, his mouth half open as if he were about to call him back. But then the old man shook his head dismissively and began to walk away.

Keela swam slowly away, keeping the child's head above water. Jessica heard the strange creature gurgle but, as the merman headed deeper into the sea, the image within the Iris shimmered and dissolved, until the water returned to its muddy state. Jessica's mournful reflection stared back at her with frightened eyes. The Iris had shown her its last.

In her stomach, Jessica felt a sensation sicklier and more disturbing than the one the witch-hunter's broth had given her the night before. It overwhelmed her. It swept away all thoughts of her duty to Jersey, or her mission to find out what Rina was. All she knew was that her mother had been murdered and the one person she had trusted to guide her through this new and disturbing world of witchcraft and horror had been shown as heartless and unforgiving. For the first time in years, Jessica allowed herself to do the one thing she had always maintained would not help her. Turning her face towards the pale morning sky, Jessica wept.

Chapter 14

The Forgotten One

Jessica wept long and loud, not caring if Old Oaky, Rosehip or the other faeries heard her. She wailed until her eyes were dry and unable to produce any more tears and her throat was sore and scratchy. Then she lay down on the damp grass and sobbed quietly to herself. It was only then she was able to hear the faerie leader's words.

'Why do you weep so, Jessica?'

Jessica propped herself up weakly on one elbow and rubbed her bloodshot eyes with the back of her hand. She could not express the insurmountable grief and uncertainty in her heart. When she did speak her words seemed futile and came out in a tone so weak and punctuated by sobs that she doubted the ancient elf would understand. 'I am crying because of what I saw. What I saw in the pool.'

The faerie got heavily to his feet and spread his tiny, wrinkled hands in a comforting gesture.

'Many great warriors and men of learning have wept after they looked into the Iris of the Ancestors,' he said. 'The memories of our elders are very often filled with heartache. Learning the truth about the past is harder than any lesson taught by human lecturer or faerie wise man, because it educates the heart and not the mind. These are the messages that hold the most value.'

Jessica wiped the cool rivers of tears from her cheeks and stared at the small faerie.

'Why didn't you tell me that before?' she asked. She felt as if Old Oaky was yet another person who had been lying to her.

The elf stroked his beard. 'Would you have gazed into the

Iris willingly if you'd known that it might cause you woe?' he asked.

Jessica shook her head.

'As I told you,' he continued, 'the Iris will only show you what you need to know, nothing more and nothing less. Sometimes it shows great horrors of bloody battles and terrible murders but never unless it can answer the questions of the one who is gazing into its heart.'

Jessica wrapped her arms around herself in a comforting hug. 'But it didn't answer my question,' she sobbed.

'Maybe, young lady,' he ventured, 'it did, only you haven't seen it yet. However, if it would heal the sadness in your heart to share with me and my young relatives what you saw, we will listen. In spite of what some humans believe, when asked politely we faeries can keep a secret.'

Jessica heard such wisdom in the elf's voice that she decided to reveal the secret of Rina's existence to him. She sniffed slightly.

'Do you promise you won't tell anyone? Please?' she begged.

All around her, the air erupted into a melody of beautiful, musical voices as the faeries seated in the surrounding bracken eagerly pledged their silence. Their voices were like a thousand tiny bells all chiming in harmony.

'We promise, Jessica. We'll keep your secret.'

'Yesterday,' she began slowly, 'Rosehip, Jake LeBlanc, Elsa Noir and I went down into the Magicroutes to see if there was any sign of witchcraft. Down there we were attacked by Black Trolls.'

A tiny gasp of horror ran through the crowd of faeriefolk.

Old Oaky looked around him at his young relatives and raised his hands to calm them. 'Now, now, there's no need to panic. Remember we have the power to hold back these forgotten souls and besides, I doubt they would venture to our part of the island. Continue, young miss.'

Jessica closed her eyes as she remembered the horror she went through the day before.

'It was terrible. We … we thought we were going to be killed. I'd hurt my leg. There was no way out. But then…' she paused for a second and rested a hand on her forehead, her brain throbbing as once again the image of Rina interrupted her thoughts, 'this creature … she came and rescued us. I don't know how but she fought off the trolls and she saved us. She cared about me. She didn't want to let me get hurt. But I don't know why and I don't even know what she was.'

Old Oaky rested his hands on the front of his scarlet tunic. 'And that was your question to the Iris,' he murmured. 'Who was this creature? And what information did the mystical pool share with you?'

Jessica bit her lip hard as she felt the tears welling up again. 'My mother's last hours,' she said. 'It showed me her just before she died and then ... and then...' She gritted her teeth and pounded her fist on the green earth with rage. 'It showed my great uncle Jim rejecting the creature who saved me when she was young. He sent her away with Keela, the merman; he said she was evil.'

Jessica began to weep again, but this time her tears were of anger not despair.

'He shouldn't have done it!' she cried to the grey faerie. 'We weren't evil. We didn't understand. It wasn't our fault.'

A gasp rose from the faeries as Jessica spoke and even Old Oaky looked slightly disturbed. He raised his wispy eyebrows.

'*We* weren't evil, Jessica?' he asked. 'Who are *we*?'

Jessica clapped her hand over her mouth. She had said it again, just as she'd done to Jake – used the plural as if she had been with Rina when she had been rejected. It scared her. It was as if the magic of Jersey itself, some of it good, some of it evil, was tying Jess and Rina together so firmly that even if Jessica wanted to she wouldn't be able to break away.

Old Oaky took a step forward, his rusty, leafed cloak shifting as he moved.

'Have you told your great uncle about meeting this Rina?' he asked.

'No,' she whispered. 'And now I'm glad I didn't. I promised her, promised her I wouldn't let anyone know where she was. The Iris proved it. If I told Jim about her he would probably have gone and dug her out, tried to kill her.' She plucked at the lush grass of the bank and muttered bitterly. 'I hate him so much right now,'

Old Oaky shook his head and his trailing whiskers danced in the breeze. 'You don't mean that, Miss Jessica. You may think you do. Right now it might feel as if you can never forgive

288

him. But you will, when the time is right. You'll understand and so will he.' The elderly faerie placed a hand on Rosehip's shoulder and stretched his cobweb-like wings, allowing them to warm in the sun. 'And what of the merman, Keela?' he asked, at last. 'An honourable gentleman of the ocean, if my memory serves me and I'm sure it does. He is very noble, with a great wisdom of the morality of things. Does he know you and this mystery of his keeping have become acquainted?'

'No,' Jessica replied. Then suddenly she realized what Old Oaky had said. 'This mystery of his keeping? I didn't say Keela *saved* the child. That means you knew about her – you knew all along. Then tell me who she is!'

Old Oaky looked very tired. 'I will not lie to you, young lady,' he said. 'I think you've endured more than enough trickery in your short life. I do know a little about the being of which you speak but it is mainly hearsay. All I am at liberty to tell you is that a long time ago your great uncle and the merman Keela took it upon themselves to make a pact regarding that which you call Rina. The pact excluded me, my kinsfolk and many others who dwell on this island. With hindsight they may both now see that it was a fateful day when they did so, but I do not have the knowledge nor the courage of conviction to say. It is between them. They hold the answer to your quest.'

With that, he sat down, yawned and wrapped his cape around him.

Jessica felt less angry though she was still confused and disturbed by what she had seen in the Iris.

'My quest?' she repeated softly to herself. 'But Jim said my quest was to save Jersey from witchcraft.'

The ancient faerie closed his eyes and snuggled down, deep into his robes, until all that was visible of him was the smooth, round dome of his head.

'Yes,' he murmured sleepily. 'But how you set about doing this is up to you.' He ceased talking and began to snore.

Rosehip, who had spent the entire time kneeling by his side, got to her feet. 'I think that's all you're going to get out of him!' she said, brushing some tiny flecks of dust from her dress. 'He does that. Wide awake one minute, snoring his head off the next.'

Jessica turned away from the Iris and started to follow the path back through the heather towards the road. She had taken only a couple of steps when Rosehip's shrill voice called after her.

'Where are you going?'

Jessica spun back on her heel. 'I ... I don't know.'

And as she spoke the words, Jessica realized they were completely true. She had no idea where she was to go. Rosehip spread her wings but made no effort to take off. The two females stood there for a second, neither one knowing what to say. When Rosehip did speak, her voice was tinged with uncertainty.

'Do you want me to come with you?'

Jessica looked out over the wild bracken and pushed a lock of stray hair behind her ear. 'No,' she said with a shake of her head. 'I want to be on my own.'

Rosehip bowed her head and looked sadly into the black pool. 'I'm sorry,' the faerie sniffed timidly. 'I'm sorry, Jessica.'

'It wasn't your fault, Rosehip. You were right to bring me here. I had to see the truth. It's hard, that's all.'

With that Jessica turned toward the faerie path away from the hurtful Iris. Her mind was numb. She found that she was running through the heather, expelling some of her anger and pain. She wasn't crying any more, didn't want to. Didn't want to waste her tears on something she couldn't yet understand. She wanted to do something, hit something, make something, she didn't know what, just anything to make her feel less helpless, less like someone who just had things happen to her and didn't fight back. She was the Guardian of Jersey, for God's sake. Didn't she at least have *some* sort of power?

She quickly reached the main road and abruptly stopped. What should she do? She didn't know, she couldn't think.

She looked up and down the road. To her left was Maison de l'hache, where her father and great uncle were. She imagined walking back into the kitchen, Martin sitting at the old pine table, Jim cooking breakfast. She felt sick as she thought of looking into Jim's shiny, dark eyes and knowing he had told Keela to slaughter the creature who had saved her life. She wondered what would happen if she asked him flat out. Would he deny it? Would he fly into a rage the moment she uttered her name, call it evil and set out to destroy it? Would he turn on Jessica for discovering his secret? She didn't know and she didn't want to find out. Everything had changed now, more than before. More than it had when Jessica had discovered the truth about her mother's identity. At least then she had believed that Jim was a decent man who knew of Jersey's perils and would be able to guide her. Now she wasn't so sure. He wasn't the Guardian. Only Jessica held that responsibility and it was her judgement alone that she could trust. At this moment her judgement was telling her it wasn't the time to return to Maison de l'hache. In fact, she doubted that she ever wanted to return to the house again. But the practicality of the situation meant that sooner or later she would have to, as there was nowhere else on the island she could go. But she would not meet Jim until it was absolutely necessary.

That decision meant she would have to take the path to her right, the one that led out into the horizon and down to the dark sea that was Keela's home.

This destination seemed, at least on the surface, to hold more hope for Jessica, even if she didn't quite know what to expect. She knew very little about the merman who had rescued her and shown her the road that destiny had to offer. But what she did know, from their one brief meeting and the vision in the Iris, was that he was fiercely loyal and honest even to those, like Jim, who betrayed him. Jessica thought that if there was one person on this mysterious and secretive island who wouldn't baffle her with lies it was Keela. It wasn't in his nature to be deceitful and by the anger he had expressed at Jessica's lack of magical knowledge, she thought he would be more than willing to reveal the truth to her about Rina.

She turned right onto the long country road that would eventually bring her to St Ouens Bay and began to walk purposefully. She was full of questions for the merman. Who was Rina and why had she protected Jessica so courageously? That was the first and most obvious one. But Jessica also needed an explanation of the exchange she had witnessed in the pool between her great uncle and his aquatic friend. It was obvious that many years ago the two of them had collaborated to keep Rina away not only from the world Jessica inhabited but from the magical world of Jersey. Keela had placed the malformed creature within the Magicroutes, away from other eyes.

'Just like me,' uttered Jessica softly as the thought struck her with harsh irony. Now that was an odd notion. It was true that her prison hadn't been as dank and brutal as the catacombs where Rina apparently dwelt but she now saw that for many years she herself had been deliberately kept away from Jersey. She had been cut off from the existence of magic and witchcraft and kept in ignorance of her title of Guardian. But there had been a reason for that, however misguided. Why did Jim wish Rina dead and equally, why was Keela determined to preserve her life? It couldn't be her hideous appearance alone that forced her underground. Jess was sure that Keela had the answers. She must find him.

However, the very second that Jessica resolved to hunt out Keela and quiz him on what had really taken place between him and Jim all that time ago, she remembered Rina's urgent injunction to her: 'No tell Keelie I sees Rina.' In her eagerness to find out what had tied her emotions so strongly to Rina she had forgotten her pledge. No, she could not ask Keela for help even if he would willingly give her the knowledge she searched for. Then, like a blinding light, it dawned on Jessica why Rina was kept hidden. Rina had been cursed, cursed by black magic in such a powerful and foul way that her very appearance in daylight would drive the witch-fearing folk of Jersey to murder her.

It was clear now where she had to head. Her own woe seemed to vanish as she realized where the path of the Guardian was to take her. It wasn't back to Jim or Keela. She had to return to Rina and tell her she knew what had happened and understood her sorrows. Neither of them would be alone.

Just then Jessica saw in the distance a large shape heading up the road towards her, its familiar growl echoing in the still morning air. Waving furiously, Jessica ran towards the bus hoping that it would stop. Her heart leapt as she saw the destination above the window: 'Grosnez'. The vehicle drew level with her and stopped with a squeal of air brakes. The door swung open and she hurried up the stairs.

Behind the wheel sat a tall man with dusty blond hair and a round, puckered face. He was clearly not happy at having to make an unscheduled stop. He slumped forward and rested his elbows on the steering wheel as the teenager fumbled in the pocket of her jeans for her purse. Holiday makers, he thought, the island was better off without them. Wearily, he said, 'Grosnez, Gorey and St Helier, as you clearly don't know the timetable.'

Jessica gave him an apologetic smile and searched through the jumble of receipts in the back of her purse for her travel card. 'Grosnez, please,' she said.

She pulled out the slightly creased ticket and placed it on the narrow partition that separated her from the driver. The weary man glanced at it and sucked his bottom lip.

'Can't take that, love,' he muttered. 'Not a Jersey travel card.'

Jessica's mind was still too full of the matter of Rina to battle with the mundane task of paying the fare. 'What?' she muttered.

The driver raised his eyebrows and prodded the small rectangle of card. 'London Travel Card,' he stated. 'We don't take them over here. You'll have to pay the fare.'

Jessica frowned at his aggressive manner and wondered whether to tell him she was the Heir of Helier so the least he could do was be polite. But she thought better of it and decided this was not the time to be petty. 'How much to Grosnez?' she asked, snapping up her travel card and stuffing it into her purse.

'Eighty-five pence,' he grumbled, staring straight in front of him.

Jessica threw him a disapproving look, scooped some spare change from her purse and dropped it with a loud clatter into the metal dish. She stepped into the aisle and the bus quickly drew away barely giving her chance to sit down.

Jessica sat in the first empty seat directly behind the driver and glanced around her. The vehicle was empty, apart from herself and four other passengers. A few seats back a young mother in her late twenties sat with a boy of seven or eight. The child clutched a red bucket and spade and had his face pressed so close to the window his nose was practically touching the glass. At the very back of the bus, a man of at least seventy perched, his legs outstretched in such a manner as to tell everyone that the entire back bench belonged to him alone. He was wearing a bright yellow sweater with diamonds of navy blue and had a wooden pipe gripped in his teeth, the stalk of which was chewed in a vaguely aggressive manner. The final passenger was a middle-aged lady with short, chestnut hair and a chubby, pink face. Jessica noted that from the moment she got on the bus, this lady had been watching her with uncontrollable curiosity and now that Jessica was looking at her she gave a half smile of recognition. Jessica responded with a polite nod of her head but then broke her gaze, feeling slightly uncomfortable at being stared at by someone she didn't know. She returned to looking at the rolling countryside as they chugged along the narrow lane. She realized then why the woman had been looking at her so intently. She must be a true Jersey person – one, like Jim, who knew of the island's magic and recognized Jessica as the Guardian. It was the first time Jessica had been aware of someone acknowledging her as special. She wondered if in her time on the island before she knew of her legacy there had been others who had realized she was the Heir and had gazed at her inquisitively without her knowing it. It was an odd feeling, to become suddenly aware that you were famous, and know that to the people of this small green gem floating in the channel you held the responsibility and power of a dynasty that went back into the mists of time. Like it or not, she held the key to something great. She only hoped she would prove herself worthy.

Jessica shook her head as if to dislodge the memory of the woman's curiosity from her mind. At the present, it would not help to pad her own ego with thoughts of her great role in history. There was more to being the Guardian than fame and recognition and in Jess's mind the important thing at present was to plan her meeting with Rina. As the bus trundled along the road towards Grosnez it was as if the strange creature were sending out magnetic waves that pulled Jessica back to her. Jessica felt no fear at returning to the entrance of Rina's subterranean home. Quite the opposite, in fact. It didn't even bother her that the Magicroutes also housed the hideous and blood-thirsty Black Trolls. All that really seemed important to Jessica was that she would soon be back with Rina.

But despite her joy, Jessica couldn't avoid a little pang of doubt that gnawed at her excitement. She wanted above all things to ask Rina who, and what, she was, but she wondered whether Rina herself knew who she was. Rina was obviously gentle and eager for Jessica's company but it was clear her intellect was somewhat limited. What kind of creature was she? Did she live all alone in the caves of Jersey or were there others like her? Had she always inhabited the scarred and malformed body she was cursed with or had she been born differently and later cursed? And why was she tied to Keela the merman? What caused him to have such a sense of duty towards her? Jessica pondered whether Rina had the capability to provide her with the answers.

She was suddenly shaken from her thoughts as the bus's brakes let out an ear-splitting squeal and the lumbering vehicle drew to a stop.

'Grosnez and Five Mile Road,' called the driver as Jessica got to her feet. She looked quickly at the woman who had watched her so intently, then got off, immediately striking out over towards the patch of gorse on the cliff top that disguised the scavenger's ladder. Parting its branches she stepped onto the rickety staircase that led to the rocks below. A brisk wind blew off the rippling ocean, filling Jessica's lungs with the fresh smell of the sea. Jessica cautiously picked her way down the steps towards the jagged rocks and pools that led down into the sea. She wondered sadly whether Rina had ever felt the sunshine on her puckered, olive skin or heard the seagulls cry or whether her entire existence had been spent hidden away from life and light in a world of gloomy half-darkness and stagnant air.

She reached the foot of the wooden stairs and stepped onto the slippery granite, taking a moment to steady herself on the uneven surface. Only a few hours ago she had been very grateful to get away from the Magicroutes but now here she was, totally alone, hurrying to get back inside. She swiftly found the inlet in the granite wall into which the sea steadily washed and bending her head slightly, moved onto the narrow ledge that bordered the left hand wall of the cave. As soon as she was inside the air felt cooler. She looked towards the back of the cave and saw at once the crooked hole that was the entrance to the treacherous network of tunnels which honeycombed the island of Jersey. It was odd but the opening that had proved such an easy exit the day before now looked too small. Jessica edged forwards until she reached the very back of the cave and knelt down on the outcrop next to the hole. The portal that led down into the blackness was now only about two feet in diameter, certainly not big enough for Jessica to get inside. She placed her hands on the rim and gently traced its circumference, pushing at the sturdy rock in the vain hope that it would, by some magical means, become larger, but it did not. There was no way she could enter the passageway. She glanced behind her to make sure no-one was watching. Then, carefully, she put her head closer to the gap and called down into the darkness.

'Rina, are you there? Can you hear me?' She could smell the moist, rotten smell that lingered in the tunnels. The bright sunlight streamed into the cave from outside, forming a narrow shaft of pale light that illuminated the area just inside. Jessica could make out the shapes of the stone that formed the slope they'd climbed up to safety from the day before but no sound or movement came from within. What if the Black Trolls had returned after their escape and ambushed Rina? What if she hadn't been strong enough to fight off another attack? Jessica closed her eyes and took a deep breath. No, she was wrong. Rina was very much alive; she could sense her close by. Jessica pressed her face closer to the rock and called out again, louder this time.

'Rina, it's me, Jessica – remember, from yesterday? If you can hear me please say something. I need to speak to you. It's important.'

Jessica held her breath, praying that Rina would answer her. Her ears seemed acutely alert and every sound from the beating sea on the rock to the cries of the seagulls resonated in her brain. She leant closer into the cavity until the whole of her head was inside the dark portal. Deep below her, in the cold blackness of the cavern, Jessica could hear a gentle padding and scraping sound; something was stirring. Her nerves prickled with anticipation. Excitement and dread wrestled each other in Jessica's brain. She knew first hand what horrors dwelt within the hidden parts of Jersey and she feared another confrontation with the Black Trolls. However, the sunshine on her back reminded her that those foul creatures thrived on darkness and would not dare venture near the surface in daylight hours.

A sound, quite unlike one that Jessica had ever heard before, echoed up from the shadows – a wet, gravelly bark like an animal coughing up mucus. Jessica's fingertips gripped the rough rim of the cave but she did not feel afraid. She knew at once that the strange yap was from Rina nestling deep in the shadows. For the third time Jessica called to her, tenderly and with encouragement.

'Rina, is that you? I can hear you. Come out where I can see you.'

There was the sound of her serpent-like body winding across the mountain of stone and of powerful hands shifting rocks. Jessica found herself grinning as she patiently waited for Rina to show herself. Then, as she stared down into the shadows, Jessica saw the gleam of two russet gems shining in the filth of the cave. For the second time that day, Jessica saw a face emerge from blackness, only this time it was solid and alive. Straggly curtains of greasy locks, inky black in the sunlight, framed the gentle irises. The small, puckered mouth buried deep in her scarred and pitted skin stretched into a dagger-toothed smile as she let out a joyful little shriek. Jessica found herself smiling.

Rina tossed back her mane of dark tangles and gurgled with laughter. 'Jecica back,' she called in her gruff voice. 'Jecica keepsie promisings.' She slapped her large hands on the walls of the tunnel excitedly.

Jessica chuckled, her heart filling with more happiness than she had felt all of that disturbing day. She shuffled her body so she was leaning against the back of the cave, her head as far in the tunnel as she could get it.

'I said I'd come back,' she told the joyful Rina. 'I had to. I never got a chance to say thank you properly for yesterday. What you did was very brave, you know. I ... we ... might not have got out alive if you hadn't shown up.'

The oily, green creature made a shy gurgle and turned her face away, resting an abnormally long digit coquettishly on her warty chin.

'No thankies to Rina is needings,' she cried. 'Rina had to be saving Jecica. 'Tis right thing. Nasty Bla-Blas all narly and snarly.'

She shuddered at the thought of the trolls. Jessica placed her elbow on the rim of the hole and rested her chin in her palm. She couldn't believe how docile and calm Rina was now. She was almost timid. Jess wondered how Jake could have doubted that Rina was female.

'Still,' Jessica continued, 'I can't believe how much you helped us. You should be proud. I'm sure Jake and Elsa feel the same.'

Rina gave a dismissive snort. 'Rina is not carings about Ake and Ellysa,' she murmured, peering out from the mass of black hair that hung over her crusty features. 'Ellysa is being prettysome and Ake is okay. But it is Jecica that means all. Jecica is all Rina

297

is carings about.' There was a tenderness in Rina's growling, that seemed to wrap around Jessica like a comforting hug from an old friend. It moved her so much that she wished the crack in the granite rock would burst asunder so she could embrace this being who was still filled with love, despite the bitterness she had been shown. But all Jessica could do was reach down through the tiny gap towards the face of the creature. She felt the cool, smooth, leathery fingertips of Rina's oversized hand caress her palm and closed her eyes. It seemed as if a memory that had long been buried was resurfacing but she could not identify it. Rina's deep voice came again in a whisper as natural and loving as the waves.

'Rina has been waitings all her lifes for Jecica come back. It is my hopes.'

Jessica opened her eyes and gazed down into the prison of stone that was Rina's home. The being gazed back up at her, the beautiful eyes shining so much Jessica could have sworn they were filled with tears. 'Rina who are you?' she asked.

The creature's face crumbled into a frown as if she couldn't understand what Jessica was asking. She dropped her head and the thick mass of dark hair fell forward over her face as she let out a soft, nasal sigh. Jessica tilted her head to one side and felt a pang of guilt. Overcome by her own intense emotions she hadn't considered Rina's feelings.

But before Jess could apologize, Rina lifted her head to looked up at the girl and her wrinkled mouth puckered tightly as she struggled to form words as clearly as she could.

'I be Rina,' she muttered, her gruff voice straining as if what she had to say carried the weight of the whole world. 'I be in the grottys all times. Kept in darkness, kept in safeness, ma Keelie say. All time here, all time till Jecica come back, Keelie says.' She bowed her head again and groaned as if in pain. Jessica's heart bled.

Rina clutched her long-fingered hands together. Her docile brown eyes twitched nervously and something in her startling appearance and anxious gestures reminded Jess of Elsa.

'But na,' continued the odd being, her voice filled with sadness. 'Rina cannot wait too longer. Time comes, Rina knows, time comes.' She extended an oversized, wart-covered hand to Jessica. 'Jecica be back so time is beings comings. But is wrong.' The

298

strange creature sucked what could loosely be called her lip and patted her chest, her hideous face constricted with frustration. 'Rina no want be alonely no more. Rina scaresome, muchly big changings happenings. Is scaresome, is scaresome and wrong beings here. No bla-blas, no want be alonely.'

Helplessness welled up inside Jessica. Rina was becoming more and more distressed by the second and the full horror of her predicament was now apparent to Jessica. She thought about the vision in the Iris and Jim's harsh words; they stung even more now she saw how lonely Rina was. She still didn't know where Rina came from but it was now clear that this was entirely the problem. Rina didn't belong anywhere; she had been left in the cave – to die most probably – because no-one, definitely not Jim, accepted her. Now the trolls had returned to Jersey, it seemed only a matter of time before they overpowered her and finished her. Jessica opened her mouth and asked the question she already knew the answer to.

'You're an orphan, aren't you?'

Rina turned her head away as if she was about to retreat into the cave below. She did not reply in words but made a melancholy purr. Jessica knew exactly how she felt because she had felt the same pain many times when thinking of her own mother – a lonely anguish too raw to be expressed in words.

Jessica rested her head against the stone of the cave and whispered, 'It hurts, doesn't it? Trying to be brave when you're lonely. I ... I know. I lost my mum when I was little.'

Rina spun round, her chocolate irises glistening in the dark. 'Da,' she said softly, a sound that was more an expression of knowing than an attempt to form a real word. 'Jecica mam-mam gone, Rina mam-mam gone. We are same, Rina know. But Jecica must fight, must put right back. Rina try, try but is weak, is body broken. Jecica is muchly importance now. Must learning from Uncly Jim, must fightsies, make Bla-Blas go.'

Ice cold pin-pricks of bitterness stabbed at Jessica's heart as she thought of her great uncle. She knew she had to fight the black magic and that Jim knew more about the threat of witchcraft than she ever could. But every time he entered her brain the words she heard from the Iris echoed back as clearly and as cruelly as if they had been spoken yesterday. Her trust in him had evaporated and it was harshly ironic that Rina was pointing her towards the one person whom Jessica now knew had rejected Rina when she was at her most helpless. She wanted to explain this but the very thought of telling Rina how cruelly she had been rejected made Jessica feel sick with horror.

She looked down at the disfigured face, at the skin scarred and covered with warts, at the reptilian nose and mouth and saw only kindness and childlike innocence. It pierced her heart with pity.

'What about you?' she asked.

Rina inhaled deeply, her narrow nostrils expanding as wide as they could. 'Rina is tryings to help Jecica how Rina can,' she murmured. 'For now must stay like ma Keelie sayings. Jecica fightsies Bla-Blas, Rina be safesy in grotties. Rina no more can do.' She shut her doe-like eyes. 'Soon time be comings,' she breathed wistfully, 'Rina be all right and prettily.'

She paused and her expression of hope was so blissful, Jessica felt that she could ignore her plight no longer.

'I'm going to get you out, Rina,' she whispered. 'I promise, I'll take you to live some place better than these horrid caves.'

For the briefest of moments Rina gave Jessica a look of complete and utter joy. Then she pouted her narrow mouth and her soft eyes took on a steely glint.

'Na, Bla-Blas go first,' she said, raising a long, tapered finger in determination. 'Jecica got muchly, great hard fightsie ahead. No more worries 'bout Rina.' She glanced behind her and shuffled her serpent-like body further into the blackness. 'Rina go now,' she whispered hastily, her features now half hidden by shadows. 'Bye-bye Jecica, we be right soon.'

Jessica strained her neck further into the tunnel as Rina slithered into the darkness. She hadn't expected her meeting with Rina to be so brief and longed to stay in her company.

'Rina,' she called after her. 'Rina, don't go. Don't leave me.'

But already she heard the sound of the stones moving as Rina crept away. Jessica found herself abandoned on the rock ledge.

She ran a wistful hand around the entrance to the caves and pondered sadly what she should do next. Rina had been deserted by everyone but Keela. Yet the cruel irony was she had placed her faith in the one person who, unbeknown to her, had turned her away. She had next to nothing and Jessica knew well the hopeless feeling of being composed of parts of a family and life that was broken and half-formed. She knew that the real tragedy of Rina lay not within her cursed and scarred body but in the world surrounding her, a world that was too cold and ignorant to see beyond the limitations of her physical form. There was nothing wrong or evil in Rina's heart – she knew the trolls were wicked, knew Jessica had a duty to save the island – yet she had been condemned to a cold and brutal prison from the time she was an infant. There was no justice in it.

Justice. The word hit Jessica like a bolt of brilliant sunlight slicing through the blackest storm clouds. Wasn't that what the Guardian of Jersey was all about? Bringing justice and right where there was discord on the island. She knew in her heart there had been a great unfairness done to Rina. A bold plan had begun to form in Jessica's mind: she would bring Rina out of the darkness of the Magicroutes into the sunlight where she truly belonged. There had to be picks and shovels back at Maison de l'hache and Jessica decided that the following day she would crack open the tunnel entrance and bring Rina back to confront Jim.

Filled with a fierce new hope, Jessica got to her feet and marched out of the cave onto the sun-drenched rocks. A resolute spring in her step, Jessica swiftly climbed the wooden steps that led up the cliff face. All the information and equipment that she needed lay back at the house with Martin and Jim and Jessica wasn't yet cool enough to return without wanting to confront Jim and tell him how despicable she thought he was for turning Rina away. That would never do. The full power of her argument had to wait until the wronged creature was brought into the open and he was made to face his responsibilities. No, the best thing that she could do right now was to rally her friends and ask for their aid.

She reached the top of the ladder and stepped out onto the grassy headland. It was midmorning by now and the day, if not Jessica's mood, was fine and breezy. She stood among the tall grass, glancing this way and that. As she gazed at the vehicles motoring up and down the long straight road, she noticed a square, slightly run down camper van parked at the side of the road and a cluster of teenaged boys standing around it, clothed in wetsuits and clutching surf-boards. As Jessica walked closer she recognized one – it was Jake. She took off at speed, calling

301

his name. As she reached the road Jake heard her and turned round, as did his two companions.

Jake's brow knitted in confusion and annoyance as Jess drew level with them. It was clear this was not a context he was prepared to see her in and he looked embarrassed. Jessica stopped, took a few deep gulps of air to get her breath back and began.

'Jake, thank God – you're just the person I needed to see.'

The lad on his right with curly, ginger hair and a face so covered in freckles that you could barely see the natural colour of his skin, gave a chuckle and nudged him. 'Ay, Jake,' he cried in a broad Jersey accent. 'Got yourself a girlfriend have you? Got yourself a bit of skirt!'

Both Jess and Jake glared at him. Jake could tell by the anxious expression in Jessica's eyes this was no time for jokes. 'Leave it, Andy,' Jake told the lad, shoving him lightly. 'It's Jess. Jessica Kent.'

Recognition dawned on the red-haired boy's face. 'Oh, Emma's daughter. I am sorry, Miss Kent, I didn't mean to be impolite.'

He bobbed his head in a small bow, though Jessica couldn't decide whether the gesture was sincere or not. She glanced at Jake's other companion, a short, round-faced youth with blond hair almost as fair as Elsa's. By his expression she realized that he too knew the significance of her role in Jersey. She felt uncomfortable in the presence of these two boys and wished very much they would leave her to tell the events of that morning to Jake in private.

Jake saw that Jessica's eyes were slightly red and he wondered if she had been crying. He hoped not. If there was one thing Jake LeBlanc was terrible at it was comforting upset women. He placed a hand on her shoulder just firmly enough to show he was concerned but not so concerned as to be thought soft in front of his mates.

'You okay?' he asked, his voice friendly but not over anxious.

Jessica quickly glanced at the two other lads making sure her gaze didn't linger long enough to form eye contact. 'Yeah,' she huffed, swallowing what seemed to be an impossibly large chunk of emotion. 'I just need to tell you something.'

She looked at him and hoped that he would motion to his friends to leave them alone but he didn't.

'It's all right,' he continued. 'Andy and Terry are Beans – they know about the witches and that.'

He gave his friends a grim smile.

Jessica gritted her teeth in frustration. Even if Jake's friends were island folk she was not comfortable telling anyone but Jake, Elsa and Rosehip about what had happened. The concern she had for Rina was a very delicate matter and Jessica definitely didn't want to share it with strangers. She fixed Jake with a knowing gaze and muttered through clenched teeth, 'It's about what happened yesterday.'

Comprehension dawned in Jake's face. Glancing up at the other two boys, he said coolly. 'Business with the Guardian. Give us a minute.'

Andy and Terry looked at each other, worried expressions etched on their faces. It was clear that Jessica's concern had made them uneasy and already their minds were conjuring nightmarish images of what might happen if the witches had returned to Jersey.

'Shouldn't ... shouldn't we know what's going on?' questioned Andy, his face suddenly pale.

Jake closed his eyes and shook his head. 'Nah, it's nothing – just boring stuff. If there's any danger I'll let you know.' He sounded tired and Jessica started to think that he wasn't seeing the situation as seriously as he should. 'Five minutes.'

Jake gestured, waving his hand as if to motion for the boys to back off. Reluctantly, they wandered off along the roadside, looking back with undisguised curiosity every few paces.

Jake glared at Jess with a look that screamed, 'How dare you show up when I'm with my friends!' He slid open the panel door to the camper.

'Inside,' he grunted, climbing into the vehicle.

The interior was cramped but well fitted. There was a padded bench along the back of the van and a small kitchen area on the right-hand side with sink, hob and kettle. Jumpers and coats were strewn around and the whole place smelt rather musty. Jessica squeezed her way to the rear and flopped down on the seat. The springs twanged as they took her weight. Jake scrabbled about in the kitchen area, fumbling clumsily with the kettle. His great height meant that he had to bend almost double to fit inside the tiny living space and even then his arched back scraped the roof. He cursed and muttered to himself and Jessica wondered whether he was annoyed because of her unexpected arrival or simply because the measurements of the camper did nothing to accommodate his lanky proportions. After a few minutes of quiet swearing and banging of mugs Jake glanced at Jess.

'You went down to see her, didn't you?' he asked. His voice was softer but there was still an edge of irritation. He dropped a teabag in each of the mugs.

'Who?' she said, though she knew that they were both aware of exactly who was being referred to, but she felt a need for Jake to say Rina's name.

Jake waved his hand vaguely and sent the bottle of milk he had just retrieved from the cooler flying, nearly spilling its contents over the draining board.

'That thing from down in the caves, Rina or whatever her name is. You got up first thing this morning and went traipsing down here to find her, didn't you? You're crackers.'

A small smile flitted over Jessica's lips the moment Jake said Rina's name. At least he had remembered what she was called, and after all she had been through she was grateful for small mercies. 'Not first thing this morning, but I have spoken to her,' she replied softly.

Jake gave a small groan of despair and poured the boiling water from the kettle into the mugs. 'I don't understand this obsession you have with that thing. We don't even know what it is.'

Jessica looked at him, her eyebrows raised, but she bit back the primal anger she felt. What she needed most at this particular time was support and she wasn't going to get that by having a go at him. 'Be fair,' she said, careful that her tone carried no hint of anger. 'She did save our lives. Even you can't deny that.'

Jake made a sound of unwilling agreement and stared down into the cups. 'You want sugar?' he asked gruffly. Jessica motioned two and the boy scooped two, uneven spoonfuls into each cup.

In the slightly calmer atmosphere, Jessica's temper ebbed and she was aware of the growling emptiness in her stomach: she had gone out with no breakfast. 'You got a biscuit or something?' she asked. 'I'm starving.'

304

Jake reached inside the hamper and pulled out a bag of crisps, which he threw to her. 'Grockles,' he muttered, his tone not quite as harsh as it had been before. 'Never plan ahead.'

Jessica caught them and opening the packet reclined as low as she could on the worn-out sofa.

'You're wrong about one thing,' she said. 'I do know what Rina is.'

Jake, who had been in the process of picking up the tea mugs, nearly dropped them with shock. 'What?' he gasped.

Jessica slipped even further back on the seat and grinned with smug satisfaction. 'Oh, *now* you're interested,' she said. 'Well good, 'cause I'm going to need your help and by your grumpy tone I was beginning to doubt I would get it!'

Jake's cheeks coloured as he handed her a mug. 'Well, I was out with my mates and didn't expect to see you. After what happened yesterday I was hoping for a break.'

Jessica gave a small smile. 'I understand, and believe me if this wasn't very important I wouldn't have disturbed you.'

Jake sat down beside her and stretched out his long, bony legs, resting his cup of tea on his stomach. 'Well what is it – I mean she – I mean Rina?' he asked.

Jessica stuffed a handful of crisps into her mouth and chewed them thoughtfully before answering. 'Well,' she said, her mouth half-full, 'to be fair, I still don't know *exactly* what she is but I've a pretty good idea of what happened to her.'

'I don't understand.'

Jess shook her head. 'I don't either,' she said, 'not completely. But I do know she was cursed by something, a witch or a warlock most probably, and she has been left alone in the Magicroutes all her life. She has no family. Everyone on the island rejected her and the only person who has been looking after her all these years is Keela.'

'How do you know all that?'

Jess licked some salt from her lips and took a sip of tea. It wasn't that nice but she was desperate to have something warm in her belly. 'Rina told me some – that she had no parents and that Keela took care of her. The curse bit I sort of figured out for myself. Well it makes sense, her looking the way she does. I don't know much about witches but to have a body that malformed it's got to be caused by some kind of black magic, hasn't it? That's why she was abandoned, people were scared she carried some sort of evil. The rest I got from the Iris.'

Jake frowned and slurped his tea. 'The Iris of the Ancestors?' he said incredulously. 'No-one on Jersey has used that for donkey's years; it's got a bit of a bad rep. Whatever made you go down there?'

Jessica leant forward, her elbows resting on her thighs. 'Rosehip told me about it. Said she remembered something that might help with Rina last night. We went down there at dawn and I asked it who Rina was.'

'Rosehip! When have you of all people taken anything Rosehip had to say seriously? You said yourself faeries are loony.'

Jessica shrugged. 'All I know is I saw things in that pool which explained a lot, even if they weren't particularly pleasant. Why? Doesn't it always tell the truth?'

In a strange way she hoped the pool was lying about Jim's rejection. It would make things a lot easier and enable her to return to Maison de l'hache without the resentment which boiled in her.

Jake took another gulp of tea and glanced at her out of the corner of his eye. 'It tells the truth all right,' he uttered darkly, 'and it doesn't sugar-coat the pill. You're a better man than me if you asked it for advice; some say it's hexed. Rumour has it a witch drowned in that pool and now it will only show you the most depressing and shameful events of your family's past. People have been known to go mad...'

He stopped. The colour had drained from Jessica's face and she looked as if she was about to vomit. She felt a heavy, warm pressure on her back as Jake rested his hand there.

'It showed you your mum's death, didn't it, Jess? I am so sorry.'

Jake's voice held more sincerity than Jessica had heard in it all that day but she was in no mood to be pitied. She shifted briskly away from Jake's hand and held her own fingers over her eyes to force back her tears; it was a personal rule she'd made never to cry in front of friends.

'Yes, but it doesn't matter,' she snapped briskly.

Jake lowered his eyes, still worried. 'But it must have been terrible seeing your mum die.'

'My mother's death wasn't the only vision I saw in the pool,' she said with forced clarity, battling to control her emotions. 'I saw Rina as a baby. She was sick and helpless. I saw Keela begging Jim to hold her, to take care of her. I saw Jim say she was evil and that Keela should murder her.' She took a deep breath and when she spoke again her voice seemed to come not from her own throat but from a place deep in her soul that was as cursed and scarred as Rina herself. 'It was Jim's responsibility to look after Rina and bring her up, Keela said. But he let him down, he let Rina down and failed in his duty. It went wrong, Jake. It all got messed up and Jim is to blame. Maybe it isn't just witches that help the black magic.'

She stood up abruptly and pressed the palms of her hands into her eyes. Jake sat quietly for a moment, his index finger resting thoughtfully on his bottom lip.

'The child still lives,' he muttered softly to himself. 'That's what Xandu told Jim at the meeting of the elders. I was so worried about the fact I was meant to be looking after you I didn't take much notice at the time. But that's who he was talking about – Rina is the child.' He wandered over to the sink his face wracked with confusion. 'That must mean Jim knew about Rina all this time. Still knows about her. Of course, of course. But it still doesn't answer anything. Why don't more people? Why has Jim kept her a secret for fourteen years? And what has Keela got to do with it? Why did he decide to save her when Jim wanted her dead?' He spun round to face Jessica. 'Have you mentioned Rina to him?' he asked.

Jessica gave a bitter laugh. 'No, and now I'm glad I didn't. I hate to think what he would do.' She paused for a second. 'But he will know tomorrow. I need your help but if you say "no" I totally understand – it's between me, Rina and Jim anyway. Tomorrow I'm coming back down here with picks and shovels and I'm going to dig Rina out. I'm going to take her back to confront Jim. He can't do anything if we face him together.' She spoke the last sentence as firmly as her voice would allow, but fear of what Jim might do trembled inside her.

Jake gazed at her with an intensity that made Jessica feel that it was her, not Rina, who was the oddity of nature. 'Has Rina had her say in this?' he asked.

Jess closed her eyes as the words and feelings of the cursed creature came back to her mind. 'She wants to get out the caves,' she said. 'Now is the time – that's what Keela told her – when I came back everything would be all right and Jim would come to her. But I honestly believe that the last thing Jim wants is Rina back in his life. He has written her off completely.' She opened her eyes. 'So what do you think?' she asked brusquely. 'Are you in or out?'

Jake scooped the plastic cup he had washed out of the sink and banged it abruptly on the draining board. 'Every instinct in my body is telling me you're crazy,' he said, not looking directly at Jess. 'But there are things happening on this island at the moment that make even someone like me, who grew up with magic, confused. Your friend, Rina, has certainly thrown the rulebook out of the window. I see no point in going up against the witches if there are secrets and hidden agendas in our own ranks. Jim has a lot of questions to answer.'

Jessica looked at him hopefully. 'Does that mean you'll come?' she asked.

'I guess so,' he replied, with a wry smile. Then, in a more business-like manner, 'But we'll have to make it early, six o'clock if possible. We don't what anybody seeing her. We'll need picks and shovels and a blanket of some kind to carry her up in. I'll bring the van so we can drive her back to Jim's. The rest is up to you.'

Jessica nodded enthusiastically. With Jake willingly on board there was no turning back now. In less than twenty-four hours Rina would be out of the danger of the Magicroutes and Jim would be forced to confront the innocent whom he had rejected and hoped had been forgotten. At least Jessica could say that in the short time she had been Guardian she had tried to put right the wrong that had been kept hidden. She drained the dregs from her mug and passed it to Jake.

'Here's to tomorrow morning and Rina's freedom,' she said.

Jake rinsed the mugs. 'Do you want us to drop you off at Jim's?' he asked.

Jessica stared thoughtfully out of the camper window. The blue sky seemed to have paled slightly in the short time she and Jake had been inside and the small, fluffy clouds which had hovered so cheerily there were clumping together more thickly in floating mountains of light slate. A chill breeze had drifted in off the sea, whisking the long grass and Andy and

Terry's hair as they stood waiting outside. A cold, hard knot of anger lay in Jessica's chest as she thought about Maison de l'hache and her great uncle. She couldn't go back, not right now. 'No,' she said. 'Don't bother. I have nothing to say to him without Rina.'

Jake looked at her wearily. 'You've got to go back sometime today. You can't wander around the island all day and all night until we can dig Rina out. I've said I'll do it tomorrow and can't do it sooner.'

Jessica remained staring out of the window, picturing Jim's stupidly grinning face. 'I know,' she breathed. 'I just can't face him this moment. Can I hang around with you and the others today? I'll be no trouble, I just need time to think.'

Jake gave a grunt. 'You've butted in on my morning and tomorrow already,' he said cheerfully. 'Why not highjack my afternoon as well?'

He slid open the door of the van and stuck his head out. 'Oi, Andy! Tel!' he yelled, his voice resonating through the cool air. 'I've done chatting to Her Nibs, you can come back.'

The two boys ambled over shivering and muttering something about 'Stuck up London bird', as they climbed inside the van.

'About bloomin' time,' muttered Terry, slumping on the sofa. 'Freezing out there now. So is there anything we should know about? Witches and that?'

Jessica felt too emotional to answer but she didn't have to worry as Jake jumped in and did it for her. 'Nah,' he replied, throwing Terry a towel. 'You know women – paranoid.'

Andy, who up until now had been staring at Jessica pensively, looked relieved. 'Well, that's good,' he said. 'Now Jake, would you ~~might~~ telling your bird to get out of the van so we can get changed.' mind

Before Jake could answer Jessica pushed past the boys and stepped outside with the comment that they had nothing of interest to look at anyway. She waited moodily, leaning on the van as the three males bumped about inside changing out of their surfing gear, and watched the vast expanse of dark cloud looming into view over the horizon as she tried to figure out what she would say to Jim when she did eventually return.

The boys took a few minutes to dress and then Jake pulled back the sliding door and beckoned Jess to enter. Jake then took his seat behind the ancient vehicle's steering wheel and the four of them were off, although the mood in the van was far from jovial. Jessica stared at the sky through the window as it grew cloudier. The effect of the weather made it even harder for her to shift her spiteful mood. Andy and Terry made stiff conversation with Jake as they travelled, clearly unsettled by both Jessica's unexpected company and her black temper. Jess swore she heard Andy make some snide comment about PMT but she couldn't be bothered to retaliate.

It seemed as if the Island of Jersey itself sensed Jessica's bad humour and the bright, sunny day that had dawned that morning vanished as midday approached. The air was close, still and warm, and seemed to thicken every second. There was no doubt about it: a storm was brewing.

Jake drove the rusty camper into the car-park of a pub. Jessica was too wrapped up in her own worries to notice what part of the island they were in. They disembarked and seated themselves in the garden. Time seemed to have slipped into a tar-pit and every second dragged. Jessica longed for dusk to fall, the next day to dawn and to free Rina so she could put right this life which now felt corrupt and filthy. She ordered fish and chips and ate it, for she had had no breakfast, but her tongue seemed dead and unable to taste. The food was like cardboard in her mouth and she only chewed and swallowed as fuel for the task ahead.

Eventually the meal was finished and paid for and they were travelling in the van again, this time to Greve de Lecq. She knew somewhere in the back of her mind, Jake was trying to keep her occupied so she would not have to return to Maison de l'hache and face Jim, and for that she was grateful.

The weather grew heavier by the minute and around three o'clock tiny spots of misty rain began to fall. Jake decided it was time to head homewards.

The sky was slate grey by the time the camper van drew up outside Jim Hellily's residence. Jessica got out and started towards the house, as if she were approaching an open grave.

'Hey,' Jake called after her, 'you sure you're ready for this?'

Jessica glanced back at the house and gave him a stiff nod. 'I'm sure,' she said, surprised at how calm her voice sounded, compared to what she was actually feeling. 'I mean, I can't very well spend the night with you, can I?'

From the back of the van, Andy and Terry made suggestive cat-calls. Jessica glared at them and the two lads fell immediately silent.

She took a deep breath to calm her temper. 'I'll be okay,' she said.

Jake raised his eyebrows doubtfully but knew better than to argue. 'I'll see you tomorrow,' he said and with that he wound up his window and drove away.

Jessica stood for a moment or two in the heavy air and comforted herself with the thought that by this time tomorrow Rina would be with her in the house and Jim would have been forced to confront his victim. She turned on her heels and crunched up the gravel drive.

As usual, the door was on the latch and she let herself in. The hall was dim and welcomingly cool.

She could hear the gentle murmurings of Jim and her father through the crack of light in the kitchen door and knew it was only a matter of moments before she would be face to face with the man for whom she felt such contempt. Jessica was torn in two, one half of her wanting to confront Jim, the other filled with longing to be with Rina once again. She stood, unmoving and stony-faced in the gloom of the hallway.

Suddenly the door to the kitchen swung open. Jessica flinched like a nocturnal animal caught unexpectedly in the light as the welcoming glow of the kitchen flooded the hallway. She was aware of Jim's heavy bulk shadowed against the bright light but could not bring herself to look at him, afraid of what she might do. Instead she remained standing as stiff and rigid as a granite statue, her head cocked at an awkward and uncomfortable angle so not one inch of his form tarnished her gaze. An angry, but oddly comforting voice, sounded in the deepest part of her brain.

Betrayer, Jim, what did we ever do to you?

Jim leaned on the doorframe and gazed at Jessica, aware she had something on her mind. 'You're back,' he stated. 'We've been wondering where you were. Your note didn't leave much of a clue.'

He chuckled softly and the light-hearted sound riled Jessica, making her dig her nails into her palms. The voice hissed in the back of her skull:

How dare you laugh at us after your betrayal! Your heart is cold and cruel.

Jessica kicked at the floor crossly in an attempt to release some of her fury. 'No business of yours where I go,' she muttered darkly. 'I'm the Guardian. I can do what I want. What do you care where I go anyway?'

You didn't care what happened to us when we were born. You wanted us killed then.

Jim's face creased with concern. He knew the burden of being the Guardian couldn't be easy for Jessica to carry and he wanted to help her as much as he could. He wondered where she had been that day and what she had seen or done to put her into this dark mood.

'Did you go back to the Magicroutes?' he asked, wishing very much that she would look at him.

Jessica didn't move the slightest bit. Rage seemed to have her in a vice-like grip. 'No,' she replied bluntly. She thought of her father and had a great desire to tell him exactly what had happened that day, to share with him her own anger in the hope he would understand.

Jim took a step forwards to approach his great-niece and watched in horror as she shrank away from him without even turning her head. 'Then where did you go?' he questioned cautiously.

'I was out with Jake,' she spat contemptuously. 'We hung around with his friends – we had a meal, it is nothing to do with you! So mind your own business!'

Attempted murderer! Prejudiced fool! Rejecter!

Jessica felt a glimmer of triumph in her fury. She saw the hurt on Jim's face and was glad. But it did nothing to quell her rage.

Jim extended his hand to comfort her but Jessica jerked away as if it was a serpent.

'Don't you ever touch me!' she shrieked with rage. 'I never want you near me again!'

She pushed past him and marched upstairs. Bursting into her bedroom she slammed the door and locked it. She threw herself on the bed, shut her eyes and blocked out everything but the angry voice in her head and her plans to save Rina. Somewhere in the dimmest corner of her mind she was aware of Jim and

312

her father beating on the door and begging her to come out and explain what was wrong, but she ignored them. So great was her rage and determination that she wasn't even aware that the rain had begun to fall steadily outside and that somewhere on the isle of Jersey an evil ten times greater than the one of which she'd accused Jim was preparing to strike.

Chapter 15

The Deepest Cut

The rain fell heavily on the lush greenness of Jersey all that night. This was unnatural weather for this was an unnatural time. The rain was too heavy, the wind too fierce, the clouds too black and close to the Earth and the people of Jersey, the true islanders, knew something terrible and magical was about to happen. It had rained like this fourteen years ago on the day Emma died.

In her bedroom, Jessica Kent sat cross-legged on her bed watching the storm. She hadn't bothered getting changed or going to bed as the anger still burned inside her making it impossible to sleep. The darkness crept into her small bedroom but Jessica didn't turn on the light. She embraced the velvety blackness. It was like the world Rina had inhabited for so long. Jessica was sure there was more to the unfortunate creature than met the eye. There was something great inside her, perhaps even greater than the poor being herself realized. Jessica knew it was her duty as Guardian to put right what had gone so very wrong.

Easing herself off the bed, she paced the room impatiently. So this was what it truly felt like to be the Guardian of Jersey. At this very moment she knew more about the burden her title carried than ever before. Being the Guardian meant you were alone, utterly alone. You walked a thin tightrope between the normal, human world and the unpredictable world of faeries, merfolk and witches. No-one from either world could know the burden of responsibility that weighed on your heart. Not even your own family could fully appreciate what drove you. It was as if you were a living ghost, not quite in touch with the real world but floating, waiting between the pages of fairy stories and just inside people's imaginations until the moment you were needed. No wonder her mother had been so keen to get married and leave Jersey.

Jessica snatched up her watch. The numbers glowed in the half-light telling her it was half past four in the morning. She had said she would meet Jake at dawn and although the rain was still beating violently against her windowpane she knew it was time to go. She marched over to her wardrobe and pulled on a thick jumper and her raincoat. The raindrops drummed heavily on the glass and with her goal so clearly in her mind she felt like a soldier donning her uniform for battle. Wrapped and bundled up, Jessica unlocked her door and slipped silently onto the landing.

It was only an hour earlier than she'd ventured out the previous day but the light was so dimmed by the thunderstorm it seemed like the middle of the night. Jessica had no inclination to turn on any lights in case the sudden brightness woke her father and great uncle. She wished Rosehip was with her. Although the faerie's insouciance was hardly appropriate for the sombre task she had to perform, Rosehip's golden light would make the shadows seem less threatening, but she would be of no practical help to the project.

Jessica tiptoed downstairs and paused for a moment in the hallway. Her intention had been to go straight out but the rattle of the rain outside and the memory of how hungry she had been the previous day made her decide to have just a small breakfast before braving the elements. After all, when she returned to the house with Rina in tow, the last thing on Jim's mind would be dinner.

She padded towards the kitchen and pushed open the heavy wooden door. The hinges creaked eerily and Jessica smiled. The storm raging outside and the old door squeaking almost made Maison de l'hache sound like the setting for a horror movie. It would have been an idea the old Jessica would have found highly amusing but she knew now there were more frightening things in her real life then a film-maker could ever dream up. The kitchen was much darker than the rest of the house as it had only a small window, but still Jessica felt unwilling to turn the light on. This morning she felt most at home in the dark. Careful that she did not trip or bump into anything, Jessica felt

315

her way round to the fridge and opened it. She took out a bottle of milk and the butter but left the door open so the artifical glow of the fridge would illuminate the room enough for her to prepare her meal. She placed the milk and the butter on the side and rummaged about until she found a slice of bread in the bread bin, which she put inside the toaster. She then filled the kettle at the sink. The water hissed noisily as it gushed from the tap and Jessica was suddenly aware of how loud everything sounded in the dark even with the rain still beating down on the roof. She hoped that the noise would not wake Jim and Martin but suspected if they could sleep through the storm, her slight clattering would not disturb them. She plugged the kettle in and found the jars in which Jim kept the coffee and sugar. The teaspoon clinked dully in her mug as she ladled the brown and white powders into it.

The kitchen felt bitterly cold with the fridge open and the icy rain lashing against the tiny window. Jessica longed for the water to boil so she could warm her hands around the steaming mug. Her mind wandered back to Rina. It was cold in the kitchen but it must be absolutely freezing deep within the Magicroutes. How on earth did she survive alone? A curious doubt crept into her mind. Was Rina human after all? Something deep in her heart told her that she was, despite all the evidence to the contrary. Fancy a human having to live within the dark and the damp since she was a baby, never knowing if or when a troll would attack? You wouldn't think it was possible. But who knew what Rina could do when she had to stay alive?

The sudden snap of the toaster as it released the bread from its slits made Jessica jump. She pondered for a moment what Jake would say about her being frightened of a toaster. No doubt something about her being a weak female or a soft Grockle – or both. There would be no time for softness when she confronted Jim with Rina. A deep hissing and a thin stream of vapour told her the kettle had boiled as well. She grabbed a knife and plunged it into the thick creaminess of the butter, scraping it onto the hard square of smouldering toast. Then Jessica poured the boiling water into the mug, allowing the fresh steam to billow up over her face like a warm blanket. She replaced the milk and butter in the fridge and booted it shut before taking

316

her place at the kitchen table, wrapped in a moody but comforting envelope of blackness.

There were two things that Jessica hoped above all else would emerge from the confrontation she was engineering. Firstly, and most importantly, she hoped that by bringing Jim and Rina face to face and telling him what had happened in the Magicroutes he would accept she was far from evil; secondly, she hoped he would explain why he had been so heartless in the first place.

Jessica shoved the last corner of burnt toast in her mouth and washed it down with the dregs of the coffee. Despite the foul weather, Jess knew it was time to set out. Just then she caught sight of something metal lying on the worktop. Jim had left his large bundle of keys there the night before. Jessica suddenly thought of a way to twist the knife in Jim's punishment. She would steal his keys. Okay, on the surface it was little more than a childish prank but the more Jessica thought about it the more appropriate it seemed. With the keys Jessica could unlock the garage and get the tools she and Jake needed to dig Rina's escape route. It also meant that her great uncle wouldn't be able to use his truck. He would be forced to sit in all day and wait until Jessica deemed the time was right for him to meet Rina. She grinned wickedly at the irony of her using Jim's tools to save the very being he had wanted to murder and of his being unable to do anything else but wait for her. Without giving it another thought, Jessica snatched up the keys and hurried back out into the hallway.

She flung open the front door and dashed out into the storm. The icy raindrops hit her like bullets the moment she was outside and the bitter wind tore through her jacket, chilling her to the bone. It was unseasonably cold weather. Jessica pulled the zipper of her coat up as far as it would go and fumbled with shivering fingers to lock the door behind her. Then, stepping off the wet doorstep on to the gravel, she swiftly crunched across to the wooden door of the garage. The howling wind blew raindrops into Jessica's face, blurring her vision as she fumbled to find the right key. Eventually she found the right one, slotted it into the lock and clambered inside.

She glanced around the garage, searching for the items she needed for her quest. Her eyes had grown used to the darkness by now and it took her only a matter of moments to find Jim's gardening equipment lying neatly against the near wall. She hurried over and grabbed the shovel, then paused for a second, her eyes resting on the other tools that lay before her. This wasn't right. She needed something else – a tool, a weapon – she didn't know what. There was something here in this garage that she needed, but for the life of her she could not remember what it was. Her determination to save Rina seemed to emanate from that item. She scavenged among the rakes and tools for a few minutes but could find nothing that fulfilled her need. The shovel would have to serve the purpose. Grabbing it firmly in both hands she swept out of the garage, back into the bitter storm.

The wind wrapped around her like an icy cloak. Turning her face away from the cruel gale, Jessica stalked bravely forward onto the slick, black snake of tarmac that was Rue de Landes. The road was almost flooded. Large puddles had formed either side. The fields and banks, which had been lush and green, were now reduced to dark swamps of thick mud. Grasses, bracken and wild flowers had all been beaten flat by the relentless force of the storm.

Jessica marched on, the shovel held across her like a musket. The rain soaked through her jacket, seeping into the wool of her jumper. Her coat was only light denim with no hood and soon her hair was plastered to her scalp. She shivered from the cutting wind but kept her eyes on the horizon where the smallest crack of grey daylight had managed to break through the leaden clouds. The water that covered the road had began to leak into her shoes and seep up her socks and jeans making them cling to her legs. The ferocious wind held in it a strange and barely detectable odour that Jessica couldn't determine. It was like something from another world, an emotion from Mother Nature herself that made the freezing atmosphere crackle with fear and anticipation. It was the scent of foreboding. The world that had existed only a few hours before seemed to have been gobbled up by this storm of primeval intensity.

Suddenly, from behind, two golden beams loomed out of the murky blackness, illuminating the road so that she could see her shadow drawn out tall and thin in front of her. The low rumble of an ancient engine sounded above the howl of the storm and Jessica spun round to see Jake's camper van.

318

Jessica ran gratefully towards it, eager for shelter and company. As she reached the side of the vehicle, the passenger door swung open and the bright interior light flickered on. Jake LeBlanc sat behind the wheel. He looked somehow different from when Jessica had seen him last but that did not surprise her in the least. Everything in Jersey seemed to have altered overnight, becoming either threatening or afraid. Dark circles ringed his eyes which, normally bright blue and full of life, were now dull and almost grey. He smiled wanly.

'Thought I would pick you up here,' he said in a tired voice.

Eager to get out of the storm, Jessica climbed into the passenger seat and shook some of the icy water from her hair.

'Thanks,' she breathed.

She leant behind her and placed her shovel in the rear of the van. She noted that there was a spade and pickaxe already there, as well as a long, coiled rope, and was glad at this evidence that Jake seemed to be taking the project so seriously.

Jake leant against the steering wheel and gazed up at the dark sky. 'I give you this, Jess,' he said dryly, 'you've picked a lovely day for it.' Then he added more seriously, 'You sure you want to go through with this?'

There was something in his voice that made Jessica doubt his caution was entirely to do with the weather. Where there had once been the gleam of mischief in his eyes Jessica now saw a very different emotion – fear. Of what, she did not know, but it was an emotion she understood. She snapped on her belt and nodded. 'I'm sure. Something tells me today's the day.'

Jake turned his head away and started the engine. 'I had a feeling you might say that.'

The camper juddered to life and they began the drive to Grosnez. Nervously, Jessica knitted her fingers together and rested them on her lap. 'I am grateful for you turning up to help me,' she said sincerely. 'I honestly didn't think you would show.'

'I always keep my word,' he said, not taking his eyes off the road. He seemed tense and Jessica could see the stringy tendons in his hands drawn taut as he gripped the wheel. Jake wasn't in the mood for small talk and with the black atmosphere around them and Rina's fate hanging in the balance, Jessica couldn't blame him. They remained in silence for a few minutes and

319

Jessica struggled to soothe her active mind by staring into the darkness, as raindrops the size of pennies exploded on the windscreen.

'Terrible weather,' she murmured quietly to herself.

'It's not natural,' Jake scowled.

Jessica looked round to face him. 'What do you mean?' she asked, her voice sounding a lot braver than she actually felt.

She saw Jake's jaw tighten as he clenched his teeth. Finally he spoke. 'It's only rained like this once before in my lifetime and thankfully I was too young to remember it.' He sounded as if he wanted to go on but stopped dead in mid-sentence and drove on in silence.

Jessica was almost too afraid to ask the question. 'When was that, Jake?'

'You don't want to know,' he whispered wearily. Jessica shuddered.

She had a good idea when that last storm had been: someone had said there had been a horrific thunderstorm the night she was born. Jake was right; there was a brooding power in the black clouds above. It was a sign. She didn't like to think about what it might portend. Maybe storms like this were the cloaked hand of Death; they only came when it was time for the Guardian to die.

'You can feel it too, can't you Jess?' Jake looked at her for a moment before his eyes returned to the road.

'Some of the old folks call it the great black dog. It's like a mass depression on the island that comes when a time of great magic approaches. That's why everyone's frightened. I'm frightened.'

Jessica shifted nervously in her seat, suddenly aware of the great pressure that seemed to surround her. It wasn't her imagination. Something was going to happen very soon and she had little idea of what that would be. She glanced at Jake again and saw how pale his skin was.

'You think it's got something to do with us rescuing Rina?' she asked.

Jake didn't answer. Jessica thought she saw a nerve in his temple twitch as if he was trying to repress something, perhaps his fear. His silence infuriated her more than she thought possible. She prodded his arm roughly and he flinched.

'Answer me, Jake? Do you think this storm has anything to do with Rina?'

Jake pursed his thin lips and ran a hand through his hair. 'I don't know,' he muttered gruffly. Jake gripped the gear stick and shifted jerkily into third. 'It could be. Then again it might be completely unrelated. All I know is something unnatural is out there and it scares the life outta me.'

Jessica's tongue felt like sandpaper in her mouth. She rested her head back on the seat as she gritted her teeth and stared into the darkness. She could barely make out the houses and fields as they passed; only the road was visible in the beam of the headlights.

'You think it could be caused by witches trying to raise the demon?' she murmured nervously.

Jake gave a humourless chuckle. 'That's a very real possibility.' Outside there was a distant rumble of thunder.

'Who do you think they are?' she inquired timidly.

Jake looked at her in amazement.

'Who do I think the witches are?' he repeated. His eyebrows were raised but his face was completely serious. 'You don't get it, do you Jess? You think you do, but you don't. It doesn't matter who I think the witches are – I don't have a clue. No-one on this island knows; that's why we're scared. Only one person can see where the black magic is coming from and only they can stop it. That person is the Guardian – that person is you.' He shifted gear again and licked his lips. 'The only reason I'm heading down to Grosnez in the middle of a thunderstorm is because you think it's the right thing to do. I am hoping that saving Rina might save the island and the only reason I believe in that is because I believe in you. Everyone is putting their faith in *you*.'

Jessica felt a heavy weight sink into her stomach like a stone. Jersey was on the brink of peril and its fate rested in her hands. Was she putting her own quarrel with Jim before hundreds of lives? At this moment the bond that drew her to Rina was pulling stronger than ever and not even the threat of witchcraft could break it.

'I have got to get Rina,' she murmured to him, closing her eyes to block out the pain. 'Please don't ask me why because I don't know. I just know it's important that Rina leaves the Magicroutes tonight.'

321

'I really hope you know what you're doing, Jess,' he said wearily.

They had circled the north west corner of the island by now, following the road that led away from St Ouens towards Grosnez and where Jess and Jake had met the previous day. It was only a short walk from here to the scavenger's ladder and Rina's grotto. Jake parked the camper van on the side of the road and switched off the engine. The two of them gazed out at the brutal landscape. Jessica could make out the outline of Grosnez lighthouse rising like a tall, narrow tombstone from the cruel sea. It was an unwelcoming scene.

'Well,' Jake said, 'there you have it. Unless, of course, you want to turn back.'

Jessica sighed and wrung her hands. 'No,' she said firmly, trying to quell her apprehension. 'We've got to do it. I can't let Rina wait a moment longer.'

Jake looked back into the rear of the vehicle where they had stored the tools to free Rina from her stone prison.

'I brought a pick and a length of rope,' he stated.

His tone was very matter-of-fact and Jessica knew that staying practical was his way of repressing fear. It was a technique she often used herself.

The lad glanced back at her, his eyes shining with concern. 'You said that the cave entrance seemed smaller when you went down there yesterday?'

Jessica nodded. Her stomach was churning as violently as the fierce ocean and for the first time her mind was filled with doubt. The storm raged all around them, waves crashing at the foot of the cliffs, strong enough to beat a human body to pulp. She began to think of all the things that could go tragically wrong. All three of them could be swept out to sea, drowned within the icy embraces of the angry ocean. A voice of warning echoed in her brain, threatening a great tragedy if she ventured onto the sheer rock face. But at the same time, all her doubts were quashed by the return of the now familiar echo from deep inside her that always brought her such comfort. '*Now is the time,*' it called to her. ' *We need to be together.*'

Jake was still chattering on, reeling off the plan in his head anxiously, his hands fiddling with a torn piece of leather on the steering wheel.

'Then we've got to chip away at the rock to make the exit bigger,' he muttered. 'I only hope that this storm hasn't flooded the cave so we can't get inside. I've about fifty feet of rope, we can lash ourselves to the top of the cliff and lower ourselves down; that should save us if we slip. It should also give us enough spare to haul Rina up from the Magicroutes. Jessica, are you listening to me?'

Jessica had shut her eyes. She could hear Jake but his voice seemed lost and muffled under the strange calling that echoed her thoughts, repeating the same five words over and over again: '*Now is the time, beware. Now is the time, beware.*'

Jessica gave her head a violent shake to try and clear her mind. 'Yes,' she barked impatiently, 'I understand. But we're wasting time. We've got to save her before it's too late.'

Jake's already wide eyes grew to the size of saucers. 'Too late for what?' he asked anxiously. 'What do you know, Jess?'

Jessica fumbled with her seat belt and tried very hard to ignore the sensation of deathly cold that swept through every fibre of her body. 'I don't know,' she said. 'Just help me to save her.'

She yanked at the van door and as it came open, a blast of cold wind hit her so hard it nearly took her breath away. Not stopping for a second, she clambered outside and was engulfed by the swirling raindrops. Jake quickly followed and together they scrambled to unload the tools from the back of the vehicle. Both were so focused on their task and so filled with fear that they didn't notice a figure, cloaked from head to toe in black, crouching in the bushes near the cliff edge.

For hours it had been lying in wait, heart pounding with anticipation. Now its victim was in its sights and every muscle in its body grew taut as adrenalin coursed through its veins. A deadly weapon rested in its grasp and it knew the slaughter would soon begin. A terrible power seized every fibre in its being, pinning it to the ground and forcing its finger on to the trigger.

Jake finished securing the rope to the base of the scavenger's ladder and got to his feet. 'Well that should hold,' he muttered grimly, checking the knot that held the line at his waist. 'No going back now.'

Jessica tightened the rope that tethered the two of them together and took a deep breath. For a second, she felt as cold and still as a corpse. It was only when Jake placed a friendly hand on her shoulder, that his warmth reminded her she was still alive.

'You ready to go?' he queried, deepening his voice as he always did when he was trying to disguise the fact that he was frightened.

Jessica nodded and gripped the rope firmly in her hand for reassurance.

Jake peered over the edge of the cliff. 'You go first,' he told her. 'That way if you slip I can use my weight to pull you back.'

Jessica shuffled to the top of the scavenger's ladder. She gazed down and the steep staircase swam up at her making her feel dizzy. The descent seemed to be a lot more dangerous than it had been two days ago. She could see the cracks and faults that riddled the ancient timber making it look as fragile as a cobweb. The route seemed steeper, almost vertical. At the bottom, briny waves smashed over the outcrop until it was almost submerged. Holding her breath, Jessica slowly stepped down onto the first rung of the ladder.

Just feet away, the hooded figure lay flat on its belly watching the perilous scene. Above the wail of the storm, it could hear the quickening beat of its heart pulsing in its ears and wondered how many heartbeats there would be before it committed murder. Its finger rested lightly in the crook of the trigger. A sudden burst of pain tore through its body and it felt as if it had been jerked up by a strong hand grabbing the back of its cape. On its feet, arms burning with agony, it lifted the crossbow and cocked it.

Jessica and Jake were now just tiny dots hovering in the mist of rain.

The crossbow was aimed, ready to kill. The assassin tightened its grip on the trigger and, with a burst of golden sparks, the arrow shot through the air.

'Jessica, look out!' Jake's voice rang through the wind, filled with panic. For the briefest of seconds Jessica lost all bearings. Two powerful and unexpected forces hit her at the same time causing the storm-drenched world around her to shake dizzyingly. The first was a sudden tug around her chest as Jake grabbed her and thrust her against the thick twine rail of the ladder. As Jessica's hands snatched wildly at the slack rope desperately trying to stop herself plunging into the untamed sea, the second force, like a flaming arrow shot past her head, not an inch away from her face. The heat was so intense compared to the bitterness of the air that, although it did not touch her skin, Jessica shrieked with pain as if she'd been burnt. She was blinded for a moment by an intense flash of golden light that blotted out everything else. Her nostrils were filled with the smell of burning and she knew with sick horror that the missile had passed close enough to singe her hair. In a fraction of a second it was gone and Jessica was just quick enough to see the blazing bolt arch down through the air and plunge into the ocean, igniting the waves momentarily with a bloody red glow, then disappearing with a hiss and a cloud of black smoke.

Jessica hung, stunned and disorientated, in the crook of Jake's arm, her eyes fixed on the spot of ocean into which the flame had fallen. If Jake hadn't grabbed her out of the way in time, the flaming shot would have struck her head.

'What was that?' she gasped, gripping the rail for support.

Jake stared up at the cliff above them, his face deathly pale.

'Assassins,' he murmured grimly. 'Witches. After you, Jess.'

Someone close by had wanted her dead and they would have got their wish if it hadn't been for Jake. So this was the evil heralded in by the storm. The witches had returned to Jersey and they were close on her tail.

Suddenly, Jake yelled. 'Up there, on the cliff. I can see them!'

Jessica followed his gaze and straightaway saw the dark figure standing on the cliff top, its face hidden inside a black hood. The figure stood as still as a statue, staring directly down at her. Then, as if snapping out of a trance, it jumped back from the edge and fled.

All thoughts of rescuing Rina vanished from Jessica's mind. Her fear and shock dissolved in a sudden burst of animal instinct to chase after her attacker. She pulled herself back onto her feet and began climbing up the stairs, no longer weak or afraid.

'We've got to stop them,' she cried to Jake.

The farmer's son didn't answer but followed her swiftly as they scrambled back up. Jessica reached the top first and glanced this way and that for signs of her attacker. She spotted the figure almost immediately, about ten yards away from her on the left, running with all its might. Rage surged within her, fueling fresh strength and energy. Casting off the lifeline around her waist, she set off at a dash in pursuit of the person in black. The witch was a fast but ungainly runner. Her cape flew out behind her as her spindly legs pounded through the long grass and scrub. Every so often she would glance over her shoulder at her pursuer before struggling onwards against the beating rain.

Jessica followed her with every ounce of strength she could muster. Every muscle in her being was focused on her goal of catching the witch. Her eyes never left the character cloaked in black as it flitted across the grassland. Her legs pumped, thrusting her forward faster than she had ever thought she could run. Her thick, dark hair flew out behind her and raindrops peppered her face but Jessica was desperate to catch her prey. She was aware that Jake was somewhere nearby but her senses were too fixed on the witch to tell her where. So great was her inner drive that even with his height and advantage in physical strength Jake couldn't catch her.

The dark figure Jessica was chasing seemed to be tiring. Her pace slowed, her arms and legs shook with exhaustion. Beneath the thick material of her cape Jessica could see the witch's shoulders rise and fall as she gasped for breath. Suddenly the figure collapsed, tumbling over its bony legs and slumping down into the bracken as if the cape no longer had anyone inside. Jessica felt a thrill of vicious triumph as she saw the witch collapse, but something in the back of her mind told her she had seen someone fall in that way before. However, so great was her desperation to see justice done that she ignored the memory.

Now the witch had fallen and was making no effort to get back up, Jessica's pace slackened as she gained on the figure lying in the wet grass. Her desperation and fear cooled into a hard stone of quiet fury as she drew closer and she prepared herself to summon all the might and reverence that her title of Guardian of Jersey possessed. She did not know what, if any, power the witch had but she was determined not to show any fear. For the sake of her deceased mother, who had lost her life at the hands of evil, Jessica would not allow the witch to see fear in her eyes. She would address it with the strength of Helier himself.

She cut through the thick bracken and came to a dead stop

before where the figure lay, gazing down with equal amounts of fear and contempt. Jessica was shocked at how small the figure was. From her position on the unsteady scavenger's ladder, the person had looked huge. Now, lying face down in the mud and grass, its body was no bigger than a child's. It lay flat out on its stomach, hooded face buried in the mud and pale white hands outstretched. The only thing that told Jessica it was still alive was the heavy rise and fall of its back as it gasped for breath.

The Guardian loomed over the creature, her fingernails pressed hard into her palms. She had never felt such fury, not even at her great uncle. This thing had tried to murder her. It had wanted to end her life and plunge the world into darkness and chaos. A strange sense of power surged in Jessica's stomach. She felt as if the pure white magic of Helier was coursing through her veins at this very second. She knew her purpose, her birthright and her destiny: to save this windswept isle from the scourge of evil. She had never known such strength.

'Get up,' she commanded. Her voice sounded deep, powerful, almost manly. The witch did not move. It lay there shivering and gasping for air, quaking under Jessica's gaze. The heavy rain soaked through the rough, black fabric of its cape revealing the frail outline of its body.

Jessica heard the steady beat of running footsteps and looked up. Jake had arrived and was gazing at her out of breath and full of trepidation. Jessica glanced at him for a moment but quickly drew her gaze back to the witch.

'She fell,' she told Jake firmly, her eyes not leaving the cloaked figure.

'I know, I saw,' came the dull answer. 'Who is it?'

Jessica barely registered his reply. Her full attention remained on the quaking person lying in the undergrowth. A new and strange feeling washed over her. It was as if her mind had been transported back through the centuries filling it with words and orders from long ago. When she spoke again her voice retained that same commanding strength but now she had the words to match it.

'In the name of Helier and our God, I, Guardian of Jersey order you to get up,' she commanded.

The witch flinched spasmodically on hearing these words as

if she was having some kind of fit. Then, slowly, shaking with fear, she clambered onto her hands and knees. The tiny figure kept its chin buried in its chest so the hood remained over its face. Above the roar of the wind Jessica thought she could hear the being sobbing, but she pushed the idea from her mind.

Jessica looked up for a moment and met Jake's eyes. They stared at each other searchingly for a few long seconds, both silently begging the other for advice on what to do. But already Jessica knew. She was just too afraid to go through with it. The witch didn't move; it knelt between them shivering.

Finally, Jessica dropped her eyes back to the crouching figure. Unwillingly, her hand reached out and came to rest on the being's head. The material of the cape felt rough and scratchy beneath her fingertips. Jessica closed her eyes and uttered a silent prayer. Then opening them again, she pulled back the hood.

The fine, baby blonde hair caught in the wind and blew about the child's face like dandelion seed. The pale face was whiter than ever, almost skull-like, the papery skin wet with tears. Huge, tired blue eyes gazed up swimming with tears of despair. The power and sense of purpose Jessica had felt moments before evaporated. She forgot that this person was a witch. She forgot she was the Guardian. She forgot everything. All she knew was a sense of grief and betrayal even more painful and real than when she'd seen Jim in the Iris. For this treachery wasn't in the past to some unfortunate who was misunderstood. It was happening here and now to Jessica herself.

Gulping down her agony and tears, she uttered one word: 'Elsa.'

Chapter 16

The Price of Friendship

Of the three young people who had ventured into the Magicroutes the day before to face the unthinkable horror of the troll attack it was Elsa Noir who had suffered the most. From the moment the beast had dragged her to the ground and attempted to murder her, a strange and disturbing sickness had fallen upon the child's already unhealthy body. It was as if the attack had somehow whisked her soul away to somewhere nightmarish, leaving her in a pain-riddled limbo. She could remember everything that had happened from the time she was attacked: how Jessica had fought off the troll; the pack of foaming, baying beasts that had surrounded them eager for blood; the strange snakelike creature that had rescued them from almost certain death and led them to safety; and their weary return to Jim's residence for healing and comfort, but it was as if she was remembering fragments of a dream. The faces of her friends metamorphosed into grotesque masks; their voices echoed in her head as screeching shouts that she had to fight hard to make sense of. And all the time, an ominous, petrifying cloud, of evil black and bloody red, floated in the back of her mind – the sum of Elsa's fears multiplied ten fold. Elsa's body longed for sleep but she knew if she allowed slumber to overwhelm her, the cloud of foreboding would swallow her and she would never wake. Her body was racked with so much pain there were indeed moments when she prayed for the release of death but she feared that even the end of her life would not banish her fear and agony. The moment she ceased living, the darkness that dwelt within her would seize her soul, leaving her forever in torment. So she kept awake, hanging numbly to consciousness like a shipwrecked survivor clinging to a raft.

In time, and after periods of near blackness, she found herself in Jim's kitchen. A shot of pure pain and vileness was poured into her mouth, shaking some of the deathly black shroud from her. One second she was drowning in a dark fog that squeezed from her all signs of life and feeling, the next a gleaming hand of burning light grabbed hold of her and dragged her violently into excruciating alertness. The vile distortion of her senses was gone and she was painfully aware of all that surrounded her. The unthinkable terror that lurked within her brain was driven back into her unconscious, hissing like a spurned cat – gone but waiting to return.

But her agony was not yet over. Without the suffocating denseness of her fears, Elsa's body was raw to the full physical sickness of her unnatural disease. The malaise was acute and as Jim drove her home that night it was all Elsa could do to bear the pain. Her stomach churned violently and even the slightest movement threatened to overwhelm her with nausea. Every muscle in her frail body clenched with stiffness so she could barely crawl. Her head throbbed and lights danced before her eyes. She somehow kept control until she was home but the moment she entered the front door, her belly lurched and battling the pain in her legs, Elsa ran to the bathroom and reached the toilet bowl just in time to vomit with such force she almost choked. She retched until her belly was dry and her throat was sore and then, with the last ounce of energy she had, she dragged herself to her tiny, attic bedroom and collapsed onto her bed.

A fitful sleep followed. Her mind and soul were caught simultaneously between a deep, deathly coma and heightened awareness. Although her eyelids remained closed, as if forced shut by invisible fingers, she saw through them into her dowdy dwelling, now infested with creatures and apparitions, brought forth from the shadows to taunt and petrify her. Their faces were reminiscent of trolls and other unholy beings she had been forced to encounter during the many pagan rituals carried out by her grandmother. These hideous ghouls lurked in the shadowy corners of her grim chamber, crouched squat and grinning atop her wardrobe and perched like vultures on the head and foot of her hard, brass bed, waiting to steal her soul. Elsa's heart pattered with terror as her tightly closed, but forever watchful, eyes scrutinized the evil phantoms. She could not tell if they were real, or figments of her imagination – nor did it really matter. If they were from some outside force, someone or something was delighting in her torture, but if they came from her own mind the horror was even worse as it meant something unnatural within her had the power to create this wickedness. There was no release either way.

Throughout the night and the following day, Elsa thrashed, tossing and turning in her stale sheets, fighting the demons that haunted her. Her pale skin was clammy with a feverish sweat; her temperature rocketed from an icy chill to searing heat and back again. Finally, after many hours, the terror and pain that laid siege to the child's malnourished form ebbed slowly away, allowing her to fall into a heavy slumber.

Elsa awoke in the late afternoon of the next day, weak and aching. She found herself lying flat out on her back staring up at the tiny, dust-covered skylight that was the only source of natural light in her room. Heavy rain beat down upon the mottled glass. The pain that had crippled her frail body was gone and all she felt now was an immense weakness and lethargy. The dusty attic was quiet and the nightmarish beings that had tormented her in the darkness hours had vanished but Elsa knew at once she was by no means alone. A soft, warm, heavy weight lay on the blankets covering her shins telling her the Siamese cat, Magiver, was nestling there, and seeing the bulky shadow that fell across her bed Elsa knew her grandmother was sitting at her side. Weakly, Elsa twisted her neck to the left to look at the squat old woman who was seated rigidly on an ancient wooden chair staring down at her grandchild.

Agatha Noir's features gave not the slightest clue to her emotions. Her deep wrinkled skin looked as hard and listless as if it were the bark of a dead tree. The thick, orange lipstick etched the outline of her mouth and clotted in small lumps in the corners. Her long, silvery hair flowed down around her face, thin and dull in the dim light. Elsa couldn't remember ever seeing her grandmother look so emotionless. Even though Elsa knew she meant nothing to the old woman there had always been some sort of feeling in her eyes when she looked at her, even if it was disdain or hatred. Now there was nothing. The

331

rain drummed dully on the roof and Magiver purred in his sleep. Elsa thought of all the chores her strange illness had stopped her doing. The fire in the kitchen wouldn't have been lit today and her grandmother might not have eaten. The hall and the doorstep hadn't been swept. She wondered if her grandmother was angry at her failure to perform the duties she expected of her but she knew that trifles such as housework were the last thing on the old hag's mind. More than anything in the world at that moment, Elsa wanted her grandmother to yell at her, to beat her and tell her how useless she was, anything brutally normal that would end this heavy silence.

The old woman turned to the battered cabinet at the side of her and picked up a steaming, china soup bowl that was resting there.

'Sit up,' she said quietly. Her voice was softer than usual but her words were still a command and as always, Elsa obeyed, pushing herself back up against the flat pillows. Mrs Noir handed her the bowl. Inside, a watery green broth steamed with powerful aromas of herbs and nettles. Without needing to be told, Elsa took the silver spoon and began to sip the warm liquid. The taste was strong and medical and filled her nose and mouth with a potent freshness so intense she knew the liquid had some property other than that of mere food.

Her grandmother sat watching her as she fed, not saying a word. Her eyes were as cold as stone. When Elsa was about halfway through her meal, Agatha did something Elsa had never seen her do before. The old woman reached out her tiny, dainty hand towards Elsa and began stroking the girl's thin, blonde hair. Elsa flinched and looked nervously at the old woman to see that she was not looking at her but staring up through the window at the dark sky, her eyes still emotionless. It was an unnerving experience for Elsa, having her grandmother touch her in such a way. It should have been such a tender, loving gesture between a child and her grandparent but although Agatha's touch was soft there was no emotion in it. She stroked her hair not as a woman cherishing her grandchild but as an owner laying claiming to an expensive and long sought-for commodity. The touch had one message alone for Elsa: 'You belong to me.'

Mrs Noir continued playing with Elsa's flyaway locks until

the girl had drained the final mouthful of soup from the dish. Then, as suddenly as she had started, Agatha stopped brushing Elsa's hair, took the bowl and spoon and placed them on the nightstand.

'How do you feel?' she asked in that same unfeeling voice.

Elsa patted her pale, thin lips on the sleeve of her nightgown. 'Better, thank you,' she whispered.

The old woman nodded, seeming pleased with this answer. She sat still for a long moment, staring into space as if waiting for the perfect moment to speak again. Elsa did not watch her grandmother but looked absent-mindedly at the sleek cream and chocolate feline as it snoozed on the floral eiderdown, its tail twitching from side to side.

Finally, Agatha Noir cleared her throat and drew her eyes toward the child's porcelain face. 'Why did you save the girl yesterday, when she was going to sit on the witches' stoop?' she said, her tone like an icy breeze in winter.

She prepared herself for the expected violence.

'I'm sorry, grandmère, please forgive me. I am no good at black magic, my spirit isn't strong enough. I left the cursed pendant the day before as you told me, but I can do no more.'

She squeezed her eyes shut and tensed her body ready to be attacked. However, the beating did not come. Agatha just continued to stare blankly at the terrified girl. She played with the silver spoon from the soup bowl.

'No matter,' she said. Elsa blinked hard. Her grandmother spoke as if the death of the Guardian, the event she had strived for so long, meant nothing to her. Then she added slowly. 'It's of no consequence now – not for you anyway.'

Elsa's fingers fiddled nervously with her rough sheets. She did not know what her grandmother was talking about but she knew something was brewing deep in the old hag's twisted brain. Why was she so calm? What did she know? Cautiously, she licked her lips.

'What do you mean, grandmère? Why is it of no consequence for me?'

The corners of Agatha Noir's brightly painted mouth twitched as she battled to repress a smile. She wanted to savour the moment of her granddaughter's ridiculous innocence but at the same time could not wait to witness her reaction at the news.

She only managed to withhold it a few seconds before allowing herself to savour the words.

'Haven't you guessed?' she said. 'Didn't the sickness you felt last night give you a clue? Elsa dear, you're dying.'

The tiny attic room swam dizzyingly before her eyes. The brutal fact of her own mortality pierced her brain with more power than any spell the old woman could have cast. It was as if her existence were a thin, silver strand of spider's web that had clung between two beams for the past twelve years but had now been ripped asunder by the heavy fingers of death. She raised her hand to her cheek and felt there the wetness of tears, she was too numb even to realize she had been crying.

'No,' she whispered hoarsely. 'You're lying. You've always been cruel to me. This is a horrid lie.'

Agatha Noir's face was unmoved. She showed no compassion as her granddaughter buried her head in her hands and wept uncontrollably. She didn't even touch her. Her eyes rested on the child's hunched form as lazily as if she had been part of the torn wallpaper.

'I am not lying Elsa and you know it,' she said dully. 'Look into your heart. Consider the weakness of your body and you will see it is true. In your soul you have always known your life would be short. Don't search for hope like a fool.'

Elsa's body felt as weak and as tattered as a rag doll. The more her grandmother spoke, the heavier the threat of death pressed down upon her sickly form. The familiar moist, fatal cloud in her lungs that had haunted her like a playground bully had returned forming a thick filter through which oxygen struggled to pass. Only now Elsa knew exactly what it meant. It was a symptom of her disease, a grim standard-bearer going before the cloaked figure of death. Her hands flew out pleadingly and gripped the thick cardigan her grandmother was wearing as she gazed up at her, trembling with fear. 'Please,' she begged, her voice high with despair. 'There must be something that can save me. Doctors...'

A bitter smile flickered on Mrs Noir's thin, bright lips. 'The doctors said there was nothing they could do. You've had this condition since birth; it was only a matter of time before it beat you. The darkness will come now, more and more often, and the pain. Your body is destroying itself Elsa, hate within you will tear at your bones, muscles and organs, damaging them until one by one they will shut down and you won't die until the last one does. And all the time,' (she paused, a glow of sick pleasure in her eyes as she caressed Elsa's sweating temple) 'your brain will be tormented with terrible thoughts until you go mad.'

Elsa slumped onto the bed weeping bitterly. Already she could feel the swirling mist of terrifying thought spread through her brain, touching every corner of her mind. But the fog of darkness did more than frighten her this time. It seeped through the keyhole of the portal in her thoughts behind which lived the darkest part of herself, the part Elsa had always denied, the side that was a reflection of Agatha's evil. In her desperation to save herself from her worst nightmare Elsa had awoken an immoral beast. Her wide eyes gazed up at her grandmother and saw through the coldness of her heart the power that could save her.

'You,' she hissed with awe. 'You have the power to cure me. You could do it with magic.'

A flame of joy ignited Agatha's black heart. She had done it, the greatest spell she had ever performed – and it had taken only the fear and imagination of a small child. She had cut through her granddaughter's stupid morality and found the core of evil. She grinned to herself. There was no such thing as good and right. Everyone had evil in them – it was just a matter of finding what would make them show it. She cleared her throat and folded her hands on her lap.

'Alas!' she uttered, her rich tones thick with mock woe. 'Such a task is beyond my power at present.' She paused and watched with deep pleasure as Elsa crumbled with despair, her face as white as the bed linen. She waited just a few more seconds to let hopelessness consume the child completely. Then she leaned forward so her lips were just an inch from Elsa's ear. 'But,' she whispered slowly, 'if the Guardian were not around to inhibit my powers, I could do it in a snap.'

A deathly cold feeling ran through Elsa's body and her stomach clenched so tightly she thought she would vomit again. She knew exactly what her grandmother was suggesting and it was so evil it made Elsa feel dirty even thinking about it. However, the primal urge had awoken within her and grasped hold of that one disgusting hope so tightly Elsa was unable to dismiss it. It whispered in her brain and the words were so simple Elsa couldn't help but listen. *'Kill Jessica,'* they said. *'Murder the Guardian and be healthy.'* Elsa shuddered. Jessica was all that held Jersey from slipping into darkness; without her who knew what terror would return? Jessica had saved her life yesterday. How could she possibly betray her? Suddenly, Elsa felt her chest tighten, forcing the breath from her as her lungs filled with mucus. Her muscles convulsed with agony and she was unable to move. *'It gets worse than this!'* hissed the voice inside her. Mrs Noir's mouth flickered into a brief smile. Elsa struggled to suck in air and forced out the words. She was in too much pain to know right from wrong.

'What will happen if I do?' she panted, clutching her sides.

Mrs Noir raised her gaze to the thundering sky outside. 'Then a new age of darkness will rain down upon this pitiful island and you and I will be most honoured servants of the Dark Lord.'

Her voice was cackling with joy and even in her agonised state Elsa could see the full wickedness of the old woman's plan. Sensing the girl's doubt Agatha grabbed hold of Elsa's arm and shook her.

'Don't be foolish child. I will have Jessica dead before the full moon tomorrow night, with or without your help. Give in to the darkness in your heart and save your soul. We will rule as queens of earth. Can you feel it? The demon has long feasted on your blood. You are already a child of evil.'

Elsa's forearm seared with pain as the puckered skin there became enflamed. The beast in her brain seemed to feed on her agony and overwhelmed her thoughts.

Lowering her head she said, 'What do I have to do?'

Agatha Noir let go of her granddaughter's arm and pushed her carelessly back onto the bed. She stooped down and picked up a small bundle of cloth from the floor, placing it on Elsa's lap. The child stared at it fearfully, not really wanting to consider what was inside.

'Open it.' The old woman ordered softly.

Fingers trembling, Elsa took hold of the folds in the thick, white linen and pulled them apart. The package fell open and Elsa found herself staring at an object both deadly and beautiful.

Inside was a crossbow so small and prettily carved it could have been a toy. The curved bar at the front was made of a rich ebony and etched with the figures of two coiled serpents, their heads coming together at the point where the bolt was placed. The body of the weapon was also engraved with a vicious wooden snake, its jaws open ready to strike. The metal screws and fixings gleamed golden in the dim light and the wood seemed to have a strange varnish to it so it almost glowed like metal. The bow was cocked and ready to be fired and the bolt was of the purest gold with a bloody scarlet ruby for its head. Elsa stared grimly at the gem. It had been cut to an impossibly sharp point and looked like a droplet of frozen blood, glittering with evil.

Nausea rose once again in Elsa's stomach. This item, however beautifully carved, had been made with one purpose: the murder of Jessica Kent, the Guardian of Jersey. Elsa turned the weapon over in her small pale hands. It was so deadly and yet so delicate, far too small to be fired by an adult. But Elsa knew it had not been designed for an adult. The crossbow would have only one victim and only one marksman. Agatha Noir had already visualized the plan and created the weapon for that purpose and now, in her desperation to save herself from death, Elsa had willingly agreed to take on the role that dark magic had decreed for her. Bitter tears filled the child's blue eyes as she wept for a death that had not yet happened. She could see an open grave with a blank gravestone waiting for one of two names – Jessica's or her own. She prayed with all her heart for the strength to break the sick bargain she had made with her grandmother but the dark fog had swamped her brain, sapping all the strength she had and torturing her body. A tiny voice in her thoughts rang vainly out, telling her this was wrong, but it was drowned by Elsa's illness. Unwilling, but unable to stop herself, Elsa raised the crossbow and looked down the sight. Her eyes were filled with so many tears she could not see.

All she could hear was her grandmother's silky tones saying: 'See what a perfect present I have given you, my darling Elsa. See how perfectly it fits. You have days of glory and darkness ahead of you. All it takes is for you to do the deed.'

But Elsa didn't care about glory or power as her grandmother did. Two great, contrasting wishes filled her heart – one was to save herself from the terrible symptoms and phantoms that tormented her mind and body, the other to keep Jessica alive and stop the blackness that was swiftly closing in around the island. She knew it was impossible to have both. Her muscles throbbed with agony and the heaviness of the bow resting on her forearm did nothing to help it. A scarlet cloud filled her every thought. Lips quivering, Elsa struggled to ask the question that she hoped would take some sting from her awful task.

'W-w-will it hurt Jessica a lot when I shoot her?'

Annoyance flared in Mrs Noir's green eyes. Even with the all-empowering darkness almost consuming her, her stupid and weak granddaughter still retained the infuriating habit of caring for others; it was a sickening trait. But Agatha cooled her temper and wet her thin lips.

'The pain for her will be...' she fought hard to repress the swelling joy she felt at the thought of the Heir of Helier being wiped out completely. She took a breath, '...momentary. The jewel at the head of this bolt is enchanted. Spear the girl's flesh with it and she will die almost immediately. But Elsa, don't allow foolish mercy to cloud your judgement. Think of your own salvation and the power that will be yours.'

Elsa lowered her eyes with shame. She would do the task, even though the very core of her soul told her it was evil. Her grandmother's fury and the torment of her unholy condition compelled her, even though she longed to turn back.

'I will do it tomorrow,' she said softly, placing the crossbow back in its white shroud. 'Where will I find her?'

Elsa knew it was one of her grandmother's many powers that at times she was able to see events before they occurred. The old witch straightened her back and shut her narrow eyes.

'The Guardian heads for Grosnez at dawn, the scavenger's ladder,' she said darkly, the corners of her mouth twitching. 'She goes to rescue the other child, a task which might have helped her. Still, that is a trifling matter. The deed shall be done there.'

Elsa slumped forward. She felt as if the doors of hope had closed behind her. She had to commit the most terrible of sins and she silently prayed to God to save her soul. Suddenly, a heavy hand fell upon her bony shoulder and she was pulled round to face the old woman once again.

'You have one bolt, one chance. Don't mess this up again. It'll be the worse for you if you do!' Her grandmother's customary harsh tones had returned She gave the child a violent shake like an angry brat with a fragile doll. 'And whatever you do, don't mention my name, understand?'

Elsa nodded weakly. She was too numb with pain, guilt and fear to do any more. Agatha Noir flung her back onto the damp sheets of the bed and picking up her mahogany walking stick, drew herself heavily onto her feet. She hobbled towards the door. Sensing the movement of his mistress, Magiver woke from his nap and gracefully followed her. Agatha paused for a moment and looked back at the child weeping bitterly on the bed.

'Remember,' she said harshly, 'Grosnez, tomorrow, dawn. Your life depends on it.'

With that she limped into the hallway and slammed the door behind her.

Elsa lay, swaddled in ghostly white sheets, staring up at the skylight for a long time.

In the hallway outside, a wide grin spread across Agatha's bright mouth. It had always been her belief that goodness and purity were paper masks that could be torn to shreds if you knew how. The wonderful force of black magic was in everyone and each human had his or her individual weakness that would set it free. For some it was the love of their family, for others it was lust for glory or power. But her granddaughter was a weak, simple soul. All it had taken to break her were an elementary sickness spell and a few lies to prey on her fears.

Chapter 17

The Witch Trial

Elsa clapped her hands over her face and wept. Great sobs of guilt and grief wracked her body. Anyone would have had their heart broken to see such a sickly child cry that way; anyone except Jessica Kent and Jake LeBlanc.

Jessica was numb. She felt nothing: no pity for the girl kneeling at her feet full of fear, no anger at the terrible crime she had tried to commit, no triumph at finding the darkness in Jersey. She felt nothing. She placed a hand on her chest to check her heart was still beating and was almost surprised to find it was. She didn't feel alive. It was as if Elsa, Jake and all that surrounded her were part of a dream, an absurd tragic comedy that had reached its ridiculous dénouement. 'Elsa is a witch, she just tried to murder you.' She repeated the sentence over and over again until she was aware that she was moving her lips to form the words. This was the reality, but the reality would not sink in. Elsa was weak, she was sickly; she had been so grateful when Jessica had offered her friendship, she couldn't want her dead. Jessica glanced this way and that along the long stretch of coastal highway. They were the only three people in sight. She had seen Elsa run away, the bolt had been fired from where she had been standing; it *had* to be her. But it didn't make sense.

Jake found his voice and spoke.

'Why, Elsa?' he said.

Elsa still remained crouched on the ground weeping bitterly. She kept taking large gulps of air as if she was trying to speak but all that came out were painful howls. Jake took a half step backwards and ran his fingers through his soaked, black hair.

'I don't believe it,' he muttered.

340

Jessica stooped down so that she was level with Elsa. She could see the red rings that circled the blue, weeping eyes, the fine bone structure that lay so evidently beneath her ghostly skin, the colourless lips.

'Tell me you didn't do it,' she pleaded.

If Elsa would just deny it, Jessica was ready to forget all that she knew to be true, just to believe in their friendship. She reached out and softly cupped Elsa's face in her hands. 'Elsa, please.'

But Elsa didn't reply. Her hands were clasped tightly, chalky white against the blackness of her cape.

Why wasn't Elsa saying anything? Why wasn't she defending herself? Did this mean she was truly guilty? That was a bitter pill in Jessica's mouth. The child's silence fuelled Jessica's rage. She drew her hand away and gripped her shoulder.

'Answer me!' she shouted, shaking her roughly.

Elsa yelped but still her pain was too great to allow her to speak. Jessica continued to shake Elsa's frail body as the child sobbed. Her fury only cleared when she felt a heavy hand on her own shoulder and heard Jake say, 'Jess, get a grip of yourself. This will do no good.'

Jessica released the small girl and Elsa flopped onto the wet grass. Jessica scrambled to her feet and turned to Jake. Placing his hands on Jessica's arms he murmured grimly, 'This isn't the way.'

Jessica bit her lip and felt her fury and frustration well up inside her. 'How then? She tried to murder me. She is a witch.'

The shock of discovering Elsa was the assassin had cut Jake deeply but he knew that the proper order of things had to be observed. 'There must be a witch trial,' he whispered as calmly as he could.

'If we suspect her of being a witch,' he said, trying very hard to keep his voice steady, 'she must be tried for her deeds. Not until then can we do anything.'

Jessica tried to grasp what Jake was telling her. In her state of shock and rage she found the formal idea of trials and courts alien. She was too emotional and she wanted to do something about it this instant. She clasped a hand to her forehead as she tried to calm herself.

'How do we put her on trial?' she asked.

341

Jake released her arms and took a step backwards. He clawed back his hair. 'You must do it,' He said firmly. 'Any witch or warlock caught on Jersey must be judged by the Guardian. You're the only one who can see if she has black magic in her.'

Jessica's anger subsided. Something inside her was disgusted at the thought of trying Elsa. She glanced at the weeping girl and pity stabbed her heart. More than anything she wanted it to be someone other than Elsa who had fired the flaming bolt at her. How could Elsa be a witch? She was only twelve; it didn't seem possible.

'I can't do it,' she breathed. 'Tell me, tell me there's another way.'

The farmer's son hung his head and wrapped his arms around himself for comfort. 'I'm sorry,' he said blankly, 'it's the only way to prove her guilt or innocence.'

Jessica hugged herself against the rain. Jake sniffed.

'Come on,' he muttered, 'we've got to take her back to your great uncle's house. Jim will tell you what the trial entails.'

He started back towards the van. Jessica paused for a moment, trying to repress the overwhelming feelings of hurt and anger that burnt inside her.

She shoved Elsa slightly with the toe of her boot.

'On your feet,' she ordered. Her voice had resumed the brusque, manly tone it had had before. Elsa made no answer but whimpered helplessly and scrambled to her feet. She kept her head bowed low and made no attempt to make eye contact with Jessica. The elder girl placed her hand firmly on her captive's shoulder and they began to march forward. Jessica's fingers closed around the material of Elsa's cape and she became painfully aware how tiny and frail the child's frame felt through the thick cloth. Elsa's physical weakness tugged at Jessica's heartstrings, but what use was that now? Jessica had felt sorry for her, tried to help her, saved her life, and Elsa had betrayed her.

Before going to the van they crossed to where Jake had left the tools near the cliff edge. The girls waited while he retrieved them. As Jake collected the items he spotted something lying beneath a bush nearby. Pulling back the branches he picked it up and turned to look at Jessica. The delicate crossbow looked ridiculously small when held by the tall lad but both he and

Jessica winced when they saw it. Jake placed the object under his arm and the group headed back to the van.

Her hand still gripping Elsa's scrawny shoulder, Jessica ushered the tiny child roughly inside. As Elsa shakily clambered up into the rear of the van, a flame of fury leapt up in Jessica and she gave the girl a vehement shove between her shoulder blades. Stumbling forward, Elsa crashed into the kitchen unit and she yelped with pain as she bruised her arm on the sharp corner of the worktop. The child stood for a moment, nursing her arm, and looked back to where Jessica stood but her desolate eyes still did not dare to meet the older girl's gaze.

'Sit down in the back!' Jessica commanded, before slamming the door and climbing into the passenger seat beside Jake. Elsa scuttled to the seat at the rear. Still she did not utter a word but continued to weep softly. The initial satisfaction Jessica had experienced from her sharp, physical outburst towards Elsa quickly ebbed away as she fumbled to fasten her seatbelt and a renewed feeling of pity took its place. 'You shouldn't have shoved her like that,' a guilty voice inside her brain chided. Jessica rested her fingertips on her brow and closed her eyes.

Once again they were chugging along the waterlogged road back to Maison de l'hache. The rain roared heavily on the thin metal body of the camper and flooded the windscreen like tears. Jake was driving slower than ever and Jessica wondered if he was simply hampered by the storm or, like herself, filled with an intense unwillingness to return to Jim and open the next ominous chapter in this sorry saga. Beneath the rattle of the raindrops, Elsa's fearful sobbing could be faintly heard, the sound fuelling both Jess's compassion and her anger. Jessica snapped on the radio to drown out her sobs. Some manufactured pop group warbled a synthetic ballad, the words and tune of which Jessica knew but couldn't identify. The music irritated her as much as Elsa's bleating. How could there be music in the world when such terrible things were happening and the threat of something greater, darker and more deadly loomed ever closer? Jessica twisted the knob angrily and the dull tune ceased abruptly.

She squirmed in her seat so she was looking at Jake, her hand cupped over her right ear to muffle Elsa's sobbing. The boy looked drawn and weary as he clutched the wheel.

'Jake,' she asked softly, desperate to break the weighty silence. 'What happens at a witch trial?'

Jake wet his lips and shifted his hands nervously on the wheel. 'I told you before,' he said. 'I don't know details. I only know what happens at the outcome.'

In the back, Elsa's crying continued and Jessica struggled to block it out. 'Tell me that then,' she said.

Jake's face twisted uncomfortably again as it always did when Jessica drew out information he was unwilling to give. He waited a few seconds before answering. 'If she is found innocent, she is released with a blessing. But if she is a witch...' he stopped and took a deep breath. 'If she is found guilty, Jessica, you must set her soul free. You must end her mortal life.'

Elsa let out a distraught howl but Jessica barely registered the sound. For the second time that day, her life seemed to stop and a cold sweat swept over her body. Jake's words filtered through her brain; he couldn't mean she had to kill Elsa, could he? She suddenly wished very much she was someone else, another person in another place or time who had nothing whatsoever to do with Jersey or witchcraft. This wasn't right, wasn't in the plan. She'd never thought being the Guardian was something as primal as this. No-one had ever mentioned killing. The Guardian kept the island safe, brought light and peace where there was evil and darkness. She thought of the title on the back of the photo of her great-grandfather, William Edward Hellily, Witch Hunter. Hunter, as in killer. Her stomach tightened. Was this her destiny? What right had she to take a life? Her idea of a witch was a dark, inhuman creature stalking the shadows, cloaked with evil thoughts. But this witch was her friend – an ill, orphaned child.

'I ... I can't...' she breathed, her voice so soft it was barely audible. 'I can't murder Elsa.'

She glanced over her shoulder at the child, curled up like a frightened animal. Jessica could only bear to look at her for a few seconds before pity overwhelmed her again and she was forced to turn away. She looked back to Jake and spoke again, pleading.

'She's twelve years old. She can't be a witch. You said yourself how ill she is. She wouldn't, she couldn't...'

She broke off suddenly, unable to find the words to form a

logical argument, and turned back to gaze out of the window, arms folded across her chest.

'I won't do it,' she declared. 'Even if she is found guilty I refuse to kill her. It would make me no better than the witches.'

Jake let out a shocked gasp and took his eyes from the road to gaze at her in horror.

'You don't understand,' he began, but Jessica's eyes flamed with fury at his words.

'That's all you ever say to me. That's all anyone's ever said to me since I got here. I'm sick of being told I don't know what's going on. I'm not stupid. I know what I feel.'

She paused for a second, but not long enough for Jake to interrupt her. When she continued her voice was hushed. 'It's true that right now I hate Elsa for what she's done but I know there's more to it somehow. So what if all the evidence says she's a witch. Don't you think there maybe a reason behind what she did? God knows she has good cause to be angry at the world.'

She muttered the last sentence so quietly that she wasn't sure Jake heard her and didn't really care one way or another.

Jake winced. 'If Elsa is a witch, her death will not be a punishment.' He placed a hand on Jess's arm. 'Witches are not human. They are an imperfect being; something malignant taints their souls. A fully committed witch can never truly be human, for the darkness drives them. They can be cured, but not by a power on this earth; only in the spirit realm can they be free, after they have gone through Purgatory. It can take hundreds of our years for a witch's soul to be cleansed. I'm not really surprised she wants to hurt the world – it hurt her. Don't you think she deserves release? If she is guilty you must destroy her body so she can move on.'

Jake spoke with compassion. Jessica thought of everything people had told her about Elsa's life, her illness, the death of her parents and the cruelty of her grandmother. Maybe she *did* deserve an escape. Maybe she *was* better off dead. But as soon as this thought entered her mind, Jessica was overcome with guilt. Her duty as Guardian collided with the feeling that there was more to Elsa's attack than met the eye. If Elsa was indeed guilty of witchcraft, Jessica doubted she had the strength of character to rectify the situation. Neither Jessica nor Jake spoke again during the journey back to Maison de L'hache.

In no time at all they drew up outside the pink stone cottage. Jake unlocked the door and stepped outside into the pouring rain. Jessica followed suit. The moment she was outside her clothes, which had just begun to dry, were drenched again. They went round to the door at the side of the van and the boy opened it. Elsa shifted nervously along the seat away from them, burying her face in her robe and staring at them like a mouse cornered by a cat.

'Come on, it's time to go,' said Jessica.

Cautiously, Elsa placed her doll-like fingers in the palm of Jessica's hand and the older girl led her outside onto the gravel path. Jake picked up the crossbow and threw Elsa a cold look.

The three young people hurried to the front door. Almost before they were inside Jessica could hear Jim muttering crossly from the living room. She shoved Elsa inside and she and Jake followed. They had barely entered the hallway before Jim emerged from the living room door, his face pink with annoyance. Jessica's father stood behind the older man; he too looked less than happy.

'There you are!' cried Jim, his arms crossed across his barrel-like chest. 'I want a word with you, young lady. What's the idea of leaving the house first thing in the morning without telling me or your father where you are going? Not to mention storming in and having a go at me last night for God knows what! And what have you done with my keys?'

Jessica was exhausted.

'Jim, please,' she begged. 'Will you just listen to me for a moment?'

'Answer your uncle,' her father chided.

Jim's dark eyes left Jessica and his initial burst of anger out the way, he realized that she was not alone.

'Jake,' he muttered, 'Elsa. What are you doing here?'

The boy's expression told him more than words ever could. The flush of anger drained from Jim's face and he became white with worry. 'Dear Lord, what has happened?'

He hurried towards Jessica. 'What's going on?' he asked urgently. 'Tell me what happened?'

Jessica melted at the sound of her great uncle's soft, Jersey voice and all the fury at the way he'd treated Rina was forgotten. She needed his guidance now more than ever.

346

'Jake and I went down to the caves this morning,' she explained wearily. 'I thought I needed to check something out, something I saw when I was down there last time.' She didn't want to mention Rina to Jim; it would complicate matters too much. 'We were on the scavenger's ladder at Grosnez. There was a flash, a flaming arrow, I'm not sure what. It came from the cliff top. It would have hit me if Jake hadn't pushed me out of the way.' She stopped and looked at Elsa.

'We saw a cloaked figure on the cliff top. A witch tried to assassinate me. Jake and I chased her across the heath. I caught her, pulled back her hood and ... and...' Her tongue felt dry and bitter in her mouth and she couldn't bring herself to form the words to finish her tale. Instead, she extended her hand towards the crying child.

The old man's bottom lip quivered and for a second Jessica thought he was going to cry. 'No,' he said softly, taking a half step towards the small girl. 'You shouldn't make things like that up, Jess. You shouldn't tell lies to your Uncle Jim.'

Jessica knew exactly how the old man was feeling because she had felt the same way.

'Jim, there was no-one else on the cliff. There was no-one else it could've been. I'm sorry. I'm so, so sorry.'

'We found this where she was standing,' Jake said, holding out the tiny, golden crossbow.

The old man took the weapon and examined it thoroughly.

'It's a warlock bow,' he declared. 'If her aim had been more accurate, you'd be dead by now, Jess. Oh Elsa, how could you?' Martin gathered Jessica in his arms and hugged her tightly.

'I'm so glad you're safe,' he whispered into her thick hair.

Jim stood motionless in the hallway, his hand clenched tightly round the bow.

'You know you must try her for witchcraft, don't you, Jess?' he said hoarsely.

Elsa fell to her knees, wailing bitterly, but no-one looked at her.

'The trial must take place at once,' Jim continued. 'I will prepare a space in the kitchen with the things you will need and take Elsa in there. Your clothes are soaking wet. I suggest you go upstairs and change before we begin.'

Jim placed a heavy hand on Elsa's shoulder and dragged her

347

to her feet. The child squeaked with panic but her cries fell upon deaf ears. Jessica began to head upstairs but her father stopped her.

'Jess...' he began, but then seemed to forget what he wanted to say.

Jess wished with all her might that they had never come to Jersey and it was still just the two of them back home in London.

'You were right, Dad,' she muttered bitterly. 'I should never have got involved. Now I have no choice.'

She pushed past him and went upstairs to change. In her room, Jessica struggled not to think about what would happen when she went back downstairs but every second brought her closer to the terrible reality. Despite herself, she felt sorry for Elsa and so she did the only thing she could think of – she got on her knees and prayed. She prayed for Elsa not to be a witch and for her soul to be saved if she was. And as she did so, Jessica knew that she wasn't the first Guardian to have prayed for a witch's soul.

A knock on the door startled her. Jim was standing outside, across his arm a large piece of midnight blue velvet. The material was ancient and moth-eaten, stained here and there with large, dark patches. 'The accused, Elsa, is ready when you are,' he informed her.

Jessica glanced at the cloth. 'What's that for?' she asked.

Jim shook some of the dust from the garment. 'It's the Hellily witch-trying vestment,' he explained. 'Been in the family for centuries. The Guardian usually wears it when...' He stopped but Jessica already knew what he intended to say. 'Your mother didn't have to wear it, nor your grandmother.'

Jessica stepped out of the bedroom. 'Then I won't wear it,' she declared.

Jim raised his eyebrows but said nothing.

'I can't believe she's a witch, Jim,' Jess whispered. 'I can't try her. She's just a child. She's too young to do any harm.'

'I know,' he replied. 'I have trouble seeing it myself. But if she did fire the bolt...' He placed a hand on Jessica's shoulder. 'I've known that girl since she was a baby. I pray with all my heart that this trial will show she's innocent. But it is the only way we can find out.'

Jim took her arm and led her downstairs. A spell seemed to

be on the house and a heavy quietness filled every corner. The rain pelted on the roof but the sound was muffled and seemed transformed into the beating of funeral drums.

Jim and Jessica reached the heavy, oak door that led to the kitchen and stopped.

'Don't make me do it alone,' she pleaded. 'I don't know how.'

'I will stay in the background,' He told her. 'You will find the witch-hunter's almanac open at the correct page. I have set up the room as you need it.' He stopped and looked directly into Jessica's eyes so intensely it shook her. 'I can't help you choose your verdict. Only the Guardian has the true knowledge to pass judgement on a witch. Look into your heart, Jess. Look into the deepest part of yourself where your hope and faith lies. That will tell you the real colour of Elsa's soul.'

He swept the door open and the two of them entered the room beyond.

The kitchen had been transformed from a warm, homely place to a chamber of pomp and sombreness. Heavy, white sheets of pristine linen draped the work-surfaces and appliances, as if the sight of trivial modern items would be an insult to the serious practice that had been performed for centuries. The electric light remained switched off and all around the room, tall, scarlet candles flickered with orange flames, throwing ghostly shadows on the walls. An exotic, spicy smell hung in the air and Jessica guessed Jim had burnt some kind of incense probably to purify the room. The floor of red tiles was, as ever, cold and hard under foot but looking down Jessica saw that a ring of freshly cut branches had been laid there; she recognized them as willow. The pine table had been moved to the back of the room but two chairs remained, facing each other in the centre of the willow circle. On one sat Elsa.

The girl gazed around with watery eyes. Her lips quivered but the only sound was a terrified mumble which Jessica could not understand. She glanced down and saw that bands of young, green willow had been tied around her wrists and ankles, binding them together. The bonds did not look particularly strong and Jessica wondered what good they would do.

Just seeing Elsa, Jessica felt her emotions bubbling up within her and she clenched her fists to fight them back until she felt her own blood seep under her nails. The girl looked so helpless

349

and pitiful but Jessica could not forget that Elsa had tried to kill her. She seethed with rage and wondered whether this image of weakness and innocence was just a mask to hide a heart as black as midnight.

'Step inside the willow ring, Jess,' said her great uncle. 'The willow stops her magic.'

Elsa's eyes grew wide with panic as Jessica slowly crossed the threshold of branches that separated them. Her mouth fell open but she seemed too frightened to make a sound.

Jessica took the seat opposite Elsa. The wooden legs of the chair scraped chillingly on the terracotta tiles. For the longest time the two girls stared at each other. Then Jessica dropped her eyes from the child's frightened face and saw the witch-hunter's almanac lying open at her feet. Beside it, a tiny silver circle glistened in the orange glow of the candles.

Jessica picked up the volume and rested it on her lap; her aching eyes flitted silently over the faded words. Jessica's voice possessed a commanding tone that throbbed with the voices of her dead relatives as she read the words that had been written so long ago.

'Elsa Noir, you are accused of witchcraft. You are suspected of wandering from the ways of holiness and entering into the realm of Dark Magic. It has come to me, the Guardian of Jersey, to decide whether your soul is pure or whether you are a child of evil. How do you plead?'

There was a long pause. Finally Elsa managed to emit a hushed whisper, 'I'm not guilty.'

You're lying, Jessica thought and, without realizing it, the words hissed from her tongue.

Elsa buried her face in the palms of her hands. 'The silver farthing,' her great uncle prompted. 'Place it on her tongue. She won't be able to lie.'

Jessica glanced at the floor. The small, shiny disc, about the size of a twenty-pence piece, sparkled against the deep red of the tiles. Jessica picked up the glistening circle, the metal icy cold against the heat of her palm, and turned it over in her fingers. On one face was a crudely carved cross and on the reverse what looked like a hatchet. Jessica was sure she had seen that axe image somewhere before, but couldn't think where.

'Place it in her mouth,' instructed Jim.

'She will choke on it,' Jessica said.

Jim's voice sounded from the shadows. 'She can't swallow it, Jess. That's not what it's for. The silver has White Magic, like the willow – it will force her to speak only the truth. Trust me, Jess. It will uncover who she really is.'

Jessica shot a harsh look at Elsa. The coin meant no more lies. With it she could tell one way or the other whether Elsa was a witch. At least she would know for sure.

Elsa wrung her pale fingers together. She kept her mouth tightly shut and flicked her head twitchily from side to side.

'Open your mouth,' Jessica ordered. Elsa tightened her face muscles so her lips were sealed and shook her head even more violently.

Before she had time to think, Jessica shot out her hand and grabbed Elsa's nose, pressing her nostrils together just as Jake had done when Jim had fed her the witch-hunter's broth. After a short time she was forced to open her mouth for air. The moment she did so, Jessica quickly shoved in the coin. There was a small flash of light as the metal passed the child's teeth, like a spark flying from flint and Elsa snapped her mouth shut, her cheeks bulging, her lips shaking as if she was struggling to stop herself speaking.

Jessica sat back and regarded Elsa. Swallowing deeply, Jessica found the strength to begin her questioning and the fact that her voice still sounded powerful and calm, helped quell her fear.

'Did you fire the crossbow?'

Elsa's lips parted and her tongue seemed to glow with an eerie, silver light as she struggled to speak.

'Yes,' she bleated woefully, her body shaking with the effort to release the word.

Jessica's worst fears were realized. Her body felt as cold as a corpse and her hand flew up to her lips in dismay as she whispered in a voice much nearer her own, 'So you are a witch, Elsa! A child of the shadows!'

The child's eyes swam with fear and urgency and she slumped forward, her bound hands outstretched towards Jessica, her fingers clawing pleadingly. 'Yes ... no,' she gasped. With each word, her face was racked with pain. 'I ... am ... not ... a ... witch,' she croaked in tones disturbingly similar to Rina's broken speech. 'I ... not ... soon ... darkness ... not ... me.' Her bony hand fell onto Jessica leg and clasped the material of her jeans.

Appalled by being touched by a witch and confused by Elsa's words, Jessica pushed the girl's fingers away.

'Do you deny you perform witchcraft?' she accused.

Elsa threw back her head and let out a howl of pain. Her hands struggled with their bonds but the willow did not snap.

'Did ... witchcraft ... but ... not ... a ... witch ... Jess ... please.'

The last two words were uttered in such a pitiful tone that Jessica was overwhelmed. She couldn't understand what Elsa was trying to tell her. She looked into her eyes, trying to see the colour of Elsa's soul.

Jessica rubbed her forehead and tried to focus on her thoughts. The kitchen was a blur of golden candlelight and midnight shadow. 'Elsa,' she begged, 'what witchcraft did you do?'

Elsa's body slumped forward. 'Arrow,' she whined, cupping her face in her hands. 'Pendant.'

Realization shot through Jessica's brain. She recalled the night she'd discovered she was the Guardian, how she'd nearly drowned in the cruel sea of St Ouens Bay. Elsa had been trying to murder her ever since their first meeting. Filled with a new rage and disgust, Jessica leapt to her feet, her eyes blazing.

'You are a witch!' she roared and before she knew what she was doing she had grabbed Elsa's hair and yanked her head back. 'You've been trying to kill me all along. Haven't you?'

Elsa's eyes rolled. Her mouth fell open – the child's entire tongue and throat glowed sparkling silver, like a polished goblet. A voice echoed from her silver throat, beautiful and weak but so unlike Elsa's own it made Jessica stumble backwards in shock.

'Care not for my soul,' it sang. 'Whether pure or dark, my fate lies at Devil's Hole – as does yours. As does yours. At Devil's Hole.' The voice seemed then to rise out of her throat transforming itself into an ear-shattering scream. The flames of the red candles rose up as if they'd been summoned by the unearthly noise, then flashed and went out, plunging the room into darkness and silence.

A burning coldness gripped Jessica's body like a fist of ice, sucking the very breath from her lungs. Suddenly the light was switched on and she heard Jim's voice.

'Jessica,' he gasped, 'what on earth was that?'

Jessica blinked and clung to her great uncle for comfort. Her eyes were fixed on the chair where Elsa had been sitting. On the floor in front of it lay the willow stems, still tied, and the silver farthing. But Elsa had vanished.

Chapter 18

Battle in the Blackness

Jessica clung to her great uncle's arm for comfort. He was shaking and she realized he was as frightened as she. Something unearthly and unnatural had just occurred and neither the old man nor the girl could explain it. But both of them knew that this was only the beginning.

Finally, Jessica slipped away from her uncle's arms and knelt on the floor in front of the chair on which Elsa had been seated moments before. Feeling hot and cold, drawn but repulsed at the same time, Jessica reached out a trembling hand and touched the wooden seat. The pine was intensely warm, though not hot enough to burn her. Gazing round the room, she hoped to see the outline of Elsa hidden behind the white linen but there was no sign of her. The heavy, oak doors leading to the cellar and out into the hall were both shut firmly and not a glimmer of light or movement showed through the tiny window which remained bolted from the inside. The red candles had dissolved into bubbling pools of scarlet wax.

'She's gone,' said Jessica in disbelief. 'Jim, please tell me I'm not going crazy. Tell me you saw it too.'

The old man timidly crept forward into the ring of branches. The foliage strewn across the red tiles was now brittle and brown. He gathered the two small loops of willow and stared down at them.

'Ay,' he said, 'I saw it all. Don't mean I understand it any more than you do. I can honestly say that in sixty-six years of being a Hellily I've never seen anything like that before.'

Jessica got to her feet and looked at him. Her heart was

354

drumming so loudly in her chest she felt he must hear it. Her mouth was dry.

'You said willow would stop her using black magic,' she sobbed. 'What happened? The doors and window are locked.'

Jim began to wander around the kitchen, wiping up the melted wax, trying to avoid her questions. 'It does,' he murmured. 'Unless there was...'

A violent knocking on the kitchen door interrupted his sentence and made Jessica scream in terror. She gasped with relief when she heard the voices of Jake and her father begging to come in. Jim hurried to unlock the door and the two men tumbled inside, their faces white with fear. Martin gathered his daughter up in his arms while Jake gazed around the kitchen, his eyes wide in bewilderment.

'I was so worried about you, Jess,' said Martin. 'Jake and I were in the living room waiting for you. We heard you shouting angrily and suddenly all the lights went out as if there'd been a power cut. Then there was this awful scream, like someone being murdered. We wondered what on Earth was happening.'

Jake started pacing about the room, staring around him as if he was trying to come to terms with the situation. 'Where did she go?' he muttered under his breath before spinning on his heel and asking Jessica out loud. 'Where is Elsa?'

'Gone,' Jessica answered, 'and don't ask me where or how, Jake, 'cause neither Jim nor I know. She said she had committed acts of witchcraft. I was furious with her. But she denied being a witch. Then she said something I didn't understand, but it wasn't her voice speaking. The candles flared and went out and when Jim turned the lights on she had disappeared. The whole thing's madness. Nothing makes sense.'

She collapsed into the chair. Jake drummed his fingers on the worktop.

'So she's a witch,' he stated coolly. 'At least we have our answer, if nothing else.'

'But we don't know that for sure, Jake. Jim told me if she was a witch she couldn't use black magic inside a ring of willow. But she must have escaped by *some* kind of magic. If she isn't a witch, what is she? And how did she disappear?'

Jessica was gazing at Jim now who had kept quiet for what seemed like an age.

'Jim,' she said, her voice deep and serious, 'you were about to say something to me before Jake and Dad came in. "Elsa couldn't escape unless..." Unless what?'

He chewed his bottom lip. 'There is a chance,' he began, 'that Elsa isn't a witch, not a fully-fledged one anyway.'

Brushing past Jessica, he gathered up the witch-hunter's almanac where she had dropped it on the floor.

'Elsa could have been manipulated,' he continued as he flicked through the pages, 'controlled by a power stronger than her own. Someone who wanted you dead, Jess, could have forced Elsa to bring you the pendant and shoot the bow. They obviously believe that their plan has succeeded and have called Elsa back to complete the work.'

He found the page he was searching for and turned the book so Jess and the others could see it. Jessica read the heading aloud. 'Familiars,' she queried. 'What? As in black cats?'

Jim gave a brisk nod and turned the book round so he could carry on reading. 'Listen to this,' he said. 'Although the use of animals as familiars such as cats, dogs, ravens, owls and other birds of prey is a common feature of witchcraft, a rarer and far more unusual kind of assistant has been recorded. The child familiar, or lost babe or changeling is a child, related to the witch or warlock or kidnapped by them. They are used because of their innocent ability to deceive the witch's victims. Fearful of their masters and commonly in poor health, human familiars will carry out evil tasks afraid of the punishment if they fail.'

Jim looked up from the page and saw Jessica slumped in the chair, her face torn with guilt. 'What have I done?' she murmured, cupping a hand to her mouth. 'It wasn't Elsa's fault after all. How awful for her.'

Jake slipped a comforting arm around Jessica's shoulder as Jim continued. 'This is the part that scares me,' the old man muttered. 'In the most potent and serious of rituals, the child familiar is a perfect candidate for human sacrifice.'

Jessica recalled the stone altar in the Great Chamber. 'They'll kill her now they think her work is done,' she gasped.

Jim snapped the book shut and placed it on the worktop. His face was drained and his eyes were desperate as he stepped towards her. 'It goes deeper than you think, Jess. It's not just

Elsa's life that's at stake, it's ours as well – in fact, everybody on this island is vulnerable.'

Jess, Jake and Martin glanced at each other. 'Don't you see?' he said. 'It isn't hard to understand. The book says human sacrifice is used in the most potent and serious of rituals.'

Jake gasped and everyone looked at him.

'Jess,' he uttered in hushed realization. 'The witches think Elsa's killed you. That means they believe there is nothing to stop them. They're going to try and raise the demon!'

Jessica was suddenly filled with an emotion quite unlike anything she had ever felt before. Her mind told her she should be fearful, angry, confused, but all these feelings were somehow dulled by an enormous strength that arose in her heart like a lion with a mane of flames. Her own life and its trivial problems seemed unimportant now; she would willingly die this moment if it would save the island. Fury raged within her but her brain was perfectly clear; her anger was like a white beam of energy, a weapon ready to pierce the heart of her enemy.

'I'm going to stop them,' she said menacingly. 'I don't care if I die trying. The evil ones will not take Jersey, not while there's breath left in this Guardian's body.'

Jessica was on her feet and pacing the kitchen like a caged tigress. Jim eyed her warily. 'Steady, my girl,' he counselled solidly. 'You are feeling the blade of Helier in your hands for the first time and it'll do you no good unless we know who is controlling Elsa.'

Jessica slammed her fist on the tabletop. 'We *must* know who it is,' she cried. 'Elsa's their familiar. Think, Jim, think. You said you've known her since she was a baby. Who would do this?'

Jim looked at the floor for a second. Then his face flushed with rage and he bellowed. 'I'll kill her! You won't have to do a thing, Jess. I'll wring that hag's neck myself.'

Pushing past Jessica and the others, he marched out into the hall, muttering furiously.

'All this time,' he hissed. 'All the times I've helped her. I thought she was a loyal islander. That old crone used me, used me for information about my own family so she could finish them off. I'll kill her.'

He let out a growl of frustration. Jessica approached him.

Jim looked at his great niece with the eyes of a broken man.

'A child related to the witch,' he quoted from the almanac. 'Her grandmother. Elsa's being controlled by Agatha Noir!'

The pieces of the puzzle slipped finally into place and Jessica saw the hideous picture unfold before her. It all made perfect sense now and she was amazed that she hadn't seen it before. Agatha Noir was the malicious being bringing evil to Jersey. No wonder Jim felt so betrayed. Who knew how many islanders might have suffered at her hands? Perhaps it had been Agatha Noir who had robbed Jessica's own mother of her life. She had to be stopped before it was too late.

Jake had followed Jim into the hallway and listened intently to what he had said. 'So the rumours were true then,' he said, echoing Jessica's thoughts. 'About what she did to Philippe, Lily, Katrina and Bill. She *did* murder them, murdered them all because they stood in her way.'

Jim nodded and ran a hand through his thin grey hair. 'I'm a stupid, stupid old man,' he lamented through gritted teeth. 'It was right under my nose too.'

Jessica's father hadn't said anything for a long time and Jessica knew that this terrible day was forcing him to remember past times. Like her mother before her, she would soon have to leave him and there was no certainty that she would come back alive. When he spoke his voice was soft and startlingly calm.

'She was probably the one who killed Emma, wasn't she Jim?' he whispered.

'Martin, please try not to think about it. We can't get emotionally involved.' The old man sighed. 'It's all my fault. Why did I trust that old witch? Why couldn't I have seen it? I'll kill her if I get my hands on her.'

Jessica pulled back her hair in a tight ponytail so that when she headed into the storm it wouldn't bother her. 'Jim,' she said, 'if Mrs Noir is a witch then she will destroy you in a second. I am the Guardian so I must face her.'

Stopping dead for a second, she shut her eyes. A sixth sense seemed to be warning her of the horror that lay in wait outside the safety of the cottage. Time was running out.

'Can you smell it?' she murmured. 'The blood. Can you sense the evil closing in around us? We have very little time.' Her eyes snapped open and she glanced around her. All three men were waiting with baited breath for her command. 'The deed will be done before the day is out,' she told them. 'But the question is, where will it happen?'

She turned away and tried desperately to focus her mind. She knew if she thought hard enough the instinct of Helier, her legacy through the mists of time and memory, would bring her the answer. Her mind conjured one, lone image – Elsa. The girl's eyes were wide and blank and her mouth was open to reveal her silver tongue and throat. Her parting words returned to Jessica now, as evidence of the child's pure heart.

' "My fate lies at Devil's Hole." That's where she was taken. Jim, where is Devil's Hole?'

'It's a steep cliff inlet to the sea not far from here. Legend has it it's where Helier banished the demon beneath the rocks and waves.'

Jessica glanced at the door.' That's where they are,' she murmured. 'I must go there and stop Agatha.'

'What do you want us to do?' Jim asked earnestly.

Jessica saw the fear in his eyes and knew that she could rely on him to guide her no longer. The fate of Jersey was entirely in her hands. Taking a deep breath she told them her plan.

'Jim,' she explained, 'I need you to get us there. Take us as far as you dare without putting yourself at risk. '

She looked to Jake. He was ghostly pale but his eyes were alive with energy.

'Do you want in on this?' she asked. 'You've saved my neck God knows how many times already.'

Jake forced a smile. 'No way am I abandoning you now, Grockle,' he said, punching her arm. 'If you mess things up we're all for it. If I'm going to die I'm going to die on the front line, cursing you all the way.'

Jessica found herself chuckling, thankful for Jake's strong character. 'Hopefully it won't come to that, mate,' she replied. 'I want you up the front with me. I need someone quick and strong. The moment you get the chance, grab Elsa and then both of you get the Hell outta there. If things get too hairy, go back with Jim.' Her eyes grew dark and cold as she added, 'You leave Mrs Noir to me.'

She then turned to her father and her face softened momentarily with the love she felt for him. She knew he felt the same and was battling with his parental instinct to stop her going. There was so much emotion in his eyes, fatherly love and fear that he might never see her again. But underneath that she saw pride and knew however much his heart was telling him to stop her facing the awful danger that awaited her at Devil's Hole, he loved her even more for following her destiny. She threw her arms around him and held him tight.

Martin brushed his lips against his daughter's forehead and remembered the love he had felt for his wife Emma. She had been a free spirit, drawn by the fates that drifted through this enchanted isle and dedicated to a legacy beyond his comprehension. He never could fully understand her soul but perhaps that was why he had loved her so deeply. Their daughter had the same connection to the mystical world and he had been wrong for so many years to keep her from her true calling. Now it was time to let her go. He stroked her thick hair as she drew back from him and gazed up into his face. He saw she was no longer a child but a young woman old enough to take hold of her own future.

'Dad,' she said gently. 'I want you to wait here where it's safe. There's no point in you risking your life. Lock the doors and windows and don't let anyone in until you see sunlight. I love you. I promise I'll be back soon.'

Martin brought his hand up to Jessica's cheek and brushed it softly. 'Are you sure there is nothing I can do to help?' he asked her, dreading the moment she would go out into the ungodly storm.

Jessica took her father's hands and pressed them together between her own. 'You can pray,' she told him and she meant that with all her heart. For in this time of heathen darkness the greatest strength Jessica could think to call on was prayer.

Jessica took a step backwards towards the door but Martin did not let go of her hand. Jim and Jake had already pulled on their jackets and were preparing to face the horror that had engulfed the island.

'Wait, just one second, Jess,' Martin said. He reached inside his jacket and took out his wallet. From a small compartment he removed a thin strand of gold. The chain was tiny and looked as if it would easily snap if pulled. From it were suspended two delicate charms of pure gold – a cross and a heart. He undid the clasp and fastened it around his daughter's neck.

'The cross and chain belonged to your mother,' he told her as he rested his hand on her chin. 'The heart is a locket I bought after she died; it has a lock of her hair in it. For the past fourteen years I've kept it close to me. But you need it now.'

'Thank you,' she whispered. Her father had given her his blessing and with this simple piece of jewellery she had her mother's strength with her.

Martin gazed down at the pendant and then looked back into his daughter's eyes.

'Look at it as *my* magic charm, Jess. No evil is stronger than the love of a family.' He paused for a moment to stroke her hair. 'Now go. You must stop the blackness.'

Jim and Jake were waiting. Jessica gave her great uncle a nod and the old man unlocked the door. A great gust of icy air billowed into the hallway. Outside, the landscape was swamped in a cloak of black fog so impenetrable that Jessica could barely make out the stone wall that surrounded the house. This was no ordinary fog; the deathly black mist swirled in clouds and miniature tornados, blown by a biting wind into hideous silhouettes of ghouls and devils. Here and there the smoky blackness was tinged with wisps of grim scarlet like vaporous blood hanging in the cold wind. The air had the odour of death and decay. The rain still rattled like invisible bones. It was only early afternoon but there was no light to be seen anywhere. Sun, moon and stars seemed to have been obliterated by dark mist.

Jessica and her companions were just about to enter the storm when a ball of glowing, white light pierced the hellish darkness and came hurtling towards them. Jessica stepped back as Rosehip zoomed inside, screeching, 'Shut the door! Shut the door! They're after me!'

Rosehip landed with an almighty crash on the side table travelling at such a speed that she skidded along its polished length and barely avoided falling off the other end. She sat up and gave her body a violent shake. Wisps of the smoky mist seemed to have clung to her and she was desperately trying to brush them off.

'I ... am ... not ... going ... out ... there ... a ... gain... leave ... me ... be ... hind ... how ... dare ... they!'

With each syllable she beat her delicate limbs with her hands as if she was trying to put out flames.

361

Rosehip glared at Jessica. 'You think I'm really stupid, don't you? I nearly died out there, no thanks to the others. They all went down in the underburrows and closed the entries off before I could follow them, leaving me out in the Devealios. I nearly got dissolved. '

True to form, Rosehip seemed to be talking nonsense and Jessica did not have the time to figure out what she was telling her.

'Rosehip,' she said, 'I don't have time for your games. There are witches about and I have to stop them.'

Rosehip let out a high-pitched squeal of frustration. 'I know there are witches trying to raise the demon,' she screamed. 'That's what I just told you! There is Devealios, Devil's mist, all over the island. It dissolves faeries like me! Everyone else is below ground, I got left behind. Nettles and brambles! I don't care if you are the Guardian, I think you must be thick!'

Resting her hands on her hips, she sighed angrily.

Jessica glanced at Jim.

'Even more proof of evil,' he muttered seriously.

Rosehip stared up at them, her blue eyes filled with peevishness. 'Duh you think so?' she asked, in a mock dumb tone. 'You humans are useless! Why aren't you out there stopping them, Jess?'

Jessica grabbed her coat off the hook and pulled it on. 'I was about to go,' she told Rosehip firmly, 'when you came zooming in, screaming "Shut the door, shut the door".'

Rosehip gave a small 'humph' and crossed her arms. Jessica angrily fastened the buttons of her coat and glared at the faerie.

'We're going now,' she informed her. 'I have to stop the witches.'

Rosehip's mouth fell open as she stared at the door. 'I'm not going back out there!' she squealed, adding melodramatically, 'I'll die.'

Peeved at the delay, Jessica slammed her hand fiercely down on the table inches away from where Rosehip was sitting.

'That's why you're not coming with us,' she barked.

The small elf jumped with shock. Jessica had gained an unmistakable air of command since Elsa had vanished and everyone could sense it. There was no doubt now that she was truly the Guardian and it seemed natural to the others not to question her authority.

362

Jess gazed down at Rosehip and proceeded to tell the faerie what she wanted her to do. 'Dad's going to stay here while Jake, Jim and I head down to Devil's Hole to try and stop them bringing the demon back to life. I want you to remain with Dad and make sure nothing happens to him. Whatever you do don't let anyone but us in. If you can, cast some sort of protection spell around the house. You think you can cope with that?'

Jessica was always doubtful of the extent and reliability of Rosehip's magical powers but as the faerie had managed to hold off the troll in the Magicroutes she figured any kind of White Magic was a bonus.

Rosehip swung her legs gaily from the edge of the table and gave Jessica a playful salute.

'Will do,' she chirped. 'This house will be safe and sound while I'm here.'

Jessica barely registered what the faerie said. She nodded briskly. The old man opened the front door and she and her two companions stepped out into the blackness.

The bitter rain and fog cloaked them the moment they stepped out into the storm. The temperature was the grim coldness of death itself and Jessica's nostrils were filled with the unmistakable stench of freshly spilt human blood. She hoped it was just a foul illusion. The fog seemed to be a living being and Jessica knew now why Rosehip had been so eager to get indoors. The mist seemed to whisper with voices beyond its own ghostly howl of the wind. She could not make out the actual words as they seemed to be in a language that no pure soul would be brave enough to speak, but Jessica knew what they were saying. They were laughing about the death of Jess's mother and taunting her own inadequacies as Guardian. Jessica covered her ears tightly so she would not have to listen to their cruel murmurings. Her eyes seemed to have grown more accustomed to the smoky darkness that engulfed her and although the billowing vapour meant she couldn't see clearly, she was able to make out dark silhouettes through the blackness. She could see behind her the two looming shadows of the house and garage. She was just beginning to wish that she could turn back and return to safety and light when she felt a large hand close around her fingers and heard Jim's voice saying, 'Come on, into the garage.'

Putting complete trust in her great uncle, Jessica allowed him to guide her. The small group shuffled inside the barn-like building. Jim didn't bother shutting the door but, strangely, the mist that twisted and billowed outside did not creep through the entrance. It was almost as if there was a barrier, a sombre and protective curtain, that hung heavy and unseen, across the doorway. The air of the garage seemed more welcoming; there was a warmth here that thawed the morbid chill in Jessica's bones and the odour of engine oil masked the stench of blood that filled the air. Jessica felt safe in this place, protected by a power and love beyond this world. It was an almost spiritual feeling.

The moment they were inside, Jim hurried over to the workbench on the right of the garage and began to scrabble around under it as if he was desperately trying to find something. Jess and Jake watched him with unease, both very aware that they had very little time to waste and should be heading to Devil's Hole this very minute.

'What are you looking for?' Jess asked him.

But the moment she had uttered these words she knew the answer even though the identity of the precious item was still a mystery to her. Just as it had done the first time she had entered the garage, a feeling of complete and utter strength swept through every fibre in her body, driving out the fear and self-doubt that had been conjured up by the evil fog. She felt an intense need to find that sacred item again and knew that Jim was experiencing the same drive. Like a tall flame of white light burning with purity and goodness, Jessica could almost feel the soul of her ancestor Helier filling her body with the bravery she needed for her quest.

Jim stopped his search and stared down at the object resting in his hands. The legacy that was rightfully hers had been found. Jim bowed his head and uttered a silent prayer as he gripped the sacred heirloom. He got to his feet and faced Jessica. The holy object was about two feet long and wrapped in thick, white cloths bound together with strands of brown leather. It was tapered at one end and looked heavy. Her great uncle held it out towards her and although she still could not picture what was concealed within the ancient material, she knew that its image had been engraved in her heart from the day she was born. Her eyes could not conjure up its image nor could her mind remember what every Hellily before her knew, but she knew with all her being that this holy artefact was the beginning and end of that most mystical and hallowed task that was her destiny. It was where blackness met light, where good met evil, where Christian and pagan faith combined. It was all that was and all that ever would be. It was the core of who she was.

Jim held the holy item out towards her.

'Take it,' he said. 'It is what has kept our family blessed for so many centuries. Helier's final gift to Romand. It belongs to the Guardian – it belongs to you.'

Jessica extended her fingers but could not bring herself to touch it. 'I dare not,' she whispered. 'I do not feel worthy.'

Jake stood close behind her, gazing with awe at the cloaked artefact.

'Is that…?' he began.

Jim nodded. The old man took a step towards his great-niece.

'Your heart has already proven itself worthy of the title bestowed upon you at birth. You have followed the spirit of goodness within you and displayed the courage and strength to do what you believe is right. Yet you cannot face your destiny without the weapon you are ordained to wield. Blood has been shed by it, but in the name of honour and righteousness that very blood can go on to protect the innocent of the isle. Take it in the name of our Lord and his faithful servant.'

Jim's words drove the last fragments of doubt from Jessica's mind and reaching out with both hands she grasped the holy item tightly. The moment her skin felt the heavy weight inside the material, intense warmth spread through Jessica's palms. It was as if the memories of many centuries of faith and courage had been wrapped inside the cloth and now were seeping out into Jessica's soul. The heat extended through her arms, making them feel as powerful as those of the strongest warrior. The taunting voices of the fog that had echoed so hurtfully in her ears faded away until they were little more than a bad memory. The heat and love enclosed in the simple cloth ran like liquid gold through every inch of her body, filling her heart with peace. She knew the item concealed inside the package was a weapon but just by holding it all desire for violence evaporated from her body. She remembered what Jake had told her about witches being trapped souls whom she must set free and she knew now

365

that that was what she must do. As the wonderful feeling of serenity engulfed her she closed her eyes and behind her lids she saw the face of a man from a time long ago but whom she immediately recognized. His face was thin and gaunt, tanned and chapped by a life spent living out in the elements. His eyes were dark and filled with inner peace and love, his hair and beard a deep shade of chestnut, tinged here and there with strands of silver. The face only appeared to her for the briefest of moments and then faded, taking with it the warmth and divine music. However, in Jessica's heart the peace and fearlessness remained.

Jessica looked up at her great uncle and saw him smiling with pride. His eyes mirrored her own thoughts and Jessica realized he knew exactly what she had felt.

'This is one of the greatest powers our family has,' he informed her. 'But it can last only a short time. Keep it close and whatever happens don't let it out of your sight. When the moment is right, free it from its bonds and release its power. Only the true Guardian can use it correctly.'

Jessica took one of the long, leather strips that tied the bundle and placed it over her shoulder. The artefact rested heavily but comfortably under her left arm and she held onto it firmly.

Jim gazed warily out into the black storm.

'We must go now,' he said. 'The Devealios grows thicker. Get in the van, you two. We have a long night ahead of us.'

Snatching up a flashlight from the workbench, the stocky Jerseyman hurried around to the driver's side of the battered truck and climbed in. Jake and Jessica followed suit, scrambled into the passenger seats and fastened their seatbelts. Through twisting blackness Jessica could barely see the wall surrounding the garden.

'Are you sure you can drive in this?' she asked Jim doubtfully.

The old man grinned triumphantly as he rummaged in his top pocket for his glasses. 'Believe me, my girl, you've no need to worry. You may be the Guardian of Jersey but as a Hellily I am not without my own magical skills. I know this island like the back of my hand and I can get you anywhere on it in five minutes if I have too. A little Devil's mist isn't going to stop me.' He put on his glasses before glancing back to the two anxious young people and shouting, 'I suggest you both hold on tight.'

The engine roared to life with a fierce growl and Jim roughly released the handbrake. The vehicle lurched forward and they took off into the blinding blackness.

Once outside, the foul Devil's mist pressed in against the windows like billowing smoke, hiding the road in front of them in a vast cloud. Despite the lack of visibility, they seemed to be travelling at a terrifying speed, much faster than Jim normally drove, and every few seconds they were thrown this way and that as Jim swerved to miss something. The old man sat hunched over the steering wheel, his stubby fingers gripping it like claws, his dark eyes straining to see through the swirling blackness. The truck bumped and jolted through the narrow roads of Jersey. Several times Jessica thought they had run over something and every time the seat seemed to lurch from under them. Jake, being the tallest, kept bumping his head on the roof of the cab. Jim seemed to be driving not by sight but by feel, and every time they slammed into an obstacle it seemed to help him guide the truck in a new direction. He seemed almost demonic in his driving. He jerked the steering wheel this way and that, careering through the blinding darkness. Every few moments, he would seize the gear stick and, with a bone-jangling judder, thrust the vehicle into a different gear, sometimes even shooting into reverse whenever the bonnet of the truck met a particularly stubborn obstruction. But however uncomfortable the ride, Jessica was in no doubt that Jim knew exactly what he was doing.

Suddenly, the truck swerved violently to the left, causing Jake and Jessica to tumble against each other. Jake clasped Jessica's hand for comfort and Jess gripped it tightly. The vehicle shuddered as it slid; cursing quietly under his breath Jim wrestled with the wheel to regain control. He slammed his foot down on the brakes and the truck skidded to a halt, throwing Jess and Jake forward in their seats. Jim fumbled with the keys and shut off the engine.

'Sorry about the bumpy ride,' he muttered, 'but nothing's going to stop Jim Hellily.' He paused for a second and regarded the two young people sitting next to him. Jake was almost green with terror as he stared around him and struggled to regain control of his senses and emotions. He was still gripping Jessica's hand for comfort. Jessica's mood, however, was in complete contrast. Her face was still and emotionless as that of a stone angel. Her eyes had lost their sparkle and were now two pieces of matt jade, hard and dark, as she stared out into the blackness that surrounded them. Jim knew this calmness was merely a mask, the disguise that all the Guardians wore when faced with unthinkable terror. Inside, her heart was a maelstrom of fears, hopes and passions – but she would not let him see this. He would only know what she truly felt when she returned from the battle. *If* she returned.

Jim glanced out of the window. The Devil's mist was thicker than ever now, almost solid in texture, and no longer an impenetrable black but a deep scarlet, the hue of anger and murder. Faces danced in the red vapour: grinning mouths with wolf-like fangs and narrow soulless eyes – the murky discharge of evil spells cast to give strength to the demon that slumbered beneath the rocks. Through the bloody air he could see the distant glow of flames, flickering sickly emerald and decaying gold in the bowl of Devil's Hole and knew that there his great-niece's fate awaited her.

'I dare go no further,' he told the others, turning his head away with the shame of his own fear. 'I am old and not brave enough to face such horror.'

Jessica looked into the wicked night. She too was afraid but the duty that burnt inside her soul was too strong to allow her fear to overwhelm her. Evil, witchcraft and death no longer held her in awe; she knew only the importance of her legacy to Jersey. The package Jim had entrusted to her was warm and heavy at her side and its weight gave her the courage she needed.

'It's okay. We'll go on alone.'

She looked up at Jake. He was deathly pale but his eyes were filled with a determination that told Jess he would not abandon her.

'You are Jessica Hellily,' Jim whispered hoarsely, 'Guardian of Jersey, my great-niece – and I love you.'

Jessica dragged her eyes away from the mystical landscape outside the window and looked to the old man sitting at her side. For the first time since she'd met him Jessica did not look for the answers to her past in the wrinkles and lines that marked Jim's face. She saw not an islander who knew more of the ancient, magical ways of Jersey than she did. She just saw an old man, proud, loving and perhaps a bit scared. The past didn't matter now and it was Jim who looked to Jessica for the truth of Helier's legend, a truth that only lay in the future.

Jessica embraced him tightly. 'I won't be the third to die,' she said.

Then, before any doubt could slip into her mind, Jessica opened the van door and she and Jake stepped out fearlessly into the realm of witchcraft.

A great hissing gasp greeted their exit from the vehicle. The gruesome fog swirled around her and Jake, gripping their bodies as if in the coils of some enormous snake. It pressed in on them, dense and thick with death, filling every one of their senses with terror. Worse than all this was the noise that pounded through her brain. The taunting voices and evil whispers she had heard before had returned but now they were louder than ever. They were singing a tuneless chant which told in hideous detail what terrors would befall innocent souls once the Dark Lord was released from his prison. Below this malevolent song Jessica could hear one lone monotone uttering a deep, repetitive chant that was at the core of the symphony of death. Jessica recognized the voice. It was Agatha Noir's.

Jessica instinctively rested her hand on the linen-wrapped bundle strapped to her side. A comforting warmth spread through her body, and in her ears the holy melody she had experienced upon first holding the bundle rang out quietly, its beautiful notes cutting through the ominous chant of the phantoms all around her. Her eyesight cleared and became more acute in the bloody darkness that engulfed her. Jessica could now make out the landscape that surrounded them.

She and Jake were standing at the top of a gravel pathway that sloped steeply downwards into a gully. Rough bracken skirted the sheer track on either side and tall trees arched their withered branches overhead. The red vapour that floated all about them seemed to be drifting up the twisting path as if its source lay at the base of the deep cavern. Jessica could discern a dull glow in the distance, at least half a mile away. From where she stood the light appeared to come from a slowly spinning disc, flickering with flames of green and gold. Whatever the shining circle was, Jessica knew it was at the very heart of the evil that gripped Jersey and she must follow the deathly beacon until she found Agatha and Elsa.

369

Keeping her right hand firmly on the precious package tied to her side, Jessica took hold of Jake's hand, guiding him forward. The youth's long, pale fingers were icy cold and when Jessica glanced at him she saw his eyes were transfixed with fear.

'Jake,' she hissed, giving his arm a violent shake. 'Jake, snap out of it. We've got to stay focused.'

The sound of her voice seemed to shake some of the crippling terror from him and he turned to face her.

'That place is unholy,' he whispered, raising a trembling finger to point at the twisting, emerald circle. 'If we go down there we'll die.'

His lip began to quiver and he looked as if he was going to cry. Jessica gave his hand a firm squeeze.

'That's just the Devil's mist getting to you. You can't let that happen,' she told him in a commanding tone, before adding, 'Nobody's going to die, I promise. I'm not going to let that happen.'

Jake's face wore an expression of frozen horror and he seemed unable to move. Jessica wondered what on earth she should do. She briefly considered leaving Jake where he was and heading down towards Devil's Hole alone but she feared that the Devil's mist would slowly eat away at his spirit. Besides which, she didn't feel capable of carrying out her plan single-handed. The weighty object bound at her right hip seemed to throb with a gentle heat and suddenly Jessica had an idea. Taking Jake's chilled hand she placed it on the bundle and knotted his fingers securely into the leather straps. Jake's eyes flickered closed for a second as the heat of the holy item soaked into his heart. He opened his eyes again.

'I'm sorry, Jess,' he murmured, shaking his head. 'I don't know what happened to me. I panicked. Horrible visions entered my brain.'

Jessica looked back down the path that led towards their treacherous goal. 'Try not to think about it; keep your mind clear and stay calm,' she told him. 'Are you ready to go now?'

Jake took a deep breath and nodded his head. Jessica entwined her own fingers with the straps tied around her treasure and together they began the long, terrifying march towards the horror that was Devil's Hole.

The hill that sloped down into the inlet was steep and long.

The ground was covered with loose flint that slipped beneath their feet like ice. Almost blinded by the dense crimson that swept around them, Jessica and Jake trembled as they picked their way down the uneven bank, their legs quaking unsteadily. The bloody cloud seeped into them through their ears, nostrils and mouths, filling their heads with unholy thoughts. They seemed to be swimming in a sea of blood and carnage that clung to their skin and would not let go. Only the heavy, reassuring heat that glowed from the bundle at Jessica's side kept them sane. The howling song of the dank vapour grew louder with every step they took until their ears began to ring and their brains throbbed with agony. Jessica could hear the broken accent of Mrs Noir's snarling cruel and powerful words spoken in some long forgotten foreign tongue as clearly as if she was standing next to her. The volume of the witch's chant told Jessica that she must have grown stronger than ever.

The pathway seemed to go on forever, drawing them ever downwards towards the grim flicker of the ghostly light. The red fog had grown so thick around them now it began to feel as if they were battling a living force. Unseen claws tore at their clothes and hair, slashing their skins. Hands grabbed at them and pulled them back, making their legs almost too heavy to lift. The rain beat down from the black heaven, heavy and thick like syrup, soaking their bodies and weighing them down. The path sloped down at an almost vertical angle and in the blinding redness it felt as if they were descending into the heart of the earth itself, right down into the pits of Hell. Oddly, despite the rain and the fog, the air around them seemed to be growing hotter as the green glow came closer. It was as if they were walking into the mouth of a great furnace, their skin almost scorching in the sweltering blaze. They stumbled forward and round a curve in the path. That's when they saw the Devil's Hole.

The deep, stone bowl scooped into the cliffs of Jersey was ablaze with flames of emerald and gold. The brilliant light thrown out onto the trees and bracken that crested the cliff top danced like a crowd of possessed phantoms whirling in a waltz of evil and death. The air stung with searing heat and the screams of thousands of tormented souls. Deep in the depth of the bay, the sea water that gushed into the cove through the small inlet had turned sickly green and spun in a twisting whirlpool which from time to time threw up great pillars of golden fire and bloody smog that became transformed into the shapes of beasts. The cove was a cauldron of bubbling evil and the gas from this huge potion spread its foul vapour throughout the island.

Jessica and Jake huddled close in the undergrowth and crept stealthily forward towards the rim of the cliff. Below them, they could see a long narrow outcrop, stretching out like a knife stuck into the side of the cliff and on the rocky base were two very different figures – Agatha and Elsa Noir.

Jessica's heart froze with terror as she saw the wicked hag. Agatha Noir was clad in flowing robes as dark as midnight that blew in the fierce hot wind like the wings of some giant bat. Her long, thin hair caught in the wind, spread out around her head like the ghostly halo of a fallen angel. Her heavy form was a shadowy silhouette against the violent gold sheen of the ignited water and her shadow fell long and black onto the chalky stone. There was no frailness in the old woman now as she stood tall and erect at the very tip of the outcrop. The weakness and illnesses of old age had vanished from her and beneath her dark vestments her body looked powerful and swollen with magic. The black material fell away from her forearms as she stretched her bony, claw-like fingers up to the moonless heaven and in the palms of her twisted hands, glowing spheres of smoky purple light formed. Every so often Agatha would hurl these pulsating, dark orbs down into the pit of the blazing cove and the churning emerald water would hiss and foam with blazing sparks and sinful vapour. The witch had her back to them but Jessica could hear her croaking tones above the howling wind as she chanted evil incantations to the boiling sea.

Far back from the possessed old woman, cowering in crippling fear against the stone wall of the cliff, lay Elsa, more sickly looking and weak than she had ever seen her. The child looked like a ghost in flesh, everything about her silvery white in the brutal blaze of Devil's Hole, her thin blonde hair blowing away from her terrified features like delicate white threads. Her face was sallow and her blue eyes rested deep in their sockets, brimming with tears. She was clothed in a floor length gown of purest white cotton, carefully embroidered with runes and symbols Jessica could not read. A heavy, steel ring had been driven into the solid rock of the ledge and a broad chain passing through it bound Elsa's thin wrists in weighty cuffs. Jessica knew now what Elsa was, a pitiful prisoner for her grandmother's warped desires, an innocent life born to be used for evil deeds and finally sacrificed as part of her mistress's blackest plan.

Jessica and Jake pressed their bodies against the singed earth and lay in the hushed cover of the thick bracken. The scene played out on the ledge below them was terrifying. Jessica felt the comforting glow of the bundle at her side and focused on it to give her strength. Now was the moment of truth.

'She's going to kill Elsa!' she muttered to Jake in horror.

The lad grimly nodded his head. 'Mrs Noir must believe you're dead. She has opened the tomb where the demon lies,' he said, his face white with terror. 'But it needs human blood to give it enough strength to awaken. If she murders Elsa and offers her body to the tomb then we're all doomed.'

Despite the searing air that engulfed them, Jessica shuddered, chilled at the thought. 'We've got to stop her,' she whispered to Jake, her eyes focused on the bulky, dark figure of Mrs Noir perched on the rim of the outcrop,

Jake lay perfectly still for a moment, breathing deeply the hot, thick air. His body tense, he looked at Jessica. 'I'm going to get her,' he told her, his voice not showing the slightest hint of fear.

Jessica stared at her friend in amazement and was shocked by the steady determination in his clear eyes. The nerves that seemed to have possessed him at the top of the hill had completely vanished and Jessica knew that he felt the same fearless devotion to Jersey that she did. She caught his arm and stared into his eyes.

'Are you sure you want to do this?' she hissed. 'You could die.'

Jake bit his lip and an expression of doubt flickered across his face but it was soon gone. He gave Jessica a firm nod and said, 'Jersey's my island. If we don't stop Agatha Noir we're all dead anyway. I'm not going out without a fight.'

Jessica gave him a half smile and felt glowing admiration for his courage. She gave his arm a reassuring squeeze and thanked God she had been blessed with such undoubting support in her quest.

'Be careful,' She told him anxiously. 'I've already lost Elsa to that evil old hag. She's not having you as well.' She shuffled deeper into the rough thicket so that she could not be seen. 'I'll wait here. If you get in trouble I'm right behind you.' She paused for a moment and then leant across and planted a quick peck on Jake's cheek.

The boy was speechless for a second before stuttering, 'Steady on, Jess. You're not my type, and even if you were this is not the most romantic place.'

Jessica frowned crossly and gave him a slap on the arm. 'Get over yourself!' she exclaimed. 'It was just for good luck. I may be facing death but I'm not lowering my standards that much. Now get on with it!'

Jake inhaled deeply to steady his nerves and crouching low to the smouldering ground began to crawl slowly on his belly towards the brim of the cliff. The crackles and howls of the black magic in the air were deafening but still every rustle of the dry, scorched heather made the young lad's nerves shake with fear that Agatha might hear him. Their hiding place was only a matter of feet from the brink of the cove but Jake crawled so slowly and carefully that it seemed to take hours for him to reached the edge.

Jessica huddled in the dense undergrowth not daring to move as she watched with unbearable trepidation as Jake crept closer to the point where the top of the cliff overhung the grim outcrop. She could hardly breathe for terror and her gaze flitted from Jake to the tall, powerful figure of Agatha Noir just a few feet away.

Finally Jake found himself lying at the very crest of the rock-face, peering down on the hellish scene below. The wind was hotter and stronger here than ever, charring his cheeks and forehead as if he was leaning over a great fire. The brilliant emerald glow that issued up from deep within the cavern cast its light over his squat form, turning his raven hair and ashen skin golden. Cautiously, he peeped down into the cove below him. The projection on which Agatha and Elsa were standing was three or four feet under him. Directly below where he knelt, huddled quaking in a petrified ball, was Elsa, so close Jake was sure that if he reached out he would be able to touch her soft blonde hair. On the brim of the outcrop, Agatha Noir, enraptured by the power she was about to unleash, hurled another smoky globe of black magic into the sizzling sea and a tower of golden flame leapt from the churning depths.

Elsa buried her face in her hands and wept with fear. She could not remember how she'd been dragged from the witch trial in Jim's kitchen to this stormy and terrifying stone altar. All she knew was that the day she had dreaded all of her short life had arrived and with her demented grandmother convinced that the Guardian of Jersey was dead, she would fully discover what terrible power the old witch had. Elsa was trapped, bound not only by the heavy chain that weighed down her feeble hands and the strong spells that exploded all around her, but by the knowledge that every last glimmer of hope and salvation was lost and the darkness she dreaded would soon arrive. She cursed her weakness, which had forced her to fire the bow and her stupid fear of the old woman who had kept her prisoner all these years. If she had found the courage to tell Jessica the truth from the start none of this would have happened. All the fury, hate and coldness that had been her grandmother was a fraction of what she had become now. Elsa had so wanted to spare her own life but what was the point of that now? Everyone in Jersey was going to perish. All was doomed.

A whisper sounded through the wailing of the magic and Elsa swore she heard it call her name. The white-faced child's heart quickened with fear. Was this the demon from the depths of the sea calling her to her demise? The voice seemed to be coming from nearby, as if it was floating above her head.

'Elsa, look up, quickly.' Elsa turned her eyes skyward. At first she saw only the thick, scarlet smoke that billowed from the churning sea and the dark, coarse shrubbery that overhung the top of the cliff. Then she noticed a movement in the thick heather and a face appeared. Jake LeBlanc was gazing down at her from just a few feet away, his eyes were urgent and filled with concern. Elsa shifted her body closer to the stony cliff face and stared up at Jake in amazement. In all the terror that had befallen her she had totally forgotten about Jessica and Jake. When Agatha had begun to cast the enchantment to set loose the unthinkable horror of Jersey's demon she was sure that the Devil's mist would stop them coming after her. Now the sight of one of the only two people Elsa felt she could call a friend filled the child with panic. They couldn't be here, in the heart of all this danger. She had caused Jake and Jessica too much grief as it was, she would not let them get hurt any more.

Her mouth lolled open in confusion and shock but finally she managed to utter the words, 'Go back, go back where it's safe.'

The farmer's son didn't budge but edged closer to the small child.

'No,' he said firmly, shaking his head. 'We've come to save you. Everything's going to be just fine. I'm here. Jessica's right behind me. We're going to set things right.'

At the sound of Jessica's name, Elsa's face crumpled and she dissolved into floods of grief-stricken sobs. 'I've betrayed her!' Elsa wailed, so loudly Jake was afraid Mrs Noir might hear. 'I betrayed you all. I fired the bow, I tried to kill the Guardian. Grandmère is right, I am useless. I deserve to die!'

Jake's heart filled with desperation. There was no time to ask Jessica for advice; he had to get Elsa to safety as fast as he could. He saw a heavy, iron key lying on the outcrop just beyond his reach and knew it would unlock Elsa's bonds but if he moved any closer the witch would be bound to see him.

'Listen,' he urged the tiny girl as she rocked on her knees, wringing her hands in despair. 'We know why you did what you did and we understand it wasn't your choice. Your grandmother used you.' He struggled to keep his voice as soft as he could. 'But Elsa, you don't have to do what your grandmother orders. You're your own person, your heart is pure. Remember the witches' stoop in the great chamber? You saved Jessica. You saved her because you knew it was right. You can do it again, Elsa. This time you can save Jersey.'

Through her fear and confusion Jake's words reached out to Elsa. She heard them and as she did, something bright and marvellous grew inside the child's lonely heart, like a rare flower opening after eleven years in bud. Jessica heard Jake's speech as well and in her hiding place she closed her eyes and prayed with all her heart that Elsa would have the strength to do what was right. Elsa placed a hand to her chest. Something was happening inside her, something warm and strange but she wasn't scared. She thought of Jake's words and of the horror that her death would unleash on Jersey. She glanced at the thick silhouette of her grandmother and her stomach churned with hatred. All her life Agatha had used and abused Elsa in the name of the black magic Elsa despised and up until now she had been too afraid to say 'no'. Soon her grandmother would command the world but as long as Elsa breathed, the old hag would no longer command her spirit.

Elsa saw the heavy key to her chains lying within her reach. Her grandmother had not bothered to put it where Elsa was unable to reach, thinking the girl would not have the courage to break free. But Elsa now found herself feeling braver than she ever thought possible. Her hands were shaking like leaves in a storm as she slowly reached for the key. Jake's eyes grew wide as he willed his friend to grasp hold of her freedom. Filled with excitement, he leant over the edge of the cliff, silently begging Elsa to take hold of the key. He leant heavily on the burnt ground that dropped down into the cove and as he did so the soil crumbled away beneath his palm.

Tiny fragments of rock tumbled onto the outcrop, clattering above the wind. Jessica gasped in horror at the sound but it was too late.

The wind roared fiercely in their ears and singed their hair with the breath of Hell itself. From her perch on the tip of the outcrop, the fearsome figure of Agatha Noir wheeled round to confront the terrified trio. Jessica cried out in horror as she saw the old woman's face, for the witch was no longer human. Her dark green eyes now glowed red like burning coals, spinning dementedly. Her face was a mask of hatred and her tongue lashed, forked, from her mouth as she screamed, 'Who dares defy me?'

Chapter 19

The Whitest of Witches

Overcome with fear and shocked by the hideous appearance of the possessed hag, Jessica jumped up from her hiding place. Her animal instinct told her to flee but once on her feet she found herself frozen to the spot with terror. Panic stricken, Jake scrambled backwards into the undergrowth repulsed by Agatha Noir's unearthly appearance. Before the powerful figure of the old woman, Elsa crouched low quaking with fear. Never before in her pitiful life had Elsa seen such pure evil smouldering in her grandmother's eyes. The girl knew that all was lost. What little humanity dwelt in the foul hag's soul before had now vanished completely and in its place was a soulless unyielding strength of darkness that swelled the old woman's stature and made her pupils and fingertips glow with glistening, crimson flames. Agatha Noir now possessed the mystical power she'd hungered for all her bitter life and for which she had given up the one thing most precious to all men – she had sold her soul.

With one hiss from the witch's twisted mouth, the emerald fire that licked the granite of Devil's Hole flared into scarlet flames as searing and fierce as the depths of Hell. The darkness that cloaked the island evaporated in a blaze of violent red light and the boiling wind howled with furious heat and force in the faces of the three terrified young people cowering before the witch. The old woman's scarlet eyes blazed with white-hot flames of demonic fury. Her silver hair caught in the storm and was blown like a tower of flame high above her head, bright orange in the light of the cavern. Her face was grotesque and twisted like the stone gargoyle that sneered down from the hearth in her front room. Her skin was a dark heavy grey as if made from granite; deeply lined it showed the cruelty of her heart. Her lips were black as beetles and her snake-like tongue coiled from between them, twisted and tasting the air, hungry for blood. Her body seemed to swell with muscle and power and all signs of weakness were gone as she stalked towards them, quaking with fury. The tips of her fingers seemed to be alight with black flame that throbbed eagerly to release their unholy might. Jake and Jessica stayed frozen where they were, their minds wracked with the awesome terror Agatha Noir inflicted on them. Only Elsa could feel something other than terror. All her life she had feared the might of the witch's powers but now when her grandmother's strength was at its most intense, all the small child felt was hatred for what her grandmother had become.

Mrs Noir's eyes bore into each of them with utter contempt and loathing. 'How dare you!' she roared. Her voice was filled with the savage bay of the demon of Jersey itself. 'How dare you lowly humans come to defile the place of sublime darkness and evil! I, Agatha Noir, hold the forces of nature in my very hands. I am the queen of all that is pagan and powerful in this isle. I command the sea and the land, the sky and the earth. Fall to your knees for there is nothing you can do to save your souls!'

The old woman threw back her head and raised her ignited hands up to the heavens. In the churning dark sky, lightning cracked like a mighty silver whip lashing the earth. Jessica took a frightened step backwards and gazed up into the heavens. Elsa's heart drummed wildly in her chest.

The witch glared at the petrified Jake kneeling at the edge of the cliff. 'You ignorant oaf!' she cawed at him. 'Why did you wander into this place of magic when you have none of your own to protect you? By the earth you lived and so by it you shall perish!'

With a swoop of her cape, Mrs Noir extended her hand and the black flames that glowed from her fingers turned brilliant green as they darted out and gripped the woody bracken surrounding Jake. The twisted branches juddered with life and movement as the black magic took hold of them. Jake gasped in horror as long, thorny stems lashed out towards him and coiled quick and tight around his wrists and ankles. He struggled

379

to free himself but the vines were as strong as steel and flexible as the lithe body of a viper. They bound up his arms and legs like living rope, their thorns slashing through his clothing and making his flesh bleed. He fell to the ground, writhing in agony. Mrs Noir's scarlet eyes gleamed with delight as she uttered softly, 'Slowly, my pretty blooms. Let him suffer before the end.' Elsa witnessed the sick torture of her friend and the burning loathing in her heart grew, stretching up into her chest like a phoenix ready to be reborn.

Overcome with horror, Jessica hurried towards the shaking body of Jake as another thick coil of wood bound around his chest, squeezing the very breath from him. Her hands reached out to grasp the prickly vines that imprisoned her friend. But before she could even attempt to release him from their grip, Agatha Noir flexed her fingers skilfully and striking the air with her palm sent a mighty block of unseen force ploughing into her. The magic hit the girl like a weighty punch to her head and she was tossed backward with a yelp. Jessica's body slammed into a tree and she lay there dazed for a moment before struggling to her feet, gripping the trunk to steady herself. A trickle of scarlet ran from the corner of her mouth and her tongue tasted of iron.

Elsa watched Jessica stumbling to master her battered body and felt her temper rocket. This beast who had for so long used Elsa for every foul task imaginable was now whipping and abusing the only two people who had ever cared for her. It was as if a knife had cut the strands of fear and duty that tied Elsa to her grandmother. She now saw without fear the monster she was. Above anything else Elsa wanted to strike out and wound the old hag the way she'd wounded her and everyone else. The fierce but beautiful white power within her burnt stronger by the second and seeped into her frail arms like a healing balm. She remembered Jake's last words to her and knew he had been right – she did have a choice.

Agatha Noir's serpent-like mouth formed a malicious grin and her hands turned purple with black magic as she raised them high like the fangs of a cobra ready to strike. Legs trembling, Jessica stood before her, her mind empty of any plan to save herself. Only the gentle throb of the bundle at her side kept her from collapsing. In the thick and twisting mass of undergrowth,

Jake battled weakly for survival. Flames blazed deep purple at the tips of the witch's fingers and her voice was gruff with fury.

'Why couldn't you just die as easily as your mother did, Jessica Hellily? Twice I sent my pathetic minion to dispose of you and twice she failed; for that she will feel my wrath. But now I have you and now the line of Hellily ends!'

As her grandmother spoke each word, Elsa felt the healing glow inside her pulse more strongly and brilliantly until so great was it she was sure it would burst through her skin and she would be transformed. She knew with all her heart that her own life did not matter but she must save Jessica at all costs. The skin beneath her shackles seared as if aflame but it did not wound Elsa. She was the heat and she knew that only she could save the Guardian.

Agatha reached back her arm as if about to hurl something at Jessica. The violet flames leapt eagerly in the palm of her hand. Elsa knew that this was the moment she had to act but she had very little idea what she should do. Her body seemed to shimmer with a power she had never felt before. She did the only thing her confused brain could think of. Just as her grandmother released the flare of pure, burning black magic from her gnarled fingers, Elsa threw back her pale golden hair and raising her own hands skywards, called in a voice clearer and stronger than her own, 'Jessica, move!'

The sphere of purple flame shot from Agatha's hand. Ever since Jessica had been hit by the first blow of the witch's power, a helpless weakness had taken hold of her body and mind and she could see no way of defeating the pure evil that possessed the old hag. She struggled to find her feet and saw with horror the twirling circle of purple evil and death hurtling towards her. Darkness was all around and she was sure that her demise was close at hand. Then a sudden burst of golden white light illuminated the cliff top and Jessica heard a ringing, strong voice call out her name. The glistening brilliance seemed to encase her, lifting her high into the air as the heinous violet globe ploughed into the earth were she had been standing, spreading across the hillside in a carpet of tiny lilac flames. Jessica felt herself drifting slowly downwards as the dazzling glow faded. She could feel her body drawing in the fresh, cool white power as it faded around her. As it did so all her physical injuries and thoughts of despair vanished and she felt once again capable of fulfilling her mission. She landed lightly among the purple fire that covered the ground and looked to the ledge where the healing light had come from.

The small figure of Elsa Noir that Jessica expected to see had vanished and in her place was another creature, so different and yet so similar Jessica gasped. Her baby blonde tresses now glowed like burnished gold, blown in gentle waves in the wind. The simple cotton gown was now finest white silk, and the runes embroidered on in twinkled like the stars of heaven. Her skin remained pale but instead of a sickly, sullen pallor it now seemed to glow with a pure light that dazzled. Her eyes were strong, dark sapphires gleaming with a mixture of peace, triumph and vengeance. Her face bore not the signs of worry and suffering it had before but was youthful, pure and full of strength in complete contrast to Agatha's malformed features. Tiny silver sparkles flashed on her newly rounded cheeks and her fingertips seemed to glow with golden flames. Her stature was still tiny compared with the witch's heavy bulk but she stood tall and proud. The chains that had held her moments before lay shattered at her side. A crown of flowers rested on her flaxen brow – lilies for purity, rue for disdain and deep, scarlet roses for the passion which now filled her heart. She looked like an avenging angel sent from Heaven and both Agatha and Jessica cowered, awestruck at her appearance.

The witch's evil face dropped with shock for a moment at her granddaughter's transformation but then her black lips twisted into a sneer of loathing and her red eyes flared with fury.

'You worthless brat!' she hissed, her forked tongue lashing. 'Yet again your foolishness has cost me valuable time. Stop trying to protect the Guardian!'

Elsa's deep blue pupils glowed like swirling pools.

'You do not frighten me any more, grandmère,' she said. Her voice was as clear and kind as it ever had been but now it rang out loud and strong like the chimes of victory. 'I am not yours to command.'

The black witch spat with disgust onto the rock and her saliva hissed and dissolved the stone like acid.

'Just like your mother,' she barked. 'Stupid! Wilful and stupid!

Always getting in my way, spoiling my plans. That's why I had to get rid of her and that idiot of a husband of hers; start afresh. No daughter of mine would refuse to take the dark arts; she had to be crushed. That's why I scarred you, crippled you to break your spirit. I offered you everything if you would obey my will and you threw it all away.'

The air around Elsa seemed to crackle with sparks of silver and electric blue.

'So it is true!' she screamed, her voice filled with fury and woe. 'You *did* kill them, killed them all to gain this cruel power. You mean nothing to me, nothing.'

Agatha raised her hands to the heaven and the boiling waters of Devil's Hole crashed their emerald might against the brutal cliffs.

'Nothing!' she howled demonically. 'Child, you should worship me as your goddess of evil and pray for mercy. Don't test my wrath!'

Elsa shook her golden mane and laughed coldly. Her laughter seemed to quell the angry waves of the cove and they sank back down.

'Pray to you for mercy?' she questioned. 'And what shall I receive? You have taken everything from me. You murdered my parents and made me an orphan. You kept me prisoner to do your evil will with spells and threats that robbed me of my health. You made me commit foul acts in the name of Darkness which filled me with fear and self-loathing.'

Elsa's eyes turned a beautiful but terrible shade of dark sapphire as her rage grew. She stepped towards her grandmother and as she walked forward her silken robe dragged behind her and everywhere it touched thick, green moss and wild flowers sprang to life.

'When I found two people who cared about me and offered me friendship, you made me betray them with lies and deceit, putting their lives in peril. If I submit to your will, I too will die. So tell me, if you dare, what have I left to lose if I defy you to defend the girl who is my friend and the Guardian of this isle?'

Mrs Noir's eyes seemed to ignite and her eyeballs became transformed into globes of fire. Fingers wide, she shot her hands forward and with an almighty cry she sent a stream of blazing orange flames straight for Elsa. The child thrust her palm out and as the blaze hit it, a silver circle spread out in front of the girl like a magnificent shield. Flames shot in every direction, hissing into a smoky haze in the blackness. Her arm still outstretched to protect herself, Elsa glance back to Jessica, who had watched the whole scene in amazement. 'Jessica,' she called, 'summon your equal. Neptune holds your shelter and Gemini will win the day. Make haste.'

Momentarily, Jessica stared into the heavenly face of her friend and any lingering doubt she may have had about Elsa disappeared. The girl had proven the true colour of her heart and Jessica trusted her words with all her soul. She knew now Elsa had become what her grandmother had always dreaded. She was the rarest of creatures and the most tortured of souls. Elsa was a white witch.

Turning her eyes away from the flashes of the battle that raged on the ledge below her, Jessica took flight. The ground all around her still crackled with purple flames and they had spread across the length of the hilltop, up to where the rock enclosed the bay from the sea beyond. The cove still curled green with evil spells but the ocean was calm and black. Jessica remembered Elsa's words and knew they were her only guidance. The sea was the only safe place. Taking off at speed, Jessica fixed her eyes on the dark expanse of water on the horizon and tried not to think about Jake caught in the snares of the enchanted brambles or what would happen if Elsa lost her power. She swore to God she would return to save them soon but knew that her true strength lay within the depths of the ocean. Elsa's magic and the warm glow of the package at her side filled her with new-found energy and she powered across the burning grassland, flames licking at her heels. The violet blaze engulfed the trees that dotted the cliff top, twisting up their trunks like foul fiery serpents and torching every leaf until they all flickered with unnatural light and life like the flames of a million enchanted candles. They blazed high above Jessica's head before tumbling one after another down towards her, caught in the searing wind that howled all around. The bewitched foliage rained down on her as she ran, like burning embers falling from the sky, singeing her thick hair and scarring her face. But Jessica could feel no pain; she dared not. To think, even for a second, of her own agony and fear of being burnt would trap her in among the flames. The package at her side dug firmly into her ribcage, warm and solid, and it was this that repressed the deathly fear within her.

It was as if the whole of Devil's Hole had sunk down into the bowels of the earth and was burning in the fires of Hell. All around Jessica, purple flames and thick reddish black smoke swirled in demonic patterns. The ground was like smouldering ashes, melting the leather of her shoes. The violet inferno that engulfed the trees destroyed the wood and sent large branches, heavy and ablaze with black magic crashing down around the young girl as she battled forwards, dodging this way and that to avoid the deadly missiles. The flames seemed to be set on devouring her and reached out like brutal, violet claws to scald her clothing and blacken her cheeks. Out of the corner of her eye, Jessica was aware of violent flashes of white, green and scarlet and she knew that the battle between the two witches still raged. Furious cries of anger and revenge filled her ears with ancient words beyond her understanding. Agatha and Elsa's voices filled the air, cursing each other as they threw spells back and forth. Jessica prayed that her friend's power would not fail. The landscape before her was unclear, crudely etched in the smoke. Jessica struggled to think what to do to save the island from destruction but her mind was so full of horror and confusion that her instincts as Guardian were lost. The only clear thought in her mind was Elsa's final words to her: 'Neptune holds your shelter and Gemini will win the day.' She had to get to the sea. The steep drop that plunged down into the ocean was only a short distance away now and Jessica was sure that she could reach it in a matter of moments. Suddenly, a huge branch blazing with fire fell from a nearby tree and landed not a foot in front of where she was standing, smashing to the ground in a shower of sparks. Jessica stumbled forward with a scream of terror and the sparks from the missile peppered her back, setting her jumper alight. The heat was so intense it wiped all but the most basic instincts of survival from her mind and wracked her body with pain. Jessica fell to the floor desperately trying to put the flames out. Over and over she rolled as the flames ate hungrily at her clothing. Before her eyes, the world was a mad blur of brilliant violet and dark smog as ash misted her vision with tears. She

385

scrabbled among the smouldering undergrowth and struggled to her feet, forcing herself onwards.

A gust of icy air blasting through the boiling atmosphere, caused Jessica to stop dead in her tracks. Wiping the ash from her eyes, she gazed out at the panorama before her and felt her heart swell with relief. She was standing on the very edge of the cliff before it swept down into the sea. The foul, black smoke and licking flames seemed to coil back with horror as they reached the precipice and the wind that blew from the billowing waves was cool and sweet. Many feet below her, the sea rippled gently, calm and black despite the raging storm, and when she looked closer, Jessica saw that just below its silvery surface, hundreds of lithe bodies and glistening tails swam back and forth as if to form a living wall between their beloved Mother Ocean and the evil of Devil's Hole. The black magic could not flow out into the purity of the seas – not yet, not while the demon was still imprisoned and the merfolk still fought for their home.

A sharp, angry cry called Jessica's attention from the merfolk and she spun back to face the horror of the duelling witches. The smoke and the flames obscured her sight but the green glow of the cove ignited the blackness so clearly that the drama on the outcrop was plain to see. Two figures, almost identical in pose and power, confronted each other, their outstretched fingertips gleaming with fire. One was cloaked in blackness so hideous that there was no soul to it, the other shone brilliant white and silver like a candle of God. The power from their hands sent interlocking beams of hateful scarlet and victorious gold across the ledge like a fishing net cast across the sky. The web twisted and turned in unfathomable designs and knots, gleaming from red to white and back again as each witch battled to defeat the other. Visions formed in the net, echoing the thoughts in their separate minds: bats, demons and ghouls from Agatha's sick imagination; butterflies, flowers and birds from Elsa's untainted mind. It was impossible to tell who possessed the stronger power and the awesome force of the fight made Jessica feel helpless and alone. She felt drawn closer and closer to the sea below her and despite the fact that she knew the fall would probably kill her, she was overwhelmed by the need to dive into its cool depths and escape the hellish heat.

Above the roar of the storm and the chants of the witches, a call echoed out to Jessica from the sea, deep, low and painful, like a great beast in distress. Jessica closed her eyes and felt the cry take her, guide her where she needed to go. It seeped under her skin and awoke that primal part of herself that she could not fathom. Nothing else mattered at that moment. The strange, woeful song had drowned out all the terror.

'I'm coming,' she whispered. Jessica turned back to face the ocean and without opening her eyes she spread her arms out before her, tipped forward and dived into the dark, cold water.

Chapter 20

Of Neptune and Gemini

Through the still, cold air and peaceful darkness, Jessica fell, body perfectly straight, like an arrow fired from a bow. Three days ago she had been forced to plummet into the fierce sea surrounding Jersey by the curse placed upon her by Agatha's pendant, but this time it was Jessica's own will that made her take the leap. The deep, soulful song that echoed up from the ocean rang loud in her ears, drowning out all the terror of the black magic of Devil's Hole. The fresh wind whistled against her face and through her hair, cooling the black burns that scarred her skin. Jessica did not open her eyes to see the lapping ocean as it hurtled up towards her. She knew that if she looked, this wonderful feeling of freedom and escape from the raging flames would vanish and she would know the full danger of what she had done. However, in her heart she knew this was her only route to safety. She spread out her arms as if they were wings and prayed that the merfolk in the sea beneath her would save her from drowning. If her faith in them was misplaced, all hope for herself and the island was lost. She held her breath and waited.

The icy water of the channel took Jessica's body to its salty bosom as she hit it and the dark waves closed in over her head blocking out the crackling evil of the land. Enclosed in the fresh marine embrace of the ocean, Jessica felt herself slip further and further away from the black magic. There was a graceful movement all around her, as if she was swimming between silken sheets. Opening her eyes, a living mosaic of glimmering silvery fins, powerful green and blue torsos and golden-eyed faces crowned with flowing locks surrounded her as she swam in among the school of elegant merfolk. Their melodic voices reverberated through the water like an angelic chorus and dozens of unseen hands supported Jessica's floating form, lifting it back up to the surface. Her head broke through the waves and she gasped for air, blinking the salt from her eyes she gazed around searching for her dear friend, Keela.

All around her, mermen and maids surfaced and dived as if to weave a magical net within the sea. The sea dweller who had brought her to the surface was a round-faced mermaid with full, sky-blue cheeks and a mane of curly dark green hair. Instinctively, Jessica turned her eyes back to the flickering light of Devil's Hole and all calmness evaporated as she saw that Elsa and Agatha were still sparring. Her stomach sank as the thought entered her mind that throwing herself into the arms of the merfork might have been a terrible idea. How was she to help anyone when she was so far away? She turned to her rescuer and was not reassured by the panic in the mermaid's glowing eyes.

'Where is Keela?' Jessica demanded, her heart jack-hammering against her ribcage with fear. 'Why are you all here? It's too dangerous. You must get back to deeper water, it's not safe here.'

A deep and woeful bellow of an unseen creature rang through the cold air, softening Jessica's fear slightly. The head of an older merman bobbed from beneath the dark waves and fixed Jessica with a stern stare.

'And let that old land hag take our home as well? Not on my father's tail!' he barked gruffly at her before diving back beneath the sea.

Jessica slumped wearily against the young mermaid's shoulder as despair and failure washed over her. She should have stayed on the cliff and faced Agatha Noir until the bitter end. Instead she had run away and expected the merfolk to save her. What kind of Guardian was she?

'I've failed everyone,' she moaned, as the low, rasping cry rang out again.

The mermaid glanced out to sea and then back to Jessica. Her face was younger than Inggot's and she couldn't have been much older than Jessica herself.

'Keela warned us that this might happened,' she said softly,

389

a tremor of nerves in her reedy voice. 'That you might come to us on this night. Xandu told him not to talk such nonsense but who listens to Xandu any more these days? Bitter old haddock!' She flicked her tail nervously and gazed out into the water, 'Where is he?' she muttered to herself. 'Jessica, you must go with Keela the moment he arrives.'

Jessica gazed at the young mermaid. She thought she knew the full role the people of the ocean had to play in her destiny but it seemed, as always, people had been making arrangements and discussing her life without her knowledge.

'What do you mean, I must go with Keela?' she said, panic and confusion making her tone sharp. 'I can't go anywhere, I've got to save the island!' She glanced fearfully at the two duelling witches before adding, 'Even if I don't know how.'

The mermaid's pretty, plump face cracked with sorrow. It was clear the evil that threatened her marine home scared her deeply and Jessica at once regretted being so sharp with her.

'I don't know,' she said, her beautiful golden eyes brimming with tears. 'I don't go anywhere near the dweller and I barely know what was said between Keela and Xandu.'

She brought a hand up and smudged a milky tear from her eye.

Jessica's heart sank lower with guilt, everything was going wrong. She swallowed her own fear and fury and stroked the mermaid's silky, moss coloured tresses.

'There, there, everything will be okay,' she soothed, hoping the sea-maiden wouldn't detect the doubt in her voice. 'Please don't cry…'

She paused, realizing she didn't know the girl's name.

'Lyurnee,' whispered the weeping maid. 'My name's Lyurnee and I don't want to die!'

Jessica cupped the mermaid's face in her hands. In her tears, the Guardian found new determination to succeed in her quest.

'No-one's going to die,' she reassured, just as she had done to Jake. 'I'm here to protect you.'

The mermaid lifted her head and gazed trustingly at Jessica for a few seconds. Then her attention was caught by something behind Jessica and she quickly gulped back her tears. 'He's here!' she exclaimed. 'Keela's here!'

Jessica spun round and saw the familiar head of her great

uncle's merman friend emerge from beneath the swells. Keela's face was darker and more solemn than Jessica had ever seen it. His golden eyes blazed with worry and grief as he gazed from the horrific glare of Devil's Hole to his fellow merfolk as they fought to keep the evil magic from seeping into their home. His eyes then came to rest on Jessica and he flinched with emotion. Quickly, he glided over and without a word, gripped Jessica in a protective hug. Jessica pressed her face into his wet, dark curls and thought of her own father, who seemed to be a million miles away.

Keela pulled back but kept his hand reassuringly on Jessica's arm. 'Jessica,' he said. 'Thank Neptune you came. I knew you would.'

A shower of sparks sizzled into the sea from the overhang where the two witches were locked in fierce combat. Jessica saw Elsa stumble backwards as if caught off balance but then regain her footing and send another beam of silver light at her grandmother.

'She can't last long,' she muttered, as another melancholy bellow rang through the air. 'Keela, I've made a horrible mistake. I've got to get back up there; I'm the only one who can stop this!'

The merman creased his forehead in a tense frown and looked away to the cliffs as if he had the weight of the whole world on his shoulders.

'That's not entirely true,' he whispered, unable to meet Jessica's gaze.

Puzzled, Jessica placed her hand on Keela's back. 'What?' she hissed, unaware that the merman was fighting hard to stop his own milky tears from falling. Keela uttered a quiet prayer to Neptune, God of his people, for forgiveness for the pact he and Jim Hellily had made a long time ago. Swallowing hard, Keela turned to face Lyurnee and Jess.

Another grief-stricken yowl echoed in the blackness as Keela inhaled ready to speak. 'If you loved your mother and want to save Jersey, come with me,' he said. His voice was cold for he was battling to control his emotions.

Jessica gazed up at the cliffs ignited with evil violet flames and froze, not wanting to flee again from her duty. Aware of her unwillingness to leave, Keela lifted her onto his back and wrapped her arms around his neck. 'Lyurnee,' he told the young mermaid battling back tears, 'go back to the sea caves with the children. You should never have come out this night, you're too young.'

The sea-maid shivered with emotion. 'I wanted to help my parents.'

Keela looked at her tenderly. 'There is nothing any of us can do now,' he whispered. 'It is the night of Gemini.'

Lyurnee fought back her sobs and with a graceful flick of her long, bronze tail, dived deep beneath the waves, back to the safety of the sea folk's submarine chambers. Keela watched her go, gripping Jessica's hands where they clung onto his shoulders. Jessica leant close to the merman's emerald back and swore she felt him shiver. Why must she go with him when she was clearly needed on land and what was the night of Gemini?

A sorrowful howl like the shuddering note of a foghorn shook the air again and Keela cocked his head to one side as if to listen.

'She calls,' he said, almost to himself, his voice choked with sadness. 'Jess, I must take you to her. Reunite you before it is too late.'

Elegantly, he turned his powerful form in the direction of the cliffs and swam towards them. Agitated, Jessica struggled to stop him taking her away from the horrors of the cove. 'Where are you taking me, Keela?' she demanded, twisting her hands to free them from his strong grip. 'Don't you understand, I'm the Guardian. I should be stopping the witchcraft!'

Keela hunched his back as if wounded by Jess's harsh words but gripped her closer to him so that the strong undercurrents that lurked in the waves did not sweep her away.

'Jessica, if you return to face the witch alone you will die,' he told her bluntly. It was clear by the tone of his voice that the merman was struggling to repress painful emotions; emotions that he had kept hidden for a very long time.

They were sailing directly to the shadowy rocks away from Devil's Hole; although jagged and dangerous they were as yet untouched by black magic. Another croaking cry echoed through the cold air, louder than before and so filled with emotion that it touched Jessica's very soul. The voice seemed to be coming from deep within the rocks as if something was trapped there.

The mournful tone floated on the fierce wind, growing louder and louder as they drew nearer to the cliffs. She wished she could put her fingers in her ears to muffle the sound but Keela was still holding her hands.

'What is making that horrible noise?' she asked the merman, her voice almost lost under the dreadful wails.

The merman caressed the back of Jessica's hands as if to calm her in readiness for the awful truth he must soon unfold to her. 'It is Marina. The one you are destined to meet this fateful night. She cries because she knows her world is changing and it will never return to the way it was before.'

Jessica shivered but it wasn't because of the chill of the deep ocean. When Keela had spoken the name, Marina, it had touched a place deep in Jessica's heart. She knew the name like a distant memory of a time long ago when she had been safe and warm; a time that had ended with such cruel trauma that her mind had buried it deep among her darkest fears so that the injury it had caused her was long forgotten. For the briefest of seconds she forgot about the terrible drama being played out behind them at Devil's Hole and was overwhelmed by the sensation that at last the darkest secret of her existence would soon be uncovered.

Keela had swum right up to the imposing rock face of the granite cliffs. Among the shadowy crevasses carved deep within the pinkish stone she could see a low, narrow inlet where the sea gushed into the rock. The opening was barely large enough for her and the merman to pass through but it was from within this very cave that the mournful cries echoed like the baying of a wounded beast.

Keela stopped dead in front of the opening and stared at it silently for a few seconds. 'I was right to bring her here this night,' he said, sounding as if he was trying to reassure himself that he had done the right thing.

Jessica thought that the merman was talking about her but wasn't sure. The whole of Jersey seemed to have been sent mad by the black magic and Jessica didn't know what was going on any more. She wished that she was back on the fiery cliff-top confronting Agatha Noir, at least then she would know what she was dealing with.

Keela shifted his head slightly as he looked at Jessica.

393

'Jess,' he said, his soft, noble voice choked with emotion, 'before we go any further I want you to promise that you will forgive me and Jim.'

Jessica blinked the salt from her eyes and stared deep into the cave before them, listening to the bitter sobbing echoing from within.

'Forgive you? Forgive you for what?' she pleaded. She felt that Keela was stopping her returning to face the witch and her patience was wearing thin. 'I wish you would just tell me what the Hell is going on, Keela! If I don't get back to the cliff top soon, we've all had it.'

She fidgeted crossly on the merman's back and once again the heavy weight of the bundle at her side throbbed with comforting warmth. She wondered how the package hadn't got lost when she'd dived into the water.

Keela gripped her hand. 'Just promise me you won't hold it against your great uncle and me,' he said urgently. 'We believed at the time we were acting for the best.'

His voice was so heavy with guilt that Jessica pondered what terrible deed hung like a stone shackle around his heart.

Jessica flexed her fingers and they brushed against Keela's thick, wet mane where it hung about his shoulders.

'I promise,' she whispered, aware that Keela's own guilt cursed him more than her hatred ever could.

The merman breathed a heavy sigh as if Jessica's words had lifted at least some of the weight from his conscience. He now seemed able to enter the cave. The sobs of the creature in the darkness filled the air all about them and now that she was nearer, Jessica could hear that the strangely familiar croaking voice was crying out the merman's name.

'Keelie,' it gurgled woefully. 'Where be you? What is these happenings?'

Keela swam through the low entrance to the cave, Jessica clinging to his back, her mind filled with fear and confusion. The inlet was so small that as they passed through it, the rough rocks caught on Jessica's hair and she had to sink her face into the water to avoid her brow being grazed.

Once they were enveloped by the still, cold darkness of the tiny grotto, the roof arched up a few feet so that the girl could lift her head and breathe in the stale air. The cave was tiny compared with the impressive structure of the Magicroutes that honeycombed the rest of the island. The sea gushed in to form a small pool, about six feet long and three feet wide, just big enough to accommodate the merman's body. The ceiling was low, leaving only a few feet of space between the water surface and the solid rock. At the far end of the cavern, a long, steep tunnel, cut into the granite, stretched diagonally upwards through the cliff. A narrow ledge extended from the bottom of the passageway and, crouched in the murky shadows, sobbing bitterly to herself was the creature. Her large, wart-covered hands were clenched in frustrated fists and her long, scaly lower limbs were curled tensely around her. Her scarred head was bowed with woe and from beneath her greasy, dark fringe her large, lonely brown eyes glinted with tears.

'Rina!' she gasped with horror at the creature's frightened state. 'What are you doing here?'

Jessica wrapped her arms around the poor creature and hugged her tight. All concern for Jersey seemed to pale and her heart was filled only with the joy of being reunited with the mysterious beast and concern for her well-being. Marina's sobs died down into a sad snuffle as she buried her blemished face in Jessica's wet hair.

'Ma Jecica,' she mewed. 'Ma Jecica is being back. Rina muchly scaredsome.'

Jessica traced her fingers through the creature's thick mass of hair.

'I know, I know,' she soothed. 'I'm scared too. Everything's gone horribly wrong, hasn't it? I'm so sorry.'

Sadly, Marina pulled away from Jessica's embrace and flicked her head shyly in Keela's direction.

'Ma Keelie bringed me here,' she muttered softly, before looking at the merman and saying crossly, 'But not sayings why, Keelie. Why Keelie puttings Rina and Jecica in danger?'

The two females turned to face Keela. The merman's obvious sadness was overridden by an expression of bewilderment as he looked from Jessica to Marina and back again. The last thing he had counted on in this painful and sorry state of affairs was that they had met already.

'You know each other?' he asked cautiously.

Jessica gave a deep sigh. All her secrets and protectiveness about her meetings with Rina seemed pointless now. The world was in turmoil with black magic and bitter secrets everywhere. What good would it do to lie any more? She leaned against the wall of the cave, her arm resting around the creature's shoulders and looked into Keela's golden eyes.

'When Jake, Elsa and I were down in the Magicroutes, we were attacked by Black Trolls,' she began slowly. 'If Rina hadn't turned up we would have been killed.'

A look of parental annoyance darted across the merman's handsome features and he stared at Marina. The whole situation was difficult enough without the added complication of Marina taking matters into her own hands. It was a capability Keela hadn't realized she had. He addressed his foster child with a brisk tone.

'I told you not to leave the grotto. You could have got hurt.'

Marina gave her thick, oily locks a defiant toss and flared her reptilian nostrils.

'Phoo!' she muttered rebelliously. 'Keelie no do what Keelie say, no bring Jecica. So Rina go do things on own.'

Keela shook his head in disbelief but Marina reached out and placed a misshapen hand on his shoulder.

'Rina no want Jecica get hurt,' she gurgled, her slurred voice filled with tenderness.

Keela didn't reply but rested his fingers on his temple as if he had a very bad headache. Marina didn't move for a moment, waiting for the merman's reply. When it was clear he was too upset to answer her Marina withdrew her rough fingers from Keela's smooth, emerald skin and slumped back against Jessica with a rejected grunt. Jessica gave her companion a comforting squeeze and brushed a strand of black hair from Marina's chocolate eyes. Despite all the horror and pain she had faced that day, despite the fact that the crackle of spells echoing outside the cave told her that all hope was truly lost, Jessica felt strangely at peace. If she had been anywhere else at this frightful moment she would want to cry with despair but, sitting in the near blackness with her head resting softly against Marina's scarred skin, she felt more at peace than she had ever done before. She closed her eyes and tried to block out the atmosphere of Keela's grief and find a place within her heart where she and this pitiful being could be safe.

396

'Why did you have a go at her?' she whispered to Keela, her soft voice tinged with bitterness. 'If Rina hadn't been in the Magicroutes we would have been killed.'

All the sadness and confusion of the past few days seemed to tumble out before she could stop it. 'I wanted to find out who she was,' she told the silent merman. 'I went down to the Iris of the Ancestors and asked it.' She paused and opened her eyes, fury burning anew in her heart. 'What happened between you and Jim? I know the two of you made a deal to keep Rina hidden. What promise did you make that you now regret so bitterly?'

Marina seemed to bristle with anger as Jessica spoke, as if their deepest feelings were in tune.

'Keelie is promisings bring Uncy Jim, but no,' she hissed. 'Why you tell fibby lie for way long?'

The merman ran his fingers through his wild, dark curls, his body trembling with emotion. He raised his head and his golden pupils swam with tears each as perfect as a pearl.

'In all the years of Helier's blessing, never was such a deed committed or such a secret kept,' he whispered. 'The power of the Guardian is stronger than anyone guessed. It is a magic stronger than hate, stronger than grief, even stronger than the darkest of witchcraft.'

Overcome with emotion, Keela reached out with his powerful, soft hands and grabbed the two females' fingers so firmly that Jessica thought he was about to drag them both back into the sea. 'You must realize that Jim and I loved your mother, he as her uncle and I as her friend. When she was lost to us, our hearts were so marred with grief that our minds were tainted and our actions wrong.'

Jessica felt her head throb with confusion. Keela's sorrow was so intense it filled her heart with fear and made her feel faint. The only thing she was aware of in the unholy blackness was the coldness of Marina's hand pressed against her own and Keela's anguished voice. The deepest chamber of the merman's heart had been flung open and the terrible story he had lived with for more than a decade spilt out.

'It was a night as foul as this when Emma returned to face the witches,' he began. 'We had no choice but to call her back from the mainland. A coven had formed and chosen a night in

397

October to perform the ritual that would bring to life the banished demon. She alone could stop them.'

Jessica's heart leapt. Why did this story haunt her so? It was the tale she most feared and yet she was told it again and again.

'I know they killed her on the night I was born!' she bleated as Marina squealed with fright in the blackness. 'Why are you telling me this again?'

'If only that was all they did,' Keela replied. 'You misjudge the intelligence of witches. They knew your mother had growing within her the next link in the Hellily chain. It would be no good to murder her and let the babe live. So they concocted a curse that would make the first child born of Emma Hellily a thing of darkness. A form that would strike fear into the hearts of man, and a life, if it was unfortunate enough to survive, condemned to pain and darkness.'

Jessica's brain span with Keela's words and her blood ran cold. She was the Guardian but until recently her life had been a happy one. What twisted form had this curse taken?

'They put a spell on me?' she asked in disbelief.

Another barking cry shattered the air, shaking Jessica from her thoughts. Marina was weeping. Keela bit his lip and caressed the woeful being's long, wart-covered hands. His heart was breaking for he had disclosed the truth he had tried to protect Marina from for so long.

'No Jess,' he whispered. 'They cursed the first born.'

A shiver, like a bolt of electricity went up Jessica's spine. With painful clarity she saw the heart-breaking truth of her own birth. Tears sprang to her eyes; so this was why she had felt so compelled to discover who Rina was. Before either of them had even existed they had been one spot in the cosmos of time. One mind, one heartbeat, one body and one soul. She looked at the girl's twisted shape, her crippled limbs and blemished skin and knew just how close she had been to taking her place.

'No,' she croaked, her voice echoing Marina's. 'It's ... it's impossible.'

Keela slowly shook his head. 'Never before in the line of Hellily had it happened. Two minds with one thought, two lives growing within the same womb. The legacy was split when you girls entered the world – weaker when split apart, but twice as strong in unison.'

Jessica bowed her head and her body shook with sobs of joy and sorrow. The merman placed a finger under her chin and gently forced her to raise her head.

'Look into her eyes,' he told her gently, 'and believe what you've always known in your heart.'

Trembling, Jessica turned to face Marina and without fear or sorrow gazed into her eyes. The brown pupils were filled with a love that Jessica had long forgotten but now came flooding back to her. For a second, Marina's ugliness seemed to melt away and Jessica saw the girl she should have been – olive-skin, chestnut hair and boyish features. Somewhere at the back of her mind, Jessica heard Keela's voice.

'Some of my people called the night you came into the world the night of Gemini. The night when the twins were born.'

A rush of love engulfed Jessica's heart and she reached out and embraced the sister that had been stolen from her so many years ago. She heard Marina's snuffling sobs and felt her tears fall into her already damp hair. It didn't matter that the witches had transformed her sister's body into something unnatural; Jessica's heart told her who she was beneath the scars and scales. Marina cried out with joy and held Jessica as if she would never let go.

'Ma Jecica,' she wept, croakily, 'ma sista.'

Jessica slowly drew away from Marina to gaze with loving awe into her twin's face. Tenderly, she ran her fingertips through Marina's thick, oily hair and pushed a knotted strand behind her malformed ear. It didn't seem to matter how her sister looked; all Jessica could see was a link to the family she had believed was lost to her forever.

'Marina was the first,' Keela went on. 'We'd all but given up hope for the line of Hellily. No-one was sure you'd survive, Marina. But, two minutes later, as the last ounce of life was extinguished from your mother's body, she pushed Jessica into the world, healthy and unscarred.'

Jessica wrapped her arms around Marina again and hugged her tight. She just couldn't get over the thrill of finding her sister again; she had discovered the part of herself that made sense of her life. There were so many questions she wanted answered. She glanced around the cold, grim cave.

'But why are you living in the caves, Marina?' she asked.

However, as soon as the words left her mouth she remembered the vision in the Iris and knew. The curse the coven had placed on her sister at her birth had been so powerful it had transformed the love Jim should have felt for her into revulsion and hate.

Keela placed a loving hand on Marina.

'My Marina,' he said softly, as the scarred girl gazed down at him, 'you know I love you with all my heart and you mean as much to me as my own children. All your life I have tried my hardest to protect you from the bitter truth. I feared it would break your heart.'

Marina's leathery face creased into a frown and she snuggled closer to her sister. Jessica stroked her rough skin; she knew what Keela was about to say.

'Ma Keelie did tell fibby-lies?' Marina queried timidly.

'In a way,' the merman said, 'yes.'

Keela gripped Marina's long-fingered hand tightly in his own. 'You are something rare and special,' he continued. 'Even on an island of magic such as Jersey, there has never been something, someone, like you. You are a survivor of the most powerful black magic. But because you are unique there are people who can't accept what you are. They don't understand you as I and Jessica understand you. And, most unfortunately of all, one of those people is your Uncle Jim.'

The elder twin's doe-like eyes grew wide and brimmed with tears of realization.

'Uncy Jim no be likey Rina?'

Marina gazed into the dark sea that gushed into the cave and a single tear dripped from her eye into the lapping waves. 'That why Uncy Jim no come see Rina. Uncy Jim think Rina badsome like Bla-Blas.' Her voice was even gruffer than usual and it was clear she was struggling to fight back tears.

Overcome with grief for her sister, Jessica gripped Marina in a tight hug. She cupped the girl's disfigured face between her hands and tenderly lifted it so she could gaze into her sad, dark eyes. At last, Jessica knew the full truth about her family and the terrible burden of guilt and grief that had haunted each member of it for the past fourteen years.

'Listen,' she whispered gently. 'He didn't have the chance to know you so he couldn't judge you. A terrible thing happened to my mother, our mother, and it broke Jim's heart. I think he would have given anything to make the pain go again, even if it meant hurting us.'

Marina gave a weak whimper and sadly shook her greasy mane.

'No with Jecica, Uncy Jim not,' she muttered. 'Rina be sent go live in icky grotty, no Jecica.'

'He lied to me too,' she said, pressing her face close to Marina's. 'They thought if I didn't know I was the Guardian, Jim and Dad could keep me safe. But they couldn't do that. When you are the Guardian, there's something inside you. I don't know what it is but it's there and it keeps you strong, even when you're scared to do what is right. It was in Mum; it's in me and I know it's in you.'

The elder twin remained silent for a few seconds and then opened her eyes. The tears she'd shed were gone and her dark pupils seemed to gleam with a determined fire that made her look stronger and more human than ever.

'Rina is good,' she declared strongly. 'Rina prove to Uncy Jim. Rina and Jecica stop Bla-Bla now! Stop for good!'

A determined smile spread across Jessica's face as she recognized the sparkle in Marina's eyes. It was the same flame of duty that ignited her soul and filled them both with the courage to face the black magic of Agatha Noir.

Suddenly, a chilling vibration shook the stale air in the cavern and in the distance Jessica swore she heard Elsa's voice cry out with pain. Fear gripped her heart, draining away all the joy of finding her sister. She remembered the two friends she had abandoned on the cliff top and the ever-mounting power of the witch. Time was running out. She glanced at Marina and could tell by the steely look in her eyes that she knew the time had come for them to enter into battle.

'Jake and Elsa!' she exclaimed to the merman, whose face had suddenly grown grim with urgency. 'I left them on the surface. Elsa's a white witch; it's her grandmother who's doing this. God, I hope they're okay!'

Keela's eyes shut and without their grim, golden light the cave was plunged into near blackness. 'It's impossible to say whether your friends are all right,' he said bleakly, 'But both of you must go to the surface and try and stop the witchcraft before it's too late.'

401

Marina squirmed agitatedly on the narrow ledge and cast her eyes towards the long, stone shaft behind them that cut up through the granite to the surface.

'Ake and Elly-sa is beings hurtings!' she stated worriedly. She began to shuffle towards the tunnel. 'Come Jecica we must be stoppings Bla-Blas!'

Marina began to climb through the steep passage. Warily, Jessica glanced back to Keela but the merman shook his head.

'That tunnel's the only way you can get back to Devil's Hole from here,' he informed her.

Jessica saw that Keela's eyes were filling with tears again and she realized that, with Marina heading into the unknown danger ahead, Keela was losing the girl who had been as much a daughter to him as his own flesh and blood.

'Take care of her for me, Jess,' he stuttered, struggling to keep his emotions in check.

'I'll protect her with my life,' she told him.

Without another word, Keela dived beneath the lapping waves and vanished.

Jessica turned to face the narrow passage which was her only route to salvation. The tunnel was just wide enough for her to crawl through on her hands and knees and climb steeply upwards at an almost vertical angle. Marina had already vanished inside and seemed to be moving at a steady pace. Breathing deeply, Jessica edged herself through the entrance and slowly began to crawl through the claustrophobic blackness. There was barely enough room for her to inch forward and she fumbled in front of her with outstretched fingertips to find crannies in the rock for leverage. Her legs seemed useless and awkward in the cramped space of the cave and she feared even bending her knees in case she became stuck and was unable to move. Marina scrambled on swiftly ahead of her, seeming to make easy work of the climb. Walls pressed in on her from every side until she could barely breathe. She pondered how her sister found the climb so easy despite her cursed form and the answer came to her in a flash. Because, frightful and unnatural as Marina's physical form might be, it had adapted perfectly to moving in the twisting caves that had been her home. Her arms and shoulders were powerful and could pull her forward with ease. Where Jessica's legs were immobile and straight, Marina's lower limbs were as supple as the bodies of two snakes and the odd grease that coated her skin eased her path across the jagged rocks. The climb was second nature to her whereas it took all of Jessica's strength to haul herself through the narrow space.

They were deep in the core of the cliff by now but still the threatening echoes of the rumbles and cracks of the black magic reverberated in Jessica's ears filling her with a desire to get back to the cliff top before it was too late. She cursed her body for being so awkward in the cramped tunnel.

A shower of pebbles fell on her from above and Marina's voice came down to her. 'Jecica,' she urged, 'why you be so slow? We must get uppy 'bove soon and stop Bla-Bla.'

'I'm trying, Rina,' she gasped, out of breath from the effort of climbing. 'But the passage is too narrow. I'm frightened I'll get stuck.'

Marina's voice came down to her again. 'It beings easy, Jecica,' she said reassuringly. 'Be as Rina!'

In her cramped space, these last three words drifted down like a magic spell. Jessica's skin tingled. She was no longer a single being existing in her own right, alone and afraid, but part of a pair, something greater than herself brought her hope in the new power within her. It was an odd feeling allowing your body and mind to become merged with another but the experience was not alien to Jessica and she felt no fear as Marina's thoughts collided with her own. Jessica remembered her first encounter with her sister during the Black Troll attack. Their minds had linked and only now Jessica realized what a great and powerful gift this was. She could absorb Marina's knowledge and memories of how to move and survive in the dark, cramped caves. More than that, Jessica felt as if Marina's thoughts were seeping into her very muscles, changing her physically. Her arms and shoulders felt stronger and her legs seemed to melt away so they no longer hampered her progress.

Jessica reached out her hands and her fingertips brushed against the cold rock. Her skin seemed to be highly sensitive and quickly she discovered sturdy cracks in the walls that allowed her to grip. She hauled herself upwards and was amazed by the strength that filled her upper body. Her arms and shoulders bore her weight easily and she was quickly able to pull herself up through the darkness to where Marina was waiting for her.

403

The tunnel widened toward its end and a sickly violet light seeped in from above. A thin layer of gorse or undergrowth seemed to hide the opening from the hostile scene outside as the terrifying cracks and bangs of Agatha Noir's spells filled the air. Jessica huddled close to her sister and thanked God she was no longer alone. In the dim light she glanced at Marina and saw her huge eyes gleam with trepidation.

'Is mighty badsome things happenings uppy 'bove,' murmured Marina, her eyes fixed on the light that shone down into the cave. Her voice quavered with fear. Jessica's heart thundered in her chest and her nerves tingled with terror at the thought of the battle ahead. Her mind was firm though and despite the dread of what lay before them and the fear that her friends might already be dead, she knew that only she and Marina could stop this unthinkable evil before it was too late. Jessica rested a hand on her sister's shoulder and swallowed hard.

'You ready?' she asked, trying to hide the fear in her voice, and failing.

'Rina and Jecica is havings no choices,' she said softly, before adding with more determination, 'Bla-Bla must be stop.'

The older twin's steady tone filled Jessica's heart with courage. She gazed up at the thin blanket of bracken that hid them from the horror and before she had time to think, reached up and pulled it apart. Together for the first time in fourteen years, the two Guardians of Jersey climbed out of the darkness and prepared to face their destiny.

Chapter 21

The Daughters of the Axe

Grim, purple light scorched Jessica's eyes as she climbed out of the comforting shadows of the tunnel. She squinted as she crawled up onto the barren earth surrounding the hole and in her temporary blindness felt the hot dry soil beneath her fingers, to try and make out just where she was. After all that time in the safe, cool cave, her eyes were not accustomed to the brilliance that now surrounded her and they watered with pain. The air all around her was burning and smoky like the smouldering plumes from a great fire. Ash peppered her face and a foul stench like cooking human flesh filled her nostrils. The atmosphere crackled with the howling and cursing of angrily cast spells and the sound of flames as they hungrily devoured everything in their path but Jessica could still make out the comforting snuffling of Marina as she climbed out beside her onto this fearful scene.

Jessica wiped the smarting tears from her eyes and battled to focus on the scene before them. Slowly her vision returned to her and as her sight cleared she gasped in horror at the living nightmare before them. The tunnel from the cliff cave had brought them out just behind a small clump of trees some way back from Devil's Hole and atop a small hillock, that meant they could look down on the bay and see at least some of the rocky outcrop where Agatha and Elsa had been. Everything in the countryside that crested the clifftops surrounding the inlet was on fire or charred to black skeletons. The ground was a blanket of tiny, angry violet flames that singed the already blackened grass. Here and there, heavy mounds of scorched bracken and fallen trees lay like newly formed graves. The few trees that remained standing had been charred to sticks of pure

405

charcoal with twisted, bare branches reaching up to the cloudy heavens. The air was streaked with wisps of curling, scarlet fog and in the centre of this horrific landscape was the demonic, searing light of Devil's Hole.

The flames of gold and green that had licked at the great chalk bowl of the bay had now turned as red as newly spilt blood. The stone outcrop appeared to be a dagger piercing the very heart of Hell itself and allowing the unquenchable evil to flow out into Jersey. A creature stood on the tip of the ledge, cloaked in billowing clouds of dark mist, its eyes gleaming like coals. At first Jessica feared that the foul apparition was the demon itself but however hideous and evil the beast was, it still clung to the tiniest thread of humanity which told Jessica it was the true form of Agatha Noir. Piercing bolts of purple lightning shot from the hag's claws into a tiny ball of white light that lay quivering but resolute against the cliff. The light Elsa illuminated was like a mirror, reflecting Agatha's spells, unmoving but slowing, growing weaker with each blow she took. Jessica's heart leapt with pride and relief. Elsa had survived – but for how much longer?

They had little time. Swallowing her fear, Jessica got to her feet and the pair headed swiftly down towards the bay. Jessica felt somehow stronger than she had done the first time she had faced the wrath of Mrs Noir. Having Marina crawling closely at her side filled her heart with hope that together there was some way to stop the frightful terror of the demon's return. The package at Jessica's side glowed stronger than ever and above the hellish noise that poisoned the air Jessica was almost sure she could hear an angelic chorus. The fierce purple flames seemed to die away as they passed over them leaving a clear path of blackened grass. Jessica stooped low, almost crawling as they came closer to the cliff edge, while Marina stayed serpent-like on her belly.

When they got within a few feet of the cliff, Marina stopped dead in her tracks, arching her head back and sniffing the air with her slit nostrils. Suddenly, she scampered over to one of the piles of burnt undergrowth that dotted the landscape and began to paw at it frantically. Jessica wondered what on earth could have caught her sister's attention.

'Rina!' she hissed urgently. 'This is no time to play games!'

Marina raised her head but kept her long fingers resting on the twisted mass of vines.

'Is not beings a game,' she replied. 'Is beings Ake!'

Gazing at the clump of undergrowth, Jessica now saw that it was an intricate knot of vines forming a tight cocoon. Quickly she hurried to Marina's side and gazed down at the tomb of her friend. A pale hand protruded from a tiny gap in the thorns, fingers curled in agony.

'Poor Jake,' Jessica whispered.

Marina's head rested on the single visible hand, her eyes closed in sorrow. Suddenly her eyes shot open and she gasped, 'Ake still alive!'

Marina squeezed the imprisoned lad's hand and then began to gnaw fiercely at the creepers that twisted about his body. Her teeth were quick and sharp and made easy work of the tough plant-life. Jessica glanced from her sister busily chewing away at Jake's bonds to the terrifying display of magical explosions that crackled just a few feet away. The charred and black bracken that stood between them and the two witches seemed very thin and Jessica could easily see the final acts of the fearful battle between grandmother and granddaughter being played out.

Elsa's human form was barely visible now; all that could be seen was a large sphere of glowing white light, like a huge pearl alive with sparks of gold lightning that flickered across its surface. The shining globe was Elsa's shield against the terrible creature that had once been Mrs Noir and that now bore down upon it like a hideous serpent. All human features in the old woman's appearance had vanished and the full wickedness of her soul was visible. Her long, silvery hair had turned coal black and twisted around her in leathery coils. Her skin had changed to dark scales and her gleaming, scarlet eyes were narrow windows into the deepest recesses of Hell.

From the tower of black muscle that was her body, a pair of twisted claws stretched out sending violent sparks of red flame raining down upon the shimmering curve of Elsa's shield. The glittering ball deflected them in showers of purple, crimson and gold across the dark sky. However, with every blast the foul being fired at her, the brilliant glow of Elsa's white magic grew weaker and the crystal refuge she had created for herself flickered

407

like a light bulb almost spent of its power revealing the frightened and battered figure of the child, no longer resplendent in gown of silk and head-dress of flowers, but as she had been before, sickly and small. Jessica knew that her young friend could not withstand the overwhelming power of Agatha Noir much longer and soon she would be unable to distract her from the presence of the Guardians.

At Jessica's side, Marina still worked furiously, disentangling Jake's body from the thorny briers. Angrily she bit through the tough stems while her long fingers worked feverishly to wrench the thicker ones away from his chest and throat. Dragging her eyes away from the deadly battle between the two witches, Jessica saw that Marina had indeed been right and despite the vice-like grip of the vines, Jake was still hanging on to the last strands of life. Marina had freed most of his writhing form and Jessica could now see the deep scarlet gashes of blood where the thorns had shredded his skin. His face was a mask of pain as he struggled to inhale precious oxygen. A last, strong tendril was coiled mercilessly around his neck, strangling him. Marina battled with all her might to break the murderous vine but it would not budge.

Instinct seized Jessica and momentarily forgetting the heinous struggle that was taking place on the ledge below them, she grabbed the evil plant and joining Marina's strength with her own, ripped it asunder. The young lad let out a rasping gasp as life-giving air filled his lungs. His eyes rolled back in his head and for one dreadful moment Jessica thought that the rescue had come too late. Overcome with panic and urgency, she took his head between her hands and shook it as if to wake him from a deep slumber.

'Come on, Jake!' she urged, 'Don't you dare die on me!'

'Jess,' he wheezed wearily, hauling himself up on one elbow. 'But how?'

His eyes flickered to Marina and his pupils grew large with confusion and disbelief. Marina grinned with triumph to see him awake again.

'How?' uttered Jake again, looking from Jess to Marina and back again.

Jessica propped him up as far as she could without allowing them to be seen above the bracken.

408

'There's no time to explain,' she whispered. She knew she must get Jake to leave this unholy place. The moment had arrived when she and Marina must face their destiny alone. 'Listen,' she told him grimly as a flurry of purple sparks blazed like a burning fan off the cliff below them. 'I know you're feeling very weak but you've got to get as far away from this place as you can. Run back and tell Jim, and leave us here to fight this evil. Do you think you're strong enough to do that?'

Jake gripped his side and winced as he climbed unsteadily onto his feet, crouching low beside Jessica.

'But what about you and her?' he queried, nodding at Marina, who was gazing at Agatha Noir with steely disdain. 'You'll die!'

Jessica placed a hand on his arm. A strange peaceful strength had settled in her heart once again and death no longer seemed to matter.

'It's all right,' she said gently. 'I finally understand everything. This is our place, Marina's and mine. We must fight. It's the way it's meant to be.'

A piercing scream echoed in the blackness and Jessica knew that Elsa's spell was almost broken and the moment had come for her to repay the white witch for saving her life. She pressed her hand on Jake's back.

'If we don't survive,' she told him, 'I want you to tell my dad and Jim that the twins love them.'

Jake gazed at the pair for a moment, his eyes bright with relief at being set free. He did not understand the impact of Jessica's message but he knew that, as Guardian, she was the only person he could trust to end this horror. He slowly backed away from the pair. His duty had been done; she was ready to take the mantle and he could protect her no longer. 'God be with you, Jessica Hellily,' he said, then swiftly hobbled away, the thick mist of black magic swirling around his form until he was but a shadow in the darkness.

From the fiery blaze within the cauldron of Devil's Hole an agonising scream rang out, cutting into Jessica like a blade. The glowing sphere of wondrous white light that cloaked Elsa's frail body shattered like delicate crystal tossed onto slate, and thousands of shards of white magic were flung outwards and devoured by the mighty black smoke that emanated from Agatha Noir's being. The blonde child was cast, broken and barely conscious, onto the stone ledge and the serpent-woman loomed down on her.

'Now,' she hissed, her forked tongue lashing like a whip, 'the glorious ritual shall be fulfilled and my master will be raised in darkness and blood.'

No longer afraid for her own life, Jessica scrambled to her feet and stepped from behind the charred bracken to confront the devilish witch. Marina reared up on her hind legs and let out a triumphant snarl, her brown pupils dancing with courage in the firelight. Jessica's heart thundered against her chest with the same strong pulse as her sister's. The burden strapped to her side infused her body with strength and knowledge.

'Leave the child,' she called out to the coiled viper poised ready to strike. 'You know it's us that you want.'

Agatha's frightful, scarlet eyes turned from the weak body of her granddaughter and bore into the two Guardians with unspeakable loathing.

'You,' she spat, her tone as cutting as daggers. 'I thought you were dead. How many times do I have to kill you?'

The air turned deathly cold as the hag spoke. Jessica glanced at Marina and clasped her hand in unity. She knew that the witch could do nothing as long as they stood firm together. Marina pulled back her puckered lips and bared her teeth.

'Bla-Bla no kill Jecica and Rina, hurt make strong, make strong for right!'

The witch's pupils glimmered with sick delight at the sight of Marina's malformed body.

'So,' she crowed, 'this is the product of the Great Curse. What a foul thing you have become, first born of Emma Hellily! I would have thought you would have been murdered years ago as an omen of the glorious black magic.'

Marina growled with rage and Jessica felt her sister's fury rise. The younger twin's eyes grew dark with anger, as her loathing for the harm the black magic had inflicted on her family mounted.

'Not all people of this island are as heartless as you,' she shouted at the beast. She felt her skin prickle, as if there was seeping from it the very essence of the blessing that protected her from Agatha Noir's rage. Her mind seemed to flood with memories and ideas. These thoughts were her legacy, the lessons

410

learned by hundreds of Guardians before her, telling her what action to take. Automatically, her free hand shot to the mysterious package at her side. A warmth seemed to ignite her fingertips as they brushed against the material that encased it. Coupled with the strong grip of Marina's fingers as they clasped her other hand, Jessica knew she had what she needed to send Agatha Noir and her evil back to the deepest pits of Hell where she belonged.

The serpent's eyes glowed with fury as she realized what Jessica had in mind.

'Oh no you don't!' spat the witch, her wide, thin-lipped mouth pulled back in a fierce sneer.

Jessica's heart leapt with fear as, caught in the snake's loathing stare, the new-found knowledge of how to conquer this hellish foe slipped from her mind. She was frozen to the ground with helpless terror and the only thing that stopped her from crumbling before the awesome might of the great, black beast was the feeling of Marina's hand clasped in her own and the myriad of beautiful voices that filled her head. She could do nothing but stand there and prepare herself for the witch's attack.

Agatha Noir's gaping jaws fell open to reveal long fangs and a throat as red as molten lava. She threw back her repulsive head and with an almighty hiss blew a stream of burning flame directly at Jessica and Marina.

Jessica felt her mind come to life with countless thoughts and feelings that overwhelmed her consciousness and drowned out her terror. The furious light and heat of the witch's burning breath engulfed her. She felt herself being swept into the air in a vortex of heat and fire. She knew that a blaze of this intensity could burn her alive but within the swirling chaos of evil, she felt the ancient and powerful strength of St Helier, her ancestor, come alive in her spirit. It roared like a sweet, autumn wind through every fibre in her body, filling her with soothing coolness and the joyous sound of angel voices, so melodious that they deafened her to the angry crackle of the flames. Her fingers interlocked tightly with Marina's as their frail forms were hurled this way and that. Through the simple touch, their dual souls united and beneath the unrelenting fury of Agatha Noir's spell, they joined spiritually as they had before in their mother's womb; the energy that had been split so long ago came together

411

again to fulfil the destiny of the Guardian. Both their minds were filled by the same mighty image of the hermit who guarded the island.

Jessica shut her eyes against the evil blaze of the vortex and saw with brilliant clarity the face of Helier, dark-eyed and with mane of chestnut hair, smiling at her. The memory of the saint was with them, reincarnated through their blood, ready to defeat the black magic in the name of Christ. She and Marina had the power to free him again. However, the twisting spiral of fire that imprisoned them was so intense that even with the holy blessing so close at hand they were not strong enough to release it.

A blow of agonising flame suddenly slammed into Jessica with such brutal force that the calming power of Helier was shaken from her body and she cried out in pain. Helplessly, she felt her hand slip from her sister's and the unity that had kept them safe from the darkness and evil vanished. Jessica's thoughts were plunged into anguish as her body was thrown as carelessly as a leaf in a thunderstorm to the stony ground. As she crumpled into a broken heap, a terrible tearing bit into her side, like a dagger ripping her flesh asunder. She cried out for mercy as she felt something that seemed to be the very essence of her soul ripped from her. Her mind was blackened as a cloud of unrelenting death swamped her brain, tipping her towards the brink of mortality. For a moment Jessica was imprisoned in a hopeless hell of fear and failure. Her pulse sang in her ears and the memory of her mother's excruciating cries came back to haunt her. Determination rekindled at the vision of Emma's last moments – she would not die the same way. Jessica forced herself to open her eyes and struggled to focus on the world around her.

She was lying on her side, her cheek crushed roughly against the blackened remains of the bracken. In a few seconds the true horror of what lay before her filtered through the haze of Devil's mist and flashing magic. She saw Marina imprisoned in a sparking net of electric blue lightning cast out from Agatha's claws. Her twin's scarred and deformed body twisted and writhed with agony as the awesome dark magic tore into her being, slowly destroying her. Her arms flailed about helplessly as she tried to strike out at the possessed hag and she let out rasping

412

screams of terror and pain. Her eyes rolled back in her head and her movements were growing weaker by the second as excruciating death slowly enclosed her in its grasp.

Panic sent a burst of adrenalin through Jessica's body. She must save her sister's life or all hope for Jersey would be lost. The stifling Devil's mist pressed down on her, hot and heavy, but somehow she forced herself onto her knees. The pain that had cut into her side still stung dully but when Jessica looked she saw no wound. Her mind leapt as she realized that what the black magic had torn from her had not been part of her physical being at all but something far more important. The mysterious artefact that Jim had fastened to her before they set out had been ripped away by the fiery vortex and in a blinding moment of realization Jessica saw why. Desperately she glanced at the smouldering ground around her frantically searching for the ancient treasure. Strands of white material and leather scattered the ground, torn asunder by the force of the witch's power but the precious relic remained intact. It stuck firm in the brittle earth like a rusty iron skeleton. Jessica crawled towards it, her body throbbing with the wounds she'd sustained from her fall. Fingers shaking, she grasped the heavy, metal handle and as her hand closed around it the blessed axe seemed to come alive. The rust and dirt of a thousand years fell away and beneath her fingers the metal turned from deepest black to burning gold, shimmering with the light and glory of heaven. It burnt with a heat, not harsh and destructive like the blaze from Devil's Hole, but a healing warmth of goodness and love. The strength from the axe flowed into Jessica's hands and spread out through her muscles, banishing any pain or weariness.

She tugged the sacred weapon from the earth with all the victory and holiness of Excalibur and as she did so an image burst on her mind. The spirit of Helier swam before her, peaceful and full of love and pride. His dark mane, beard and simple robes drifted in a gentle breeze and his eyes sparkled with knowledge. A golden halo of holy light crowned his head and his arms were outstretched, guiding Jessica wordlessly. The Saint was real and alive in Jessica's soul, the true protector of Jersey living again within his descendant. Jessica gazed down at the hatchet in her hands and saw that the glistening head was tinged with blood. She knew this redness was not a mark of horror or

413

despair, but a holy sign of the Saint's final sacrifice to Jersey. This was the axe that had stolen his life and now, through Jessica and her sister, he would purge this island again of the evil that plagued it.

Gripping the hallowed weapon tightly and with Helier's pure presence resting in her soul, Jessica walked towards the tortured form of Marina, bound in the witch's sick spell. The black magic sparked violently as she drew closer. It leapt out and caught hold of Jessica, like the burning tendrils of some enormous sea beast. The axe throbbed powerfully in her hands and she was not afraid as the evil sucked her into its grip. Her body ached as the blue lightning whipped around her, thrashing her this way and that, but in the girl's spirit Helier drew into himself the cruelty and horror of the black magic. Jessica struggled against the evil power that battled to overwhelm her body and desperately sought out her twin's help in the chaotic blur of white and black magic. Helier existed within her but Jessica knew that he could not stop the black magic unless both she and Marina held the axe. She saw her sister's unconscious body floating, locked in the unrelenting grasp of the darkness, and used every fibre within her to call out to her and bring them together. Agatha Noir's demonic red eyes flashed before her and with all the strength she could muster, Jessica forced her-self towards her lifeless sister. Their two bodies collided and Jessica embraced her twin tightly. Their minds and bodies seemed to engulf each other and through the might of Helier they were once again one soul. Jessica pressed the handle of the magical axe into Marina's palm and suddenly the whirling heat of death that gripped them was transformed into an icy blast. The witch's eyes grew wide with terror and she let out a soulless scream.

'No!'

Within herself, Jessica felt Helier released from the shackles of time and live once again. The Saint was raised up through the twins' spirits and they clasped each other tightly as his awesome presence shook all that surrounded him, shattering the prison of the witch's spell to pieces. The great serpent hissed with terror as the essence of the Saint swept towards it in a blaze of white light. Grasping the witch, Helier flung himself into the depths of the swirling water of Devil's Hole and

414

screaming with horror, Agatha Noir was dragged down into the blazing vortex of her own creation.

The water erupted as the snake's body met it and the bitter air that whirled around the sisters' bodies turned into a sucking vacuum that drew all the evil Agatha Noir had unleashed deep into the Devil's Hole. Jessica curled herself into a tight ball around Marina as the storm swept over them. She felt the air pulling at the precious axe and grasped it to her more firmly. The storm was unbearable; it was as if the whole earth was being sucked into the bowels of the ocean. Wind blasted in Jessica's ears until she thought that surely this must be the end of Jersey. The last spark of purple flame plummeted into the churning water of Devil's Hole and the spinning whirlpool swallowed it up with a gasp before the waves calmed again. Jessica felt the wind stop as suddenly as it had begun and fearfully opened her eyes.

The black clouds that had blanketed the sky had vanished and the sea beat gently against the pink walls of Devil's Hole. The trees and bracken were fresh and green once more and the air was sweet. In the blue sky, the late afternoon sun shone down on Jersey with pale, warm light. Jessica threw back her head and laughed with joy as the breeze caught her long, chestnut hair.

'We did it!' she screamed. 'Rina, look, it's all over!'

But Jessica's twin did not look. She didn't even move. Jessica looked down at where her sister lay. The cursed child's skin was papery and had lost all moisture. Her dark eyes were closed and her puckered lips dry and white. She sucked in tiny, weak gulps of air with great effort. Gently, Jessica shook her sister to wake her.

'Rina,' she called softly.

She was sure that the girl would open her beautiful eyes and smile with triumph at their victory. But she just lay there, still and weak, a rattling sigh caught in her chest. Beneath the warts and scars that marked her skin, there was a dullness that hadn't been there before, a sickly pallor that covered her face like a veil of death. Jessica felt her pulse quicken with panic. She brushed Marina's matted hair from her face.

'Rina!' she cried again, more desperately this time. 'Wake up! Why aren't you waking up?'

Her twin remained motionless, her breath shallow and gasping. Bitter tears filled Jessica's eyes – once again the witchcraft had been driven away at a terrible price to her family. Fourteen years ago it was her mother who had made the sacrifice and now her own sister, whom she had only just found, would be the one to die.

Chapter 22

A Greater Magic

A sweet wind blew off the sparkling billows of the bay of Devil's Hole. It caught in the trees making their newly green leaves rustle like the sweeping gown of an unseen lady passing along the cliff top. On a stark, broad ledge reaching out across the silvery water from the cliffs high above, the body of a small pale-faced girl lay, peacefully sleeping. Her hair spread out around her like a soft halo of white gold though the cotton gown she was wearing was ripped and stained with ash. The small graze that marked her right temple was the only wound she bore from her great battle. The soft, summer wind swept some leaves from the ground, swirling them around in a graceful waltz before dropping them on the face of the white witch. Elsa felt the damp foliage brush against her cheek and woke gently from her deep slumber to face a life she never thought she would live. Elsa had changed.

Such loathing had filled her soul, cursing the years she had spent as a helpless slave. The dark magic had felt overwhelming and yet it was in that hour of unspeakable blackness that Elsa's spirit had finally cast off the shackles of terror that had bound her to her grandmother's will for so long. She had known her death was inevitable and in that moment of reckless fury decided that her last moments would not be spent in the unwilling service of evil. A white-hot flame of fury had begun to glow inside her. Elsa had never felt anything like it before and yet the light was so familiar and comforting, it was as if it had been with her all her life, locked behind a secret door in her heart which her grandmother had forced her to keep shut with fear and illness. When Elsa realized her fear was futile, that if she spent the final moments of her life cowering in terror she would die as she'd always lived, a helpless slave to her grandmother's evil will, the white light burst from her as radiantly as the sun. Its heat and light was intense, a beautiful sparkle, warm but powerful – pride, tinged with hate, reckless and free, the silver light of a star. It took hold of Elsa like rivers of mercury running through her veins, shimmering with the force of nature and youth. She was frightened of it at first, but the transformation of Elsa's body and soul felt so wonderful that her heart lifted with joy. Her body felt strong and powerful, filled with a magic that Elsa alone could command. She felt her soul become transformed into a winged lion, noble and true, ready to be sacrificed, not to the Dark beast that dwelt in the rocks of the cursed bay, but as a soldier for peace. She had been ready to die to save Jessica's life.

Elsa couldn't remember how she knew the spells she had cast at her grandmother to stop her wicked deeds. Perhaps they had always been in her, etched on her heart in a language she hadn't understood until the moment she needed it. It was as if her mind had been wiped clean of all the spite, self-loathing and poison Agatha had planted there and all Elsa knew was the wonder of the magic of nature. Flowers and birds and all living things. And so she used these things as her shield, hurling the beauty and love her grandmother so despised back in her face. Elsa's fingers had sparkled like firecrackers and she discovered that she could recreate the loveliness of the living earth in dancing dreams and flaming images. The witch had fought back with vicious hate-filled curses. Elsa bore the force of each blow of black magic. But much as these foul images wounded Elsa, the silver brilliance that glowed from her soul did not leave her. Elsa had felt her body slowly weaken beneath the onslaught of evil that rained down on her. Darkness crept into her brain, filling it with fear. However, the perfect flame of purity still burnt strong in her soul. The fire Agatha had secretly feared would grow inside her granddaughter had been ignited and now nothing could ever extinguish it. Even when Elsa's body could take no more and she crumpled like a helpless doll, her last conscious thought had been that, finally, she had given her all in the name of good, and she prayed for Jessica to save the island. Then there had been nothing but blackness.

The sun was warm on Elsa's face and beneath her she could feel the hard granite of the shelf. She could hear the gentle beating of the waves below and felt the wind brush her cheek. Was she in heaven? A slight soreness throbbed in her temple, telling her that she was still very much in the physical world. Something had changed inside her but she couldn't work out what. Cautiously, she opened her eyes. The sky was a pale blue and she could make out the light green bracken and grass where it curled over the cliff top a few feet above her head. Elsa sat up and gazed at the horizon. The sky was bright and the sea was calm. There wasn't a sign of magic to be seen and all the horror and evil that had filled this place had vanished like the memory of a nightmare. Frightened for a second, Elsa looked around for her grandmother, but the old woman was nowhere in sight.

Elsa sat and rested her hand upon her chest. Everything had returned to the way it should be but in the child's heart a transformation had taken place that could never be reversed. Elsa felt different. She couldn't describe it; the feeling was too wonderful for mere human words. It was as if she had become herself – not a quaking minion, fearful of her grandmother's fury, not a frail body that would fall ill at any second. Elsa was Elsa. She wasn't afraid any more, because with Agatha dead there was nothing to be afraid of and she didn't feel guilty because she knew she was no longer a pawn of evil. Her body didn't ache or throb with pain as it had done before and when she inhaled the sweet sea air, her lungs filled without any sign of weakness. The white-hot blaze that had transformed her spirit had cooled but Elsa still felt it like a golden halo ringing her heart. She turned her face towards the sun as she realized for the first time in her life she was free. Elsa didn't know what to call this emotion that overwhelmed her because she'd never felt it before: it was Hope.

If her grandmother was dead, Jessica had succeeded. She must find her and make sure she was okay. Close by, someone was weeping bitterly.

'Jess?' she called out, scrambling to her feet. 'Where are you? It's all right. You did it!'

Elsa's voice sounded louder than it ever had and was full of confidence.

The sobbing stopped; Jessica called from the top of the cliff. 'Elsa, Elsa, we need help. I don't know what to do.'

Her words tugged at Elsa's heart. Nimbly, she hurried over to the rock-face and hitching up her white gown, began to climb. To her delight, the aching weakness that had haunted her muscles all her life had vanished and her arms and legs worked swiftly as she hauled herself up towards the top of the cliff. With one last effort she pulled her slim form onto the soft grass of the cliff top.

Pausing for a second, Elsa adjusted the thin material of her dress and looked around. The damage and charring of the magic fire caused by her grandmother's spells had vanished along with the old woman and the trees and bracken were once again fresh and green. The only sign of the brutal damage Agatha Noir had caused was the sorry sight of two figures, bruised and woeful, on the grass. Jessica was kneeling. Her clothes were soaking wet and blackened with soot. Her hair was a matted tangle and her face so smudged with ash and mud that the only pink skin that could be seen were the two watery tracks that ran from her eyes. She sat nursing Marina, who lay mortally wounded on her lap. Elsa recognized the creature they had encountered days before, deep in the hopeless shadows of the Magicroutes, now even more hideous and sickly in the warm glow of day. The blisters on her scarred skin looked red and painful and her snakelike body lay limply on the damp ground. Her face was a mask of ill health, her huge brown eyes closed and her thin lips white and dry. A horrid, rasping sound came from her chest every time she inhaled and her body showed little sign of life. Tenderly, Jessica was stroking the creature's pockmarked cheek.

Filled with compassion, Elsa hurried over to her friend and knelt by her side. She did not know why the strange being from the caves beneath Jersey was here but her relief at seeing Jessica alive drowned out such questions. She placed a tender hand on the older girl's shoulder.

'Jessica,' she whispered gently, 'it's all right. It's over. You banished grandmère.'

Jessica violently shook her head and continued to stare down into the tortured face of the dying Marina.

'No,' she croaked, 'I didn't ... I'm not ... Marina ... I couldn't have ... she's dying.'

Elsa struggled to make sense of what had happened.

Suddenly, as if waking from a horrid dream, Jessica realized Elsa was there. She looked straight into the small girl's face and her eyes were filled with such sorrow that it nearly broke Elsa's heart.

'She tried so hard, Elsa,' Jessica bleated desperately, her voice brimming with tears. 'I couldn't have stopped the black magic without her. And now ... and now she's going to die.'

Jessica scrabbled around in the mud, desperately searching for something. Shaking with emotion, the Guardian clasped the sacred axe of Helier. The weapon was no longer a lustrous gold, but a rusty and ancient lump of metal with no sign of the power it had held. Frantically, Jessica shook it, trying to bring it back to life. Throwing back her head she wailed to the clear sky.

'Helier!' she screamed. 'Where are you? You can't do this to me! You can't let them take my mum and my sister!'

Jessica's voice faded into bitter sobs and the axe tumbled from her fingers, landing with a dull thud on the muddy ground.

A chill clasped Elsa's heart as she gazed down at the rapidly weakening creature. Jessica's words had sparked a memory in Elsa's brain, the recollection of something her grandmother had said long ago and which, until this moment, had made no sense to her. Agatha had spoken with triumph of the other child, as if it had been some great victory for the forces of black magic. Now Elsa could see with brutal clarity what she meant. The coven of many years ago had succeeded in cursing the first born of Emma Hellily and it had been only a fluke of nature that Jessica had been born minutes later to take her place. Elsa swallowed hard; her throat was very dry. She wished she had seen it earlier, when Rina had rescued them in the Magicroutes. Maybe then she could have said something and this would never have happened to Jessica's twin.

'Jessica,' she whispered, 'I'm so, so sorry. No-one knew for sure she was still alive. We all thought the story about there being twins was a myth.' Elsa's words failed her and she could not think of anything else to say to console her friend. Sadly, she gazed down at the cursed body of Marina Hellily.

Elsa placed her palm to Marina's wart-covered forehead. The weeping skin was cool at first to the touch, wet with sweat and pus, but quickly the young witch detected the angry burn of

421

fever. Elsa pressed her ear to the girl's chest. It took her several seconds to detect a heartbeat and when she did it was weak and irregular. All the time, Jessica cradled the limp body of her twin, crying helplessly. 'She's going to die, isn't she?'

Elsa's familiarity with sickness and witchcraft extended beyond her years, as a result of many frightful experiences with her grandmother, not to mention the number of spell books she had pored over behind the old woman's back in a vain search for relief from her own malady. The symptoms did not look promising. Her mind whirled with half-remembered spells and vague potions as she tried to think of something that would aid Marina's suffering.

'Don't say that,' she begged Jessica, her voice struggling to sound positive. 'Black magic thrives on negativity; if we think she's going to die, it will make her worse. Stay positive.' She combed her fingers through Marina's tangled, wiry hair to try and comfort her. 'She needs to be kept warm,' Elsa began, 'and liquids – she must take plenty of liquids.' She gazed up into her friend's tear-stained face. 'You have got to keep talking to her, Jess. Don't let her slip away. You're her twin. You can reach her when others cannot.'

Jessica nodded. She knew Elsa spoke the truth. She bent close to her sister's ear.

'Please don't die!' she murmured. 'Never leave me.'

Marina let out a sickly splutter and twitched her head so it moved closer to Jessica's.

Elsa got to her feet and glanced around as she tried to work out what to do next.

'Where are the others?' she asked. 'Jake and Jim? Are they okay? If we can get Marina back to Maison de l'hache I may be able to make a tonic to ease the black magic.'

Jessica didn't reply. She just hugged Marina tightly and prayed.

Elsa looked down the long path leading away from Devil's Hole, her heart thumping with urgency. After a few moments, she saw two figures hurrying towards her up the slope – it was Jim and Jake.

Jim led the way. His head was down and he was running as fast as his bulky frame would allow. Jake followed him several feet behind, limping and clasping his side. Elsa's heart leapt when she saw them and she began to call out, frantically waving her arms to get their attention. Jim heard her and turned his eyes towards the top of the hill. He quickened his pace. Jake attempted to match his speed but was handicapped by his injuries.

Elsa scurried down the path and met the pair just before they reached the peak. Her feet were bare and the stony ground cut them, but the child was too worried to notice. She met Jim with outstretched arms. 'Elsa,' he cried, 'you're all right. Jake told me what happened to you but to be honest I found it hard to believe.'

Elsa shook her head dismissively. 'I don't matter now,' she said. 'There's too much else for you to worry about.' Her eyes flitted to Jake who was gasping for breath and gripping his side. 'Are you all right, Jake?' she asked.

The young lad didn't answer for a moment but continued to take deep breaths and nurse the right of his rib cage.

'I'll be okay,' he wheezed finally, 'but I don't think much of your grandma's gardening!' Jake was joking again and Elsa took that as a sign he couldn't be too badly injured.

Jim tried to hurry past but Elsa kept firm hold of his hand and tried with all her might to stop him.

'What happened?' he asked. 'It's Jess, isn't it? Dear God, what has happened to her? Is she dead? Is she injured? Tell me Elsa!' Jim's voice grew from a worried murmur into a desperate shout. His sparkling eyes filled with tears as he struggled to pass Elsa and reach the top of the hill. He seemed dazed and confused as he wandered, zigzagging across the path to get around her.

'Jim, stop, please,' she said firmly in a tone so alien to the way she had spoken before that the old man did indeed stop, taken aback by the gravity of her voice.

'Jessica's fine – she's alive and relatively unharmed,' she told him. But Jim detected a note in her voice that told him worse news was to come. Elsa lowered her eyes to the gravel road as she fought hard to find the words to explain about Marina. She thought about the battle in the Magicroutes as well as all that had occurred that day. There was so much Jim didn't know and so much pain he had tried to forget. Now it was up to Elsa to cut open old wounds that had healed so poisonously. It wasn't really her place to speak about such hurtful secrets; this should be a matter for Jim and his family. But what choice did she have? Marina might die and then the bitterness and grief would start all over again. Elsa took a deep breath and spoke.

'Jessica didn't defeat my grandmère alone. Only one person could give her the help she needed to rid this place of such evil. Marina helped her. Please don't ask me how she got here or how I know who she is – Jessica knows too. And now Marina's dying. I might be able to save her if we get her back to the house, but I don't know.'

'Marina!' Jim sobbed, his body shaking. 'Oh, God forgive me, what have I done?'

He hugged himself tightly and turned his stricken face towards the heavens whispering, 'Emma, I'm so sorry. I failed you and your daughters.'

The blonde-haired child looked towards Jake. 'So Jess was right,' he said. 'That creature in the Magicroutes *did* have something to do with Jim and the Guardian. But what, Jim?'

'Leave him, Jake,' Elsa whispered. 'It's not for us to be involved any more. This is a family matter.'

But Jim had already heard him. 'That *thing*,' he said thickly, 'is my other great-niece, Jessica's older sister. They were born two minutes apart. A foul spell was placed on Marina's head, for being the Heir of Helier. She was transformed into a creature all God-fearing Jerseymen would be repulsed by. And it worked. For fourteen long years I hated her, thought she was a thing of evil, placed all my hopes in Jess and told myself that Marina was not worth anything. I cast her out of my life and only the kindness of my good friend Keela and his fellows stopped her from dying.'

Jim Hellily faced them. He stared directly at Elsa and the girl saw fourteen long years of suffering in his hollow eyes.

'I hold no grudge against you, Elsa. I have no right to condemn you for whatever foul acts your grandmother forced you to perform – because I have done worse. I have willingly rejected the true Guardian of Jersey. I have betrayed my own niece and wounded both her daughters. And now that I have finally seen my sins, despite the bravery she has shown to prove her heart is pure, it is too late to ask Marina for her forgiveness. She is dying.'

'Like I said,' Elsa replied, 'there is a chance she could be saved. No matter what has gone before, Marina is still a Hellily,

424

is still the Guardian. Whatever effect the black magic has had on her body, her spirit is strong. You owe it to her to help her. You owe it to Jessica, too.'

Jim gazed up to the pinnacle of the hill, at the bracken behind which Jessica was hidden in lonely isolation, nursing her sickly twin.

'She hates me now,' he said sadly, 'and with good cause, after what I've done to her sister. No wonder she was furious with me last night. When did she find out?'

Jake stiffly straightened up and limped forward to come to Jim's side. The young lad was struggling to comprehend this strange and sorrowful turn of events and knew that he hated seeing both Jim and Jess this upset. He cursed himself for not being able to fit the pieces together when Jessica had explained to him what she saw in the Iris, but this was futile. No-one on Jersey apart from Jim, Keela and Marina herself had known Jess was a twin. All he and Elsa could do now was reveal what they knew and hope for the best.

'It's wasn't me who fought off the Black Trolls in the Magicroutes, Jim. It was Marina,' he said. 'Jess was sure she had something to do with the magic but she wanted to find out more before we told anyone. I wish now I had told you.'

Jim raised his hand to his face and wiped the tears from his eyes. 'And what would I have done? Denied everything like I've done for the past fourteen years. That's what you were doing down at Grosnez this morning, wasn't it Jake? You and Jessica were trying to undo my mistake when...'

He stopped dead and clapped a hand over his mouth as his eyes rested on Elsa's face. The child stared up at him with stern, blue eyes. She looked older than she had done before, more mature. The frightened child that had cowered in terror at her grandmother's evil was dead now and in her place was a girl whose sad life had brought her wisdom beyond her years.

'Say it, Jim,' she said, her voice without a shred of self-pity. 'I tried to murder Jessica. I do not deny the awful things I have done so why should you? I betrayed my only friend in the name of evil. I filled her heart with betrayal and hatred for me. I thought all goodness in my soul had been lost because of these deeds. But Jessica saw. She saw decency in me when even I myself could not. This is why I'm still alive. Jessica forgave

425

me and gave me the strength to come from the darkness into the light. Yes, she hated you for what you did but she knows now your actions were born out of grief and suffering. That's why you have to believe me when I say you can save yourself but only if you attempt to save Marina. It's the only way.'

Without another word, Jim Hellily brushed Elsa gently aside and began to climb the hill to reach the two girls whose forgiveness he sought. His heavy work boots clattered noisily on the gravel as he trudged onwards. His mind had been wiped clear of the revulsion he remembered at seeing Marina for the first time. He did not care what hideous beast would appear to him when he reached the top of the hill; he would see her only with his heart now. He would gaze upon her as he had gazed upon Jess, as an echo of the beloved niece he had lost and a beacon of hope for Jersey. He prayed that now he had put his bitterness aside, fate would let him know Marina before she died.

Elsa and Jake watched him go but hung back for a few moments before they followed. Both were aware that no matter how deeply their fates were tied to the family of Hellily they could not fully understand the pain that gripped the hearts of Jim and Jessica at this moment. The existence of Marina had been a dark and upsetting secret that Jim had kept and now it was up to the old Jerseyman to make his peace. For their part, all that the farmer's son and the white witch could do was stand on the edge of the shadow of grief that blanketed their friends and offer what support they could. Hand in hand they followed Jim up the hill, their minds filled with thoughts of pity.

Jessica cradled her sister's head in her arms and rocked her tenderly in rhythm with the melody of her sobs. Her body felt cold and numb from her despair. Her soul cried out silently to her twin to grip on to the slivers of life that were quickly slipping away. Marina's hoarse gasps rang in Jessica's ears, each one sounding as if it would be her last. Slowly the warm, safe, sacred link that bound their minds together was closing, like a candle reaching the end of its wick. Jessica was finding it harder and harder to sense her twin's emotions and knew that this meant Marina was losing the will to fight.

'Stay with me,' she sobbed weakly. 'For God's sake, stay.'

Jessica wanted to scoop Marina up in her arms and run with her back to Maison de l'hache where she could be safe and warm but her grief and the battle had left her own body so fatigued, she was barely able to hold herself up, let alone bear Marina's weight. She thought hopefully that if her sister died she might also perish and then she would not suffer the agony of their being torn apart again. Just when Jessica thought she would faint from sorrow and hopelessness she felt a presence at her side that was so warm and familiar that it soothed her grief. A pair of thick, strong arms coiled round both her and Marina in a loving embrace and she smelt engine oil and the sea. A deep, gentle voice reached out to her in her grief.

'Jess,' it said, 'it's okay, I'm here. I'm sorry.'

Jessica forced her eyes to open and looked up into the sad face of her Uncle Jim. The old man's eyes were brimming with tears. Jessica forgot all the hatred she had felt towards him and the way he'd abandoned Marina. She buried her head against his bulky shoulder and sobbed.

Jim gripped his youngest niece close and tried to comfort her. He gazed down at where Marina lay and saw with painful clarity the severity of her illness. He witnessed her pock-marked skin and malformed limbs. He heard her laboured breathing. But despite her ailments, Jim saw something in Marina that he hadn't when he looked at the creature in Keela's arms all those years ago. He saw she was human.

'Jess,' he repeated softly, as he rocked the teenaged girl against his shoulder, 'Elsa and Jake told me everything. I don't know what to say. You have the right to hate me. So does Marina. I cannot make excuses for what I did. I wish I'd kept you both with me.'

The old man felt a sob catch in his chest but stifled it. This was no time for his sorrow, he must now make up for the lost years.

Jessica pulled back from Jim sadly and gazed down at Marina's pale face.

'She...' she croaked through the sobs, 'she was so brave. I love her and I don't want her to die.'

Jim nodded his head and ran his hand through Jessica's dark locks.

'You are both heroines to me,' he whispered gently. 'Just as your mother was.' He lowered his eyes to Marina and took her hand in his. 'I never gave you enough credit, did I?' he uttered hollowly.

Jessica knew that he was speaking directly to Marina and prayed that she could hear him. In the Jerseyman's rough palm, Marina's fingers twitched weakly. Jessica wondered whether this was a response to Jim's words or just a spasm of agony. She placed her arm under Marina's head, lifting it slightly off the ground. Marina spluttered hoarsely as Jessica moved her.

'She saved my life,' Jessica whispered. 'Twice. Now she's dying.'

'I won't let it happen,' Jim hissed, squeezing Marina's hand. 'I swear before God and Helier, nothing will harm you two girls as long as I live.'

'What can we do?' Jessica moaned. 'Marina's been through so much, her body can't take any more.'

Jim placed a tender hand on Jessica's head. The warmth from it seemed to soothe the pain in her body. 'Faith,' uttered the old man simply. 'Faith saved our ancestor Helier from the wrath of his father. Faith has kept this island safe down the centuries and faith will bring Marina back to us if God wills it.'

Jessica gripped her uncle's arm and wept with hope and sorrow. She looked down at her twin and placed a hand on her cheek. Marina's skin was dry and hard like battered leather and she felt hotter than she had before.

'Come on,' whispered Jess to her sister. 'Don't give up the fight.' Marina sighed deeply, gulping in air with a ragged gasp.

Jim glanced behind him. A few feet away from where they sat, Jake and Elsa stood close together, gazing nervously at the family.

'You two,' he said trying to sound calm. 'It's best that we take Marina back to the house. I don't know exactly what we can do for her but it looks like it's going to be a long night. You can stay if you want. I think Jessica and Marina would appreciate the company, but if you want to go home we understand.'

The pair glanced at each other. Fate had decided that their lives would be tied to the Hellilys. There was no way Jessica, Jake and Elsa could survive what they'd been through and then walk away from each other. Their friendship had been forged under the heat of Hell and the coldness of fear. They would support Jess and Rina no matter what.

'We'll stay,' said Jake, 'as long as you need us.'

Jim turned back to Marina and regarded the sickly girl. Slowly, carefully the Jerseyman cradled Marina in his arms. The cursed child's head rested heavily against his arm and her flaking, lower limbs flopped wearily as he lifted her up. Getting to his feet he whispered tenderly, 'Don't worry, little one. We're going home now.'

Mustering all their strength, Jim and Jessica began to head down the steep slope back to the car park. Jessica clung to her uncle's arm tightly as they shuffled across the gravel and whispered words of comfort in Marina's ear. Elsa and Jake followed, bringing the sacred axe of Helier with them.

About half way down the hill, Elsa stopped quite still and gazed into the knotted undergrowth at the side of the path. A memory had come flooding back and hurrying over she swiftly began to gather the white flowers that grew among the lush grass.

Jake looked at her puzzled. 'What are you doing?' he hissed.

Elsa finished her chore and dashed back to him, the blooms cupped in her palm. 'Repaying a debt,' she answered. 'If I can.'

Jake didn't understand what she meant but didn't like to ask. He knew Elsa had her reasons and that her life was more complex than he understood. After all that she had been through he couldn't blame her for wanting to do something to show she was grateful for the salvation she had been granted.

He nodded and placed a comforting arm around her shoulder, as together they followed the winding path down to the car park where Jim and Jessica were waiting for them beside the truck. Jim had laid Marina's frail body carefully in the back, her heavy head resting on a pile of old blankets that he kept there. The girl seemed to be growing weaker by the second and her skin had turned from its usual glossy olive to a sickly lime colour. Her dry lips puckered as she sucked in air and she looked badly dehydrated. Jessica stood close to the vehicle gazing down at her twin, her tear-filled eyes begging her to hold onto life. In an unusual way, Jessica's body seemed to have taken on the same sickly appearance that had cursed Elsa. She looked thinner, weaker than the dusky teenager who had arrived on

429

the island only a week before. Maybe the black magic had cursed her too – not directly perhaps, but the grief of watching her twin in such a helpless state would scar her for the rest of her life. She had been in the darkest heat of battle and had come out the other side. Jessica had earned the right of the title of Guardian and was truly part of Jersey but it came at an awful price.

Jake left Elsa's side and approached the Hellilys. He brushed Jim's hand with his own to offer his old friend some support before placing his arm around Jessica's shoulder. He felt as if he was at a funeral even though Marina was not yet dead. It was only a matter of time. Elsa had told all of them to stay positive, that if they thought Marina would survive it would help the infection pass from her body. But now that seemed impossible. The intensity of Marina's sickness was clear and no amount of faith or supernatural power, be it Christian, black magic or white magic, could hide the facts.

Jessica shrank away from Jake's touch. The lad knew that this rejection was not a personal slight. His comfort had been an expression of sorrow and pity and by accepting it Jessica would be admitting there was no hope left. She had to believe, no matter what her eyes told her, that Marina would survive. That thought was their life raft, holding Marina to this world and Jessica to sanity. But it was hard to think that her sister would recover when Jessica seemed to see Marina's corpse in everyone's eyes. Her mind felt numb to her twin's feelings and her body was cold and weak. Tiredly she raised her head.

'I want to ride in the back with her,' she told Jim. She climbed up into the rear of the truck and settled herself among the rags next to her sister. Wrapping her arms tightly round the girl, Jessica nuzzled her nose into Marina's matted mane and squeezed her eyes shut to block out the cruel truth of the world.

No-one spoke during the short journey back to Maison de l'hache. A heavy sadness filled the cab, suffocating the three passengers with their own thoughts. Elsa had laid the small posy of white blooms out on her cotton dress and carefully set about separating the snowy petals from the blood-coloured stamens. She sang softly to herself as she did this in words of an ancient tongue. Jake stared out of the window, his thoughts drifting like the thin mist over the sea. He felt helpless and mortal, not knowing what to do or say to ease his friends' sorrow. He thought about Martin, Jess's father, and his blood chilled with grief. Did he even know he had another daughter and if not, was he only to learn of her existence hours before she died? The bruising around Jake's ribs made him wince with pain. He made the decision that whatever happened to Marina, when he returned to his own home he would find his mother, father, older brothers and grandfather and hug them all very tightly. He knew now the value of family.

Jessica was barely aware of the movement of the truck as it rolled through the narrow roads of Jersey. She had entered another world and was almost in a trance, away from the horrors of all that had happened, where only she and Marina existed. She tried very hard to remember what it had been like to be safe and warm with Marina as they were cradled in the belly of their mother. Three bodies living as one, filled with love and hope. If only she could take her twin back to that place, to that small, safe patch of darkness, it would mean that their lives were one, strong and new, and Marina wouldn't be this horrid crippled being edging closer and closer to death. Marina's laboured breathing rattled in Jess's ear, reminding her with each desperate gasp how ill she was. Jessica felt a heartbeat but could not tell whether it was Marina's, her own, or both, so tightly bound together were they that even their pulses beat with the same rhythm. Jessica's mind was full of thoughts, prayers and fears and she desperately clung to any feeling or notion that seemed to be coming from Marina's spirit. For the briefest of moments, she could have sworn that she saw an image of their mother, arms outstretched and smiling. Jessica squeezed her sister tightly and wept.

But then the vision was gone, fading like the sun at dusk and Jessica felt again the pain of her sister. It told her Marina was still alive but only just and the agony that ripped the crippled girl's body was so acute that it burnt into Jessica. Marina's skin felt like paper, as if all the moisture was being drawn from her body. Beneath her pale, flaking skin, Marina's muscles contracted in agonising spasms and she strained her throat to cry out in pain but even that was too much for her.

The journey back to Jim's home from Devil's Hole took only a few minutes, but to all the travellers, especially Jessica,

431

every second they were on the road was a second too long. No-one knew what could be done to save Marina but somehow they all believed that getting her back to Maison de l'hache would help somehow. It was a futile thought, the kind people only have when they are clinging to hope against insurmountable odds. The warmth and the comfort of Jim's stone cottage could not ease Marina's suffering – nothing could, not even witchcraft.

The truck shuddered to a halt outside the pink stone building. Now all trace of evil was removed from the island, the house once again looked warm and homely. The peachy walls overrun with lush ivy looked so pretty against the periwinkle sky. A golden light glowed from within the downstairs window and the dark outline of a man could be seen waiting nervously inside. Jessica gazed up at the house and her heart ached. It looked so beautiful Marina would have thought it was a fairytale castle. Now her sister would never see it. Jessica knew that their father was waiting inside, praying and hoping for her return. How was she going to explain that, while she was unharmed, Marina, the daughter he didn't know existed, was dying? Slowly their family was being ripped to shreds. No wonder Martin had hated Jersey.

Jim switched off the engine and got out of the cab. Jake and Elsa followed him around to the rear of the vehicle. All three wore grim expressions and no-one knew quite what to say. Jessica felt cold and clung even closer to her sister's shaking body. She was scared to let Marina go, scared that if they were physically parted again it would be just enough to tip Marina into the shadow of death. She buried her face against her twin's damp hair and yelped with fear.

'No,' she whimpered, 'I don't want to.'

She knew her words made no sense but so cutting was her grief and fear she couldn't express herself. She no longer felt like the Guardian of Jersey, but a lost and confused child trapped in a world beyond her understanding.

Jim bit his lip. Tenderly, he stooped and gathered up the twisted body of the dying twin in his arms and lifted her out of the truck. Marina cried out in agony as she was moved and her muscles contorted in pain. Seeing her sister's aguish, Jessica screamed and fell down sobbing hysterically.

432

Jake reached out and offered Jess his hand. 'Come on,' he murmured, ' let's go inside.'

Jessica felt too weak to move. Jim was trudging towards the front door with Marina cradled in his arms. Jessica wanted to be close to her family but was terrified of witnessing the death of her newly found sibling. She needed the comfort of her father's embrace for only he knew the suffering of losing someone you loved dearly to the wickedness of black magic.

'Daddy,' she bleated. 'I want my Daddy.'

Elsa shuffled her bare feet on the cold, stony ground. In her cupped hands were the fragments of the blooms she had gathered at Devil's Hole. Her face gazed up at Jessica and there was a calm warmth in her blue eyes. Only someone who had suffered as much as Elsa had could wear an expression of such empathy.

'Your papa's inside, Jess,' she whispered softly. 'Marina will be okay soon, I know it, I feel it. Her pain will end.'

Elsa spoke in a voice so tender and beautiful, it quelled even Jessica's grief. Silently, the older girl allowed Jake to help her down from the truck and lead her towards the house. Jim was waiting for them on the doorstep, holding Marina in his arms. Jim had not rung the doorbell and Jess knew why. Guilt still gripped the old man's heart. It had been Jim's actions that had finally led to the injury of Martin's eldest daughter. He had placed both the writer's wife and children in mortal peril. Emma had died the last time Martin came to Jersey and if anything did happen to Marina, all forgiveness Martin had felt for Jim would be washed away. He would detest the Jerseyman and with good cause.

Elsa stepped forward and pressed the bell. A weak chime came from within the house and Jessica heard the hurried footsteps of her father as he came to greet them. Her heart froze with fear and dread as she contemplated his reaction to Marina, his lost child, so sick and close to death. She feared it would bring back cruel and haunting memories of the death of his wife. Jessica could not deal with so much heartache. The prospect of losing her twin was agony enough but if it rekindled the bitter spite between the two men, what little security remained for her from her family would be shattered beyond repair.

The door swung open and Jessica stared up at the pale and anxious face of Martin. The man seemed to have aged in the

433

last few hours and the redness around his eyes told her he had been weeping ever since they'd left him. His face crumbled into an expression of relief when he saw his daughter. A great sob of grief caught in Jessica's chest and, unable to find the words to tell of her hollow victory, she flung her arms around his neck and wept against his shoulder. Now and here, in the safety of her father's arms, she was once again just a young girl caught in a family tragedy.

Martin held his daughter close. For the longest time he had prayed to God for her return and stared out of the windows into the impenetrable blackness for the slightest sign of hope or life. Minutes ticked by into hours but time meant nothing to him as long as the world remained in unnatural night and his daughter was standing at the gateway to Hell. Finally, the dim light of late afternoon had returned but nothing could quell his terror until he knew that Jessica was alive. Now she was here he could at last rejoice.

'Jess,' he wept into her thick hair, 'you're all right. I was so worried. You were gone for a very long time.'

Jessica drank in the warmth of her father's embrace and it calmed her fears.

'I know,' she whispered. 'I love you, Dad.' She wiped the tears from her eyes and struggled with all her might to turn her thoughts back to her sister and the awful truth she must divulge to him. She pulled back from her father's embrace and gazed intently at him. Jim had already hurried inside with Marina lying weakly in his arms. Elsa and Jake had followed but Martin had been so taken up with seeing Jessica home safe again he had barely noticed the others.

'Jess?' he queried, studying his daughter's disturbed expression. 'Whatever has happened? Tell me, sweetheart, are you all right?'

'Dad,' she breathed wearily. 'Something ... something awful has happened.'

'Whatever do you mean, Jess?' he soothed. 'The black magic's gone and you're safe and well.'

'I don't matter,' she said, straining her weeping eyes to look over her father's shoulder to see what was happening in the hallway.

'What do you mean?' Martin said, half laughing. 'Of course

you matter. You're my daughter and the Guardian of Jersey. You matter a great deal.'

But Jessica pushed past him into the house. The hallway was warm and the atmosphere claustrophobic with so many people crowding into the small space. Through her grief, Jessica was aware of the glittering, golden light of the faerie Rosehip flittering about, observing the scene with candid curiosity. Martin hurried after Jessica. His daughter glanced back at him and uttered hoarsely, 'I'm not the true Guardian.'

The elder twin lying cradled in Jim's arms seemed to be edging closer to death by the second. Her hands and limbs lashed out weakly in pain and her face twisted as if she was crying, yet no sound came from her mouth.

Rosehip fluttered low over Jim's shoulder.

'What's that thing doing here?' she asked in a disgusted tone.

Elsa looked at the faerie reproachfully and pressed a finger to her lips to silence the sprite. Jim had his back turned towards Martin, his body tense. He dreaded the younger man seeing the sickly twin in his arms. She was the last hurtful secret of the Hellily family and keeping her away from her father for so long was Jim's greatest sin. If he wished to, Jim could excuse the deceit he played on Jessica as mercy, hiding the knowledge of the magic of Jersey so that she could live a normal and happy life. But sending Marina away was unforgivable; it had been a selfish act of fear and prejudice.

Martin's face had grown ghostly white once more. He noticed the scarred and wan figure resting in Jim's arms. In the darkest corner of Martin's mind, a grieving and terrible memory stirred. A memory so horrific and painful that he had, until this moment, forced himself to forget. It cut him deeper than any other sorrow, greater even than the death of his wife. Even now the terrible event was cloudy to his recollection and all he was conscious of was the overwhelming fear and sorrow that he had denied for so long.

'Tell me, Jim,' he said, his voice shaking with emotion. 'I know who it is in my heart but I am too frightened to remember. Are my nightmares true?'

Slowly Jim turned to face Martin, his head bowed in sorrow. In his arms, Marina gasped for breath and turned her face away from her great uncle so that her father could see the full severity of the evil that had been inflicted on her physical form for so long. Martin's face was expressionless; so great was the agony of being reunited with his estranged crippled daughter he felt his heart would stop.

'It's Marina,' sobbed the old man.

Martin approached his eldest daughter silently and placed a tender hand on her blemished cheek. He felt the dryness of her skin and the angry warts that thrived off her flesh. She was hot and feverish. Martin remembered the pain he'd felt when he discovered his wife had died and his first-born child had been cursed. It had been as if a vast, black void had swallowed his heart. Jersey and all that had come from it had been dead and decaying in his eyes. So great had the tragedy been he never wanted to return to the island. His one comfort had been Jessica. The fact that she'd survived, healthy and carefree, soothed his tortured soul and stopped him from living in a hate-filled, hopeless world. He had despised Jim for many years after Emma's death. Hating him for surviving, for keeping alive the ancient ways that had brought so much sorrow to his family. But as the years past his loathing had cooled. In the past week Martin saw again the mystical ways that were intertwined with the island. He saw them living in Jessica as an echo of the woman he had loved, and now he saw that by trying to forget what had gone before he had also forgotten about his other daughter. He could no longer blame Jim for the events that had injured their family.

'You told me she died when she was a couple of months old.'

'I believed,' Jim whispered tensely, 'that she had. I didn't think a person could survive a spell so powerful.'

Jessica caressed her sister's matted hair and sobbed.

'Marina could,' she said softly. 'She was so brave and strong. I wouldn't be here if it hadn't been for her. It was Marina, not Jake, who saved us from the Black Trolls and tonight I couldn't have stopped Agatha Noir if it hadn't been for her.'

Martin winced at Jessica's words. Marina had suffered so greatly and fought Black Magic in so many ways. Even her body and her own family had become enemies against her. She had survived against all odds for fourteen thankless years without comfort or love from those who shared her blood, and what was her reward? Dying slowly and painfully after her greatest

436

triumph just when all that she wished for was so close to coming true.

Martin brushed a strand of thick, greasy hair from Marina's face. The child's face creased as if this softest touch caused her pain. 'Isn't there anything we can do?' queried Martin, a tear rolling down his cheek.

Jim closed his eyes and shook his head. 'She lived with black magic all her life. To deal with any more would be impossible. What happened tonight will kill her.'

Jessica's body became deathly cold. The light in the hallway seemed to dim and all hope and brightness in the world was extinguished. Agatha Noir was dead and the demon still imprisoned safely below the crashing waves of Devil's Hole but the evil of the black magic had laid one last devastating blow on the Hellilys. It seemed, in their duty to save Jersey, the descendants of Romand must always sacrifice their own joy.

Aside from the unhappy quartet, Elsa Noir stared at the dissected blooms in her palms. She and Jake had remained silent for a long time, neither of them wishing to disturb the grieving family. But now, the tiny seed of an idea which had been planted in the young witch's brain when she had seen the strange, white flowers at Devil's Hole, budded and Elsa knew it was time to pay for her own salvation.

'Please,' she said softly, in a voice full of gentle strength. 'Perhaps, there is something that can be done for Marina.'

Jessica was stirred from her sorrow and slowly turned to look at Elsa. Everyone stared at the tiny figure in white. At this time of great darkness it was hard to believe anything could save Jessica's poorly twin. Jess held her breath and gazed at Elsa. Dare she hope that her friend had the knowledge to save her sister? Elsa shifted her feet uncomfortably; she didn't like being the centre of attention. It made her doubt her own abilities and wonder whether she should've spoken up at all. Clearing her throat she began.

'I cannot promise it'll save Marina's life but it may at least ease her suffering. Long ago, I read of a spell in one of grandmère's books. It is a very old magic charm and I can't even remember whether it's black or white magic. But the book said it could give strength to the very weak and save those who had been cursed in the act of great bravery.'

Jessica smudged her tear-stained cheek on the back of her hand and gazed at Elsa. Then she looked back to her sister shivering in Jim's arms. She would gladly give her own life if it meant Marina would get better. She was just about to ask Elsa what the spell was when there was a sudden burst of golden light and Rosehip flapped down from where she had been perched on the lampshade.

'Are you mad?' she chirped in disbelief. 'Jess, your dad told me what happened today at Corbiere. Elsa is a witch! If you want to save this horrible, ugly thing, though God knows why; you shouldn't let that bony hag anywhere near her!'

'Shut up, Rosehip!' Jessica yelled, trembling with fury.

Rosehip let out a sigh of disbelief and landed on the sideboard. Elsa lowered her eyes. She knew the faerie was right. If she hadn't had some magical power within her she would have perished on that cold rock at Devil's Hole. What saved her was the gift that her grandmother had inadvertently given her, the gift of power and magic. It ran through her veins and as much as Elsa hated the evil it had brought when her grandmother used it she couldn't deny it was part of who she was.

'I'm afraid Rosehip is right for once,' Jake said dejectedly. 'You saw what happened today. There's no doubt Elsa's a witch.'

Jessica drew back towards Marina and leant close to her sister. It seemed that even if Elsa knew all the spells in the world, none would be powerful enough to rescue Marina.

Elsa looked at Jake and Rosehip with calm, sapphire eyes. 'I do not deny what I am,' she said surely. 'As long as I can remember, there has been something inside me that made me different from everyone else. I watched my grandmère and feared that the evil that was in her was also in me. But I am no longer afraid, for I know I cannot use this power for myself as my evil grandmère did. I must pay back the harm she caused, if Jessica allows me to. She is the Guardian and only she can judge this witch.'

Elsa's words reached out to Jessica through the darkness of her sorrow. Until that moment, all hope for Marina's salvation seemed to be lost and yet in Jessica's heart she could not bear to believe that there was nothing to be done. Jessica was willing to give anything if it would bring her twin back from the brink of death. So great was her desperation that all awareness of right and wrong seemed to melt away. Jessica was even willing to consider black magic if it would save her sister. What did the legacy of Helier matter now? The true Guardian was dying anyway. But a memory pierced Jessica's selfish sorrow and filled her heart with the duty of Helier. Before the horror and tragedy of the battle at Devil's Hole, Elsa had been on trial for witchcraft. Jessica still hadn't passed judgement. She knew now that she didn't have to quiz Elsa to see whether her heart had been blackened by evil. The truth lay in the child's eyes and she realized that there too she would find the mercy that might save Marina.

Jessica gave her sister one last lingering glance before turning to face Elsa. The small girl stared at her with an openness and confidence Jessica had never seen in her before. For the first time since the battle, Jessica really looked at her friend and saw that she had changed. Her face was no longer frightened and careworn but had an aura about it of a woman far beyond her years. There was so much within Elsa's pale blue eyes that when Jessica gazed into them she could see a knowledge of mystic ways far beyond her comprehension, perhaps beyond Elsa's too. It was like looking into two mirrors that reflected all the horror and pain of the young girl's childhood. Countless cruel words and hateful deeds were captured there and Jessica knew that although her grandmother was dead the memories of what she had been through would haunt Elsa forever. Yet from these scars and wrong doings there shone a new and warm light, in Elsa's soul. Elsa's life had been a living nightmare from the day she was born but she had survived. Something deep within her had stayed strong and pure no matter how her body had suffered or her mind been filled with haunting terror. However powerful Mrs Noir had been, her evil and her witchcraft could not touch Elsa's purity. Jessica knew now that no matter what Elsa had done to hurt her in the past, her heart had never done it willingly. If she did have any magic within her it was of the purest kind and that could save Marina.

Silently, Jessica stepped forward and placed a hand on Elsa's cheek. 'Do whatever you can to save Marina,' she said tenderly. 'You are my friend and I have faith in you.' Jessica paused for a moment before leaning close to Elsa's fair hair and whispering, 'I find you not guilty.'

Emotion flickered across Elsa's face and she looked for the

briefest of moments as if she was going to cry. The woman who had blighted her life was dead and despite all that had happened Jessica, the Guardian of Jersey, her closest friend, had forgiven her. She was truly free. She wanted to weep with joy but there was too much sorrow to be undone. Swallowing her tears she glanced up at Jessica.

'Take Marina upstairs and make her comfortable,' Elsa instructed.

Jessica hurried back to her family where Jim still had the unconscious Marina cradled in his arms. She motioned for her great uncle to follow the child's instructions. The old man looked slightly doubtful that Jessica was placing so much faith in the granddaughter of her enemy.

'Jess,' he hissed gently, 'are you sure?'

Jessica placed a hand on Marina's forehead. She was extremely dry and burning up with fever.

'I'm sure,' she said resolutely.

However, Jim didn't move. Doubt filled his mind and his experience told him witches were not to be trusted.

Jessica glared at him and anger bit through her sorrow. 'Jim,' she told him firmly, 'I've forgiven you once for the wrong you did to Marina. If you do not allow me to place my trust in Elsa and Marina dies...' The word stuck in her throat and it was all she could do to continue. 'I will not forgive you twice.'

The statement came like a slap across the Jerseyman's weathered face and he needed no other incentive. He turned on his heels and began to carry Marina upstairs. Martin and Jessica followed close behind him, their eyes and minds fixed on the sickly girl cradled in his arms. Marina's breathing was so faint now and yet in the sorrowful stillness of the small cottage it echoed with a volume and clarity, filling every heart with the pain that Marina was suffering. It told all who heard it that the eldest twin of Emma Hellily was close to joining her mother in the afterlife. Jake and Elsa watched the mournful family climb the stairs and enter Jess's room. Both felt momentarily that they shouldn't be there, as if they were intruding on something very private. But the feeling lasted only for a moment – for Elsa at least. She knew her part in this saga was not yet over.

Sighing deeply, Elsa stared down at the fragments of flowers she held in her cupped palms. Then summoning up all her reserves she headed towards the kitchen. Jake watched her intently. He had felt quite useless for a long while now and it didn't sit well with him. He was by nature a man of action and in times of crisis it unsettled him even more not being able to do something to help. He was very aware that he was the only one of them who had no real magical powers. That and the throbbing pain in his side made him feel helpless. He could always make his excuses and go home to nurse his own wounds but he felt that was unthinkable. He liked Jessica and hated to leave when she was so upset. He liked Elsa too, surprisingly more than he had realized. Whatever he knew, or thought he'd known about her, didn't alter the fact that he admired the girl and her courage. He shuffled his feet and tried to think of something to say.

'You sure you know what you're doing?' he called out to Elsa just as she was about to enter the kitchen.

The fair-haired girl paused but didn't look round. 'No,' she said softly, 'but isn't that what life is? Hoping. Putting your faith in something. I understand if you want to go, if you don't trust me. Like you said, I am a witch.'

Jake felt his heart lurch. In that moment he understood just why Jessica had forgiven Elsa. That was the trouble with legends and magic: they grew so large it was easy to forget about the small things that went into making them. Guardians and witches, merfolk and faeries – at the end of the day they were all people with feelings and sorrows. Elsa's gift – and he saw now that her magical power was indeed a gift – didn't change the pure, gentle person she was. The word 'witch' seemed such an unjust name for what she was. She had been as brave as any of them that night, perhaps braver.

Rosehip gazed at Elsa from where she was seated on the sideboard. Her bright, blue eyes drank in the girl's slim figure and quiet manner. She certainly didn't look like a witch, but nowadays who could tell. All the humans seemed to have gone mad and to her the world looked all upside down. Jessica was trying to save that horrid thing they had met in the Magicroutes and the person she had been told was a witch had been found innocent. It was just too much for Rosehip to understand. Still, she wasn't going to give her opinion on the whole matter. Every time she did that she seemed to be told to shut up. Screwing up her elfin face thoughtfully, Rosehip swung her legs off the edge of the sideboard.

'I don't know,' she muttered musically. 'If it was my decision I wouldn't trust her. Once a witch, always a witch, I say. What with that thing upstairs, huh, I don't know what to make of it all. I might as well go home.'

Jake looked at Rosehip crossly. Her constant twittering was beginning to tell on his nerves.

'Then why don't you,' he muttered under his breath. He turned back to Elsa and tried to find the right words.

'I . . .' he began, 'I trust you, Elsa. Jessica cleared you of witchcraft and that's good enough for me. It's not my place to judge.'

He saw Elsa take another deep breath and lift her head slightly and he took this as a gesture that she bore him no malice. The strange feeling of uselessness washed over Jake once more. He had made his peace with Elsa by placing Marina's fate in her hands; there was nothing else really he could do. Dumbly, he wandered over to the door of the lounge and was just about to enter when Elsa called out.

'I want you to help me, Jake.'

Jake's mouth fell open. Doing nothing had made him feel helpless but being asked to aid Elsa in such an important task shrunk his confidence even more. He knew nothing about spells and witchcraft so what use could he be?

'I'm . . . I'm not a warlock,' he stuttered.

Elsa turned round. Her expression was open and held none of the hostility Jake expected it to.

'It's not that kind of spell,' she continued gently. 'I want – no, I need – both you and Rosehip to help me. It's hard to explain but I won't force you if you don't want to. You have to do it willingly.'

Pride rose in Jake's heart. Finally there was a way he could support Jessica.

'Sure,' he agreed. 'I'll help you, if you think I'm able to. How about you, Rosehip?'

The faerie looked at him doubtfully and flexed her fragile wings. 'I don't know,' she chirped. 'Whatever you say, she *is* a witch.'

Jake's face soured and his eyes filled with disappointment in the faerie.

'Come on, Elsa,' he muttered bitterly, turning his back on Rosehip. 'I'll help you at least.'

With that, the two of them entered the kitchen leaving Rosehip muttering to herself. The faerie shrugged dismissively. She'd done the right thing, hadn't she? Of course she had, Elsa was a witch and as for that thing upstairs ... Rosehip thought about the creature and how ugly it had been but, funnily, all she could remember was its soft, brown eyes. A strangely unpleasant feeling surrounded Rosehip's heart. It didn't mean anything, she was sure. She could go home now and let Jessica handle the whole messy business. Rosehip gazed at the letterbox in Jim's front door. Back to the fields and woods then, back to where it was safe. She could fly through the letterbox easily; however, her wings didn't seem to want to work. There was a soft sound in the air, drifting down from the upper landing. Rosehip knew it was the sound of Jessica crying. The pricking feeling gripping the faerie's heart tightened and she glanced curiously at the kitchen door. Stupid humans, always changing their minds! She wished this strange emotion would go away. It was stopping her from leaving the house and going back to her own kind, and making her want to follow the humans into the kitchen. Rosehip spread her wings and fluttered towards the open kitchen door.

Jake and Elsa barely noticed her as she flew into the small room. Jim's kitchen remained almost exactly as they had left it from Elsa's witch trial but in the stark light of the electric bulb the room seemed to have lost it reverence. The pale linen that covered the appliances and worktops looked messy and untidy and here and there, pools of scarlet wax scarred the ghostly material. Elsa had retrieved two small bowls from the cupboard and deposited the blood red stamens in one and the delicate, pale petals in the other. Then she and Jake swiftly went about the kitchen tidying away all signs of the witch trial. They took down the white sheets and folded them. The floor was swept of willow branches and Jake carried the heavy, pine table back to its usual spot in the centre of the room. Rosehip watched all of this with great curiosity from the top of the doorframe. When the room was tidy again, Elsa carried the two bowls containing the dissected flowers to the table and placed them side by side. She then paused for a moment, struggling to remember what to do next.

Jake looked at the young girl expectantly. He had no clue what the spell would involve and was more than a little nervous. This magic may be about to determine whether Marina lived or died and it worried him that Elsa looked so unsure. Finally the white witch spoke.

'Right,' she said, trying to sound confident. 'First of all we need some milk.'

'Milk?' queried Jake, surprised at the request for such a mundane item. Elsa nodded and without another word, Jake hurried over to the fridge and opened the door. He found a half-empty milk bottle on the shelf and pulled it out. 'There isn't much left,' he informed Elsa, giving the creamy liquid a sniff, 'and I think it's on the turn.'

Elsa was busy at the stove. She placed a small pan on the hob and the blue flame of gas caressed it.

'We can't be picky,' she said with a sigh. 'Hand it here, please, Jake and, if you can, try and see if one of these candles will still burn.'

The lad passed her the milk and hurried over to the worktop where the malformed candles still drooped in pools of wax. The wax was still pliable to the touch and Jake scooped the yielding, red substance into his palms and moulded it as best he could back into a short, lopsided tower. Rummaging in his pockets, he found a length of string and squeezed the wax around it to form a new wick. It was a crude effort and he prayed it would serve the purpose for which Elsa needed it.

While Jake crafted the candle, Elsa stood at the stove clasping the bottle of milk in her hands and searching her memory for the words she had read in her grandmother's spell book long ago. The charm flickered in and out of her mind in half-forgotten phrases and she strained to grasp the knowledge hidden in her mind. After a few moments her thoughts rested on a chant she hoped was correct. Hands trembling slightly, she poured the milk slowly into the warming pan.

'Hail be to Mother Nature,' she murmured softly as the cool white fluid hissed against the heat of the metal. 'Be with us always, Lady of the Green. Flow into the heart of your servant wounded in battle in the name of purity. Her heart is chaste and her being is injured. Let this nourishment be the cream of your teat. Let it fill her again with the life wrongly stolen. We

444

serve you with passive hearts and our worship is to the Lord of goodness. Answer our prayers.'

The milk swilled gently in the pot as Elsa finished her chant but no change could be seen to indicate that any great magic had been performed. Elsa gave the simmering milk one last hopeful stir before turning back to face Jake.

The farmer's son had placed the roughly crafted candle in the centre of the table, between the two bowls Elsa had left. Elsa gave him a hopeful half smile. 'The milk must be left to boil,' she informed him moving towards the table.

From her seat high on the top of the doorframe, Rosehip shifted impatiently. Her initial fear of witchcraft had been overcome by her natural curiosity and she was just itching to know exactly what Elsa was doing. Eventually, her inquisitiveness wiped out all her pride and fear and she fluttered down from her hiding place to get a better look.

'What *is* happening?' she queried impatiently as she landed lightly on the tabletop and strode over to inspect the contents of the two bowls. Elsa and Jake looked at each other and Jake raised his eyebrows. The appearance of the faerie came as a shock to both of them and if there hadn't been far more serious matters to be dealt with, her return would have annoyed Jake even more. But for now both humans silently agreed that the most useful course of action would be to ignore her completely.

The faerie wandered over to the vessel containing the bright, scarlet stamens and pollen and peered inside. The plant particles looked almost like dried blood against the white crockery. The stamens curled slightly and a fine powder of pollen drifted over them like a delicate vapour.

'Ew!' stated the faerie in a mixture of disgust and interest. 'What is that? It looks like some kind of flower but it can't be. I know all the flowers that grow in Jersey and I've never seen that one before!' The elf reached out a delicate hand but Elsa snatched the dish away, sending the faerie tumbling backwards.

'Don't touch it!' she warned. 'It's a very rare and sensitive herb.'

She stared intently into the bowl.

His curiosity piqued, Jake asked, 'What is it?' and leaned across the table to get a better look at the odd plant.

'Didn't I say?' Elsa replied, her voice resuming its normal

tone. 'I'm sorry. It has many names but I can't remember them all. Saint's Hope is one, Dragon's Heartstrings another. Some even call it Witches' Blessing.'

Jake leaned on the table and listened intently to what Elsa was saying. The child caressed the rim of the dish with her fingertips.

'It hasn't bloomed in Jersey for many years. It can only grow on the battlefield of a great fight between good and evil. Some say it's the last sign of a witch's humanity.'

Jake frowned. 'What does that mean?' he asked.

Elsa closed her eyes. 'It means this plant, if administered correctly, can undo the darkest of spells, as long as the victim has a pure heart.'

Jake stared at the wispy, scarlet tendrils and shook his head. 'But isn't that what witch-hunter's broth does?' he said softly. 'Can't we just give Marina some of that?'

Elsa shook her head. Her expression was so mournful that Jake thought she was going to cry.

'It would kill her,' she said. 'I know because it almost killed me. You see Jake, Marina and I share something in common. Although our souls are good our lives have been so linked to black magic that if that power dies within us we die too. That's what cripples Marina's body and what made me fear grandmère for so long. Witch-hunter's broth will destroy black magic and make her weaker than ever. Our only hope is to turn what is evil into something good. That's what this herb does.'

Jake stared at Elsa, awestruck. Once again he felt very small and weak; he knew so little about the complex arts of magic. He had always assumed, as did most true islanders, that the divide between white and black magic was clear-cut. Black magic was always evil and should be destroyed – that is what he'd always been told. He never thought that witches and witchcraft could mean anything more than death and destruction. But in Elsa's and Marina's case black magic had existed alongside something good. It had been repressed and controlled, and perhaps it was the awesome power that Agatha Noir had lusted after that had kept Elsa and Marina strong through their unhappy lives. Both of them bore the scars of curses and hexes – maybe these made them even stronger. Jake licked his lips nervously.

'What do we have to do?' he questioned.

The fair child closed her eyes and battled to push her own sorrows out of her mind.

'The potion comes in three parts,' she explained. 'The milk is to nourish her body, the red pollen is to replace the life and blood that has been wasted and finally, the petals are added to bless her soul and keep her on this plane. It must be done in that order.'

Jake nodded and tried to look as if he understood all that Elsa had said but the girl could tell he was lost. She gestured to the malformed candle that stood on the table between them. 'Light it,' she instructed.

Jake nervously reached for the box of matches. Fingers trembling, he took one out and struck it. Jake ignited the wick of the candle and the flame cast its orange light across the table. Elsa took the dish containing the scarlet stamens and cupped it between her hands.

'Fire and life will turn these seeds into the blood of rebirth,' she explained to Jake. 'Place your hands over mine and we'll heat the pollen over the flame.'

Cautiously, Jake took hold of the bowl and together he and Elsa lowered it over the flickering candle. The flame licked the base of the vessel, tingeing the white china black with smoke. The powder inside seemed to darken and burn as the dish warmed but nothing that could be called magical happened. Jake gazed at the smouldering remnants of the plant and his heart sank.

'It doesn't look like it's working,' he sighed.

The white witch didn't answer him straightaway. She seemed to have entered into some kind of trance. Her eyes were closed and her face wore a strained expression. A small frown creased her forehead and she looked frightened.

'Elsa!' called Jake.

The girl let out a disappointed sigh and opened her eyes.

'The candle isn't enough to release the magic,' she told him sadly. 'It's needs to absorb the strength of true life. We must give ourselves to the spell. We must die a little to give Marina life.'

Jake gasped and let go of the bowl. The vessel tilted and Elsa was just quick enough to stop it tumbling from her hands. From where she was seated, cross-legged beside the candle, Rosehip leapt up with a triumphant squeal and fluttered onto Jake's shoulder.

'I knew it!' she chirped. 'Black magic, just like her grandmother. She wants to kill us all!'

Jake eyed Elsa warily. The faerie's words had struck fear into his heart. Up until now he thought she had been interested in saving Marina's life; now he wasn't sure.

'No,' he said. 'I thought this was about life not death!'

Elsa's face crumpled with pain. 'I knew this would happen. I knew when the moment came for you to give something of yourself to help Jess you wouldn't.' She dropped her eyes to the smoking ashes in the bowl. 'Leave now,' she said bitterly. 'The gift must be given willingly and I cannot force you. I shall help Marina alone if I can. The potion will be the weaker for it but it'll have to do. She shall take part of me.' The girl's fingers tightened angrily around the bowl but her blue eyes showed frustration, not malice.

Jake looked at her and guilt filled his heart. After the great victory they had won along with Jess and Marina he had believed all the sorrow and mistrust in Jersey had gone. But was he right? His friend's sister lay upstairs dying and if her life came to an end, Jessica's heart would be broken forever and Jersey, her family and her responsibility as Guardian would be meaningless. Jake couldn't repress the fear of black magic that had been instilled in him since birth but when he looked into Elsa's pure blue eyes he knew that if he turned down the offer to save Marina, guilt would haunt him for the rest of his life. He would become like Jim, battling to hide the memory of what he had done and living every day with the knowledge that he could have done more if he hadn't been such a coward. Was a life like that really worth living?

'What do you mean, give part of yourselves?' he asked slowly.

'We all live,' said Elsa simply. 'Whether we are creatures of magic or not, the power of existence flows through all of us until the day we are destined to die.' She paused and gripped the bowl hard as if she was trying to hold something back. 'We also all know pain and the fear of death. It is possible for anyone, not just a witch or a warlock, to give their life to save another. If you embrace the memory of that moment when you were closest to death while holding the pollen of the Saint's

448

Hope flower, the magic of the plant will absorb part of your life and it can be given to another. It will not kill you, but if you can do that you may be able to save Marina's life.'

A cold chill invaded Jake's heart as he listened to Elsa's words. The thought of willingly coming that close to death terrified him but he knew he could never forgive himself if Marina died and he had done nothing to help. Taking a deep breath, he tried to prepare himself for the unknown.

'What must I do?' he asked in a hushed voice.

Elsa once again held the small dish of pollen over the flickering candle flame. Nervously, Jake cupped his hands around the bowl and felt the gentle heat of the tiny blaze. Elsa closed her eyes and began to focus her thoughts.

'You've got to find the memory that most terrifies you,' she explained, 'and relive it. Relive it until you know the pain Marina's feeling and are able to let go of part of your life.'

Jake knew exactly the moment he must focus on. Tonight, when Elsa's grandmother had ensnared him in the twisted vines he'd felt as if the very life was being squeezed from his body. Now he must experience again that chilling terror. The image of the gnarled tendrils flowed into his mind with such clarity it was easy for him to imagine he was back at Devil's Hole, being sucked down into the undergrowth. The pain throbbing in his bruised ribs flared again. The bright light of the kitchen never faded but, as Jake entered deeper into his nightmares and memories, a deathly blackness seeped into his thoughts.

The room swam before his eyes, colours and images swirling until all that was safe and familiar faded and the terror of his past torture closed in on him. Jake gazed down into the dish and saw the pollen sparkle like scarlet stars and the stamens wiggling like maggots. Then his eyes clouded over and he was plunged into a void of fear and death. His body felt ice cold. The only part of him that retained any warmth was his hands. His fingertips clasped the bowl securely; the dish seemed to smoulder like volcanic rock in his grasp. The tips of his fingers tingled and twitched as if something powerful was flowing out of them and into the blazing vessel. The terror of the enchanted vines returned to him; he felt again the strong, leathery tendrils knot around him. He was no longer in the physical world but in a domain that existed only in fear and memory. The strength of his own terror overwhelmed him. Then, suddenly, everything was gone and a familiar voice echoed through the dark, recalling him to his earthly life.

'It is done,' Elsa whispered from somewhere in the shadows.

Jake felt as if he was plummeting through blinding blackness at a terrifying speed. As he fell, memories, thoughts and feelings flooded back to him in a flickering montage of colour and image. Like tiny pieces of a jigsaw, the fragments of Jake's mind reassembled at breathtaking speed as he grew closer to the world of the living. An almighty impact hit him, like a tidal wave of sensation as he once again found himself back in the mundane setting of Jim's kitchen. His shaking hands were still wrapped around the china bowl and he had to try very hard to steady them so he didn't drop it. The pain from the bruising in his ribs throbbed dully and somewhere on the floor above he could hear the gentle sobbing and hushed voices of Jessica and her family as they nursed Marina. Jake gazed across the table at Elsa who was standing opposite him. The girl looked shaken and pale but otherwise unharmed.

'Elsa,' he said, his voice trembling, 'what just happened? Everything kinda went black for a moment.'

'Well,' she said, 'for a second, we both died. But just for a second. It's okay – we're back now.'

Jake felt he was going to faint. He'd died – for a second, so Elsa said, but died nevertheless. He felt as if he had been away on an amazing journey lasting many months, but no time had past at all. He knew that he had seen and experienced many marvellous things in the past few seconds but he couldn't remember what they were. Elsa carefully took the bowl from his hands.

'A second!' he said in awe. 'It seemed so much longer.'

But Elsa was not listening to him. The girl was staring into the small bowl, transfixed with joy. A healthy, pink light emanated from the dish and fell in a radiant glow upon Elsa's face.

Rosehip, who had been sitting on the tabletop watching, looked closely at Elsa. Whatever was in the dish was ablaze with a soft, roseate flame. The faerie's curiosity overcame her, as it usually did, and she fluttered up to sit on Elsa's shoulder and stared into the dish.

Her blue eyes grew wide with childlike amazement and a blissful smile played on her lips.

'It's beautiful,' she sang. 'It's the most beautiful thing I've ever seen.'

Jake wondered what magic had occurred while he had been transported to the edge of life and was eager to see it for himself.

'What is it?' he asked cautiously.

'Take a look for yourself,' Elsa said and gently tipped the bowl towards Jake.

The fine powder of the Saint's Hope pollen had vanished and in its place was a thick, scarlet liquid which undulated and rippled despite Elsa's steady hands. Within the pool of scarlet, other shades glistened of burnished gold, rich amber and vivid amethyst like the essence of precious gems. These sparkling fragments of brilliant colour seemed to be actual living beings, twisting and dancing in the crimson sea to an unheard melody. They evolved and changed before his eyes, becoming shining images of dolphins, tigers and glorious birds of paradise. For one brief second Jake thought he saw a vision of himself formed from these curling shapes.

'What is it?' he asked.

'It's the blood of life,' Elsa explained. 'It comes from all living things. When you and I died for that brief moment the magic in the Saint's Hope pollen absorbed the life we momentarily sacrificed and made it into a separate essence.'

A golden dolphin leapt from the ruby waves and burst in a shower of jewelled fireworks that rained back down into the redness.

'I can't believe part of me is in there,' Jake murmured.

He regarded Elsa and saw that a melancholy expression had fallen on her face. It was as if performing this spell was the end of a very long journey for her and she was not sure what was going to happen next. She looked back and smiled a strange smile.

'But Jake,' she half laughed, 'you of all people should know that every one of us has power to help others. You are the one who made me believe I had the strength to stand up to grandmère tonight. So why do you doubt your own strength?'

'Of course he doesn't have magic,' Rosehip interrupted. 'He's a mortal. I don't trust all this new magic and white witchcraft. It used to be faerie and Guardian magic good – witches' magic evil. Now there's a witch doing spells to help the Guardian and that thing upstairs. I don't know where I am any more!'

451

Elsa sighed wearily at Rosehip's outburst and turned to face the cooker, the precious blood clutched in her hands. The milk simmering on the stove had reached boiling point and sensing that Elsa was about to complete the spell, Jake watched her avidly. Elsa paused in front of the stove and looked back at Rosehip.

'Times are changing,' she told the faerie in a matter-of-fact tone. 'Jessica's back in Jersey now; there is a new balance. The problem is, none of us is quite sure what that is going to be.'

The kitchen fell silent. Somewhere in the house Jake could hear Jessica weeping. 'Whatever happens with Marina, we have to accept things are going to be different now and we can't go back to how it was before,' Elsa continued. She cast Rosehip a cold glance. 'Perhaps this time change is for the better.'

Rosehip squirmed uneasily on the table and pouted. The strange, prickly feeling around her heart had returned at Elsa's words and she didn't like it one little bit.

The girl gazed at the simmering milk in the pan and inhaled deeply.

'It is time,' she breathed.

Jake watched as Elsa carefully poured the jewelled liquid into the milk. A glistening waterfall of birds, flowers and fish poured into the hot milk. The white liquid let out an almost human gasp of steam as it enveloped the blood. Jake, peering over Elsa's shoulder, could see that the clean whiteness in the pan now glittered with tiny flecks of crimson and gold.

A sweet odour of honey, vanilla and summer flowers rose from the pan – the essence of all things good and full of life. Elsa stirred the mixture with a wooden spoon, her lips forming words from a long forgotten tongue. Jake strained his ears to try and make out what she was saying but it was futile. Behind them, Rosehip crawled to the edge of the table to try and get a better look.

Finally Elsa stopped her quiet chanting and looked up at Jake. The lad raised his eyebrows expectantly. This spell seemed to be taking a very long time and every minute that past brought Marina closer to death.

'Well?' he asked, nervously. 'Is it done?'

'Not yet. We need to bless the potion.'

She scurried back over to the kitchen table and scooped up

452

the delicate petals of the Saint's Hope in her hand. Elsa motioned for him to hold out his hand. She placed some of the silky petals into his outstretched palm, saying, 'This is very important. We must utter the invocation so that the spell will be cast with love for Marina.'

'We barely know Marina, how can we love her?'

Elsa glanced up. 'You do care for Jersey, don't you?' she asked bluntly.

'Of course, it's my home. I'd do anything to save it.'

'So you believe in the old ways?'

'If I didn't, all we've been through this past week would seem a bit pointless.'

'Then we must learn to see Marina for who she is, the Guardian of Jersey.' She plucked a petal from the small pile in her palm. 'Repeat after me and do as I do,' she told him. 'I give this pulse so her heart may beat again.'

She dropped the fragile bloom into the milk. It rested on the surface which blushed a deep pink, then sank.

'I give this pulse so that her heart may beat again,' he muttered nervously, dropping the petal into the brew. Once again the liquid turned pink for a moment before the flower melted from sight.

Elsa smiled gratefully at him before uttering the next phrase. 'This blessing is pure as is the soul that receives it.'

Jake copied her and two more petals were added. The ritual carried on, Elsa saying the enchantment and Jake repeating it. With each phrase two more white blooms were added. As it proceeded, Jake noticed a warmth filling the room, lifting his heart and making him truly believe that Marina could be saved.

The spell was completed with the line, 'Bring her back to us once more.' And Jake felt convinced that this powerful magic would heal Marina. He dropped the final bloom into the brew.

'Is it ready now?'

Elsa gave the silvery mixture one last stir and removed it from the heat. She cast a sour glance in the direction of Rosehip as she carried the saucepan over to the table. 'It'll do,' she said briskly.

'It'll do?' Jake repeated doubtfully. 'We want this potion to be the best for Marina, don't we?'

Elsa continued to stare at Rosehip for a few moments before looking away in disgust.

'There is one final ingredient that would set the magic more strongly,' she muttered, 'but I can't see us finding it now.'

Rosehip shifted uneasily. Elsa's gaze unnerved her and made the odd prickling around her heart return more intensely. She felt dirty and uncomfortable and wished very much that she was back home. However, she doubted that if she were to leave now the heavy feeling in her heart would ever go away. A tiny voice at the back of her head seemed to be telling her that if this spell didn't work and Marina died it would be her fault. She was angry with the voice and kicked her feet nervously against the edge of the table. 'What is the missing ingredient?' she asked barely audibly.

She had a pretty good idea what would complete the spell and her stomach churned at the thought. She really didn't want to be involved with witchcraft. The two humans didn't seem to hear her but before Rosehip could breath a sigh of relief, the little voice at the back of her mind started pestering her. 'Come on,' it urged. 'Speak up. You know if you don't help them you'll feel awful for the rest of your life.' Rosehip frowned and stamped her foot crossly. What an awkward time to develop a conscience! She coughed unnecessarily loudly to get their attention.

'I said, what is the missing ingredient?'

'To fix the spell,' Elsa began reluctantly, 'we should really add faerie's blood to the mixture. It's a powerful ingredient. Grandmère used it all the time.' She gazed at Jake and the two of them exchanged knowing looks before Elsa added bluntly. 'But in a spell such as this, the faerie would have to donate her blood willingly or the spell wouldn't work.'

Elsa's words confirmed Rosehip's fears and the faerie shuddered involuntarily. 'It doesn't matter,' Elsa went on brusquely. 'It'll work without it. I don't expect you to do anything, Rosehip.'

Rosehip bowed her head and gripped her hands around the edge of the tabletop. There was a rough splinter on the under-side of the table and Rosehip absentmindedly rubbed her palm against it. Her fear of all things to do with witchcraft would not leave her but in the heavy silence of the hot kitchen she couldn't help but hear the plaintive sobs of Jessica upstairs and she was forced to wonder how long Marina would survive without Elsa's spell.

'I don't like witchcraft,' she squeaked loudly.

Elsa removed the wooden spoon from the pan and dropped it onto the table with an angry bang.

'We know,' stated the white witch sharply. She looked at Jake. 'Pass me a bowl and spoon, please,' she said. 'We'd better take the potion up to Marina.'

Rosehip bit her lip with remorse and pressed her palm hard against the jagged fragment of pine beneath the table. The action was painful but she felt it was what she deserved for her selfishness.

'Suppose there was a faerie,' she began with trepidation, 'who was willing to donate her blood. How much would you need?'

Elsa lifted the pan and began to pour the enchanted milk into the dish Jake had brought her. Rosehip gazed as it cascaded forth and heard the tender, almost human, gasp of the sweetly perfumed steam filling the bowl.

'A drop would be enough,' Elsa murmured.

Rosehip knew what had to be done and braced herself. Neither Elsa nor Jake saw the faerie stab the palm of her delicate hand onto the spike of wood beneath the table. Rosehip let out a tiny bleat of pain and cupped her wounded hand. In her palm, a small pool of shimmering, silver blood had formed.

The white witch looked at the faerie. She saw the knowing look in her brilliant sapphire eyes and the freshly bleeding wound on her right hand.

Rosehip cleared her throat and took half a step forwards. 'I cut myself on the table,' she chirped. 'So I suppose you might as well use the blood.'

Jake stooped low to get a better look at Rosehip's injury but the elf snatched her hand away 'Sicko!' she squealed at him in disgust, as she stalked over to the bowl containing the milk. 'And before you say anything, I cut myself entirely by accident. I still think that thing upstairs is weird, I still think witches are evil, and if you say anything to the contrary I'll deny it!'

The glistening elixir shimmered with silver and pink as Rosehip's blood flowed into it. For a second the enchanted milk looked like a brilliant full moon captured in the bowl. Then the light faded and the potion returned to its creamy state.

Rosehip gazed down at her palm. Where she'd expected to see a painful gash of open, silver flesh, the skin had healed and was flawless. The faerie ran her fingertip across her palm and felt a prickle of nerves run up her spine. Not even faeries could heal that quickly. She began to believe there was perhaps a more powerful magic than she could ever have dreamed of. She struggled with the notion that maybe not all witchcraft was evil after all.

Elsa scooped up the bowl and its precious contents. 'The spell is complete. We must feed the potion to Marina before it's too late.'

For a second, faerie and white witch stared at each other, both knowing that the sacrifice Rosehip had made was more than a few drops of blood. A slight smile played on Elsa's lips and without Jake noticing she mouthed two simple words to the faerie to make absolutely sure she knew what she had done. 'Thank you.'

Jake and Elsa stepped into the hallway, leaving Rosehip alone to contemplate life, magic and witchcraft. A strange coldness cloaked them as the door swung shut.

They climbed the creaking stairs that led to the bedrooms. The light was dim but it seemed rude to let the stark glare of electricity flood this house of sadness. In Elsa's hands, the mystical brew simmered with warmth and life but so sombre was the atmosphere in Maison de l'hache that even she found it hard to believe that the pearly liquid held any more power than hot milk.

Jake knocked softly on the door. It creaked open a crack and Jim peeped sorrowfully out. He looked old and confused, as if he couldn't quite remember why the two young people were there.

'She's still with us,' he murmured. 'Though I don't know for how much longer. Come in,' he said hoarsely.

Jake and Elsa slipped inside.

The bedroom was as dimly lit as the rest of the house and the air was heavy with the grief of the family. Only a small lamp was alight; it cast long, black shadows across the room. The air stank of infection.

Jessica sat curled on the very edge of the bed, her sister lying weakly in her arms. Her clothes were torn to shreds and stained with the mud and ash of battle. Her skin was so muddied and charred it was as if the blight that had scarred Marina had been transferred to her. She seemed unaware of anything happening

456

around her as her shaking fingers caressed her beloved sister's hair and with trembling lips she whispered words of comfort to the cursed girl. It was hard to believe this pathetic scrap of youthful womanhood had been the hero who had fought for Jersey so bravely.

Elsa stepped forward bearing the shimmering bowl. No-one spoke. She knelt at the side of the bed.

'Jess,' Elsa said, 'this is the potion I told you about. It's ready. It will help her if she could drink a little.'

Jessica's heart leapt at this fragment of hope represented by the creamy liquid. Her arms shaking, Jessica propped Marina's head in the crook of her elbow. Trembling fingers grasped the spoon and held it to Marina's blackened lips. But Marina didn't open her mouth.

'Come on, Marina.' Jessica begged. 'Swallow it. It will make you better.'

An angry sob caught in her throat and she forced the spoon between her sister's lips in furious desperation. 'Drink it!' she urged fiercely. 'Don't you dare give up on me now!'

For a second, the elixir seemed to fill Marina's mouth. Then the girl's heavy head lolled forward and a pitiful trickle of milky drool dribbled from her lips. The air was eerily silent. Marina had stopped breathing. Jessica's fingers fumbled at Marina's throat to find a pulse but she failed. Martin and Jim hurried to the bed as they realized what had happened. Elsa's shoulders slumped; her worst nightmare had come true. Jake moved to comfort her, his spirits exhausted.

On the bed, Jessica clung to Marina's lifeless body. The witches had won after all. The last Guardian of Jersey was dead.

Black despair overwhelmed her. She was aware of the cries and comforting words of her family and friends but they were like phantoms existing just beyond the corners of her mind. Darkness had fallen.

Suddenly, something sparkling and golden glistened before Jessica's tear-filled eyes. She struggled to make out what it was. The fine gold chain hung with a heart and crucifix, the charm her father had given her before she fought Mrs Noir, glowed like a warm sunbeam. Fingers shaking, she reached out and touched it. She had never been very religious but now she began to pray.

'God,' she begged as the tears rolled down her cheeks, 'I don't understand. Why are You letting these horrid things happen? You sent Helier to save Jersey. Why are You hurting his descendants?'

She stopped, hoping for some divine answer to her question but none came. Only the memory of her mother and sister filled her mind.

'You know they did nothing wrong,' she pleaded. 'All they ever wanted was to bring goodness to Jersey and You let those evil witches kill them. It isn't fair!'

'What do You want from me!' she screamed. 'I've done everything I was told to. I was willing to die for Jersey. I am not the Guardian. I cannot help anyone. I tried but I can't do any more. If You want to kill somebody, kill me and let Marina live! I don't matter. She does!'

Bending her head wearily, she gazed at the cross lying in her hands. It was glowing red hot, the intense heat seeping into her skin, burning her until her hands felt they had been thrust into hot coals. She saw Marina's face dance before her eyes and remembered how she had healed her broken leg.

Suddenly, she was back in the bedroom, her twin's lifeless body lying beside her. Jessica's palms were still burning but she knew what she had to do. Tenderly, she cupped her sister's head in her hands and felt the fire flow into her. Through the heat, she could feel the very essence of Marina's being. Her sister's soul reached out to her from beyond the grave. It grew stronger by the second until Jessica could hear Marina's croaky voice in her ears. The stronger Marina's spirit grew, the more intense was the fire that filled Jessica's palms. The heat was so fierce that Jessica was in agony. It flowed through her veins like liquid fire and into Marina's body. The cold skin absorbed the powerful blaze. Jessica's vision was blurred; painful specks of silver light flickered at the corners of her sight and her head pounded. But through her distorted vision she could see a definite change in Marina's appearance. The olive hue was returning to her leathery skin and the shadows that had ringed her eyes were vanishing.

Her fingers trembled with a force that overwhelmed her and Jessica no longer felt in control of her own body. The power that was calling Marina back into her earthly form came from a place far beyond the mere magic of Jersey.

Suddenly, the blaze that ignited Jessica's palms vanished. Overcome with exhaustion she let go of Marina and the girl's head flopped back onto the pillow. Giddily, she slumped backwards onto her heels and Elsa and Jake hurried forward to support her.

She heard her father's voice gasp, 'She's breathing!' Life had once again returned to Marina's crippled form. Her lips were moist again and she was taking deep gulps of air. Wearily she moved her arms and flippers as if waking from a dream.

'It's a miracle,' Jim gulped.

Overwhelmed with happiness, Jessica seated herself once more beside Marina, supporting her fragile body in her arms. 'Come on,' she smiled. 'That's it Marina, you can do it!'

A spluttering cough shook the older twin's body and mucus dribbled from her mouth. Her heavy eyelids flickered open.

'Ma Jecica,' she said softly.

'Oh Rina,' Jessica wept, 'I thought I'd lost you again.'

Marina cupped her twin's cheek in the palm of her oversized hand. 'Rina never leave Jecica,' she declared, tapping her sister's chest gently. 'Always together, here. Always.'

The Guardian's beautiful eyes left her sister's face and gazed about her. 'Where be I?' she quizzed. 'Badsome witchy go bye-bye, yes?'

Jessica wiped a tear from her eyes. 'Yes,' she soothed. 'She can't hurt anyone any more. You're home, Marina. We're home.'

Marina smiled.

At the end of the bed, Jim and Martin exchanged happy glances. All the bitterness that Emma's death had brought was washed away and all that mattered was that two very special girls were safe. The miracle that had brought Marina back to life had not healed her scarred and twisted form but it had brought peace to the hearts of her family. For now, that was enough.

'Rina,' Jessica said, 'I want you to meet our family.'

Marina gazed at her father and uncle. All her life she'd hoped that her family would return for her.

Martin knelt beside his daughters. He wrapped them in his arms and thanked God he had been given a second chance.

Jim, however, hung back. His abandonment of Marina preyed on his mind and it weighed heavy on his heart to think back

459

over the many years he'd denied her existence. However much he was relieved to see Marina's return to life, her impairments still unnerved him.

Marina's blissful expression became tinged with sorrow as she regarded her great uncle. Jim shuffled his feet nervously. Marina cocked her head thoughtfully to one side.

'Uncly Jim,' she said in a small, breathy voice as the beginnings of a smile creased her lips.

There was something in that smile that reached down into the old man's memory, raising thoughts of happier times. The angle of her head and glimmer of her eye had echoes of her mother.

Jim fell to his knees beside the bed. He reached out and clutched Marina's hand. 'Forgive me, Marina,' he cried. 'I was so wrong about you. You are the Guardian, you are Emma's child. I shouldn't have cast you out. Keela was a better parent to you than me.'

Fearfully he raised his head to gaze at her. Marina looked at the old man with childlike fascination. With tender, long fingers she traced the lines of his weathered face and stroked his soft, white hair. Jim recoiled slightly, not out of repulsion at her malformed hands but out of disbelief that the child he had wronged so greatly could express such affection towards him.

'She doesn't understand what you want forgiveness for,' Jessica whispered. 'She has waited all her life to find you and now you are here. All she ever wanted was a family; she has that now. We both have.'

'Rina wait way long time to see Uncly Jim.'

'Me, too,' he told her.

Marina hugged her uncle for a moment and then let go, reclining wearily on the bed.

'Sleepiesome now,' she murmured with a gurgling yawn.

Jim and Martin smiled knowingly and eased their weight off the bed. Marina was safe now but it would take some days of heavy rest before she would fully recover from the battle. Jessica stayed lying snugly by her side, not wanting to lose the safe, warm feeling she had found.

'I'll sleep here,' she sighed, nestling onto the edge of the bed beside her slumbering sister.

Jake gazed longingly towards the door. He had a family of

his own to return to, maybe not as mystical as the Hellilys, but dear to him nonetheless, and after all the horror of that night he longed to be with them.

'Well,' said the farmer's son, hiding his own emotions as he always did when they threatened to overwhelm him. 'I'd better be getting back. I'm glad Marina's on the mend but that won't milk them chickens.' He was rambling again as he often did, filling his words with humour when he didn't quite know what to say.

Jim realized his awkwardness and smiled at him with affection. Jake was a good lad, with more courage and compassion than he allowed himself to show. Jim shook his hand warmly. 'Take care,' he told him. Jim knew just how much Jake's friendship meant to Jess; she would've told him herself had she not been so drained from the day's events.

Jake blushed slightly at Jim's gratitude and hurried out of the door, leaving the Hellilys alone with Elsa. The white witch had been even more contemplative than Jake after Marina's escape from the grim clutches of death and with good cause. She'd always had the ability to sink into the background and she had done this now to be with her own, very private thoughts. She was happy that by some miracle Marina was alive again but standing in the presence of such a family reunion had touched her heart with a sadness that she could not ignore. Now her debt to Jessica had been repaid, Elsa allowed her thoughts to return to her own future and she struggled to see what could possibly lie in store for her. Her grandmother was dead, a joyous thing for all the sorrow and terror she had caused, but still a fact that unnerved her. Cruel as Agatha Noir had been to Elsa she had still been the girl's only living relative and now she was gone Elsa was very aware she was completely alone in the world. With the black magic defeated, Elsa had been given back her freedom but just what she should do with it she didn't know. All her life her home had been the dark and loveless house at Gorey. It was an abode full of evil tools of black magic and spiteful memories and the last place Elsa wanted to return to. Could she really build a home for herself in such a heartless place? But if not there, where else could she go?

And it wasn't just the sense of physical belonging that eluded Elsa. The discovery of her ability to do white magic had shocked

461

her. Even now, with Marina's recovery and the battle against her grandmother far behind them, Elsa could feel the warmth and goodness of the white magic throbbing through her veins where before there had been only sickness and self loathing. Elsa didn't need anyone to tell her what that meant. She was a witch, a being not wholly human but connected to the ancient ways of paganism and magic, just as her grandmother had been. The forces of nature had touched Elsa's spirit but did not fill her with hatred or a lust for power as they had done with the old hag. So what was her destiny to be now that she had been pardoned by Jess and her debt to the Guardian been paid? Marina was alive and back where she belonged in Maison de l'hache. With Jim's guidance and Jessica's aid it was she who would be the warrior against black magic and keeper of the ancient ways of Helier; that was not Elsa's place. White witches were as forgotten and fictional as dragons for the people of Jersey, so how could Elsa live among them? For the first time in her life Elsa truly felt like a child, lost and alone.

Her brooding silence had not gone unnoticed by Jim Hellily and it had not taken the man much effort to guess what was on her mind. The battle at Devil's Hole had altered many things in the lives of all who knew of it and as the oldest of the party he felt responsible for the future. However, he was physically and emotionally drained at present and it would take him many hours of thought to come up with an appropriate plan. For now he would take only the most practical steps. Jim placed a hand on her shoulder.

'And what are we going to do with you, Miss Noir?' he said softly. 'Have you thought what you are going to do now?'

Elsa let her shoulders slump.

'The truth is I don't have a clue, Mr Hellily,' she said. 'The important thing is that Jessica and Marina are safe. As for me,' she looked towards the door and gave a small shudder, 'I don't want to go back to that house – not tonight, anyway.'

'You don't have to go anywhere just now,' he told her. 'You can sleep in my room. I'll take the sofa. You are a remarkable young woman, Elsa Noir. I never want you to forget that. One day, you'll be rewarded – you'll see.'

From the bed, Jessica shifted out of her drowsy half slumber to look round at the white witch. She had been half listening to everything that had been said but had been more concerned with nursing Marina than joining in the conversation, but now she felt she must speak to her friend.

'Elsa,' she called quietly.

The child hurried over to the bedside and took her friend's hand.

'What is it, Jess?'

Jessica struggled to find the words to express just how much Elsa meant to her. The small girl had suffered so much hardship in her short life and yet her heart had been strong enough to overcome her fears and save Jessica from evil. 'Thank you for saving my life.'

A distant look appeared in Elsa's eyes. 'No,' she whispered. 'It was you who saved mine.'

Chapter 23

Destiny Will Decide

A strange and refreshing calm settled over Jersey as dawn awoke the isle after the great storm. The weather was fair and warm and for several days there was a tranquillity on the island that few could remember ever feeling before. The thoughts of its people became serene and even the hottest of tempers was cooled. In the graveyards, mourners returned to forgotten tombs to clear away the dead foliage and lay fresh flowers as they recalled loved ones. Within families, petty arguments and spite seemed childish, and meaningful 'sorrys' were uttered as the past was forgotten. Strangers passing as they hurried about their daily business would hold eye contact longer than usual with their fellows and smile. Even the hearts of faeries and merfolk were moved to peace and the following eve saw bright specks of golden light darting in gay dances around the brim of Devil's Hole while the haunting melody of a merfolk chorus echoed from beneath the waves.

For nearly five days Marina slept heavily, waking only for short periods of an hour or so in the early afternoon when she would chat to Jessica and her father and drink a little of the blood of life as well as a few spoonfuls of soup. Each day her spirits grew brighter and although her physical appearance did not improve she seemed to be growing stronger; by the third day she was eagerly asking questions about her new environment.

It was Jessica who answered her questions as she was the one who was usually at her bedside. She'd hardly moved from Marina's side since the battle and it took Elsa all her powers of persuasion to make Jess take some breaks. Jessica simply did not want to be parted from her twin for more than a few seconds.

It was impossible to keep her mind on the present and worries about Marina's future filled all her waking thoughts. Her holiday in Jersey was swiftly drawing to an end and although she would have given anything to remain in the new magical life she had found she knew that realistically she had to return to London. Her school, her father's work, their home, everything was there and it was childish fancy to hope that she could stay on the island. As Marina slept, Jessica studied her cursed body and felt helpless. Marina's strange appearance and crippled form meant she would never be accepted in the non-magical world of Jess's home so it was foolish to think that she would ever be able to leave Jersey. She was tied to the island just as Jess was tied to her old life on the mainland.

While Jessica kept her daily vigil beside Marina's bed, Elsa made herself busy with cleaning and cooking for the Hellily clan, all of whom had greater things on their minds than such mundane tasks. The white witch did return to the house at Gorey the morning after her grandmother's death and had it in her mind to stay there so that Jim, Jess and the others would have some time alone. However, the building had such a cold and hateful atmosphere Elsa found it impossible to stay for more than a few minutes. The memory of her evil grandmother hung in the bricks and cement of the dank residence and the moment Elsa was inside, it was as if the ghost of Agatha Noir had returned to haunt her. The smell of the herbs she had used in her wicked spells scented the air and her tweed cape and wooden cane hung next to the front door as if to taunt Elsa with the threat that the old woman might come back from the dead. This had been Agatha's domain and her memory would always be here as long as Elsa remained. The house held nothing for the girl but recollections of a time she was glad had past. With Jim's blessing, Elsa collected a few sets of clean clothing as well as some personal belongings and returned to Maison de l'hache where she remained for the rest of the week. She dreaded the time when her welcome in Jim's home would wear out and she would have to return to the loveless house that now, as Agatha's only relative, was hers. She had nothing but the prison of her childhood to call her home. Where else was she to spend her days?

Elsa was far from naïve. She was all too aware that she was

465

still a child and as soon as the authorities learnt of her grandmother's death she would be whisked into the great machine that was the care system. In the past, Elsa had dreamt of someone taking her into a loving foster home, away from her grandmother's cruelty. However, the white magic throbbed through her veins with every heartbeat and her instincts were alive with countless healing spells. Elsa could never be a normal child. If she was placed in a foster home on the mainland where magic and witchcraft were seen as nothing more than childish fantasies, Elsa knew she would wither and die. She prayed that there were foster parents among the community of true Jersey people who would take her in, but even that could be fraught with problems. True Jersey people did not trust witches and Elsa felt that she would surely be shunned by the islanders once they knew what had happened at Devil's Hole. As she gazed out of the window before she fell asleep, Elsa contemplated gathering her grandmother's herbs and books of spells and running off into the night to become a travelling healer, going from place to place, helping people where she could. There didn't seem to be a place for her anywhere – but then there never really had been.

Elsa wasn't the only person who seemed uncertain of her future. Ever since Marina's escape from death, Jim Hellily had been very withdrawn. The old man seemed very unwilling to be in the house, making all kinds of excuses to go out. Jessica got the feeling that he was finding any excuse to avoid Marina and this needled her. She had hoped that after her twin's recovery the bitter mistakes of the past would be forgotten and Jim would welcome Marina as the true Guardian, but she was beginning to doubt this. Jim didn't seem to want to be in the same room as her, let alone speak to his great-niece. However, on the third evening after the battle, as Jessica dozed lightly in the chair beside her sister, she could have sworn she sensed Jim's presence in the doorway, gazing at them. Jessica tried very hard to guess at what her great uncle was thinking but after all that had happened it was difficult to know.

One day, towards the end of the week, Jim finished his dinner muttering that he had to meet some people and disappeared until the early hours of the next morning. Jessica had a pretty good idea where he had gone. Like Jessica herself, Jim seemed

466

to want to speak with Keela about Marina and she wished more than anything that she could have gone with him. She had a horrible feeling that Jim was making arrangements for Marina to go back into the caves under the charge of the merman again. This thought angered her beyond belief.

A new routine settled on the house during the last week of Jessica's stay. Most of the time, Jessica and her father stayed in the bedroom looking after Marina while Elsa made herself busy downstairs, only coming upstairs a couple of times a day to check on her friends and bring them their meals. With Jim being out most of the time no-one spoke much about the future but it preyed heavily on all their minds. On a couple of occasions, Jake dropped by. The injuries suffered by the farmer's son during the battle were painful but nothing that severely disabled the healthy seventeen-year-old. On his welcome return home, Jake had informed his family – in particular his grandfather, who was on the council of elders – of the events at Devil's Hole. The story of Marina's salvation was difficult to take in, even by true Jersey folk like the LeBlancs, and gave the family a great deal to be grateful for. If Jake's mother had had her way the lad would have stayed in bed for the rest of the week and recovered properly but he insisted on going round to see Jess and the others nearly every other day. He could sense the unease in Jim's home and knew that a decision was yet to be made on how to deal with the aftermath of the battle. He thought of asking Jess herself what was happening but knew that if she heard anything she would tell him anyway. Jake had decided that he would continue these visits even after Jessica had left for the mainland, just to keep an eye on Elsa and Marina. It was the least he could do after all that had happened. He had a duty to them and it would be unkind to end it now the terror was over.

On his third visit to Maison de l'hache, Jake found the house unnervingly quiet. Jim was in the living room smoking his pipe, a habit he only adopted in times of stress, while Elsa had settled herself at the kitchen table to polish the horse brasses that hung around the fire.

Marina lay on the bed, snoring softly to herself while Jessica tiptoed around collecting clothes from drawers and placing them in a suitcase. Jake watched her sadly for a few minutes. He

467

knew that Jessica would have to leave sometime but hadn't realized it was going to be so soon.

'You're packing,' he observed, at a loss what else to say.

Jessica looked up from her task and Jake expected her to make some sarcastic comment about him stating the obvious. However, her expression made it clear she had no time for humour.

'I fly back to London tomorrow,' she said dully, placing a pile of t-shirts in the case.

Jake noted that she didn't say 'I fly home', and he had a good idea why – London wasn't home any more. He stepped inside the room and shut the door. Jess pressed a finger to her lips and gestured towards Marina.

'Don't wake her.'

Jake nodded and felt his throat go dry. It was a difficult time and he didn't know quite what to say. He had got the impression that Jessica was feeling so stressed that if he said the wrong thing she would bite his head off. Finally he settled for, 'Does Rina know you're going?'

'I haven't told her yet,' she admitted reluctantly. 'When she wakes I'll explain everything to her.'

Jake's stomach tightened with nerves. This must mean Jim and the elders had come to a decision on what should be done about Marina. He noted Jess's mood and wondered whether it had been bad news. His heart sank; neither of them deserved to suffer any more. He cleared his throat and shuffled over to where Jess was collecting her things from the open wardrobe.

'I'm guessing that the council has come to a decision, then?' he ventured.

Jessica stared at him. Her eyes had a glassy sheen and for a moment he thought she was going to cry. Instead, she turned back to the suitcase and flung in another bundle of clothes.

'I don't know.'

A resolution had to be made before Jessica left; it just wasn't right to leave her in the dark. He wondered suspiciously if Jim was deliberately holding out until Jessica had gone so he could dump Marina back on Keela without a fuss.

'Jim hasn't spoken to me for two days,' she said, fiddling with the catches on the trunk. 'He's been out all the time, sorting stuff out, he says. He must know something.' She paused before adding more timidly, 'When he is at home I'm too scared to ask anything in case he says she has to go back to the caves. I know he's meeting with the elders.'

Jake bit his lip and looked stern. He thought of his grandfather, the elder of the Jerseymen and council member. Arthur LeBlanc had listened to Jake very seriously when he told him about Marina. He had praised his grandson for his bravery but said very little else. Jake's father had told him that several nights that week his grandfather had had important business to attend to and Jake knew that the council were making plans for his friends' future. For the first time Jake truly understood how Jessica must have felt when everyone was keeping the secret of who her mother had been from her. There were many things regarding Marina and Elsa that Jake had wanted to know but no-one would tell him. His grandfather had reassured him that everything would turn out for the best and that he had nothing to worry about, but that wasn't enough for Jake. 'Grandpa sits on the council,' he told her.

'I know,' she whispered. 'Jake, if you know anything, anything your grandfather's said, I'd be grateful if you'd tell me. I won't hold it against you if it's bad news.'

She walked over to him and let her hand brush against his. Jake pulled a dejected face. He hated to let her down but how could he help her?

'They haven't said anything to me.'

'They're treating us like children!' Jessica hissed crossly. 'Like they always do. Marina's the Guardian, for Christ's sake. They could show a bit of respect. It was the four of us who went down to Devil's Hole, not them! The least they could do is to be honest with us.'

In her sleep, Marina stirred and rolled over, growling to herself. Jessica clawed back her thick hair.

'I'm sorry. I'm just worried about Marina. If Jim does anything to harm her, I'll ring his neck, whether he's my great uncle or not!'

Jake chuckled and placed an arm round Jess's shoulder.

'You're tired,' he said. 'You know Jim wouldn't do anything to hurt Marina, not after all that's happened. Besides, I'll keep an eye on her while you're away, I promise.'

Jessica gave a half smile as she returned Jake's hug. 'You're a good mate, Jake.'

469

At that moment a snuffling noise from the bed told them that Marina had awoken. Jessica quickly shut her suitcase and went over to see if her sister was okay. Jake saw that the cursed girl had grown noticeably stronger since his last visit. Her skin, although still deep green and scarred with warts, seemed to have a healthier glow to it and her warm, dark eyes had regained their sparkle. Shuffling amongst the cotton sheets, Marina sat up and opened her puckered mouth in a yawn. Jessica perched on the bed beside her sister and wrapped her arm round her shoulder.

'Good morning, sleepy head,' said Jessica affectionately. 'And how are we feeling today?'

Marina made a contented growling sound in her throat and gave Jessica a peck on her cheek.

'Rina is beings muchly better, thankings you,' she croaked happily. Her eyes drifted round the room and seeing Jake, let out an excited squeal. 'Ake!' she called, waving an oversized hand. 'Hellos to you.'

'Hi,' he grinned, taking her hand. 'You're looking healthier than when I saw you last.'

Marina nodded earnestly and flicked her unkempt locks. 'Rina is feelings muchly healthily now,' she declared seriously. 'For way long time, Rina's head is a-throbbings, chesty all ucksome and ick, body muchly flopsome. But now...' her deep, chestnut eyes glistened as a broad grin spread across her face. 'But now, Rina is beings full of the goodsome and heathliness.'

She chuckled merrily, bouncing up and down on the bed before launching herself at Jessica and Jake and tickling them as hard as she could.

The two friends fell about giggling under Marina's playful attack. Marina gurgled with joy but then suddenly stopped the game as if she'd remembered something.

Turning to Jessica she exclaimed, 'Is beings muchly busisome day, ma Jecica.' She patted her sister's arm. 'Rina must be makings readisome. Yesterday, ma Jecica say Uncy Jim is talksies to important people about Rina coming home. He tells Jecica what happenings, yes?'

Jessica forced an awkward smile as her heart sank. She knew this moment had been coming and had hoped that it wouldn't arrive until Jim had explained to her what the council had decided. Telling Marina that she and her father had to leave Jersey for the mainland was bad enough but the situation was made even worse by her not knowing where Marina was going to live when they had left. Marina was so happy right now it didn't seem fair to break her heart like this. How could Jess explain why she had to leave when she herself didn't want to go? Suddenly Jessica was aware of a familiar sensation in the darkest corner of her mind. She looked at her twin and saw that Marina's eyes were closed and an expression of understanding smoothed her features. Without Jessica even speaking, Marina had known what was in her heart.

'Ma Jecica and Da not be at home in Jersey,' murmured Marina, a note of sad acceptance quavering in her voice. 'They must live way far away, Rina know.'

She let out a sorrowful sigh. Jessica bit her lip and tried very hard to stay strong for her sister.

'I don't *want* to leave you,' she said, terrified her twin would think she was being rejected again. 'It's complicated, but there are things that mean I can't stay here. Important things.' She struggled to find an example to give but all thoughts of her home, school and friends seemed trivial compared to Marina and the magic of Jersey. Instead she cupped Marina's leathery face in her hands and told her: 'We'll visit whenever we can.'

She looked into Marina's chocolate pupils expecting to see tears. But to her surprise, Marina looked happy and a smile played on her lips. She held Jessica's hand in her own and pressed it to her chest. 'Ma Jecica no really all go away,' she said softly. 'Always here always.'

Jessica nodded sadly and flushed with embarrassment. There was she, worried about how she was going to break the news of her return to the mainland to Marina and it was Marina who was comforting her. Jessica realized now that her sister had an advantage. All her life, Marina had known about Jess and loved her even when they were apart. Jess's leaving saddened Marina but she knew that they would always be together in each other's hearts. This sisterly bond was new to Jess and her feelings were still raw. She had to learn, as her twin had done, that physical distance couldn't break the bond formed in their mother's womb.

'You'll be okay,' said Jess knowingly. 'You have friends here to look after you while I'm gone. Jake and Keela.'

Marina sat bolt upright in bed and let go of Jess's hand.

'Ma Keelie!' she cried. 'Rina must be makings plans. So muchly do, so muchly do!' She counted out the chores on her long, tapered fingers. 'Ask Uncly Jim what important peoples say 'bout Rina and Jecica; tell ma Keelie way important newsies; say bye-byes to Da; check on prettysome ickle Elly-sa.'

A soft rapping on the door interrupted this recital. Jake got up and went to open it.

Outside on the landing, Elsa stood pale and nervous. She was wringing her hands and her eyes were bright with concern. She peered behind Jake into the room, eager to catch Jess's eye.

'Is Jess there?' she asked. 'Her uncle wants to speak with her.'

Jessica heard her friend's anxious tone and hurried to the door. Just by looking at Elsa Jessica knew her message was important and she had a pretty good idea what it would be. Elsa was so fretful that she could barely stand still. 'Your uncle wants to see you, Jess. He and the elders have come to a decision.'

Jessica felt her stomach lurch with fear. This was what she had been waiting for. Marina's fate had been sealed. She uttered a silent prayer that they would let her sister stay with their great uncle.

Elsa watched her friend, almost green with panic. She knew it wasn't just Marina the council had been discussing. Jim would have told them about her witchcraft and Elsa's heart pounded at the thought of what her fate may be. Would she be punished despite Jessica clearing her name?

'Oh dear!' she bleated, gasping for breath. 'Oh dear! Everything has been so confusing since Jessica banished Grandmère!'

Jake looked from the shivering Elsa to the angst-ridden Jess and tutted. Women had no control over their emotions!

'Stay calm,' he told them in his gentlest voice. 'Please, both of you. It'll do no good getting all worked up about things that might be.'

'You're right,' she said, before grabbing his hand and begging, 'Will you come down with us? Please, Jake?'

The lad was surprised. This matter was a private and serious issue and he hadn't expected to hear about the council's decision until it had been told to him second hand. However, he could hardly abandoned Jessica when she was in such a state. 'Okay,

I'll stay. It'll be all right.' He patted her hand calmingly.

Worried, Jessica looked back at her sister. Marina was sitting very still, head cocked to one side, listening intently to all that had been said. She looked a great deal calmer than Jess and Elsa. Elsa glanced at Marina and fiddled with the hem of her skirt.

'That was the other thing,' she murmured tensely. 'Jim wants to speak to Rina as well.'

Jessica hadn't expected this. Jim had barely spoken to Marina since her recovery and now he wanted her involved she was quite shocked. It was very out of character. Did this mean the news was good or bad? There was no way of telling and Jess didn't know her uncle well enough to judge what he was thinking. All she did know was that the old man wouldn't mince his words and God knows how Marina would cope if Jim rejected her once again.

Elsa noted her friend's shocked expression and her brow furrowed in sympathy.

'It is *her* life,' she reminded Jess. 'Of any of us, she has the most right to be there.'

Jessica lowered her eyes and felt Jake stroke her hand comfortingly.

'You're right, Els.' She looked to Marina who had crawled down to the end of the bed and was staring at her sister, pleading to be included in the conversation. 'Uncle Jim wants to talk to us both,' she said.

Marina knelt back on her flippers and folded her huge hands in front of her in a solemn pose.

'Talksies now,' she murmured, sounding very serious. 'Ya.'

Jake left Jess's side and strolled back towards Marina, lifting her off the bed to carry her downstairs. Marina didn't acknowledge Jake's aid and her face was tense and full of worry. Elsa gave Jessica a grim smile that did not dilute the concern in her pale eyes and taking the older girl's hand, led her out of the bedroom and down the stairs. Jake and Marina followed.

The silent troop reached the ground floor and headed towards the door that led into the living room. Cautiously, Elsa pushed it and they went inside.

Jim and Jessica's father were already there. Martin stood tensely before the fireplace, nervously prodding the smouldering embers

473

with the poker. As they entered, he looked up and gave his daughters a hopeful smile. Jess studied her father's eyes carefully for any sign that he might know what had been decided but his expression told her that he was as ignorant as she. At the fireside, Jim Hellily sat in his usual armchair. He looked older somehow; the spirit of youth that usually made his dark eyes sparkle was gone and he wore a deeply thoughtful expression. His stubby, black pipe drooped from his lip and the smoke hung like heavy vapour in the air. The smell of the Virginia tobacco made Jessica's chest tighten. She crossed to the two-seater sofa directly opposite the fire and sat down. Jake followed her into the smoky room and settled Marina next to her sister before taking the chair opposite Jim. Marina's wide eyes stared at her uncle and for the first time Jessica saw that her twin was truly afraid. Jess clutched her sister's hand and tried to comfort her.

Elsa didn't move from the doorway. Too scared to enter, she gazed into the room with terrified eyes. Jim's gaze wandered over each one of his guests broodingly before coming to rest on the child in the doorway.

'Come inside, Elsa,' he muttered. 'This concerns you too.'

The pale girl scuttled across to the sofa and perched on the arm beside Jess, trembling like a baby animal. Jessica took her friend's hand but Elsa didn't respond. She remained staring blankly at the floor.

Jim removed the pipe from his lips and emptied the tobacco into a small, resin ashtray.

'You all know why I have called you here,' he said gruffly.

Despite her nerves, Jessica stifled a small smile. The situation they were in was most odd. The smoke, the collection of anxious players, Jim's grim tone; it all reminded her of some period murder mystery. It seemed so removed from the events of the past fortnight she wished Jim would just get on and say what he had to.

Jim inhaled deeply. 'The council had to be called. The events of the recent past have been most unsettling to many islanders.' His eyes drifted to Marina's face and Jessica noticed an awkwardness in his expression. Jessica's temper rose, sore from nervous anticipation. This whole charade was ridiculous! She didn't see what the council had to consider; it was a black and white situation. Mrs Noir was dead and Jersey was free from her

474

threat; Marina had returned to her rightful place as Guardian. If some stuffy old traditionalists were going to be upset because their lives weren't saved in the correct way she thought them most ungrateful.

'For God's sake, you're making it seem like we're the villains here, Jim,' she said, giving Elsa's hand a little squeeze.

Jim shifted uncomfortably in his seat at Jess's words and Martin looked up from the fire.

'Jess,' he chided, 'let your great uncle speak.'

Jess flashed her dark eyes crossly in her father's direction. She was sick of the so-called elders making decisions about her and her friends when it wasn't them who'd risked their lives. Treating them like immature children when it was they who had battled to save the island.

'No I won't listen, Dad,' she retorted. 'Not if he's going to sit there and pick on me and my friends after all we've done. Elsa, Jake, Rina and I nearly died to save the people of this island but when it comes to deciding about what the outcome of our triumphs should be we are pushed out and it's wrong. Jake agrees with me, don't you, Jake?'

All eyes fell on the youth sitting opposite Jim. Jake squirmed in his seat; he hated it when Jess dragged him into her arguments. True, he did agree that they should have been more involved in the days after the battle but it was against his nature to go storming into a quarrel. He felt Jess's gaze burn into him as she waited for his agreement and swallowed hard.

'Well,' he began tactfully, struggling to find the most diplomatic way of agreeing with Jess. But he didn't get any further as Jess had not yet finished.

'You've got a nerve, Jim Hellily,' she went on, glaring at the old man. 'Sitting there like you're an expert on the ancient ways of magic. I hope these elders know about the mistakes you've made, mistakes that put us in this position in the first place.'

Despite her anger, she chose her words carefully. She saw no point in reminding Marina about Jim's rejection of her. But that didn't mean she could completely forget all that she had seen in the Iris of the Ancestors. It would always be a sore matter between her and Jim. She glared at the old man and prepared for him to defend himself. But instead of looking cross or shocked

475

by her onslaught, Jim bowed his head and his eyes softened. The austere hostility that had shadowed his face before seemed to melt away and once again he became the warm-hearted islander Jess knew.

'Aye, lass,' he said in his soft, Jersey accent, 'you're right. I haven't always had the best of judgements.' He turned to gaze into the glowing ashes of the fire as Jess felt her anger ebb. 'Maybe, that's why the council took so long coming to a decision. Maybe they didn't trust me as once they would have.'

Marina turned to her sister. 'Why Uncly Jim so sadsome?' she asked.

Jessica lowered her eyes, not really knowing how to answer. There was a moment of silence as Jim tried to collect his thoughts. Finally, taking a deep breath he turned back to Jess.

'Okay,' he began, sounding friendlier than before though still serious. 'You are right when you say that you should be treated as an adult and so I will explain just what was said at the meeting. Jersey is an island full of beliefs and traditions – this you know. People here don't like change. Despite the fact that all four of you have shown great bravery in the defeat of Agatha Noir, her death has brought to surface facts we can't ignore.' The old man paused and let his eyes drift across the three girls sitting on the sofa. 'Twins born of the last Guardian, the next Guardian cursed by a witch, a white witch living among them. These things unsettle the balance of the old ways.'

Elsa bowed her head and began to weep bitter tears of shame. She felt as if her death sentence was being read. Jess slipped her arm around her crying friend.

'Rina and I won't let them hurt you, I promise,' she soothed.

Marina reached across to place her hand on Elsa's knee. 'Elly-sa no bad. Elly-sa goodsome.'

Jim cleared his throat to regain the room's attention. 'It is true that the old ways must be respected, but that doesn't mean that they are always right.'

'You will not know,' he whispered to Marina, 'all the guilt that has rested on my heart. I pray that you will allow me to help you to fulfil your destiny. You may call this house your home because that is what it is from now on.'

Marina sat perfectly still for a moment, clasping her great uncle's hands. The expression on her face was so subtle it was hard for Jim to know what she was feeling. Jessica knew however. The mystical link that bonded the twins' thoughts and feelings opened wide in Jess's mind and through it flooded overwhelming joy and a sense of belonging. After fourteen years of loneliness she was finally coming home.

Marina leant forwards and rested her head upon Jim's shoulder. Without fear of her malformed body, Jim embraced his great-niece.

'Rina be home now,' she said with a happy sigh.

Jessica gazed at her sister and great uncle and peace flowed through her heart. She had faith that Jim was now willing to accept Marina as his flesh and blood and Jess no longer felt so guilty about leaving Jersey. Her place, like Jim's, was on the edge of the legend of St Helier, aiding the Guardian in her role. It was a task that would forever tie her to her sibling and the mystical ways of this tiny island. She was glad that she had found her destiny.

Elsa watched Marina's welcome with a heavy heart. Jessica and Marina had been given their family back and Elsa knew that was a gift she could never share. All had been put right in the house of Hellily and she had no purpose. She was like a white shadow, floating at the edge of their happiness. Jim, Jess and Marina were so joyful they didn't see Elsa stand up and walk silently over to the door. It was only when Jake heard the creak of the hinges that anyone saw she had moved.

'Where are you going, Elsa?' asked the young lad.

She stood still, her hand resting on the door handle, a single tear bleeding from her eye. She could not answer Jake's question for she simply didn't know where the path ahead lay. Elsa didn't exist, not in the way that Jess or Jake or even Marina did. She had been just a tool for her grandmother's evil power. Now that power was gone, Elsa was empty and alone. The thought of death that had always tormented her before no longer seemed such a frightening option. She had died once to create the blood of life and in that blissful darkness all her problems had vanished. Was it wrong to enter that happy void again when there was nowhere else for her?

'I don't belong here,' she whispered sadly. 'I don't belong. I must go.'

Jim got to his feet and turned to Elsa. 'There was one condition the elders made when they said Marina could come to live with me,' he said.

Elsa quivered. 'I know,' she wept. 'They want me dead! I'm a witch and all witches must die. Jess's judgement will mean nothing. There is something inside me that I can't hide and it must be destroyed.'

Ignoring Elsa's pleas for death, Jim continued. 'The elders decided that although Marina would reside with me, her care would not be my sole responsibility. They said there was a need for a being with powers greater than a mortal. An individual with an understanding of black magic but whose heart was pure. They've put Marina under the guard of a white witch and they know only one on this island. They want you to help me look after her, Elsa.'

Jim's words swam in her head. It didn't seem real. To protect the Guardian was an honour she did not deserve. She stopped crying for it seemed that her wish had been granted. Had she died already? There could be no other explanation for such clemency.

A blossom of hope flowered in Elsa's heart, watered by her tears and warmed by Jessica's friendship. It grew from the garden of the girl's lost childhood, a place she locked tightly away from herself in the expectation she would never freely roam there.

'A home,' she murmured. 'People who like me, who'll take care of me. I don't want to be frightened any more.'

From her seat on the floor, Marina reached up and brushed Elsa's palm.

'Prettysome Elly-sa come be with Rina and Uncly Jim,' she murmured.

'Yes,' she whispered happily. 'I will, Marina.'

Jessica's heart found peace as she saw her friend smile. She was no longer afraid of returning to the mainland, for now she had found in Jersey what her heart had searched for all her life. Her beloved twin sister, her great uncle, her friends Jake and Elsa, the faeries that danced among the heather and bracken, the merfolk who had done so much to protect her, the ghost of the saint who would haunt her heart always. These were her real family.

* * *

478

The full moon shone upon the sands of St Ouens Bay as four figures launched a small rowing boat into the silky waves. The air was sweet and warm and the sky was a blanket of blackness hung with diamond stars.

The rest of the day at Maison de l'hache had been full of happiness as Jessica and the others set about arranging to move Elsa into the upstairs bedroom. Jess, Jake and Elsa returned to Gorey to collect what remained of her meagre belongings. For Elsa, the house seemed no longer as threatening or chilling as it had done. It was as if by moving away from her grandmother's gloomy abode, she had cut off the supernatural power that fed the old hag's memory. As she walked through the empty halls and rooms, Elsa gazed at the dust and cobwebs that coated the unhappy dwelling. There was no life there now, good or evil. What had once been a prison was now an empty shell. Even Magiver, Mrs Noir's Siamese cat, had vanished without so much as a coffee coloured hair to tell he had ever been real. Elsa walked tall and proud through the house and knew nothing within it could ever harm her again. With her friends' help she collected the rest of her clothes, along with a selection of spell books and herbs she felt might be useful, and left never to return.

The day had drawn long and lazily into nightfall and as dusk settled over the island, Jessica's contented thoughts turned to melancholy as she realized that in just a few short hours she must leave this beautiful, mystic isle to return to the grey normality that was London. Marina's well-being no longer worried her as her sister was healthier than ever and Jessica knew she was now in the best of care. Jess's sadness was more selfish than that. She felt that she belonged in Jersey and her old life back in the smoky gloom of the city was mundane in comparison. In her short time on the island she had formed many bonds to the place and its people, deeper than she ever believed was possible. She might not be the Guardian but she loved Jersey with all her heart and now saw why her mother had been so unwilling to leave. After what would be her final dinner with Jim and the others, Jessica strode out into the garden and sat down on the lush, green lawn beside the rhododendron bushes to feel the soft summer air on her face one last time, pondering all that had happened in the past two weeks and what the future held in store. Marina must have been having similar, reflective thoughts for after a short while she hobbled out of the back door and approached Jessica with the request that she wanted to visit Keela to say goodbye before starting her new life on land with her great uncle. Jessica too, wished to say farewell and thank the merman for all he had done. So, as darkness fell, Jim drove Jess, Marina, Jake and Elsa down to the bay where they launched the boat and set out to find Keela.

Jessica and Jake sat side by side on the centre bench of the boat, rowing it out to sea. In the stern of the vessel Marina and Elsa rested, gazing out at the ocean, enjoying the beautiful night. Marina turned her face happily to the starry sky above and the silvery light shone down on her, making her deep, chocolate eyes sparkle.

'Keelie, ma Keelie, we go and see ma Keelie,' she sang playfully to herself as the boat rocked gently to and fro.

Jessica's eyes wandered from her twin's smiling face to Elsa who was seated by her side. The white witch was gazing sorrowfully down into the ocean, a brooding frown creasing her brow. She was trailing her hand in the water and watching, as from her pale fingertips a faint mist of white magic filtered into the waves, like the last smoke from a forgotten fire. She looked so sad Jess couldn't help wondering what was wrong.

'Els,' she called softly. 'Is there anything the matter?'

The small girl lifted her head and forced an unconvincing smile.

'I'm fine, Jess, really,' she replied, her voice sounding as if her thoughts were elsewhere.

Marina stopped her singing and turned to face Elsa.

'Elly-sa sadsome,' she said knowingly, reaching up to brush Elsa's fine, blonde hair. 'Elly-sa is tellings friends what is beings the matter.'

Elsa knew it was futile to hold anything back from her three friends, they had shared so much.

'It's grandmère,' she said with a sigh. 'I can still feel her with me.'

Jessica moaned wearily at her friend's burden and rested her oar on the side of the boat. 'Oh, Elsa,' she said. 'You really have to let her go. She can't hurt you any more.'

Elsa straightened her neck and arched her fine eyebrows.

'It isn't that. I know I'm safe now. It's just...' she inhaled and gazed down at her delicate hands. 'I've lived with witchcraft all my life. I hated it and hated my grandmother for using it. All I've ever wanted was to be as far away from magic as possible. But now I know that can never happen. Even though you've pardoned me, Jess.' She rested her hand on her chest. 'Even though everyone on the island accepts me, I can't accept myself. The thing that I've always hated is now inside me and no-one can make it go away. Part of grandmère will always live on because of me. We're both witches.'

Elsa dropped her gaze to her shoes and Marina lovingly placed her arm around her to comfort her. Jake groaned and rested his chin in the palm of his hand.

'You can't carry this guilt around with you for ever, Elsa,' he told her. 'You'll make yourself ill again.'

Jessica barely noticed him. Her attention had drifted upwards and she was now gazing at the uncountable stars that spread out high above them, still and unchanging. In the breathless warmth of the Jersey night, Jessica felt a presence within those stars, a power of love too limitless to be defined by mere human words. God? Nature? She did not know what that never-ending force was; all she did know was that it moved all of them along paths and threads in a great tapestry.

'You remind me of Helier,' she told Elsa.

Elsa looked at her shocked. 'Jess,' she hissed, as if she feared someone might hear them. 'You mustn't say such things. Comparing me to the great Helier.' She briskly shook her head as if the very idea was unthinkable.

'No, I mean it,' she smiled. 'Think about it, Elsa. Helier was the son of a warlock who did a great many evil things. He was ill as a child; he nearly died. It was only after he escaped from his family and proved to others that his heart was pure that he was able to help people. Sure, your grandmother passed her witchcraft on to you, but you can choose how to use it.'

Elsa contemplated her friend's words. Jessica looked out over the dark sea and watched the glistening ripples of the moon as they sailed on the cresting waves.

'I've been thinking,' she said, almost to herself. 'Christianity, paganism, saints, warlocks, witches. Maybe they all boil down to the same thing. The power for what we choose to do doesn't come from out there somewhere – it's inside us, all of us. It doesn't matter if you're human, a merperson or a faerie – all of us can make a difference.'

Jake gave a little sniff as if he wasn't sure he agreed.

'That's all very well and good for you and Marina. You're descended from Helier. And Elsa is a white witch. But for the likes of me, let's face it, I'm just a farmer's son. There's more cow's muck in my blood than magic.'

Jessica glared at him. Here was she divulging her innermost beliefs and all Jake could do was pooh-pooh them. Before Jessica could chide him Elsa did it for her.

'How can you say that, Jake?' she piped, 'Why, in the last fortnight you've saved Jessica from falling off a cliff, from being shot by a cursed arrow, and you've stood by her through thick and thin. You've been more than just a friend to Jess!'

The strength of Elsa's speech shook them both. Jessica found herself blushing and unable to look Jake in the eye. It was easy to tell Jake off when he was being cocky or foolish but somehow Jess found it very to hard thank him for all that he had done. Elsa was right: he had saved her life and she was very grateful. She just felt stupid saying it.

'Yeah, you're right,' Jessica muttered. 'Thanks, you're a good mate.'

Jake seemed equally awkward. He squirmed on the narrow, wooden seat and fiddled with the oar.

'No problem,' he grunted finally.

There was an awkward silence that seemed to go on forever. All four of them sat in the small boat gazing out into the peaceful darkness as the waves caressed the hull of the vessel. Jessica was finding it very difficult to look at Jake and even harder to think of something to say. Her speech about the meaning of life had been her big effort to open up to her friends and now that it had been said she found herself at a loss for words. She very much wished someone would say something – anything, to break this deafening silence.

Suddenly, Jess's wish was granted by Marina pointing out to sea and crowing excitedly, 'Keelie, ma Keelie!'

The others followed Marina's gaze and saw that from beneath the gentle swells a few feet to the left of them, the head and shoulders of the merman had emerged. The starlight glistened on his dark locks and although he was quite a long way off Jess could see he was smiling, welcoming them. He raised a strong, green skinned arm and waved, calling. 'Ahoy, my friends!'

Marina let out a gurgling laugh as she and the others waved back to him. Swiftly, Keela began to cut through the water towards the boat leaving not the slightest wake upon the surface of the ocean. Within a few seconds he had reached them and floated peacefully beside the boat, gazing up at the glistening stars high above.

'The Heavens,' he said happily. 'They say it is a night for celebration. The order of things is restored. They are right.' He lowered his gaze to look kindly at Marina. 'My Marina,' he said paternally. 'I am so happy for you. You will make a marvellous Guardian.'

Marina purred affectionately and tilted her head to look down at her foster parent. 'Rina will be missings ma Keelie,' she said, reaching down to stroke the merman's thick mane.

Keela looked as if he might burst in to floods of proud tears at any moment but somehow he managed to maintain his composure. 'You do know that I still want to see you,' he told her. 'You can visit any time.'

The handsome merman had done so much good, not only by looking after Marina but also by guiding Jessica back to the life she longed for and yet he asked for nothing in return. The words of Old Oaky, the faerie elder, came back to her. Truly, Keela was the noblest of creatures.

'Thank you, Keela. I don't know what I would have done without you.'

Keela let out a peaceful sigh as the sweet sea breeze caressed his smooth skin.

'I have always seen myself as in debt to the Hellilys for protecting the island that is my home, and I always will,' he told her simply, fixing her with his kind, golden eyes. 'Marina may be the Guardian, Jess, but never underestimate the importance of what you have done. All four of you are heroes, true of heart and strong of spirit.'

Jessica bowed her head, flattered by his kind words. There was a peace in her soul such as she had never felt before. The gentle wind sang in her ears and the salty smell of the ocean filled her nostrils. She looked at her beloved sister and her two

483

dear friends and saw in their eyes a reflection of the love she had longed for from her mother. She would never yearn for her lost parent again for she had found her spirit. Emma's heart had always been in Jersey and now it was the place Jessica would always call home.